NO SANCTUARY

The Complete Series

MIKE KRAUS

NO SANCTUARY

The Complete Series
Books 1-6

By
Mike Kraus

Contents

Part One
BOOK ONE

Part Two

BOOK TWO

Part Three

BOOK THREE

Part Six
BOOK SIX

Stay in Touch

Stay updated on Mike's books by signing up for the Mike Kraus
Reading List.

Just visit www.MikeKra.us and click on the big red button.

You'll be added to my reading list and I'll also send you a copy of
some of my other books to say thank you!
(I hate spam with the burning passion of a thousand suns and
promise that I'll never spam you.)

Special Thanks

This book wouldn't be possible without the help and support of my amazing beta reading team. Thank you all so very much for all of your support and advice.

Read More from Mike Kraus

Final Dawn: The Complete Series

Clocking in at nearly 300,000 words with over 250,000 copies sold, this is the complete collection of the original bestselling post-apocalyptic Final Dawn series. If you enjoy gripping, thrilling post-apocalyptic action with compelling and well-written characters you'll love Final Dawn.

Final Dawn: Arkhangelsk

The Arkhangelsk Trilogy is the first follow-up series set in the bestselling Final Dawn universe and delivers more thrills, fun and just a few scares. The crew of the Russian Typhoon submarine *Arkhangelsk* travel to a foreign shore in search of survivors, but what the find threatens their fragile rebuilding efforts in the post-apocalyptic world.

Surviving the Fall

Surviving the Fall is an episodic post-apocalyptic series that follows Rick and Dianne Waters as they struggle to survive after a devastating and mysterious worldwide attack. Trapped on the opposite side of the country from his family, Rick must fight to get home while his wife and children struggle to survive as danger lurks around every corner.

Prip'Yat: The Beast of Chernobyl

Two teens and two Spetsnaz officers travel to the town of Prip'Yat set just outside the remains of the Chernobyl power plant. The teens are there for a night of exploration. The special forces are there to pursue a creature that shouldn't exist. This short thriller set around the site of the Chernobyl nuclear disaster will keep your heart racing right through to the very end.

Zero Hour

A devastating attack. A family separated. A desperate struggle to survive. Jackson Block is trapped far from his family and those he loves when a rogue state unleashes a devastating attack on the United States. To reunite with his loved ones, he must fight through streets that have turned into a war zone as survivors and government agents alike threaten not only his existence, but that of the entire nation.

Darkness Rising

The unthinkable has happened. A North Korean nuclear attack has wiped out most of the west coast and portions of the Midwest and east coasts along with it. As the county reels from the devastation, one family struggling to survive discovers that they may have a closer connection to the disaster than anyone else. The price for potentially ending the crisis before the country completely collapses? That of their eldest child.

Preface

Frank sipped on his coffee and sighed. Twelve straight hours on the road had taken their toll on his eyes and he had to rub them several times to keep from seeing double on the menu. The small greasy spoon at which he'd stopped at was quintessentially American. He sat at the long, wrap-around bar with a view into the kitchen and there were a few other people scattered around the bar as well. A handful of couples and a trio of road workers were spread across the booths where waitresses with beehive hairdos took orders with a drawl and the frequent use of the word "hon." If not for the chilled weather outside and the falling leaves, he would have sworn he was somewhere in Alabama or Texas instead of Maine.

Twelve hours. Frank took another sip and shook his head. *I'm not cut out for this.* Having been behind the wheel of a tractor-trailer for less than a month, Frank wasn't adjusting well.

He started his life in a much different place as an accountant for a large technology company where he had managed to stay on for his entire adult life. As the economy started to tank, though, he lost his job and there were few companies looking to hire someone in their late thirties when they could pick up a college graduate at a quarter the cost.

After moving back in with his parents for a few months, Frank managed to find the only job that was available—driving a rig cross-country. It wasn't glamorous and the pay was terrible, but he had a clean record and had been able to get a commercial driver's license fairly easily.

"Any dessert, hon?" Frank looked up at a face caked with far too much makeup that was smiling down at him.

"No thanks, just the check. And a coffee to go. A tall one, please."

The waitress nodded sympathetically. "New to this, are you?"

Frank nodded. "That obvious is it?"

"Most of 'em do speed to stay awake. Try to stay off that stuff as long as you can, okay hon?" She flipped through her order pad and tore out a page.

Frank looked at the check, glanced at his watch and sighed. He had spent less than twenty minutes at the diner, but he knew based on experience that the computer inside his truck was going haywire with alerts from his dispatcher.

Mandatory maximums for time spent behind the wheel as defined by federal and state law meant nothing to his company. They pushed their drivers for up to eighteen hours a day, six days a week since that was the optimal balance—according to their calculations—between speed and keeping the number of accidents to an "acceptable minimum." As new as he was, Frank couldn't risk any more long stops for a couple more days, and he was counting on the next fueling station to have some decent food to see him through.

So far the transition from an office job to unemployment to driving a truck all hours of the day and night was rough to say the least. Frank felt like he hadn't gotten a handle on any aspects of the new job, and his body felt like it was being run through a meat grinder day in and day out.

Frank threw down a few crumpled bills and drained the last of his coffee. He met the waitress halfway to the door and took the Styrofoam cup from her and nodded in appreciation. "Thanks."

"Stay safe out there, hon."

As Frank pulled open the door, he glanced around the parking lot to locate his truck. As he walked towards it, a far-off sound caught his attention. It sounded—at first—like a gunshot or series of fireworks going off, though he soon discovered what it actually was.

Frank's truck exploded in a fireball a hundred feet in front of him, the force of the explosion throwing him back against the wall of the diner. Frank's truck wasn't the only one to explode, though. Three other 18-wheelers in the lot exploded within seconds of his, sending pieces of metal, glass and the contents of their trailers flying through the air.

Frank sat still on the ground for several seconds, dazed and confused about what had just happened. Stunned by the blast, he fought to catch his breath and comprehend what had just happened. Just then he heard more explosions from the highway in front of the diner. A passing truck was incinerated instantly and the trailer behind it flipped up into the air before crashing back down.

Several cars and SUVs driving behind the truck and trailer smashed into it, while others further back careened off the road as they tried to avoid the crash. As much as Frank hoped that the explosions would stop, they didn't even slow down. There were distant echoes from down the highway and on roads in the small town off to the west, though the sounds eventually faded some minutes later until they again sounded like gunshots and fireworks.

Frank struggled to his feet, bracing himself against the diner wall as he stood. His legs felt unsteady, his vision was blurry and his mind felt clouded and overwhelmed with sensory input. Inside the diner, people rushed in and out, screaming and crying and shout-ing. Several drivers and passengers had been in their cars when the large trucks exploded, and were instantly killed by the blasts. Others had been walking to or from the nearby gas station, the diner and their vehicles and had been injured.

Frank lurched forward instinctively, still dazed as he started towards his truck. After a few steps he felt a hand on his shoulder that turned him around. Frank blinked a few times and a concerned face came into focus. "Are you okay?" The man speaking to him had been sitting a few seats down from Frank at the bar munching on a chicken sandwich.

Frank looked down and held a hand against his head as he felt a sharp pain in response to the movement. "I… I think so."

The man looked down at Frank's head and shook his own. That's a nasty wound you've got there. Come on, let's get you inside and sat down." The man put his arm around Frank's shoulder and started guiding him back towards the diner.

Frank went along willingly, still trying to get a handle on what was going on. Just as they reached the diner steps the stranger ran off to try and help two other men pull open the door to a burning car. Smoke filled the air as Frank trudged up the steps and all he could hear was an endless array of screaming and shouting.

Inside, Frank slumped into one of the back booths, pulled out a wad of napkins from the dispenser on the table and pressed them against his head. As the destruction continued to rage outside, he looked up at the television above the bar as he tried to get his eyes to focus.

The overly chipper daytime talk show host that had been on the television earlier was now replaced by the pale face of a well-dressed reporter. The reporter sat behind a desk in a studio, shuffling through pieces of paper that the crew were running and handing to him as he tried to compose himself.

"We've—uh…I'm sorry. I'm sorry, ladies and gentlemen. One moment please." The reporter leaned off-camera and held a hurried, whispered conversation. "My apologies. We're doing our best to get all the facts here. This is an active story right now and what we tell you may radically change based on new information that comes in. However, as we understand it right now there's been a nationwide terrorist attack the likes of which we've never seen. We're reporting that there have been dozens and perhaps even hundreds of explosions at key rail and air facilities around the country. We're also receiving reports of thousands of smaller incidents that seem to involve 18-wheelers and—" The reporter stopped mid-sentence while someone wearing a headset came on-camera and whispered in the reporter's ear.

"What the hell is going on?" Frank mumbled to himself. He pulled the wad of blood-soaked napkins off of his head and tossed them on the table before getting a fresh handful.

The reporter nodded a few times to the person talking to him before turning back to the camera. "Folks, we're going to be cutting to a live announcement from the White House in just a few minutes. Before that, though, we wanted to update you on an AP update that just came out with some disturbing claims from the radical terrorist organization—"

The television flickered and powered off, along with the lights in the diner. Frank looked around, then glanced outside. Several people who had been in the lot and survived the explosions were sitting on the grass nearby, talking on their phones when they all took them from their ears and glanced at the screens. Remembering his own phone, Frank reached into his pocket, only to frown as he felt nothing. He dug in another pocket and frowned again, then started patting his jacket, shirt and pants to no avail.

"What the…" Not only could Frank not find his phone, but his wallet was gone as well. He turned around to see if they had fallen out into the booth or the floor below, but couldn't find any sign of them. As Frank stood up, he turned to look out the window and saw the man who had helped him. The man had his arm around another person and was helping them walk back to the diner. From his vantage point, though, Frank could see what else the man was doing—reaching into the other person's pocket.

Frank lurched forward and put one knee on the booth seat while the other banged into the table, causing him to fall forward. He barely caught himself on the window with his free hand, then regained his balance and started banging on it. "Hey! Asshole! Give me my stuff back!"

The man looked up at him, his eyes wide as he saw Frank shouting at him from inside the diner. Not waiting around to find out what Frank was saying, the man took off like a shot, disappearing a moment later beyond the gas station down the road.

Inside the diner, Frank stopped banging on the window and dropped back into his seat. He shook his head and instantly regretted the movement as a wave of pain shot through his head and neck. The waitress that had served him before came running up to him, concern written on her face. "You okay, hon?"

"I... I don't know. I'm pretty sure that guy took my phone and wallet and I think he was stealing from that lady sitting out there." Frank pulled the napkins off of his head and touched the wound gently.

The waitress gasped at the sight and ran back behind the counter to fetch a first aid kit. She sat down next to Frank and began bandaging his head, all while looking out the window and talking to him.

"I was in the walk-in taking stock until the power went off a minute ago. What happened out there? Did a gas truck explode?

Frank winced as she scrubbed his wound with antiseptic wipes. "I don't know. I was walking out to my truck when it exploded. Several others did, too. Then I came back in here and the news was on, talking about some terrorist attack when the power cut out."

The waitress's face turned white. "Terrorists? Oh God, not nine-eleven again."

Frank shrugged. "All I heard was that this is all over the country, apparently. I was—" Frank was cut off mid-sentence by a shout from the other side of the diner.

"Lucille! You got the first aid? Get over here, quick!"

The waitress glanced at Frank's head and gave him a pat on the shoulder. "I was a nurse for a few years before the hospital closed down. You'll be fine. Just try and stay off your feet as much as you can." With that, the waitress was up and moving.

Frank turned away from the billowing smoke outside the diner as he realized how much noise was coming from inside. Several of the injured had been brought inside, and all of them were crying and moaning as a few others tried to tend to their wounds. Frank stood up, still unsteady, and walked down the length of the diner, unsure of where he was going. He headed outside and walked towards his truck, shielding his face from smoke and flames as he reached the parking lot.

The trailer on Frank's truck was engulfed in flames, but the cab was still mostly intact, though it was masked by plumes of smoke. Frank broke into a run, hoping he could get up into the cab and grab some of his personal belongings before they were destroyed. When he reached the passenger door to the truck he hopped up, opened the door and ducked inside. Smoke had been leaking into the cab but it was otherwise untouched. He reached into the sleeper compartment and grabbed his backpack and threw it out onto the ground, then dug around on the floor for his spare pair of shoes and his computer.

He found his boots just as the flames found their way into the cab, fueled by the fresh supply of oxygen from when he had opened the door. Frank nearly fell backwards out onto the asphalt as he tried to get away, catching himself at the last second by the door and swinging outward. As the flames continued their slow, steady journey across the truck, Frank grabbed his backpack and shoes and broke into a run back towards the diner.

Just as Frank reached the steps to the diner, a fireball consumed the cab as the flames finally found their way into the fuel lines and tanks. Already damaged by the initial explosion in the trailer, the lines were easily compromised by the heat from the fire. Frank dropped his belongings on the ground and shielded his face with his hands, watching the fire through the cracks between his fingers. A single thought ran through Frank's mind as the flames consumed his job, his home and his life.

"What now?"

Introduction

The United States of America runs on tractor-trailers. Eighty percent of the country relies exclusively on these trucks to deliver all of their essential supplies including food, medicine, clothing and other manufactured and raw goods. Trains and planes help to transport a modest amount of our goods, but if all of the tractor-trailers in the USA vanished overnight, our country would plunge into chaos.

Over the last few decades we've transitioned from a country that transports goods in regular, moderate intervals to one where every single business—grocery stores, hardware stores and even hospitals—depend on what's known as "just in time" transit.

These businesses do not keep large amounts of stock on hand, but instead rely on small, more frequent deliveries to keep goods in stock "just in time" for when they are needed. This helps reduce cost for companies since they don't have to store large quantities of goods on-site in a warehouse. It also helps companies respond faster to fluctuations in market demand than they otherwise could.

So what would happen if tractor-trailers *did* vanish overnight? What if a terrorist organization were to—with the snap of a finger

—disrupt the single biggest and most important piece of our national shipping system?

The results would be unimaginably disastrous.

Without constant deliveries, grocery stores would run out of food in a matter of hours or perhaps a day or two at most. Hospitals would be unable to provide essential care as they would run out of basic supplies in a few days. Fuel would quickly run out as tanker trucks would no longer be able to make their daily or more frequent deliveries. Families—most of whom have no more than a few days' worth of food on hand at a time—would starve.

Our modern society operates on a razor's edge. All it would take to plunge us into chaos, anarchy and total societal collapse is the smallest of nudges one way or the other into a world where there is no sanctuary.

BOOK ONE

NO SANCTUARY

Chapter One

Inside the diner, a triage station of sorts had been set up, with Lucille moving from her position as head waitress to impromptu doctor. Her skills as a nurse hadn't been forgotten, and she was clearly in her element as she gave out instructions, forming the other waitresses into a squad of makeshift nurses under her command.

Frank, for his part, stayed as far from the commotion as he could. After dragging his backpack inside, he made a beeline for a booth at the far back corner of the diner near the bathrooms. The power had flickered back on half an hour after he came in, though the only thing showing on the TV screens was static. After searching for and locating the remote control for the television behind the counter, he spent several minutes flipping through each and every channel, but couldn't find anything except white noise.

"Damn!" Frank sighed and tossed the remote onto the table. He turned to his backpack and opened the flap and began rifling through its contents. In addition to the boots he had pulled from the backseat, he also had three other changes of undergarments, a couple of shirts, an extra pair of pants, enough toiletries for a month, a couple packs of beef jerky and a large tin of peanuts. He pulled each item out and placed it on the table in front of him, making a mental note of everything as he went along.

Though Frank wasn't too fond of the title, he was what most people called a "prepper" and as such he carried his "go bag" with him wherever he went. His go bag was his backpack, and in addition to clothing, toiletries and some emergency food, it also contained a large, flat pan at the bottom that had a watertight lid affixed. Inside the pan was a full survival kit that included matches, water purifying tablets, fishing line and lures, a signaling mirror, a magnifying glass and a whole host of other odds and ends that could be used in case of emergency.

While Frank had been an accountant, he had never subscribed to the notion of preparing for "the end of the world as we know it" or "TEOTWAWKI," but after he lost his job he started to realize just how fragile life really was. The fact that his parents were both born and bred preppers was enough to send him over the edge. In between job hunting he had helped his parents with all sorts of tasks on their Texas ranch, including restocking their emergency larder, reloading ammunition and performing maintenance on the various gadgets and appliances around their house.

Frank soon fell in love with the prepper lifestyle, and even after he was hired as a truck driver he continued practicing what he had learned. The survival case he put together was entirely of his own creation, inspired by watching a myriad of videos online and taking advice from his parents, too.

In spite of all of the time he had spent preparing for a theoretical "end of the world" scenario, Frank wasn't entirely certain what to do now that he was *in* one. In fact, he was having trouble believing that what was going on was really all that serious—but one quick glance out the window reaffirmed that whatever was going on wasn't only real, but incredibly serious.

The metal survival case was left safely tucked away inside his pack to avoid drawing attention, but Frank popped the top off while it was still inside the backpack to visually check what was inside. Once he had verified the rest of the contents of the pack, he quickly refolded the clothing and put them and the other items back into the bag.

Frank slung the backpack over his shoulder as he stood up. He walked slowly back through the diner, looking around until he spotted Lucille. She glanced at him and he waved, then she held up a finger and mouthed for him to wait. Frank sat down at the bar and watched as she held up the leg of a young boy, no older than seven, and helped his parents wrap a thick layer of gauze around a burn on his leg. When she finished, she stood up and took off a pair of disposable gloves before walking around behind the bar and heading toward Frank.

"Sorry, hon; we're not cooking anything now. We'll probably start something in an hour or so, if you want to wait."

Frank shook his head and smiled. "No, thanks, I'm good. Listen, I was wondering—do you have a phone or something I can use? My phone was kind of... stolen. And my wallet, too."

Lucille glanced at the phone on the wall behind her. "They went out a while ago, hon." She pulled a cellphone from her apron pocket and turned it on, shook her head and turned the screen around to face Frank. "See, no signal."

Frank groaned. "So there's no way to get in touch with my company? Or the cops?"

Lucille blinked at him a few times before responding. "You don't know what's going on, do you?" Frank's blank stare was all the answer she needed. She motioned down to the other end of the bar and he followed along. When they got to the other end, away from everyone else, she leaned forward and whispered to him.

"We heard some calls come in from some guys with portable CBs. They said that this thing is *everywhere*. There are trucks going up in flames all across the state and the country. Nobody's driving anywhere right now. Even folks with regular cars are too scared to drive. All the planes are grounded and apparently even some boats were hit. Whoever did this has everyone all scared." Lucille stood back up and gave Frank a sad smile. "I'm sorry, sugar. We're all stuck here for the time being. This is bigger than... well, bigger than *anything*."

Frank sat on the barstool and rubbed his eyes as he tried to comprehend what she was saying. "So there's like… no way to contact the company, then?"

"Hon." Lucille put her hand on Frank's arm. "You must have hit your head harder than I thought. I'm telling you that your company is probably gone. Yours isn't the only rig that's burning right now. They're burning across the whole *country*. This is some kind of big terrorist attack or something."

Lucille's words finally hit home, and when combined with what he remembered from the brief newscast earlier, he suddenly felt a wave of nausea hit him. Lucille looked at him with concern, but one of the other waitresses ran up to her before she could say anything else.

"Lucy—they brought another one in. He's hurt bad."

Lucille glanced back at Frank and gave him another sympathetic pat on the arm. "Take it easy there, hon. You should go sit back down in a booth, give your head some time to catch up with you."

Frank nodded slowly as Lucille dashed off, then promptly ignored her suggestion as he stood up and headed toward the front door. Outside once again, Frank breathed deeply of the smoke-filled air, wrinkling his nose at the taste and smell. Across the parking lot were the scattered remains of burned and damaged vehicles, though not a single one of them looked drivable.

Frank started walking in the direction of the gas station, not entirely certain where he was going, but knowing that he didn't want to stay in the diner any longer. Being cooped up in the place was making his head hurt, and he wanted some space to try and get a handle on his thoughts.

If what Lucille said was true, and whatever happened to his rig had happened to others, he was most certainly without a job. The feeling of unemployment, though, meant nothing in the face of being stuck in a remote part of a state where he had never been, and over a thousand miles away from his closest family.

Frank picked up his pace as he neared the gas station, and a plan started forming in his mind. It was still early in the afternoon, and he had passed a larger town a few miles back, before the diner. He could get to it before the sun went down and they would surely have some sort of phone service that he could use to contact his employer. If things really were as bad as Lucille had predicted, Frank would have to find some way of getting back to Texas and his parents. How he would do that, though, was a problem he wasn't entirely certain how to solve.

Chapter Two

The small newsroom is—for the first time in its existence—consumed in chaos. Not even the string of tornadoes that hit the region a few years prior caused as large of a stir. After the power shuts off and the emergency generators kick in, reports begin flooding in across the newswire. The journalists are too stunned to speak, merely standing and reading silently as the reports stream across the monitors.

FOUR HUNDRED DEAD on a highway in Los Angeles during rush hour after two tractor-trailers explode.

Fifty-nine dead and scores injured after a freight train carrying toxic chemical waste is derailed into a residential neighborhood.

Three separate explosions shake the main east coast sorting hubs for two of the nation's largest logistics and shipping companies.

Hundreds feared dead at seven different ports; Customs and Border Patrol have yet to release official numbers.

Three oil refineries along the Gulf Coast are in flames after vehicles at the facilities burst into flames.

White House orders immediate deployment of Coast Guard and reserve units to four major metropolitan cities as part of a wide scale search and rescue mission.

Civilians are advised to stay in their homes and avoid public areas.

Martial law has been declared in Manhattan, Los Angeles, Miami and dozens of other cities after widespread damage.

The reporters and staff in the newsroom can scarcely believe their eyes. Their small town has yet to see any of the horrors described in the incoming reports, but there is no denying the fact that something terrible is happening.

"Listen up, everyone." The station manager claps his hands and motions for everyone in the room to circle up around him. "The main phone lines are dead right now, but we've still got web access—for now. I want everyone to their computers gathering as much information as you can. Call, video chat, talk to your sources. I don't care what you have to do to get more info. Just do it!"

A flurry of activity begins as staff and reporters alike begin scouring the web, piecing together what information they can. The station's backup generators hold a few days' worth of fuel, but once that fails, they won't be able to broadcast anymore. The station manager checks his watch. An hour till prime time. With any luck, they'll have something concrete to pass on to their viewers, though he doubts it will matter. The reports continue to stream in and he studies them intently. 'Things,' he thinks, 'are only going to get worse, aren't they?'

Chapter Three

Frank moved down the highway at a fast pace until he saw the smoking wreckage of a large pileup ahead of him. A lone ambulance was on the scene, its lights flashing, and multiple people were running around, trying to use bottles of water and small fire extinguishers to put out the massive blaze. He thought about trying to help, but the sight of another ambulance racing down the opposite side of the highway and stopping near the wreckage was enough to prompt him to keep moving.

After climbing over a short fence that separated the highway from the median, Frank moved to a service road that appeared to be abandoned and disused. Grass and weeds grew from cracks in the asphalt and the service road wound between small hills, keeping parallel with the highway but meandering along instead of cutting a straight path. The air was brisk and fresh, but every time the wind changed Frank picked up on the scent of something new that was burning on the highway nearby.

Frank completely missed the name of the small town after passing the sign for it, but as he walked down the idyllic streets, he was sure it was something that ended in "-ville" or "-burg." Wide-trunked oak trees sat in every yard, and the leaves they had long since shed in preparation for winter were scattered about in the yards and streets, adding stunning red and orange accents to the neighborhoods. Frank wasn't used to much physical exertion and the two-hour walk left him out of breath and tired. He trudged along through the residential neighborhood, keeping his eyes open for any signs of movement nearby.

When the first car drove past, it turned out to be an electric vehicle, and it startled him as it appeared out of the corner of his eye. He tried waving and shouting at the driver, but they accelerated instead of slowing down, blowing through a stop sign and turning at the next street up.

"Asshole." Frank grumbled and then sighed as he begrudgingly admitted to himself that he would probably do the same thing. "I guess it's good that there are still cars that are running, though. Means that whatever happened wasn't some kind of EMP or something crazy like that."

The thought, while initially comforting, became a source of discomfort as Frank thought back to the news announcement he had seen in the diner. A terrorist attack that was large enough to disrupt the entire country would have to have been absolutely massive in scope and scale. If trucks and other transportation-related hubs were attacked first, he wondered what targets would be next.

Most of the houses that Frank passed didn't have any cars outside, though their garage doors were closed shut and he assumed their vehicles were inside. He stopped at the first house he saw with a car parked outside and walked up the driveway, crossed the yard to the front porch and stood nervously at the front door. He was more than aware of how he looked, but he didn't have much of choice but to start ringing doorbells and asking for help.

Bzzzzz.

The doorbell was metallic in sound, though hearing it meant that the power outage at the diner had been isolated. *Maybe a truck hit a power pole along the highway.* He waited at the door for a full minute before pressing the button again, then followed it up with a few loud knocks on the door.

"Hello?" Frank shouted as loudly as felt comfortable. "If anyone's home, I could really use some help. I just need to make a phone call!"

There was no response, and after two more attempts at knocking and ringing the bell, Frank sighed and headed back to the street, giving the car in the driveway a longing glance as he went. Three more houses with cars parked outside went the same way, and Frank started getting nervous about the fact that no one was answering their doors.

"Oh come on, people." Frank threw up his hands in frustration at the fourth house and stomped through the yard. "How can it be that *nobody's* home?"

Several gunshots from further down the street were the answer to his question. Frank ducked and scurried to the side of the street, looking around as he tried to identify where the shots were coming from. Three more followed in rapid succession, and though they didn't appear to be aimed in his direction, they sounded very close by. While Frank initially hesitated to head in the direction of the shots, he still needed to find a phone or transportation, and given the lack of response he had gotten so far in the town, he didn't see many other options.

"Lovely." Frank grumbled as he picked up his pace and began jogging in the general direction of the shots. Guns weren't a stranger to Frank, though he had found little use for them in his day-to-day life. On his parent's ranch he had practiced with everything from Derringers to a 50 caliber Barrett, but once he took a job with the trucking company, he hadn't gotten enough time off the road to catch up on sleep, much less to have any sort of fun at the range.

As Frank drew closer to the source of the gunshots, he started to hear other loud noises, too. More than a few vehicles were revving their engines and dozens of people were shouting and screaming at each other. Frank emerged from a road leading from the residential neighborhood into the commercial part of town. The city was apparently larger than he had originally thought, as there was a divided four-lane highway a short way ahead of him. A narrow two-lane road ran parallel to the highway, and there were periodic intersections that allowed drivers on one road to reach the other.

The two-lane road led to a variety of small shops to the left and right of where Frank was located, and the sound seemed to be coming to his right, down toward a gas station. Leaving the relative peace of the residential neighborhood behind, Frank turned off of the street and ran along the thick wooded area that acted as a noise and visual barrier between the commercial area of the city and the residential neighborhood. The road, being open and providing little in the way of protection, was a far less appealing route when there were gunshots and shouting involved.

Two more shots went off, confirming for Frank that the source for them was, indeed, the gas station up ahead. He kept to the trees as he approached the station from the side until he was close enough to clearly make out what was going on.

Dozens of cars crowded the station, their drivers revving their engines and honking furiously. The lucky few near the pumps tried to ignore the noise around them and fill their tanks. As one driver opened his trunk and pulled out a small red plastic gas can, the person sitting in the vehicle behind him opened his door and shouted at him. "No cans! Just your car, asshole!"

The man tried to ignore the shout, but the word "cans" was like a dinner bell to the surrounding vehicles. The man pumping his gas barely had time to close his trunk and hop back into his car before he was surrounded by a swarm of people beating on his windows and shouting at him. So many people had tried to pull into the station that there was no way in or out, forcing the man to crouch down in his car and hope that the anger from the surrounding people would die down.

Another gunshot rang out and Frank ducked, though the people at the pumps acted like they didn't even hear it. At a small outbuilding along the side of the gas station, though, a group of four people jumped back and began shouting wildly. Frank looked closer and saw that there was a woman inside the outbuilding though he couldn't make out any details about her. What he could make out, however, was the heated shouting match she was having with the small group outside her building.

"I said leave me the hell alone!"

"Lady, you took *way* too much gas! Hand over your keys, let us empty out your truck and you can go!"

"Like hell! I keep telling you assholes I was here before this whole shitshow started! That gas is mine—bought and paid for, unlike what you morons are trying to do!"

One of the four, a tall muscular man in a t-shirt advanced on the door, holding a metal pipe in his hands. He tried to be sneaky, but the building had a wraparound window and the woman spotted him before he got close.

BANG!

The shot threw up a spray of asphalt in the man's face as the ground in front of him exploded. He dropped the pipe and threw his hands up to his eyes as he backed up, and the shouting began anew.

"We're not leaving here till you give us those keys, lady!"

"Screw you!"

The four gathered in a huddle, with the tall man keeping a wary eye on the outbuilding. They held a hasty conversation before the older woman cast an evil grin toward the outbuilding and the woman trapped inside. "Don't say we didn't try to do this the nice way!"

The woman inside the outbuilding frowned as the group of four backed up, away from the outbuilding, and then shouted at the crowd near the pumps. "Hey! There's gas over here! This lady's got her truck and this building loaded down with cans!"

It took a moment, but the crowd slowly responded to the cries of the four, and several more people began migrating toward the outbuilding. Frank's eyes narrowed as he watched the situation rapidly devolve, wondering what he could do to help. The woman had managed to hold off the four without much trouble, but with a larger crowd it would only be a matter of time before they rushed her. At best she would lose her vehicle and at worst... well, Frank didn't want to consider that.

"Dammit." Frank whispered to himself as he looked around for a way to help the woman trapped inside the outbuilding. The crowd was becoming increasingly hostile, and he was afraid of what might happen if she started shooting again.

Up the hill from the gas station, a few dozen feet away from Frank, sat a beige sedan. The paint was peeling and it looked like it had been out in the elements for a few years. It was parked in the grass off of the feeder road and pointed at the direction of the outhouse, which gave Frank an idea. He ran to the sedan and peered inside, noting with great satisfaction that it had a manual transmission. Frank tossed his backpack on the ground next to the sedan and pulled on the driver's side door, which opened with ease.

"I guess if you have a car this ugly you don't worry about somebody stealing it." Frank mumbled to himself as he slid into the seat, his pants scraping over layers of old duct tape that were the only thing holding the upholstery together. The interior of the car was caked in a greasy yellow film while cigarette butts and ash were overflowing from the ashtray next to the shifter.

Frank glanced up at the outbuilding one last time as if to confirm his decision. The original four were now climbing on and inside the woman's truck, having broken the driver's side window to gain access to the interior. The woman inside the outbuilding wasn't able to do anything about it, though, as the larger crowd was still shouting at her and harassing her. The only thing that appeared to be holding them back from rushing at the outbuilding and the gasoline they thought was inside was her gun, which she kept pointed at the crowd as she shouted for them to back off.

"Why is it I'm doing this?" Frank shook his head and put his foot on the sedan's brake. "Because if I don't, they're going to kill her." He popped the emergency brake off. "Of course, she might kill one of them first. Or me." The shifter stuck as he jammed it out of first gear and into neutral. "Then again this might kill me, her and any of those assholes, too."

Frank sighed in resignation as he let off the brake. The car began rolling forward slowly and he held tight to the wheel, trying to keep the car moving straight. When it was going a few miles an hour, he opened the driver's side door and jammed his arm down on the horn. The noise cut through the shouting of the crowd like a knife, and they turned in unison to see the source.

Frank jumped out of the sedan and rolled twice on the grass before he could stop. He turned and watched as the crowd parted like an ocean, their attention immediately drawn to both the car and the man who had driven it into their midst. Frank cupped his hands and shouted at the woman as the car bounced along the pavement. "Run!"

Already sensing the opening, the woman was halfway out the door by the time Frank called out to her. She chased after the sedan as it rolled across the parking lot toward her truck, then impacted against the back side, bouncing off and continuing its path out behind the gas station. Two of the people in the crowd had been slow to get out of the way, and had been grazed by the sedan's mirrors as it hurtled through their midst.

The ones who really suffered, though, were the original four who were in the midst of ransacking the woman's truck when the sedan hit it. The two who were standing in the back throwing gas cans out onto the ground were knocked off the truck immediately, and fell to the ground with howls of pain. One was standing near the front of the truck when the sedan struck, and the truck moved several inches forward from the impact, knocking him down.

The older woman who had been shouting with the owner of the truck was in the driver's seat, feeling around under the seats. After the sedan bounced off the side of the truck she opened the door, only to find a shotgun inches from her face.

"Get out of my truck. Now."

The older woman snarled as she climbed out, and the owner of the truck clambered in. She locked the doors and started the truck, threw it into reverse and hit the gas as hard as she could. The wheels of the truck shrieked against the ground, throwing smoke into the air as they bit into the pavement and strove to find traction.

After watching the sedan make the crowd near the outbuilding scatter, Frank had hurried back up the hill to grab his backpack.

He was planning to try and slip away when he heard the roar of an engine heading towards him. He turned to see the large green truck flying up the hill, sending dirt and grass into the air as it skidded to a stop next to him.

"Hop in, quick!" The woman gestured to the seat beside her. Frank hesitated for a split second as he looked at the crowd down at the gas station. The group that had been scattered by the sedan had regrouped. Led by the four people who were originally harassing the owner of the truck, they were streaming up the hill, shouting obscenities.

"You going to get in, or should I leave you here to talk to them?" The woman shouted at Frank again and he leapt into action, scrambling around the front of her truck and climbing in just as she hit the gas again. The truck continued backward, following the same general path Frank had taken to reach the gas station, until they hit the road. The woman spun the wheel and the truck skidded around to face the neighborhood before she put the transmission into second gear and took off.

With his pack still on his back, Frank sat sideways in his seat, awkwardly trying to keep from sliding onto the floor, bouncing up against the roof and falling sideways against the woman driving. His fingers and knuckles were bone white by the time the truck started to slow down and finally stopped after making several turns over the course of a mile.

Frank looked up at the woman, opening his mouth to comment on her driving skills when he saw the barrel of a pistol pointed straight at his chest.

"Get out."

Frank raised his hands slowly and scooted back across the seat until he felt his pack press up against the window and door. "Hey, whoa, what're you doing?"

"Nothing personal. I appreciate the help back there, but I don't need any passengers."

Frank snorted in derision and shook his head. "What the hell, lady? You were about to get eaten alive back there and this is the kind of thanks I get?"

The woman shrugged. "Like I said, nothing personal."

"So you're going to leave me here with… what? Nothing? To just walk? Where am I supposed to go, exactly? Back into town for one of those maniacs to see me and remember who I am?"

The woman's eyes narrowed and Frank saw the barrel of the gun waver ever so slightly as she weighed what he said. After a long, harrowing minute, she lowered the gun and nodded at him. "Fine. You can ride along as far as the state border. After that, though, you're on your own."

Frank dropped his hands slowly and let out a long sigh of relief. "I'll take that over a hole in my chest, thanks."

The woman slid the pistol beneath her left leg, leaving it in a position where she could easily grab it again. She motioned at Frank with a roll of her head. "Better get your pack off and on the floor and get a seatbelt on. No telling how bumpy this ride's gonna get."

Frank unclipped the waist strap for his backpack and shrugged it off, then slid it down onto the floor between his feet. As he reached for his seatbelt, he gave the woman a long glance, studying her in depth.

She was taller than he thought at first at around six feet, slender and sporting light tan and blonde hair pulled up into a tight ponytail. She was wearing jeans with mud and grass stains around the cuffs and a button-down long-sleeved work shirt that was rolled up to her elbows. The woman looked to be in her early thirties and she and her truck both smelled like motor oil and gasoline. The stains on her arms and the backs of her hands spoke to the fact that she had been working on some sort of vehicle recently.

Frank stuck out his hand as she jammed the truck into gear and coughed. "My name's Frank, by the way. Frank Richards."

The woman glanced at him, then at his hand, then back at him without taking it. "Linda Rollins."

Frank withdrew his hand slowly and turned away to look at the window, rolling his eyes as he did. "Great to meet you, Linda. Thanks for the ride, by the way."

Linda merely grunted in response, and the pair sat in silence as she drove through the neighborhood, winding her way out to the feeder road where Frank had come in. When he saw where they were going, he spoke up again. "Uh, why are we going back to the highway?"

"It's the fastest way out of here."

"Yeah… see, I kind of need to get to a phone. I was a few miles down the road eating lunch when my truck just sort of…"

"Exploded?"

Frank nodded. "Yeah, basically."

Linda grunted again.

"You, uh, saw it yourself?" Frank probed gently, hoping to get her to open up a bit.

Linda didn't say anything for a few seconds as she swerved around the remnants of a tractor-trailer that was spread out across the highway. When the truck stopped weaving and was driving straight again, she glanced over at Frank. "You don't know much about what's going on here, do you?"

Frank shook his head slowly. "I… I don't know. I saw a few seconds of the news before the power went out. Some kind of big terrorist attack."

Linda snorted. "Some kind? This is *the* attack." Frank felt a shiver go down his spine as she continued. "My brother's a SIGINT analyst down in Washington."

"What's SIGINT?"

"Signals intelligence. Intercepting electronic communications. He called me yesterday, out of the blue, haven't talked to him in weeks. He sounded freaked out on the phone. Said I needed to get as much fuel as I could and then get as far away from the major cities as possible. He couldn't tell me any more, but he sounded genuine. I woke up this morning and packed a few things, went to the station and started filling up cans. Next thing I know half the trucks driving by are exploding, the power's flickering and everyone starts going insane."

Frank nodded silently as he recalled the panic that had gripped those in and around the diner. "Is that when you got stuck there?"

Linda rolled her eyes and sighed. "No. I was an idiot. I had plenty of gas to get to my parents' place down in Tennessee. But I wanted to make extra sure I was prepared. So I stopped back at the station after getting a few more things from my house. I thought I'd be able to fill up another can but... well. Yeah. You saw."

"It was insanity."

"That's not even the worst of it." Linda reached down to the radio and turned it on, then spun the dial as she tried to find a station within range. "I don't think anybody's still broadcasting, or if they are they're the ones lucky enough to still have power. After I fueled up the first time and headed back home I stayed glued to the radio."

She stopped speaking for a moment as she navigated another wreck on the highway and Frank asked the obvious question. "And? What did you hear?"

"That this is a hell of a lot bigger than a few trucks blowing up."

Chapter Four

"Anything new coming in?"

A balding man with a sweat-stained collar and loosened tie shakes his head without looking up from the screen of his computer. "Nothing new. More places are losing power from the cascading failures. If the Texas or California grids take another hit then nobody will be able to get them back online."

"Got a source for that?"

The balding man grabs a piece of paper off of the desk next to him and hands it over his shoulder to the woman standing behind him. She pats him on the back. "Keep doing what you can. I'll get this on air ASAP."

The woman carries the paper out of the dimly lit room and down the hall. The air in the building is stifling hot. Though it's already autumn the weather is in the nineties, and the small Kansas town is wilting under the intense heat. Fuel in the station's backup generator is dangerously low, leaving the station manager a choice between extending their broadcasting abilities by a few more hours or cooling down the building.

As the woman enters the broadcast room, she slows down and circles around the ring of cameras that are pointed at the two on-air personalities. With the small station one of the few left with power in the region, it has become a central hub of information that is being rebroadcast across the nation. A station that once counted a story about a new restaurant opening in town as *its story of the year is now responsible for disseminating information about the breakdown of society itself.*

The pair that sit in front of the cameras are out of their element. The bright studio lights cause their makeup to run, they are sweating, stumbling over their words and unable to cope with what they are reading. Their broadcast goes out over radio, television and the internet. It is coarse and imprecise but it is one of the few sources of information left.

"We, uh, just got this in." The woman holding the paper walks quickly up to the desk, drops it in front of the hosts and leaves. The man sitting at the desk glances nervously at his co-anchor, then picks up the paper.

"We're looking at reports from power companies in both Texas and, uhh… California. They're reporting that the cascading blackouts are only going to get worse, and a total failure of the electrical grid isn't far away." The man wipes the sweat from his brow with an already-soaked handkerchief and looks at the camera.

"For those of you out there who can still hear us, we've got about three more hours until our generator is dry and we can't broadcast anymore. If you're in a large city, we encourage you to shelter in place and follow the instructions of your local law enforcement and government officials. We have no new information on…" The man glanced down at a few other pieces of paper. "No updated information on FEMA and the Army Corps of Engineering and their attempts to restore power, but we believe they are still working with power companies to get things working as quickly as possible."

The man glances at his co-anchor and she nods, then picks up where he left off. They ad-lib what they are saying, as the teleprompter isn't functioning. "If you're in one of the affected areas, we want to remind you again, to shelter in place. If you need supplies like medicine, food or water, federal and state agencies are working to set up distribution points, so you shouldn't try to venture out on your own. Also please keep in mind that the White House and FBI have declared the ongoing situation as active, meaning that they believe that more terrorist actions may be forthcoming. For that reason you should stay away from heavily populated areas, avoid vehicles and any forms of transportation."

"That's right, Lacey." Her co-anchor takes over again. "Most major public transportation systems have been shut down after the devastation caused in Manhattan's subway system and, of course, all flights have been grounded indefinitely until we can figure out what's going on."

The woman who delivered the piece of paper to the anchors watches them for a moment before slipping out of the broadcast room. She heads back down the hall, doing another round to pick up any new information gathered by the journalists who are scattered about the building. With only a precious few hours left, every single piece of information that comes in may prove useful.

Chapter Five

"Wait a second. What do you mean *nobody's* driving?" Frank stared out the front windshield of the truck as it barreled down the highway, slowing only when there happened to be an odd car or wreck in their way.

"Okay, so there are a few people still driving—like us, for example. But that's what I heard earlier, and you can see it now. We're pretty much the only car on a highway that should be packed to the gills."

Frank rubbed his eyes and shook his head, having trouble coming to terms with what Linda had spent the last half hour explaining to him. Earlier in the day she had picked up a radio broadcast from a New York station that was rebroadcasting from a station that was in the Washington, D.C. area. The broadcast was a mixture of informational reports and cautionary tales from stories across the country.

One of the most frightening bits of news she passed on to Frank was that the destruction he had heard about on the television was far greater than he realized. Enough bombs had been planted and then remotely detonated in shipping containers, tractor-trailers, trains and even in a few private vehicles that the transportation grid in the country had effectively ground to a halt.

Truck drivers that hadn't been affected were refusing to even go near their vehicles. The federal government had grounded all planes. Trains and mass transportation grids in larger cities had shut down. Even the general population, as they started to learn about what had happened, was beginning to rapidly abandon their vehicles, afraid that they might be one of the unfortunate few to have been targeted.

"Did you hear about any sort of pattern to the attacks? I mean, it sounds like whoever did this was just trying to shut everything down." Frank moved around in his seat, trying to find a more comfortable position.

"I don't think there was a pattern except to try and shut everything down. Whoever did this caused just enough destruction to scare everyone. And now that people won't travel and shipments of basically everything are shut down, things are going to get very bad, very fast."

"No kidding, and especially with the power outages. How long do you think that'll take to get fixed?"

Linda raised an eyebrow and glanced over at Frank. "Months? Years? The little dab I heard before the station went dead was that the rolling blackouts were caused by physical damage to plants and infrastructure. Some of those parts can take several years to replace. Whoever did this was smart—really smart. They chose the perfect way to cause a tremendous amount of chaos."

"I just...I don't understand." Frank struggled to form the words. "How... how could anyone—or any organization—manage to destroy a few hundred trucks. I mean, I understand the effect. I wouldn't go within a hundred feet of one right now. But the sheer logistics of managing that, and remaining undetected... it's mind-boggling."

"No kidding. Not to mention hitting everything else." Linda sighed and clenched her jaw. "Whatever. I just need to get home, make sure my parents are fine and then I'll figure out what to do from there."

The way that Linda managed to cycle between sounding friendly and sounding aloof was still a mystery to Frank. He felt like he was being open, forthright and transparent with her, but was receiving nothing but a stone wall with the minimum required amount of human interaction back. *Maybe if I'm nice to her she won't kick me out.*

"So your parents are where? Tennessee?"

"Pigeon Forge."

"Hey, that's a nice place! I remember visiting Dollywood when I was a kid. The cabin we stayed in had a lot of spiders." Linda's face remained stoic, but Frank swore he heard her snort in slight amusement. "What do they do down there?"

"They're…" Linda licked her lips hesitantly. "They're retired."

Frank could sense the uneasiness and worry in Linda's answer. "I'm sure they're fine."

"Yeah, I don't know about that. That's why I need to get there." Linda shook her head slightly and glanced over at Frank. "So what's your story? You said you were a trucker?"

Frank laughed. "Barely. I started a month ago. I was an accountant for most of my life. Everything dried up and I moved in with my folks in Texas for a while, then got a job with a little trucking company. Not exactly my cup of tea but hey, I've gotta work at something."

Linda nodded approvingly. "Nicely done. Not a lot of folks would take that kind of a downgrade. How's life been treating you on the road?"

"Almost no sleep, long hours, barely any pay." Frank smiled. "Better than nothing, I guess."

They rode in silence for several more minutes before Frank spoke up again. "So what's your plan for everything once you get back to your parents? Do you have any kids?"

Linda kept her eyes on the road as she replied. "No kids. Never found the time or the person. As for a plan, that's hard to say. My folks still own a bit of land down there a few miles from the city, as long as they haven't sold it yet. I can take them there, take care of them and ride this out as best as I can."

"They don't live on the land?" Frank asked.

Linda responded hesitantly. "They don't live on it. No. Mom had a stroke three years ago, then dad had one a year after her. They're in a nursing home right now."

"Oh wow. I'm really sorry."

Linda coughed and shifted in her seat, her expression hardening. "I don't need you to feel bad for me or them."

"Huh?" Frank started to protest. "I'm really sorry I asked. Forget about it, okay?"

"It is what it is." Linda tightened her grip on the steering wheel and twisted it sharply. "What about your parents?"

"They're down in Texas. They're uh… 'preppers' I guess you could call them." Frank noticed Linda's expression softening at the sound of this, and he continued. "I never really bought into all that stuff till I stayed with them for a few months before I got my new job."

"Did they turn you into one?"

Frank laughed and patted his bag. "I don't think I could ever be on their level. But yeah, they wore off on me a bit and I learned a few things." Frank eyed Linda closely. "Something tells me you're familiar with their way of life."

Linda slid her eyes over to look at him, studying him closely. "Something like that, yeah."

"Awesome." Frank nodded with satisfaction, then turned back to look at the road. The hills and trees whipped by at eighty miles an hour as Linda kept the truck speeding along. Frank counted the number of other vehicles he saw driving and in the course of three hours saw five in total. None of them were commercial, and they were all loaded down with people and luggage, indicating that the passengers inside were trying to get away from or to somewhere.

Darkness soon crept up as the sun slipped beyond the horizon, putting an end to the worst day that Frank could remember in a very long time. As tired as he had been earlier at the diner, he hadn't been able to sleep at all in the truck. A few short conversations had passed between Linda and himself, but for the most part they stayed quiet, each of them lost in their own thoughts.

Frank smiled slightly as he thought about his parents on their ranch and how they would have undoubtedly reacted to the disaster that was unfolding across the country. Unlike most other people, his parents wouldn't have panicked, since they had a plan for every single potential societal breakdown possible. *Hell*, he thought, *they're probably happier than they've been in a long time.* Being stuck on the other side of the country from his only family was a problem, but with a bit of luck he'd be seeing them again before too many more days passed. *Besides, it can't be as bad as Linda's making it out to be.*

The encroachment of artificial lighting into the most remote places in the United States meant that there were few places left where the majesty of the night sky could be fully enjoyed. National parks and isolated patches of wilderness were the last bastions of freedom from light pollution where one could look up at the sky and see the vastness of the universe laid out as if for one's personal benefit.

Frank leaned forward and looked up through the windshield, shaking his head and whistling softly. The inky blackness of the sky was punctuated by innumerable pinpoints of bright twinkling light that were more majestic than he had seen before. "Wow." He muttered softly to himself, taking in the majesty of the sight.

Next to him, Linda leaned forward slightly and smiled. "I guess that's one benefit of the power being out everywhere."

"You think this means the blackouts are nationwide?"

Linda shrugged. "That's what it sounded like on the radio. I know there are towns all over the place on either side of this highway, so if we're seeing the sky like this, I'm pretty sure the power's out pretty much everywhere around here. Wouldn't surprise me if it's the same across the country."

A soft chime rang out and Linda sighed. "Getting low on gas. I'll have to pull over and fill the tank."

Frank could sense the tension in her voice and tried to put her at ease. "I'll get out and fill it up, if that'll make you feel more comfortable." He watched her grip on the steering wheel relax and she nodded.

"Thanks, that'd be great."

"No problem."

There were no exits anywhere in the next several miles, so Linda pulled over when the shoulder of the road grew wide and there was enough room to get the truck completely off the highway. "Doubt we'll see any traffic, but better to be safe, especially in the dark." She nodded at Frank. "Cans are in the back."

Frank hopped out and dutifully walked around to the back of the truck. Linda's continued distrust of him was starting to wear thin, but the last thing he wanted to do was to piss her off and get stranded out in the middle of nowhere. He pulled a couple of gas cans out of the back of the truck and brought them around to the side. The cap cover popped open as Linda pulled the lever inside the truck, then he heard the driver's side door open.

"Hey." Linda hopped out of her seat and Frank could see that her pistol was tucked into the side of her pants. "Look, I'm sorry for treating you like this." She walked up to him and took the can he was holding and unscrewed the cap, flipped the spout over and began pouring it into the tank.

Frank took a step back and eyed her warily. "You don't need to trust me; I can understand the reluctance."

"It's not that I don't trust you…"

Frank snorted and crossed his arms. "I think the gun says differently. But I understand, and it's okay. I appreciate you taking me as far as you can south. I'll figure something else out when you're ready for me to leave."

Linda threw the empty gas can into the back of the truck and uncapped the second can. "Let's just take this one step at a time, all right?"

Frank watched Linda finish filling the truck, wondering what was going on inside her head. After the second can went into the back of the truck, Linda glanced at Frank. "Let's get going. A couple more hours and we can look for a place to stop and rest."

Chapter Six

Frank realized he was dozing on and off when he kept bumping his head against the window and waking himself up. He didn't fight it, but was starting to get frustrated by his inability to completely fall asleep when the truck took a sharp turn to the right, pushing him against his seatbelt and causing him to reach out for the dashboard to keep from falling sideways.

"Sorry." Linda yawned from the driver's seat and nodded in the direction they were going. "I saw a place that looked good to stop for the night."

"Where are we anyway?" Frank stretched and rubbed his eyes. "Seems like we've been going for more than a few hours."

Linda glanced in the rearview mirror and nodded. "Yeah, I haven't liked the look of any of the places we've passed."

"Wasn't there a rest area or two that we went by? I was sort of falling asleep so maybe I missed something."

"Rest areas are going to be a prime target for the kind of folks we want to steer clear of." The road grew bumpier as the truck rolled along a rough dirt road. Ahead of them a few hundred feet the headlights picked up the shape of a large wooden building with peeling red paint and a disturbingly angled roof.

"What is this place?" Frank squinted at the building and the area surrounding it, trying to figure out where they were.

"Looks like a farm, but nobody's been back here in a while based on the condition of the road and the overgrowth. It's a perfect place to get a few hours of sleep."

Frank raised an eyebrow. "Out in an isolated place like this? You sure about that?"

Linda's right hand fell off the steering wheel and lingered near her hip. "I'm not saying I trust you, Frank, but I'd rather rest up with someone who hasn't been trying to kill me all day than take my chance with people I know absolutely nothing about. Besides, I'll be sleeping in the truck with the doors locked while you take your shift."

Frank laughed and shook his head. "Whatever you say, Linda. I'm just along for the ride."

The truck eased to a stop and Frank unbuckled his seatbelt. "I'll go check it out." Linda nodded and shut off the engine, though she kept the lights on.

Frank slipped out of the truck and closed the door gently, raising his head to look at the building in front of him. The barn was old, at least thirty or forty years, and was in rough shape. The grass and brush growing up against it hadn't been trimmed in several months and one of the two doors on the front hung at an odd angle, offering a glimpse of the interior. Trees butted up against the back side of the barn while fields, brush and under-growth surrounded it on the other three sides. If there was a house on the property it wasn't nearby or was hidden by the woods on the opposite side of the barn.

Frank approached the entrance to the barn cautiously, and peeked inside, using the light from the truck to see. The interior looked surprisingly clean and neat compared to the outside, with a couple of older tractors parked next to each other and several farming attachments for the tractors arranged on the floor of the barn. Several bales of hay were stacked near the front, giving off a familiar odor that Frank remembered from his parents' ranch.

He put his shoulder up against the crooked door and gave it a push. The rails at the top and bottom squealed in protest, but with a bit of effort he was able to slide it open a few feet. Behind him, Linda stepped out of the car and walked up next to him carrying two flashlights. She handed one to him and peered inside the barn. "Looks cozy."

Frank laughed and looked back at the truck. "Better than trying to sleep in the front seat of that thing. Anyway, do you want to take the first watch, or me, or just both try and get some sleep at the same time?"

Linda turned and pointed at a long black and brown object that was hanging from her shoulder. "Here, take this." Frank raised his eyebrows as he saw the shape of a hunting rifle hanging from a strap. He grabbed the barrel and pulled it from her shoulder, then eyed her with confusion.

"I'm sorry, but I thought you didn't trust me."

"I don't." She took a small bag off her other shoulder and held it out. "Extra ammo and some batteries for your light."

"Why are you giving me all this?" Frank was completely confused, and wasn't sure what was going on.

"Like I said, I don't trust you. But you haven't tried to kill me yet, and you're going to be useless while you're on watch if you don't have a weapon." Linda turned and headed back to the truck. "I'm going to get a couple hours sleep. Come wake me up if you hear or see anything."

Linda climbed back in the truck, closed the door and shut off the headlights. Frank could hear the click of the locks engaging and could just barely make out Linda leaning over to lay across the seats. He put the small bag of ammo and the rifle over his shoulder and wandered into the barn, using his light to examine every inch of it as he slowly walked around.

Linda's behavior went beyond confusing and Frank had no idea what to make of it. She fully admitted that she didn't trust him, but she was still willing to give him a weapon and apparently go to sleep while he took the first watch. He suspected she was up to something, but wasn't sure what it was yet. He took a few moments to check the ammunition she had given him for the rifle, and couldn't find any problems with either the gun or the ammo. He was tempted to take a test shot just to be sure, but thought better of it.

In the back of Frank's mind was the lingering temptation to betray Linda's seeming trust by taking her truck, leaving her behind and heading for Texas. As much as he wanted to get back on the road, he wasn't willing to go that far. *Then again, I did nearly kill a few people by pushing a car into the midst of them.*

After exploring the rest of the barn, Frank went back outside and scanned the woods and fields around the building with his flashlight. The highway off to his left was eerily quiet, and with no sign of artificial lights anywhere, he suddenly felt extremely isolated. He occupied the following two hours by exploring the barn more, wandering up and down the dirt road they had driven in on and leaning against the side of the truck to watch the stars.

When Frank finally heard the click of a door opening, it startled him and he whirled around, turning on his flashlight while he fumbled to get the rifle off of his shoulder.

"Not bad." Linda smiled at him as she stepped out of the car, making a show of stretching her arms and back while yawning. There were still bags under her eyes, though, and her whole face and demeanor betrayed the fact that she hadn't slept a wink.

"Yeah, well." Frank relaxed and lowered his light. "There's been absolutely nothing going on tonight. Not even a car going by on the highway that I've heard."

"That's good." Linda looked up at the sky and checked her watch before circling around to the other side of the truck. "You ready to get a couple hours sleep before we move on?"

Frank followed Linda slowly, trying to figure out what she was up to. "Nah, I'm feeling a lot better now. I wouldn't mind sleeping in the car, to be honest."

"Oh, I wouldn't do that." Linda opened the passenger door and glanced at Frank. "We're going to go through a big city next, and we both need to be rested up in case something happens." She reached into the truck and pulled out Frank's pack before holding it out to him with a smile that Frank swore looked forced. "Here; in case you want a change of clothes or something."

Frank took the bag slowly, keeping his eyes locked with Linda's. "Thanks. So… I'll be in the barn? The bales look comfy enough. You'll be fine out here?"

"Yeah, I'm good. And that sounds good. You can grab a blanket out of the truck to put down on the hay if you want."

Frank shook his head. "Nah, I'm good. Just make sure to wake me in two hours, okay?"

Linda nodded and turned back to the truck without saying anything. Frank backed slowly towards the barn, watching as Linda busied herself with something inside the truck, not bothering to even look back in his direction.

"What the hell is going on here?" Frank shook his head as he mumbled to himself. He headed into the barn and into one of the small rooms near the back where he had stacked several inches of hay and laid out a cleanish-looking tarp while he was wandering around before. The room had a door and a bolt on it, both of which sounded incredibly helpful given how odd Linda was behaving.

He sat down on a stool that was in the room, leaning his pack against one leg and the rifle against the wall behind him. He had absolutely no intention of going to sleep in case Linda's odd behavior was a precursor to her trying to do something to him, but his body had other ideas. The light sleep he had gotten in the truck while they were driving earlier had had nearly no effect on him and he fell fast asleep within seconds.

Chapter Seven

The Mississippi River is on fire. Crude oil spills from the Alliance refinery in Belle Chase into the water, spreading the fires from the refinery downstream. With a two hundred and fifty thousand barrel per day refining capacity, the Alliance refinery is the largest in the state. Its pipelines have ruptured, its holding tanks burst and its emergency response capabilities had been crippled by the explosion that occurred three hours earlier.

Massive plumes of thick black smoke billow into the sky and are pulled to the northeast by light winds. The smoke is filled with toxins that slowly drift over residential areas, coating the buildings and people inside and out. To those living near the refinery the smoke is a sight they see on an infrequent basis, but never in such volume or for so long. If they weren't already dealing with the sounds of explosions from nearby highways and the terrifying announcements being made on the news then they would be more concerned with the smoke than they otherwise are.

Rescue workers triage the wounded that are pulled from the buildings on the refinery grounds that still stand, though the smoke and heat from the flames make each rescue more difficult. There are still dozens of workers unaccounted for, trapped beneath burning rubble or swallowed by mammoth amounts of crude oil.

From the air, a news helicopter circles the scene, broadcasting the footage *live to local news stations. If it was the only disaster of the day it would make national headlines, but the headlines are already swamped. Five other refineries have been hit in the last three hours and many more are yet to come. Government officials and law enforcement still do not know the vector of the explosions, and are powerless to stop them from happening.*

Refineries and distribution stations that have not been hit are ordering emergency shutdowns, some of which are physically damaging to the processing and transportation equipment. These plants suffer the least of all, but will still require weeks and months of work to return to full operation—assuming that day ever comes.

Local radio stations struggle to make sense of the destruction. They receive conflicting instructions from local, state and federal officials as emergency services, law enforcement and response agencies struggle to cope with a scenario that they never imagined could take place.

Chapter Eight

W hen Frank woke up, it was still dark in the small room inside the barn, with only the moon and starlight peeking through the cracks in the wall and ceiling. He wondered at first why he was awake, where he was and what was going on, until a noise from outside the barn snapped him back to reality.

"Shit!" Frank leapt up and unbolted the door, leaving the rifle and his pack behind as he ran down the length of the barn. The front door to the barn was still partially open and he ran outside, slowing to a stop on the dirt path in front of the building as he saw the source of the noise that he had feared.

"What the hell?" He shouted at the top of his lungs as Linda's truck bounced and bucked on the bumps in the dirt road, driving away at a high rate of speed. Dust swirled into the air and Frank ran his hands through his hair, trying to make sense of what had just happened. As he turned around and kicked at the ground in frustration, he spotted a red object near the front of the barn and a piece of paper stuck in one of the barn door's handles.

Frank grabbed the piece of paper from the barn door and stalked back inside, feeling a significant amount of anger rising inside of him. He returned to the room where he had slept and found the flashlight Linda had left for him, turned it on and spread the paper out on the floor.

The paper turned out to be a few pages from an old grocery store sales flyer with a prominent advertisement for half off ground chuck, blackberries and store-brand milk on the front. Over the brightly colored images, though, was scribbled—in bright blue marker and large lettering—a message that spanned several pages.

Frank – Sorry to leave you like this. You're clearly trustworthy but I prefer to travel alone. Half a mile back up the road is a car with the keys in it. I left you enough gas to get a few hours more south. Good luck. –Linda

"What the hell, lady?" Frank crumpled the flyer into a ball and threw it against the wall in frustration. He paced around the room for a few minutes, trying to think of what to do before he sat back down and sighed. "At least she didn't shoot me, I guess. You'd think she could be *slightly* less paranoid though." Frank picked the paper up and smoothed it out, re-reading it again now that he was feeling less angry.

"A car half a mile back down the road?" Frank thought back to the bumps and swerves he had felt while dozing on and off right before they turned off to the farmhouse. He snorted and shook his head as he realized how far back she had planned to ditch him. "She must have been keeping her eyes open for a car that looked like it was in half-drivable condition."

Frank sighed again and slipped his pack over his shoulders, then buckled the waist straps. He had already tucked the extra batteries and ammunition into the top of the pack, and he grabbed the rifle that Linda had left for him and checked the small ten-round magazine to make sure it was still loaded. *Still can't believe she trusted me with a gun but not to ride along with her. She's got some kind of crazy issues.*

With there being no real point in lingering at the barn any longer, Frank slung the rifle on his shoulder and headed out of the building. He picked up the gas can with a grunt and set off down the dirt road leading back towards the highway.

The first rays of dawn were just starting to peek over the horizon when Frank made it back to the highway. He cast a longing look to the south in the direction where Linda and he had been driving before she turned off before trudging back to the north. The weather was cold and he was glad he still had a jacket even though it was barely adequate for the early morning temperature. Still tired from the activities of the previous day and the lack of decent sleep, it took Frank a full hour—and several stops—to make it to the vehicle that Linda had pointed out in her note.

While Frank had passed several other cars on the side of the road earlier, all of them had either been involved in a crash, were overturned or didn't have the keys inside of them. When he reached the small, two-door blue sedan, he pointed his flashlight through the window and couldn't help but smile at the sight of a set of keys that were still inserted into the dash-mounted ignition.

Both of the car's doors were locked but the trunk was slightly ajar, and Frank opened it to find it empty. He looked around, seeing nothing of interest aside from the pink and purple hues of the sunrise, and took off his rifle and backpack and put them on the ground right behind the vehicle. He sat the gas can down next to them as well, then began the arduous process of slithering his way through the trunk and into the front of the car.

A few inches above average, Frank's six-foot two-inch frame was bulky, and he thought more than a few times that he was going to get wedged between the seats as he crawled forward through the sedan. With the upper half of his body twisted around on top of the vehicle's shifter next to the front seats, Frank realized that there wasn't enough room for him to actually get into the seats without turning into some sort of circus contortionist.

He reached for the lock on the driver's side door and slid it up, then started backing out of the car. The amount of grumbling and cursing that came from him doubled during the reverse expedition until, finally, he fell a few feet onto the hard pavement and let out a groan. "Dammit." Frank stood up slowly and walked around the driver's side door and pulled on the handle. The door opened freely, and he rolled his eyes with relief.

After adjusting the seat back so that he could fit his legs into the car, Frank got in and turned the key halfway in the ignition. The dashboard lit up and he pushed the starter button next to the ignition, but all he heard was the sputtering of the engine as it tried to draw in fuel that didn't exist.

"Huh." Frank pulled the lever to release the gas cap cover before getting out and heading back to the can behind the vehicle. "I wonder how she knew it was out of gas. Or maybe she just assumed it was." It took a few minutes to drain the can of gas into the sedan. Once he was done, Frank put the empty can into the back of the sedan and loaded his backpack and rifle into the front passenger seat.

"All right, you piece of crap. Don't make me walk." Frank turned the key and pressed the start button. At first, the engine coughed and sputtered again, but after a few seconds the lights on the dashboard flickered and the engine hummed to life. "Yes!" Frank shouted in glee and shut his door.

The gas indicator showed that he had about a third of a tank, and as long as he moderated his speed and stayed on the highway, he figured he'd be able to get fairly far. "Oh." Frank glanced up and saw a set of numbers displayed on the corner of the rearview mirror. "Thirty-five miles to the gallon?" He nodded approvingly. "Not bad. That was, what, a five gallon can? So a bit over a hundred and fifty miles."

Frank realized then that he had no idea where in Maine he was —if he was even in the state still—but figured that his best bet would be to head south along the highway until he hit a major town. "Hopefully they'll give me a warmer welcome then in the last place I was at." Frank mumbled to himself as he put the sedan into gear and slowly took off down the road. It was the first time that he had driven anything smaller than a tractor-trailer in weeks, but he was glad for the fact that it had a manual transmission since it made the transition slightly less jarring.

The first few minutes of the drive went by at a snail's pace as Frank adjusted to driving the smaller vehicle. As the morning wore on, though, he quickly got used to the differences and even began to enjoy himself. Driving on an empty highway in a vehicle that he could maneuver without worrying about tipping over was something he had forgotten about in the last month.

After the initial fun of driving the small car wore off, Frank's thoughts drifted back to Linda and the situation that he found himself in. He glanced at the rifle sitting next to him and shook his head in amazement yet again. He was glad that she had left him the gun—and it was one of the reasons he wasn't all that upset about her leaving him behind—though he hoped he wouldn't have to use it.

Despite her description of how bad things were, the newscast he had seen and the nearly rabid behavior of the people at the gas station, Frank tried to understand how the country really could have ground to a halt in a matter of hours. "The truckers," he said, talking aloud to himself, "I get. A few hundred of their trucks explode and nobody's going to want to hop in one and drive around. I sure as hell wouldn't touch one again."

Frank suddenly remembered Linda talking about how she had gotten her information from a radio station before it went dead and he glanced at the large flat panel that was sitting in the middle of the vehicle's dash. He tapped a large red power button on the display and it instantly flared to life with several large virtual buttons and dials on display. He tapped the one labeled "RADIO" and the car was filled with the sound of static. He cringed and turned down the volume, then began skipping through the AM and FM bands, trying to find a station that was still broadcasting.

Disturbingly though, even after several minutes of carefully picking through each and every frequency, Frank couldn't find a single channel that gave even the hint of broadcasting more than just static. He switched to the car's satellite antenna, but although it showed him as receiving a signal, there was only dead air on every station he selected. The realization was slow to come, but as he thought more, it dawned on him what that meant.

"There's not a single place still broadcasting? How is that even possible?" Not picking anything up on the radio stations made sense, but to not hear anything on the satellite broadcasts—even on foreign-based channels—was extremely odd unless a significant amount of infrastructure had been wiped out. Frank shook his head and switched the radio and center display back off. He gripped the steering wheel tightly and set his jaw as he pressed down on the accelerator. He didn't know what was happening but he was finally convinced that, whatever it was, it was worse than he could have imagined.

Chapter Nine

F rank had been driving for just over half an hour when he saw the first signs of major wreckage and chaos on the highway. The blackened wreckage of several overturned trucks caused him to slow down and he wove between them, looking in the cabs of the vehicles for any signs of survivors. Occupied as he was with paying attention to the road directly around him, Frank didn't see the line of intact trailers overturned on the road ahead until he was only a few hundred feet away. He jammed on the brakes and the sedan slid to a stop, and he stared through the windshield, wondering what was going on.

Five or six intact trucks and trailers were overturned on both sides of the highway. Between them the median dipped sharply downward, making it impossible to bypass the obstruction. The obstacles were laid out in such a way that they were directly next to an exit off of the highway on both sides, which was the sole path available for Frank to take. "Huh. Guess I'm taking a detour." Frank turned the center console back on and scrolled through the menu until he found a button that read "NAVIGATION." He tapped it and an overhead map sprang to life, showing his position and the roads nearby.

The satellite imagery and mapping data showed that the exit ran through a small town nearby, though it eventually looped back around a few miles down the road and went back onto the highway. Frank sighed and drove forward again, angling off to the right to take the required detour. The map data on the screen showed that there was a gas station and two small restaurants in the town —both with mostly two and three-star reviews—and though Frank doubted he'd be able to get more gas, he figured it was worth checking out anyway.

"I just hope these people are nicer than the ones in the last town. Freaking savages." How ordinary people could allow their behaviors and ways of thinking to degenerate in less than a day was beyond him. "Maybe they're just scared. But still, no need to act like that just because a few—wait, what the hell?"

Frank stopped his muttering as he noticed a pair of cars that had run off into the ditch by the side of the road. The first vehicle was on its wheels, but the windows were broken out and it had hit a tree hard enough to crumple the hood. The second, larger vehicle was overturned and the taillights were still blinking, indicating that it had flipped very recently. One of the back tires was shredded and what looked like a metal net was wrapped around the wheel. Sharp spikes stuck out of the net, a few of them still holding pieces of rubber from the tire.

The sight was odd, but a car or two on the side of the road wasn't unusual given what he had seen in the last day. The larger concern was that he recognized the second, overturned vehicle. He eased the sedan to a stop and pulled over to the side of the road, trying to figure out where he had seen it before when he saw several red gas cans scattered in the ditch next to the upside-down vehicle.

"Linda's truck? What the…" Frank felt his heart pick up speed and the hairs on the back of his neck stood on end. Linda had proved to be more than a capable driver, and the odd spiked netting wrapped around the wheel of her truck indicated that something bad had happened when she had taken the same detour as him.

Frank parked the sedan and rolled down both windows before climbing out. It was an old habit he developed years ago when he used to drive. Anytime he had to hop out of the car for a few seconds and didn't want to take the keys with him he would roll down the windows just to make certain he didn't lock them in the car. It only took one time of that happening for him to ensure it never did again.

He half-walked, half-slid down into the ditch and knelt down next to the window of the truck and looked inside. No one was inside, but the seatbelt had been cut, the glass to the driver's side window was shattered and there was a dark red bloodstain on the back of the driver's side cushion. Linda's bags and other equipment that he had seen in the back of her truck were nowhere to be seen, and the only contents of the vehicle that appeared to be left were the empty gas cans that had been scattered along the ditch.

Frank stood up and put his hands on his hips as he looked around. He was about to cup his hands and start shouting Linda's name when a series of gunshots from nearby made him duck back to the ground and press himself up against the truck. It was hard to judge where the shots came from at first, but several more came in rapid succession and Frank realized that they were coming from further down the road where it bent off to the right. The area was thickly wooded and from what he remembered on the map in the sedan the only areas that were clear were the road and the town.

Frank squatted next to the truck for a long moment, debating what to do. He could always go back on the highway and head north to find another route around the entire area, but he doubted he had enough gas in the sedan to get very far. Beyond that, though, was a sense of obligation he felt to try and find the person who had abandoned him and make sure she was still okay.

"Son of a…" Frank turned around and clawed his way out of the ditch and ran back to the sedan. He grabbed his pack and opened it up to pull out an extra box of ammunition, then put the pack on his back and grabbed the rifle. He reached in and shut off the sedan before grabbing the keys and locking the doors, then shoved the keys into his pocket and cycled the bolt on the rifle, ensuring there was a cartridge in the chamber.

After checking to make sure he had everything, Frank took off down the road at a jog, trying not to think about what he was doing for fear that he might change his mind. While he wasn't entirely certain, the gunshots he had heard sounded like the same type he heard when Linda had been shooting previously. "How does that woman manage to get herself into two gunfights in less than twenty-four hours?"

Rather than following the road all the way into town, as soon as he saw a few buildings ahead through the trees, Frank immediately headed several yards into the woods and slowed his approach. After the burst of gunfire earlier, he hadn't heard anything else. The town—if it could even be called that—was more of a motley collection of buildings on either side of the road. There were no residential homes in sight and the only buildings Frank could recognize were the gas station, one of the restaurants—a place called "Bud's Steak Shack"—and what looked like a combination laundromat and arcade, though the sign was too faded to make out.

Frank crouched in the woods and watched the buildings for a moment, looking for any signs of movement. He was getting ready to move forward when he saw a figure dart out from behind the gas station on the other side of the road and head towards one of the buildings on his side. He squinted as he watched the figure running, then realized who it was.

"Linda?" Frank whispered to himself as he watched her running along, hunched over as she tried to keep her body tucked as low to the ground as possible. She ducked inside the back of the building just as two men charged out the front, heading towards the restaurant located next to the gas station. The pair were both holding guns, wearing jeans and jackets and woolen hats that appeared far too warm for the time of year. They were talking to each other about something and were clearly agitated, but they weren't loud enough for Frank to make out what they were saying.

Without thinking, Frank bolted for the door that Linda had left open on the back side of the building. It took him several seconds to cover the small bit of open ground between the woods and the building, and he cringed as his feet crunched on the gravel behind the structure. He had no idea what was going on or who was at fault for whatever was happening, but there was still no sense in drawing attention to himself.

The door on the back of the building was slightly ajar and Frank opened it quietly, praying that the hinges weren't going to squeak. Inside, the building was mostly dark, though several candles and a lantern were spread out on the floor and tables that offered a faint glow that he could barely see by. The building appeared to be the second restaurant he had seen on the map of the town, though he couldn't remember what cuisine they served and the interior offered up no clues, either.

Frank stealthily walked through the kitchen and into the dining area, keeping both shaking hands on the rifle. A rustling noise from the dining area made him turn in surprise and he saw the form of a woman on one knee as she manipulated an object in front of her. Taking a chance, Frank whispered at her. "Linda?"

The woman whirled and raised a pistol, searching for the source of the voice. When she spotted Frank her eyes grew wide and she lowered the gun, her eyebrows scrunched into a mixture of confusion and angered surprise. "Frank? What the hell are you doing here?"

Frank scuttled across the floor to her and saw that she was collecting items off of the ground and putting them into a backpack. "I had to turn off the road because of all the trucks. Never mind, that, though; why did you leave me behind?"

Linda shook her head in frustration and turned back to her packing. "Frank, you need to get out of here right now, okay? I don't need you on my conscience if something happens."

Frank grabbed Linda's shoulder and spun her back around, hissing at her as he tried to remain quiet, though he was still unsure why. He glanced at her shirt and saw a large bloodstain on her left shoulder and several scrapes across her face and arms. "If something happens? What am I, a child? I helped you out once before, and you look like you could use it again. What happened, did you piss somebody off about fuel again?"

Linda pushed Frank's arm away and glowered at him. "Stay off me, Frank. And keep your voice down. These assholes mean business."

Frank rolled his eyes and looked out the front window of the restaurant. Across the street he could see the gas station and Bob's Steak Shack, but there was no sign of the two men that had spotted previously. "Who do you mean, the two I saw running out a minute ago?"

"You mean the two opportunistic assholes who decided to set up a roadblock on the highway to catch any travelers unawares?" Linda scowled as she glanced out the window. "Yeah, them. I think they must have towed those trailers there, blocked up the road so that anyone on the highway would have to pass through here. When I pulled off I hit some kind of spike trap. Blew out my tire and rolled the truck."

"Yeah, I saw. That's how I knew you were here. Well that and the gunshots."

Linda shook her head. "Yeah. Anyway. When I came to, they had cut me out of my seatbelt—and sliced my shoulder up something good—and dragged me back to this little hellhole. They were in the midst of tying me up when they heard another car down the road."

Frank snorted. "Probably me."

"Well that's another one I owe you for. I got loose, grabbed my gun and winged one of them. Then I managed to get around to here where they said they dumped my stuff."

"Nicely done." Frank nodded approvingly. "One question for you. How is it that everyone's decided to go crazy in less than twenty-four hours?"

Linda looked at Frank as though he was speaking another language. "What're you talking about? Frank, people are animals. The shit just hit the fan and they're freaking out. By now every fuel station outside of places like this is going to be dry. Every store will be completely out of food by tomorrow. People are panicking and when people start to panic the vipers come out of their holes and start trying to take advantage of the situation."

Frank listened quietly as Linda whispered to him before zipping up her pack and throwing it on her shoulders. "So what is it you want to do now?"

Linda looked at the rifle Frank still held. "Now? Now I think it's time we cut the heads off a couple of vipers."

Frank recoiled, clutching the rifle. "You want to kill those two? Why don't we just run?"

Linda fixed him with a gaze and spoke with a tone that chilled him to the bone. "I'm not the first one to come through here, Frank. If you want to get an opinion from the other people who came through, you'd better call a psychic."

The blood drained from Frank's face, both at the realization of what Linda was saying as well as how casually she was saying it. "What... how... who are you?"

Linda stood up and walked over to Frank. She took the rifle from his hands, then handed him her pistol in return. "I'm the one who's *not* going to turn into a corpse."

Chapter Ten

Frank followed Linda out the back of the restaurant and they slipped far enough into the woods that they couldn't easily be seen. Now that he was back outside he could hear the shouts coming from town as the two men searched high and low for Linda.

"You're seriously going to kill them in cold blood?"

"Cold blood? They killed two people already and were getting ready to kill me, too. They're not getting the chance to do it to anyone else."

Frank groaned. "I can't believe this is happening."

"Shut up." Linda elbowed Frank in the ribs and pointed down the tree line. "Get down there to that defilade. If you see them, give a whistle."

"Get to the what?" Frank looked down where Linda had pointed, confused about what she meant.

"Defilade. The protected area, up on that incline." Linda pointed again and Frank saw what she meant.

"Right. On my way." He slunk off through the woods, keeping an eye on the town. When he got to the spot Linda had indicated, he settled down into the dead leaves and surveyed the town. He could still hear the two men talking to each other, though it was impossible to make out exactly what they were saying. He looked back down to his left and watched as Linda crept away from him, keeping the rifle at the ready. Her every movement was that of a trained killer, and Frank suddenly felt incredibly nervous about the previous night when he had fallen asleep in the barn.

After a moment he turned his attention back to the town and saw the two men crossing back over the street to a building directly down and in front of him. Nearly panicking at the sight, Frank whistled awkwardly, intending to make a sound like a bird but instead giving off a warbled sound like that of a parrot caught in the spin cycle of a washing machine.

The two men whirled at the noise, bringing their weapons to bear as they searched for the source. Frank lowered his head and tried to blend in with the leaves and brush as much as possible, though he felt like he was sticking out like a sore thumb. As terrible as his whistling had been, it had the desired effect. From his left, Frank heard a shot ring out and saw a spray of blood from one of the two men as a large portion of his skull turned into a fine pink mist.

The man's friend jumped back and screamed at the sight, then began shooting in random directions with his shotgun. Frank ducked down as pellets sprayed over his head. When the man finally stopped shooting Frank peeked back over the defilade and saw the man running for cover across the road. Down to his left, Linda was laying down just off of the road, using a large bush and a slight incline to help hide her position.

When the man with the shotgun stopped he was behind the last building down and across the road. He was breathing heavily and kept glancing between the body of his friend and his shotgun that he was desperately trying to reload. Even from across the street Frank could see the man's hands shaking from fear. Frank started second-guessing the whole affair, wondering if Linda was really right about what the two men were doing. *Maybe she's lying about it. She was pretty scraped up, though… but what if these guys are innocent. Hell, what if the people at the gas station yesterday weren't what she said, either?*

Frank was on the verge of standing up and shouting at the man to try and negotiate with him when another shot rang out from the hunting rifle. The edge of the building where the man tried to hide split open and a shower of splinters rained down as the bullet passed through the thin strips of wood and through the man's upper torso. He howled in pain and dropped the rifle, clutching at the wound like a desperate animal.

"No!" Frank jumped up and ran across the street towards the man. By the time Frank arrived, the man was lying on his side on the ground, the shotgun a few feet away. The man's breathing was shallow and ragged and blood dripped from his mouth and pooled on the ground from the chest wound. Linda ran up a few seconds later and stared down at the man with a blank expression on her face.

"Why did you have you kill them both?" Frank whirled and shouted at Linda. "Couldn't you have just wounded them or something?"

Linda shifted her gaze to Frank and looked at him for a few seconds before turning to point at a building down the road. "Go inside, up the stairs and through the first door on your right. I'll wait for you out here."

By the time Frank returned several minutes later his face was ashen and he walked along slowly, shaking his head. Linda was busy dragging the bodies of the men into the gas station when he arrived and she stopped when she saw him and wiped the blood from her hands onto some rags.

"Well?" Linda raised an eyebrow.

"Those people were..." Frank shook his head.

"Yep."

"And those two... they did all of *that?*"

"Yep."

"I still don't understand how people can be acting like this. It's not even been a day! Has the entire world gone mad?"

Linda gave a sympathetic smile and sighed. "Not the entire world, Frank. Look—there are plenty of bad people in it. We see that all the time. There are always people who are looking for any opportunity to take advantage of others no matter the situation. That's where you get scum-suckers like this who crawl out of the woodwork the instant they get the chance. Then you have others, like the people at the gas station yesterday. They're not bad people, they're just desperate and scared and surrounded by other people who are desperate and scared."

"So where are the good people?"

"Look in a mirror, Frank. Folks like yourself or the people you told me about who were helping others at the diner you were at yesterday. You got to see the best and worst of everyone right there at the start. People giving selflessly and people taking advantage of the situation." Linda shrugged and turned away from Frank to look at the bodies lying on the floor. "For what it's worth, though, I'm sorry I left you behind at the barn. It wasn't right. I knew you were one of the good ones just based on how you acted at the gas station. I have… issues with trusting people. I'm sorry."

"Thanks. I just want to get back to Texas, to my folks. Somehow I don't think I'm going to get any more assignments from the company I work for." Frank shifted his gaze to look at the pair on the floor and shuddered. "You weren't kidding about those two."

Linda looked at Frank for a long minute before responding. "Yeah, well, without your help it would have been two against one. I don't like those odds even when I'm confident in myself. So thanks. I appreciate it."

Frank nodded and turned away, looking down the road that led off into the trees. "So, uh… what do we do now? Find a police station and report these guys to the cops?"

Linda laughed. "I think the local constabulary have their hands full with other issues at the moment. No, I think we need to get moving."

"I parked the car you left for me—thanks for that by the way—back up the road a ways."

"You get all your stuff out of it?"

"Yeah. Why?"

Linda motioned for Frank to follow her. "Come on. I'm pretty sure I saw a truck out behind one of the buildings."

As the pair walked along, a thought occurred to Frank. "How is it that this pair was alone here—well, aside from the couple who they... yeah."

Linda shrugged. "Small place like this isn't so much a town as it is an economic center. Owners of the businesses here probably cleared out yesterday when everything hit the fan and went back to their homes. There are plenty of farms and isolated homes out here in the woods. These two assholes probably spent all of yesterday blocking up the highway and snagged their first catch late last night or before I drove through this morning."

"Jesus..." Frank shook his head at the cavalier way in which Linda talked about the two bodies Frank had seen in the second floor of the building. "Who are you, anyway? You barely told me anything about yourself before. And now all of this." Frank was flabbergasted and began to sputter and stutter as he tried to express his exasperation.

"We should get moving, Frank." Linda walked on ahead, not bothering to answer his question. He stood in the road for a moment watching her go before finally walking after her, shaking his head and wondering if it was such a good idea to go with her after all.

Chapter Eleven

"*Come on, rookie. Get your shit together!*"

Men wearing bulky padded armor and carrying tall shields and rifles pour into the armored personnel carrier. One of the first aboard, Dean Wilson, had his hiring ceremony three days ago. Hired to work as a patrol officer he's now been inducted into the riot control squad, handed a shield and tear gas launcher and told to hold the line no matter the cost.

He struggles to move his shield and rifle aside as the other, more experienced officers shuffle and push their way onto the vehicle. One of them sits next to him and pats him on the leg sympathetically.

"Name's Jim. You're Dean, right?"

Dean nods nervously.

"Yeah, thought so. You're the new guy. Shit break you got here, kid. Listen, just stick close to me, all right? We'll make it out of this mess before you know it."

Dean gulps and nods again, though there is little reassurance to be found in the older officer's words.

"We're moving out! Everybody hold on!" The announcement comes over the speakers as the vehicle roars to life and lurches forward. Dean clings to his rifle and his shield as though they are the only things keeping him alive. Fifteen minutes later the vehicle stops and the back drops open. Harsh sunlight pierces

*the interior, and Dean is suddenly grateful for the dark glasses he wears under-
neath his riot helmet.*

*"Move, move, move!" The officers pour out of the APC and begin running
down the street. A block away stands a line of riot police that have been on duty
for only a few hours, but their lines are starting to break. Tens of thousands of
people surge forward against the officers. Tear gas is fired into the crowd but it
does little good. Rocks and flaming bottles of alcohol are launched in long arcs
against the police, injuring a few and rattling their nerves. There is shouting
from bullhorns that order the people back to their homes, though these instructions are completely ignored.*

*Dean looks around in amazement at the chaos as he runs to help support
the line. Everywhere he looks there are people engaged in both acts of violence
and acts of compassion. A small group of volunteers wearing bright red crosses
on their shirts helps remove the helmet from an officer who was injured. Lying
next to him is a rioter whose heavily bleeding arm is bandaged before he is put
on a stretcher.*

*The five minute briefing before the new reinforcements were sent out has
long been forgotten by Dean, though it was never clear in the first place. They
are instructed to restore peace to the city. 'But how,' he wonders, 'do you restore
peace in a time like this?'*

Chapter Twelve

Highways, in general, aren't peaceful places. At night, when the traffic dies down they can be quieter than usual, but there are still plenty of cars and trucks going back and forth, delivering people and goods across cities and states. During the day, when traffic reaches its peak, the business is often offset by the stunning views that lie in between stops along the road. Sweeping plains, majestic mountains, thick forests and scorching deserts offer unparalleled beauty and majesty observable from within the comfort and safety of a multi-ton vehicle equipped with air conditioning, televised entertainment and heated seats.

As the small red and white truck zipped along the highway, Frank thought nothing of the sights around him. There were no other cars on the road, the sights mattered little due to his state of mind and the comforts of the truck were sorely lacking. He stared out the window, his eyes glazed over as he replayed the events from hours prior over and over again, wondering what—if anything—he could have done differently.

The truck—with its peeling paint, cracked windshield and smell like the inside of a smoker's lungs—had been parked out behind one of the buildings in the small town just as Linda had said. It took Linda and Frank a few minutes to scrape out the piles of trash and debris from the seats, floorboards and back of the vehicle to make room for the two of them and their gear. Before they got in, Linda had swapped out their weapons again, giving Frank the rifle and taking back her pistol. Though his shooting abilities were no match for what she had displayed in the town before, he didn't argue as he was too lost in his own thoughts to give the matter any consideration.

Linda had mostly stayed quiet as they drove, leaving Frank to do his thinking in peace. After an hour or so he finally spoke up. "Why is it you're taking me with you again?"

Linda looked at him with a mildly confused expression. "I thought I already explained that."

"Not really. You said that I'm one of the 'good ones' but that you already suspected that beforehand. So what's changed now?"

Linda's grip tightened on the steering wheel as she stared out the front of the truck. "I… it's a long story that I don't really want to delve into at this point. I was in trouble several years ago, though. One of my best friends—or someone I thought was my best friend—ended up abandoning me in a firefight in Ahvaz. I barely survived. Never managed to get over that, though." Linda took a deep breath and glanced back at Frank. "So I don't like trusting people. But at this point going alone isn't the smartest thing to do for either of us."

"I'm… sorry to hear that. But thank you." Frank didn't really know what to say in response to Linda's revelation that she had been in the armed forces or her admission of why she had left him behind at the barn the night before. The new information put a startling new light on her, though, and explained a lot about her actions and mentality.

"Let's just get to Tennessee. Once we're there and I make sure my parents are okay, I'll help you get whatever you need to get back to Texas."

Frank nodded and turned back to look out the window, mulling over what Linda had said. Lost in thought, he didn't notice that she had turned the truck's radio on and was cycling through stations until a garbled voice cut through the static.

...unconfirmed reports of----detonations at the-------along the border of Vermont and Massachusetts. Authorities believe that-----------------but residents are advised to stay clear of the area. Clouds of fumes are currently blowing to the east and anyone------------of the facility are advised to evacuate immediately before----------

Frank turned to look at the radio on the dashboard, then over at Linda. "What the hell was that about?"

"I don't know." She shook her head. "Sounds like another explosion, though. Somewhere along the border of Vermont and Massachusetts."

Frank scratched his chin as he mused. "I wonder if it's the new fuel refinery they were building. I had a couple of deliveries there during my first week. Had a hell of a time getting through security since I was so new. It was right on the border and it was a huge place, too."

Linda shrugged. "You'd know better than I. Should we keep going south, though?"

"Where are we right now?"

"Last mile marker looked like we're about thirty miles from the border. We've got enough gas in the tank and in my cans they threw in the back to get down to the northern part of West Virginia, if we keep going straight south."

"The problem with that," Frank said, "is this highway's going to take us straight by that refinery. We can risk it, but if I were you, I'd say we should cut west into upstate New York and head south down through Pennsylvania. That'll keep us clear of the highways which are only going to get even more treacherous as we get into the more densely populated areas."

"You think that's why the roads have been mostly clear so far?"

Frank stretched his back and neck, feeling and hearing the satisfying cracks as he talked. "I do, yeah. If you think about it, what are people going to be doing when they see a bunch of trucks on the road exploding? They're going to get off the roads and back to their homes as soon as possible. Most people probably had less than a half tank of gas left, and with food shortages and a lack of fuel it's going to force them to move on foot before too long. The closer we get to the larger cities, though, the more cars will have been destroyed by the explosions of the trucks and the more people will be driving around trying to find food and supplies."

"All right, then. Upstate it is. Do you know the area?"

"I lived in the area for a couple years. I don't know every road but I know the general layout of the area."

"Anything we need to worry about?"

Frank shrugged. "Not particularly. Most folks are going to be keeping to themselves, I'd guess. I think we'll run into the same problems no matter what high-population center we visit. Like you said, there are a lot of scared people out there. Scared, desperate and soon to be hungry and willing to do anything for a meal."

"This couldn't have happened at a worse time, too." Linda looked up at the sky and shook her head. "Going into autumn and winter with transportation networks down is going to add a whole new twist to this whole thing if people can't get electricity or fuel deliveries for their heating."

Frank whistled softly. "Damn. I hadn't even thought of that. But still, I mean come on—give it a week or two and you'd think the government will have things back under control."

Linda snorted. "Really? Frank, I'd have thought that if your parents were preppers you'd have learned a few things from them."

Frank shrugged. "Anytime I wasn't helping them I was busy applying for jobs. I didn't exactly have time to attend Prepper 101 classes."

Linda's laugh was genuine, and Frank couldn't help but smile in response. "All right, fair enough. Consider this, then; if it takes around two weeks for the government to come up with and imple-ment a response, what do you think they'll be able to do?"

"I don't know, implement some better checks for explosives on the tractor-trailers? Come up with some temporary repairs to the electric grid to get power back for some people? Maybe start airlifting food supplies to towns?"

"Think about it, Frank. No trucker is going to go back on the road anytime soon, even if somebody wearing a badge says their truck is safe. And even if everyone did, there are hundreds—maybe thousands—of trucks destroyed. That's small potatoes compared to how many are in use across the country, but it's going to force every single company to recalculate their logistics and figure out how to get deliveries going again. That'll take more than a couple weeks to smooth out."

"Okay…" Frank frowned. "So why not work on the grid? Surely that can get straightened out a bit so that at least people in major cities can get power back."

"No way in hell." Linda shook her head. "The power grid in the United States has been perpetually on the verge of collapse for decades. Beyond the problem of getting new parts that take years to manufacturer, if enough of the grid is down it can't just be brought back online. The grid in the United States is incredibly complicated and interconnected. It takes a massive amount of work—most of it computerized—to keep everything coordinated and to respond to constantly changing power demands."

"Food deliveries, then. We give enough foreign aid to other countries. We can feed our own people for weeks or months until we start getting things straightened out."

"You think so? There are over three hundred and fifty million people living in this country. We're spread out so far that even if the Air Force was working nonstop and we somehow had enough emergency food supplies there simply aren't enough aircraft that could get food to people before a lot of them start starving and dying. And that doesn't even bring up the problem of people who need medication or who are in the hospital who'll go first."

Frank couldn't recall how many times in the last day he felt dwarfed by the magnitude of what was going on, but it was happening again. He felt his head spinning and he pressed it against the window and closed his eyes. "How is it you can say all of this and sound so calm?"

Linda gave Frank a sympathetic look. "Some of us figured something like this would happen one day. Honestly I thought things would be worse than this. At least nobody's lobbed any missiles. Well." Linda hesitated. "At least none that we know of, anyway."

Frank groaned. "Oh boy. Something else to look forward to."

Chapter Thirteen

Jim Collins, the manager of Tony's Sports World, watches from his small office at the top of the back of the store, staring out at the chaos below through a heavily tinted piece of glass. Behind him, on the floor of the office, are several of the sales associates who are tending to their wounds. Two of them are standing guard at the door to the office, holding baseball bats and looking nervous as the sounds of fighting and looting grow louder down in the warehouse and on the sales floor.

Jim takes another drink from a small bottle of Tennessee whiskey he pulled out of his desk drawer and glances at the young sales associate standing next to him. Her hair is disheveled, her clothing is wrinkled and she stands watching through the window with a hand on her mouth, horrified by what she sees below.

Dozens of people flood through the store, sweeping over its contents like starving locusts on a field of wheat. Fistfights break out between pairs and groups of individuals as the people fight over scraps that they aren't even sure they need.

Most of the useful supplies are long gone, including camping and fishing equipment, coolers, dried food packets and warm clothing. The guns are still under lock and key, though several individuals have brought in bolt cutters and are working to break the thick cables that hold the weapons fast. Not a single bullet remains in the store as the ammunition was first to disappear. It is no small miracle that there have yet to be any gunshots, though the tension is still rising and panic is palpable in the air.

Jim glances over at the young sales associate and puts his arm around her. She is crying now, and she manages to get out a few words in between the sobs. "My brother… my parents… what do we do, Mr. Collins?"

Jim takes another drink from his bottle and grits his teeth. "I don't know, Sarah. I don't know. Why don't you go sit down and try to rest. Hopefully they'll be done down there soon and we can all go home."

Another of the sales associates speaks up from the back of the room, an older man who works in the fishing department. His hair is stained with white and grey flecks and he groans as he stands to his feet, feeling the effects of his age and weight. "What makes you think home is going to be any better?"

Sarah turns to look at him, her face smudged with makeup as she tries to wipe the tears away. Jim walks over to the older man and speaks softly to him. "Come on, Sam. Can't you keep quiet for just a while? People are already scared enough here. They don't need anything else to be afraid of right now."

"People deserve to hear the truth!" The older man raises his voice louder and Jim steps aside, shaking his head. "It's the end times, people! Repent from your sins and turn away from your wickedness!"

"Sam! For pity's sake, shut up and sit the hell down!" Jim turns back around as he shouts at the older man who is taken aback by the harsh tone. He glowers at the store manager but he eventually sits back down, though not without muttering a few choice words under his breath.

Jim walks back to the mirror and takes another drink from his bottle. The chaos below has reached its apex and is beginning to die down as people realize there isn't much left to steal. A pair of teenage boys stand on a high shelf, pulling at a canoe that is mounted to the wall. Several women cluster around near the front of the store, talking about where to go next. In the gun department, another set of bolt cutters is foiled by the security cable and the would-be thieves throw down their tools and traipse towards the exit in disgust.

Jim turns around and sits down at his desk and looks at the pictures sitting on it. He touches the pictures and picks up the phone on his desk, hoping to hear something other than silence on the other end. He has picked up the phone more times than he can remember since the chaos began. Each time it has been silent.

The silence persists once again.

Chapter Fourteen

Upstate New York is a wondrous sight with its rivers, lakes, farms and seemingly untouched landscape that stretches for miles in every direction. In the autumn the colors change between dark green to orange to yellow to red in a shifting kaleidoscope of richness and beauty. The back country roads twist and meander through the forests and towns, offering a view of an entirely different universe from the one most people think of when they hear "New York."

A light breeze rustled the trees as Linda leaned against the truck, tilting another gas can up to drain its contents into the truck. The rolling hills, mountains and lushness of the multi-colored foliage made her feel at peace and she very nearly forgot about the events of earlier that day. She and Frank had taken turns spending the rest of the day driving through Vermont and Massachusetts and by the time they entered New York the afternoon was giving way to the evening. As the sun began to sink off in the west, the orange and purple hues from the sunset made the sight of the autumn leaves all the more wondrous to behold.

After the third can had been emptied into the truck, Linda threw the empty container into the back and walked around the vehicle to inspect the tires. A rustle in the brush off the side of the road caught her attention and she glanced over to see Frank walking out of the woods.

"Freaking poison ivy *everywhere* out here." Frank zipped up his fly and rubbed his hands on his pants. Linda laughed and shook her head, then walked back around to the driver's side of the truck.

"Come on and get in. We don't have long till it gets dark."

Frank opened the passenger door and climbed inside. "So when do you want to stop for the night and leave me behind again?"

Linda rolled her eyes. "Do we really have to keep rehashing this?"

Frank laughed. "Anyway, when do you want to stop? Some of these roads get pretty twisty and I'd rather not damage our only means of transportation."

"Honestly I'd rather not stop at all." Linda started up the truck and slowly pulled back onto the road. "It's gorgeous up in here, but there's something about this place that gives me the creeps. Let's just take it slow, keep going till it's dark and then figure out what to do from there."

Frank buckled his seatbelt and settled in. "Works for me."

As the pair drove along, Frank kept Linda's pistol tucked in a holster beneath his right leg, ready to grab at a moment's notice. Her pronouncement that she found the area they were driving through to be creepy had initially surprised Frank, but the more they drove along the more he started to feel the same way.

Before they had gotten off of the highways and started taking back roads, they had started to see more vehicles driving on the highway as they passed through Vermont and Massachusetts. All of them had been passenger vehicles, but the fact that there were still other people driving around had brought some small comfort to both him and Linda. They had tried to flag a few of the cars down, but no one stopped, and every single driver they caught a glimpse of looked paranoid, terrified and like they were on a desperate mission to get somewhere without delay.

After leaving the highway, though, the number of other vehicles they had seen had dropped to zero and they were once again alone. The feeling of solitude didn't exist on a wide highway where there were at least the remnants of destroyed vehicles to remind them about the existence of other people. Being on a back country road surrounded with woods and fields and little to no sign of other people grated on Linda's nerves and Frank was finally realizing that it had been grating on his as well.

The arrival of darkness brought with it some small relief from the anxious feelings, but it also brought along a new set of challenges. The map that Frank had found wedged behind the seats in the truck had helped them navigate the roads easily enough in the daylight. In the darkness, however, each intersection and street sign turned into an agonizingly long stop as they studied the map, verifying their location and ensuring they were still on the correct path.

It was around midnight, after Frank had taken the wheel for a couple of hours before giving it back to Linda, when he spotted a light in the distance. "Do you see that?" Frank rubbed his eyes as he spoke, wondering if he was imagining things.

Linda looked to where Frank was pointing and nodded. "Looks like a fire to me."

"Want to go check it out?"

Linda looked at Frank like he had grown a second head. "Are you insane?"

"What?"

"Did you suddenly forget what happened earlier today?"

"Hey, you were the one who said that not everyone's bad. We should at least check it out, and see what it is. If there are people there, they might be friendly. We could stand to talk to someone else and see if they know anything about what's going on."

Linda rubbed her eyes. "Dammit, Frank…"

"Park the truck along the road somewhere and we'll hike up to it. If it looks clear we'll talk to them. If things don't look right we'll get back to the truck and keep moving."

Linda wanted nothing more than to get away from the source of the light as fast as possible, though Frank's argument did have some merits of its own. "I swear to you, if we end up getting killed out here…"

"Yeah, yeah. And if it turns out to be okay then you owe me one."

Linda sighed and continued driving while Frank rolled down his window and listened intently. The light source was still too far away to hear anyone who might be near it, but the closer they got, the more he thought he was hearing music coming from that general direction. His suspicion was confirmed as Linda pulled the truck over to the side of the road and turned off the engine. Without the wind and vehicle noise he heard the faint warbles of the music through the trees and he grinned.

"Steppenwolf! I can get down with that!"

Linda rolled her eyes yet again in what was fast becoming a habit. "Can we at least get a look at them before we decide whether they're friendly or not?"

Frank and Linda both grabbed their backpacks and Linda handed him the rifle. "Here. You carry this."

He looked at her warily as he took the rifle and handed over the pistol. "Uh. I'm thinking you should be the one carrying this, given your shooting skills."

Linda didn't look at him as she tucked the pistol into her waistband. "I'd rather not use it unless I have to. You'll do fine." She walked ahead down the road towards the lights at a fast pace leaving Frank to stand and stare at her with a confused expression for several seconds before he followed after her.

"Can you explain that for me?" Frank caught up with Linda and probed again.

"Just leave it, Frank. Besides, we need to be quiet if we want to actually be stealthy."

Frank said nothing else but made a mental note of the odd exchange and hoped he could get a more satisfactory answer at some point later.

The two walked down the edge of the road until they came to the base of a small hill. A gravel road branched off from the paved one and went up the hill in the direction of the lights and music.

Frank could just see the sparks and smoke thrown into the air by the fire and intermingled with the music he heard people talking and laughing. As the wind changed direction to blow in his and Linda's direction, the smell of cooking meat made him realize that he had eaten nothing but energy bars and water since his stop at the diner.

"Something smells divine." Frank whispered to Linda and she held a finger to her lips.

"This way." She whispered and headed up the gravel road. When they were halfway up the hill she turned and headed into the trees with Frank following close behind. They stopped just short of the top of the hill and crouched down, hiding behind a pair of pine trees as they watched the activity going on in front of them.

At the top of the hill stood an old strip motel that had undergone a serious amount of change and now appeared to be a home rather than a commercial building. The outside had been repainted, there were copious amounts of plants and flowers around the building and the strip of pavement where visitors would have parked had been turned into a large vegetable garden. The roof of the building was covered in solar panels that appeared worn but still usable and each of the windows was decorated with colorful patterned curtains and the doors to what used to be the individual rooms had either been sealed over with bricks or had been painted bright colors.

In front of the building, beyond the gardens, was a large circle of rocks surrounding a shallow pit in which was burning an enormous fire. A spit with several medium and large sized pieces of meat hung over the fire and were slowly being turned by a person sitting nearby. Tables and chairs were arranged around the fire and Linda counted at least fifteen people sitting and standing, with more going back and forth between the building and the fire.

There were smiles on each person's face as they talked and laughed. A few were dancing near the fire as the music played and others sat in the grass nearby, holding hands as they talked. There were several children playing as well, and each of the adults worked to ensure that the children didn't stray too close to the fire. Clothing appeared to be the common thread between everyone in the group. Every shirt and pair of pants was brightly colored and most of the men and women had long hair, though each appeared to have their own personal hairstyles.

The atmosphere in the group was, in a word, joyous, and Linda and Frank looked at each other with raised eyebrows. "Do you think they're all high or something?" Linda whispered to Frank and he nearly choked as he stifled a laugh.

"I doubt it, but maybe. I think regardless we can assume these are pretty safe people. They've got kids running around for Pete's sake."

Linda's eyes narrowed as she studied the people milling around outside the building. "Just because they have kids nearby doesn't mean anything."

Frank gave Linda an odd look and shrugged. "I think we should risk saying hello. Worst case we can just hold them off with our guns as we get back to the truck."

"I still don't know if it's a good idea." Linda sighed and stood up slowly. "But what the hell, right?"

Frank kept his rifle on his shoulder and Linda kept her pistol tucked away in her waistband as they slowly stepped out from the trees and into the light. The first person to spot them was a man in his early twenties wearing a long-sleeved tie-died shirt, wrinkled blue jeans and flip-flops. When he saw the two strangers emerge just a few dozen feet away from the building, he immediately dropped to a knee and reached behind him to pull out a pistol which he leveled at Frank and Linda. At the same time he gave a loud yell and shouted at the others near the fire.

"Oy! Intruders! Form up!"

The response to the call was instantaneous. Several of the women rounded up the children and took them around to the back of the building away from Frank and Linda while the men clustered together, each of them producing a firearm of some sort from a holster strapped to the inside of their pants. The men moved quickly as they drew their weapons, forming a firing line and a protective barrier between the two strangers and the building.

"Holy shit." Linda whispered. "I thought they were a bunch of hippies! How the hell do they all have guns?"

"Now what?" Frank replied.

"You two!" One of the men at the end of the line stepped forward, lowering his gun slightly as he shouted at Linda and Frank. "What business do you have here?"

Linda was reaching for the gun tucked in the small of her back but Frank put a hand on her shoulder and shook his head. "Just let me handle this." He whispered to her then took a step forward. He reached for the rifle strap on his shoulder slowly, noticing that nearly every gun in front of him shifted slightly to focus on him over Linda.

"Hey, easy there. I'm just going to lay this on the ground. That okay with you?"

"It would be a great relief to us all, brother." The man who was advancing stopped and watched Frank closely. Frank's movements were slow and steady as he slipped the rifle off of his shoulder, put it on the ground and then raised both hands to chest level.

"There we go. Look, we're sorry for startling you. We've been on the road for a long time and have barely seen anyone else. We're exhausted, saw your lights and heard the music and figured we'd see what was going on."

"Why the sneaking around in the trees?" The man glanced between Linda and Frank.

"We had a pretty bad experience with a couple of fellows who decided to take advantage of whatever's going on out there right now. Figured it was better to play it safe than sorry. What's your name, by the way? I'm Frank and this is Linda."

The man slipped his gun from his right hand to his left and lowered it farther towards the ground. "I'm Jacob. Nice to meet you, Frank and Linda." Behind Frank, Linda slowly walked forward until she was even with Frank. The two of them shook Jacob's hand and the man holstered his gun. Behind him the line of men with guns out lowered theirs as well and put them away before slowly turning back to their previous activities.

"Sorry for the scare there, Jacob. We were just trying to protect ourselves and not get into a tight spot."

"I understand." Jacob smiled and glanced at Linda. "I noticed you reaching behind your back a moment ago. Are you carrying?"

Linda glanced at Frank and nodded. "Yes. Is that a problem?"

"Only if you intend to try and visit harm on any of us. If you do not intend to do so, however…" Jacob walked over to Frank's rifle, picked it up and held it out. "Then it is not a problem whatsoever. Each and every adult here is armed and capable of defending themselves."

Frank accepted the rifle with a nod and slung it across his back. "I'm sorry, Jacob, but I have to ask—what is this place? And who are you people?"

"Looks like a cult to me." Linda mumbled under her breath and it was Frank's turn to jab her in the ribs.

Jacob laughed and turned around, waving for them to follow him. "I'm sorry to disappoint you, but we're not a cult. At least I hope not."

"Hippies, then?" Linda spoke louder this time and Frank jabbed her again and gave Jacob an apologetic look.

Frank leaned in to Linda and whispered in her ear. "What the hell's your problem?"

"I don't like hippies, Frank!" Linda hissed back at him. Jacob turned back and smiled at them again as he shrugged.

"I'm not sure that's an accurate description of our shared community here. We do embrace a peaceful way of living and try to keep to ourselves and work together as a group."

"You call everyone walking around with guns peaceful?" Linda scoffed at Jacob's comment.

"Living peacefully doesn't mean that we won't defend ourselves. We will do so violently if we must, but we prefer other methods if at all possible."

"So, uh, you all live here at this motel?" Frank tried to change the subject.

"It was once a motel, yes. A few of us pooled our resources and purchased it and the surrounding land several years ago. We spent a great deal of time, money and effort on turning it into a place that would be a self-sustaining home away from the world." Jacob sighed and his face darkened. "Recent events seem to show that our plan may have been fortuitous, but not in the way in which we would have hoped."

"You mean all the destruction that started a couple days ago?"

"Indeed. But allow me to ask a few questions of my own, if you would."

Frank suddenly realized how well-spoken Jacob was and wondered what that indicated. "Sure, ask away."

"Where are you two from?"

Frank looked at Linda and she glanced uncomfortably at the two men. "I have a small place up in Maine. Been living there for a while now and I'm trying to get to Tennessee."

"I'm a trucker. New at it, too. I was an accountant but had to take a job driving eighteen-wheelers. I'm trying to get to Texas."

"Ah." Jacob nodded sagely. "So you two don't know each other?"

"Not before yesterday we didn't."

"Interesting." Jacob smiled again and Linda raised an eyebrow but decided not to inquire further.

"So, Jacob." Frank spoke again. "What do you know about all of this stuff that's going on? I saw some of it happen firsthand and Linda's heard about a lot of it on the radio."

Jacob sat down at a table near the fire and motioned for Linda and Frank to join him. "We've heard a great deal on the radio as well. None of it good, I'm afraid."

"You can still get radio transmissions out here?" Linda sat up in her chair. "How far out can you get them?"

Jacob motioned upward and Frank and Linda looked up above the motel. "We have a reasonably powerful transmitter and receiver setup. We've been monitoring transmissions from across the world." Linda stared at Jacob, her mouth agape as he continued. "Most of what we've heard has been about the United States and Canada. Our brothers up north were hit pretty hard. Not as hard as us, but with all the trade back and forth they took a heavy beating. Mexico, too, though not as much."

"Any word on how the military's been responding?" Linda leaned forward as Jacob spoke.

"There were troop withdrawals from several fronts overseas and the National Guard's been deployed to most major metropolitan cities to try and quell the uprisings. Food shortages are the worst part right now, but with the power out to pretty much everywhere it's going to get ugly in the next day or two."

"It's been ugly since it started." Linda said, edging even farther forward in her seat. "People were basically rioting within hours. I can only imagine what it's like in the cities with the power out."

Jacob was about to reply when one of the women who had taken the children inside earlier came running up to him. She whispered something in his ear, he glanced at Frank and Linda and then nodded at the woman. She cast a quick glance at the duo before running back to the motel.

"Sorry about that. The children wanted to come back outside."

"We appreciate you trusting us like this, Jacob." Frank smiled. "Even after that awkward first impression."

"I fancy myself a good discerner of persons, Frank. It's all right." Jacob stood up. "Come on, I think you'll find this interesting."

Frank and Linda followed Jacob into the motel and were shocked at what was inside. Although the exterior appeared run down the interior was anything but. The walls appeared freshly painted and the carpet and hardwood floors were immaculate. Clothing, toys and personal belongings in the rooms they passed were all clean and the building had a fresh, lived-in scent to it that made Frank feel instantly at ease and comfortable with the place.

The biggest surprise, though, was the fact that the lights inside the building were on, as was a heat pump that was keeping the building warm and comfortable against the cool of the autumn night. After walking halfway down the building, Jacob opened a door and stepped through. "In here."

Frank and Linda walked through the door and nearly gasped in astonishment. Computer monitors lined an entire wall from waist-height all the way up to the ceiling. A long desk stretched beneath them and two people—one man and one woman—sat in chairs at the desk, both wearing headphones and speaking quietly into microphones that sat in front of them. On the wall opposite the monitors was a row of computers set behind a glass barrier that were whirring away.

Jacob tapped the shoulder of the woman sitting at the desk and she turned around and took off her headphones. "Jacob! We have guests?"

Jacob smiled. "Liz, this is Frank and Linda. Frank, Linda this is my wife, Liz. They had some questions about the information we've been gathering on the Collapse." Jacob turned back to Frank and Linda. "That's what we've been calling it around here. 'The Collapse.' It sounds a bit ominous but then again the situation is pretty dire, isn't it Liz?"

Liz swiveled around in her chair and picked up a notepad from the desk. "I think that's an understatement. There are riots in most cities, fires breaking out all over the place, no power and no way to get anything back up and running. The National Guard is mostly just standing around trying to keep people focused on destroying things and not each other. There's an emergency order currently being debated in Washington that would effectively put the entire country under martial law and deploy the army to keep order."

Frank shook his head while Linda's eyes grew wide in horror. "How do you know all of this? Where are you getting it from?"

Liz pointed to the monitors above the desk. "We're off the grid here but our antenna is powerful enough to pick up just about anything. There are scattered stations going on and off all the time as power plants are trying to restart." Liz sighed and flipped through her notebook. "Unless they get system coordination back online, though, they'll never get the power restored."

"Any word on what's happening south of us, Liz? These folks are trying to get down to Tennessee and Texas."

Liz furrowed her brow as she skimmed through her notes.

"Nothing beyond what appears to be the norm. Looting, rioting and such. I imagine that's only going to get worse though, and if you're driving a working vehicle you'll be an even bigger target. Once you get into the more populated areas you should stick to back roads as much as possible and only use highways if absolutely necessary."

Linda nodded. "That's what we were thinking too."

Liz smiled. "I'd be happy to talk to you more in the morning, before you leave." She glanced at her husband questioningly. "They are staying, right? Don't tell me you didn't offer them a room for the night!"

Jacob chuckled and looked at Frank and Linda. "We do have a spare room for guests if you'd like to stay."

"What are you talking about, 'if you'd like to stay'—no, you're staying and that's final. We'll get some food into you, get you rested up and you can leave in the morning with provisions and all the help we can provide."

Linda started to protest but Liz held up her hands. "Nope, not another word. Jacob, get them fed and help them with whatever they need." Jacob smiled and kissed Liz, then motioned towards the door.

"I'm afraid you're staying for the night; I hope you don't mind."

"We'd love to, thank you both." Frank smiled and shook Liz's hand.

"Yeah, thank you very much." Linda forced out a smile even though she was still distracted by the new information and the equipment in the room. "And I'd like to talk to you tomorrow about the routes down south if you don't mind, Liz."

"Of course. Talk to you both then!"

Frank, Linda and Frank walked back down the length of the motel before Jacob stopped at another door and opened it. "Here's your room. Feel free to leave your things here; they won't be touched. Once you get settled please come back outside and get some food and drink and we can continue talking." Jacob walked off before Frank or Linda could say anything. They glanced at each other before entering the room and closing the door.

Standing in the middle of the colorful room with a ceiling fan turning lazily overhead, Frank was the first to speak.

"What in the hell *is* this place?"

Chapter Fifteen

The soft 'thunk' of tear gas grenades being launched through the air is lost amid the screams and shouts of the shoppers inside Gristedes super-market at the south end of Manhattan Island. It has taken just under a day for riots to break out across the city as the power has gone out, fires are still spreading and food is dangerously short. The small supermarket is packed dangerously full of people and just outside fights have broken out as others desperately try to get inside to secure some sort of food for themselves. In a city where every square inch of space is at a premium, no one has food on hand for more than a few days at best and most have less than that.

Nearby, at the Brooklyn Bridge, the walking and driving lanes are packed with people walking, jogging and running as they try to get off the island as quickly as possible. A few brave souls still try and drive their cars, but the amount of people on foot makes it nigh on impossible to get anywhere quickly. Up ahead, halfway along the bridge, the people come to an abrupt stop at a series of barriers set up by NYPD and the National Guard. One officer, speaking through a bullhorn, orders the people to turn around and return to your homes.

"Emergency relief supplies are being airlifted into the city!" He sounds confident as he speaks, though he is trembling inside. The crowd is not happy about being stopped and they look anxious enough to force the issue. "Return to your homes and places of business for your own safety! No traffic is being allowed on or off the island until proper security measures can be implemented!"

The crowd pushes against the barriers, shouting and yelling in frustration and anger. Most of them do not live on the island and all want to return to their families, not the stores and shops and offices where they work. Behind the barrier, one of the members of the National Guard speaks into a radio in hushed tones, his expression growing nervous as he hears the replies.

"I don't think we can hold people back much longer sir."

"Keep them there, dammit! Between the fires and the looting there's nowhere for these people to go!"

"They need supplies, sir. Any idea when the food drops are coming in?"

At the other end of the radio, at a nearby military airbase, a Lieutenant leans back in his chair and sighs as he rubs his eyes. He has been without sleep since the incident occurred and it's likely to be another twelve hours before he can get any rest.

"We're working as fast as possible. Just do your best out there, son."

The radio goes silent with a click and the officer at the airbase stands up and stretches his back. He looks out the window at the people below on the airfield and the organized chaos that is still ongoing. After a civilian truck detonated on the base and destroyed two buildings in the process, there have been no flights authorized to take off or land until a complete check has been made of every vehicle, aircraft and piece of equipment. This scene is replicated across civilian and military airports and airbases across the country. Emergency supplies sit in hangers, ready to be loaded onto aircraft, but it will be days before the brass feel comfortable with sending them out.

By then, deaths will number in the hundreds of thousands as the most vulnerable and weak fall prey to hunger and become victims of the underbelly of society as the fight for survival begins in earnest.

Chapter Sixteen

"I really don't think it's a good idea to leave the rifle behind."

"Linda, it's going to look *really* awkward if we go back out and I've got it over my shoulder. You've got your pistol and besides, every single freaking one of these people is armed. It doesn't matter how many guns we've got."

"Ugh." Linda sighed and shook her head. "You're right. But dammit, this has got to be the weirdest place I've ever been."

"No kidding. Bunch of pseudo-hippies with guns, computers, solar panels and a whole self-sustaining setup in the middle of nowhere upstate New York. It boggles the mind."

"So let's go get some answers." Linda picked up her jacket off of the floor and looked around the room one last time. There were two beds on opposite sides of the room with a colorful curtain hanging from the ceiling that could be pulled back or stretched out to provide privacy to the beds.

The walls were painted a bright blue, the ceiling was stark white and the slowly turning fan overhead had each of its blades painted a different primary color. A small bathroom sat off on one side of the room with a toilet, sink and shower and the main window for the room looked out over the rolling hills beyond, though it was hard to see anything at night.

Linda and Frank stepped out of their room and closed the door behind them. Frank had been initially worried about leaving all of their things behind, but based on his interactions with Jacob so far, he felt a strange sense of calmness about the entire place. That plus the knowledge that the people at the commune could have over-powered them at any instant gave him a sense of relief that was hard to explain.

Outside the building on a table near the fire, Jacob was sitting down in front of three plates of food and large cups filled with water. A thick slab of roast pork, fresh vegetables and steaming potatoes just pulled from the coals of the fire sat on each plate. He was in the midst of taking a bite when Linda and Frank emerged from the building and he waved them over as he stood and wiped his mouth.

"Hello you two!" He smiled broadly as they sat down at the table. "I hope this is satisfactory. If you have any allergies or intol-erances to anything, just let me know; don't be shy about it, please!"

Frank and Linda both shook their heads. "No, I think I'm good." Frank said.

"Yeah, same here."

Frank picked up a fork and glanced at Jacob. "Thanks for this, by the way. You guys really didn't need to feed us or give us a place to stay for the night."

Jacob smiled again as he cut another piece of pork. "Nonsense. I'd be a terrible host if I didn't at least do that. But that's not why you're here. You're here for information, I know. Please, eat until you're full and then ask whatever questions you have."

Frank and Linda wasted no time in filling their growling stom-achs. Frank knew in the back of his mind that the food tasted so good due to how little he had eaten in the last couple of days but he still swore that it was the best meal he had in his entire life. He and Linda both said nothing as they ate, and a few minutes later when their plates were clean, she sat back and nodded appreciatively at Jacob.

"Thank you again. That was amazing."

Jacob smiled and looked behind him. "The vegetables and potatoes all come from our gardens. We have the ones you see there in front of the building plus several more large patches in fields behind us."

"Can we ask you about that, Jacob?"

"Of course, Linda. Please ask away."

"Who *are* you people? You live like hippies on the outside but you all carry guns and your computer setup is like nothing I've seen before. Plus you have enough solar panels and battery capacity to run everything off the grid. How did you do all of this?"

Jacob took a long drink from his cup as he studied the pair before replying. "I was one of the five original founders of this place. We were originally from the Boston area and we were entrepreneurs, starting and selling off companies to larger organizations. We were quite good at our jobs. It became apparent to one of my friends first that he was getting tired of the constant cycle of creating something only to sell it off and have to start anew. So he, I and three others sat down one weekend and brainstormed about what we wanted to do." Jacob spread his arms and motioned around. "This was the result. We don't have a formal name for this place, but it's our home and our way of life now."

"You were all tech guys?" Frank raised an eyebrow. "Startup founders and stuff like that?"

"Hard to believe, yes, but we were. The challenges we were facing had grown too mundane so we collectively decided that we wanted to challenge ourselves in a different way. We brought ten others to this place with us and we've grown to twice that size. Mostly families live here now and we all work together to keep this place free from the cares of the outside world and focused on what really matters."

"So why all the guns? And the computers and all that?"

Jacob laughed. "Having money makes it easy to get permits for things like firearms here, even with the recent changes to the laws. That happened a month after we arrived, when some unscrupulous individuals decided to vandalize the building and scared one woman half to death that they were going to kidnap her or do something far worse. We agreed that we would act as our own protection from that day forward. I'm thankful every day that we don't have to use them."

"What about the computers?" Linda repeated the second half of Frank's question.

"We're still very much technology-oriented. Everything we grow is optimized by computerized systems we developed."

Linda chuckled. "Doesn't that sort of negate the point of living off the land?"

Jacob shrugged. "Remember who we are. We're people who made our living in the city, working on computer systems all day. Tackling something like this even when it's augmented with computer systems is a challenge for us. But that's the point and that's what we set out to do—challenge ourselves to create a small community that could flourish. If I had to be completely honest about it, we also wanted to keep some comforts from our old lives. Things like air conditioning and occupying some of our time with the systems we've built. But we don't believe that negates what we've done in any way."

"Fair enough." Frank nodded, impressed by Jacob's open answers.

"So what's with all the monitoring you were doing? That's what I assume you were doing anyway; I think your wife and that other person were monitoring radio transmissions?"

"Yes, that's something we started as soon as we realized something was going on. We decided to try and monitor and record as much information as possible about what's going on so that we can analyze it at a later date and use that information for good." Jacob shrugged. "Who knows if anything will come of it, but we've already discovered some limited uses, such as finding out what's going on between here and your destinations. We'll have something for you in the morning that should prove useful, I hope."

"That would be amazing." Linda was taken aback. As she

started to ask another question, a man walked up to Jacob and tapped him on the shoulder.

"Your shift's about to start, Jacob."

"Ah! Of course." Jacob pushed back his chair and stood. "All of us are taking turns monitoring for transmissions. I'll be doing that for a few hours if you need me, but you should feel free to speak to anyone else, as well. Everyone here is more than capable of helping should you need anything. I'll talk to you both in the morning."

With that, Jacob was off, heading back into the motel. Frank and Linda sat in silence at their table for several minutes as they watched the fire and the other people around them. Finally, after a long sigh, Frank spoke.

"Well then. This place is something else, isn't it?"

"No kidding." Linda shook her head. "I'm not sure what to think of it. It seems like it shouldn't even be real but... it is? I think?"

"It's an oddity here for certain. But I don't want to look a gift horse in the mouth since it sounds like they're going to be setting us up nicely tomorrow."

Linda snorted. "Either that or they're going to skin us while we're sleeping."

Frank laughed. "Speaking of sleep, we should get a few hours. I'd like to make as much progress tomorrow as we can."

"Agreed." Linda lowered her voice and looked around. "I want to keep watch in shifts tonight, though. Just to be absolutely certain we're safe."

"That sounds fine to me. I'll take first watch as long as you promise not to run off without me."

"If I do then you can just join them here and start gardening."

Frank chortled and they both stood and headed back to the motel. It took them a few minutes to find their room again and once inside they were pleased to see that their belongings were exactly where they had left them.

Frank stayed up for a few hours, sitting on the edge of one bed while Linda slept in the other. His thoughts wandered as he stared out the window at the darkness beyond. He still felt confident that his parents were doing well on their ranch. Linda's parents, though, he wondered about. She told him that they were in a nursing home but he had no idea how their health was. Every time he had probed about her personal life she had given him the minimum amount of information required to answer the question and then either changed the subject or refused to go into any more details.

Oh well. We'll be in Tennessee before too long and then she can take care of her folks while I get to Texas.

———

FRANK WOKE Linda a few hours before dawn and she kept watch while he slept. The bed was firm but comfortable and it felt like heaven after a month of sleeping in the back of his truck. When he woke up, the room was empty and he had a sinking feeling in the pit of his stomach as he got out of bed. "Great." Frank grumbled to himself as he stood up and rubbed the sleep from his eyes. "She took off again. What a—"

"What a what, Frank?" Linda popped her head out of the bathroom and flashed him a smile.

Frank rolled his eyes. "What a lovely person you are to not leave me here."

"Oh come on, Frank. It's not so bad here." Linda stepped out, running a brush through her hair before pulling it up into a pony-tail again. "They have power, running water and lots of food. Plus everyone seems creepily friendly. It's the perfect place to spend the rest of your life before they pass you a cup of off-brand Kool-Aid and tell you to drink up."

Frank laughed and grabbed his backpack off of the floor and rifled through the contents to double-check that everything was there. "No thanks, I'm good. And besides, they're not that bad."

"Yeah, I know. It's actually scary how nice this place is. Makes me wish we could stay here some more and get to know these people better. I'm sure they're doing a lot better than most."

Frank stepped into the bathroom after Linda went out. "Still, though, we have places to go. Let's find Jacob and see about that information he promised us."

After both Linda and Jacob were refreshed and had their backpacks on, they headed outside. The morning was foggy and overcast with more warmth than they had felt for the last few days. The fire in the pit had died down over the night, though it was still being fed wood as the small group tending to it started to set up equipment for cooking breakfast. Jacob was nearby talking to his wife, Liz, and he smiled at Frank and Linda as they approached.

"There are our guests! How did you two sleep last night?"

"Very well, thanks." Frank shook hands with Jacob and Liz and Linda nodded in agreement.

"Excellent. I'll leave you two for a few minutes while I get your promised provisions. Liz has some information that you'll no doubt find useful for your trip."

"Oh you don't need to give us anything—you've been generous enough already." Frank protested but Jacob waved him off.

"Nonsense. I'll be back in a jiffy." Jacob jogged off leaving Frank and Linda to talk with Liz who pulled a manila folder out of a small bag she kept on her shoulder.

"You two are heading to Tennessee, right?"

"Yeah, Tennessee for me and then Frank's going on to Texas from there."

"Right. Well. I don't have much in the way on information between Tennessee and Texas. All I can do is advise you to stick to back roads near cities and take highways in between, and only when you have to. As far as getting from here to Tennessee, though..." Liz opened the folder and pulled out a colorful map of the northeastern portion of the country with several colorful lines drawn between New York and Tennessee. She ran her finger down each of the lines as she spoke.

"Here are the routes you could take. I advise staying away from Washington as much as possible. It's a hellhole right there, as is the rest of the northern Virginia area. I'd say to get down through Pennsylvania and West Virginia using the back roads as much as possible, then crossing through the western tip of Virginia before you hit Tennessee. Where is it in Tennessee that you're going?"

"Pigeon Forge." Linda studied the map as she answered, not seeing the look of shock going across Liz's face.

"Pigeon Forge you said?" Liz asked the question hesitantly.

"Yeah… why, what's wrong?" Linda picked up on Liz's concern and was suddenly worried herself.

"That whole area of Tennessee was hit by a nasty storm two nights ago. Three or four feet of snow with more expected tonight, if the forecast from a few days ago still holds true. You're in for a rough time once you get there."

Linda's thoughts immediately flew to her parents and the potential danger they were in. "How long do you think it'll take us to get there if we use the back roads?"

Liz shrugged. "Hard to say, really. It depends on what's happening along the way. If you get lucky and avoid running into anyone you could get there in a day. If things continue to deteriorate, though…" Liz trailed off and looked at Linda. "I'm sorry I have so little information for you to go on."

Linda shook her head. "No, no this is incredible. It's perfect. Exactly what we need. I'd rather know now before we get there than be surprised."

"Preparation is everything." Liz smiled and patted Linda on the shoulder. "I truly hope your parents are safe." She glanced at Frank. "And yours as well. And I hope the two of you make it safely to your destinations. Here—take this. There's more information inside. Transcripts of radio transmissions and such. It should help you understand what's going on right now. Whether it's of value or not I don't know, but more information is always better than less."

Liz held out the manila envelope and Frank accepted it with a nod. "Thanks, Liz. We can't tell you enough how much all of this means to us."

"Revisit the kindness on others, Frank." Liz smiled. "We'll need a great deal of kindness to see us through all of this before it's over."

Liz embraced Linda and Frank before leaving, and the duo stood together for a moment not knowing what to do next. It didn't take long before Jacob returned carrying a large canvas bag with two other men behind him, each of them toting a small gas can in each hand.

"Sorry for the delay there!" Jacob smiled and held out the bag in his hand. "Enough nonperishables to last you until you get to Tennessee. Plus I put some fresh vegetables and smoked meat in there and we have several gallons of gasoline for you. I'm afraid it won't be enough to get you all the way there, but it should help. We have an emergency generator and couldn't afford to take more than this."

To say that Frank and Linda were shocked by Jacob's generosity was an understatement. "We can't accept all of this, Jacob." Frank shook his head, but Jacob rebuffed him.

"Nonsense. You two have many more miles to travel. The least we can do is help you out. Now come on. You parked down the road a bit, yes?"

Jacob took off with the two men behind him in tow. Frank and Linda watched him for a few seconds before they got their feet into gear and trotted off after him. When they arrived at the truck, Jacob loaded the canvas bag into the back and secured the gas cans next to the two remaining full ones and the several empty ones. "Excellent! Looks like you'll be able to make it farther than I thought since you have some gas already in there."

"Jacob—we're sorry, again. And thank you. Again. You've shown unbelievable generosity to two strangers who walked in one night."

"Nonsense. You'd have done the same thing, I'm sure of it." Jacob smiled and shook the pair's hands before stepping away. "Stay safe on your travels, you two. And once all of this mess clears up and you get a chance to travel again, please come back to visit."

As Frank drove the truck down the road, Linda watched Jacob and the others disappear around a bend through the rearview mirror. She sat back in her seat and shook her head in amazement.

"Unbelievable that people like that exist. Especially right now. Simply unbelievable."

Frank grinned. "Sounds like somebody didn't exactly believe her little speech about there still being good people left in the world." He sighed and his smile faded. "Try to hold onto that feeling, though. I have a feeling we're going to need to remember it here before too long."

Chapter Seventeen

The journey south through New York was beautiful, though it was not without its downsides. As Frank and Linda wound their way to the south and west, it became increasingly necessary to stop at every intersection and study their map. The roads seemed to have an almost magnetic attraction to taking them towards New York City, and there was no way that either of them wanted to head in that direction.

After a day of driving and a night spent trading off keeping watch and stretching out across the front seats of the truck for a few hours of sleep, they realized that they were getting close to the Pennsylvania border. Unfortunately that realization came with a price.

"See that?" Linda put her hand over her eyes and squinted as she looked east.

"I see it and smell it. That's got to be one hell of a fire. Think somebody started it on purpose?"

Linda shrugged. "Who knows. We need to get off these back roads though. If that thing's spreading very fast then it'll be easy for us to get trapped by the blaze." She looked up at the canopy of trees that spread across the road. "And these little roads don't exactly work as good firebreaks.

"What are you thinking? Go west towards a highway?" Frank opened the map and spread it out across the hood of the car. "We're not that far from interstate 81. We could head there, take that down through Binghamton, maybe see if we can get some fuel there."

"Ugh." Linda looked in the back of the truck at the two small cans of gas they had left. "I hate the idea of heading into a city to look for gas. We might as well, though."

"Think we can make it there?"

Linda walked back and looked at the map, tracing out their route with her finger. She nodded. "Yeah. Yeah I think so. It'll be close but if we run out then we'll have to find some other solution."

Frank folded up the map and looked back to the east. The sky was blue and clear for the most part, except for in the east, when it turned into a roiling black mass of smoke and ash. The hills and mountains of the area made it difficult to tell how close the fire was or how large it actually was, but the amount of smoke made it seem far larger than what Frank or Linda wanted to tangle with.

"Good." Frank walked to the driver's side door and hopped in. "Let's get going, then."

As Linda got into the passenger's side of the truck, Frank noted with satisfaction that she didn't give him a look. She had initially been uncomfortable with him driving and though she hadn't said anything he could tell by her body language that she preferred being in control of the vehicle. After their visit to the "techno-commune" (as they were now calling it) she seemed to no longer mind him driving, and didn't seem as nervous or worried about it.

Linda took the map from Frank and navigated as he drove, and the truck was quiet except for those moments. Frank began thinking about some of the previous conversations that he and Linda had and remembered something she had said.

"Did you say you were in Ahvaz? Was that during the invasion?" Linda was staring out the window but Frank could see her entire body tense up at the question and he immediately apologized. "You know what, I'm sorry. I shouldn't have asked that."

Linda didn't reply for another few minutes and Frank shifted uncomfortably in his seat, wishing he could take the question back. When she finally did speak, her voice was quiet enough that Frank had to slow down the truck to reduce the engine noise enough to hear her.

"Yeah, I was part of the first wave that rolled into Ahvaz. We were tasked with taking over the governmental and administrative buildings on the left bank of the river, to the west. We were supposed to leave the residential buildings on the opposite side of the river intact and not cross over, but we started taking heavy mortar fire from emplacements they had set up on the tops of people's homes."

Linda sighed and shook her head. "We weren't expecting them to have the capabilities they had. I'd still like to know who supplied their weapons, because those weren't dumb mortars. Those were new, state-of-the-art smart mortars. The ones that can adjust themselves in flight and target vehicles and people. We were unprepared." Linda stopped talking and Frank glanced over at her.

"I'm sorry. For asking, and for what you went through."

Linda turned back to look out the windshield, wearing a mask of determination on her face. "Yeah, well, that's what I get for joining the Marines. Mom said I was crazy and Dad called me an idiot. I guess they were right after all."

"Well I'm sorry, again. I shouldn't have asked."

"Nah." Linda shrugged. "It's been long enough I should be able to talk about it."

"Not necessarily. My dad went through some pretty crazy stuff during his time in the sand. I remember waking up to him screaming in the middle of the night because somebody drove a loud motorcycle by the house."

"Shit." Linda nodded. "I knew guys like that."

"All I'm trying to say is that if you don't want to talk about it, don't. If you do… well, I listened to my dad enough that I'm decent at listening."

Linda nodded and patted Frank on the shoulder. "Thanks, Frank. I appreciate it."

The pair lapsed back into silence for the next half hour until they saw the first sign for the interstate. As the major north/south corridor for the eastern seaboard, interstate 81 had seen several upgrades over the years, including an expansion to 4 lanes per side in the entirety of Virginia, Pennsylvania and New York. The expansion was necessary due to the amount of traffic seen on the road, though that turned out to be a not-so-good thing for Frank and Linda.

When they arrived at the first onramp to the interstate, they were forced to continue on a service road for three more ramps until they found one that wasn't clogged with abandoned or destroyed vehicles. The amount of traffic on the interstate was much greater than on the highways in Maine and they were finally starting to get a sense for just how much of an impact the attacks had caused.

Driving on the interstate was incredibly difficult—much more so than they had thought—due to the sheer amount of obstacles they encountered. Remnants of destroyed tractor-trailers sat every few hundred feet, though they were not alone. Damaged cars, vans, trucks and SUVs clustered around the trucks, giving evidence of how tight traffic had been in some areas when the bombs went off. Frank tried to keep his eyes forward and not look inside the vehicles for fear of what he might see, though Linda studied them closely, squaring her jaw and gritting her teeth at the sight of more than a few blackened skeletons.

At more than a few points Frank had to take the truck off of the road entirely, going through the median or onto the grassy shoulders to get around portions of the road that were completely blocked. Deep scars in the soft earth testified to how many other people had been forced to go the same way, and in a few places Frank almost couldn't make it since more than one person had gotten their vehicle stuck and had to abandon it.

As they drove along, Linda and Frank salvaged a length of garden hose from an abandoned car and siphoned gas from several vehicles into their gas cans and the tank of the truck. Contrary to what they expected, though, most of the vehicles were out of gas or so low that they weren't able to get much. In the end they managed to pull twenty gallons out, which Linda estimated would help make up for how much extra they were burning as they were going so slowly.

"If we make it to this city," she said, "we need to fill up somehow. Beg, borrow, steal. I don't care which."

Frank looked at where she had pointed. "You ever been there before?"

"Binghamton?" Linda shook her head. "No. Why?"

"Decades ago it used to be quite the place. Good schools, booming economy and a technology center thanks to IBM and some other companies. When they moved away the place started to dry up. Last time I went through was probably five years ago, on a business trip." Frank shook his head. "It wasn't the worst of places, but it wasn't the best either. I remember seeing a news bulletin about a rise in drug and gang activity the area. Meth dealers and stuff like that. I'm not sure I want to see what it's like now after all of this."

Linda folded the map up and tossed it onto the dashboard before leaning up against the window and closing her eyes. "Well, whatever's there we'll be fine. We just need to get fuel and go. I'm going to take fifteen to rest up before we get there."

"Sounds good." Frank drove on in silence, weaving his way down the interstate as he thought about what might be waiting for them in the city ahead.

Chapter Eighteen

The Port of Oakland is in shambles. Fires spread from Molotov cocktails consume buildings in and around the port while dozens of people sift through the containers, opening them with bolt cutters and rifling through the contents. Anything useful or valuable is loaded into one of the many vans parked nearby and is driven away to be stashed in the city.

The thieves work their way through the shipping containers quickly, and after two hours they've finished combing through all of the ones that are on the dock. Several container ships are still loaded down with goods leaving and arriving, though, and they are the next targets.

As the thieves climb onto the first ship and fan out among the shipping containers, one of them opens one to find a curious sight. The container is empty save for a single crate the length and half the width of a small car strapped down in the center. The man cuts through the straps holding the crate down and cracks it open to reveal a block of metal with a silvery finish and a small display on the top. The display appears damaged and flickers on and off so quickly that it's impossible to tell what it says.

The object looks valuable and the man calls over his cohorts to help him move it out of the crate and towards the ramp leading down to the port. While carrying the heavy object, one of the men loses his grip and drops his corner of the object onto the hard metal of the container ship. The clang of metal on metal is loud and reverberates across the length of the ship.

The jolt from the drop forces back together the two circuits inside the object that came loose during a storm while the container ship was at sea. When the circuits align, the object's internal computer reboots and immediately performs a time check. The deadline was a week ago and the trigger is past due.

The object explodes instantly. The fireball vaporizes the men standing around and carrying the object and launches the shipping containers on the ship into the air. The fury of the explosion is so great that the thieves standing too close to the ship on the dock are killed by the force of the blast. Those standing farther away clutch their ears in agony as the compression wave washes over them. Every window in the port is blown out and the container ship itself lists to the side and begins to sink.

Several security officers and half a dozen CPB officers lie dead near the entrance to the port, having been overwhelmed by gunfire from the group ransacking the port. More officers and workers hide inside, tending to wounded and desperately calling for backup that will never arrive. The city behind them is on fire, and emergency services are overwhelmed. As the detonation rips apart the container ship and a large portion of the port, the surviving officers and workers gasp in shock, wondering what could have happened to cause such a terrifying explosion.

Chapter Nineteen

W hen Linda and Frank arrived in Binghamton, the city was not at all what they expected. Contrary to Frank's assumptions, the area had seen a remarkable boom in the last two years as the city enacted tax breaks that drew several large technology companies back. The area had grown immensely, adding new roads, shopping centers and several new neighborhoods as well.

What was most peculiar about the town, though, was how calm it was. Shells of burned-out tractor trailers were still scattered about on the roads and hardly anyone was out driving but the buildings were still intact and some of them even appeared to have power.

"How on earth do they have power still?" Linda shook her head as she looked out the window and up at a tall building with the logo of an obscure computer chip manufacturer on the side.

"Maybe they've got a power plant nearby or the buildings are running on generators still?" Frank shrugged. "I have no idea, but I'm loving the lack of people running around rioting and looting."

The lack of chaos in the city gave Frank hope, but Linda had a funny feeling in the pit of her stomach. "Doesn't this seem *too* calm to you?"

"Meh. I'd rather this than deal with the people at that gas station or those two guys who you… yeah."

"I suppose so." The mention of the two men Linda killed didn't faze her. "Still, keep your eyes open."

As they drove through the town they kept on alert not just for signs of danger but for a gas station, as they were still in desperate need of enough to get them to Tennessee. They passed multiple gas stations, but all of them were out of fuel as evidenced by the "NO GAS" signs. Most of the stations were dark and empty, but when Frank spotted one with the lights on he decided to pull into the empty parking lot.

"What exactly are we doing here?" Linda pointed to the sign hanging from the front door. "They're out of gas."

"I know. But I want to talk to whoever's inside and see if they know of anywhere in town that still has some."

Linda sighed and nodded. "All right. Just be quick about it." She glanced around the parking lot. "I don't want to sit still here any longer than I have to."

Frank hopped out of the car and ran inside to the front counter. Linda watched as he spoke with the clerk for a moment before running back out and jumping in the car. "He said there's still one place in town with gas. They're rationing how much they sell to each person to just ten gallons each."

"That'll get us a ways down the road, I guess."

"He also said they don't take cash. They're bartering for the fuel."

Linda rolled her eyes. "Oh great. We've already devolved to a bartering-based economy. Perfect."

"Want to skip it and try our luck siphoning from cars on the highway?"

Linda shook her head. "Nah. Let's go there and try our luck. How far is it?"

"The guy inside said to keep following the main road and we'd spot it when we got there."

After a few more minutes of driving, Frank and Linda did indeed spot the gas station in question. It was a large place with wide lanes, ample parking and the building had a clean, fresh look except for the copious amounts of barbed wire and sandbags that had been stacked around the perimeter of the building and parking lot.

"What the hell…" Frank hit the brakes and stopped the truck a few hundred feet from the gas station as he and Linda gazed in shock. Behind the hastily-constructed barriers were several wooden platforms that each held a pair of people wielding rifles. They didn't act in an aggressive manner, but appeared to merely be keeping watch over the station.

As Frank and Linda stared at the station, a car pulled up to the narrow gap in the sandbags and barbed wire that acted as the entrance. The person in the car rolled down his window and spoke to one of the guards who waved him through. After parking next to a pump, the person in the car went inside for a moment before returning with a woman wearing a shirt with the gas station's logo on it. The clerk and the driver of the car spoke while the clerk filled up a small can of gas, then the driver handed the clerk a small bag and drove back out.

The whole exchange only took a few minutes, and by the end of it Frank wasn't sure how to feel about the whole affair. "Um. So do we still want to try this? I mean it seems pretty orderly and everything. And we could do with the fuel."

Linda didn't answer immediately as she was busy studying the layout of the guards. "Whoever put up those barriers did a terrible job. And the guards are half-assed at best. They don't even have a full view of the grounds outside and inside the barriers." She snorted and nodded. "Yeah, let's do this. If things get hairy just get down. From the way most of those guys are carrying their guns they've never handled one before."

Frank eyed Linda carefully as he stepped back on the accelerator. He approached the entrance to the gas station slowly and rolled down his window well before he got to the entrance. A wiry young man no older than 18 with a full camo outfit on that was three sizes too big for him walked up to the window.

"Can I help you?"

"Yeah, we're just passing through and could use some gasoline. A guy down the street said you're still selling some. That true?"

"Absolutely, though we don't take cash, credit or check. You'll have to trade something. Gold, silver, things like that."

Frank glanced at Linda who spoke up. "How about bullets? You taking bullets in trade?"

The young man frowned and stepped back. "Just a second." He turned around and spoke quietly into a radio pulled from his belt. After a whispered conversation he turned around and nodded. "Yes, ma'am, that'll work. Just pull through, go inside and talk to the folks in there and they'll get you squared away."

Frank rolled up the window and pulled forward slowly as he looked over at Linda. "Bullets? You have them to spare?"

Linda chuckled. "Just stay here and watch the truck. I'll be back in a minute."

After Frank stopped next to one of the gas pumps, Linda hopped out of the truck and dug around in one of her bags that was in the back. She took out a handful of small boxes and carried them with her into the gas station where she talked to both the woman they had seen earlier and a man who came from a room in the back.

"Jeff said you wanted to trade bullets?" The man didn't bother to tell Linda his name or greet her as he came out.

"Yep. Nine millimeter. Three boxes for ten gallons."

The man took one of the boxes and opened it, examining the bullets inside. "Five boxes."

"Four, and we'll use our own gas cans."

"Done."

Linda passed the four boxes of bullets to the man and he nodded at the woman behind the counter. She and Linda walked out and Linda grabbed two five-gallon cans from the back of the truck and placed them on the ground. Frank rolled down his window as the attendant filled the cans and whispered to Linda.

"How'd it go?"

She smiled. "Just fine. The guy had no idea how to haggle.

Makes me glad I spent a while in the sandbox over there; every vendor in the city wanted to rip off the white American girl. I had to learn pretty quickly how to avoid that kind of BS."

"All done." The attendant interrupted Linda and started walking back to the gas station.

"Thanks. Say, know of any place to stay around here for the night?"

The girl either didn't hear Linda's question or, if she did, she didn't bother answering. Before Linda could ask again the attendant had run back inside and was back behind her counter.

"Huh." Linda scratched her head. She stepped out of the way as Frank hopped out of the truck and put the filled cans into the back, then walked around to the passenger door.

"You drive for a while, okay?"

"Hm?" Linda looked over at Frank. "Oh, right. Yeah." Linda started the car and slowly turned around in the parking lot of the gas station and began heading out. Linda watched the guards in the gas station in the rearview mirror and frowned. "Weird place that was."

"Think they were doing something shady?"

"Mm." Linda furrowed her brow. "Not sure. They didn't seem shady but now that I think about it, something was definitely off."

———

BEHIND, at the gas station, a figure watched the red and white truck pulling out from a small window at the far end of the store. When the truck was gone, the figure exited his office and went to the attendant at the counter. She bore a nervous expression as the figure advanced on her, and gulped audibly when he stopped and spoke.

"Did you plant the transmitter?" The man's voice was soft and smooth with a touch of malice running through it that could easily be mistaken for something more benign if the listener wasn't paying attention.

The attendant bobbed her head up and down gently. "In the back, while they weren't watching."

The man smiled, exposing rows of blackened rotting teeth. "Good."

Chapter Twenty

The source of the power for the city soon became evident as they saw the signs for the "Binghamton Wind & Geothermal Power Project" pointing to a location just outside town. Several power trucks were parked along the road near the plant and people wearing hard hats and working in buckets were replacing transformers on poles.

"Huh." Frank nodded approvingly as he saw the sign. "I guess that explains the source of the electricity. I didn't know there were geothermal sources around here."

Linda raised an eyebrow. "I'm just surprised that they can put out enough juice to power the town."

"Want to go check it out? If they have power they might have some more information on conditions around here."

Linda patted the set of notes that Liz had provided and shook her head. "I think we're good on that front. Besides, I wish that sky looked better." Linda looked up through the windshield at the blackening clouds that were gathering overhead. The clouds had started forming as they pulled into town, but they were starting to take on a decidedly dangerous look. The wind was picking up as well, buffeting the truck as they drove along and sending plastic bags, newspapers and other trash and debris tumbling through the air.

"You want to find a place to stop for the night?" Frank looked at the buildings around where they were driving. "I don't see any hotels. We could try closer to the edge of town, though."

"I think I'd rather stay away from hotels at this point." Linda gripped the steering wheel tightly as a gust of wind buffeted the car. "I do think we need to get off the road, though. Let's get out of town a ways and see what's out there."

Frank nodded in agreement. "Sounds good."

The darkening sky and roaring winds were soon accompanied by sheets of driving rain. The downpour came at a sharp angle, tapping at the glass on Frank's side of the car like so many skeletal fingers trying to pry their way in. As they approached the outskirts of the city on the eastern side, Frank and Linda had to shout in order to make themselves heard. "I sure hope that storage box in the back is watertight!"

"I doubt it!" Linda shouted back. Her knuckles were white from her grip on the steering wheel.

"We need to pull over soon!"

"I know, Frank, I know!"

"What about there?" Frank pointed to a house off of the street. The windows were shuttered and the door boarded up and the fence in front of the house had a small sign on it indicating that the home had been foreclosed on. While other homes they had passed had a few lights on, this one did not. There were no vehicles outside, the grass was overgrown and vines had made it nearly to the second story, though there was still one more floor left for them to ascend.

"An abandoned house in a storm?" Linda shook her head as she shouted. "Sounds like a classic horror movie mistake to me!"

"It's either that or trying to drive in this!" A bolt of lightning cracked a tree less than a block away as Frank finished his sentence as if to emphasize his point.

"Screw it!" Linda turned the wheel sharply and headed up the driveway to the house at the end. She and Frank hopped out, grabbed their guns and opened the storage case in the back of the truck. Water was seeping in, but not seriously, and they both grabbed their backpacks and Linda grabbed one of her other bags.

"Just leave the rest!" She shouted at Frank. "It'll survive in the rain!"

Frank ran towards the front door and skidded to a stop once he was on the porch. Linda followed close behind and threw her bags on the porch and took several deep breaths. "Where on earth did this storm come from?" Linda brushed the water from her jacket and shivered involuntarily. "It's *freezing* out here."

Frank, meanwhile, was digging through the bottom of his bag. After a minute's frantic searching he stood up with a smile on his face. "Ha!"

The small pry bar was only six inches long, but he was able to put enough leverage on it to start pulling away the boards that were nailed across the front of the house. Linda put a hand on his arm to stop him.

"Wait a second." She walked across the porch and motioned for Frank to follow her. "There's a side door here. Better to go in here than right out in front, eh?"

Frank nodded and walked along the porch to the smaller door that was set on the corner of the house. Linda looked to the left and right at the boarded-up windows and shook her head. "You know, this place creeps me the hell out. Maybe we should have just gone to a hotel."

Another bolt of lightning cracked nearby, causing both her and Frank to jump in surprise. "Be my guest!" Frank tossed one of the boards out into the yard off the side of the house and leaned in to wrench the other off. The second board came off with significantly less effort and Frank threw it out into the yard after the first board. He put his shoulder against the door and stepped back, preparing to throw himself at it when Linda held up her hands.

"Whoa, hang on!" She stepped up to the door and twisted the handle. When it didn't budge, she took a step back and forced her weight into a step forward, raising her right foot and bringing it to bear on the door directly next to the handle. The motion was enough to cause the deadbolt and door latch to tear through the cheap wooden frame of the door on the inside and it opened freely. Linda caught herself on the frame before she fell forward, then turned to smile at Frank.

"Never use your shoulder. A boot right at the weak point takes care of it every time."

Frank raised an eyebrow as he picked up his backpack and Linda's spare bag. "Nicely done, GI Jane. Let's get inside and see what we're dealing with."

Linda took her backpack and pulled her pistol out of its holster as Frank held the rifle in one hand. As they walked inside, Linda pushed the door closed and looked around at the foyer. "Put my bag by the door," she whispered, "and let's clear the house and make sure we're alone."

Frank kept his backpack on but held tight to the rifle as he followed Linda through the house. She held one of her flashlights in one hand and the pistol in the other, sweeping each room in the house that they went through with the weapon as they checked for any signs that someone was in the residence with them.

The rooms were barren save for dust and a few scraps of packing paper, though, and it didn't take more than fifteen minutes for them to sweep the basement and the three floors above. When they returned to the foyer Linda looked visibly more relaxed, a fact that Frank decided to ask her about.

"You do a lot of this house sweeping stuff when you were overseas?"

Linda stiffened slightly at the question but answered after a few seconds of hesitation. "Yeah, you could say that. If I'm alone somewhere I like to *know* I'm alone."

Frank nodded. "Makes sense. Especially now. Say, speaking of alone, why didn't we think of knocking on some doors where the lights were on and seeing if someone would take us in?"

Linda gave Frank a look like she was staring at a potato. "What would *you* say if two strangers showed up in the middle of a storm demanding to be put up for the night?"

"Well, if I was Jacob I'd welcome them in." Frank sighed.

"You're right, though. Still, it'd be nice if we had some warmth. It's going to get crazy cold tonight with all this rain."

Linda walked over to the nearest switch and flicked it up. The lights in the foyer immediately sprung to life and she laughed. "A foreclosed house that's all boarded up but the power is still connected? What kind of a crazy town *is* this?"

"Hey don't look a gift horse in the mouth. Let's get the heat cranked up before it gets colder."

"Yeah, yeah." Linda waved over her shoulder as she headed down the hall. "I'm on it."

Chapter Twenty-One

"What's the status of the Russian naval fleet?"

"Heavy movement in the Pacific. No real changes since they began assembling."

"China?"

"No changes there, either."

"Anything new from our European allies?"

"Germany's sent twenty thousand as a show of strength to the east. Russian 'exercises' are still ongoing. The Chinese appear to be staying out of that particular dick-measuring contest for the moment. Britain's being finicky with their commitment. On a side note, Australia committed another ten thousand should we need them."

"Hm. Good. And the homeland? What new developments?"

"We're still awaiting official authorization to begin deploying the Army into a total of thirty-seven major metropolitan cities to act as peacekeeping and aid personnel. National guard and local law enforcement's been doing a shit job of keeping things together. Hospitals are overwhelmed and we've seen scattered attempts to break into bases and training camps but so far the majority of people are sticking it out at home. Almost no one is on the roads due to fear of being another victim."

"Do you have the latest casualty projections?"

"I believe so. Yes, there. On the screen now."

"Hm. And these are accurate?"

"Absolutely, sir."

"Damn. The Air Force still doesn't have a time frame for when they'll be through with their security checks, do they?"

"I'm afraid not."

"All right. Send this summary up the chain to the President. Attach a memo with my personal recommendations I sent earlier."

"No changes to them?"

"None."

"Very good, sir. I'll take care of it."

Chapter Twenty-Two

It was around one in the morning as Linda and Frank were both dozing on the floor of a carpeted room when she suddenly woke up with goosebumps rising on her arms and legs.

"Frank." Linda crawled across to the other side of the room and tapped Frank on the leg. "Frank, get up!" Her whisper was frantic and hurried.

"Wh—what? Huh?" Frank opened his eyes and sat up quickly when he saw the look on Linda's face.

"We need to sweep the house again."

"Why?" Frank yawned. "What's wrong?"

"I'm pretty sure I heard something downstairs."

Frank raised an eyebrow and looked out the window. "Are you sure? It's raining pretty hard out there right now. Could have just been the wind or something."

"Let's just do a quick sweep of the house. Also, one of us needs to be awake tonight."

Groaning, Frank got to his feet, put on his jacket that he had been using as a makeshift blanket and grabbed the rifle. "All right, let's do this."

Linda led their sweep through the top floor of the house with

Frank following stiffly behind, though he was only paying half attention and continued yawning every few seconds. When they reached the second floor, though, Frank suddenly stopped and cocked his head at the sound of a creak coming from the floor below. "What the hell was that?" Frank whispered to Linda, who had frozen in place at the sound as well.

Linda shook her head and put her finger over her lips as she quietly made her way towards the stairs. She took them one at a time, keeping her feet as far to the edges as possible to minimize the sound coming from the boards. Frank followed close behind her, and when they got halfway down the stairs to the landing, they both stopped and listened intently.

Several seconds went by in silence, then came the sound of a car door shutting from somewhere outside the house. The noise was faint and barely audible behind the noise of the pouring rain, but it was unmistakable.

Linda's jaw clenched and she continued moving down the stairs with Frank close behind her. They had turned off all of the lights in the house before moving upstairs to rest, but as Linda and Frank moved onto the ground floor, they could both see a faint glow shining up the next set of stairs that led down to the ground floor.

"Stay behind me and watch our backs, okay?" Linda whispered into Frank's ear and he nodded, wide-eyed and no longer feeling sleepy. His heart pounded in his chest and he could hear each beat thudding against his ears.

As the pair descended the stairs, one of the boards suddenly let off a loud groan and they both froze. There was a sudden, frenzied clatter from one of the rooms on the ground floor and they heard the sound of the front door being thrown open, the rush of rain, then the sound of the door being slammed closed.

Linda moved quickly down the stairs, no longer bothering with stealth, glancing inside each room they passed as she made her way forward. Behind her Frank hurried to keep up the pace, and he nearly ran into her as she stopped at the front door and crouched to peek out through one of the windows next to it.

"Who was it?" Frank whispered to Linda.

"I have no idea. Whoever it was, I think they're gone now." She stood up from looking out the window and turned back to talk to Frank when a bright light pierced through the windows of the house in multiple directions. The loud *click* of floodlights turning on accompanied the brightness, and the duo shielded their eyes from the sudden assault.

"What the hell?" Frank held his arm up as he stepped away from the front door and windows.

From outside the house, a static-laden squawk cut through the rain like a knife, followed by the amplified voice of someone speaking into a bullhorn.

"You two in the house! Come out with your hands up!"

Frank glanced at Linda. "The cops? Really?"

Linda shook her head. "No way. They wouldn't bother with sitting outside or not announcing themselves as such. Has to be something else."

After a few seconds of silence, the voice spoke again. "I said come out with your—oh, what the hell, Josh? Can you not hold an umbrella straight for two minutes? Fucking hell, get out of here!" The voice wavered and the bullhorn crackled followed by the sound of a loud *thunk* and someone crying in pain. "You! Yeah, you. Get over here and hold this thing up over me. Damned rain making everything complicated tonight."

Linda moved into one of the side rooms where the lights coming in were dimmer and looked out the window through a crack in between the boards. It was difficult to see out through the windows as the array of floodlights pointed at the windows kept Linda and Frank from seeing most of the people milling about outside.

A man dressed in a black leather trench coat sat in a cheap plastic lawn chair that was set up in the back of Frank and Linda's red and white truck. His face was impossible to make out, but he held a bullhorn in one hand while the other had a large black umbrella that he was holding out to a second man who was trying to climb up into the back of the vehicle. After a few slips and false starts the second man finally got into the back of the truck, took the umbrella from the man in the trench coat and held it over their heads.

"No, you idiot; over *my* head! What's the point of having someone holding an umbrella for you if they're going to try and share it?" The man in the trench coat jabbed the one standing behind him, who moved the umbrella forward.

"There. That's better." The trench-coated man adjusted himself in his seat, then held the bullhorn back up to his mouth and shouted again. "As I was saying, you two in the house come out right now! We want to have a word with you!" Even while seated, the man was shifting around in his seat constantly, moving with an impossible amount of vigor and energy. The series of floodlights shone around him, overwhelming Linda and Frank's vision and making it nigh-on impossible to get off a clean shot.

As the man spoke, Frank dashed into the room next to Linda and spoke to her breathlessly. "We've got a big problem."

"No kidding. He's sitting in the back of our truck."

"No, bigger than that."

"What?"

Frank nodded and gulped. "I was just checking the other windows. There are a *lot* of lights out there moving around. Like… at least ten, maybe more. They're all around the house, on every side."

Linda closed her eyes and swore. "Shit!"

"Who are they, anyway?" Frank looked out the window at the man in the trench coat who was slapping at the man holding the umbrella behind him. "And what's with this idiot?"

"I have no idea." Linda looked back out the window as the man started talking through the bullhorn again.

"Okay, so you two don't want to come out. Fair enough. Listen —here's what I want. We already looked in your truck, found a few things that don't look all that special. What I want is that nice big bag of ammunition you've got stashed in the house there."

"Ammunition?" Linda narrowed her eyes and glanced at Frank. "The gas station. These must be the people from the gas station."

As if on cue, a young woman holding a small piece of plastic over her head as a makeshift umbrella came running up to the truck. Frank shook his head as he watched her talking to the man with the trench coat. "That's the attendant; the one who filled the gas cans."

"Son of a…" Linda sighed. "How did they track us down to here?"

"Anyway!" The man in the trench coat started talking again. "I may have started off a little rude there what with all the demands. My name is Thomas Peters! I don't know your names but I know you're in the house. Now, we have the house surrounded and the only way you're getting out alive is by tossing out your ammo and all of your guns. After that we'll leave you alone and you can continue on your way!"

"Oh. Lovely." Frank snorted. "Is that all he wants? And what's with their teeth anyway?"

"Their teeth?" Linda raised an eyebrow.

"Yeah, I could see the teeth of a few of the people walking around the sides of the house. They're all black and stuff. They look like they're half-starved, too."

A lightbulb went off in Linda's head as she recalled the look of the attendant and a few of the "guards" that had been positioned around the gas station. "DAMMIT!" Linda shouted in fury and annoyance with herself for not paying more attention when she had the chance.

"What? What is it?"

"They're meth heads, Frank. The teeth, the gaunt faces and everything? Meth heads. Dammit. I knew the signs. I *know* the signs but I missed them. Two plus two was staring at me in the face and I just smiled and said 'five.'"

"So… we're surrounded by a gang of druggies who want our guns and ammo. Oh yes, this should end well. Can't you just shoot him?"

Linda peeked out the window, wincing at the light. "I can try, but he's hopped up on something and keeps moving around. That plus those lights and… I don't know. If I don't take him down on the first shot it might make things even worse."

Frank started chuckling to himself and, after a few seconds, it turned into a full-blown belly laugh. As he wiped the tears from his eyes, Linda stared at him like he had grown a second head.

"You okay there, Frank?"

"Yeah, sorry. It's just… how much more absurd can you get than trapped in an abandoned house in a thunderstorm with a gang of meth addicts outside? I mean… really?"

Outside, in the back of the truck, Thomas Peters was holding a bottle full of clear liquid with a rag sticking out of the top. In his other hand was a lighter which he was flicking, trying to get a flame going in the driving wind while the person behind him crouched down to cover the lighter and bottle with the umbrella. After several attempts the lighter finally caught and the alcohol-soaked rag erupted in flames. The man holding the umbrella nearly fell out of the truck as he jumped up in surprise, but steadied himself at the last second.

Peters held the Molotov cocktail up in the air, then pulled it back under the umbrella as the rain hissed against the flames. He then picked up the bullhorn and began shouting again. "This is your last chance! Either you toss out everything you've got in there or we'll just set the place on fire!"

Frank noticed Linda's body stiffening. "Are you okay?"

She nodded curtly. "Yep. Just don't like the idea of burning alive."

"I don't know who would, but yeah. Shit. Any ideas?"

"You said there were lights all around the house?"

"I didn't look out of *every* window but I think they were every-where, yeah."

"We need to go check. Right now. If there's a potential way to get out, we need to take it. We might be able to escape through the rain without them even noticing."

"Why not just… kill them?"

"He's got, what, a dozen or more spread out? We've got two. We're not exactly in the best situation to be handing out free naps. If the situation changes and we can get any kind of advantage then we'll take every last one of them out. For now let's try not to get our arms torn off by a bunch of druggies."

"Fair enough. You check the windows. I'll go grab our stuff from upstairs."

Linda nodded and she and Frank split up, each of them going about their tasks. While Frank bounded up the stairs to grab his backpack, Linda's backpack and her spare bag, she ran from window to window, peeking through the slots in between the boards at the figures that were standing out in the darkness. By the time she had finished running from room to room on the first floor she counted a total of eight figures holding flashlights, plus three or four more that she wasn't sure of but that might have been out there.

By the time Frank got back downstairs, Linda was at the front door listening to the apparent leader of the gang as he talked to a couple of his cohorts. Keeping her pistol hidden behind her back, she cracked the front door and shouted out at the man, startling him enough that he nearly dropped the flaming bottle into the back of the truck.

"Hey! We're not giving you shit! So why don't you and your lackeys run back to your gas station and keep pretending to do honest work!"

Thomas laughed at Linda's words, and picked up his bullhorn again. "You hear that, fellas? Kitty has some claws! Too bad those won't help you when you're dead!" He raised his arm and threw the bottle, failing to account for the umbrella still over his head. The edge of the bottle caught on the umbrella and instead of hitting a window on the second floor of the building as he had intended, it burst harmlessly all over the wet front porch. The flames futilely licked at the wet wood, finding no purchase and quickly went out as another gust of wind blew a torrent of rain up against the house.

"Get it out of my way!" Thomas backhanded the man holding the umbrella behind him and the man tumbled out of the truck. Thomas hopped down after him and snarled at him before picking up the bullhorn and shouting again. "Last chance, missy! Just throw everything out and we'll leave!"

Linda looked back at Frank. "You ready to run?"

He nodded nervously and held out her backpack. "Yeah, I think so."

"Good." Linda quickly put on her backpack and cracked the front door open again. "Hey asshole!" Linda stuck out her arm and extended her middle finger. "Here you go!"

An enraged, unintelligible shout was all Linda and Frank heard before Thomas gathered his senses enough to shout at the others spread around the house. "Get in there and kill them! Burn the place down if you have to!"

Linda closed the door and Frank looked at her with a scared expression. "Are you sure you know what you're doing?"

"Nope. No idea. I'm winging it as I go." Linda looked at Frank as she ran for the back of the house. "Come on, let's get up the stairs. I want the high ground on these idiots."

"What if they set the place on fire?"

"While they're inside of it? I doubt they're that stupid, but if so then we'll figure something out. I changed my mind; I'd rather deal with that than get shot by a meth-head in the pouring rain!"

Linda and Frank ran up the stairs to the second story. Frank stood guard at the top of the stairs, listening for movement below while Linda ran to a nearby room and looked through the window at the ground below. The second and third story windows weren't boarded up and she could see figures still standing in the darkness, holding flashlights. She ran to the closest window overlooking the yard in front of the house and looked down to see Thomas and three other people all clustered together in a group. After a minute of frantic pointing, nodding and shaking of their heads, the group disbanded and Thomas shouted into the bullhorn one last time. "All right, little lady! You had your chance!"

Thomas and two others with him opened the door to the red and white truck and threw another Molotov cocktail inside. They followed it by opening one of the cans of gasoline in the back of the truck and tossing it in as well. The resulting conflagration engulfed the truck almost instantly, the heat and flames being too intense for the driving rain to extinguish. Linda felt her gut twist as her and Frank's sole source of transport—along with her spare bags containing clothing and a variety of personal effects—went up in flames.

"What's going on out there?" Frank shouted from down the hall and Linda turned to look at him.

"Bastards just destroyed the truck!"

"What?" Frank shook his head and gritted his teeth. "Son of a whore!"

"Get ready because I'm pretty sure they're coming in here next."

"What do they expect to get from us? A stockpile of ammunition from a military bunker?"

"I don't have a clue; just be ready!"

Frank adjusted his grip on his rifle and looked back down the stairs. Out front in the yard the commotion had died down and Linda couldn't see any sign of Thomas or the others. She moved to one of the side rooms and saw no sign of any of the people that had been standing around outside.

"Frank! They're in the house!"

"I haven't heard anything!" Frank continued to watch and listen down the stairs, but everything continued to be quiet for the next few minutes. Linda, meanwhile, continued moving from room to room as she watched out the windows for any signs of movement. After seeing nothing, she went back to Frank near the stairs and paused by his side, listening along with him for movement downstairs.

"Where are they?" Frank whispered to Linda and she shook her head.

"No idea." She mouthed.

Frank felt his heart racing again as a feeling of lightheadedness passed over him. His vision began to blur and he stumbled backwards, only able to remain standing because Linda caught his arm.

"Are you okay?" Linda asked him. Frank tried to speak, but found it hard to focus and concentrate. As Linda watched him flounder, she realized that she was starting to feel dizzy as well. She lurched for one of the side rooms, pulling Frank along with her, then she grabbed the rifle and swung the stock at the window. The glass shattered outward and a gust a wind burst through, bringing with it a breath of air so fresh she could scarcely believe it. Linda and Frank both stood near the window sucking as much air in as they could before Frank turned and gasped out a question.

"Carbon monoxide?"

Linda nodded. "They must have set a fire or something downstairs in the basement. Or they started a car and are piping it in. Either way we need to get out of here before they decide to do something even more drastic."

"Can't we just make a run for the back door?"

"I have no idea where they're at, Frank. They could all be huddled on the porch or spread out in every room downstairs or in the basement or who the hell knows where!"

"Oh little missy!" The voice that floated up the stairs was stilted and hollow, but Linda instantly recognized it despite it being muffled by some type of mask. "Where are you?"

Chapter Twenty-Three

Two men sit in a darkened apartment on Manhattan island. The windows are covered with solar panels that block the light from entering. The panels are connected to a series of batteries stashed under a table covered with old takeout boxes and dirty dishes that have yet to be washed. One of the two bedrooms is filled from floor to ceiling with boxes of non-perishable food while the other has a pair of narrow mattresses and stacks of five-gallon jugs of water. More water is piled out in the small living room and several large bottles of propane sit next to a small oven. The exhaust for the oven runs through a small metal pipe and out through a hole in one of the windows.

The only light in the apartment comes from a single lamp sitting on the floor of the living room and the screens of two laptop computers. Each of the men works on his own computer, pausing only to take a sip from a glass of water or ask one another a question. The men speak in a foreign tongue and they make sure to only whisper. Their apartment building is mostly empty but they dare not speak loudly for fear of attracting attention.

Outside their building the world is consumed in chaos. Inside there is peace, silence and tranquility. One of the men pulls up pictures on his computer and swings the machine around so that the other man can see the screen. A large shipping vessel is on fire in the photograph on the screen and there is a cloud of black smoke rising into the air.

The two men grin at the sight and return to their typing. Their communications are encrypted and passed along through shortwave communications, bouncing off relays set up across the country. More reports on the damage done to the country flow in and out, forming a more complete view of what has taken place.

After two days of carefully sifting through the data coming in, one of the men opens a folder on his computer. The contents of the folder are displayed in a foreign language but the name of the folder itself is in English:

"Phase 2"

BOOK TWO

THE PRECIPICE

Chapter Twenty-Four

"Oh little missy!" The voice that floated up the stairs was stilted and hollow, but Linda instantly recognized it despite it being muffled by some type of mask. "Where are you?"

"That's that guy!" Frank whispered to Linda as he continued to take in deep breaths of fresh air through the broken window.

"No shit, Frank." Linda whispered back to him.

"Any thoughts on what to do?"

Linda's eyes flashed across the room and out the window as if a solution was sitting somewhere nearby. "Yeah. I should have shot his rotting teeth out of his head the moment he showed up."

"It's a little late for that now!"

"Says who?"

Frank rolled his eyes. "You know what I mean. They're in the house now, so what do you want to do?"

Heavy footsteps in the next room cut through their whispers and the noise of the pounding rain and they both froze and turned to look at the door. "You three head upstairs!" The muffled voice spoke again. "These tanks have ten minutes so let's be fast, hm? The rest of you with me on this floor. They're in one of these rooms so spread out and shoot on sight!"

Linda and Frank glanced at each other and Linda held a finger up to her lips. She took several deep breaths from the window before moving back to the doorway into the bedroom and crouched down near the side. Frank copied her movements and crouched behind her, doing his best not to breathe in any of the lung-choking fumes that were filling the building.

Footsteps pounded throughout the house as the men began to fan out. As one set of steps grew closer to the bedroom where they were hiding, Linda tensed the muscles in her legs and arms, waiting like a coiled serpent. The moment a dark shape loomed through the doorway she attacked, jumping up and forward with her left arm bringing the man's head up while her right hand slammed a knife into his throat, tearing apart his arteries and vocal cords with one swift motion.

The sound of the man's body thumping against the wall of the room and then falling to the floor was masked by the sound of the rain and Linda picked up one of his still-flailing arms and began pulling him across the room. "Frank!" Linda kicked at Frank's leg as he sat staring at the man, trying to comprehend what he had just witnessed. "Give me a hand here!"

Frank stood and took the man's other hand, helping Linda drag his body across the floor and dumping it against a wall. Frank took a step back and stared wide-eyed as Linda ripped off the man's mask and looked it over. The man looked like he was in his early twenties and he clutched weakly at his throat, trying to stem the loss of blood.

Air passed through the gash in his neck as he sucked in the poisoned air, though the air quality made no difference either way. Frank locked eyes with the man as blood pooled out in thick ribbons, staining the carpet in the room. As the man finally died, Frank watched the light leave his eyes and shuddered involuntarily.

"Frank." Linda stood up and patted him on the shoulder. "We need to go."

"You just…" Frank looked at Linda and pointed at the man that she killed.

"Let's go, Frank. There's a lot more of these guys in the house."

"How did you do that?" Frank kept looking between Linda's bloodied hand and the body of the man on the floor. The way she jumped between extremes of passiveness and extreme violence not only confused him but it terrified him, too.

"Frank. Shut up and let's go, okay? We can play twenty questions once we're out of the house filled with *murderous meth-heads!*"

The reminder that they were still in mortal danger snapped Frank back to reality. He took his rifle and nodded to Linda, who was busy fitting the mask onto her face. "What's that?"

"Oxygen mask. Captain meth-head says it's got a ten-minute supply. They probably use them when they're cooking. We'll have to trade back and forth as we go—wait. Sh!" Linda cocked her head as a few pairs of steps converged just down the hall.

"Any luck?"

"Damned house is like a maze."

"Where haven't you searched?"

"Jack's supposed to be looking down there."

"Well then let's get the other end. Idiots."

Any further responses were too muffled to hear. Linda peeked her head around the corner and saw three shapes heading down the hall away from the stairs. "Let's go!"

Linda charged forward and Frank followed quickly, confused about what they were doing but eager to escape the house. The stairs down to the ground floor were close by and they both ran down them at full speed, leaving behind any semblance of stealth as they hurried forward as quickly as possible.

By the time Frank and Linda were both on the ground floor the leader of the group of men had heard them and was running back towards the stairs to follow them down. "Follow them!" Linda grinned as she pulled off the mask and handed it to Frank who took a few deep breaths before handing it back.

"Where are we going?" Frank looked around the hall and pointed at the front door. "Out there?"

Linda shook her head and pulled at Frank's arm. "This way. Hurry!" Linda turned the corner and ran down another set of stairs, heading for the basement. Frank was about to argue with her when he saw two men open the front door. By the time they began pointing and shouting in his direction, though, Frank was halfway down the stairs behind Linda.

"They're right behind us!" Frank shouted at Linda. He scarcely got the words out before he began coughing and retching. The fumes in the basement were thicker than in any other part of the house and he could barely see let alone breathe.

"Put this on!" Linda shoved an oxygen mask into Frank's hands and he held it up to his face, sucking in the precious bottled air.

"Don't you need it?" Frank's eyes were watering from the fumes and he could barely see anything even through the thick plastic eyepieces of the oxygen mask.

"Found an extra!" Linda shouted at him from the other side of the room and he stumbled towards her.

"Why's it so bad down here?" Frank waved his hands in front of his face to try and clear the smoke and fumes away, though it did little good.

"Looks like the bastards hooked up garden hoses to their car exhaust and ran them through into here." Linda pointed at the windows in the small basement that had holes in them through which rubber hoses had been inserted. "The only place the fumes had to go was up."

Frank glanced behind him, readying his rifle for the inevitable onslaught of people that would be running down the stairs at any second. When none arrived, he looked over at Linda. "They were right behind me! Where are they?"

Linda looked back at the stairs. "I don't know, but keep me covered. They locked this door from the out—oh hell, screw it. We'll go out through a window." Linda looked around the room before grabbing the first heavy object she saw and hefting it into the air. "Be ready to go as soon as I—"

Just as Linda was about to take a swing at the nearest window with a fireplace poker a series of shots from outside broke the window for her. Bullets whizzed past both Linda and Frank and they both ducked down, crawling along the floor until they got to the wall beneath the window.

"So much for that!" Frank still kept his eyes trained on the stairs on the other side of the room, just waiting for someone to walk down. "Any more ideas?"

Linda's response was cut short by the familiar—and now not muffled—voice of the man they had been listening to for longer than either of them desired. "No way out, babycakes! You and your little friend are going to be out of oxygen soon and then we'll be in to collect ya!"

Linda leaned her head back against the wall and closed her eyes. After a few seconds Frank nudged her and spoke again. "Linda? Any more ideas?"

She shook her head and sighed. "Fresh out for now."

"I have one."

Linda cracked an eyelid and looked at Frank. "Do tell."

"It sounds like most of them are outside the basement here, right?"

Linda tilted her head, listening to the raucous laughter and conversations that were taking place against the backdrop of the thunderstorm. "Yeah, probably. They seem stupid enough to do something like that."

"I only saw two upstairs when I ran down. If I had to guess they left one guy upstairs, maybe two. If we could get up there and out the front door they probably left one of their cars out front."

Linda nodded. "It's a shit plan that'll get us killed, but I like it. Let's go."

Frank merely nodded in response as Linda got up and started moving towards the stairs. He had expected a conversation or an argument or *something*. Getting instant agreement from Linda was something entirely new and he wasn't sure what to make of it.

"Stay behind me." Linda's voice was cold and Frank felt a chill run down his spine.

"You sure? I can help with—"

"Frank." Linda turned and glared at him. Her voice, even beneath the mask, was layered with precision and an icy coolness that was hard to describe. Frank wasn't sure what she was about to do, but he knew that he didn't want to be on the receiving end.

Chapter Twenty-Five

L inda moved up the basement stairs like a ghost. Her breaths were shallow and measured, her footsteps were quiet and every movement she made was fluid and precise. Her flashlight was jammed in her back pocket though she no longer needed it. Keeping her pistol locked against her chest and her knife tucked up next to it, she was ready to strike at the first sign of movement.

Frank waited at the bottom of the stairs for her to reach the top first. When she motioned for him to follow he tried to move quietly, but only succeeded in slightly dampening the sound of his movements. Linda crouched at the top stair, waiting inside the entrance as she had done in the bedroom upstairs a few minutes prior, listening carefully for any hint that someone was waiting on the other side.

When Frank got halfway up the stairs he accidentally tripped and tumbled forward, catching himself with an "oof!" and banging the barrel of the rifle against the wood of the stair. Linda jerked her head around to look at him before turning back to the door. Frank's noise was loud enough for the two men on the ground floor to hear and they peeked out from their hiding places across the hall to see if their intended prey was trying to escape.

The brief flash of movement across the hall was all Linda needed. She brought the pistol up and fired twice at the man directly across the hall, striking him in the ear with the first shot and dead between the eyes with the second. The noise caused the second man, farther down the hall, to jump out and fire his shotgun towards Linda. She, however, was already on the move, scrambling across the hall on all fours and tucking herself up in an alcove.

The man with the shotgun screamed as he charged the stairs, incorrectly assuming she was on them as he ran forward. He fired the shotgun twice more before Linda's knife found his neck, then he joined his comrade in death as Linda brought him to the floor, pressing her full body weight against his chest until he stopped moving.

"Jesus." Frank stood at the top of the stairs, breathing heavily as he glanced between the two bodies. Linda wiped her blade on the shirt of the man she was sitting on before she stood up and spoke.

"We need to go before they send someone else to see what the shots were about."

Frank nodded wordlessly and followed Linda to the front door of the house. After checking to make sure no one was positioned directly outside, the pair hurried out onto the porch where Linda pointed at a car sitting just beyond the smoldering ruins of their truck.

"There. We'll take that."

"What about the stuff in the back of the truck?"

"It's all gone now." Linda shook her head. "Come on, let's get to the—"

Linda cried out in pain as a shot rang out from the side of the house. Frank turned to look in the direction of the shot and saw several figures walking along in the rain next to the house. More shots rang out and Frank dove behind the burned out truck. He grabbed Linda's backpack and pulled her towards him to move her out of the line of fire as the shooting intensified.

"That's right!" The same voice shouted from the direction of the shooting. "Pin them down! We'll have us some fun tonight one way or the other!"

"Linda!" Frank whispered to Linda as he pulled her into a sitting position. She was still conscious, but her face was a mask of pain. Frank began checking her over when he saw a dark stain growing in size on the outside of her upper right thigh. Much of the blood was washing away in the rain, but enough of it was pouring out and staining her pants that he was able to easily identify where she had been shot.

"Goddamn it!" Linda ground her teeth together as Frank turned her over to examine the wound.

"Stay still!" Frank was by no means a trauma specialist, but he knew the general response for any sort of traumatic wound: apply pressure and keep it clean. While there wasn't much he could do to keep it clean while they were under fire in the rain while crouched in a muddy yard, he at least wanted to make sure she wouldn't bleed out before they got to the car.

"It's not deep, I don't think!" Frank turned her back over and grabbed her hand. "You're going to need to walk! Can you do that?"

Linda nodded and ground her teeth together again. "We need to go before they get any closer, though!"

Frank picked up his rifle from where he had dropped it a moment earlier and wiped a glob of mud out from around the trigger guard. He peeked through a crack in the burned out truck to see that Thomas Peters—the man in the trench coat—was still advancing on the truck with his cronies, though they were slowing down as they got closer.

With the thunderstorm still in full effect and his mind still panicked and racing, Frank assumed that any shots he took in the driving wind and rain would be terribly inaccurate. He failed to take into account, however, how close the advancing group was as well as how confident they were that they had caught their prey.

"Move!" Frank shouted at Linda and she started to stand up and move towards the car. As she did, Frank rose to one knee and rested the barrel of the rifle on the side of the truck. He aimed it in

the general direction of the closest meth-head and pulled the trigger. Not having fired the rifle previously, he was surprised by how
little kick he felt in his shoulder. The bullet was on target and
pierced through the chest and left lung of the man he aimed at,
causing him to double over in agony and drop to the ground.

Caught off guard, Thomas fumbled with his pistol as he shot
first at Frank and then at Linda. All of his shots went wide, disappearing into the rain or sending up small puffs of water as they hit
the ground. When Frank heard the distinct *click* of a trigger pull
behind which there was no more ammunition, he swung back up
and fired again.

Frank's shot caught Thomas in the shoulder and he howled in
pain and dropped his pistol as he grabbed at the wound. He tried
to duck behind one of his fellow meth-heads, but the sight of one
of their own bleeding out on the ground had caused their bravado
to leave them. All of Thomas's accomplices fled after the first shot,
stumbling down the wet grass as they ran for the back of the house
where they had left most of their cars.

"I've got you covered. Get moving!"

The shout came from behind Frank and he turned to see Linda
crouched between the open passenger's side doors. She held up her
pistol and fired three shots at Thomas, who dove for the ground
and crawled behind a large oak tree.

"Get up here, you cowards! Bring the cars!" Thomas screamed
at the men who had gone down behind the hill, and a moment
later one car and one truck wound their way up the slight incline,
tearing deep gashes in the wet dirt and grass. Thomas dove into
the back of the truck at the same time as Frank and Linda both got
into the car. Linda laid her right leg across the back seat and
wrapped her left arm around and put pressure on the wound. She
leaned up at the same time and looked out the back window before
shouting at Frank.

"Get us out of here, Frank! Now!"

Chapter Twenty-Six

Frank slammed the small car into gear and tore down the driveway, kicking rocks and mud into the air as he went. The car fishtailed and nearly slammed into a tree as he spun the wheel sharply to the left at the end of the driveway. As they slid out into the road, Thomas's truck and the car behind him followed closely in hot pursuit.

"Gah!" Linda tried to lean up to peer out the back window, but she sank back against the door and breathed heavily. "Son of a bitch!" She pulled her hand away from her leg and made a face at the blood on it before reapplying and doubling the pressure.

"How are you doing back there?" Frank glanced in the rearview mirror.

"I don't think they hit a vein, but it hurts like hell!"

"Just try to hold out. I can't exactly stop right now with them behind us!"

Linda leaned up again just enough to get a glance of the two vehicles chasing them. With the truck directly behind them, Linda could make out Thomas's face as he stood up in the back of the truck, wearing his face mask to protect his eyes from the rain and wind. Bright lights on the sides and back of the truck illuminated everything in and around the vehicle, and Linda dearly wished she could get a clear shot on it. A rifle appeared in Thomas's hands and he tried to steady it on the roof of the truck, but it was clear even through the darkness and rain that he was having trouble with his shoulder wound.

He fired several times, missing Frank and Linda's car wildly with each shot. Frank began swerving along the road as he drove, trying to ensure that Thomas continued to miss. Each bump and swerve made Linda groan, until she finally sat up and hooked her arm around the headrest of the driver's seat. "Frank, you've got to lose them."

"No kidding!" Frank removed one hand from the wheel to wipe a trickle of sweat and water from his brow. "Got any suggestions on where to go?" Several more shots came from behind them, with one ricocheting off of the trunk.

"I don't know!"

Frank glanced back and looked at Linda's leg. The flow of blood had slowed slightly, but Linda's face was pale and Frank could tell she had lost a sizeable amount of blood. "Are you sure they didn't hit anything critical?"

"I'd be dead right now if an artery had been nicked. I'll be fine so long as we get somewhere soon where I can get this wound cleaned up."

"Great." Frank mumbled to himself and shook his head. "No pressure or anything."

"What about that turn up ahead?" Linda pointed at a traffic circle down the road. "Go through and take the right-hand turn. We can probably lose them on the country roads with how terrible their driving is."

Frank looked at the rearview mirror and nodded. "They're pretty bad, aren't they?" The truck and car behind it had both been fishtailing wildly nearly the entire way, and Thomas had almost been thrown from the truck several times. The condition of the drivers and the terrible weather made it difficult for them to stay on the road, though Frank didn't want to admit out loud that he wasn't doing all that much better.

"Hold on!" Frank entered the traffic circle at twice the speed he should have on a sunny day with a dry road for the car's tires to grip. The car hydroplaned briefly, sliding several feet to the left onto the grass in the center of the traffic circle. The deep puddle ended and the car jolted forward towards the turn Linda had pointed out.

Behind them, the truck carrying Thomas and three others entered the traffic circle even faster than Frank. As the truck hit the puddle that caused Frank and Linda's car to hydroplane, it did so as well, though its greater speed meant that not only did it drift farther across into the grass at the center of the traffic circle, but it lost all semblance and hope of regaining traction.

The truck slid sideways through the grass and then back onto the pavement on the opposite side of the circle without slowing down. The car behind it behaved in exactly the same way, and within seconds it was sliding along towards the truck with nothing to slow it down. Both the driver of the truck and the car panicked and threw their steering wheels in every direction while they slammed on the brakes as they tried to break out of their slides. This merely exacerbated the problem, though, and it only took an instant longer for the car to slam headlong into the side of the truck. The speed difference between the vehicles was only around twenty miles per hour, but when combined with the way in which they were turning and spinning along, it might as well have been a hundred mile an hour difference.

Thomas was ejected from the back of the truck like a cannon-ball, flying through the air as he screamed at the pain that was soon to come. The three passengers in the truck slammed against each other before being thrown forward and then backward. All three weren't wearing seatbelts and suffered concussions and whiplash from the forces involved in the collision.

The four in the car that hit the truck had it the worst. As none of them were wearing seatbelts either, when they impacted head-on with the side of the truck the two in the front seat had their heads thrown against the windshield as the airbags for the car had long ago been torn out and sold for scrap. The pair in the backseat were flung violently forward and then to the side as the car turned. The two on the left side of the car were the first to have their heads smashed against the windows. As the car jerked around the pair on the right side did as well.

"Stop!" Linda shouted. Frank slammed on the brake and winced as he felt the pedal drop down to the floor with very little resistance. The ABS module throbbed under the car, but with barely any pads left on the brakes it took a long time for the car to finally come to a halt.

"What is it?" Frank looked back at Linda, afraid that she had been injured again. In the backseat Linda thrashed her limbs, trying to pull herself up and open one of the back doors. Finally she gave up and looked at Frank.

"Get the rifle, get out there and kill whoever survived that wreck."

"What?" Frank blinked a few times, wondering if he had misheard her.

"Frank, this is just like that pair of assholes who grabbed me."

Frank looked back at the wreckage of the two vehicles on the side of the road. "Are you kidding me? If any of them survived that they're going to be too injured to do anything to us!"

"Just do it!"

"You want me to go down there? In the dark? To face an unknown number of assailants? Alone? When we have a perfectly good means of escape right now and we need to get somewhere safe to get your leg looked at?"

Linda stared at Frank for a long moment before licking her lips, closing her eyes, sighing and nodding curtly. "You're right. I'm sorry. If I could do anything except crawl around then I think we should do it. But… yeah."

Frank took a deep breath and turned back around. He put the car into gear and continued down the road, easing down on the speed to ensure that he could slow down and stop with the spongy brakes if needed. The right-hand turn did, indeed, lead into more back country roads as Linda had predicted, and he soon became lost in their twists and turns. He kept to the wider roads with a yellow line as he went along, avoiding the narrower roads that branched off into dead ends and driveways, and after fifteen minutes or so he pulled the car over.

"There's a barn over there. Looks pretty old. I think we should get in there for the night, take a look at your leg and see what the weather's like in the morning."

Linda's face was even paler than before and she nodded slowly. "Sounds good."

A few minutes later the car was parked beneath an awning off to the side of the barn and Frank was out with his rifle, creeping through the unlocked door into the barn to make sure it was empty. He emerged a moment later and slung the rifle over his shoulder, then opened the back door to the car and held out a hand for Linda. "Looks clear. Pretty clean, too. Let's get you inside."

After wrapping her arm around his neck and shoulder, Frank helped Linda hobble inside before lowering her carefully to the ground. "Flashlight. In my pocket." Linda mumbled weakly and tried to point at her pants. Frank put her backpack on the ground and grabbed her flashlight before helping her lower her head back onto the pack. He placed his flashlight and hers on a footstool he had found nearby and pointed them at her leg. He then slipped off his backpack and began digging through it to find his first aid kit, which he pulled out and placed on the ground and opened up.

"This is going to hurt."

Linda glanced at the bottle Frank held in his hand and rolled her eyes. "Bring it on."

Frank chuckled and unscrewed the bottle of isopropyl alcohol and set it to the side. He pulled out a small pair of razor-sharp shears and cut away a large section of Linda's jeans around the wound while doing his best not to touch it directly. After picking up one of the flashlights Frank examined the wound closely and pressed at the flesh around it.

"Jesus, Frank. Just sanitize it and put some gauze on it. Stop trying to make out with it."

Frank didn't bother to look at her as he replied. "I'm no expert but it looks like it went in the back side and out the front. Clean pass. You're not bleeding too badly anymore, either."

"Good. Now will you plea—gah!" Linda tried—and failed—to hold in a muffled groan of pain as Frank poured a copious amount of alcohol over the wound, ensuring that as much as possible went into and through the wound as he could. With an extremely high percentage of alcohol by volume, the isopropyl alcohol made an excellent field antiseptic. Frank wasn't sure how well it would work considering they had been driving for a short time after she had been shot, but he figured it was better than doing nothing.

"I thought you wanted me to bring it on?" Frank smiled at Linda and she shook her head.

"Little warning next time would help."

"Nah." Frank gave one last pour of the liquid over Linda's wound before squirting some into his hand and then rubbing it across the surface of his hands and between his fingers. He then opened a few disinfectant wipes and began cleaning the skin around the wound, rubbing away the dried blood and bits of dirt that were still stuck to it. When he was finished, he pulled out a large piece of gauze and pressed it over the wound, then used several strips of medical tape to affix the gauze to her leg.

"There." Frank sat back and wiped his hands on his pants. "Not perfect but the best I can do. I don't have anything to suture it up with, but I think it'll be okay if you take it easy. If you have a pair of spare pants you should get changed when the rain stops and we'll change the bandage and secure it a little better. This should hold for the night, though." Frank was busying himself with repacking his first aid kit into his backpack when he noticed that Linda wasn't responding. He turned to see her eyes closed and her head leaning to the side. Her skin was still pale but her breathing was regular as she slept. Frank smiled again and shook his head before rummaging through his bag until he found a couple of flannel shirts which he draped over her chest, arms and legs.

Frank whispered to himself as he stood slowly, feeling a burning in his calves and thighs. "Yeah, I'll take first watch." He felt somewhat odd about spending the night in yet another barn. He figured that Linda wouldn't try to ditch him again, but her condition gave him an extra sense of relief on that front. With the car parked out of view of the road and him keeping their flashlights off inside, he was hopeful that no one would know they were in the barn.

As Frank settled down into a sitting position with the rifle lying next to him, he ran over the events of that evening again and again. Of all the questions he had, there were two that bubbled to the top that he couldn't answer no matter how hard he tried. The first of the questions had to do with Linda, her skills and the way in which she had interacted with the meth-heads, both when they were outside and inside the house.

The second had to do with the meth-heads themselves and just how they had managed to find where Frank and Linda had stopped. The pair had chosen the seemingly-abandoned house because it was far enough off the main road that they wouldn't easily be seen. Frank assumed that someone had been following them or that a neighbor living near the house who knew the gang had tipped them off.

The truth, though, had ramifications far beyond what Frank could imagine.

Chapter Twenty-Seven

I n the basement of a bombed out building, underneath piles of rubble and debris, sits a curious operation. The basement is well-lit and furnished with enough food and running water for the residents to last for months. The walls are sparse with thick coats of antibacterial paint covering their entirety. Each fluorescent light in the ceiling is accompanied by a pair of ultraviolet lights, and the hundreds of UV lights are coupled to a series of emergency switches spread out throughout the room. More emergency switches are connected to sprinkler systems set in the ceiling as well, with some holding water and others holding caustic chemicals designed to thoroughly cleanse the room of all biological materials.

The floor of the basement is divided into two sections. The first consists of one fourth of the room and is a living area. Space is cramped and the smell of body odor is overwhelming. Racks of beds four high are stacked against the walls and groups of women and children huddle together, whispering, talking and quietly playing with each other. Each of them has a manacle on their wrist or leg attached to a long chain that stretches back to their bed, where it is connected. Chains are easily tangled and the prisoners must move slowly and cautiously to avoid injuring themselves and each other.

The rest of the basement of the building is divided from the living quarters by a thick transparent sheet that stretches from the top of the ceiling down to the floor. The sheet is designed specifically to be sturdy and stable but still weak enough that it can be pierced with a bullet or sharp knife. On the side of the sheet opposite the living quarters sits an advanced laboratory filled with the latest genetic sequencing and alteration technologies. Large machines sit in rows on tables and nearly every one of them has a man wearing a white lab coat in front of it.

The men in lab coats are tired. Their faces are gaunt, their hair is greasy and unwashed and the clothing beneath their coats is wrinkled and soiled. Some of the men wear rubber gloves that cover their hands. Others wear gloves that reach up to their elbows. A few work in a small room in an isolated corner of the lab, wearing full rubber suits as they administer shots to animals and collect data on the results of previous experiments.

Most of the scientists sit at machines, performing mind-numbing research as they work for their kidnappers who stand as guards around them. The guards all wear full face masks with independent oxygen supplies that are changed out every hour. Each of them carries a large blade, a revolver and a submachine gun. They walk slowly up and down the aisles, ensuring that the scientists are spending every waking moment working. Seventeen hours per day are set aside for work, one hour is split between short breaks and meals and the remaining six are when the scientists are allowed to rejoin their families and choose between visiting with them and sleeping.

Even as the men sitting at the machines work frantically they still find time every few minutes to glance up at the other side of the room, catching the eye of their wife or child and smiling bravely. Many of these glances are unnoticed or ignored by the guards. If they occur too frequently, though, the guards begin shouting, threatening to pierce the barrier between the two rooms and expose every woman and child to the diseases that are under development in the laboratory.

Three months into their work, one of the scientists tries to escape. With no family to use as leverage against him, he has only his own life to risk. He attacks a guard with a handheld pipette, piercing the man through the neck. The guard is severely injured, but does not succumb to his injuries quickly. He shoots the rebelling scientist six times in the chest with his revolver before the other guards converge. The injured guard is carried away, never to be seen again.

The dead scientist's body is taken away an hour later and the scientists are *forced to clean the environment before they are shuffled off to the sleeping area and the UV lights are turned on to complete the sterilization.*

The brutality of the killing and the extra labor ensures that one attempt at rebellion is all that will take place.

Nearly a year into their work, a group of scientists approach a guard. They hand him a clipboard and he looks it over. He nods and shouts to the head guard, handing him the clipboard. The head guard takes the information out of the room, returning twenty minutes later with a wicker basket. Inside is a pile of fresh fruit, cheese and bread. The food is given to the scientists who presented the information and the entire group is given the rest of the day off in celebration of their accomplishment.

Three weeks later, when the information on the clipboard is confirmed to be accurate, the scientists and their families are released. They are closely monitored to ensure they do not tell anyone about the work they performed and their families' lives are threatened if they speak a word about their imprisonment. Each one of the scientists knows the terror created in the basement laboratory but none of them dare to risk their lives or the lives of their families by approaching the authorities.

Inside the empty laboratory, a small group of men in suits gather around the animal quarantine area in the basement. They watch as a man dressed in white robes and headpiece presses a button on the outside of the quarantined room. A small aerosol container inside the room is remotely triggered at the touch of the button, filling the space with an invisible substance. The rats and monkeys inside the small area don't react initially. Thirty minutes later, though, and they are all coughing up blood. Three hours later and they are dead, blood pouring from their bodies and pooling on the floor of the room.

"You have a human-compatible variant?" One of the men wearing a suit asks the man in white robes.

The man in robes points across the room. The group walks across to look through the transparent barrier into the area where the scientists' families were held. An older man and woman are strapped down in two of the beds in the room with manacles on their limbs and chains across their bodies. Their eyes are glazed over from the sedatives they were given, but they still attempt to turn their heads to watch the approaching men.

"Yes." The man in the white robes finally responds to the earlier question

with a flat, emotionless voice as he watches the pair struggle against their chains. "I have a human-compatible variant."

The man in white robes presses a small button installed on the side of the transparent barrier and another aerosol can releases its invisible gas. The man and woman begin struggling against their bonds, but the chains and sedatives are too much to overcome. Within half an hour a trickle of blood begins to run from their eyes and ears. Half a day later both are too sick to struggle against their chains. A day later and the woman is dead while the man waits at death's doorstep.

Chapter Twenty-Eight

E very bone and piece of flesh in Liam Peters' body felt broken and bruised. He opened his eyes only to screw them shut again in pain as the morning sun came piercing through the broken windshield of the truck like a knife. The son of Thomas Peters, Liam was a tall, wiry man barely out of his teens. The son of a long-gone relationship between Thomas and a woman whose name he could no longer remember, Liam had taken to his father's work and way of life with gusto.

While Thomas acted as the overall head of the meth-amphetamine production facilities located in Binghamton, Liam was involved in the payment collection and protection side of the business. If someone owed them money, was threatening their operation or simply happened to glance at Liam the wrong way, he enacted swift, brutal and permanent revenge upon them.

"What in the fuck..." Liam opened an eye and moved his head to look away from the sunlight, feeling a fresh lance of pain shoot through his neck and back. He moved slowly, cautiously, exploring the pain as he tried to determine what was broken and what still worked. He could still feel his legs and move his toes and his arms worked, but two of his fingers were bent and twisted and there was a sharp pain in his chest every time he took in a breath.

Liam set his jaw as he grabbed the two fingers and popped them back into their sockets. A fresh surge of adrenaline flowed through his body and he kicked at the window in front of him, removing the last remnants of the windshield with a few blows. As Liam crawled out of the overturned truck, he suddenly felt overwhelmed with exhaustion and dropped to the ground for a few moments. His breaths were ragged and shallow and he touched his chest, probing for any signs that something had penetrated through. "Fucking ribs." Even whispering brought on pain and he closed his eyes and mouth for a few moments more before struggling up to his knees, using the truck as a support.

All around him were the mangled remains of the pickup truck, the car and the bodies of those that had been driving and riding in them. It took Liam a solid minute of staring at the bodies and twisted metal wrecks to realize what had happened, and when the memories finally came back in a flash his eyes widened and he grunted out his father's name. "Thomas."

Never one to call his father "dad" or any of the other standard names a child calls a father, Liam had always been on a strict first-name basis with Thomas. There were never many overt displays of affection or love shown between the pair, and they treated each other as colleagues and equals more than anything else. Deep inside, though, past the pain, the poor upbringing, the drugs and the myriad of emotional and mental issues, Liam cared for his father in some twisted way. When he spotted Thomas' body lying on the grass a few dozen feet away, he pushed himself to his feet and staggered towards it, repeating the name over and over through the pain he felt in his chest.

"Thomas?" Liam prodded his father's arm a few times before noticing that Thomas' neck was at an impossible angle and he wasn't breathing. Liam sat next to his father's body, concentrating on breathing, as he tried to figure out what to do next. The sun was nearly overhead in the sky when a noise behind Liam made him slowly turn to locate the source. Two of Thomas' men who had survived the wreck were slowly walking toward Liam, holding onto each other for support. Dried blood covered their heads, faces and various limbs, and they looked like they were in just as bad shape as Liam was.

"Where's the boss?" Josh, one of the two men, coughed as he asked the question. Liam raised an unsteady hand and pointed at his father's body lying next to him.

"Dead?" The second man, Reggie, asked.

Liam nodded slowly before standing to his feet. "As a doornail." There was no respect for his dead father in his voice, and in his mind all trace of the brief feeling of caring he had for his father was gone as well. All that was left was rage, though it wasn't over the loss of Thomas. "Are you two all that's left?"

The two men nodded in response.

"Those bastards killed him." Liam pointed down the road in the direction that Frank and Linda had fled. "We lost a lot of good men to those two. Plus our vehicles. And with Thomas gone our whole operation's on hold till we find more recruits and get more of 'em trained." Liam shook his head, then winced at the pain.

"What do you want to do?" Reggie asked.

"Let's get back to the station. We'll round up a few of the regulars and persuade them to help us. Long as the transmitter in the car's working we can find 'em if they're within a few hundred miles. No way they'll get that far before we get on their tails."

Josh and Reggie both nodded and hobbled along after Liam as he headed back towards town. The journey took the entire afternoon, and by evening they finally arrived at the gas station. Their legs were tired, their bodies were somehow even more sore than they had been after the wreck and they were parched and hungry beyond belief.

With most of their vehicles either destroyed or left behind at the abandoned house, Liam didn't have a lot of options left. While Reggie and Josh limped back inside the station, Liam circled around the back to a small garage and opened the door. The rusted frame of a green 1986 convertible Corvette stared back at him. The tan top was torn in several places that had been temporarily patched with a variety of tape and glue more times than he could recall. The brakes were shot and the clutch was nearly burned out, but the engine was sound, if a little rough. Dents, scrapes and scratches covered the entire exterior of the vehicle, making it look like it had just rolled in from a Mad Max movie.

The interior of the car was barren, the result of multiple upgrade projects that had been derailed and never completed. Aside from bare metal seats, a sagging roof liner and windows that had been jury-rigged to allow for partial opening when the need arose, the dashboard of the Corvette was completely gone. The radio, vents, air conditioning and heater controls were gone along with the dashboard dials and gauges, making it impossible to know exactly how fast you were going.

Despite its flaws, the Corvette was Liam's favorite car, and he felt a certain sense of nostalgia and poetic justice knowing that he would be taking the first car his father bought for him out to kill those that were responsible for his death. The fact that Thomas had ambushed and attacked Frank and Linda first meant nothing to Liam, and the thought didn't even enter his mind. He was consumed with the idea of revenge, and nothing else would satisfy him.

"Liam?" The woman working the register came outside and grimaced as she saw him. "Are you okay?"

"The tracker." He didn't bother looking at the woman as he ignored her question. "Do you have it?"

"I can go get it. Shouldn't you come inside and sit down?"

"No. Bring me the tracker and tell Josh and Reggie to get out here. Make sure they're armed. We're leaving right now."

"But—"

"Get going!" Liam screamed, then clutched at his chest as pain exploded outward. The woman turned and ran back into the gas station, returning a moment later with a small black box in her hand. Liam was still hunched over, leaning against the car with one hand as he wheezed.

"Please, Liam…" The woman placed the box on the hood of

the car next to Liam before taking a few steps back. "Please just come inside for a while? You need someone to look you over!"

Liam slowly lifted his head to glare at the woman. Fire danced in his eyes and—had he not been in severe pain—he would have inflicted physical harm upon her. "Get Josh and Reggie out here now. We leave in five minutes."

As the woman ran back into the gas station, Liam took the small black device in his hand and flipped a few switches on the side. A series of lights on the face of the device lit up in series, then all but the bottom one vanished. Liam held the device in the air and moved it slowly around in a circle until the other lights began to turn on as well. An evil grin spread across his face and he turned the device back off and slipped it back into his pocket.

"We're coming, you two. We're coming…"

Chapter Twenty-Nine

Though the weather is unusually chilly so early in the season, the Pittsburgh Zoo and PPG Aquarium is bustling with activity. Visitors swarm the labyrinth of tunnels in the recently upgraded aquarium and zoo complex, allowing them never-before-seen access to the animals inhabiting both land and water. The majority of the visitors are children, either with their parents or on school field trips. There are several such field trips going on at once and the grounds of the zoo and aquarium are packed.

In a white panel van in a parking lot near the zoo, a trio of men sit in the back, huddled together as they whisper to one another. Each man wears a different set of clothing. One wears the uniform of the local police department, another wears an EMT's uniform and the third wears a firefighter's jacket and pants. The nametags on the clothing are fake, though each man calls the others by their fake names as a joke to help distract themselves from their nervousness.

Each man carries six small aerosol containers in their clothing. Even though the containers are secured and virtually unbreakable, all three men treat the containers with care, knowing that their deaths are assured if one of the containers is deployed prematurely.

"How long?" The man in the police uniform whispers.

"Two more hours." The doctor leans back in his seat in the back of the van. "It's time for us to go."

"Remember your destinations, brothers." The firefighter looks the other two in the eyes and they nod solemnly. "Do not let anyone stop you. Stay well hidden in plain sight."

The three nod at each other and pile out of the van, quickly separating and going in different directions. Once they are away from each other they slow down and walk naturally, heading for different areas of the city where they can do the most damage.

Two hours later, the doctor is on the third floor of the UPMC Presbyterian hospital, a few miles south of the zoo. The officer is making small talk with real officers outside a local station while the firefighter uses his disguise to gain access to businesses under the pretense of performing fire extinguisher checks. All three men blend in with their surroundings, offering up no reason for anyone to suspect them of anything.

Two hours after leaving their van, the city of Pittsburgh—and the nation at large—is rocked by explosions. Three bombs placed on school buses outside the zoo turn the yellow vehicles into twisted piles of metal. Dump trucks carrying debris from a construction site on the north side of the city explode, sending rocks high into the air before they begin raining down on nearby cars and pedestrians. A series of explosives set along the tracks at the train station cause an incoming passenger line to derail, killing dozens and injuring scores more.

As deaths and injuries continue to pile up the three men continue to blend in with the activity as they assist with treating the injured and rescuing those who are trapped. As they move about, though, each man plants an aerosol can in a strategic location. One goes into a storage closet at the hospital. Another goes into the locker room at the police station. Yet another is placed near a temporary shelter being erected to help treat victims.

The aerosol cans are placed in locations where the men expect large numbers of people to pass through in the next several days. The cans themselves are nondescript and easy to overlook, but each consists not only of a can but of a timing device that counts down the seconds to when it automatically deploys. Each canister is set on a timer to randomly deploy. Some of them deploy hours after the initial explosions. Most deploy a day or two later, when the citizens of the city are in a full-blown panic and people are desperately searching every-where for food and medicine.

One of the later canisters to deploy is at a school building near the zoo that *was undamaged by the detonation of several buses outside. The school has undergone a radical transformation in the last few days and is now an emergency shelter, filled with residents who desperately need food, water and medical attention. The man dressed as a police officer placed the canister under a teacher's desk in one of the classrooms when he was helping organize the relief efforts at the school. He is long gone now, having slipped away under the cover of night to reunite with his two co-conspirators.*

The classroom containing the canister, like most of the other classrooms, now serves as a sleeping area for families staying in the shelter. Personal effects are pushed under cots and sheets are hung from the ceiling in an effort to muffle the sounds of snoring and whispering as well as to afford a shred of privacy.

It is three o'clock in the morning when the canister deploys with no more noise than someone gently sniffing. Ten seconds after the noise starts, though, it stops and the contents of the canister are fully expended into the room. Across the city—and nation—more canisters deploy. A few of them are nowhere near any people, as their placement was misjudged. Most, however, deploy around dozens or more people at once. The results are catastrophic.

Chapter Thirty

"It *hurts*, dammit! That's what it feels like! It feels like somebody poured a bunch of booze all over an open wound then left it to sit all night!"

Frank stifled a chuckle as he ripped off another strip of tape from Linda's leg. "Hey, it's a valid question! Does it feel infected?"

"Will you—give me that already!" Linda grabbed at the final strips of tape and yanked them off of her leg with a sudden motion. "I thought this crap was supposed to come off easily!"

"Seems pretty easy to me." Frank couldn't stifle his next chuckle and was rewarded with a ball of tape and a bloody lump of gauze being thrown at his face.

"If I had some kind of disease I'd be praying for you to get it right now. Asshole."

As Linda gently probed the skin around the wound on her leg, Frank collected the tape and gauze and stood up. He stretched his back, neck, arms and legs as he walked along, trying to get the circulation going through them. The barn had been colder than he had expected, though Linda had recovered substantially through the night and was mostly back to herself by morning.

After a quick peek outside the barn to make sure no one had

come up during the night, Frank and Linda ate a brief breakfast of
bits of packaged food from the bottom of their backpacks that they
had thankfully stuffed into them. While Frank still had his backpack and all of the gear that went along with it, Linda had suffered
substantially. She still had her backpack and a bag with ammunition and a few stray pieces of food, but the other bags that they
had transferred from her wrecked truck into the white and red one
days earlier had been burned by Thomas and his associates.

Thankfully Linda had a spare change of clothing in her backpack
and after she and Frank ate, she stripped off her pants without warning
and propped up her leg for Frank to change the bandage. He had taken
the unexpected moment of vulnerability in stride and did his best to
ignore it and act professionally while helping her dress the wound and
then affix a bandage that would survive light to moderate movement.

"What's the matter, Frank?" Linda grinned. "Do I look *that*
bad?" Frank rolled his eyes and sighed.

"You know what? I really don't get you." Frank turned around
and started to repack his backpack while Linda put on a fresh—
and bullet-hole-less—pair of jeans.

"What's not to get?" Linda stood up slowly and finished
buttoning her pants, then took a few slow steps to test how her
leg felt.

"You go from joking to serious in a heartbeat. You go from
trying to wait out a guy who's threatening to kill us to slicing and
dicing everyone in your path." Frank turned around and shook his
head as he put his pack on. He could hear his voice getting louder
as he spoke, but he didn't bother trying to be quiet. "I've been
trying to keep my mouth shut about it all for the most part but I
can't do that anymore. What the hell's your deal?"

Linda stood for a moment with her weight awkwardly on her
good leg before hobbling over to a hay bale and powering herself
onto it. "When I started this whole thing, I wasn't exactly planning
on taking on any passengers. I've tried not to be standoffish but
trying to trust someone when you're in my position is a little bit
difficult."

"What position is that, eh?" Frank threw his arms in the air. "Can you name one thing I've done to give you reason to distrust me? I've tried to help you in every possible way since we met. I understand that it hasn't been all that long, but come on already! What's your deal with me?"

Linda looked down at the floor of the barn and squeezed her lips together, shutting her eyes as she submerged herself in memories of the past. "You've heard of Operation Iranian Liberation, right? I think I told you I was part of the invasion, with the Marines."

Linda had mentioned her military service previously, but Frank had completely forgotten about it until she mentioned the name of the massive military operation that had taken place several years prior. "Oh hell." Frank's frustration instantly evaporated and he ran his hands through his hair. "You were part of the Liberation operation? Not just the invasion itself?"

Linda gave a bemused snort. "Yeah."

Frank sat down quietly across from Linda and watched her closely for several seconds before speaking again. "My grandfather was a veteran. So is my dad. My mother always said that asking them about their service, because of what they'd seen and done, wasn't the best idea, so I won't ask you. I'm sorry, though. For everything you went through, whatever it was, and whatever you're dealing with now. I'm sorry. I didn't realize, but I apologize regardless. I—"

"Frank. Shut up and listen."

Frank closed his mouth and stared at Linda as she took a deep breath and spoke.

"I told you I was abandoned by someone who I thought was my best friend. That... wasn't quite the truth." Linda looked up at the ceiling and bit her lip, closing her eyes as the sights, smells and sounds of the past came rushing back. "My squad was together from boot camp and special training exercises right through when we deployed. We lived together, breathed together and we knew each other inside out. We were part of MARSOC – Marine Corps

Special Operations Command. The Marine Raiders. Think SEALs but for the Marines instead of the Navy."

"That sounds insane."

Linda chuckled and shook her head. "Yeah it was. And I was even more insane for joining up."

"Heh." Frank cracked a slight grin as Linda continued.

"We went through everything together, us eight. When we deployed, we were given a modified Bradley IFV and sent in to secure the western side of the river."

"The government and administrative buildings, right? You had mentioned that before."

"Yep. Then the mortars started coming in from across the river, right in the heart of the residential buildings. The Iranian army was taking over people's homes and setting up smart mortars on the tops to target us. Three other squads went down before we got the okay to move across the river."

"Right into the residential area?"

"Right into the heart. We moved past the apartments and directly into the thick of the neighborhoods. It was a terrible choice for all the reasons you can imagine but we didn't have a choice. Smart mortars can punch through an IFV's top armor like a hot knife through butter and there's no way to hide from them except to get out of range or get right on top of them."

Frank shook his head. "So you drove right into the heart of them."

Linda nodded slowly. "We fought for sixteen hours straight. Cleared probably three dozen mortar nests. That was before they punched a hole in the side of the Bradley. Then we had to move out on foot. I think we went on for another twelve hours and a dozen more mortar nests before we got pinned down."

"Was this when…" Frank trailed off, not wanting to ask the question.

"Yeah." Linda steepled her fingers and took a deep breath. "It was a beautiful neighborhood. Most of the war hadn't reached them yet, so aside from the odd tank track or three it was actually gorgeous. Like most of the country, before the war." She took another deep breath before continuing. "We had been hearing mortar fire all morning from a nest that was well hidden. Turned out to be in a small park. They had set up sandbags and camouflage in between some swing sets and stuff.

"We were moving through houses and porches, using the roofs to mask our approach from the air so the mortars couldn't target us. We took out the nest easily enough but as soon as the last man went down we started taking suppressing fire from all sides."

"A trap?" Frank's eyes widened.

"You got it. It wasn't an ordinary trap, though. They were using us as live target practice for some nasty new weapons."

"Who, the Iranian army?"

"Sort of." Linda's upper lip curled in disgust. "His name's Farhad Omar, director of the Iranian army's special weapons division."

"Special weapons?" Frank raised an eyebrow. "What kind of special weapons?"

"Name something that's not a conventional weapon and Omar's probably had his hand in it. His specialties, though, are chemical and biological weapons."

"I thought Iran was staunchly against the use of chemical weapons."

"That was decades ago." Linda shook her head. "Omar used some sort of connections or blackmail or voodoo magic to convince the government to sanction the development of new biological and chemical weapons. The speed at which he developed them made it obvious that he had been working on them in secret for some time."

"Holy shit. So your squad…"

"Four of us died in the first thirty seconds from the gas. I don't know how half of us survived long enough to get our masks on. Maybe Omar engineered it that way. We couldn't move for the gunfire, though, and we knew that there would be something else coming in soon. I radioed in for backup, but they wouldn't be able to get birds on our location for another ten minutes at least." Linda stopped talking for a moment and closed her eyes.

"You really don't have to talk about this, you know." Frank spoke gently.

"We... uh... we were pinned down. No reinforcements. Then Chad got a rocket off at one of the emplacements to our west and made an opening through one of the houses. We were able to move out of the park and into the cover of the house. That's when the shit hit the fan. They tossed these weird orange canisters into the house and our masks started beeping warnings about the filters being compromised. We moved out to the back of the house into an alley with decent cover and had to decide whether to move or stay and defend our position until reinforcements could arrive."

"What happened?"

"I had command of the squad but panic was running rampant among everyone else. I made the call to stay and... the other three fled. They didn't make it beyond the end of the alley before they were cut down. Two minutes later reinforcements showed up in the form of half a dozen IFVs. Those were two minutes of my life I'll never forget. I used a dumpster as cover from one end of the alley and laid down fire on the other end. They tore me up pretty good before the IFVs rolled in."

Linda spoke so matter-of-factly about the situation that Frank began to realize how much of an effect it had really had upon her. "Were they able to help your squad?"

"No. All of them died. The IFVs secured the area, recovered the bodies and then we got out of there. A few weeks later the doctors got around to looking at tissue samples from the ones who died to the gas and started putting two and two together. It was a while before I got word through the grapevine about Omar being the one responsible."

"Linda. I'm sorry for what I said." Frank shook his head as he put it in his hands.

"It's okay. You didn't know. Just... understand that it's not about you, all right? Like I said before, you're one of the good ones. But so were they. And when the pressure was cranked to eleven they snapped and ran." Linda took a deep breath and stood up, shaking her head and chuckling. "Anyway. Way more details than you wanted or needed. You're not my therapist and we barely know each other. I'm going to take a leak then we should get going. Could you grab my stuff and throw it in the car?"

Frank nodded and watched Linda as she limped across the barn and out the door. The sum of all she had shared with him filled his mind with a cacophony of noise so loud and violent that he had trouble processing it all.

Chapter Thirty-One

While Frank busied himself with cleaning up his and Linda's effects from the barn and packing everything up, she relieved herself out of sight nearby. When she returned, Frank was loading his and her backpacks into the back seat of the car. Once he finished, he took the keys and popped open the trunk just to check and see what was inside.

"Holy mother of pearl…" Frank whistled as he lifted the trunk, marveling at the flat trays of fuel that were stacked in the trunk, nearly completely filling it up. A coiled length of tubing was on top of the packs and as he gently jostled them, he could hear a large quantity of liquid sloshing around.

"What've you got?" Linda strode over to the back of the car, then whistled just as he had. "Damn! Nice find! This should get us all the way to Pigeon Forge and then some, you think?"

Frank nodded slowly. "Absolutely. Makes you wonder, though, why they would have so much fuel in one of their cars."

"Mad Max purists? Maybe this was their 'tanker' that they were planning to use for something?"

"I'm still amazed at how fast these people degenerated into… this."

"Opportunists are everywhere." Linda looked inside the car, then back at Frank. "You ready to go?"

"Yep, all set."

"Good. Let's get out of here."

"Where are we heading to now, anyway?" Frank helped Linda into the front passenger's seat before slipping behind the wheel.

"I don't know about you, but I could use some clothes. Most of my stuff was burned up in the truck."

"Any suggestions on where to go?" Frank pulled around the barn and headed back out to the road. Once there he turned towards the south and began cruising down the back country highway.

"Someplace… out of the way. No shopping malls or big cities, obviously."

"What else do we need?"

"Food would be good. I had more than enough but again… fire. Burned up. Poof. Gone."

"At least you were able to hang on to your bag of extra ammunition."

"Thank goodness for small favors." Linda turned around and patted the bag in the backseat. "I wonder how they made out in that wreck."

"Who knows. Hopefully we never find out."

Linda nodded quietly and they lapsed into silence. As the day wore on, the weather took a turn for the worse as dark clouds rolled in over the horizon. The oscillation between warm and cold weather seemed to be waning as the temperature steadily dropped to the point where Frank had to switch the car's sorry excuse for air conditioning off and switch on the heater.

Most of the rest of the day was spent winding through the back roads and trying to guess at where they were based on landmarks, road names and what type of road surface they were on. By the time they realized that they had left the state of New York and were well into Pennsylvania, the darkened sky was becoming rapidly dimmer as night set in.

"Where do you want to stop for the night?" Frank yawned as

he spoke and rubbed his eyes. "It's nearly seven and your bandage needs changing."

A worried look crossed Linda's face as she studied the road ahead of them. "I don't know that we should stop just yet. We still need to find some spare clothes and food of some sort."

"Well unless you want to go back to the national park we just went through, kill a bear and skin it, I don't know of anywhere nearby where we can go."

Frank eased the car to a stop at a T-junction and looked at the sign standing next to the road. "Ever heard of a town called Brockway?"

Linda shook her head. "Nope."

"Good. Hopefully it's small enough that nobody will have looted it."

Linda laughed as Frank turned to the right, following the sign. "Yet."

"What do you—oh. Hey, no, I'm no looter. I'm…" Frank wrinkled his brow. "I'm a strategic acquirer of necessary supplies."

"You're a scrounger."

"Call me whatever you like if we make it out of this town with some clothing and food. Besides, we won't need to steal anything. If anybody's left there we can trade them some fuel for what we need."

"I hope they're as polite as you're imagining."

Linda and Frank remained silent for the next few minutes as they drove towards town, until Frank finally slowed down and stopped the car. "There it is, up ahead. Looks quaint."

Though difficult to see with no stars or moon to offer light, the bright beams from the car illuminated the close side of the town with ease. It appeared to be extremely small, with one main road running down the center and small clusters of homes and businesses branching off to the side. Two large school buildings sat on the far western side of the town, visible only because there were bright lights illuminating their exteriors and because Frank and Linda's car sat atop a slight rise just outside town, affording them a view of the entire place. No movement was visible inside the town, and the only lights appeared to be those at the middle school and high school buildings.

"Quaint and creepy." Linda shook her head and raised an eyebrow. "Do you really want to drive down main street with the lights on?"

Frank shut off the lights on the car and eased forward down the road, waiting for his eyes to adjust to the darkness before speeding up. "What I'd like to do is turn around and go somewhere else, but my stomach is telling me that we need to stop here."

"All hail Frank's mighty stomach." Linda deadpanned the joke before giggling. "Sorry. I've got a bad habit of cracking jokes at the worst possible times."

"Beats the hell out of getting grumpy, I guess."

"Well, if you want to go through town and see if we can spot a dollar store or grocer or something I'm game. I wouldn't mind just leaving a flat pack of fuel on the counter for trade and avoiding all contact if possible."

"I'm okay with that." Frank nodded. "Looks like the clouds are breaking up some, too. Should make things easier."

Frank increased the speed of the car and he and Linda both began scanning to the left, right and front of the vehicle as they crept towards town. The engine noise was quiet enough that Frank felt confident it would be masked by the distant booms of thunder, but he and Linda still remained vigilant.

After passing by the first few rows of houses, the buildings turned from strictly residential into a mix of residential and light commercial. A small flower shop was on the left, followed by a BBQ stand on the right, then a laundromat on the left nestled in between two single-story rows of apartments.

Linda used her flashlight sparingly, pointing it out the window and turning it on in brief intervals to look down streets or into shops they passed by, but never leaving it on long enough to easily give away their position. The quintessential small town was filled with mostly two-story houses painted white with large porches and sharply angled roofs.

Most of the lawns were large and covered with a layer of leaves that had fallen from the storms passing through, and none of them looked raked. A few cars were parked along the side of the road, but none of them appeared damaged in any way. Frank was beginning to think that the town had been spared from the destruction wrought by the attacks when Linda pointed at a small muffler shop they were driving past.

"Looks like the whole place went up in flames when that tractor-trailer exploded. Sheesh."

Frank shook his head. "Damn. And here I thought these folks might have been spared from all this mess."

"What I'd like to know, though, is where everyone is." Linda frowned. "The whole town seems deserted except for the lights at the schools."

"We'll know soon, I guess. I think they're coming up soon."

"Mm. Hey! Stop for a second!" Linda pointed out to the left and Frank hit the brakes.

"What?"

Linda smiled and motioned with the flashlight for him to look. "Jackpot."

Frank turned and saw a large glass front to a small shop with the name "Angel Wings Thrift Store" written on the front and grinned. "Want to stop?"

"Hell yes. Pull around back and kill the engine. We'll see if the back doors are unlocked, then check the front, then break in through the back if we have to."

Frank shifted in his seat. "Not sure I'm entirely comfortable with breaking and entering."

"Desperate times, Frank. I'm not the B and E type myself, either, but it's getting cold as hell around here and we—well, mostly me, but you do too—need clothing."

"Fine." Frank sighed and pulled around to the back of the shop. He backed into an empty space near the back of the building that would afford them a fast escape if that became necessary, then cut off the engine. He got out of the car first, shivering involuntarily as a gust of cold wind caught him by surprise, then went over to Linda's side of the car. She was trying to get out on her own and he extended a hand, which she begrudgingly took.

"Thanks. I hate relying on people for basic stuff like this."

"You'll be fine soon enough. Speaking of that, don't you need a fresh bandage soon?"

"I'd rather wait till we're out of town."

Frank shrugged. "Fair enough." He headed for the back door to the thrift store and pulled on the handle, finding it locked as he had expected. He glanced at Linda who was still limping towards the door. "Locked up tight. Hang here with the car while I go around front and check to see if it's open, okay?"

Linda reached into her waistband to check that her pistol was still there and nodded. "Sounds good."

Frank walked slowly around the building, keeping the noise from his footsteps to a bare minimum. He kept his rifle low, the barrel pointed at the ground and his finger away from the trigger, not wanting to appear like he was being aggressive just in case there was anyone friendly around. He was halfway around the side of the building when he realized that his flashlight was in the car, but he pressed onward, using the light from the moon to guide his path.

When Frank arrived at the front, he looked in through the main window before turning his attention to the door. He stared at a sign hanging in the door for a long moment before nearly laughing out loud. He pushed on the door and it squeaked open, a small bell hidden above tinkling as he went inside. Once in, he grabbed the sign off of the door and crept through the shop floor and into the back, where he quickly located the back door thanks to the faint light streaming in through a pair of skylights.

Around the back of the shop, Linda started getting antsy when Frank didn't show back up for a few minutes. She was getting ready to head around to the front to search for him when she heard a click and the back door slowly swung open.

"Linda? Where—what the hell, it's me!"

Linda breathed a sigh of relief and lowered her pistol. "Dammit, Frank. Why didn't you come back around?"

"Seemed easier to open the back. Less walking for you."

"Did you break in through the front door?"

Frank grinned and held up the sign he had taken off of the inside of the front door. "Nope. Check this out."

The sign was handwritten in black marker against cream-colored paper with a small pair of wings in the upper right corner over which the name of the store was printed.

TO ALL VISITORS,

If no one is available to assist you, please take what you need and leave whatever you find fair in trade. In this troubling time we ask you kindly to only take what you need and leave the rest for others.

Thank you.

LINDA HELD the sign as she read it, then handed it back to Frank with a puzzled look on her face. "That has got to be the most polite sign I've ever read. They even laminated it and put a suction cup on the back, too."

"I'd love to shake their hand but I'll settle for doing exactly what the sign says. I'll grab one of the fuel containers and bring it inside while you start looking for something your size."

Linda nodded, handed Frank the keys to the car and hobbled inside while he held the door open. Once she was in, he grabbed his flashlight from the car, then went to the trunk and pulled out one of the flat plastic containers filled with gasoline. "Five gallons seems like a fair trade for some clothes." He mumbled to himself as he carried one of the packs in through the back door of the shop and placed it behind the counter.

After affixing the sign back on the front door, he searched behind the counter for a pen and paper and wrote a short note thanking the store's owner for their generosity and left it on top of the fuel container. He then began browsing through the store, trying to find some long pants, shirts and a pair of gloves to go with his jacket and undergarments that were in his backpack.

It took Frank and Linda just over half an hour of browsing to get everything they needed, and even though they were in an unknown shop in the middle of a strange town at night, neither of them felt wary of the situation. There was something about the town, the store or perhaps the blatant generosity and goodwill of whomever owned the establishment that put both of their minds at ease.

"You find anything?" Frank walked over to the women's clothing side of the small shop with three shirts, a pair of gloves and two pairs of pants draped over his arm.

"Yeah, this should help a lot." Linda held up an armful of clothing. "Got a couple jackets, some more pants and shirts. Found a pair of shoes that fit me, too."

"I'm jealous. I looked for shoes but there was nothing in my size."

"We should go, if you're ready."

"Yep." Frank nodded and headed for the back of the shop. He held the door open for Linda and they walked out to the car together. "You know," he said, "this has to be the slowest-paced breaking and entering that's ever been performed."

Linda looked back at the store as she tossed the clothing into the back of the car. "This whole town seems so… I don't know."

"Peaceful?"

"Abnormally so. But without the creepy psycho-murderer vibe. It feels wholesome."

"So we're at, what, two for five if you count that little place where you shot those two guys?"

"Yeah. Well. We'll see, I guess. We're still not out of the town yet."

"True enough." Frank threw his clothes into the back of the car and helped Linda into her seat. "Think it's worth visiting those schools to the west, or should we just blow past them? We still need food and I'm not seeing a grocery store around here so it's probably not on the main road."

"I think I have enough for another day. Maybe two if we

stretch it. But we need water, too. We could always try to find a rest stop and raid the vending machines instead."

Frank shook his head and got in the car. "Those're just going to be on the big highways. I think we're far enough into the state and away from the major highways that we won't find anything like that."

Linda leaned her head back against the seat and sighed. "Dammit. Fine. Let's see what's going on at the schools. Worst case we can just drive like a bat out of hell if things get sketchy."

.

Chapter Thirty-Two

With the deployment of the eighteen canisters the city of Pittsburgh is doomed. Infection sets in almost immediately after deployment and the initial symptoms take less than thirty minutes to appear. People taking shelter in the school building begin to cough up blood in their sleep. They wake up, startled, and rub their eyes to find blood oozing from there as well. Panic sets in as each person realizes that they are not alone in their symptoms.

As groups of infected start to panic, they begin running to and fro, spreading the infectious disease far and wide. The rate at which the disease tears through their bodies is wholly unnatural and unprecedented. Within two hours ten percent of the population of the city is infected. Twenty-four hours later and one hundred thousand—a full third of the city's total population—are infected.

While the disease kills quickly, the rate at which it burns through its victims is both a blessing and a curse to its survival. The panic caused by the rapid onset of symptoms causes victims to seek help, thus spreading the disease far and wide. Once medical personnel begin to understand what is going on and enact basic quarantine procedures, though, the death rate plummets.

Martial law is declared and individuals are told to remain in their homes. Public workers out in the field don respirators to protect themselves, but infections still run rampant as the virus enters through small cuts and tears in their *skin. As the number of new infections drops, the disease all but wipes itself out within a few days of when it began. This fact, however, is impossible to know.*

State and federal agencies across the country—already strained to their breaking point by the explosions that rocked the transportation industry—are ill-equipped to handle a biological attack. Though the attack is over with nearly as soon as it begins, the states and feds set up massive quarantine perimeters around cities that are both infected and not infected.

Infected cities are off-limits to anyone going in or out and teams of scientists work tirelessly with samples of the contagion to identify its nature and how to combat it. Bomb disposal robots are refitted with biological sensors and sent out to roam the streets, measuring the air and any bodies they come across for evidence of infection. Cities that are not infected are fortified and act as region-wide emergency shelters. Broadcasts are put out on every working television and radio station, calling anyone and everyone to mass at what are quickly known as Shelter Cities.

After long delays the Shelter Cities are the first to benefit from food and medical airdrops from the United States military as their planes and convoys start moving again. People who hear about the cities begin walking towards them or, if they are lucky, are carried by military transport. With tens of millions of people slowly relocating to Shelter Cities, resources are strained to their breaking point, and martial law is put into permanent effect in the cities. Across the United States, the population distribution is shifting and the face of the nation is changing. People struggle to survive in the harsh new world, not knowing that the worst is still yet to come.

Chapter Thirty-Three

After passing over a narrow bridge, Frank slowed the car to a crawl while he spoke with Linda, confirming that she wanted to go there.

"For the last time, Frank, yes. The town seems like it's in good shape so I think food is the most important thing here."

"I don't see why you don't want to try and sneak in like we did with the hippy camp."

Linda chuckled. "Call it intuition. I don't think we're going to find trouble here."

Frank sighed and gunned the engine as he made a turn into the long, winding road that led onto the school grounds. "I sure hope not."

The two-lane road leading into the school was framed on either side by wide fields of grass. A few scattered trees dotted the landscape, but it was well-maintained, plain and extremely clean. Farther to the west past the second school building was a football field and a few playgrounds. The winding road opened into a large parking lot in front of the schools that was barren aside from half a dozen vehicles parked right up next to the entrance.

Located to the south of the school buildings, the large parking area was separated from the main road out of town by a short wooden fence and a long strip of tall grass. The main road sat on an incline looking over the parking lot and school buildings, but the slope was gentle enough that it could easily be walked without trouble.

"Where do you want me to pull up?"

"Turn the lights on first and honk the horn a couple times. Then pull up slowly in front of the high school. There are a lot of lights on inside there. Try to keep the left half of the building shielded by the cars next to us, though. If trouble breaks out I want you to pull behind those cars, then head for the slope behind us to get back onto the main road."

Frank glanced around, trying to put the pieces together for all of what she had just said. "Put us in partial cover, use the cover in case we start getting shot at, then go straight for the road and hope we don't take a bullet. Got it."

"You're doing fine, Frank. We want them to know we're here but we don't want to make ourselves completely vulnerable." Linda patted Frank on the shoulder and pulled her pistol out of her waistband before tucking it under her leg.

As Frank eased the car up into the parking spot Linda had pointed out, he turned on the lights to the car and honked the horn twice. Before he could do anything else, the double doors to the front of the high school exploded outward as a pair of uniformed police officers ran out. They stopped halfway between the school and the car and raised a pair of shotguns, bringing them to bear on Frank and Linda.

"Oh shit!" Frank put his hand on the shifter and was about to throw the car into reverse when the shorter of the two officers, a woman with brown hair pulled into a tight bun, shouted at them.

"Stop right there! What do you want?"

Frank glanced at Linda who was already in the process of rolling down her window. She whispered to Frank as she raised her hands, keeping them up near her face and in plain view of the officers. "Keep your hands down and ready to get us out of here if this goes south."

"Hi there!" Linda cracked a big smile and tried to sound as friendly as she possibly could. "I'm Linda and my friend here is Frank. We're just passing through and were hoping we could trade for some food."

The taller officer, a man with short-cropped greying hair, eyed Frank and Linda suspiciously. "Where are you from?"

"Maine!" Linda shouted back, still keeping her hands raised.

"Mighty long way from Maine. How'd you find yourself in our town?"

Linda shouted, "That is a *very* long story. Look, do you mind if we get out of our car?"

The two officers glanced at each other and the taller one leaned down and whispered in his partner's ear. She shook her head and frowned, then looked back at Frank and Linda as she whispered something back. He, in turn, shook his head and rolled his eyes before glaring at Frank and Linda. Both of the officers lowered their guns slightly and the woman began walking slowly towards Frank and Linda's car.

"You got any weapons in there?" The woman spoke loudly.

Linda nodded and the man raised his gun again, his entire body stiffening. "Keep your hands up, both of you!"

Frank looked at Linda who nodded at him and whispered. "Just do what he says. Leave the talking to me."

The woman stepped down from the sidewalk into the parking lot, keeping a few feet away from the car as she eased closer. "Look, I'm sorry about all of this." The woman shrugged sheepishly and motioned at her partner. "Everybody's on edge, Officer Jackson especially."

Linda smiled and nodded. "I completely understand. Look, we've got a rifle and a handgun in here. The pistol's under my left leg and the rifle's in the back seat. Both are loaded and there are rounds in the chamber."

The woman nodded. "Thanks. I appreciate that. Just do what he said and keep your hands up so he doesn't get nervous. Now you said you wanted to trade? We don't have a market here, you know."

"We have fuel. Gasoline. We'd be happy to give you some in exchange for a few days' worth of food. We're trying to get to Pigeon Forge, where my parents live."

The woman eyed Linda and Frank carefully for several seconds before nodding slowly. "I'll see what we can do for you. You ex-military?"

"Marines. How'd you know?"

The woman gave Linda a faint smile. "You talk like one. Stay here for a minute, okay?"

Linda nodded and the woman walked back to her partner. They held a brief whispered conversation that involved a lot of gesticulating and looks being thrown at Linda and Frank. Finally, after a long minute, the woman walked back to the car. Her stance was visibly relaxed and while she still held on to her rifle, it was loose in her hands and pointed at the ground. Her partner's gun was still at the ready, but he appeared to be somewhat more relaxed as well, but still vigilant about the new arrivals.

"Come on out, guys." The woman waved to Frank and Linda. "Just… leave the guns in your car, please."

Linda pushed open her door and swiveled her legs out. Frank got out slowly and walked around the front of the car to help Linda, and the woman backed up a few paces and looked at him warily. He caught her glance and held up his hands. "She was shot in the leg. Just helping her out of the car."

The woman nodded but stayed back until Frank had helped Linda out and they both stood in front of the car. She reached out and shook Linda's hand first, then Frank's. "Linda, Frank, I'm Caroline. The guy who looks like he's got a stick up his rear end is Percival."

"Perry." The other officer grunted and shook his head at Caroline. "Only my mother calls me Percival."

"Right. How do I manage to keep forgetting that?" Caroline cracked another smile, then gave Linda a concerned look. "You mind leaving your piece in the car?"

Linda raised an eyebrow, impressed that Caroline had managed to see when Linda stealthily slipped her pistol back into her waistband. "I really would rather not, if it's all the same to you. We're happy to do a quick trade out here and then leave, if you don't want us to bring our weapons inside."

"Yeah, Perry's not going to like it if you're carrying inside the building."

"Nope." Another grunt followed Perry's blunt pronouncement.

"I wouldn't mind going inside and seeing what we'd be willing to trade, then bringing it out here, though." Linda swore she could hear Perry growl at Caroline's suggestion, but the man made no move to put a halt to the offer.

Linda nodded quickly. "That'd be great, thanks."

"You got the fuel in the back?" Caroline motioned towards the back of the car.

"Yeah." Linda limped around to the trunk with Frank following close behind. Caroline, despite her upbeat demeanor and pleasant smiles, was cautious to stay several steps away from Frank and Linda. As the three of them circled around to the back of the car, Perry walked along the sidewalk, watching them intently.

Linda noticed Perry's movement and spoke quietly to Caroline. "Your partner there; is he former military, too?"

"Yeah, part of a SEAL team."

Linda nodded. "That was my first guess."

"It's good for you that you were in the Marines. Otherwise he'd have sent you packing and probably put a few holes in the back of the car, too."

Frank unlocked the trunk and opened it with a flourish. "That would've sucked."

Caroline took a step forward, raising her eyebrows and nodding appreciatively. "No kidding. That's a lot of fuel. In flat packs, no less. You guys preppers or do you just like driving around with a bunch of gas in your trunk?"

Frank started to speak but Linda cut him off. "We had a run-in with some less than savory types. They torched our truck so we borrowed one of their cars. We were lucky that it had all of this in it, otherwise we wouldn't be able to make it to Pigeon Forge."

"Very nice." Caroline nodded and looked over at Perry, giving him a thumbs-up. "So how much can you spare?"

Linda glanced at Frank. "What do you think?"

He shrugged. "Ten, maybe twenty gallons? Depends on what you have to trade."

"Hm. That's less than I was expecting. Just hang tight, though, all right? I'll go inside and see what we can do for you."

Caroline was walking back towards Perry when the sound of a rifle shot was accompanied by her crying out in pain and falling to the ground as she clutched her shoulder. Linda immediately whipped her head around to locate the source of the shot before grabbing Frank's arm and pulling him towards the front of the car. "Get down, Frank!" Linda limped along for a few feet before ducking down in front of the car just as another shot rang out.

Concrete exploded from the sidewalk next to Perry where he squatted over Caroline's body, trying to identify where she had been shot. "Get her over here!" Linda shouted at Perry and he quickly scooped up Caroline and gently laid her back down behind the large truck parked next to Frank and Linda's car.

"What the hell is this?" Perry glared menacingly at Linda and Frank.

"How would I know?" Linda shouted back. She flinched as a shot passed through the back window of their car and struck the front floorboard.

"Nobody's been shooting at us until you two showed up!"

"Can we divvy up the blame later and get inside the school first?" Frank looked back and forth between Linda and Perry as he spoke. "Don't you two think there's probably more than one of them? Plus she needs to be looked at!" Frank pointed at Caroline, who was groaning in pain.

Perry clenched his jaw and nodded curtly. "I'm taking her inside first. I want suppressive fire laid down to cover us."

"Frank, grab the rifle."

"The hell?" Frank looked at Linda with a wide-eyed expression. Another bullet came whizzing in, hitting the back of the truck sitting next to the car.

"Whatever that shooter's got, it's a bolt-action. You have a few seconds in between shots. As soon as the next one comes in, get in between that truck and the car and grab the rifle and my bag of ammo!" Linda pulled out her pistol. "I'll try to give you a few extra seconds of cover."

Frank groaned but moved to the front left corner of the car, getting ready to run to the back door as soon as the next shot came. When it did, ricocheting off of the top of the car, he ran for the side of the car and opened the door as Linda leaned up and fired several shots at the small rise next to the main road. Unbidden, Perry did the same, placing several evenly paced rounds at the top of the ridge in a line as they both tried to scare whoever was up there into waiting for the next shot.

"Got it!" Frank scurried back around the car and Linda grabbed the bag from his hands. Frank glanced at Perry and Caroline before speaking to the tall officer. "I'll stay here and try to buy you guys a minute to get inside, but I need you to get Linda in, too."

Perry glanced at Linda before shaking his head. "Sorry. We're going in first, then we'll allow you two to come inside."

Frank pointed at Linda's leg and nearly shouted back at the man. "She was shot yesterday and needs help getting inside, asshole! If we had known your idyllic town was going to turn into a shooting gallery we would have never stopped!"

"Perry." Caroline's voice was full of pain and the others could see a dark red stain spreading out across her shoulder. "I can walk just fine. She can't. Do what he says."

"Caroline…" Perry shook his head but Caroline reached up with her good arm and put a shaking hand on him.

"Just trust me, okay?"

Perry closed his eyes and sighed deeply. "I hope she's right about you two. Fine. Get over here. You—as soon as the next shot comes we're going to get moving. I think there's just one shooter, directly up the hill next to the cluster of bushes around the big sign."

Frank peeked up and squinted, trying to make out the location.

The light from the moon had grown brighter as more clouds dissipated and after a few seconds of searching he saw what Perry was talking about. "Right. Shots on the bushes. Got it." Frank felt the sudden weight of responsibility on his shoulders as another shot turned a chunk of sidewalk a few feet behind him into a cloud of dust.

"Let's go!" Perry pulled Caroline up by her good arm, then yanked Linda into a standing position. He pushed Caroline forward and she began running for the school building, clutching at her right shoulder with her left hand. Before Linda could even take a step he had already picked her up and began running forward.

As Perry, Caroline and Linda made for the entrance to the school, Frank popped up and leaned against the side of the car. He peered through the rifle scope, trying to calm his breathing as he searched for the cluster of bushes in the narrow field of view. He swore silently as the seconds ticked past until, finally, he found what he was looking for.

A brief flash of movement in the bushes caught his eye and he loosed a round, sending it slightly off target. It passed through the sign near the bushes and the movement stopped as the shooter retreated from taking his next shot. Frank fired twice more into the bushes with no effect except to further delay the shooter from firing upon the other three. Frank glanced back after his last shot and saw the doors of the school swing open as Linda, Perry and Caroline ran inside.

"Okay then. Now what?" Frank talked to himself as he fired a few more shots into and around the bushes at the top of the ridge. Behind him, from inside the school, he heard more shots and glanced back to see Perry crouched inside the entrance.

"Get in here!" Perry bellowed at Frank who started moving towards the entrance of the school when a better idea flashed through his head.

"Hang on!" Frank threw the rifle through the open passenger's side window of the car before running around to the driver's side. He jumped in, jammed a key into the ignition and started the car. As it sputtered to life he threw it into gear and it lurched forward, bouncing on the curb and scraping the undercarriage as he drove it up out of the parking lot and towards the school building. When he was halfway there he slammed on the brakes and pulled the emergency brake, sending the car sliding through the soft grass towards the entrance. It stopped a few feet from the doors and Frank grabbed his rifle and backpack before jumping out, pulling his belongings along after him.

Perry moved out of the way of Frank as he dove through the entrance, the brief lapse in Perry's suppressive fire giving the ridge shooter enough time to fire another shot that sent splinters of wood exploding from the door a few inches from Perry's head.

Frank pulled the door shut behind him as he rolled away from it, yanking back his fingers just in time to keep them from getting pinched. Several more rounds hit the front door, but the material was thick enough that none could penetrate through.

Lying on his back, Frank closed his eyes and took several breaths before he felt something hard poking him in the shoulder. He opened his eyes slowly to see Perry taking a step back, his rifle trained on Frank's chest and a frown etched across his face.

"So." Perry glanced down at Caroline and then over at Linda, who was being held at gunpoint by a woman in blue jeans and a grey polo shirt. "Why don't you stay still right there on the floor, keep your hands away from your gun and explain to me just who you are and what kind of storm you've brought down upon our town."

Chapter Thirty-Four

Liam Kevin Peters had a headache. As each bump in the road revealed new aches and sores from the car wreck earlier in the morning, the pain in his head continued to grow. Building off of a lack of sleep and food and compounded by the stress of trying to search down a spider web of back country roads for his prey, he knew that it wouldn't be much longer before the headache turned into a full-blown migraine.

"Reggie." Liam spoke quietly, though there was menace in his tone.

"What's up?"

"I need something."

"Oh. Sure. One second."

"Mm." Liam twisted his hands around the steering wheel as another bump jostled his body, making his ribs, legs and arms feel as though someone was stabbing them with sewing needles.

"Here you go." Reggie dug through a baggie pulled out of his coat pocket and held up a small opaque shard of methamphetamine. Liam accepted the shard with a grunt and popped it in his mouth, crunching it between his teeth. Reggie grimaced as

he listened to the sound and, from the back seat, Josh shook his
head in disgust.

"Why do you do that?"

"Do what?" Liam looked at Josh in the rearview mirror.

"Eat it. You're not supposed to eat it."

"It helps me focus."

"Yeah, but smoking it is *way* better."

"You take it how you want and I'll take it how I want." Liam
sighed as he felt the pain in his head receding as the meth-
amphetamine penetrated into his bloodstream, releasing vast
amounts of dopamine from his brain that helped to block out the
headache. Oral ingestion of meth, while uncommon, was Liam's
father's favorite way to take the drug, and Liam had picked up on
the habit early in life.

For some reason, despite the fact that most of the people who
worked for and with them were hopelessly addicted to injecting
and smoking methamphetamine, Liam and his father had never
truly been addicted to it. They had gone through periods of days
or weeks where they ate or smoked it, but when they got tired of it
they stopped for long stretches with no noticeable withdrawal
symptoms.

"Give me a reading." Liam felt stronger and more confident
with the pain in his head gone and he looked back at Josh who was
holding the small black box.

"Still dead ahead."

"Hm." Liam abruptly swung the Corvette onto a side road,
taking a sharp right that threw Josh and Reggie against their seatbelts that Liam had insisted they all wear. "Keep an eye on it."
Liam looked down at the map on Reggie's map and nodded.
"Mark the signal strength so we can triangulate their position."

Liam's search for Frank and Linda had yielded no results for
the first few hours of the day except for the intermittent detection
of the transponder's signal. The mountainous terrain and the fact
that they had no other detectors with which to triangulate the
precise direction of the signal meant that they had to constantly
change direction in order to determine where their targets were.

A plan cooked up by Thomas years prior, each of the vehicles owned or operated by the gang had been outfitted with basic transponders that allowed him to know their exact location thanks to a series of antennas scattered in and around Binghamton. A few bribes and extortions later and he had outfitted the local police force with the same transponders without them knowing, making it possible for him and his crew to enjoy high levels of freedom while performing their illicit activities.

With the car that Frank and Linda took out of range of the antennas in Binghamton, the only way to track the vehicle was to use the handheld receiver. A combination of guesswork, common sense and a lot of back-and-forth driving gave Liam a rough estimate of the direction that they were headed, though he wasn't sure how long it would take for him to catch up.

The hit-or-miss signal of the car finally started growing stronger late in the day as they passed out of the hilly areas of New York and into Pennsylvania. Liam chuckled as he realized where they were and remembered more than a few trips he had taken to the area while in search of new markets where they could sell their goods.

Several small operations overseen by associates of his father had sprung up and all were supplied by the Peters gang. The death of Thomas would no doubt have a huge impact on the regions around Binghamton, especially in light of the recent events in the world, and Liam grinned as he realized the opportunity that was laid out in front of him.

It was after dark before Liam realized that they were closing in on the car, just as they entered the outskirts of a small town. Liam kept the engine noise to a minimum by coasting along wherever possible. He shut off all but the running lights on the vehicle and rolled back the tattered top to make it easier to see, hear and—he hoped—shoot.

After driving straight through town, Liam headed for the lights on the western end that he had seen when they were driving in. Instead of driving down to the schools, though, he stayed on the main road that traveled up a modest hill. He parked at the top of the hill and got out of his car, taking a pair of binoculars and a rifle with him. He crouched behind the metal barricade at the edge of the road and looked down at the school through his binoculars.

The car that Liam, Reggie and Josh had been chasing was parked at the school and two extremely familiar figures were stepping out of it. In front of them, fanned out on the sidewalk, were two police officers. The larger of the two, a tall man, was pointing a rifle at the couple getting out of the car. The other, a shorter woman, was talking to the couple, though she wasn't aiming at them.

The sight of the car and the couple he had been pursuing filled Liam with a sickening joy and he felt his heartbeat race. *Got you.* Liam smiled coldly before dashing back to Josh and Reggie, both of whom were still standing over by the car.

"Josh!" Liam snapped at the man. "Get your gun and get ready to start shooting. Reggie, you and I are going to flank the school. I'm taking the left side, you take the right."

"What?" Josh looked confused and Liam slapped him across the face without warning.

"Those two are down there! You're going to keep them pinned down while Reggie and I flank them. There's a couple of cops there, too. Kill the cops if you want but make sure the two from before are left alive. You got it?"

Josh's eyes were wide as he rubbed the side of his face. "Sure thing, Liam. Anything you say."

"Reggie, grab a shotgun. If things go south just keep on the right side of the building and watch for anyone trying to leave. Stay out of sight, though. We don't have the advantage of numbers or superior positioning this time. We'll burn the place down with whoever's in it if we have to."

Reggie nodded and grabbed his shotgun from the back seat. Josh took his rifle and uncapped the scope while Liam pulled a small bullhorn from the trunk. He smiled deviously at it and shook his head in appreciation. *Never thought I'd have use for this. Guess you were right about that.*

"I'm ready." Josh held up his rifle and Liam nodded.

"Good. Get in position. Reggie, get running. Go as wide as you can and sneak in towards the sides of the lot without being seen. Josh, keep them pinned down for as long as it takes for us to get there."

"Got it." Josh ran forward to the edge of the road and crouched down. He laid the barrel of the rifle on the guardrail and began sighting his targets while Liam and Reggie took off running in opposite directions down the road. They both ran for a good thirty seconds before heading back to the edge of the road and finding cover for their descent down towards the school.

On the left-hand side bordering the school was a collection of bushes and trees that offered Liam excellent concealment as he ran down the slope. Reggie, meanwhile, found a defilade along the length of the slope that provided concealment as long as he crouched the entire way down.

The first rifle shot came just as Liam and Reggie began their descent and it was accompanied by a cry of pain from near where Liam had seen the four people earlier. He scowled as he realized it was a woman's cry, hoping that Josh hadn't just killed one of the couple. Liam and Reggie increased their speed as they went down the hill until, finally, they arrived at the edge of the school. With nothing to provide concealment or cover in the parking lot, Liam realized that they were in a bad position if they wanted to advance on the couple. He decided to just try and see what was going on before he made any further moves.

Liam peeked out from the trees and brush as several shots rang out one after the other, though instead of coming from the hill they came from the direction of the parking lot. "What?" Liam muttered to himself as he tried to get a better view on whatever was going on. Finally he spotted movement out near the parking lot and watched helplessly as three figures ran into the school. The fourth waited at the cars for a moment and Liam hesitated, trying to decide if he wanted to engage or wait to see what happened next.

When the fourth figure jumped into the car and drove it towards the school entrance, Liam cursed as he realized that he had completely lost the element of surprise. As the car slid in front of the door, the fourth figure hopped out and ran inside. Anger clouded Liam's face as he realized that his targets were inside the school and he would have to rely on his backup plan to flush them out.

Chapter Thirty-Five

"Percival! For pity's sake, leave the man alone!" Caroline struggled to sit up but a small cluster of people ran down the hall towards her and placed her on a makeshift stretcher before carrying her off. "Dammit, Perry!" Caroline's shouts were lost as she was carted off to a back room to have her wound examined.

The rapidly changing events had caused Frank to instinctively freeze in place, neither speaking nor moving except to glance around and look for a way to gain the upper hand. Perry had ensured that he was far enough away from Frank to prevent any sort of surprise attack and Frank's rifle was entirely out of reach as well.

Linda, for her part, seemed more pissed off than anything else, and she shook her head slowly, keeping her hands raised but not even bothering to look at the person who had a gun pointed at her. Perry, she had determined, was one of—if not *the*—ringleader in whatever circus she and Frank had stumbled upon. Caroline's apparent kindness aside, Perry was the one they would have to deal with.

"Do you mind if I sit down?" Linda was balancing the majority of her weight on her good leg. Perry looked her over and nodded curtly. "Do it slowly. No sudden moves. Barb—step away from her."

The woman pointing a gun at Linda took a few steps back, glancing nervously between Perry and Linda. Perry watched Linda closely as she slid down to the floor, her face awash with relief as the pressure was lifted from her leg.

"How bad is your wound?"

"Not nearly as bad as your partner back there." Linda could barely repress a sneer as she snapped back at Perry.

"Yeah, we need to have a talk about that. Who's that who shot her, anyway? One of your friends, trying to take us out so you could loot this place unopposed?" Perry's voice was commanding and forceful but without any trace of anger. What he said was stated as cold hard facts and he wasn't about to let anything come between himself and his search for the truth.

Frank, still on his back on the floor, shook his head. "We have no idea. We got into town just a little while ago, on our way south to Pigeon Forge. We saw the sign in the thrift shop and left some fuel there in exchange for some clothes we took. We figured that given the sign, we'd try and see if we could trade for some food."

Perry's eyes narrowed. "South to Pigeon Forge? The road through town goes east to west. There's nothing going south to Tennessee for a long way around here."

"No kidding." Linda rolled her eyes, not even attempting to mask her frustration. "Glad to see you understand basic geography."

"Linda…" Frank shook his head at her. "Now's not the time."

"Bullshit it's not. Don't give me that crap, Frank!" Linda looked back at Perry. "We were waylaid in Binghamton. Barely got out with our asses intact. We stole a car from a group of meth-heads—"

"After they torched your truck. Yeah. I heard the short version you gave to Caroline."

"Yeah, so after we stole their car we decided to head down some back roads to try and lose them if they came after us…" The anger on Linda's face evaporated as she realized what she was saying. She turned to look at Frank, his concern mirroring her own.

"Linda. Is this… do you think he survived?"

"No way in hell."

"Who survived?" Perry's eye twitched as he looked back and forth between the pair, growing increasingly annoyed as the conversation evolved without his input.

"The leader of the meth-heads, a guy named Thomas Peters." Linda's mind raced as she put together the pieces from the last several hours. "Somehow he tracked us down at an abandoned house outside town." Linda shook her head. "You don't think…"

"GPS?" Frank furrowed his eyebrows. "If there are satellites still working I guess that would explain it, but they'd need some kind of data signal to track and I'm pretty sure the cell towers are still offline. Or maybe something more basic. If they tracked us here, it's probably someone from his gang taking shots at us."

"You said Thomas Peters?" Perry lowered his rifle ever so slightly as he asked the question.

"Yeah." Linda nodded. "Why?"

Perry shook his head and ran a hand across his brow before adjusting his grip on his rifle. "We had a couple guys associated with him coming down to the towns around here over the last few years trying to get folks hooked on their stuff. We ran them off but I heard he got his claws into more than a few places."

"Unless he could survive a high speed car crash while riding in the bed of a pickup I don't think you have to worry about him anymore." Frank slowly eased himself up into a sitting position, watching Perry carefully as he went.

As if on cue, the electric crackle of a bullhorn sounded from outside the school. Perry glanced at the woman holding the gun on Linda and whispered to her before moving into one of the side rooms. "Watch them both." In the first classroom just inside the school, Perry peered through the boarded-up windows, looking for the source of the sound. The crackle finally—mostly—went away and was replaced by a flat and emotionless voice.

"Listen up, you in the school! You're giving refuge to two

people, a man and woman. Send them out and we'll leave you in peace. Don't and we'll burn the place to the ground with everyone in it."

Throughout the school building Frank could hear the gasps, cries and faint murmuring of the townsfolk as they all reacted to the statement from the man outside. Frank glanced at Linda and shook his head. "That's not Thomas."

"Definitely not. This guy sounds halfway sane, if not a little bit bored with everything."

Perry started to speak but the voice outside crackled to life again. "You have ten minutes to send out the pair inside. At that point, if you don't listen, we'll set fire to the building."

Despite moving from room to room and looking out various windows to locate the man who was speaking, Perry couldn't see him anywhere. He finally shouted out through a crack in a window in the general direction that the voice had come from. "Who the hell are you and what do you want?"

"The name's Peters. Those two in there stole one of our cars and are responsible for killing several of my... friends." The last word was spoken hesitantly, as though the speaker had some trouble with it. "Now send them out and we'll be on our way. You've got ten minutes to decide."

Frank stood slowly, not going for his rifle as the woman holding the pistol was still glancing back and forth between him and Linda. He looked at Linda and shook his head. "Peters, huh?"

"His brother or son or something? The guy sounds young and it's definitely not Thomas."

Perry stepped out into the hall and put his hand on the arm of the woman who was pointing her gun at Frank. He whispered in her ear for a moment as her face grew more confused until he finally stopped and she spoke. "Are you sure, Perry?"

"Just do it, Barb."

The woman lowered her gun and nodded at him before heading down the hallway. When she was out of earshot, Perry turned to Linda and Frank, licking his lips and shaking his head slowly. "Listen. I'm sorry. Clearly I was wrong about you two. If the Peters are after you then you can't be all that bad."

Perry slung his rifle over his shoulder and held a hand out to Linda. She stood and nodded before he turned and did the same to Frank. Perry then picked up Frank's rifle and handed it to him. "Sorry about all of that. No hard feelings?"

Frank shook Perry's proffered hand and nodded. "None at all."

"Good." Perry took a deep breath and rubbed his hands together. "So then, any thoughts on how to deal with this?"

Chapter Thirty-Six

"Look. I'm just saying that I don't understand why these meth-heads are so obsessed with burning things down. First it was the house, now it's the school."

"I don't know, Linda. Maybe it's all the *meth* that's made them slightly out of their gourd."

Linda scowled at Frank and gave him a friendly shove. He shook his head and chuckled. The pair walked as quickly as Linda could manage down the hall deeper into the school. After the pronouncement from the person outside the school and the conversation with Perry that followed, Perry decided that they needed to go check on Caroline before deciding what to do.

Linda's first instinct was to wage an all-out war on whoever was outside, but Frank managed to talk her down. There were too many people in the school and too many unknowns about who was outside for them to risk anyone's lives during a fight. More than that, though, it was clear that Perry and Caroline were running the show and once Frank emphasized that to Linda she finally relented and agreed to go along with what they decided.

Perry was already far ahead of them as he jogged down the hallway and Frank had to restrain Linda to keep her from trying to run after him. Perry stopped and slowly pushed open the door to a classroom on the right-hand side of the hall. Linda and Frank entered a moment after him and walked up slowly behind to see what he was looking at.

On a table in the center of the room, beneath the glow of half a dozen flashlights duct-taped to a tall lamp, was the form of Caroline. She was lying on her stomach on the table, her breaths coming slowly and evenly despite the fact that the person standing over her had a pair of long metal tweezers that he was using to probe the wound in her shoulder.

"What's the prognosis, doc?" Perry whispered and the man holding the tweezers glanced up at him.

"She's pumped full of morphine and she may never be able to lift anything with her right arm again. But she'll live." He spoke softly as he worked, pulling out a sliver of metal and dropping it into a nearby pan a few seconds later.

"You sure you should be doing that?" Linda nodded at the tweezers. "Most of the time they leave the bullets in if they're not in danger of causing more harm."

"That's very true." The doctor nodded at Linda before going back to probing Caroline's wound. "I am trying to give her the best possible chance at recovery though, and these loose pieces of metal rolling around near her tendons and bones in the shoulder make a full recovery somewhat less than likely."

"Yeah, but—"

"Relax, Ms…"

"Just call me Linda."

"Very well. Please relax, Linda." The doctor said Linda's name with a slight edge of discomfort, unused to calling anyone by their first name. "I'm only going after the largest pieces. The rest will be left alone and her body will deal with them."

"Doc." Perry took a step forward and leaned in. "We're in a time crunch right now. I need to talk to Caroline."

The doctor pulled out another piece of metal and raised one eyebrow before shaking his head firmly. "Not possible. She'll be under for a couple hours."

"We don't have that kind of time."

"I don't think you understand, Perry." The doctor tapped one of his gloved fingers against a bag hanging from a slender metal stand. "It's not that I don't want you to talk to her. It's that she's out. You *can't* talk to her because she's not in any position to communicate."

"Is she going to be okay?"

"She'll be fine, Perry."

As if on cue, Caroline let out a groan and tried to speak and move. A pair of assistants next to the doctor ran forward and gently held her down. "Perrnh?" Caroline slurred Perry's name a single time before dozing off again and the doctor gently inserted the tweezers again.

"Sorry Officer Perry. If you want to talk to her, come back later."

Perry shook his head and turned around, pointing to the entrance of the room. "Out. Now." Linda and Frank hurried back and Perry stomped forward, slamming the door shut behind him. His face was a mix of confused emotions and as Linda watched him she suddenly felt incredibly sad for him.

"What's wrong?" Linda gave him a concerned look.

"Caroline's the one who's... better at things like this."

Frank looked at Linda with a raised eyebrow. "You want to give us up, you're saying?"

Perry shook his head firmly. "No. I'm not a monster. But I have several hundred people here that I need to protect for who-knows-how-long. I can't risk all of their lives for two strangers who rolled into town." Perry sighed deeply. "I could just use Caroline's advice on this one."

Linda looked at Frank who nodded in agreement to the unspoken question that passed between them. "No need to do that, Perry." Linda straightened her back and nodded at him. "You have way too many people here for us to be putting you and all of them in danger. Just give us some covering fire and we'll draw those guys away from the building."

"How're you going to do that?"

"I think the car that Frank so expertly drove up here is the perfect solution to that little problem."

Perry nodded. "Good thinking. I don't want to be the one to tell you that you have to leave, though."

Frank unslung the rifle from his shoulder and gripped it firmly. "You don't have to. Any thoughts on keeping them occupied? There's got to be at least two but I don't know how many more they brought."

Perry scratched his chin. "There's a tall barrier going around the edge of the roof and plenty of ductwork and such to hide behind. I could get up there, spy things out and start giving you cover. Caroline's going to kill me for letting you leave under these conditions, though. Just… wait here a moment." Perry glanced at the face of his watch on the underside of his wrist. "We still have seven minutes left. Come on; hurry and follow me."

"Go with him, Frank. I'll wait here near the front." Linda limped back towards the front door while Frank and Perry raced down the halls of the school until they reached the cafeteria. Set in the middle of the school with no windows looking in, the open room was filled with supplies that the residents of the town had brought in and stored for future use.

Stacks of perishable and non-perishable food lined the wall while a large plastic container half-filled with water sat nearby. A few dozen people were scattered through the building, with most of them quietly talking with each other while the rest slowly worked their way through the food supplies with clipboards in hand, taking careful notes on what they had.

"Wow." Frank nodded in surprise. "You have quite the operation going on here."

"We have Caroline to thank for that." Perry slowed down and began scanning the room as he spoke, looking for one person in particular. "Caroline's been the pillar of this community for years. When all of that… *stuff* happened, she was the one who everyone rallied around."

"I'm impressed that you've been able to keep everyone together and working through all of this."

"Folks here are pretty down to earth, Frank." Perry lowered his voice slightly and glanced around. "I'm probably the one most out of place here. It took a few years for all of this to grow on me but it's been worth it."

Frank started to reply when Perry finally spotted who he was looking for and shouted out. "Jason!"

A short, balding man carrying a clipboard turned and smiled at Perry before making a quizzical expression as he caught sight of Frank. "Perry? Do we have a visitor?"

"Something like that." Perry took Jason by the arm and led him into a corner of the room with Frank following close behind. "Listen, I need you to get me a week's worth of nonperishable food. I need it right now, okay?"

"A week? For how many people?"

Perry looked at Frank. "Two?" Frank nodded and Perry confirmed the number. "Two. Please, Jason, no questions. We're trying to deal with a situation."

Jason shuffled his feet nervously. "Yes, we all heard what that person outside said. What're you going to do about it?"

"Come on, Frank." Perry ignored the question. "Jason, have those supplies in a spare backpack by the front door in two minutes. Got it?" The slightly menacing undertone in Perry's voice was enough to cause Jason to leap into action. As he raced across the cafeteria shouting at several people to help him, Frank and Perry headed back down the hall towards the front entrance.

"Four minutes left." Perry shook his head. "Assuming that these idiots can actually count time properly. I'm going to head up to the roof. Once your supplies get here I want you to fire a single shot out the front. That'll let me know that you're ready to go and we can get this party started."

Despite the danger that they found themselves in, Frank couldn't suppress a smile as he realized that Perry was actually feeling excited about what was going on. "You don't see a lot of action around here, do you?"

Perry ejected the magazine from his rifle and swapped in a full one as he grinned. "How could you tell?"

"What's going on, boys?" Linda looked up at Frank and Perry as they stopped in front of her.

"I'll let you fill her in, Frank. Best of luck to both of you."

"You as well. We'll make sure to draw them off."

"I'll do my best to take them out. If they make it through, though, just keep heading west and south towards Pittsburgh. I've been hearing all day on the radio about a huge military presence they have there. You should be able to get plenty of help there."

Linda's eyes widened and she started to ask the first of many questions but Perry turned and ran back down the hall before she could speak to him. "Frank? What the hell's he talking about?"

"I have no idea. But we're getting out of here."

"So I gathered. Perry's going to draw their attention while we get to the car?"

"Yep."

"Thank goodness." Linda patted her leg gingerly. "It's hurting like hell from all this movement but I can make it to the car at least."

"Good." Frank turned at the sound of footsteps and saw a man carrying a backpack running up to him. The man handed the backpack to Frank before turning and running back in the opposite direction.

"Uh." Linda's eyes darted back and forth. "What just happened?"

"A present. Courtesy of Perry." Frank unzipped the bag to reveal a stash of rations along with a water purifier. Frank closed the bag and put it on one shoulder before taking the bag of ammunition near the front entrance and looping it on his shoulder as well. "You ready for this?"

"Not really." Linda sighed and Frank could see the exhaustion behind her eyes. "I want to stay here and get some damned sleep."

"Hopefully we'll find that soon. Maybe we should stop by Pittsburgh before turning south. You still have some military connections, right?"

Linda shrugged. "Eh. Maybe."

Frank was about to probe further when they heard the electronic crackle of a bullhorn outside. It was followed a second later by the same voice they had heard ten minutes earlier. "Your ten minutes are up! What's it going to be?"

Frank cracked the front door and was about to fire a shot out into the parking lot when he was surprised by gunfire that originated from on top of the building. Five stories up, on the roof, Perry kneeled down at the edge of the building with his rifle aiming down into the trees on one side. Firing in three-round bursts, he sent a hailstorm of bullets into the thick bushes at the base of the trees, working his way down the line in an effort to flush out the source of the voice.

"I guess he's going to give the signal! Let's go!" Frank shoved open the door to the front of the building and ran headlong towards the car. While he had managed to shut off the vehicle during his mad rush to get out of it and into the building earlier, the keys had fallen out of his hand. He thought they might be on the floor of the car or on the ground just outside the driver's side door and wasn't looking forward to having to locate them.

Shots from the roof continued to snap across the empty parking lot, echoing out into the darkness as Frank ran the short distance to the car. He opened the right-side back door and threw their bags and backpacks in. His rifle followed and he slammed the door shut, then flung open the passenger door. Behind him, Linda limped forward as fast as she could, her pistol out and at the ready.

Perry's gunfire thankfully offered enough of a distraction that Frank and Linda were both able to make it to the car without taking fire. Once they started climbing in, though, all hell broke loose.

While Reggie and Liam were distracted with locating the shooter on top of the school, Josh had quickly overcome his initial surprise and began searching for the source of the shots. Dim flashes of light from the muzzle of Perry's rifle illuminated the top of the school, and Josh quickly zeroed in on them with his rifle. Their source was hidden behind a large piece of ductwork but Josh took aim anyway, hoping that the bullet would penetrate through the duct and strike his target on the other side. Although he fancied himself a crack shot due to the fact that he had hit Caroline in the shoulder earlier, the shot had actually been more due to blind luck than anything else.

Josh fired at Perry and the bullet went soaring off into the night, his aim having been wildly off. The crack of the rifle made Perry spin around and search for the source, his elevated position making it easy to see where the shot was coming from. He had hidden himself behind the duct on purpose, expecting a shot from the person on the ridge, and was pleased that the person had both revealed themselves and that they were such a terrible shot.

Perry peeked out from behind the duct and saw a figure standing on the hill beyond the parking lot. He flipped the fire mode switch on his rifle back to single fire and ducked low behind the ducts and barrier at the edge of the roof. After crawling several feet to the side he took a deep breath and rose to one knee. His rifle went up to his shoulder and he instantly sighted his target.

While Josh's shot hadn't even come close to hitting Perry, Perry's first shot and the immediate follow-up were both on target. Josh reeled back in pain as the first round passed through his right arm. He dropped his rifle in pain and the second shot nicked the top of his head due to his sudden movement. Three more shots came next, with two of them passing through Josh's leg and the third passing through his right lung.

As shock overtook his body, Josh went from writhing in pain to lying still on the ground, taking in short breaths of air as he fought hopelessly against the inexorable embrace of death. "Asshole." Perry muttered under his breath as he watched Josh through his scope, making sure that the man was truly down. A burst of fire to Perry's left made him duck low until he realized that it wasn't directed at him but at the car carrying Frank and Linda that was peeling out of the parking lot.

On the ground, Linda struggled to fasten her seatbelt and Frank clung to the steering wheel as he tore across the parking lot, heading for a section near the edge where the curb had worn away over the years. The area offered easy access to the slope above and Frank approached it at full speed. The car lurched as it went from the hard flat surface of the parking lot and into the rising slope of grass, but their decrease in speed was barely perceptible as Frank kept the gas pedal to the floor.

Gunfire cracked from behind the car, but instead of coming from the rooftop it came from the ground, off to the side of the school. Frank spun the wheel and the car swerved sharply, sliding across the grass at the top of the slope and broadsiding the guardrail. The car jerked back to the right but Frank managed to keep it at the top of the slope until the guardrail abruptly ended and he could pull back onto the road.

While Reggie was busying himself with firing at the car, Liam was crouched behind a tree trying to spot the person on top of the school who had been pinning him down. There hadn't been shots for a long moment and as he heard the car pulling out across the parking lot he realized what was going on. "Shit! They're getting away!"

Liam ran through the trees back up towards the road, being careful to stay far enough into the woods that the person on top of the school wouldn't be able to fire upon him. On the other side of the school, Reggie also realized that the car was getting away and assumed that Liam would want to pursue it. As he ran for the top of the slope he briefly forgot to hide behind the slight ridge and Perry was able to get a few shots at him. None of them impacted, though, and Reggie quickly ducked into cover and followed the ridge up to the top of the slope.

Liam was the first to arrive at the car and he saw Josh slowly pulling himself along the ground to try and reach the vehicle. Liam flipped Josh's body over with a kick and snarled at the wounds dotting the dying man's body.

"Help…" Josh barely managed to whisper the words as Liam stepped over him and into the car. Reggie showed up a few seconds later and jumped into the car before glancing out the window and gasping at the sight of Josh.

"Liam, aren't we going to help him?"

"He's already dead. And we have a job to do." As Liam pulled away, he didn't so much as glance back at Josh's body. His attention was focused completely on the car that was barely a few minutes ahead of them and the two passengers that were inside.

With the car being just out of sight of the top of the school, Perry could do no more to try and stop the shooters from reaching it. He ground his teeth in frustration as he heard their vehicle start up and watched the glow of their headlights recede into the distance as they gave chase to Frank and Linda.

"Good luck, you two." Perry shook his head wearily. "You'll sure as hell need it."

Chapter Thirty-Seven

"Fucking hell." Linda watched in the rearview mirror as the small town receded into the distance, slamming a fist against the dashboard in frustration.

"What is it?" Frank didn't take his eyes off the road as he replied to Linda's outburst.

"I'm sick of running! This is twice that we've turned tail and fled from these bastards."

Frank was quiet for a moment before replying. "What do you want to do about it?"

Behind them a pair of headlights flared to life in the darkness. The sight of the lights made Linda smile slyly. "I want to end this nonsense."

Frank glanced in the mirror. "That them?"

"It has to be."

"So what do you want to do?"

Linda's tone was deadly serious as she replied and Frank felt a cold chill run up his spine at her response. "Kill them all."

"Fair enough." Frank laughed nervously. "How do you want to do it?"

Linda didn't answer for a few moments as she kept an eye on

both the road ahead and on the car behind them. It was somewhere in the early morning hours before dawn and the sky and
road were both dark. The only illumination came from their car's
headlights as they raced down the highway, dodging wrecked tractor-trailers and abandoned cars that were strewn in the road.

The vehicle behind them was neither gaining distance nor
receding, and at Linda's prompting Frank had slowed their speed
enough to allow the car to catch up. It was still far enough back
that whoever was in it wasn't taking shots at them but the margin
of error for their driving no longer existed. One wrong turn or slip
of the wheel would mean that their pursuers would catch up to
them in no time at all.

"Take the bypass here. Skirt around the edge of this
city ahead."

"Bypass around Brookville. Got it."

As Frank merged onto the bypass from the highway, a sign
caught Linda's eye and she nodded thoughtfully. "That
might work."

"What might work for what?"

Linda focused on reading the road signs as they drove along,
trying to form a mental picture of the area despite the fact that
they didn't have the benefit of a map. "We're on the road to Pittsburgh now, once you turn off on the exit a couple miles down
the road."

"You want to try and make it all the way there and let the military handle them?"

"Hell no. I want to set a trap on the bridge that'll cross back
over this river."

"Say what now?"

"Look at how the roads are laid out. We just went over some
big river and we're looping around the city. By the time we get to
the next exit we'll have to cross over another bridge and that's
where we'll spring the trap."

"What kind of a trap?"

Linda smiled. "We're going to make good use of all that gasoline and motor oil back there. We'll need a good two minutes lead

on them to get it ready, though. Think you can pull ahead of them by that much?"

Frank grimaced. "Maybe? Depends on how long this overpass is and—shit!"

Frank pulled the wheel sharply to the right as the car lurched left. The screech of metal-on-metal made his skin crawl as the car scraped against a piece of a trailer that was sticking farther out into the road than he had thought at first glance. The sharp bits of metal sliced into the side of the car, causing jagged tears down the side. A loud *pop* accompanied the screech of metal and Frank fought with the wheel again as the car swung wildly to the left.

"Dammit!" Frank shouted as he wrestled with the car, trying to reduce their speed and get it back under control before they spun out of control or—even worse—flipped over off the side of the road.

"Keep it straight and hit the gas!" Linda shouted and Frank did as he was instructed. The car's wild fishtailing gradually evened out as Frank increased their speed, though the ride was considerably bumpier than it had been before.

"Now ease up on the accelerator!" Frank again did as Linda instructed and the car gradually slowed down.

"Good call there." Frank let out the breath he had been holding and glanced over at Linda.

"That was all you; kickass driving there, Frank."

"Yeah, but we've got a problem." Frank kept a death grip on the steering wheel, wrestling with it as they continued down the highway. "I think we lost both of the wheels on the left side. There's no way we can do whatever it was you wanted with the whole trap thing."

"No, we need to get off the highway. Take the next exit; I don't care what it is."

"Got it." Frank continued reducing their speed in order to maneuver around the cars and debris in the road ahead. While he dared not take his eyes off the road, he could tell due to Linda's uncomfortable shifting around in her seat and the increasing brightness above his right eye that their pursuers were gaining on them.

"Hold on tight, we're taking this exit at speed." Frank drifted into the shoulder and then turned, taking the exit far faster than was safe even if the car had all four wheels. A loud thump and a bump from the front of the car indicated that the last of the rubber from the front left tire had just been ejected from the wheel. Metal groaned as it met the surface of the road, giving Frank even less traction to work with.

"Any suggestions on where we should go would be great right about now!" Frank shouted above the noise of the car and Linda held out her hand to point at a building just off to their right.

"There! The radio station! Pull in there!"

"A radio station?"

"Closest defensible building we can get to unless you've got a couple wheels you can pull out of your ass!"

Frank mumbled a string of curses under his breath and turned the wheel of the car, fighting against the metal behemoth to get it off of the road and into the parking lot in front of the radio station. A massive metal tower sat just behind the squat, single-story brick building whose roof was covered in antennas and satellite dishes.

Frank hit the brakes as they slid into the parking lot, but the brakes did next to nothing and the car smashed into another vehicle in the parking lot before finally coming to a rest. The right headlight was broken, the left was blinking on and off sporadically, the engine was coughing and sputtering as it slowly died and the car's horn blared uncontrollably. Frank and Linda, however, were alive.

Linda grunted in pain as she shoved her door open and jumped out, pistol in hand. Frank unbuckled his seatbelt and tried to open his door, but it wouldn't budge until he threw his weight against it several times. After he hopped out he could see the jagged tears in the metal on the side of the car and realized what a close call their accident had truly been.

"Get inside, Frank! They'll be here soon!" Linda shouted over the deafening sound of the car horn and waved for Frank to follow her. While Linda limped as fast as she could towards the building, Frank grabbed his rifle, his and Linda's bags, the bag of food and the bag of ammunition from the back of the car. He felt like a pack mule as he stumbled into the building after Linda but he wasn't about to leave any of their precious gear behind again.

The radio station building was smaller than he had expected with most of its space devoted to the lobby and the large broadcast booth just inside. The broadcast booth was the only enclosed area inside the building as the rest of the space was taken up by small offices divided by flimsy cubicle walls. The front section of the broadcast booth facing the lobby entrance had a large, thick multi-layered sheet of plastic and glass and a single door made from the same material.

After a quick look around the inside of the station Linda headed for the broadcast booth, first pulling on the door before realizing it only opened inward. Once she was inside she motioned for Frank to follow her in and he dropped their bags with a thump.

"Frank, they're going to be here any second." Linda fixed Frank with a steely gaze and he nodded in affirmation.

"Yep, and I've got a plan."

Linda raised her eyebrows in surprise. "Let's hear it."

"You saw all the stuff on the roof? Satellite dishes and what-not. There's gotta be roof access either outside or inside. I'm going to head up to the roof while you barricade yourself inside here. Get hidden and protected. You lure them in and then I'll ambush them from the roof. If you flip that table over and push it up against the door and window it'll provide excellent cover. Once you hear me shooting you can fire directly out through the front doors at them."

"It's a shit plan. Let's do it." Linda nodded and turned to the table. She began shoving the computer and audio equipment off of it onto the floor. Frank, meanwhile, headed back through the door and looked out through the lobby into the parking lot out front. The single light on their car was still blinking on and off and the horn was still blaring. Out behind their car he could see a pair of headlights growing steadily brighter and he realized that they were nearly out of time.

"Dammit!" Frank ran through the building as Linda pushed the large wooden table up against the door to the broadcast booth. She sat down in one of the rolling chairs once she was done and began checking her pistol and reloading a spare magazine with ammunition from her bag.

Frank kept his eyes on the ceiling, using his flashlight sparingly to avoid giving away his position to the people approaching from outside. There was no obvious access to the roof from inside the building and he was starting to think he would have to go outside and look for a ladder when a sign on a door at the back of the building made him pause.

Rooftop Access - Authorized Employees Only

"Jackpot." Frank smiled and pushed open the door, finding a metal ladder on the wall leading up to the roof. A door leading out behind the back of the building was open and Frank realized that aside from the front entrance the back exit was the only other way into the building. Thinking quickly he grabbed a broom and mop that were standing up in the corner and jammed them through the handle of the door after pulling it closed. He then twisted the lock for extra security before swinging his rifle over his shoulder and starting his ascent up the ladder.

Loose rounds of ammo jingled in his pockets with each step until he reached a small hatch in the roof. The hatch had a simple bolt locking it in place and he slid it to the side, pushed the hatch open and emerged onto the roof. The shrill sound of the car's horn once again filled his ears, but it was accompanied by the sound of a roaring engine as well. Frank crouched down low as he headed for the edge of the roof where he hid behind a satellite dish before peeking down at the parking lot below.

In the parking lot sat an old Corvette convertible with the top down and two figures running from it towards the damaged car. Frank unshouldered his rifle and took aim at the figures when one of them opened fire on the damaged car, sending a burst of fire into the passenger and engine compartments. A few seconds later the sound of the horn finally died and the two figures ran towards the front entrance to the building. As they stood directly beneath Frank he no longer had a clear shot on them though he could hear them talking to each other as they discussed their impromptu plans.

"Go around back, see if there's another way in."

"What if there's not?"

"Then meet me back here, dumbass!"

"Right. On my way."

One of the two figures ran around to the side of the small building and Frank crossed his fingers, hoping that the locked and barricaded door would remain shut. He crept around on the roof for a moment, hoping he could get into a better angle to see the figure still standing at the front entrance, but the roof's overhang stuck out far enough that it was impossible to see where the person was standing.

It only took a minute for the person who had gone around to the back of the building to return, where he and the person who had remained out front held another brief conversation.

"Well?"

"There's a door but it's locked tight."

"Didn't you try breaking it in?"

"I tried, but I couldn't!"

"Worthless." A loud sigh was interjected into the conversation. "Fine. We're going inside. They're holed up somewhere in here, no doubt. You go in first and watch the left. I'll watch the right."

From inside the broadcast booth Linda couldn't hear a word of the conversation outside but she could see the blindingly bright light from the vehicle's headlights and the moving shadows from the figures standing near the door.

"Dammit, Frank. Where's the ambush?" Linda whispered to herself as she watched the shadows and the lights outside. Without knowing how many were outside or their precise locations she didn't dare risk giving her position away prematurely. Instead she kept herself tucked into a corner on the floor of the broadcast booth, waiting to see what happened next.

"One. Two. Three." The whispered countdown was followed by a loud slam as Liam and Reggie flung open the front doors and stormed in, waving their rifles and flashlights wildly in all directions. Reggie jumped over the receptionist's desk in the front lobby before continuing on, bypassing the broadcast booth completely to start checking the small cubicle workspaces. Liam did the same thing on the right side of the room, and by the time the pair met in the back they were starting to wonder where their prey had hidden themselves away.

As Liam glanced at the large series of walls set in the center of the room he realized where they both must be and grinned. He circled around to the side again and aimed his flashlight through the window, revealing the mess of equipment scattered on the floor and the large wooden table pressed up against the window and door.

"Hello in there!" Liam called out in a singsong voice. Linda ground her teeth together, still tucked away in a corner and waiting for the source of the voice to emerge. The flashlights that Liam and Reggie were holding were bouncing around the station and making it look like there were half a dozen people instead of just two. Linda didn't dare to turn on her light to confirm how many there were lest she give away her exact position.

"Hello!" Liam called out again as he advanced slowly on the broadcasting booth. "Anybody in there?"

From the rooftop, Frank could barely hear what was going on inside the building. The fact that there weren't any more lights or sounds outside, though, told him all he needed to know. He crept back to the hatch in the roof and lifted it slightly only to see a bright beam of light in the room below. He closed the hatch back and his eyes grew wide as he tried to figure out what to do.

While Frank crouched on the roof trying to figure out what to do, Linda scrunched in behind a pair of chairs in the broadcast booth, keeping her pistol in hand and ready to fire. The light and mocking voice came from around the corner out of sight, and she could feel her heartrate increasing as the light drew closer.

"Now come on, you two!" The voice was unnaturally cheery in

a way that made Linda's skin crawl. "You can't stay hidden in here forever!" Liam punctuated the last word in his sentence with a gunshot that shattered the glass on a window. He laughed as shards of glass fell to the floor, waiting for someone inside the building to cry out or try to talk or fire back. His laugh dissipated as he realized that no one was responding to his attempt to rile them up.

"Reggie." Liam didn't bother trying to be discreet, so confident was he that he had the upper hand in firepower and positioning. "Check the booth."

Several seconds before the gunshot and the sound of shattering glass cut through the still night air, Frank had been standing at the edge of the building looking down at the parking lot. Upon hearing the sounds he set his jaw, adjusted his belt and tightened the strap on the rifle slung over his back. He climbed up over the ledge of the side of the building and jumped off, steeling himself for the pain that was sure to follow.

Not knowing enough to try and tuck and roll to dissipate some of the energy from his landing, Frank collapsed into a groaning pile as he hit the dirt and grass before slowly picking himself up, taking the rifle off of his back and charging in through the front door.

Responding to Liam's order, Reggie was slowly going around the left side of the broadcasting booth with his flashlight held high and his rifle ready to fire upon the first person he saw. Liam was still out of sight of the window and door to the booth on the right side as he kept an eye on the back portion of the building.

When Frank charged through the door with gun raised and a guttural scream bursting forth, Reggie was taken completely by surprise. Frank fired two shots into Reggie's back before the man could turn around. The second shot passed through his soft tissues and broke large chunks of glass on the front of the broadcast booth, sending Linda ducking and rolling to the side as she avoided the glass and any further gunshots.

As Reggie collapsed to the floor Liam came running around the side of the booth firing wildly at the front of the building.

Frank got one more shot off before ducking behind the receptionist desk to shield himself from Liam's fire.

"There you are!" Liam continued shooting at the desk, advancing on it one step at a time until he was out of line of sight to the broadcast booth. Linda, who had been watching the shadowy figures moving around with all the attention of a cat keeping an eye on a mouse, finally figured out exactly how many enemies were in the building. Once Reggie went down and Liam started firing, Linda rose to her feet, aimed and fired upon Liam.

The glass and plastic were thick, but they still shattered from the impact of the rounds. The shot was easy enough and didn't require every single round in the magazine, but Linda used each of them. She fired evenly, pacing each shot to ensure that every one was precisely on target. Her breathing was steady and she squeezed the trigger firmly with each pull, controlling the recoil with the ease of a practiced marksman.

Liam screamed in pain as the bullets entered his body. Some passed through out the other side while others tumbled and rolled, tearing through and ripping apart his organs. He gasped fruitlessly for air as his lungs collapsed from the perforations made by the bullets and his legs rapidly turned to anchors that pulled him down to the ground.

Blood oozed from the edges of Liam's mouth. His tongue and lips moved but without air to expel from his lungs he could form no words to verbally express his anger. Even in death Liam was defiant, but defiance could not overcome the sheer amount of damage done to his body.

Forgetting the pain in her leg due to a rush of adrenaline, Linda climbed out through the empty window and reloaded her pistol. She stood over Liam and aimed directly at his head as Frank stood up and shouted at her. "Down!"

Acting on pure instinct Linda dropped to the ground and Frank fired two more shots, hitting Reggie in the neck and face. Liam's accomplice had managed to pull himself to his feet and was aiming his rifle in Linda's direction when Frank noticed what was going on and took the man down. Linda turned to look at Reggie's body before nodding her appreciation at Frank. She took aim at Liam's head again but when she saw that he was no longer moving she lowered her arm.

Acrid smoke filled the air, playing in the light of the flashlights. Linda tried to stand up but collapsed back down to the ground as her leg buckled in pain. Frank stepped over Liam's body and took her arm. He guided her into one of the chairs in the lobby and sat down next to her, all the while keeping his rifle pointed in the direction of the two bodies. Frank and Linda both remained quiet for several minutes as they took slow, deep breaths, each of them processing what had just happened. Frank was the first to speak, not taking his eyes off of the bodies as he did.

"That didn't exactly go like I had hoped."

Linda snorted and shook her head. "It's your turn to play bait next time."

"Oh come on. You handled it perfectly."

"It was still an absolute shit plan."

"If it's stupid and it works, then it isn't stupid."

Linda was quiet for several seconds before she started chuckling. "Fair point. Come on. Let's get the hell out of here."

After getting their bags out of the building and into the parking lot, Frank helped Linda get outside. He brought one of the chairs from the lobby out for her and she pulled her pants down partway before easing into the seat. Frank took off his jacket for her to cover her good leg from the cold while he checked her wound. It was bleeding moderately again and the bandage was thoroughly soaked. Frank pulled off the bandage, scrubbed around the wound with antiseptic wipes and slathered on another layer of antibiotics before applying another bandage.

"How's it look?" Linda shivered as a cold breeze cut across the parking lot.

"You really need to stop moving around and let it heal for a while. It doesn't look infected, though."

"Good. I'll drive." Linda chuckled for a second before frowning. "Speaking of driving, what are we going to have to—oh what the hell is *that* thing?" As Frank helped Linda to her feet she caught sight of the Corvette that Liam and Reggie were driving. She grimaced at the sight of the beaten up old car and shook her head. "Hell no. No, no, no. That thing looks like a death trap!"

"At least it runs." Frank held tight to Linda as they walked towards the car. The interior was worse than he had anticipated despite his already lowered expectations upon viewing the exterior.

"Do you think the top even goes up?"

"I hope so. Otherwise it's going to be a cold ride to Pittsburgh."

"Are you set on going there?" Linda leaned against the side of the car as Frank started loading their bags into the backseats.

"You don't think it's a good call? It's to our south and we've got a long way left to go before we hit Pigeon Forge. If the military's there maybe we—well, maybe *you* can talk to someone higher-up and see about getting us a ride that looks like it won't fall apart thirty seconds in."

"You do realize that I don't know every single person in every branch of the military, right?"

Frank shrugged as he slid the last bag into the back of the car. "I get that. But the alternative is trying to beg, borrow or steal another vehicle on our way to Pigeon Forge or taking this thing. And I don't know about you, but if the military's massing at a city I'd like to find out why. It might shed some light on what's going on."

Linda sighed deeply and nodded. "You're right. It's on the way and shouldn't take that long anyway. If we're going to do that, though, I don't want to make any more stops. Let's get whatever fuel packs we can salvage from the back of the other car and stay on the road. No more stopping in cities, no more talking to people, no more anything. We get to Pittsburgh, see what's going on, see if we can get a new car or something and then we continue on to Pigeon Forge. Okay?"

Frank nodded. "Okay."

Chapter Thirty-Eight

The drive through the rolling hills, back country roads and major highways took the rest of the day. While only a two-hour drive under normal circumstances, profound changes had taken hold in the few days since the attacks.

Avoiding every small town and city was a tremendous chore and Linda and Frank spent more than an hour stopped by the side of the road while they studied a map they found in Liam's vehicle. On the few occasions they passed through a city or town they did so at a high rate of speed, avoiding the main roads and cruising through as quickly as possible.

The town of Brockway had, from what they had seen throughout the day, been an isolated anomaly. Fires appeared with alarming regularity as survivors struggled to stay warm in the rapidly dropping temperatures. Food supplies—nearly all of which had been bought or stolen in the first twenty-four hours—were completely gone. The discovery of a single can of food was enough to cause a fistfight to break out. If a vending machine stocked with snacks and drinks in the back of a building was found there would undoubtedly be more than one person who would die in an attempt to possess its contents.

Bits and pieces of these fierce conflicts bled over into public actions that Frank and Linda picked up on as they sped along to their destination. Each and every one of them reminded the pair of how fortunate they had been in their journey as well as how fragile their existence really was. The tribulations they faced had been nearly evenly matched by the generosity shown to them. As they neared Pittsburgh in the late evening, it was this topic that weighed heavily on both Frank and Linda.

"The commune makes sense, right? A small group who basically prepared for this exact kind of situation could certainly be friendly towards outsiders."

Linda nodded. "Yep. I kind of wish we had stayed there."

"Ha." Frank smiled. "You and me both. Those people I understand. But those people in Brockway… how were they so well prepared and friendly and helpful?"

"Eh." Linda shrugged. "They weren't all *that* friendly. Not Perry, anyway. Caroline was friendly, but I think she's the reason why the town was prepared and functioning instead of devolving into a hellhole."

"How do you figure that?"

"People naturally want a leader to follow, especially in a time of crisis. If there's someone strong who they trust and look up to then they'll follow that person to hell and back. I get the sense that Caroline was that type of person."

Frank shook his head and sighed sadly. "I hope they don't lose her. Especially Perry. I think she's the only thing holding him back from turning into some kind of post-apocalyptic overlord."

Linda snorted and laughed. "Post-apocalyptic, eh? Did you ever think you'd be living through the apocalypse?"

"Are you joking? When I was a kid I would have *killed* to be in my position right now. Living on the edge and traveling across a destroyed country with no rules where only the fittest survive? I sure don't like it but kid-version of me would have loved it."

"I was more into ponies when I was a little girl."

Frank bit his tongue at first but burst out laughing when Linda failed to contain her own giggle. "Ponies? Is that a common thing for every girl? Because all the ones I went to school with were obsessed with them too."

Linda pursed her lips and nodded thoughtfully. "Yeah, I think every little girl goes through a horse and pony phase."

Frank was about to make another joke when he saw that they were heading for an overpass. "Heads up." He nodded at a sign above the road. "We're a few miles out from the edge of the city."

"Hey, slow down and pull into the far right lane for a second." Linda was craning her neck to see out her window as she tried to get a better look at a building below the overpass.

"What's going on down there?" Frank glanced out her window but kept his eyes mostly on the road.

"It's a hospital with… my God. Is that… are those bodies?" Linda's eyes grew wide as she realized what she was looking at. The tone of her voice got to Frank and he slowed the Corvette to a stop and clambered out. He walked to the edge of the overpass and looked over the side at the building below. The main building was in the shape of a large "H" and there were several other buildings surrounding it. In front of the main building sat a large grassy area dotted with benches, walking paths and trees that—at one point in time—was most likely a gorgeous place to sit and relax.

As Frank looked over the complex and the grassy area, though, he realized that there was something off about it. Instead of being covered in green or brown grass, the ground in front of the hospital was stark black. He squinted at the sight, trying to process what he was seeing until Linda's words struck home.

The grassy area's walking paths and benches were left uncovered but amongst them—stacked three feet tall and covering the entirety of the grass—were rows upon rows of black body bags. The thick plastic barely moved in the evening breeze but every now and then as a particularly strong gust picked up Frank could see the edges of the bags shifting. As the wind turned toward the overpass for a moment Frank nearly doubled over, gagging from the smell of the rotting corpses. He hurried back to the car, got in and wordlessly took off, trying to push the sight and smell from his mind.

Several more minutes passed before he felt confident that

opening his mouth to speak would not automatically include vomiting. "How… how are there so many bodies?"

"Without basic supplies even the most basic wounds could kill. Hospitals have been relying on just-in-time deliveries for a while now."

"That many people, though? In this short amount of time?"

Linda shook her head slowly. "Maybe that's where they decided to put the mass grave and they're not all from the hospital. Regardless, though, it makes sense… in a very messed up way."

"I just don't see how so many could have died already."

"It's like we talked about before, Frank. We're balanced on the edge of a razor and someone just pushed us off."

Frank sighed but didn't say anything else as he and Linda remained quiet for the next half hour. As they passed through increasingly urban areas on their final approach to Pittsburgh, Frank began to notice that the occasional signs of people living in the area were no longer present. Trails of smoke that signified fires vanished and the sight of small clusters of people in and around various buildings grew less and less frequent. Frank was about to comment on the odd decline in the visible population when something on the road ahead prompted him to slow the car.

"What the hell's that?" Frank pointed at a large metal object with a tall sign mounted on top. The metal object was armored and painted a dark green while the sign was tan in color with a large solar panel mounted on the side. The sign was at least thirty feet tall—though it appeared as though it could be extended even higher—and at the top was a large LCD panel flashing messages in both English and Spanish.

ATTENTION
BY FEDERAL ORDER
ALL PERSONS
AND VEHICLES
SUBJECT TO SEARCH

"Looks like the outer perimeter of a military cordon." Linda pointed at the sign as they slowly drove past. "They probably set those up along all the major roads. I guess Perry was right about there being a—holy shit."

Linda stopped talking and stared as they crested a hill. The city of Pittsburgh was still off in the distance, but midway between their car and the tall buildings in the heart of the city sat a seemingly endless expanse of military vehicles, tents and soldiers. A pair of UH-60 Black Hawks flew low and fast across the city in a manner that made Frank feel incredibly uncomfortable. On the ground, outside the perimeter that the military had set up, Frank could see Humvees and APCs patrolling along streets and through empty fields, their spotlights swinging back and forth to illuminate the ground and buildings around them.

Frank pulled the Corvette to a stop at the top of the hill and Linda opened her door and jabbed him in the side with her elbow. "Get the rifle and help me get out." Frank grabbed their hunting rifle from the back of the car and pulled Linda out of the car. She took the rifle and steadied herself against the car before peering through the scope. As she swept it across the expanse of the city and military perimeter surrounding it, she shook her head.

"Unbelievable."

"What is it?" Frank shielded his eyes from the setting sun beyond the city but couldn't make out very many details.

"They've completely surrounded the city."

"How? That would take… more soldiers than I can imagine."

"Nah. They've probably got a dozen drones circling the area all focused on watching the city. It looks like a lot from here because of all the barricades and tents they have set up but it's not." Linda switched from watching the perimeter around the city to looking at the city itself. It took her a few seconds to realize what she was seeing before she gasped. "Holy hell. The city's flooded."

"What?"

"The water mains must have burst or something because half the roads are underwater."

"You think that's why there's a perimeter around the city?"

Linda shook her head firmly. "Nah. No way. I can't see any sign of them sending troops in past the perimeter. Those Black Hawks are the only things going in over the city and they're flying like they're doing reconnaissance."

Frank cast an uneasy eye to the sky, squinting as though he could see the drones thousands of feet up in the air. "Shouldn't we be worried about the drones watching us right now and seeing you pointing a rifle down at those guys?"

Linda glanced up before peering back through the scope. "I'll take my chances. The way they're focused on the city so much almost makes it seem like they're trying to keep people from getting out." Linda lowered the rifle and frowned. "We should get moving. There's a forward operating base down the road towards the city."

"Wait a second." Frank held his hands up. "You want to go *towards* the guys with guns who've surrounded an *entire freaking city*— which, by the way, is flooded—and just say 'what's up' to them?"

"We'll approach slowly and make it clear we're not a threat."

"Christ." Frank rubbed his hands through his hair and took several deep breaths. "You're the boss on this one, I guess."

Linda slid the rifle into the backseat of the car and held out her hand. "Here, let me drive us in."

"You? Drive? With your leg like it is?"

"Yep."

"How do you figure that's a good idea?"

"Frank." Linda sighed and looked back out at the city. "I don't want to get shot any more than you do. I'd feel a lot more comfortable if I drove us into what seems like certain doom given that it's my idea. I suspect you'd feel more comfortable too."

Frank shook his head and threw up his hands. "Whatever. If you start bleeding out again or run us off the road or something don't look at me."

Linda rolled her eyes and limped around to the driver's side of the car. She and Frank got into their seats and Linda put the car into gear, taking them in towards the city. "Keep your hands up on the dashboard when we get close and do exactly what I tell you to do. Follow my lead here and we'll be fine."

"Got it." Frank remained quiet for the rest of the fifteen-minute drive. When they were just outside the city the mess of vehicles on the highway abruptly vanished and the road was clear.

"Get ready." Linda slowed down the car and rolled down her window, motioning for Frank to do the same. As they approached the perimeter series of loudspeakers squealed to life and a voice barked at them.

"Stop your vehicle immediately! Lethal force is authorized!"

Linda immediately stopped the car, put it in park and turned off the engine. She removed the keys next and placed them on the dashboard before whispering to Frank. "Hands on the dash, Frank. Don't move a muscle unless they tell you to."

Frank nodded as the voice shouted at them again. "Step slowly out of the vehicle, walk to the front and sit on the ground!"

"You gonna be okay getting out?" He gave Linda a concerned look.

"Be quiet and listen to them." Linda and Frank opened their doors and stepped out. Linda winced in pain and nearly lowered her hand to put it on her wound but managed to resist. They both walked to the front of the car and sat down with their hands raised.

"Make no movements while you are approached! If you move then lethal force may be used!"

Frank and Linda glanced at each other, their arms already starting to feel sore from holding them up. Several more minutes ticked by before movement at the perimeter caught Frank's eye and a pair of Humvees began driving toward them.

"Here we go." Linda whispered, her eyes glued on the Humvees. "Remember to follow my lead and do what they tell you."

The Humvees squealed to a stop a good fifty feet from Linda and Frank. When the doors opened, Linda's eyes widened in surprise. Instead of the typical soldiers clad in camouflage the people who jumped out were dressed in full-body hazmat suits and carrying small black boxes attached to long wands. Four such men began running down the road toward Frank and Linda while six more soldiers piled out of the vehicles and followed behind. The other six soldiers were also clad in hazmat suits but four of them carried rifles and the other two carried flamethrowers.

"Linda?" Frank's eyes were wide with panic as he watched the soldiers running toward them. "What the hell is going on?"

"Stay still!" One of the six soldiers carrying rifles shouted at Frank and Linda. The four carrying the strange devices stopped a few feet away and began waving the wands on the devices in the air. After a few seconds one of them pointed at Frank.

"You! Extend your arm and hold it still!" Frank looked at Linda as he slowly held out his arm. The man who shouted at him pressed the wand up against Frank's hand and Frank felt a sharp pinch. He pulled his hand back and saw that his finger was bleeding.

"What the hell?" Frank balled his fingers into a fist and held it against his chest. The soldiers wielding rifles bristled at his action but two of the men carrying the strange devices held up their hands.

"Wait!" The man who had pricked Frank's finger with the wand nodded as he looked at the box in his hand. "He's clean. Check the woman, too, just to be safe."

Linda held out her arm before being asked and the procedure was repeated on her. A few seconds later the man who performed the procedure held up his thumb. "She's clean. No sign of infection."

The men in the hazmat suits and carrying the strange devices turned and ran back to the Humvees while one of the soldiers wielding a rifle stepped forward and pulled off his hood. "Sir. Ma'am. Stand up, hands in the air."

"What's going on, soldier?" Linda grunted as she slowly stood to her feet.

The soldier who had spoken to them raised an eyebrow. "Are you not aware of the quarantine?"

"What quarantine?" Frank asked.

"What's your name, soldier?" Linda ignored Frank's question

and adopted a harsher, more formal tone as she addressed the soldier speaking to her. The shift in her tone and facial expressions surprised him and he nearly stammered as he replied.

"Corporal Simmons, ma'am. Are you two—"

"Simmons. Good. I'm Sergeant Linda Rollins, USMC Raiders, retired. I need to speak to your commanding officer immediately."

Corporal Simmons visibly relaxed and glanced at his fellow soldiers. "Ma'am, I'm going to need to clear this with base."

"Corporal, I'll make this very simple for you. My friend and I have been on the road for days. We've been to hell, visited all the sights and made it back. We are in desperate need of some information and then we'll be on our way and out of your hair. The soonest you get us to whoever's in charge around there the sooner we'll be gone and the less paperwork you'll have to deal with surrounding our presence."

Simmons audibly gulped before looking back and forth between his fellow soldiers. "We'll need to search you, ma'am. And you'll have to leave your... vehicle behind."

Linda nodded. "Carry on."

After a brief search of their persons Simmons directed the soldiers to secure the Corvette before he and two others escorted Frank and Linda back to the Humvees. Directions given by the soldiers during and after the search were brief and as they walked back to the Humvees Frank whispered quietly to Linda.

"They don't talk much, do they?"

"Heh." Linda shook her head. "No. You're doing fine, though."

Frank was quiet for a moment before whispering again. "What's with the suits and shit anyway?"

"Some kind of biological quarantine from the look and sound of it. I dunno, though. I'm hoping we can see whoever's in charge and figure out what's going on."

The soldiers loaded Frank and Linda into the back of one of the Humvees and Frank noticed that while he and Linda were being treated far gentler than he would have expected, the soldiers were still keeping their rifles and sidearms at the ready. Their somewhat casual demeanor didn't fool him in the slightest and he was certain that they could easily dispatch both himself and Linda if either of them made a wrong move.

The Humvee carrying Frank, Linda and a group of the soldiers headed towards the city while the other military vehicle rolled forward to the Corvette to link up with the soldiers tasked by Simmons. Frank kept his head on a swivel, watching the buildings fly past as the Humvee sped along.

The highway was still remarkable clear, though Frank finally understood why. A large section of it had been cleared with massive bulldozers to make a zone free of obstacles that the military could use as a zone to stop any vehicles passing through. As they got closer to the city he saw that the bulldozers had moved to clearing a single lane on each side of the highway nearest the median, making it easy for the military to move in and out on the road.

The main forward operating base (FOB) was situated in an industrial complex on the eastern edge of the city just off of the main highway. Guards were posted on the roof of the tallest building in the complex overlooking the river to the south. Inside the gate in a parking lot sat a large tent under which several drones were being repaired and refitted. Several large canvas-covered trucks were parked near the back of the complex and dozens of soldiers ran back and forth between the trucks and the buildings as they offloaded and delivered supplies.

The hustle and bustle of activity was moderately overwhelming for Frank but for Linda it felt like she was back home. After the Humvee stopped and the soldiers inside stepped out, the rest of them took off their hazmat suits. Simmons kept his on as he led Linda and Frank inside the warehouse. He escorted them to the back office of the warehouse and rapped on the door. Another soldier glanced out, gave Simmons a questioning look and then opened the door.

"Simmons. Who're the civilians?"

"They're clean. And here to see Colonel Garland."

The soldier holding the door gave Linda and Frank a long look before nodding once. "Sir. Ma'am. Step inside, please."

A small cluster of soldiers and officers were gathered around a table in the room as the soldier announced Linda and Frank's presence. "Colonel Garland? Corporal Simmons sent these two in to see you, sir."

Lieutenant Colonel James Garland was a tall, broad-shouldered man with the build of an ox and the demeanor to go along with it. His eyes were narrow and full of fire, his voice was low and gravely and he carried himself with the demeanor of a man who was in full control of both himself and those under his command.

"What the hell are two civilians doing in here?"

Linda jumped in with an answer before Garland could get it from anyone else. "Colonel Garland? Pleasure to meet you. Sergeant Linda Rollins, Marine Raiders, retired. This is a friend of mine, Frank Richards."

The mix of suspicion and anger in Garland's eyes evaporated almost instantly as he stuck out his hand to shake Frank and Linda's hands one after the other. "Raider Rollins? You must've had more than a few jokes made about that, I'll bet."

Linda nodded and gave a slight smile. "That's an understatement."

"So what the hell's a jarhead doing out here in the middle of all this shit anyway?"

"Long story, Colonel. I'm trying to get back home to Tennessee to my parents. Frank's trying to get back to Texas."

"A Texas man!" Garland smiled proudly. "You ever serve, son?"

Frank shook his head. "Afraid not, sir. My father did, though, as did my grandfather. Both were very proud to serve in the Army."

"Ha!" Garland smiled and chuckled as he eyed the pair standing in front of him. "Damn straight. So you're both trying to get home?" Garland's smile evaporated and he scratched his chin. "I'm afraid you came to the wrong place if you're looking for transportation. We've got just enough wheels running to keep the city locked down. The only birds cleared for flight are the two we've got running recon. Everything else is still being triple-checked before it's being allowed into the air or on the ground."

"Colonel, forgive me for sounding ignorant, but just what's going on here? Why's there a perimeter around the city?"

One of the Colonel's bushy eyebrows went up and he looked around the room at the other officers and soldiers present. "Everyone take ten to get updates and get your bio breaks out. We'll finish the planning shortly." A moment later the room was empty and Garland motioned to a cluster of chairs in the corner. Linda tried to make it to the seats without limping but failed on the last few steps and both Frank and Garland reached out to steady her.

"You all right there, Rollins?"

"Just fine, Colonel. A meth-head tried to take my leg off. Only succeeded partially."

"So you've seen this insanity up close, eh?" Garland nodded. "Good. Saves me the trouble of starting from square one."

"We've seen plenty, yes." Frank jumped in, glancing at Linda as he continued. "But you were going to tell us about the city, yes?"

"Hm. Yes. What've you two heard about what's going on?"

Frank shrugged. "We heard bits and pieces on the radio and television. Some sort of massive terrorist attack. I was up in Maine when it happened—my truck was one of the ones hit."

"Consider yourself lucky, then. Unofficial estimates peg the loss of our country's truckers at over seventy percent. So not only did we lose a huge chunk of the trucks but we lost a lot of those who can drive them, too."

"Good God." Linda shook her head. "Do you know what's going on with all this or who's behind it all?"

"Most of it's classified. Sorry. But I can tell you about the city, though it doesn't much matter anymore. The virus has all but burned out at this point."

"Virus?" Frank had a note of disbelief in his voice. "What kind of a virus?"

Garland took off his cap and rubbed his head and Linda detected a trace of sadness in his voice. "Right after the shit hit the fan the alphabet agencies started feeding us all sorts of information about the attacks. Both the ones that had already occurred and ones that were coming down the pipe. I'd wonder why they didn't stop the first attacks but that's way past my pay grade.

"A few hours in and we started getting orders to head out and start securing major cities. Most of them were in the Midwest, but more than a few were in the west, northeast and central south."

"Securing the cities… against biological attacks?"

Garland nodded. "You got it, Rollins." Garland stretched the next word out, exaggerating the syllables. "Bi-o-logi-cal attacks. Some kind of crazy shit. Makes Ebola look like the common cold. Lucky for us, though, it burns through the victims so fast that they're gone before they can infect very many people."

"So your perimeter is for… what?" Frank looked at Linda then back at Garland. "Keeping people inside the city until the virus burns itself out?"

Garland nodded slowly, clenching his jaw. "That's correct."

"What the…" Frank could scarcely believe what he was hearing. "So, what, you guys weren't sent here to help these people?"

"What is it you'd like us to do, exactly, Mr. Richards? Pass out blankets and chicken noodle soup? Half the city was dead before we even got here. Most of the other half's dead by now. We have twenty-four more hours before we sweep the city, pick up any survivors and start cleaning up the corpses."

"I don't know… what about vaccines or something?"

"Vaccines? For some sort of mysterious disease that nobody's ever seen or heard of and can kill in hours?" Garland scoffed.

"How widespread is this?"

Garland licked his lips. "I'm afraid that's classified. But it's not isolated here, I can tell you that much."

"Any particular places where it's the most prevalent?"

"So far it seems to be every major city that isn't on the east, west or gulf coasts."

"Really? So LA, DC, New York—those haven't been hit by it?"

Garland shook his head. "While I can't confirm or deny that I can tell you that they're having a lot of problems of their own. Nobody's willing to risk driving a car, airports are all shut down, food stores are gone, water mains are broken. The warzone is on our doorsteps."

"Holy shit." Frank whispered to himself.

"No kidding." Garland sighed.

As Frank continued to ask for details and Garland continued to provide occasional snippets of additional information, Linda quickly found herself lost in her own thoughts. It wasn't until a few minutes later, after Frank had said her name three times in a row to get her attention, that he tapped her on the shoulder and she jumped in surprise.

"Linda?"

"What?" Linda's eyes grew wide as she looked between Frank and Garland.

"You all right over there, Rollins?" Garland leaned forward in the chair he had finally planted himself in.

"Yeah, no, I'm fine. Listen, when you said it's a fast-burning virus, do you happen to have any sort of research notes on it?"

"Nothing of any use. Why?"

"Just curious. I spent some time after I got out learning about that sort of thing."

"Never met too many Marines interested in learning." Garland grinned, then the smile evaporated. "Sorry about that. Old habits die hard."

"I wouldn't expect any less from a grunt like yourself." Linda returned the grin and Garland nodded and smiled.

"Rollins, I don't know why you're here but you're welcome to stay. You and Richards both. We're stretched thin enough that we need every able-bodied pair of hands available."

"If the circumstances were any different, Colonel, I'd stay in a heartbeat. But we need to keep going to Tennessee."

Garland frowned. "Where in Tennessee are you heading, anyway?"

"My parents are in Pigeon Forge. I'm planning to——" Linda stopped talking as she saw Garland's expression change. The roughness disappeared and it was replaced with an awkward feeling of remorse that quickly grew until it was all she could see. "Colonel? What's wrong?"

"Rollins…" Garland hesitated. "Pigeon Forge is gone."

Chapter Thirty-Nine

Despite her initial lack of verbal response, the sudden drop in Linda's stomach was palpable across the room. She blinked several times and swallowed hard against the bile rising in her throat before managing to choke out a response. "It's... gone? How can an entire city be gone?"

The distant boom of thunder shook the warehouse and Colonel Garland looked out through the nearby window. "Christ... just what we need." He shook his head then looked back at Linda. "How can a city be gone? A perfect-fucking-storm. That's how. The city took an extra hard beating during the initial attack. The wildfire north of the city got absolutely fuck-all for attention after that and spread out of control. Whoever didn't die in the fires or from the virus is half-frozen."

"Half-frozen?" Frank asked.

Garland snorted and nodded. "Sorry, I forget sometimes the radios and TVs are out. Massive snowstorm. Blew through in and out in a day and dumped two feet of snow on the ground." Garland's look grew distant. "They've been one of the hardest hit cities. Them and Salt Lake. Drone flyovers project less than half a percent of the residents could have survived."

"Holy shit." Frank whispered, shaking his head in disbelief. "How is that even possible?"

"Perfect storm, like I keep saying. Doesn't help that we're still being forced to check every single vehicle in the entire United States military before we're authorized to send them out. It'll be weeks before we have rescue operations fully staffed, plus we're spread so thin right now we can't do jack shit."

"Colonel." Linda stood up slowly from her seat and spoke with a stiff, robotic voice. "Thank you for the information. Do you have a pair of cots we can use for the night? We'll be out of your hair by morning."

Garland gave Frank an odd look and nodded slowly at Linda. "Not a problem, Rollins. If you need anything just ask."

Thunder rumbled again, shaking the warehouse even harder. A few seconds later the sound was accompanied by the noise of rain-drops hitting the metal roof. "Shit." Garland stood up and headed for the door, shouting as he ran out. "Simmons! Get these two some food and beds. Give them their vehicle and whatever else you confiscated as well."

"Yes, sir!" A distant reply came and was followed by the thud of boot steps racing across the warehouse floor. Corporal Simmons showed up a moment later and looked at Frank and Linda.

"Please, follow me."

Frank and Linda followed behind Simmons and Frank watched with interest as the flurry of activity in the warehouse continued to explode. "Corporal, what's up with everyone here?"

"Rain protocol."

"Rain protocol? What's that mean?"

Simmons looked around and shook his head. "Water mains in the city broke and the floods are wreaking havoc with our robots on the ground."

"What're they for? Recon?"

"Yeah, something like that. Mostly to test the air and figure out where any survivors are holed up. They're not equipped for the rain, though, so we have to get them back as fast as possible. That plus the fact that even the slightest amount of extra water's going to mean flooding in even more areas."

"Jeez. Sounds rough. Anything we—I—can do to help? I don't want to just be an imposition."

Simmons motioned for Frank and Linda to go ahead of him into a large tent set up in a corner of the industrial complex. "No, thank you, though. We have it under control. We'll have your vehicle and equipment back to you by morning. Meals are in the cupboard under the table, water's on top and you can heat whatever you'd like in the microwave. We've only got instant coffee at the moment."

"Sounds like heaven after the last few days. Thank you, Simmons."

Corporal Simmons nodded and ducked back out of the tent. Frank waited until he was gone before shaking his head and nudging Linda. "Under control my ass. Did you see how they were running around out there?"

When Linda didn't reply Frank guided her to an empty cot in the tent and helped her sit down. She looked at him blankly for several seconds before focusing on him and blinking a few times in surprise. "Hm? Oh. Yeah. It's chaos out there."

"Linda, are you—"

"Let's talk tomorrow, Frank. I've got a lot to think about tonight. You should get something to eat and drink and get some sleep. I'll let you know if I need any help with the bandage." With that pronouncement Linda laid down on the cot, rolled over to face the side of the tent and closed her eyes.

Frank backed up slowly, taken aback by what she said and did and not sure how to interpret it. After microwaving a suspicious packet of rice and some sort of unidentifiable meat Frank sat at a small table across the tent and ate, keeping a close eye on Linda the entire time. She didn't make any sounds and barely moved at all, shifting only slightly as she tried to get into a more comfortable position.

While Frank sat quietly in the tent wondering what was going on with Linda, she was not sleeping at all. On the contrary, she was deep in thought, her mind racing as she tried to put pieces together from the last few days and merge them with the information that she had learned a short time before.

The news about Pigeon Forge had come as a surprise, but her stilted speech and faraway look had been little more than a ruse designed to get her out of the Colonel's office as quickly as possible so she could have time to think to herself. Linda was worried about her parents, but in the face of such a devastating threat she fell back on her training, seeking to prioritize the threats she faced and systematically eliminate them one by one.

While in Garland's office, as Frank was chatting with the Colonel, Linda had taken an opportunity to steal a few glances at papers scattered across the table. Linda was somewhat surprised that Garland had left the papers out while chatting with her and Frank, but while he could have just been incompetent, she wondered if he was actually trying to share the information with them in the first place without being overt about it.

The papers all had a top secret stamp across the tops and bottoms and most described troop movements, locations of temporary bases set up around the city and detailed plans for the next few days split up into hour-by-hour sections. The paper that had intrigued her the most, though, was one that contained more detailed information about the perpetrators of the attacks as well as warnings for what was coming next.

In the hours before the first bombs went off, six canisters containing the virus that was ravaging Pittsburgh were found by local police officers in three different cities. The canisters were innocuous-looking enough, though, that they were simply bagged and placed into an evidence holding area for later processing. An eagle-eyed police chief spotted one of the canisters activating inside of the evidence bag and sent out a description of the device which was forwarded on to the military.

Soda can size with a plain white label, screw-off pressurized top and lime-green seals. The gas was light orange or tan in color at first. The evidence bag nearly popped from the pressure and after the device expended the gas contained inside, the electronic mechanism that triggered the release seemed to shut down.

The description of the canister had caught Linda's eye and at the time she wasn't sure why. Mulling it over as she rested on the cot, though, reminded her of why she found the canister so eerily familiar. *Is it the same thing? The lime-green seals and the label match. But there weren't any electronic components... I think.* Linda ground her teeth together and squeezed her eyes even tighter as she tried to remember the details from that fateful day so many years prior.

Linda played the fragments from the scene back in her mind, watching the metal canisters bounce across the ground towards her squad. Thick lime-green seals were wrapped around both ends and a plain white label with Arabic writing ran along the side. The canisters spewed a white smoky gas as they tumbled across the ground and Linda grimaced as the screams of her squad mate burned in her ear.

"From beyond the grave you spit at me." Linda whispered to herself on the cot. Across the room Frank's head jerked up and he looked around, trying to figure out if he had been imagining things or if Linda had really just spoken.

"Saywhuh?" Frank rubbed his eyes and yawned, then stood up and walked over near Linda. She rolled over in bed and slowly sat up, staring him in the eyes.

"From beyond the grave he spits at me." Linda sighed and pointed at the cot across from hers. "Sit down, Frank. It's time to lay my cards on the table."

"What, about being a Raider? I'm not an idiot, you know. I wasn't a typical Army brat but I know a thing or three."

Linda sighed again and shook her head. "No." Linda ran her fingers through her hair, pulling it back into a tight ponytail. "I think I know who's responsible for all of this."

Frank felt a chill run down his spine as he asked the obvious question. "Who?"

"Farhad Omar. The same bastard that was behind the slaughter of my unit."

Chapter Forty

It has been eighteen months since the invasion began and Linda Rollins has been a civilian for three months. As she leans against the tight harness in the back of a privately contracted Osprey flying over the desert sands, the same thought goes through her head that has passed through it a thousand times in the last three months.

"Am I insane?"

Immediately after being shipped back home and receiving a medical discharge Linda Rollins set her mind on one goal: avenging the dead. The fact that some had abandoned her meant nothing. Her mind was fixed on a singular purpose and nothing would dissuade her.

When Linda Rollins knocked on the door of Talon Creek, LLC she was hired on the spot. Her pay was a quarter million per deployment and she was promised access to every toy she could ever dream of. The Private Military Contractor was one of hundreds employed by the United States to perform work in Iran during and after the invasion. For most employed by the PMCs it was a chance to blow things up and get paid a lot of money to do it.

For Linda Rollins it was a chance for revenge.

"Wheels down in thirty seconds!" A voice screams over Linda's headset and she paws for the volume control to turn down the volume. "We are in a live *fire zone! Upon landing you are to proceed immediately to the rendezvous and proceed with your patrols!"*

Linda looks around at the others strapped in to the back of the Osprey. Most are men with tattoos, goatees, wraparound sunglasses and too much attitude. The few women that comprise the rest are nearly as masculine as the men, carousing and joking with them as though they've known each other for years.

Linda has purposefully kept to herself the last three months. Kept her head low, stayed out of the limelight and ensured she isn't noticed. All while working in the background to influence where she goes on her first assignment. Her hard work pays off ten minutes after the Osprey touches down and the group in the back charges out into the sandstorm that blankets the city.

The first nine minutes of the patrol are spent establishing locations and objectives, identifying where enemy fire is originating and making plans to destroy emplaced weapon positions. The tenth minute, once the plans are established and the group moves out, is spent falling to the back of the group and slipping away into the shadows.

The fierce wind and sand-filled air make breathing without a mask or filter impossible. Communications are next to impossible. Somehow, though, Linda solves the communications problem. She ducks into a small home, checking each room with a quick sweep of her rifle before squatting down and putting on a headset from her bag.

"Eagle, this is Badger. I am in position. Please confirm and advise."

The seconds tick by in agony without a response and Linda nearly repeats her message when the earpiece crackles to life.

"Badger, this is Eagle. Message confirmed. Transmitting rendezvous location. Good luck, Raider."

Linda pulls off the headset and stuffs it into her bag. Picking her way through the city to the indicated location takes nearly two hours, though that's an hour less than she estimated. When she arrives at the burned out buildings she searches through the rubble until she finds the unmarred steel trapdoor, just as it was described. The lock on the door has already been cut and she kicks it away before pulling on one of the handles.

A few steps down the stairs and Linda is forced to switch on her headlamp and the light attached to the barrel of her rifle. She heads down slowly, sweeping each turn with an excess amount of caution and care. She knows who *should already be awaiting her arrival in the basement but an abundance of caution is the difference between life and death.*

A faint glow appears at the bottom of the stairs and Linda slows down and peers at the source through the scope on her rifle. A tall figure dressed in a long leather coat and headwrap squats on the floor.

"Munir?" Linda says the name in a stage whisper and the figure shifts position to look in her direction. The figure appears unthreatening, but in the soft light of the lantern Linda catches a glimpse of a submachine gun in the man's hand, tucked back beneath his jacket. He looks at Linda for a long second before lowering the gun and standing to his feet.

"Linda. You're early."

Linda pulls off her mask and smiles at the lanky man. The only portions of his olive skin that are visible are his hands, face and neck. His hair and top of his head are wrapped in a thin covering and his typically long, flowing robes are nowhere to be seen, having been replaced by cargo pants and a long-sleeved shirt.

"Better than late. What've you got for me?"

Munir holds up his lantern and gestures at the room. "Not much, I'm afraid. What you see here is what's already been cleaned out and picked over by scavengers a dozen times over."

"You wouldn't call me here unless you had something more than an empty room."

A slight smile passes across Munir's lips and his hazel eyes twinkle with a mischievous air. "You are correct. Come, this way."

Munir leads Linda across the basement, passing bits of broken machinery, smashed tabletops and overturned lockers. Near the side of the room Munir stops and gestures at the ceiling. "Illuminate that, please."

Linda turns her head and rifle toward the ceiling, sending twin beams of light flashing across a strip of torn plastic that dangles from above. Half an inch thick, the plastic is shredded like it was torn apart with great force. Bullet holes riddle the bits of plastic that hang close to the floor.

"You see it, yes?" Munir sweeps his hand across the path of the sheet.

"Huh." Linda nods. "A contamination shield. Separating this section of the room." She looks at Munir. "For testing?"

Munir shakes his head. "For the families."

"Families? Of—oh. Oh my." Linda casts her lights across the floor behind

where the thick plastic sheet once hung. The beds and linens that once covered the area are gone, having long ago been looted. Holes in the floor where bolts held the stacked beds in place are still visible, though, and Linda crouches down and sweeps a gloved hand across the floor. "Bastards. How long since they were here?"

"A month, perhaps two or three. It is difficult to tell. No one is willing to speak of it for fear of what will happen to their families."

"Wait, you mean he let the scientists go?"

"Every one of them. Their families as well."

"Why the hell would he do that?"

Munir's eyes grow sad. "He has total control over them. If they whisper a word of what they know then their families will be slaughtered in front of them."

"Can we extract any of the scientists and their families? Get them out of the country and to safety?"

"They will not be willing. And if you were to try to move on them, I fear he would see it coming and prepare a counterattack. All elements of surprise would be gone."

Linda stands and slowly walks through the room. "So this was a bust, eh?"

Munir tilts his head. "In some respects, yes. In others, no. We now know he was here and we have confirmation of the biological testing he guided."

"Without specifics I'm not going to be able to get anyone to believe me much less send in some cavalry." *The watch on Linda's wrist lights up and it vibrates softly against her skin. She looks at the face and curses.* "Shit. I have to go. They're wrapping up their patrol early."

"I will let you know when I have more information."

"Thanks, Munir." *Linda embraces the man in a brief hug and pats him on the back.* "If you need anything you just call."

Munir smiles at her as she puts her mask back on. "Take care of yourself out there."

Chapter Forty-One

"Back up for a second. You spent how long trying to find this Farhad guy?"

"I've been working on it in some capacity since I was discharged."

"Damn." Frank nodded. "That's some dedication. And you think he's the mastermind behind all of what's going on?"

"If there's one thing I've learned it's that Omar has a unique hatred for our country. He's the one who drew us into the initial invasion."

Frank frowned. "I thought we went in because of the attacks. Everyone said those were government-sanctioned by the Iranians."

"That's what it looked like, didn't it? I actually got to see some of the so-called evidence that supported that theory. It was bullshit. When I started going after Omar that's one of the first things that came to light."

"So this guy pulls us into an invasion that ravages his country for... what?"

"They weren't the only ones who suffered. And I'm not just talking about the loss of life. You remember how our standing changed and the policy changes that happened after we pulled out of that quagmire."

"Fair point. If he's the mastermind then why didn't the military pursue it, though?"

"After that clusterfuck of an invasion? The last thing anyone wanted to do was get any more involved in that sand trap. I'm sure a few eggheads in the alphabet agencies figured out the truth but it would have been political suicide to try and go in there again, even if it was to get the guy who was behind the attacks."

"I have to say—and don't take this the wrong way—this all sounds incredibly…"

"Paranoid?"

"I was going to say insane. But that works, too."

Linda snorted in amusement. "Yeah, I know. I've spent a long time chasing this guy, though."

"What is it that makes you so convinced he's the one behind all of this stuff?"

"It's not any one thing in particular. It just all adds up. Omar's a wealthy and connected man. He could easily afford to have people loyal to him snuck across our borders who then set up a self-contained group of cells here in the country that don't need any external resources. With that you eliminate the typical way for the FBI or others to infiltrate terrorist cells. He was also very much into biological weapons as a tool for shaping populations." Linda shook her head. "It's no accident that so many cities in specific locations are being hit. It's all part of something larger."

Frank scratched his head and stood up, pacing back and forth in the tent. "This is crazy. You sound crazy and I feel crazy for listening to it and even crazier for starting to believe it."

"Believe it or not, Frank, it doesn't really matter to me. This has Omar's fingerprints all over it. It's his MO and he has the resources, knowledge and motivation to pull it all off. If you believe me or not, I don't care. I know what I know, and what I know is true."

"All right. So what do you want us to do?"

"Us?" Linda shook her head. "You've done more than enough,

Frank, and I haven't thanked you enough for what you've done. You need to take the Corvette to Texas."

"I'm sorry... what?" Frank could barely believe what he was hearing. "You want me to leave? What about your parents? What about all of what you just told me?"

"You heard Garland. Pigeon Forge is gone." Linda pressed her fingers against the bridge of her nose.

"And you're just going to leave it at that? You won't even go there to check for yourself?"

Linda nearly growled at Frank in response. "Do you really think I owe you an explanation for my choices?"

"Fuck yes you do! I've been traveling with you since this started and while it may not be that long in terms of the amount of time I think you owe someone whose life you've saved and who's saved your life *some* kind of explanation for why, suddenly, you decided that your parents aren't worth trying to save!"

Linda hadn't been expecting such a forceful response from Frank. Taken aback, she shook her head and gritted her teeth. "You heard Garland."

"Yes, I did. And maybe he's right! Why is this guy so important that you'd chase after him instead of trying to get to your parents?"

"My parents are in a nursing home, Frank. I haven't spoken to them in years. The city already got hit by a storm days ago. Liz told us that. Then another storm blows in, plus a viral outbreak plus fires?" Linda shook her head. "They're gone, Frank. Under the circumstances, if there was nothing else going on, I'd want to go there and find them and give them a proper burial."

Frank's voice softened. "But?"

"But this is just the tip of the iceberg. And I'm in a position to potentially do something about it."

"So you're going to run off and traipse around looking for this mystery man?"

Linda scoffed. "Screw you. You have no concept of what I've done in my life and the things I've seen. He is out there right now and I'm one of the few people who know enough to do something about it. If he can be found and stopped then millions of lives can be spared and this horror can finally stop. You can fuck right off."

"You have no concept of how pretentious you sound right now. Even if you're right about all of this you don't need to play the victim card and act like you're one person against the world. You can ask for help. You should ask for help." Frank threw his hands in the air.

"I don't need your help, Frank."

"Whatever. You know, we've been working together for days and I thought we were finally starting to become friends on some level. But hey, I've been wrong before and I guess I'm wrong again. You want me to fuck off so I'll fuck off. Take the Corvette yourself or throw it in a trash heap where it belongs. I'll figure out how to get south myself."

Linda crossed her arms and stared at him. "Fine then. Take care of yourself, Frank."

"Yeah. You too."

With that, Frank turned and left the tent, heading off to find Simmons, get his gear and some transportation before he started heading for Texas. Behind him, in the tent, Linda fought with herself, wrestling in her mind with the things Frank had told her along with her realizations about the horrors that were unfolding.

Her singular devotion to chasing Omar had cost her a relationship with her parents, a career and any hope at a normal life. Now it had just cost her a budding friendship with someone whom she could trust—a true rarity in the world. As Linda's anger gradually subsided and reason began to take back over she put her head in her hands and hissed through her teeth.

"Fuck."

Chapter Forty-Two

The two men in their Manhattan apartment building are exhausted. Monitoring the effects of Phase 2 has taken every ounce of their concentration, but the data they have gathered is exactly what they have been instructed to get. With the data summarized, packaged together and encrypted, they send it to an orbiting satellite which then relays the data to three more satellites before finally sending the information back down to the other side of the planet.

The man in the white robes examines the data carefully, looking for any signs that things have gone wrong. He allows himself a rare self-congratulatory smile as he realizes that his plan is working perfectly. The initial biological attack has had the predicted effect and the "Shelter Cities" are forming in exactly the locations he predicted.

After a final look-over of the data, the man closes his eyes and sits back in his chair. Organizing the coordination of hundreds of intricate precise pieces has taken every waking moment of his life for decades on end but the fruit of his labor is truly glorious to see. Bombs followed by the outbreak of a virus has had the intended effect of panicking the populace, causing them to harm themselves far more than any bomb or biological outbreak could ever hope to achieve.

The final phase of the man's plan will take weeks more before it can be executed and there are still many more moving pieces in play. He allows himself five minutes of relaxation before resuming his work. Hours later, after yet *another document is finished and sent off to a subordinate, a buzzer rings. The man stands and walks to the door of his building, opening it to the small group outside.*

"Gentlemen." The man in the white robes nods to each of the suited figures as they step inside. Once the group is assembled the man in the white robes claps his hands and a cluster of servants appear. They take jackets from the suited men, bring out bottles of water and cups of tea and coffee and lay out napkins at a round table in the living room of the home.

"It goes well?" The thick accent of a portly, red-faced man is Slavic, though it's hard to place the exact region.

"Very well." The man in the white robes smiles slyly.

"Then why have you called us here?" A dark-skinned man glances at the figure to his right, then at the figure to his left. "Our presence here is a danger to all of us."

"This is very true." The man in the white robes nods. "However, there are some... changes that we must discuss."

The group of men in suits mumble and murmur in dissatisfaction. "What types of changes?"

"The addition of a third phase."

The murmurs grow louder. "What third phase?" The portly man shouts. "We were told there were two phases! There was never a mention of a third phase!"

"Gentlemen." The man in the white robes lifts his hands and waits for the grumbling to settle down. "Gentlemen, I assure you. The third phase is one that you will appreciate far more than the first two. And all we need to complete it is a bit of help from each of your countries."

BOOK THREE

THE FRACTURE

Chapter Forty-Three

Linda laid still on her cot for a few more hours, until dawn broke, without getting the faintest hint of sleep. Her mind was racing with a variety of thoughts. Her revelations about Omar, her argument with Frank and the fate of her parents all mixed and jumbled together, making it difficult to focus on any one thing.

It was a hell of a lot simpler before today. It was all about getting to my parents. And now... all of this. Linda shook her head and sighed before standing up. She headed out of the tent and glanced around at the flurry of activity unfolding around her. The rain was still falling, though it had lightened up somewhat from the heavy thunderstorms. It wasn't affecting the soldiers and Marines who were running back and forth across the factory lot, though. Some of them were carrying supplies, others looked like they were getting ready to go out on patrol and a few were trying to play some basketball in a back corner.

Linda headed for the main building where she and Frank had met with Colonel Garland. On her way there she ran into Corporal Simmons who was standing with his men around a small table while they discussed point on a map of the city. Linda tried to slip past Simmons but he noticed her and called out. "Ms. Rollins! Something I can help you with?"

"Just looking for the Colonel." Linda threw a thumb in the direction of Garland's office. "He still in there?"

A look of panic crossed Corporal Simmons' face. "Uh, I believe so, but he's in a meeting at the moment."

Linda smiled and kept walking towards the office as she replied. "No problem. I'll just wait outside until he's done."

"Ma'am, if you need something I can—"

"I appreciate it, Corporal, but I need to speak with him." Linda didn't bother looking back at Simmons. Behind her Simmons looked as though he was going to protest again but it was clear she was on a mission and nothing was going to stop her.

Outside the Colonel's office Linda peeked through the window and saw him sitting alone and going through paperwork. She knocked on the door and he glanced up, saw that it was her and motioned for her to come inside.

"Rollins!" The Colonel stood and shook her hand before motioning for her to sit down. "What can I do for you?"

"I was actually wondering if you had seen Frank. He uh… we had a bit of a disagreement yesterday. I wanted to talk to him to try and patch things up."

"Huh." Garland rubbed his nose and watched Linda closely with a quizzical look. "Richards left about an hour ago. He was going to take that piece of shit you both drove in here with but we've got more vehicles to spare than we can count so we gave him a Humvee and enough fuel to get most of the way to Texas."

"Oh." Linda looked down at the floor, not sure what to think about the news. She didn't realize it until just then but she had been secretly hoping that he hadn't left yet so that they could have at least one more conversation before splitting up. Shaking off the emotions she was starting to feel, Linda looked back up at the Colonel. "I had another question, Colonel."

"Spit it out."

"Do you know if there are any plans to go into Pigeon Forge? Once it's safe to do so, I mean."

Garland leaned back in his chair and narrowed his eyes at her. "I'm sure you know I can't divulge any information on what we may or may not be doing. Why do you want to know?"

Linda leaned forward and plucked a pen and pad of paper from Garland's desk. She scribbled on the pad before handing it and the pen back to him. "That's the address of my parents' nursing home. If you happen to be going into the city I'd consider it a personal favor if you were to make that address a priority. I know the chances of anyone there surviving are extremely low but…"

"Say no more." The Colonel tore off the top piece of paper, folded it up and slipped it into his pocket. "*If* we have any convoys passing by the area on a regular basis and *if* they happen to take a wrong turn into the city I'll be sure to ask them to swing by this location. Hypothetically, of course."

"Thank you." Linda meant the words she spoke and swallowed hard before her next request. "One other thing."

Garland raised an eyebrow. "More favors?"

"Just a vehicle."

"Ha. Help yourself. I've got more of those than I know what to do with."

"How's that?"

Garland shook his head. "It's going to take forever to check all of them for IEDs. I know they don't have them and you know they don't have them but that's the order right now. Everything has to be stripped down and searched front to back before it can be used in the field. I've got men sitting around with their thumbs up their asses and nothing to do because of it."

"I appreciate it, Colonel."

"No problem. Talk to Simmons on your way out. He'll make sure you get some extra ammo, a rifle if you want and some food and water to keep you through to… well, where is it you're going, anyway?

I need to get to Washington."

"State?"

"D.C."

Garland's other eyebrow went up. "You had to get to Tennessee yesterday. Why the hell would you be going to D.C. all of a sudden?"

"I have a contact in Washington. They may know something about what's going on right now."

"You mean about all of this?" The Colonel waved his hand above his head in a dramatic fashion.

"That's right." Linda was trying extremely hard to *not* sound evasive but doing a terrible job at it.

"Mind if I ask what it is you're meeting this contact about?"

Linda licked her lips, trying to determine how much of her past to divulge to the Colonel. "Some of what we discussed yesterday reminded me of information I gathered in my past, after I was discharged."

"You did intelligence work?"

Linda made a face. "Eh… sort of. It was personal, though. Had to do with an incident that occurred when I was deployed. There was a man who I found out was responsible for the incident. There's a decent chance he's behind what's going on now."

"Have you reported this to anyone?"

Linda chuckled. "Colonel I literally just came up with this theory a few hours ago. You're the first person I've talked to about it besides Frank."

Garland frowned. "Still, if you have any sort of information I'm going to need to ask you to give me all the details so we can run it up the chain of command. Not that I think they'll do anything about it given how fractured this whole damned situation—"

The door to Garland's office slammed against the wall as it was thrown open. One of Garland's subordinates came running in, a panicked look on his face. "Sir! I'm sorry, but we need you out here right now!"

"What is it?" The Colonel rose from his seat, a scowl on his face.

"The floodwaters are rising fast and they're nearly here. We're going to need to evacuate and head for higher ground, sir!"

"Hrmph." Garland growled and shook his head. He looked down at Linda, still in her seat, and nodded to her. "Go find Simmons. Have him get you some supplies and whatever else you need. Give him a report on what you know before you go." The Colonel left his office without another word, rushing out to give directions on what to do about the flooding situation.

Linda sat in her chair for a long moment, trying to decide what to do next. She doubted that any good would come of telling anyone within the Army about her suspicions about Farhad Omar but decided to give it a shot just because of how helpful Garland had been.

Linda exited Colonel Garland's office to a sea of chaos. Soldiers and Marines ran back and forth as they loaded supplies into vehicles. Only the most critical and vital supplies such as food, medicine and ammunition were being loaded. The infrastructure that had been setup in the form of shelters, office spaces, communications lines and other similar equipment were being abandoned to the flood waters due to the urgency of the situation.

While much of the rain had passed by the city, overflowing rivers and the fact that the city's water mains had yet to be shut down meant that water levels of only a few inches twenty-four hours ago were now several feet in depth in some places. Linda jogged to the edge of the compound and looked down the street towards the city, her eyes widening as she realized she could actually see the waters quickly approaching the factory compound.

"Ms. Rollins?" Linda heard her name called and she turned to find Corporal Simmons running up to her. "Ma'am, the Colonel said you needed transport?"

Linda nodded. "Transport, my gear, a bit of food, some ammunition and a rifle is what he promised."

"You'd better get over here quick, then. We're packing up the last of the food stores now."

Linda followed Simmons through the compound to a warehouse near the back. Inside were a couple dozen soldiers scurrying about like ants as they worked to load crate after crate of food into the back of several trucks parked outside. Simmons tapped Linda on the shoulder and pointed to a green Humvee parked nearby. "That's yours. We haven't checked it, but Colonel Garland said—"

Linda patted Simmons on the shoulder and nodded. "He already explained it to me. It'll be fine."

"I took the liberty of getting you some food, ammunition and a weapon. Take as much food as you want and get it in there quick." Corporal Simmons glanced behind him at a cluster of soldiers struggling to free a vehicle from some mud near the edge of the compound. "Was there anything else? The Colonel mentioned something about you having information?"

Before Linda could reply one of the soldiers in the cluster called out for Simmons and he ran off to help them. Linda watched him go, her finger in the air and her mouth open as she debated trying to stop him and relay her theory to him. "Screw it." Linda whispered to herself before running into the warehouse. She made three trips back and forth to her vehicle before the last of the supplies was loaded up. Water on the ground in the compound was already up to her ankles and she realized that if she didn't get moving soon she wouldn't be able to get out at all.

Unfortunately, though, the soldiers were coming to the same realization as their shouts and calls to each other grew louder and more frantic. The floodwaters had come upon their base faster than they had expected. The organized chaos was swiftly dissolving into chaos as the soldiers and Marines jockeyed to be the first out of the compound, each group prioritizing their gear and equipment as number one. Linda shook her head at the madness, wondering where Colonel Garland was and why he was allowing his men to continue acting in such a manner.

Linda jumped into the Humvee that Simmons had set aside for her and fired it up. The throaty diesel engine roared to life and she pulled away from the warehouse and aimed for the exit from the factory compound. As she rounded a corner about halfway through, though, she slammed on the brakes to avoid hitting a group of soldiers who were running in front of her. In front of them sat a line of vehicles trying to get out of the compound, though each of them was moving slowly so that they could take on more gear, supplies or personnel.

It only took a few minutes for Linda to find herself trapped between a large covered truck behind and a pair of Humvees in front. With no way to get around them she was forced to sit and watch the water level continue to slowly rise. A light shower started, dotting the Humvee with water droplets and she put a palm to her forehead in frustration.

"Come on..." Linda groaned through gritted teeth. She glanced out the window down at the ground and saw that the water level was rising much faster than it had been just a few minutes prior. After glancing around again at the clogged escape from the compound, she decided that a second exit from the place needed to be created.

Linda threw the Humvee into reverse and slammed into the truck behind her, eliciting a couple of angry shouts in response. She paid the soldiers no mind as she turned the wheel and put the vehicle into drive, jolting forward and to the right while taking off a few layers of paint from one of the Humvees in the process. Another shout came from behind her as she pulled off, heading to the side of the compound at a rapidly increasing speed.

"I hope to hell this works!" Linda gripped the steering wheel tightly and winced as the Humvee struck the faux brick wall that surrounded the compound. Designed to look intimidating and discourage casual passersby, the wall crumbled easily under the force of the armored vehicle. The chain link fence a few feet beyond didn't stand a chance either and Linda turned the wheel again as she bounced over spilled brick and metal and came to a stop.

Upon seeing the secondary exit from the compound the vehicles that were already ready to go immediately pulled out of line and raced towards it. Linda pressed down on the accelerator and winced again as she heard metal scraping against the Humvee as the chain link fence was ground between the wheels and frame until it finally popped free. As she pulled away from the factory compound she glanced into the rearview mirror and gave a slight smile.

The vehicles were pouring out of the compound in droves through the exit she had created, escaping the rapidly rising flood waters. With any luck the soldiers and marines would be able to quickly relocate to a new location without losing too many supplies or any men. What would happen next, though, was something she didn't want to ponder. Sending soldiers into a city full of a viral plague sounded like certain death for those involved.

Chapter Forty-Four

Driving down the road wouldn't have felt like such a waste of time had Linda been traveling on literally any other road in the entire country. The road she and Frank had taken into Philadelphia was the best one—initially at least—to take back east, though, and she begrudgingly took it. It was hard not to feel like the last few days had been a waste, though, and in more ways than one.

With all of the disasters to have befallen Pigeon Forge she was certain beyond a doubt that her parents—the chief reason for her travel south—were gone. She had also spent a great deal of time and energy working with Frank and while she had expected them to go separate ways at some point she felt emotionally exhausted by the entire situation thanks to their argument.

The larger, overarching reason for feeling like her time had been wasted was Omar. Linda couldn't help but feel responsible for the terrorist attacks taking place. She reasoned that if she had somehow managed to work a little harder or make just one or two more contacts then she could have gotten to Omar and stopped him before he had a chance to unleash his violence upon the United States.

Her injury, all but forgotten during the commotion at the base, was bothering her as she drove and she did her best to ignore it. It wasn't bleeding and she doubted it was infected but she wished she had remembered to get a medic there to check it out. The half-assed patch job done by Frank and herself had held it together, but she didn't know what sort of physical labor was going to be required in the days ahead.

With the torrential downpours well behind her, Linda tried to enjoy the sunny skies while they lasted. The sky was blue with few clouds, the trees were still shedding their colorful autumn leaves and everything—aside from the destruction scattered here and there on the road—seemed serene and peaceful. If Linda hadn't been driving a three-ton armored military vehicle that handled like the Titanic then she could have almost believed that it was just another average day.

Linda's attempts to focus on the positives of her drive were soon derailed when she heard a sound in the distance behind her. She looked in the mirror and saw a vehicle far behind her honking its horn and flashing its lights. As it got closer she realized that it was another Humvee, though dark green in color. It was impossible to identify who was driving or riding inside, but the vehicle drove erratically, swerving all over the road. Whoever was driving it was experienced with handling large vehicles, though, as Linda thought more than once it was going to flip or crash only to be surprised as it stayed firmly on the road.

"What the hell?" Linda's eyes flicked back and forth between the mirror and the road as she tried to figure out what was going on. No one from the Army or Marines surrounding the city would have been driving like the person behind her and with all the commotion and confusion going on she wouldn't have been surprised if someone had stolen a vehicle. Already feeling paranoid by her recent theories about Omar, Linda immediately jumped to the assumption that the person behind her was going to try and run her off the road.

Looking ahead and to the sides, Linda saw that the clearing on the left side of the road was nearly at an end and a line of fencing and large trees was at the end of it. The road going along past that point was clear as well so she eased off the accelerator, letting the massive vehicle slow itself down as she shifted into second gear.

The vehicle behind her didn't slow down with her, though, and it swerved to the left to overtake her. Right before it drew neck-and-neck with her Humvee she hit the brakes and turned the wheel to the left. She braced herself as her Humvee slammed into the one that had been following her. The driver, while skilled, was taken completely by surprise by her maneuver. She saw the driver's form flailing about in the driver's seat, struggling to keep the vehicle under control, but the impact was too great to handle.

The green Humvee went flying off the road into the thick grass and dirt, slowing down dramatically as the wheels dug into the wet soil. The green Humvee didn't slow down enough to avoid slamming into one of the large oak trees at the edge of the field, though, and the sound of the impact was a sickening crunch that made a grim smile of satisfaction cross Linda's face.

She hit the brakes on her vehicle and pulled to the side of the road before parking her Humvee, grabbing her rifle and jumping out. She headed down into the field, walking slowly with her weapon at the ready. Linda circled around the back of the Humvee, keeping it at a safe distance while she tried to get a view of the driver to see what condition he was in.

As Linda drew close the driver's side door flew open and she moved her finger to the trigger, ready to fire. The person that emerged did so slowly and haphazardly, groaning as they slid out and onto the ground. The figure was a man, though his back was towards Linda, and he was clutching his chest in pain as he coughed weakly.

"God... dammit..." The man's voice was faint but Linda recognized it instantly. She lowered her rifle and broke into a run as the mask of anger and suspicion left her face and was replaced by worry.

"Frank?" Linda shouted as she ran up to Frank and turned him over. He coughed again and winced, his body shaking from the pain and shock of the wreck.

"What the *fuck*, Linda?" Frank spat the words out at her, looking at her with an expression of betrayal in his eyes.

"Holy shit, Frank! I didn't know it was you!"

"Who else did you think it was who would be driving after you and honking and flashing their lights?" Frank started trying to push himself up to his feet but stopped and clutched at his chest again. "If I broke a rib I'm going to tear it out and stab you in the face with it, you asshole."

Watching Frank lying on his back in the grass with the Humvee's radiator hissing steam and listening to the birds and the wind in the background suddenly seemed extremely amusing. Linda tried to hold back a giggle but couldn't, then broke into a full-blown laugh as she plopped down onto the ground next to Frank. He, in turn, gave up on trying to sit up and put his head back, breathing heavily for a minute before he looked at her.

"What the hell's so funny?"

"You. Being so indignant right now. I'm just wondering what made you think that it was a good idea to come driving up on me like one of those meth-heads."

Frank snorted, his temper waning as he listened to Linda still chuckling next to him. "I had been driving for a while and when I saw you I wanted to get your attention." He shifted positions on the ground, moving a few inches to the side to get his back off of a tree branch and groaned from the pain. "I'd say it worked."

Linda nodded. "Sure did." Her laughter died out and her smile faded as they sat for several more minutes in silence while Frank continued to catch his breath and assess his injuries. When she finally spoke she did so without looking down at Frank, choosing instead to look out across the grassy field. "So why are you here, Frank?"

Frank sighed. "Because I'm a stubborn son of a bitch."

"I can see that. Why, though?"

"After our argument I got my stuff, got a vehicle from the Colonel and started heading south. It took me an hour or two of driving before I calmed down and realized that you needed me to come along with you so I turned around and came back." Frank slowly pushed himself into a sitting position and turned around to sit next to Linda with his back to the Humvee.

Linda scoffed at his statement and shook her head. "Me… needing you? Ha. For what?"

"Well I did save your ass… how many times was it? At least three. Maybe more than that?"

Linda rolled her eyes. "I had those situations under control. Besides, what about your parents?"

"You ever see the movie Tremors?"

Linda frowned as she thought. "I think so. Years ago. It was about those underground grabber things, right?"

"Graboids. Yeah. I watched it all the time growing up. There was a character on the show named Burt. I can't remember his last name. But he was the kind of guy my parents are. Lived in the middle of nowhere, had enough food and water to last years and enough guns in his basement to outfit a small South American country."

Linda chuckled. "So they're well-armed, huh?"

"That's an understatement." Frank took a deep breath and opened his jacket and pulled up his shirt. His chest was red and there were already several small bruises showing up along the line where his seat belt had been located. "Dammit. That's going to leave a hell of a mark." Frank gingerly touched his rib cage, wincing in pain. "I don't think anything's broken. Hurts, though."

Linda glanced at Frank's chest and patted her leg. "I keep forgetting about this stupid thing till it hurts so bad I feel like I couldn't walk if I had to."

"You should've gotten it checked out back there at the base."

"Yeah. I should've done a lot back there at the base."

Frank and Linda lapsed into silence for a moment until she spoke again. "So what happened to the whole 'don't abandon your parents' shtick?"

Frank shook his head. "My parents don't need help from me or anyone else. Your parents, though…" Frank paused and sighed. "I'm not going to pretend I think you made the right choice to leave."

Linda could feel herself getting angrier with each passing word and she tried to talk but Frank cut her off. "Just shut up and listen to me, okay? I don't think you made the right choice but maybe you did. That's for you to deal with. I shouldn't have said some of what I said to you. While I was driving I did a lot of thinking and realized that if what you're saying is true, about this Obar guy—"

"Omar." Linda slipped the word in quietly.

"Omar, yes. If your ideas about him are true and everything you told me about you pursuing him is true then you need my help. And I have to help you."

"What makes you think I need your help?"

"Because if you screw up and fail then that'll be on my head."

Linda snorted and turned to look at Frank. "You sure don't seem confident in my abilities to handle myself."

"Lady," Frank said, smiling at Linda, "if the last few days is anything to go on you need somebody there watching you twenty-four seven. I'm surprised you didn't run off the road already." Linda slugged Frank in the arm and he toppled over, barely holding in a laugh through the pain in his chest.

"I really don't want you here, you know." Linda pulled Frank back up. "This is my war, not yours."

The smile disappeared from Frank's face and he grew deadly serious. "Every single red-blooded American is in this war now. Including me. I'm not a soldier. I'm a pencil-pushing accountant who got laid off and had to drive eighteen-wheelers to pay the bills. I was lucky enough to have parents who showed me how to handle a gun and I can take care of myself. All things being equal I'd rather live on the grid than off. But this?" Frank shook his head defiantly. "No way. I'm not letting this slide. No, I'm with you. If you know who did this and if they're planning something even worse then I'm with you every step of the way."

When Frank got to the end of his impromptu speech he realized he was out of breath and Linda was staring at him with an odd look on her face. He gasped for air a few times until he stopped feeling light-headed and Linda replied.

"I'm sorry, Frank. I don't say that often but I mean it. I

shouldn't have said some of the things I did. And maybe you're right about Pigeon Forge. But I think I'm making the right call given the situation. And if I am right and I... *we* can figure a way to stop this asshole then a lot of people *won't* have to die like so many have."

"Apology accepted." Frank nodded and ground his teeth together. He pushed off from the vehicle and stood up swiftly, grabbing for the open door of the vehicle to keep from doubling over from the pain. He held out a hand to Linda and she took it, standing awkwardly as she favored her injured leg.

"Good." Linda nodded. "Grab your stuff. We've got a war to fight."

Chapter Forty-Five

"Follow me, please."

The statement is simple, but it is more than a request. It is an order with an implication that if it is not obeyed then there will be severe consequences. Linda stays close to the secretary she is following, ensuring she doesn't fall behind by more than a few feet. She knows full well what the implication of disobedience entails inside the normal-looking office building.

Sitting on the bank of the Potomac River just a few miles from the CIA's headquarters in Langley, the building is seven stories high—ten if the basement levels are included. Its exterior is faux brick and the windows are for appearances only. No signals are allowed in or out of the building except through monitored hard lines.

Security, to the layman, appears lax but Linda knows it to be anything but. Electronic monitoring of the physical and digital world inside the building is at an unprecedented level due to the extreme level of secrecy required for the work that goes on. The building also functions as a test bed of sorts for deploying advanced monitoring techniques to other facilities both within the CIA and other government bodies.

While no armed guards are visible from the halls, Linda is well aware that a small army of them are located on and around the building. Any attempts to disrupt security, steal anything or even piss off the wrong person will be met

MIKE KRAUS

with varying degrees of force. Due to her background she knows that she's being watched extremely carefully so she makes sure to keep her hands visible at all times and do everything she's told to do.

After passing through numerous halls and up two flights—one by elevator and the other by stairs—Linda and the man she is following arrive at their destination. A nondescript door with a keypad and simple numeric identification number on a tag above the keypad are the only indications that they have arrived at their destination.

The secretary turns to Linda. "Turn around, please, and place both of your hands on the wall in the designated positions." She obliges the request by placing her hands on two handprints and the secretary knocks on the door one time before entering a code on the keypad. A biometric scan is performed of both the secretary and Linda using scanners in the keypad and on the far wall, ensuring that both of them are who they say they are before the door opens.

Linda turns around at the sound of the opening door and the secretary steps aside, motioning for her to enter the room. She won't be allowed out of the room without an escort out of the building and the secretary must ensure the door is closed and locked before he can return to his duties.

Inside the small office a woman sits at a computer, furiously pounding on a keyboard. Linda steps inside and nods at the secretary who pulls the door shut and locks it. The woman at the desk doesn't look up at Linda, continuing to type for a full two minutes before finally stopping. She turns and glances at Linda before nodding at her.

"Ms. Rollins, I presume?"

"Call me Linda, please. You're Mrs. Callahan?"

Sarah Callahan, a fifteen-year veteran of the Central Intelligence Agency, stands up from her desk and extends her hand. "Pleased to meet you, Linda. Call me Sarah. Have a seat, won't you?" Sarah walks around the desk to a coffee pot sitting on a table. "Forgive my manners. We don't typically get visitors and I don't get out much these days."

"No worries at all." Linda flashes a smile and accepts a paper cup filled with coffee with a nod. "Jack said they work you hard here."

Sarah sits back down behind her desk and sighs wearily. The intense, focused look that was on her face when Linda walked in is gone, replaced by a look of someone who is about to fall asleep from sheer exhaustion. "It's been hell lately, I don't mind telling you. But that's not why you're here." Sarah *straightens in her chair and looks at Linda. "You must have something juicy on Jack for him to get you clearance to be brought in here."*

Linda laughs. "Yeah, well, they didn't exactly make it easy on me. I'm pretty sure my time in the Marines worked against me."

"That makes sense, I'm sorry to say." Sarah takes a sip from her cup of coffee. "So what is it I can help you with?"

Linda glances around and licks her lips, still unsure about sharing the information she has brought. Sarah, immediately understanding her nervousness, points at the ceiling. "It's unmonitored in here for video and audio. Shocking, I know, but we get a tiny bit of privacy at least."

Linda nods with relief. "I'm glad for that. There's no easy way to talk about this so I'll try to give you the highlights first and you tell me what details you think might be important."

Sarah remains silent as she sips on her coffee so Linda clears her throat and continues. "As you're probably aware my squad was a victim of an unorthodox attack during the invasion. It's my belief that we were essentially used as guinea pigs to test new weapons tech developed by Farhad Omar. I've done some digging but all I've been able to come up with is tenuous proof that he did it. Which is something I already know. What I'm trying to find out is how to catch the bastard and bring him to justice."

Sarah sits quietly, watching and listening with intense interest to every syllable Linda utters and every movement she makes. Trained for years on how to spot someone lying as well as how to read a person Sarah is convinced that her initial impression of Linda was correct. She finishes her cup of coffee and throws the paper cup into a trash can before pulling her chair back up to her desk and placing her hands on the desk.

"Linda, I have to tell you that what you're asking for is something I can't do."

There is a long pause and Linda's heart sinks. Sarah Callahan was recommended to her as someone who could and potentially would be able to help track down Omar, but it is clear that she cannot help. Until she speaks again.

"Officially."

Linda looks up from her paperwork that she was starting to put away in preparation of leaving. "Huh?"

"I can't help you officially with what you're asking. I'm sorry. However, if you want to meet tomorrow evening I can look over what you have and offer a

few unofficial opinions. Here's my cell. Give me a call sometime tomorrow and we'll meet."

Linda is shocked by the turn of events and can't understand her good fortune. She thanks Sarah and leaves the building in the same manner she came in. A day passes and she calls Sarah but there is no answer. After two hours and three more calls go unanswered and without a return of two messages she grows frustrated. She is about to call Jack and ask him about Sarah's reliability when there is a knock on the apartment door.

Linda opens the door to find Sarah, wrapped in a long coat, standing on the doorstep. Without saying a word Sarah pushes past Linda and enters the apartment. She glances around as she unbuttons her coat and throws it across the couch. "Nice place."

Taken aback by what is happening, Linda looks at Sarah with a confused expression. "Sarah? Why… what are you doing here?"

Sarah takes a briefcase and sets it down on the small kitchen table before taking a seat. She opens the briefcase and pulls out two large stacks of folders and paperwork before looking up at Linda. "You gonna sit down or what?"

Linda closes the door to her apartment and sits down slowly, unsure of what is going on. She watches as Sarah works for a few minutes, arranging the paperwork into neat stacks on the table. When she finally finishes she places the briefcase on the floor and looks at Linda.

"Here you go."

"What? Here I go what? What's all this?"

Sarah sits back in her seat and gestures to the stacks of paper with a flourish. "This is the sum total of what I've been able to pull on Omar from nonclassified files. I'm not even going to try getting a classified file out but there's about three pages worth of that information on Omar and I can tell you that from memory."

"Wait a second, time out. Slow down." Linda shakes her head and raises her hands. "Are you telling me you're helping me and you're giving me all of this?"

Sarah nods. "Yes."

"Why? I mean I appreciate it, I think, but I was looking for more of a lead or a name or something."

The corners of Sarah's mouth turn up slightly. "I doubt that. After you came by yesterday I did some digging into your past first. Very interesting stuff. Next I checked on Omar. Also very interesting, though in a horrifying way."

"I—I don't follow you."

"Omar's an enigma. There are bits and pieces of intel on him scattered all over the place but nothing solid. Which is very odd for a man of his reputation. I dug around and found a few intel operations we have on him but none ever went anywhere." Sarah closed a folder she was leafing through and looked at Linda. "Somebody's gone to great lengths to hide this guy. Somebody inside the United States government. That kind of bullshit doesn't sit well with me."

Linda gulps and feels the hairs on the back of her neck stand on end. "Omar's well-connected enough for that?"

"Either that or we just suddenly don't care about a mass-murderer who likes to experiment with biological, chemical and other unconventional weapons." Sarah shakes her head. "No, something's going on. So here's the deal. I'll help you where I can, but I'm not turning into a leaker who gets arrested. I like my job. I like my work. I'm not risking that for you, Jack or anyone else. Got it?"

Linda nods. "Absolutely. One hundred percent."

"Good." Sarah sighs. "I looked through the documents Jack forwarded from you before I came over. You did a stint with a PMC to gather intel, huh?"

"Yeah. It sucked but I think the intel was worth it."

"More than worth it. Watch yourself, though. I may or may not have seen some signals indicating they figured out you were using them for your own benefits."

Linda nods and laughs. "Yeah, I think so too. Thanks, I appreciate it. I can handle them, though."

Sarah shrugs. "Your life. Anyway. You got some good info. Way better than anything we ever got on Omar. Which, again, speaks volumes in and of itself. One thing you flagged as a question for Jack was the lab you found in the basement underground, correct?"

"That's right, yeah."

"Mm." Sarah flips through more papers until she finds what she is looking for. "Here's the redacted version of what was found. It confirms your suspicions. Omar was absolutely using that lab. Ownership of the building had been transferred over to an oil sheik shortly before the estimated timeframe that the lab was set up. Omar has a familial and business relationship with said sheik."

Linda skims through the papers and shakes her head. "This is astounding. But everything about the equipment in the lab and what they were trying to create has been redacted. Isn't there any way I can get more information?"

Sarah sits back in her chair and studies Linda closely. "I want you to listen to me very carefully, okay? We both know Jack, but I don't know you from a hole in the wall. I've already taken the risk of being asked some very uncomfortable questions by bringing you this redacted information through a fairly streamlined internal FOIA request. I'm not going to be breaking the law and risking my job for you, though."

"I know, you said that. I was just—"

"But here's what I will tell you. This guy is on my radar now. He's not on the CIA's radar for some reason so that limits what I can do but I'll do what I can. And as much as I can I will help you wherever possible. If I get intel on him that's unclassified you'll be the first to know. But I need you to not come to me about it, okay? All of this stuff should keep you occupied for a few weeks. Chase whatever leads you want. Just don't try and cross a line with me."

"I won't. But you need to tell me where the lines are if I start trying to cross them inadvertently." Linda stares Sarah in the eyes as she speaks. "I don't want you risking your job and your freedom for me, but I'm not going to back down on anything for anyone. This is personal for me and I'll do anything it takes to find this son of a bitch.'

Sarah nods. "I don't blame you." She stands and looks at the stack of papers. "Good luck with this. I won't be in touch for another month at least. If I have anything I'll email or call you."

Linda stands up and holds out her hand before giving a half-shrug and wrapping her arms around Sarah. "Thank you," Linda whispers, in an uncharacteristically emotional tone.

Sarah squeezes her gently and smiles before hurrying out of the apartment, leaving Linda to slowly sink back into her chair. She stares at the paperwork in front of her, wondering which bits of information to devour first.

Chapter Forty-Six

While Linda's Humvee was loaded down with enough supplies for both her and Frank, both of them spent half an hour laboriously moving over food, water, ammunition and spare fuel from his damaged vehicle to her intact one. The journey to Washington was, under normal circumstances, around four hours from Pittsburgh, but both of them were fully aware of the fact that nothing was guaranteed in the new, darker world they now lived in.

Working through the pain in her leg with the help of some pain medication from a bag of first aid supplies that Frank had been smart enough to grab, Linda took the first shift of driving. They wound their way east and south, traveling through the southern portion of Pennsylvania as they headed for northern Virginia, Maryland and the outskirts of the capital.

The storms that were ravaging the central portions of the country hadn't yet made it as far east as they were traveling and the weather was surprisingly pleasant. Both Linda and Frank wore jackets they had received from Corporal Simmons back at the base but they weren't necessary for the seventy-five-degree weather.

With the windows down Frank rested his head against the door of the Humvee, watching out the side and front as he tried to keep from dozing off. It had been a long few days and an even longer last several hours. A few hours prior he had been on his way to Texas to hunker down with his family and wait out the disaster that was unfolding across the country. Instead of being in relative safety, though, he was on his way to meet some mysterious contact that Linda had in Washington after discovering that the bombs and viral outbreaks weren't the full extent of the terrorist attacks that were taking place.

Decades of hearing government officials on both sides of the aisle talk up the idea of "fighting terrorists" had calloused Frank—and much of the rest of the population—to the concept. While small attacks happened across the country from time to time, people were safer in the US than many other places in the world. The constant cries of terrorism warnings eventually fell on deaf ears as the public ignored their elected leaders, some of whom were sincere and many of whom used the concept as a way to get funding for their pet projects.

All of this added up to a population—including Frank—who were ill-prepared for a true, nationwide attack. Even days after the first bombs went off Frank was still flabbergasted both by the attack itself and by how quickly things had gone south. As he thought more about the situation he asked Linda a question.

"How is it that we had hundreds or more bombs go off with none of them being found? For that matter how did enough people get into the country to plant the damned things without being discovered by the FBI or something?"

"Back when I first met Sarah she told me that it seemed like Omar was being shielded by someone within our government."

Frank turned to look at her. "Someone within the United States government was helping this guy?"

"That's what she said."

"How? Why?!"

Linda shrugged. "We never found out. Over the years we spent digging around pursuing him she tried to bring him up on the FBI and CIA's radars multiple times but nobody would pursue it. Every time someone new would get the case file they would back down shortly thereafter. My guess is whoever was shielding him was also the one helping get people into the country to carry out the actual attacks, too."

"Good grief." Frank shook his head in disbelief. "You're talking about someone systematically betraying their country for years. How's that possible?"

Linda shrugged again. "I don't know. And it could have been a lot longer than just years. It's been seven years since I went in with the invasion. I've spent most of my time since then chasing after this guy, but he was active long before then. Maybe years. Maybe decades."

"Decades of people living here, just biding their time?" Frank let out a whistle. "That sounds impossible."

"Under normal circumstances I would agree. But if they had someone protecting them here and keeping the feds off their backs…" Linda trailed off. "Anyway I'm not saying that's what happened. But it's plausible."

Frank sat quietly for several more minutes, digesting the information from Linda before speaking again. "How do you know this Sarah person's still in Washington?"

"She worked out of Langley for years. Last time I talked to her was a couple months ago. She was still working there, in an annex to the CIA headquarters. With any luck she'll still be there."

Frank blanched. "Seriously? We're going into the CIA's headquarters? Are you crazy?"

"Why's it crazy?"

Frank shifted in his seat and stared at Linda. "Going into the capital when tensions are as high as they are right now seems pretty crazy. You've seen how even the tiniest towns are; that's going to be ten times worse! But on top of it you want to go visit the CIA? Don't you need an appointment or something?"

Linda shrugged. "I doubt she's at her office. I know where she lives. And if she's not at home then we can find her at her office. She worked in an annex. They had high security but it wouldn't be like strolling up to the main headquarters."

"Wouldn't she have evacuated?"

Linda glanced at Frank and shook her head. "Not in a million years. She's a career worker. Loves her country more than anything else. She wouldn't abandon her work for something like this. In fact this is probably the *last* thing she'd abandon her work for. No, she'll be there doing one thing or another." Linda sighed. "I just hope she'll be willing to tell me everything she knows this time, given the situation."

"Come again?"

"For all the help and clues and leads she gave me to help me try and track down Omar she never compromised her rules. She never gave me classified information or leaked anything to me. I understand why she did it but right now's not the time for holding back information."

Frank rubbed his eyes and pushed back against his seat as he tried to find a more comfortable position. "This sounds stupid."

Linda smiled at him and raised an eyebrow. "I'd be happy to chuck you out on the side of the road and let you walk to Texas if you'd like."

Frank closed his eyes and leaned his head against the door again. "Just shut up and drive."

Chapter Forty-Seven

T he scent of death hangs in the air. The death is several years old, existing solely in the memories of the woman who walks down the narrow alley, but she can still smell it. She covers her nose with her sleeve, hoping to filter out the scent but because the scent is in her mind it does not change.

The alley is dark and hot even though the late afternoon sun is hidden behind the tall buildings. Dust swirls in the air as a warm breeze rushes down between the buildings. The woman pulls her shemagh up to cover her mouth and nose and squints, not wanting to put on sunglasses due to the low light in the alley.

She steps lightly on the uneven stones, brushing her gloved hand against the side of the nearest building. The first building on her right in the alley is new but the second and third are not. The first is made from steel and concrete but the others are made out of adobe bricks. She stops partway down the alley and pauses with her hand on a wall, staring at the ground. A dumpster that once sat in the alley years ago is no longer there but she remembers the spot nonetheless.

The pattern of bricks on the wall from when her face was pressed against them. The long scars from where the buckles on her uniform scraped as she took cover behind the dumpster. The smooth spot where she knelt as she waited for death's embrace.

Linda traces the line of one of the scars on the brick with a finger before the distant shout of a man talking to someone jolts her back to the present. She moves on, eyes flicking to the left and right as she traces the backward journey of her steps from years past. She walks another twenty meters down the alley and stops to look at a building to her left. The house has been completely renovated. It looks like nothing she remembers but it is the right house.

"Hello?" Linda speaks in Persian as she knocks on the door and looks through the open window. A child appears at the window and responds with a snaggle-toothed smile.

"Hello! Who are you?"

Linda lowers her shemagh and smiles at the child. "I'm a visitor. Is your mother or father home?"

The child looks behind her as a woman walks into the room. She wears a head covering and long robes and her face is plain with a quizzical expression. She takes her daughter by the shoulders and speaks.

"Can I help you?"

"I'm a visitor. Do you have something to drink?"

The woman nods and opens the door, looking both ways down the alley before stepping to the side. "Please, come in." Linda enters the house and the woman beckons for her to follow. "Come. This way."

"Thank you."

Linda studies the interior of the house carefully as she walks through, noting with grim satisfaction that it is, indeed, the same building she remembers. There have been extensive repairs and renovations and changes to the inside and outside but there is no question about which building it is.

The woman retrieves a jug of water and pours it into a simple cup on the table. She sits down at the table and holds her daughter in her lap while Linda sits down on the opposite end and drinks deeply of the cool liquid.

"What are you doing here?" The woman asks, not sure if Linda knows enough of the language to converse fluently.

"I was here once, years ago, and wanted to visit again. I remember there being a small park near here and I hoped to see it. Do you know the place?"

The woman nods. "I can take you there if you'd like."

Linda smiles. "If you can just tell me the way I'll find my way there."

The woman gives Linda directions and they speak for a few moments longer. Linda remains coy about her reasons for being in the country and the *woman does not press her for details. Visitors are rare in the area and the woman is fascinated by every piece of information that Linda provides. When their conversation is done the small girl jumps off of her mother's lap and runs to open the front door. Linda reaches into her pocket and pulls out a packet of chewing gum she had been saving and hands it to the girl.*

"Thank you for your kindness. Be sure to share these with your mother?"

The little girl beams at the treat and proudly displays the gum to her mother. The woman smiles and nods in appreciation to Linda. "Thank you!"

Linda smiles back and speaks to the girl's mother. "No, thank you. I appreciate your kindness."

The woman and her daughter watch as the mysterious stranger leaves as quickly as she arrived. The little girl looks up at her mother with a questioning expression. "Who was she, mama?"

The girl's mother watches the stranger disappear down the street and closes the front door. "Someone very sad. Someone very, very sad."

Chapter Forty-Eight

The four-hour drive under normal conditions stretched into twelve hours due to various delays and it was the late evening before Frank and Linda began nearing the capital. While the cities and towns they passed by were all dark, as they approached Washington Frank could see that there was a glow on the horizon that grew brighter the closer they got.

"Are those lights?" Frank squinted at the tree line and rubbed one eye.

"Sure looks that way." Linda adjusted her grip on the steering wheel as she turned off of the road onto the shoulder. Sitting atop a hill far outside town Linda parked the Humvee and switched off the engine. She got out first, taking her rifle with her, and climbed up on top of the roof of the vehicle for a better view.

"What can you see?" Frank stood below, watching as she scanned the area with her rifle scope to see what the situation was like.

"Huh." Linda muttered to herself as she took in the sight below. From their position north of the Potomac River she could see that most of Washington, Langley and a good portion of Arlington were bathed in the warm yellow glow of artificial lighting. The area aglow was roughly seventy square miles and covered most of the main government buildings as well as huge swaths of residential areas and undeveloped land on both sides of the river.

As Linda examined the edges of the areas with power compared to those without she realized that electricity wasn't the only thing that set the area apart. The sections of the cities that had power were mostly ringed by roads and highways that formed natural barriers between the areas. Light armor and foot patrols were clearly visible along the roads, along with the construction of guard towers that stood twenty feet high and were equipped with spotlights and cameras.

In areas with open fields, residential homes or places where there were no roads to separate the lit from the unlit sections, fifteen-foot high barriers were actively being pushed into place. While the barriers were largely unfinished there were enough boots on the ground from local, state and federal law enforcement—as well as from the Army—that Linda could see what they were doing quite plainly.

"They're setting up a survivor city."

"What?" Frank scrunched his eyebrows in curiosity and confusion. "What's a survivor city?"

Linda didn't look away from her scope as she replied. "They're setting up a perimeter around Washington and half of Arlington. It's a huge area of land they're cordoning off."

"Wait, they're surrounding the capital? Like with Pittsburgh?"

So caught up in what she was doing, Linda didn't hear Frank's question. After she had examined the edge of the region with power she turned her attention into the heart of the area. As she watched she saw covered vehicles traversing the streets, stopping in front of houses and offloading crates of supplies. Residents of the houses collected the contents of the crates and took them into their homes under the watchful eye of police officers that looked like they were deployed on every street corner.

In some of the homes that were on the northern side of the river and close enough to see inside Linda could make out the shapes of people milling about. Some looked like they were eating dinner, others were sitting and talking around their tables and some were even watching their televisions.

"Linda?" Frank climbed up on the Humvee and stood next to her, squinting as he looked out over the city. "Are they doing what they did in Pittsburgh?"

Linda shook her head. "No, this is different. This is definitely a survivor city." She lowered her rifle and sat down on the hood of the vehicle.

Frank sat down next to her and poked her in the arm with a finger. "What's a survivor city and why are you so distracted by it?"

"Hm?" Lost in thought again, Linda turned to Frank as she processed his question. "Oh. Right. Sorry. I learned about them years ago, part of basic training. It was a relatively new concept they were teaching everyone. Biological warfare was on the rise and they figured that it was only a matter of time before something —either man-made or natural—swept across the country. So some egghead in a lab came up with the idea of survivor cities."

"So they're refugee camps?"

"Sort of. Not really." Linda raised her rifle again to look at a long line of vehicles waiting at a makeshift gate that had been set up on one of the highways. "There are a couple dozen sites in the country that were designated as survivor cities. If a national disaster ever occurred that shut down the power grid or disrupted our transportation systems the plan was to pull people from other areas of the country into the survivor cities. That would make it easier to take care of people by limiting the distance supplies and such would have to be distributed."

"I'm surprised they still have power."

Linda shrugged. "Probably part of the emergency protocols. If they have that many vehicles, up, though, then I bet they're starting to relax the requirements around checking every nut and bolt before they're allowed out." Linda frowned as she watched the activity below. "This is really odd, though. It doesn't look like they were hit by the virus. I'm seeing biological scanning equipment around the perimeter where they're screening people coming in but that's it. No body bags, nobody in isolation suits and no signs that anything's wrong." She lowered the rifle and cocked her head to the side. "Why the hell would Omar hit a place like Pittsburgh with a virus but not hit the capital?"

"That does seem weird. Do you think they were supposed to get hit by it but didn't because something went wrong with the attack?"

"I have no idea. This would probably make a lot more sense if I knew which cities were targeted and which weren't."

Frank reached for Linda's rifle and he looked at the area through the scope as well. "So where are we going?"

"See the curve in the river, over there? That big building's the CIA headquarters. Just a bit upriver from there is a small complex with a brick building. That's where we have to go."

Frank zeroed in on the area and nodded. "Looks easy enough. It's close, too. Can we just drive in?"

Linda chuckled as she hopped off the hood of the car. "No way."

"Why not? They've got that road open into the city and it looks like they're letting people through, right?"

"We're not going through the checkpoint."

"Why not?"

Linda crossed her arms and shook her head as she looked at Frank. "Look at what you're sitting on. Do you really think that a couple of random people in a military vehicle are going to just drive through the gate? They'll be all over us before we get within half a mile of the place wanting to know where we got it, where we've been and where we're going. And—assuming they don't shoot us on sight for suspicion of stealing military hardware—I somehow doubt they'll be enamored with us for wanting to visit the Central Intelligence Agency in the middle of a national disaster."

Frank's shoulder's slumped farther and farther throughout Linda's rant. When she finished he slid off of the car and handed her rifle back to her. "All right, fine. So what's your plan?"

Linda's eyes sparkled as she grinned. "We sneak in."

"ARE YOU *FREAKING* INSANE?" Frank hissed under his breath to Linda as they crouched together behind a row of hedges. Twenty minutes prior they had parked the Humvee behind a house in a residential neighborhood half a mile from the edge of the perimeter. Linda's insistence that they sneak into the city past the patrols rather than simply going in with everyone else didn't sit well with Frank mostly because he figured the consequences for being caught sneaking in would be far worse.

"Keep quiet and be still!" Linda was at the end of the row, peeking around the corner. A patrol consisting of one LAV and a pair of Humvees was rolling slowly down the street. One soldier was atop the LAV swinging a spotlight back and forth while the Humvees each had a soldier atop them with handheld flashlights.

"As soon as these guys pass we'll make a run across the road, okay?"

Frank closed his eyes and suppressed a groan. "Where are we going after that?"

"There's a white two-story house with blue trim. We'll head around that, through the gate on the side and into the backyard. From there we'll wait for the patrol to round the next corner before continuing on."

Frank crawled up next to Linda and looked out across the street to see the house she was talking about. "Got it. I'll follow your lead."

The next few minutes went by with agonizing slowness as they waited for the patrol to continue on out of sight. During their walk from where they stashed the Humvee down to the neighborhood where they were hiding Linda had assured Frank that sneaking in was the best possible choice they could make.

Getting caught sneaking in would likely result in them being taken to an intake center where they would be delayed with biological scans before being released with a slap on the wrist. Because they weren't carrying any heavy weapons or illegal materials on them they would be much less likely to be thrown into a holding cell or—at worst—shot than they would if they drove in. Frank still didn't buy her explanation but her military experience outweighed his protests so he followed behind, doing his best to help keep them both safe.

Crouched behind Linda, Frank noticed her shifting uncomfortably as she rubbed her injured leg. He tapped her on the shoulder and whispered to her. "Are you okay?"

"I'm fine." She nodded. "Stop worrying about it."

Frank had asked her the question repeatedly as he noticed her having trouble working the pedals in the Humvee and while they were walking but her answer was the same each time. "I'm fine. Stop worrying about it." The relative severity of the injury was still fresh in his mind and she hadn't let him take a look at it since they had linked back up together outside of Pittsburgh.

"You should really let me take a look at it and redress the bandages." Frank whispered again, pushing back against her protests.

"Frank." Linda glared at him. "It's fine. Drop it, okay?" Frank shook his head and sighed as he sat cross-legged on the ground next to her. A moment later she stood up and motioned at him. "Get ready. They're almost far enough away."

Frank stood next to Linda and watched the patrol as they made the turn at the end of the street. Linda took off without a word, moving across the front yard of the house they had been hiding near. Frank followed her, ready to reach out and help if she looked like she was going to fall. On the other side of the street Frank reached out and opened the gate to the backyard she was going for, then closed it once both of them were inside the wooden fence.

The house next to them was abandoned like many of the others in the neighborhood as many of the residents had died or gone elsewhere in the first few days after the attacks. Based on looking at the contents of the backyard and house, though, Frank couldn't tell that anything was amiss. A swing set and small wooden castle sat on freshly mown grass while a patio set with large cushions and a round glass table sat on the back porch.

Frank peeked inside a window as they walked through the yard, noticing that the interior of the house looked lived in but not damaged in any noticeable way. Linda was at the rear of the yard, standing next to the fence with her head tilted by the time he caught up to her.

"Hey." Frank whispered to her as he looked back at the house. "This place looks like there are still people living here."

Linda shook her head. "Nope."

"How do you know?"

"There was a sticker on the front door. Green for occupied, purple for unoccupied and red for uninhabitable. This one has a purple tag."

"I guess we shouldn't turn on the lights, huh?"

Linda rolled her eyes. "Not the best idea, no." She stretched up to see over the fence and immediately grunted in pain before grabbing onto the fence to steady herself.

"Okay, seriously?" Frank grabbed Linda's arm. "You need to stop and let me take a look at that leg."

"I'm fine, Frank, really."

"No you're not. Stop trying to hide it and let me take a look and help, okay?"

Linda slid slowly to the ground, gritting her teeth from the pain. Frank took a look at her leg and noticed a dark red stain that hadn't been there earlier in the day. "Hell's bells, Linda. It's bleeding again. When were you going to tell me this?"

Linda shrugged. "It's not a big deal. Besides, we have more important things to worry about."

"No, actually we don't. Not right now."

"Frank—"

"No, don't you try and argue with me. We've been going all day. It's time to stop for a while and gather our strength before we continue. It's only one in the morning. We can get inside the house, get some food, get your leg cleaned up and have a few hours of rest and leave before sunrise, okay?"

Linda looked for a moment like she was going to argue with Frank but in the end she sighed and nodded. "Fine. Help me up and let's get inside. We'll need to find someplace away from the windows if we're going to have our lights on, though." Frank nodded and helped Linda to her feet before the pair headed to the back door of the house. Linda was ready to break the glass when Frank reached out and twisted the knob to find it already unlocked.

"In we go." Frank helped Linda inside where she made a beeline for a nearby couch and threw her backpack down before flopping down on it.

"Can you check the house?" Frank already had his pistol out and was taking off his backpack in preparation to sweep the house when Linda posed the question.

"Already on it."

Chapter Forty-Nine

A quick check of the house confirmed it was empty. Electricity was still on and Frank found a pot in the cabinets though he had been unable to locate anything more than a few crumbs in the pantry. He pulled a can of soup from his pack and combined it with the contents of an MRE to form a late dinner for Linda and himself. Twenty minutes after they arrived, Frank had a pot of canned soup bubbling on the stove and was busy heating up a pair of side dishes from the MRE in a pan. It was only another minute before he was scooping it all onto plates and bowls.

He limited his use of his flashlight to very brief intervals while stirring the food and once he was done he took the food back into the living room and placed it on the coffee table. "One second, I'll get some water."

Linda looked at him and shook her head. "No. Not tap water. Get bottled water from our packs."

Frank shook his head and frowned. "Not tap? How come?"

Linda was midway through slurping down a spoonful of soup when she replied. "Water might be bad."

Frank eased onto the couch next to her and looked at her as he took his plate and bowl. "The water might be bad?"

Linda nodded, breathing through her mouth to cool down the hot food before responding. "Public water treatment usually requires a lot of chemicals to make it sanitary. Those chemicals are trucked in and water treatment plants only have a week or two worth of chemicals on hand at any time."

Frank's eyes widened as he realized what she was saying. "Oh. So if they haven't gotten any shipments, which they probably haven't, then... yikes."

"Yeah. I mean it's *probably* safe to drink but I'd rather not take the risk. Packaged food and bottled water is the name of the game right now. We could always boil some if we had to but we've got enough that I'd rather not take the time."

After finishing their meal Frank insisted that Linda let him take a look at her leg. She protested at first but finally relented, and when she slid down her pants Frank winced. "Shit. This is starting to look infected."

Linda leaned up on the couch and looked at the wound before putting her head back and closing her eyes. "I'm sure it'll be fine. Can you just clean it up a bit?"

Frank helped Linda roll over onto her side and sat on the coffee table with his light a few inches from her leg as he looked it over. "I don't know; this could get serious pretty fast. I need to get in there and clean it out some."

Linda grunted. "Do whatever you think you need to. There might be some topical treatments there, but if not we'll need to find a medic and convince them to hand over some antibiotics."

"Something tells me that'll be more difficult than it sounds." Frank pulled out the first aid kit from his backpack and set it on the couch. He cracked it open and put on a pair of rubber gloves before getting tweezers and rifling through the bandages. A kit had been in each of their Humvees and Frank had insisted on carrying one with them despite its bulky size and weight.

Frank shook his head as he carefully picked at the edges of the wound, squeezing out the pus that was building up and applying liberal amounts of topical antibiotic cream over and inside the edges. "You really need to stay off of this thing. One side's starting to heal but the other burst open again and is infected." After opening one of the half-dozen butterfly bandages he applied it to the center of the wound and worked his way outward. When he was done and was certain they were going to stick he applied another layer of antibiotic cream and finished by wrapping a few layers of gauze around her thigh and taping it down so it couldn't move.

"Finished?" Linda moved around on the couch and looked down at the bandage. "Sheesh, use enough gauze there?"

Frank shrugged. "It'd be nice if the silly thing would actually stay closed so it could heal a bit, y'know?"

Linda smiled and started pulling her pants up while still laying down. She gave up after a few seconds of struggling and slouched back. "I'll just stay here for a while."

Frank looked around the room and grabbed a decorative quilt from near the fireplace and spread it out over her legs and chest. "You need to get some sleep."

"Nah, I'll take first—"

"Like hell you will." Frank pushed Linda back down as she tried to sit up and wagged a finger at her. "Close your eyes and get some sleep. You look like hell."

"So do you!"

"I'm not having to deal with an infection on top of everything else. Get a couple hours of sleep and I'll wake you up and you can keep watch till dawn. Okay?"

Linda started to argue but sighed and closed her eyes instead. "Fine. Two hours."

"Deal." Frank grabbed another quilt and sat down in an easy chair on the other side of the room. After spreading out the quilt he placed his pistol on his lap and leaned back in the chair. He realized that it was the first time in days that he had gotten a chance to really sit back and relax in a comfortable chair. While the feeling made him happy at first his joy soon waned as he wondered how many more times he would be able to perform such a simple action.

Minutes ticked by as Frank slowly rocked back and forth in the

304 MIKE KRAUS

chair, watching out the glass back door of the house. He had drawn the blinds after they first entered the house though they were thin enough that he could easily see out into the yard and over the fence to the neighborhood beyond. Every twenty minutes or so a new patrol rolled down the street in front of the house, the engines of the vehicles rattling the windows.

The first two patrols that went by while Frank was on watch made him nervous enough that he got out of his chair and crouched near the front door, listening to hear if any of the soldiers were coming towards the house. Once he realized that they were paying almost no attention to the buildings inside the patrol zone he relaxed and stayed in his chair each time they went by.

Three in the morning came and went and Frank started feeling drowsy. He got up from his chair and knelt down next to Linda, putting the back of his hand against her head. She didn't feel like she had a temperature and she was sleeping deeply so he left her alone and walked back into the kitchen. He began rummaging through the cabinets in the kitchen and moved into the bathroom, dining room and then the upstairs level.

After half an hour of quiet searching Frank headed back downstairs with a small medical kit and four more bottles of water in hand that he had pulled from the back of a closet. The house had been cleaned out of any other useful supplies and all of the clothing in the closets were too small to fit either of them. Frank packed the new supplies into his backpack before sitting back down in his chair.

The soft glow of the distant sun was barely visible when Linda began to stir. Frank stood up quickly and went to sit on the couch next to her, restraining her from moving around too much until she got her bearings.

"Hey. Keep quiet. A patrol should be coming by any minute."

"A patrol?" Linda rubbed her eyes and looked at Frank with a confused expression before she remembered where she was and what was going on. "Right. Patrol. What time is it, anyway?"

Frank handed Linda a bottle of water and pulled the edge of the blanket back from her leg. "Time to get moving. First I'm just gonna take a peek under the gauze and see how it's looking." Frank lifted up the edge of the gauze in between the strips of tape and pointed his light at her leg. "Still a bit red but not like it was earlier." He sighed with relief and pulled the blanket back over Linda's leg. "I think it's looking better, honestly. We need to change the bandage again tonight, though."

"Good. What did you mean by its 'time to get moving,' though?"

Frank was already up and shouldering his pack as he answered. "It's just past six. The sun'll be up soon and we have a fair distance to go, don't we?"

Linda blinked a few times and shook her head. "Did you get any sleep last night?"

"Nope. Now get your pants on and grab your backpack."

Linda was quiet as she got dressed, took a few more sips of water and put her backpack on. Frank was already out in the backyard, listening for patrols as he tried to remember where they were relative to what he remembered of the city when they had looked at it on the hill the day before. Linda slowly walked up to him and peeked over the fence at a patrol that was moving away from the house before she whispered to him.

"How long is it between patrols?"

"About twenty minutes. That one just left so we can go anytime now."

"Thanks."

Frank glanced at her. "For what?"

Linda kept her gaze locked on the vehicles. "For the extra rest. I appreciate it."

Frank shrugged and nodded. "No problem. You're the one with the hole in your leg still. I figured you needed it more than I do."

"Thanks all the same."

Frank nodded and grunted in affirmation before motioning his head at the fence. "You think you can make it over?"

"Yep. Just give me a boost. I'll try not to tear the bandages off when I land."

Frank rolled his eyes. "Great. But, uh, where are we going after this?"

"Deeper into the city."

"What?"

"Trust me, okay? I'll lead, you follow. Stick close to me and keep your gun hidden. We don't want to start a firefight with the military. If I crouch low, do the same. If I walk normally, do the same and pretend like we're talking to each other."

"Say what now?"

"Frank, we're inside the patrol area. If we get deeper into the city and we're spotted then they'll think we were already admitted through the main entrance and that we're just out walking around. If they see us this near the edge then we'll have an issue."

Frank groaned and leaned up against the fence. "I'm not liking this plan at all right now."

"Duly noted. Give me a boost?"

Linda moved slowly through the neighborhood, keeping as much weight off of her injured leg as possible. Frank followed close behind, watching behind them for any patrols or residents in the city. While the pair had their handguns well hidden and they didn't appear too out of place, Frank felt like they stuck out like sore thumbs.

Being as close to the edge of the survivor city as they were, Linda told Frank that their chances of getting away with being seen were slim to none. The farther into the city they moved, though, the less suspicious it would be if a patrol or resident spotted them walking around with backpacks on.

Halfway between the outer loop of the beltway and the Langley High School Linda spotted a green sticker on a house across the street. "Thank heavens." She turned to Frank and patted him on the shoulder. "I think we're in the clear. Let's try to look like we belong here, okay?"

Chapter Fifty

S*ometime in the Past*

THE WOMAN *with short blonde hair pulled into a tight ponytail looks out from under her umbrella. The streetlights are blinding even in the heavy downpour, though neither disguise the bright glow of the sign above the building in front of her. The blonde woman enters the building, folding her umbrella and sliding it into a canister in the lobby. She shakes raindrops from her overcoat as she walks quickly across the tile, her high heels clicking with each confident step.*

The woman stops at the center of the counter at the other side of the lobby. Behind the desk atop tall stools sit half a dozen men and women in uniforms. A young man is in one of the center seats and he looks up at the blonde woman as she stops.

"Can I help you, madam?" The man speaks in German.

"I'm here to see a prisoner." The woman responds in German with almost no hesitation, though her accent is clearly from out of the country.

"Which prisoner, madam?"

"Rahim Namazi." The officer behind the counter is looking down at his

computer when she speaks and upon hearing the name he glances up at her with an odd look on his face.

"Rahim Namazi? May I ask the reason for the visit, madam?"

The woman answers by sliding an unsealed envelope across the counter. The officer glances at the envelope with a raised eyebrow before taking it. He opens it and unfolds the single sheet of paper on the inside. By the time he reaches the bottom of the letter his expression has changed from one of suspicion and curiosity to one of stone-cold professionalism.

"You understand, madam, that this is highly irregular?"

"Indeed."

The officer rubs his hand across his brow and scratches his head as he considers the letter's contents. After a moment's thought he gives a soft sigh and taps at the keyboard. "I will need your name, madam."

"Linda Rollins."

"You are American?"

"Yes."

The man gives her a slight smile. "Your German is exquisite."

Linda returns the smile with a nod. "Thank you."

The officer continues to tap away at his keyboard until, a few seconds later, a small printer on the desk spins up. It spits out a label with a barcode beneath Linda's name. The officer hands her the label and points to her chest. "Peel it off and stick it there. Make sure it's visible at all times."

Linda does as the officer instructs and he nods. "Thank you, madam. Have a seat, please, while I arrange for the visit."

Linda walks to the side of the lobby and sits at the end of a row of chairs. Her overcoat hangs low, revealing the dark red dress that goes just below her knees. A small clutch is in her hands, the strap wound around her left wrist, and she slowly untangles it and places the bag on her lap. Her external confidence and cool demeanor is merely a façade. In truth she is uncomfortable and worried about how she appears. Every movement she makes is being recorded and she wants to ensure that there is absolutely no reason for anyone to question why she is at the station.

She glances around as she pulls out a phone from her clutch. She unlocks it and opens an encrypted messaging application and types out a brief message to an unnamed contact, shielding the screen between her leg and her hand.

'It worked.'

The reply comes a few seconds after she sends her message.

'You're in?'

'Nearly. Waiting for meeting.'

'Any questions about letter?'

'None.'

'Good. Don't take long. In case they start asking.'

'I won't. Any info on his ties? Flying blind here.'

'Still nothing. Pushing hard but red tape is thick.

'Understand. Will message when done. Thank you.'

'Good luck.'

Linda sighs and turns the phone off, locking its contents behind a layer of encryption impossible to break without the correct passphrase. She slips it back into her clutch and straightens her back. She starts to tilt her head to crack her neck when she remembers where she is and how she is dressed and slowly stops. As the minutes of waiting drag on she feels every blister on her toes and heels from the tight shoes. Each time the front doors open she feels a draft on her exposed legs and represses the urge to shiver. She focuses every ounce of her being on appearing as casual and in-charge as possible.

Finally, when she is about to go back to the counter to ask what's taking so long, an officer approaches her. He is different from the first, wearing markings on his uniform that indicate his higher rank. She stands as he approaches and he nods to her.

"Madam." He speaks in German as well. "Come this way, please."

The officer turns without hesitation and walks away. Linda is frozen in shock for half a second before she moves to follow him. After days of planning how to talk her way out of a dozen different possible situations that could arise she is shocked to find that none of it was needed.

Linda and the officer walk through a side door and into a wide hallway. Supply closets are on either side, followed by small offices and conference rooms. After a few turns they arrive at an elevator and the officer motions for Linda to step inside. "After you, madam."

Linda nods to him and steps inside. The elevator is clean but sparse, with no controls or handholds or anything mundane or remarkable visible. The design appears to be solid steel or aluminum on the floor and sides. The lights built into the top of the elevator are set behind an inch of composite glass and a small camera is mounted in one corner next to the lights.

The station on the west side of Berlin is one of the main processing stations for illegal immigrants into the country as well as the location where potentially high-value 'agents of terror' are brought for questioning. Although Rahim Namazi has not committed any acts of terror that the government is aware of his place of origin places a high degree of suspicion upon him.

The officer steps into the elevator and opens a small panel next to the door. He inserts a key into a hole inside the panel and taps out a code on a numeric pad. "Mind your hands and feet, madam."

The doors close swiftly with a whoosh and a clang and the elevator starts moving. It descends two floors, down past the holding cells and into the interrogation area. The officer looks at a small tablet computer in his hand and speaks as the elevator moves downward at an agonizingly slow pace.

"Are you familiar with the particulars of Mr. Namazi's entry into Germany, madam?"

"Just the highlights, I'm afraid. He was denied entry so he came over illegally. I'm not sure why he was denied or what his reasons were for trying to immigrate."

"Correct, madam. That is, essentially, all we know. He's refused to speak to us or counsel so we have very little to go on. He is from a region of Iran that has produced a high number of suspected and confirmed agents of terror, though, so we're holding him until we get more information."

Linda nods politely, not hearing anything she doesn't already know. She does, in fact, know a great deal more than what she told the officer but the success of her mission relies upon her keeping that a secret. "There will be no recording devices active in the interrogation room, correct?"

"Yes, madam, as requested."

"And no external viewers?"

The officer hesitates. "Yes, madam. Although it's most irregular that—"

"So I've been told." Linda's tone remains cordial even as she speaks bluntly to the officer. He clears his throat and nods in response.

"Very good, madam."

Another minute passes in silence until the elevator finally stops. The officer enters another code on the pad and twists his key and the doors open, revealing a brightly-lit corridor. The officer steps out of the elevator first. "Follow me, please, madam."

Linda follows him, cringing internally with each step. Each step in her high heels echoes harshly in the enclosed space and she finds herself wishing she was back in a pair of sneakers or combat boots. Her attire is necessary for the ruse, however, as it both adds legitimacy to what she claims and provides a visual distraction for those around her who might otherwise notice that all of the points of her story don't quite add up.

Halfway down the hall the officer stops and motions to a small room to the side. "The interrogation room, madam."

Linda stops at the door and tilts her head. "Is he inside?"

"He will be brought in momentarily."

"Very good." Linda brushes past the officer, pushes open the door and enters the room. She walks to the seat with its back to the large mirror on the side wall. Her overcoat slips off with a shrug and she folds it over the back of the seat. Her clutch is carefully placed on the corner of the table and she gently adjusts its position.

As she sits down the door opens and three people appear. The first and third are both officers, though the man in between them is not. He is dressed in plain clothes—a button down shirt and khakis—and carries a nervous expression on his face. The officers escort him to the seat opposite Linda, point to it and then step back behind him.

"Gentlemen." Linda raises an eyebrow as she speaks to them in German. "Please leave us. There is to be absolutely no monitoring of this conversation."

The officers, already knowing full well what she has told them, slowly walk out of the room. They each cast a wary glance at the man seated across from Linda and the first man stops and speaks to her as he watches the man. "We'll be right outside, madam. Should you need anything."

Linda makes a show of adjusting her burgundy dress as she runs her tongue across her teeth. "Should I need anything I will let you know. Until then I expect to be left in peace." The officer nods and exits the room, closing and locking the door behind him.

With the officers out of the room and—she desperately hopes—no one watching from the room behind the mirror Linda turns her attention to the man seated across from her.

"Mr. Namazi, is it?"

Chapter Fifty-One

As Frank and Linda meandered down the road they began to see more residents of the survivor city. Most were in their homes, watching out the windows or talking on their front porches. Others carried bags and boxes stamped with military codes from the road into their houses and Frank nudged Linda and whispered to her.

"What's with the boxes?"

"Looks like rations. Two, maybe three days' worth could fit into a box of that size for a family of five."

Frank nodded. "Makes sense. Smaller, more condensed distribution inside a place like this versus trying to deliver emergency supplies to every Tom, Dick and Harry across the country. Makes you wonder why they aren't having the people walk to pick them up, though."

"Probably for disease and population management. You get a big group together in one place and even the smallest problem turns into something major."

A few seconds later, as Linda turned to look down the opposite street, she stopped and snorted. "Or because of that."

Frank looked off to his side and his eyebrows shot up. Half a dozen large covered military vehicles were parked on the street in front of a row of stately white houses with large lawns and white picket fences. On the other side of the street from the houses sat a wide field that normally would have been empty.

Today, though, the field was filled with soldiers who were working to assemble a dozen or more structures. The structures were dark green in color, one story tall and looked like they were made out of a combination of aluminum and plastic. A door sat in each end of the structure and the roof had a slight slope to it. Through one of the open doors of a finished building Frank and Linda could see a row of bare metal cots lined up on one side.

"Are those emergency shelters?" Frank whispered to Linda, not wanting to attract the attention of the soldiers.

"Not just emergency shelters. Long-term shelters." Linda shook her head in disbelief. "That sort of verifies that they're setting this place up as a survivor city. I bet it's another reason for supply deliveries, too. They're going to be filling up every square inch of free space in the area they've selected with shelters and they're making sure their distribution points are up to the challenge."

"How many people do you think they'll cram in here?" Frank tugged at Linda's sleeve as he asked the question, prompting her to keep moving. One of the soldiers had noticed them standing in the middle of the road and Frank wanted to stay out of any trouble.

"As many as they can. There's already something like six million people in DC and the surrounding areas. You could probably squeeze five times that many in here if they set things up properly."

"People who live here won't like that, will they?"

"No. No they will not. Especially if they're forced to give up space in their homes to house people."

Frank glanced at Linda. "They'd do that?"

She nodded. "Absolutely. National emergency, martial law, suspension of habeas corpus. All the good stuff."

"Lovely." Frank sneered in disgust.

"Come on, now." Linda slapped him on the back, adding a thick layer of sarcasm to her words. "It can't be that bad, right?"

THEY CONTINUED down the two-lane road that wound along like a country road with stands of trees and large fields on both sides. Linda's assurance that they would blend in better walking on the road—and therefore looking like they belonged there—made sense even if doing so made him extremely nervous.

At times, though, it felt like they were out in the middle of nowhere as they walked for minutes without seeing any sign of homes or other people. At other times it was clear they were moving into a more populated area as the houses—most of them two stories or taller—grew more frequent. If it wasn't for the increased frequency of these homes along with manicured lawns, pruned trees and immaculately painted wooden fences Frank would have thought he was about to hear banjo music. The thought that he was just a few miles from the capital made him rethink how he saw the Northern Virginia area.

After cutting across a few streets and fields the pair drew closer to Langley High School. It had been a while since Linda had visited the area but she remembered using the school as a land-mark more than once when she was driving around and was certain she could find her way to the CIA annex from there.

"How much farther?" Frank leaned up against a tree to take off his shoe. He smacked it against the tree a few times and a pebble fell out.

"The school's not far from the main building." Linda pointed out to the east as she shielded her eyes with her left hand from the sun that was still low in the sky. "We can cut down through the neighborhood next to it and out towards the parkway and the river."

"Linda." Frank sat down slowly and motioned for her to join him. "Let's take a break. I could use some rest." Frank had noticed that Linda's limp was growing worse and wanted to get her to stop and give her leg a break before she hurt it even further. He figured that mentioning her injury would only lead to an argument about how it wasn't really hurting.

"We really should keep moving."

"Just twenty minutes. We've been walking all morning and I'm beat."

Linda gave him a sideways glance before nodding in agreement. "Ten minutes. Then we keep going."

She sat down slowly, trying to hide the pain in her leg, and sighed as she hit the ground. The wide-trunked oak was at the edge of the last field before they would reach the school. The wide, squat set of brick buildings sat just over half a mile away past a few more roads and groves of trees beyond the field, just out of sight of Frank and Linda from where they were sitting.

Glad for the moment's respite not only for Linda but for himself, Frank leaned his head back against the tree and closed his eyes. A cool autumn breeze was gently shaking the leaves above, lending a serenity to their rest that he found to be both surprising and relaxing. Events of the last several days had grown far beyond anything he could have ever imagined. When he had stared at the burning wreck of his truck wondering just what was going on the thought that he'd be traipsing across half the country with a stranger would have never entered his wildest dreams.

"Linda?" Frank kept his head back and his eyes closed as he spoke.

"Hm?"

"What if this contact of yours isn't there?"

"Hm." Linda thought about the question for a long moment before responding. "She lives in a townhouse somewhere in Wildwood Hills, north of the river near the Westfield shopping mall. I don't know her exact address but we can search there."

Frank opened one eye and turned his head to look at Linda. "You know where she lives?"

"Mhm. The general area."

"Were you two friends?"

"Nope."

Frank paused. "How do you know where she lives?"

"I have my ways. Or, should I say, *had* my ways. I was involved with more than a few clandestine missions in my pursuit of Omar."

"Were any of them government sanctioned?"

"Nope. All of them were self-funded. Sarah gave me a bit of support but it was never very much and never official."

"Huh."

"What is it?"

Frank shrugged, scratching his head and brushing off a leaf that had fallen from the branches overhead. "That's just a completely different world for me. It's hard for me to imagine devoting my life to pursuing one person for years and years."

"Well, you're part of the club now. Though we don't have 'years and years' left to get this guy."

"Is there a membership card?"

Linda chuckled and leaned back against the tree. She closed her eyes and took a deep breath, focusing for a few moments on the cool air and the smells of autumn. The decaying leaves mixed with the chill in the air, taking her back to the falls she had spent in Maine.

Her hunt for Omar had turned her into a hermit, causing her to shun her friends, abandon her family and spend her days poring over pilfered documents, satellite images and internet message boards. She spent thousands of hours talking with other veterans, extracting information from obscure papers and learning how to speak three different languages all in the effort to track down Omar's location.

She rarely left the house, heading out once every few weeks to get food. The only exceptions were the occasions she was forced outside to do work on her house to fix a broken shingle, replace the boards on the back deck or drain the swamp that used to be her swimming pool. A few of those times had been in the fall and winter and it was that smell she could recall— along with the feel of her rough denim jeans and soft flannel of her shirt—as if it was only yesterday.

Not wanting to dwell on the past for fear of letting old emotions worm their way back in, Linda sat up and went through her backpack. "Energy bar?" She held one out to Frank and he accepted it gratefully.

"Thanks." He unwrapped the bar and ate it quickly before balling up the wrapper and putting it into his pocket. He looked at the lump under Linda's pants where her bandage was and nodded at it. "How's that doing?"

"It's…" Linda paused for a second. "It hurts like hell. But I'll make it."

Frank did his best not to show surprise over the small admission of weakness and nodded thoughtfully. "I know you will. We shouldn't have much farther to go."

"Nope." Linda nodded. "We'll head north from the school to the river. The annex is within sight of the main building so we'll be fine."

"Hey!" The shout came from behind Frank and Linda and they both turned, reaching for their pistols at the same time. They had been so engrossed in both their conversation and their own thoughts that they hadn't noticed the sound of a car driving by, stopping and shutting off.

Frank was the first to see that the source of the voice was a police officer standing near the road, his hand on his gun. Frank pulled his right hand back around to his side slowly, glad that he hadn't yet taken his pistol out. He waved at the officer and smiled. "Hi there!"

The officer didn't return the smile and shouted back at them instead. "I need to see your admission papers!"

Frank turned to glance at Linda, keeping a forced smile on his face as his eyes grew wide and he hissed at her through clenched teeth.

"What now?!"

Chapter Fifty-Two

The man seated across from Linda Rollins is afraid. That much is certain. There is a fear in his eyes that is genuine, the type of fear that cannot be manufactured except from raw, pure emotion. He is afraid of something. What that something is, though, is what she hopes to discover.

"Mr. Namazi?" Linda speaks his name again after waiting several seconds for him to respond.

He takes a short breath and looks at her, nods and speaks in broken German. "Yes. I am Namazi. Who you are?"

Linda smiles at him, switching languages. "Mr. Namazi, perhaps English would be better?"

The man is clearly startled and caught off guard by her words and he narrows his eyes. His response is hesitant but smooth with a deep middle eastern accent. "English is preferable, thank you. But who are you? Why are we speaking without my counsel present?"

Linda eyes Namazi coolly. "You are from Iran, yes?" She doesn't give him a chance to answer. "Of course you are. Sixty-four years old as of three months ago, born in the north and selected to receive a state-funded education after scoring at the top of the charts on the national tests."

Rahim Namazi audibly gulps. His heartbeat increases and a few beads of sweat break out on his forehead. Linda continues, rattling off fact after fact about him that she memorized only a few hours prior to arriving in Germany until, finally, he has enough. He slams his palms on the table and stands halfway out of his chair.

"Who are you, woman?! What is it you want?"

Linda leans back in her chair, a thin smile on her lips. "My name's not important, Mr. Namazi. What is important, however, is something you know." She leans forward again, across the table, lowering her voice to a confidential whisper. "And if you tell me what you know then I can help you.

Namazi sneers, trying to appear tough but still rattled by Linda's knowledge of his past. "You? An American? Helping me? I don't believe you."

Linda shrugs. "I'm here on behalf of our government, Mr. Namazi. We need to know something about someone you once worked for. In exchange we're ready to offer you immediate immigration into the United States and set you up with a home and a job in any city you'd like."

Namazi's eye twitches at the corner and he sinks back into his chair. He struggles with what he hears, somehow knowing what question will come next and trying to decide if the potential reward is worth the risk of answering said question. He murmurs a prayer beneath his breath and pushes his fingers through his hair before looking up at Linda again.

"What do you want to know?"

"Tell me about Farhad Omar."

There it is. The question Rahim Namazi expected.

"Who is that?" He resists it at first, though he knows his attempt is ultimately futile.

Linda sighs. "Mr. Namazi. I already know the answers to many of the questions I'm going to ask you." This is not entirely accurate but the lie is convincing. "If you try to dodge the questions or deceive me then I will walk out of here and you will spend the rest of your life rotting in a cell or you'll be shipped home where Omar will have you killed within a week. Do you understand?"

Namazi hesitates before giving in. When he gives in, though, he does it in his own way, knowing that the woman from America can't possibly know every single thing about his time spent with Omar.

"I was one of his scientists."

"Go on."

"Our goal was to create pathogens that had different properties. Some *infected quickly. Some had no symptoms. Some could live for weeks or months in hostile environments."*

"What was the purpose for this?"

Namazi shrugs. "I don't know. He kept us segmented from each other. We were not allowed to speak with anyone who wasn't in our group."

"Mm." Linda nods. She already knows everything Namazi has told her. The next question will, if he answers, reveal new truths. "Where is Omar now?"

Namazi looks puzzled by the question. "Where is he? How would I know?"

Linda keeps her expression steady. "You worked under the man for months. Surely you heard things."

Namazi shakes his head. "I was kept under lock and key, along with the rest of the scientists. We knew only our work."

"Mr. Namazi." Linda sits up straight in her chair and leans forward. "We have reason to believe that you were more than a simple scientist working under Omar." Namazi's eyes grow large as Linda speaks. "We have reason to believe that you worked with him and that you have intimate knowledge of what he was doing and where he might be right now."

Panic grips Namazi's heart and etches itself across his face. He stutters nervously as he tries to speak. "I—I don't kn—know what you're—"

Linda opens her clutch and pulls out her phone. She presses the power button and the screen lights up, displaying the time for both herself and Namazi. "In ten minutes I'm going to receive a text message. It's going to contain information from a contact that will either confirm or deny our suspicions about your connections to Omar. If you tell me the truth—right here and now—then my deal still stands. If you don't, however…" Linda trails off, leaving the implication hanging in the air.

Namazi licks his lips nervously. He had expected to face off against the American woman holding information that she did not have, but the tables have been turned. "I—"

Linda's phone buzzes with an incoming call. She glances at the screen and stands up, grabbing her clutch before she walks towards the door. "Excuse me while I answer this, won't you? You can have an extra moment to think over my offer."

Outside in the hall the pair of officers that escorted Namazi to the interro-

gation room are standing twenty feet away. They are holding a quiet conversation when they notice Linda step out and hold her phone to her ear.

"Hello?"

"We have a confirmation."

Linda's eyes narrow. "Why the call instead of a message?"

"Not safe. Have to go offline. Contact you in three days."

The line goes dead before Linda can respond. She turns to look back through the door, her eyes meeting Namazi's. He shivers as he sees her expression, knowing that his only advantage is gone. She knows who he is and has all the leverage over him that she needs.

Linda turns and walks down the hall to the two officers and interrupts their conversation. "Excuse me, gentlemen."

"Yes, madam?"

"Pursuant to the orders dictated in the letter I gave your superior earlier, I'll be taking the prisoner with me to a secure location for immediate deportation to the United States."

"Madam, you can't just do that. You have to go through the courts."

Linda reaches into her clutch and pulls out a second letter bearing the forged signature of the German Chancellor. "Take me to your commanding officer. I want to see him immediately to arrange transport of the prisoner."

The officer looks at Linda blankly before taking the letter she is holding out. The officer skims the letter, gulps, and nods nervously. The next several minutes consist of another slow elevator ride back upstairs, the passing of the letter to a superior officer and a slow elevator ride back downstairs. As Linda dives deeper into her act of subterfuge she is surprised to find that she is feeling less nervous instead of more so. She tempers her confidence with caution, though, lest she overstep herself and reveal the charade.

When the elevator doors open Linda's confidence vanishes as she hears the shouts of a pair of officers from a room down the hall. She and the group of officers with her dash down the hallway and stop near the open door to the interrogation room. The two officers in front of the door are throwing themselves at it as they try to force it open, but it will not budge. Linda cannot hear what is going on inside the room due to the shouts of the officers so she stays out of the way as she nervously glances around, wondering if she should just abandon her mission.

It takes four minutes for the officers to realize they cannot break the door *down by themselves, to shatter the small glass window, and use a pole to release the chair wedged on the inside of the door. When the chair comes loose the door opens and the officers pour into the room. Linda follows close behind, stopping at the entrance. She looks into the room and feels a wave of defeat pass through her.*

The body of Rahim Namazi hangs from the ceiling, his neck at an odd angle and his corpse slowly twisting in circles. A thin piece of wire secreted away days ago on the inside of his belt is looped around his neck and fastened to a thick pipe running above the ceiling tiles. The officers quickly pull him down and begin resuscitation efforts.

Linda doesn't bother sticking around to watch them fail. She leaves the building through a fire exit and quickly heads back down the street. The commotion at the station over Namazi's suicide is enough to cover her tracks. When she arrives at her car she pulls out her phone and taps out a short message. When she's done she turns off the phone, puts it back in her clutch and closes her eyes.

With the death of Namazi another lead connected to Omar is gone. Another thread and another clue is irreparably removed and there is nothing she can do to fix it.

Linda grabs the steering wheel with both hands, squeezing until her fingers tingle and her hands are white before she lets out one short, shrill shout.

"Dammit!"

Chapter Fifty-Three

"Hey!" The officer shouted at them again and advanced a few steps. "Did you hear what I said? I need to see the admission papers from you two!"

Linda was about to step forward and reply, but Frank took her by the arm and held her back. "Let me try." He whispered in her ear and immediately stepped in front of her, giving the police officer a big smile.

"Hello there, officer! I'm sorry but we're just out for a walk." Frank looked back at Linda and gave her a quizzical look. "Did you remember to bring our papers?"

Linda patted her pockets and jacket and shrugged. "Ugh, I think I forgot."

Frank turned back and gave an exaggerated shrug of his own. "I'm sorry, officer. We'd be happy to take you back and get them."

The police officer's eyes narrowed. "Travel anywhere outside of your domicile without your admission paperwork is strictly forbidden. When did you arrive here?"

Linda was about to reply when Frank cut her off. "Arrive? We've lived here for about five years now." The officer's gaze shifted between Frank and Linda and his right hand relaxed slightly as he kept it resting on his holster.

"What're your names?"

"I'm Frank, this is Linda." Frank took a half-step to the right and turned to gesture to Linda. He noticed that her right hand was still behind her back and quickly stepped back in front of her.

"Where's your place?"

Frank turned and pointed back the way he and Linda had come from. "Lawton street, last house on the left." The officer looked down the road and rubbed his hand across his nose, considering what Frank was saying. Frank could see the man wavering as he tried to decide what to do and decided to press the issue slightly further.

"We've been so cooped up in the house that we just plain forgot about the papers. I'm really sorry, and like I said we'd be happy to take you back there to get them and show you."

The police officer looked at Frank and Linda and sighed as he shook his head and took his right hand off of his holster. "No, don't bother. But you two need to get back right now and make sure you never leave without them. If those military assholes stop you then you'll be looking at the inside of a cell until they strip search you and stick needles in your arms enough times to be satisfied you're not carrying a virus."

Frank smiled again and stuck out his hand. "Thank you so much, officer. I really appreciate it."

The police officer took Frank's hand and shook it, then touched the brim of his hat as he looked at Linda. "Ma'am. You two have a nice day."

The officer took a few steps back before turning around and heading back to his car, glancing around as he did. Frank kept still with a smile on his face until the car had started and was out of sight, then turned to see Linda still had her hand behind her back.

"Seriously?" Frank hissed at her before turning back to the tree to grab his backpack. "You were going to shoot him?"

Linda lowered her arm and shrugged. "It seemed better than letting him take us in."

"Yes. Great idea. Shoot your gun off in the middle of a military-controlled city. And kill a cop. What could *possibly* go wrong?"

Linda was quiet for several seconds before she, too, reached for her backpack to put it on. "You did well there. I'm impressed."

"Mom always said I was a people person." Frank snorted as he adjusted the straps on his bag. "Can we just get out of here now? Maybe stay away from the roads since we don't have whatever the hell 'admission papers' are?"

"Yep." Linda pointed off across the field. "We'll head that way. The terrain looks rougher but the annex is straight that way. We can stick to the woods and backyards as long as possible."

Frank didn't say anything else until they were safely in the woods, and even then he kept his voice low for fear of drawing unwanted attention. "What's with the admission papers thing anyway? Have we devolved to Nazi Germany levels already? That's terrifying."

"It sure sounds like it, doesn't it?" Linda shook her head. "It's probably how they're keeping track of people who've been cleared by the patrols for any biological contaminations and just to make sure they're supposed to be here. My guess is that it was set up by the feds and they're tasking all local law enforcement with performing random checks." She gave Frank an odd look. "How'd you come up with that street name, anyway?"

"I noticed it while we were walking by and it stuck in my head for some reason."

"Yeah, but that was quite a risk, telling him we lived on a nearby street. What if he had taken us there in the back of his car?"

Frank chuckled. "That would have been the point to start shooting."

"I'll keep that in mind if we get stopped again." Linda smiled at Frank's joke before her face fell again. "You're right about one thing, though."

"What's that?"

"This is terrifying."

HIGH WOODEN FENCES separated the backyards of the stately
homes from the overgrown woods behind them. Located less than
a mile from the CIA headquarters Frank had expected the entire
area to be well-manicured and show signs of... something. As he
thought about it he realized he didn't know what he had expected.
An affluent, relatively normal-looking neighborhood right next to
the spy center of the United States was definitely not it, though.

There were signs of activity in nearly all of the homes they
passed but the soldiers had not yet gotten to the point of setting up
shelters that close to the CIA's headquarters. Eventually, though, a
reinforced fence would go up around the building and shelters
would be built up to that point. Every square inch of free space in
the cordoned-off area was to be used for shelter except the most
vital portions that ensured some form of governance continued.

Truth be told, though, the governance that still existed was
merely a shell of what it had been only weeks prior. The façade of
ordered chaos within the survivor cities was necessary to keep the
civilian population from panicking any more than they already
were. Federal and state resources were stretched past their breaking
point and any further disruptions would ensure that there would be
no recovery from the attacks.

Every possible stop was being pulled out to keep life inside the
cities as normal as possible but those in charge knew it would only
last so long. Direction from those higher up was nonexistent as all
three branches of government were still reeling from the attacks.
Trying to govern was impossible under the circumstances. Those
who were watching the chaos unfold from the shadows knew this
and were biding their time as they eagerly waited for the opportunity to unleash their final blow.

While Frank remained relatively unaware of much of what was
going on behind the scenes Linda's mind was racing with a mixture
of fact and fiction. Her years of service and pursuit of Omar had
endowed her with a unique grasp of what the government and
Omar were both capable of. She had initially expected the govern-

ment's response to the attacks to be far better than it was, though, and as each day passed she realized more and more that Omar's plans had been an unmitigated success. This caused the same question to go through her mind over and over.

What's he going to do next?

Chapter Fifty-Four

"You are ready?" *The question posed seems simple. The taking of life is rarely simple, though, even to those who have been trained for years to take it without question. The taking of dozens or hundreds of lives is even less simple. To some it looks easy. Walk in, press a button, die a hero to a few and a villain to most. The truth is far more complex.*

"Yes." *The answer is given without hesitation. Hesitation is weakness and weakness is culled without hesitation.* "I am ready."

The asker of the question nods and pats the answerer on the shoulders before moving on to ask the same question of yet another. The man asking the questions is tall and slender with a long white beard and hair completely covered by a simple white keffiyeh. His tan robes brush against the floor as he walks. Splitting sandals filled with darkly tanned and calloused toes peek out from beneath the robes as he moves from person to person, each of them dressed far differently than he.

Each of the thirty men being asked the same question is from the same region as the man with the robes but all hide their origins in different ways. Some shave their heads while others dye their hair and skin. Some are fairer-skinned than others thanks to their genetics and blend in naturally wearing blue jeans, a polo shirt and a windbreaker.

Each of the thirty men—and dozens more like them in key areas across the country—have trained for the question for the last ten years. Each man arrived in the country at a different point in time and then slowly the men began to link up into groups of three and four. These cells were kept small and discreet on purpose to avoid detection by authorities. Of the nearly three hundred men in the country only six ever became involved in activities that attracted enough attention for them to be caught. The cellular structure of the men ensured that even when they were caught there was no possibility of them divulging the ten-year plan.

Every six months the cells received a visit from their handlers. Some visits would be accompanied by new information and training regimens. Some visits were merely check-ups to ensure that the men were getting along and following the orders. For most of the ten years any orders that were issued to the cells consisted of seemingly mundane activities.

Go to this location. Work this job. Begin this exercise routine. Move to this state.

Issued from the top of the food chain and disseminated through a network of lieutenants, the orders remained mundane for years. Their chief purpose was to ensure loyalty and train obedience. The orders that were not mundane came in the final few months.

The thirty men standing in a circle, each in normal clothing, look at each other. There is fear in every man's eyes but that fear is overpowered by their sense of loyalty and duty and commitment to their orders.

After the question is asked to each of the thirty, the man in the robes issues his final order, "Gather your tools and use them with righteous fury!"

The thirty men obey the command without hesitation. Some pick up guns. Others carry small explosive charges in backpacks and satchels. Others carry knives. Two take no weapons but climb into large trucks, instead, each with reinforced bumpers and doors that cannot be opened with anything less than a wrecking ball.

IN THE CITY of Pittsburgh the death toll is unfathomable. Bodies litter the streets and buildings and the survivors dare not leave their homes for fear of contracting the horrific disease that has laid waste to the city. The disease is incredibly lethal and fast-acting and cannot survive outside the human body for long, though. It burns through the population at speeds greater than any plague ever seen and then dies out just as quickly.

Thunderstorms sweeping across the region do little to help with sanitation as the corpses in the street begin to swell and burst. Flooding is prolific and quickly overwhelms the city's sewer systems, causing the water levels in the streets to rapidly rise. Bodies, trash and raw sewage are carried throughout the city streets and into the rivers that are overflowing their banks.

Outside in the perimeter set up by the Army and Marines, the situation is more fluid than that of the rising flood waters. Patrol routes are constantly changing due to the water levels and there are gaps in the perimeter through which people and the remnants of the disease can escape. Drones—both land and air-based—are knocked out of commission by the water, leading to a forced delay in the search for survivors.

The delay and disruption caused by the rains is a boon to the thirty men. They had originally planned on having to smash through the perimeter to bring down even more horror upon the city but they are able to slip in unnoticed in between patrols. They no longer fear the disease that ravaged the city both because it has burned out and because even if they somehow become infected they won't live long enough for the disease to do them much harm.

Chapter Fifty-Five

"Dammit!" Frank jerked his arm around towards his chest, hearing a tearing in the fabric of his jacket. Linda stopped ahead of him and turned around to see what was going on and raised an eyebrow.

"You okay there?"

Frank picked at the tear in his jacket before sighing and taking off his backpack. "Yeah, just give me a second to put a piece of tape over this. Stupid fence."

The fence Frank was referring to was a tall length of chain link that wrapped around the perimeter of the annex building, the building's parking lot and the small grassy areas and pond that sat next to it. The fence sat a couple hundred feet from the building at its closest point which was near the edge of the parking lot. A nearby dumpster provided the perfect aid for Linda to scale the fence first and land gingerly on a car parked just a few feet away. Once she was safely across Frank went next, but in his rush to make sure his backpack didn't get caught on the top of the fence he inadvertently got his jacket snagged instead.

Linda walked slowly back to Frank, taking it easy on her leg as the pain had started to return. "Are you hurt?"

"Nah. Just my jacket."

"Good." Linda looked back at the building as she leaned against a nearby car to take the weight off of her leg. "When you're done we'll keep going."

As Frank pulled out a roll of duct tape he had stuffed into his bag a day or so earlier, he watched Linda carefully. She was sweating profusely, breathing hard and kept her right hand hovering near the wound on her thigh as though she was subconsciously protecting it.

"How's the leg?" Frank mumbled as he tore a piece of tape with his teeth.

"Probably should have walked around to find an easier way in." Linda touched her leg gingerly and winced. "It sure doesn't feel great."

Frank slipped off his jacket and put a few strips of tape over the tear. He put the tape away, put his jacket back on and picked up his backpack. "Come on." He reached for Linda's backpack and began pulling it off of her back.

"What are you doing?" Linda tried to grab her pack but Frank had already gotten it off of both arms before she could stop him.

"You need to stop for a while and rest. I don't think this is the best spot, though, so we need to get you inside."

"Frank… honestly I'm fine. Really. Just feeling tired."

"You're still fighting an infection. That much is clear. You need to get inside so you can get some rest."

"Frank—" Linda tried to argue with him but she felt a wave of dizziness wash over her and she nodded. She had been fighting how she felt for the last couple of hours out of pure stubbornness but she could no longer deny the fact that something felt wrong inside her body.

With Frank's help Linda moved slowly towards the building. When they reached the front entrance Frank pulled on the door handle. To his surprise it swung open freely and he looked back at Linda in surprise.

"It's unlocked."

Linda shook her head. "Just for the lobby. The secure areas are farther inside."

The lobby of the building was dark and sparsely decorated and furnished, akin to a small business in an office park. A few paintings hung on the walls, limp-leafed potted plants were scattered about in the corners and there were a few thinly-cushioned chairs sitting across from the receptionist's desk.

Frank stood in the lobby for a few seconds with Linda at his side before a ragged breath from her drew his attention back to her situation. "Here, sit down." He guided her into a seat in the corner and put her pack at her feet.

After digging his flashlight out of his bag, Frank helped Linda slide her pants down and peeled back the bandage on her leg. The wound was slightly inflamed and red but didn't look bad enough to be causing her symptoms. He probed around the wound with his fingers, watching her for any reactions.

"Hey!" Linda pulled her leg away and swatted at his hand. "What the hell are you doing?"

"How much does that hurt on a scale of one to eleven?"

"Bad enough that I'll punch you in the mouth if you do it again!"

Frank sat back and ran a hand across his head and down the side of his face. "It honestly doesn't look that bad. I'm no medical expert but I wonder if the infection moved somewhere else. Or maybe it's just deeper in your leg."

"I know how to shoot things, Frank. Your guess is as good as mine."

Frank put his hand to Linda's forehead and nodded. "You've got a fever. Looks like your 'recovery' back at the house was only temporary."

Linda shook her head. "Never mind that. Let's get moving. Sarah's office is upstairs and we need to see if she's there."

Frank looked up at the ceiling. "Given that the lights are all off I sincerely doubt anyone's here."

"Doesn't matter. We still need to check."

Frank squeezed his eyes shut, pressing his thumb and index

finger against them until his photoreceptors started triggering and bright lights appeared on his vision. He suddenly wished that he had stayed on the road to Texas instead of coming back to help Linda given that her plan—which had been flimsy from the start— was rapidly falling apart.

"Linda…"

"Frank. Don't you say it."

"Maybe we should take a break from this." He turned and gestured to the dark room. "Nobody's here. And despite whatever protestations you may make you are not doing well. I can go back into town and try to find some medicine for you, some antibiotics of some sort maybe?"

"No." Linda shook her head. "Not happening. We can't stop. Omar—"

"Omar what?" Frank licked his lips, not wanting to get into another argument but tired of following Linda into hell with nothing to show for it. "This guy you've been chasing isn't going anywhere in the next few hours. We should just—"

It was Linda's turn to interrupt Frank as she jerked forward, her pants still halfway down and sweat pouring down her face. Strands of blonde hair that had come loose from her ponytail were stuck to her forehead and cheeks and her eyes were full of a fiery passion that both inspired and terrified Frank. Linda grabbed Frank by the shirt and pulled him forward, whispering to him as she spoke slowly, over-enunciating every syllable.

"Frank. Listen to me carefully. I did not survive all the shit I've survived, get shot multiple times—the latest by a fucking *meth head* —break multiple laws and risk life in prison just to *give up* when we're so close." Linda wheezed slightly and sat back, releasing Frank's shirt as she started to topple over.

"Jesus…" Frank muttered as he stood up and grabbed Linda to keep her from falling over onto the hard floor. "Dammit, Linda, this is why I said you need to take it easy."

Frank looked around the room for a few seconds before easing Linda down out of the chair and over to a rug nearby. "Come on.

This isn't going to be comfy but it's better than cracking your skull on the tile."

"Whuh?" Linda's eyes were fluttering open and closed as Frank helped her down. He pushed her backpack under her head and stood up over her, wondering what to do. Her fever worried him and without a thermometer he was at a loss for what to do. "Need to cool you down somehow…" Frank whispered to himself before reaching for her jacket and unzipping it. He pulled her arms out and slid her shirt up a few inches, exposing her stomach. He glanced at the half-dozen scars on her abdomen before unzipping his backpack and pulling out a spare pair of socks and a bottle of water.

"What the hell have you gone through, lady?" Frank quietly talked to himself as he soaked the socks with water and placed one on her stomach and one on her forehead. Linda's eyes flew open at the feel of the cold cloth on her body and she reached for Frank's arm and grabbed his wrist with a vice grip as she stared at him.

"Up two flights. Three eight seven's the door number. I don't know the code to get in. If it defaults to locked on a power outage you'll have to break in somehow. Hopefully the doors auto-unlocked, though."

"No," Frank started, "I'm not going anywhere except to get you help."

"Other than you, Sarah's the only person I trust to help right now. You need to find her. If she's not in her office then I guarantee you she left a clue about where she is."

"I thought you said you know where she lives."

"She's far more clever than you or I, Frank. She might have gone somewhere else. Or she might be hiding in the basement. You need to go up there and grab everything you see. Every scrap of paper, every hard disk. Everything. You understand me?"

"What about you? We have to get you something to treat this infection!"

"This is way more important than me."

"I don't know anything about all of this grand conspiracy bullshit!" Frank gesticulated wildly. "You're the person who has all the information!"

"Twenty minutes, Frank." Linda's voice began to waver. "If you hurry it'll take you twenty minutes. Then we can find Sarah and she can help us with all of this. Including whatever's wrong with me."

Frank clenched his jaw until he was certain he was about to chip a tooth. "Dammit!" He slammed his fist down on a nearby table, immediately regretting the decision as pain shot through his hand. "Three eight seven, right?"

Linda nodded weakly as she put her head on the backpack again. "Remember to grab everything. Just in case she couldn't take something with her. We may need it."

Frank stood up and took his knife out of his bag and stuck it between his belt and pants. He pulled out his pistol and adjusted his grip on his flashlight as he looked down at Linda. "I'm looking for twenty minutes. If I don't find anything then I'm heading straight into town and finding someone to take care of you."

When Linda didn't respond Frank shook his head and cursed silently as he headed toward the doors behind the registration desk.

We are so fucking screwed.

Chapter Fifty-Six

The original run from the park to the house took less than a minute all those years ago. Linda walks slowly now, though, ruminating on the past as she traces a path to the park. She didn't need directions from the woman in the house but asking for the directions and a drink of water gave her a chance to look around the building and confirm she was in the right place.

Even with the distraction provided by the woman and her daughter, the house felt uncomfortable for Linda. The scent of death pushed at her again and she could hear screams in the background as the woman spoke to her. The beeping of gas masks alerting to filter failures was more than she could handle and she had ended her conversation with the woman abruptly just to get out of the building as quickly as possible.

The jumble of thoughts and emotions is more than Linda expected to deal with. Outside, in the street, she pauses and leans against the side of a building with her eyes closed. She takes a deep breath and steadies herself. The screams slowly dissipate and the smell of death recedes. She opens her eyes and pulls the shemagh back up over her mouth and nose. She notices that the sun is hot and bright out in the street and she slips on a pair of reflective sunglasses as well.

Beneath the face and head coverings and the loose fabric she wears over her long-sleeved shirt and jeans, Linda blends in surprisingly well. From a distance she looks like a man who is protecting himself from the elements and thus avoids most stares and questions from those passing by. The westernization of Ahvaz and the country in general has proceeded rapidly in the years since the ill-advised invasion but there are still many who resist change and are happy to see those representing the change "disappear."

Linda continues her slow walk until she finds the place she was searching for. The park, like the house, has changed greatly over the years but it is obviously still the same place. The playground equipment, benches and many of the plants were replaced but there are still remnants of it that line up with Linda's hazy memories.

She walks the edge of the park slowly. Each time she nearly puts a foot onto the prickly green and brown grass she stops. The fresh memories from the alley and the house burn inside her and she doesn't want to relive the memories from the park as well.

No matter what, though, she has a job to do.

Linda reaches inside a pouch beneath her robes and pulls out a small glass sample container. Using a small removable piece of her belt buckle she scrapes a piece of bark off of a tall tree and deposits it in the container. She carefully uses the sharp edge of the metal to carve out a sizeable chunk of the tree beneath where she stripped the bark. The second tree sample goes in a new container. The next three sample jars are filled with dirt and stone from several inches below the topsoil from different areas of the park. The final container is filled with trimmings from bushes and other small plants.

When the sample jars are filled, sealed and slipped back into her pouch Linda exits the park. She heads away from the area in a different direction than she arrived. The possibility of her being followed by someone is slim but she doubles back on her path more than once to ensure that no one is tailing her.

Twelve hours later, after slipping the containers into an international shipment sent by a private courier, she arrives back in the United States. The containers take several days to arrive and thankfully they pass through customs. When Linda picks them up she guards them carefully as she drives to a laboratory three states away.

She visits the laboratory after hours, when two technicians stay after everyone else closes. She enters through a back door in the building and greets the pair with a nod as she holds out a padded bag containing the samples.

"You got everything?" The shorter of the two technicians asks her the question as he takes the bag.

"Everything I could. A lot's changed over there."

"And you're sure it's from the site?" The taller technician reaches into the bag and pulls out one of the sample containers.

"Everything's from the park. The house changed way too much. There's no way there's any residue left there."

"Mm." The shorter technician shakes his head. "You'd be surprised."

Linda shrugs. "There were people there. I wasn't about to start drilling core samples of their walls and floor with them watching."

"You got bark and wood?"

"Soil from three separate spots, too."

The taller technician nods approvingly. "This is excellent. We can work with this."

Linda rubs her arms and looks around, finally noticing the low temperature in the building. "It'd be better if the bodies were still here."

The technicians glance at each other, shuffling nervously. "We're really sorry about that. The cameras never caught who it was, though. And we still haven't gotten an answer from upstairs."

Linda shakes her head at them in an understanding gesture. "Yeah, yeah. I know. You won't get an answer, either. Believe me." Linda sighs and nods at the containers. "Just do what you can with these. I need as much information on whatever was used in the attack."

"We'll try. Finding chemicals from years past is tricky but these look like good samples."

Linda nods. "How long do you figure?"

The taller technician checks his watch. "We'll have the soil samples analyzed right quick. Couple hours max. The plants and tree will take longer. Probably tomorrow night."

"I'm still good to camp out here?" Linda throws her thumb in the direction of a back room of the lab.

The shorter technician nods. "Good to go. You don't have to stay, though. Really. We'll keep this under lock and key."

Linda gives the two men a wistful smile and pats them both on the shoulder as she heads to the back room. "I trust the pair of you. I wouldn't be here if I didn't. But everyone else? No. Not a chance." She stops at the door to the back room and looks back at them before going in. "I'm going to grab a couple hours of shuteye. If you find anything out of place you'd better wake me up."

The two technicians nod rapidly. "We will."

———

THE SOIL SAMPLE *results are completed in one hour, though the technicians wait until a total of three hours pass before they wake Linda. At first she is angry over the delay but their explanation rapidly cools her temper and her attitude turns into concern and fear.*

"I'm sorry." Linda puts her head in her hands and sighs. "I'm jet lagged to hell and back but this still doesn't make sense."

The two technicians look at each other nervously. "What doesn't make sense?" The taller one asks nervously.

"If I understand what you told me correctly, you're saying that you've never seen some of these chemicals before. Right?"

"The spectrograph identified a few. But there are several that are mysteries. Their masses aren't something we've come across before."

Linda sighs and sips on her can of iced coffee she got out of a vending machine. "What's it going to take to identify them?"

Both technicians look down at their feet. The answer to Linda's question is not one they wish to speak out loud for fear of her response.

"Well? Come on, I won't bite your heads off." Linda forces a smile to try and coax them into speaking.

"We don't have the tools required to analyze these samples here. And based on what little we can tell about them… well…"

The shorter technician jumps in to take over for his taller comrade. "They would probably trigger alarm bells at whatever lab took a look at them. You'd need a very sophisticated setup to pull them apart and figure out what they are since there's not much left of whatever they are. Any setup like that's going to have protocols requiring them to report stuff like this to the CDC and who knows how many other agencies."

Linda flexes her toes in her shoes as she tries to restrain herself from showing any outward signs of anger. "So this is another dead end?"

"I'm afraid so." The taller technician shuffles papers on his desk and passes a stack to Linda. "The one thing I can tell you is that the bodies of your team contained chemicals that look very similar to the ones in the soil. They're most likely identical."

Linda snorts. *"That doesn't tell me anything I didn't already know. What about the tree and plant samples?"*

"It'll take a while more for those but I can tell you already that we won't get anything useful out of them." The taller technician's face is crestfallen. *"I am very sorry. And we'll keep doing the tests just to see if we can find anything else out. But just... I wouldn't hold out much hope. I'm sorry."*

"It's fine." Linda takes a sip from her drink. *"Don't worry about the rest of the tests. You two have done more than I deserve."*

The shorter technician goes to a filing cabinet, pulls out a thin folder and returns to Linda with it. He pushes his glasses up on his nose as he passes it to her. *"Since you're here and we're already giving you bad news I might as well save a few stamps and give this to you in person."*

She looks at the label on the folder and raises an eyebrow at the technician. *"A final report on the disappearance of the bodies, eh? I'm surprised they bothered after all this time."* Linda touches the folder to her forehead and closes her eyes. *"Let me guess: an unknown intruder broke in and absconded with the bodies, likely for illegal body part harvesting or other purposes."* Linda cracks open the folder and skims the top page, laughing as her guess is confirmed.

"What a bunch of bullshit." Linda closes the folder and throws it onto the table. *"Body part harvesting. What kind of idiot decides that should be the official excuse?"*

"We're still trying what we can, but..." The taller technician trails off and shrugs.

"I appreciate that. Don't worry about it, though. If their official line is that the bodies were stolen by someone wanting to sell their months-old livers and lungs then we won't find anything else out." Linda taps the folder on the table and shakes her head. *"This is a message, you know. Whoever's behind this cover-up is sending me a message. They think they can make up whatever they want and get away with it."* She pauses for a second and shrugs with reluctant acceptance. *"And you know what? They can."*

Linda closes her eyes and leans back in her chair. Her mind is tired and her body is weak. She has spent years chasing her tail around in circles, trying to track down every lead possible. Each one that she finds holds enormous promise but is eventually extinguished. Sometimes time is the enemy. Sometimes the enemy is some unknown adversary, like whoever absconded with the bodies of her fellow Marines before they could be fully examined.

The ultimate enemy, in her mind, is still at large. And she will continue to do whatever she can to find him.

Linda finishes her drink and crushes the can before throwing it into the trash. She stands up and gives a hug to each of the technicians. "Thank you both. I know you risked a lot to do this. If you ever need anything you know how to reach me."

The technicians nod and smile at her. She gathers her things and departs from the lab to head home and lick her wounds of defeat. She needs a long rest and some time to think about her next move. Being repeatedly forced back to square one after years of effort is exhausting and she is tempted yet again to give up. The memories of that day so many years ago haunt her every step, though, and she can not—will not—give up.

Chapter Fifty-Seven

Frank found it odd that the annex building was completely deserted and the feeling that there might be someone else inside with him made him exceptionally nervous. Traipsing around in old barns had its own dangers including the possibility of being shot by the owner. Had he been wandering around the CIA-run building before the attacks when it was staffed, though, he would have most certainly been shot, arrested or—in his imagination at least—taken to some black site in some foreign country to be interrogated for years.

Fortunately, though, while the empty building did have an exceptionally eerie feel about it he hadn't heard or seen any sign of anyone else around. In fact, as he whipped his flashlight back and forth along the main corridor on the first floor, he noticed that each room he walked past appeared exceptionally empty. A few of the rooms were conference rooms while others looked like supply rooms or offices but all were both unlocked—a fact he was relieved to discover—and devoid of both people and all but the most basic of office equipment.

Frank stepped into one of the offices and pointed his light at the desk, a small side table and then at a filing cabinet in the corner. Each of the cabinet's drawers were open and a key was still inserted in the lock at the top. Instead of being filled with paperwork, though, the cabinets were utterly empty. As Frank glanced around further he noticed that there wasn't a sign of paperwork or personally identifying items anywhere else in the room, either.

"What the hell's going on here?" He pulled open each drawer on the desk, finding only a few pencils and pens rolling around inside. He went across the hall to the next office and found it to be virtually identical to the first. All of the drawers and cabinets were empty, nothing identifiable was visible and it had the look and feel of a room that had been systematically cleared out.

Frank headed back to the hall to continue searching for a way up to the next floor. Signs were posted on the wall every few feet that contained ominous warnings to visitors about what would happen if they were caught with a camera, recording device or even glancing in the general direction of something they weren't explicitly authorized to view. After circling the main floor twice in search of some stairs Frank finally found them behind a closed door down the main hall near the back of the building.

Frank stepped out onto the second floor and looked at the numbers on the wall next to each door. The numbers on the first floor had all started with one while the numbers on the second floor all started with two. "Guess I'll go up another flight, huh?" Frank muttered to himself as he turned back to the stairs before stopping and looking into an open office next to the stairwell. While all of the others had been empty he noticed a gleam of metal inside office one two zero. Frank scooped the source of the glint off of the desk in the office and held it up in front of his flashlight, giving a slight grin as he realized what he had found.

"Hello there. I wonder why someone left you behind." He slipped the set of keys into his pocket and looked through the drawers in the office, but found nothing else of interest besides a few framed photos and some discarded coffee cups. The sight of the personal items made him wonder if the offices on the first floor hadn't actually ever been used and he decided to take a slight detour to check the rest of the rooms on the second floor.

Five minutes later, after hurrying from room to room, Frank had decided that the offices on the first floor were, in fact, never used. The filing cabinets in the offices on the second floor were all twice as wide as the ones below and the locks were much larger. They too, though, were left open and were all empty, but there were bits of plastic tabs and a few metal supports inside the cabinets that gave the impression that they had actually been used before. Some of the locks, too, were missing keys while others had their keys inserted.

It looks like they cleaned out every single piece of information this place ever held. Frank mused to himself as he walked around. *I bet they were ordered to evacuate and this was part of the process. Makes sense, too. Destroy any sensitive data and it doesn't matter if a couple of random people break in and look around. I bet the headquarters still has power and is locked up tight, though.*

Despite the less sterile and more lived-in look of the rooms on the second floor Frank failed to find anything of value in any of the offices he checked besides the car keys he had noticed earlier. A quick glance at his watch to check the time made his stomach churn as he remembered Linda lying downstairs and he ran back towards the stairs in an effort to make up for lost time.

On the third floor it took Frank less than thirty seconds to find room three eighty-seven. It, like all the others, was open and Frank could see before he even walked in that it was more like the rooms on the first floor than the second. There were no personal photos anywhere in the room, the trash can only had a few torn pieces of paper wrapper from some sort of food and the filing cabinets and drawers were completely empty.

Not wanting to fail Linda, though, Frank did his due diligence and methodically searched through the office, combing each drawer, nook and cranny for any signs of information. After a few minutes of searching he plopped down in the chair behind the desk and shook his head, wondering just what he had gotten himself into.

"I could be in Texas right now." Frank scrunched his nose up as he responded to himself in a mocking tone.

"You could! But nooo. You had to go after the crazy lady to try and help her save the world."

Frank sighed and turned slowly in the chair as he wondered what to do next. Going for help would, at best, result in he and Linda being taken into custody but it would also mean that she would get medical treatment. When she recovered, though, he was certain she would kill him for ruining her quest to stop the man she believed was behind everything.

He leaned back as the chair turned and idly looked around the office when his gaze fell on the computer monitor. His eyes narrowed as he looked at the corner of the monitor and he sat up suddenly, pointing his flashlight at it. "What on earth?" Frank reached out and plucked a small yellow sticky note from the corner of the monitor, holding it close to read the tiny handwriting that covered the entirety of the scrap of paper.

L – We were right. I hope I'm right about you coming here. If you are reading this, come to 2854. I know you know the street.

The note was unsigned but knowing what he knew it was easy for Frank to figure out who wrote it. "She knew Linda would come here." Frank sat back in the chair, still holding the sticky note as he thought about everything Linda had told him.

While he would have never said it to her face he had started to consider her as something of a crackpot. It was true that the terrorist attacks were quite real but her stories about pursuing a mysterious seemingly all-powerful person across the globe were a strain to believe. When she added in the theory that the person she had spent years pursuing was behind the attacks Frank had found it frighteningly difficult to believe that what she said was true.

He had still gone along with her, though, going as far as abandoning his own journey home to help her. Doubt had clouded his mind but it was there no more. The small scrap of paper with four sentences on it somehow made more of an impact on him than all of what she had told him herself. All trace of doubt was gone and his thoughts reeled as he struggled to figure out what to do next.

"Crap!" Frank scrambled up out of the chair as he remembered that Linda was still downstairs. He ran down the hall and stairwell and burst back out into the hallway on the main floor. He skidded to a stop in the lobby where he knelt down next to Linda's still form and put his hand to her forehead.

She still felt hot to the touch but was breathing relatively normally though there was a certain amount of extra effort in her inhalations that he hadn't noticed before. He took the socks off of her forehead and stomach and shuddered as he felt how hot they were before pouring more water over them and placing them back on her body.

"Hey." Frank whispered to Linda as he took her hand. "Hey, you still with me?"

Linda's eyes fluttered open and she moved her lips quietly for a few seconds as she tried to speak. "Yeah." Her voice was hoarse and she closed her eyes again after speaking.

"Hey! Don't go to sleep on me! Listen, your friend, Sarah Cala-whatever—I found her office. It was empty, just like the rest of them. They must have cleaned out all the files before the employees left. But she left something up there for you."

Linda opened her eyes again and Frank held the note in front of her face, shining his flashlight at it. "Apparently she thought you'd be coming here to find her. What was the name of the street she lived on again?"

"In Wildwood hills. North of the river." Linda took the note with a shaking grasp, flicking her eyes across it as she tried to read the words through her blurred vision. She dropped the paper and Frank took it, then she grabbed him by the arm with a surprisingly strong grip. "Get us there."

Frank shook his head. "No way. We are going to find you a doctor right now."

"Frank." Linda's grip grew stronger and Frank found himself unable to shake free. "Get. Us. There. Now."

"You've got a fever! You could die!"

"She will help. Just get there. Twenty minutes if you find a car. Just hurry." Linda's grip faded and she slumped back onto the floor, closing her eyes as she drew in fast wheezing breaths. She had expended all of her energy in the span of a few seconds. Frank watched her closely, placing the wet sock back on her forehead where it had slipped off when she was pulling on his arm.

Standing up, he walked over to the front door of the lobby and looked out at the parking lot and the grass and trees beyond. It was a beautiful day outside, but the sight meant nothing to him. His stomach churned as he tried to decide on the best course of action. Whatever choice he made would be one that he could not come back from.

If he took Linda to those who were in charge of the survivor city then she would most likely survive, but she and he would both end up trapped in the city for an indefinite amount of time. If, on the other hand, he took her to try and find her contact from the CIA then Linda could perish regardless of whether they found this "Sarah" person or not.

In all of Frank's thinking, the one thought that was no longer present was the question of whether Linda was right about Omar or not. The simple note from Sarah proved that Linda was telling the truth. It also proved that the threat, as radical and crazy and impossible as it seemed, was real. And somehow he had gotten himself tangled up with the only person who had put enough pieces together to possibly disarm the threat.

In a choice between saving Linda's life but rendering it impossible to stop Omar or giving her a chance to stop Omar but risking her life on someone who might not even be there, Frank was at an impasse. Every second that ticked by while he wrestled with his decision was another second that Linda slowly slipped toward the abyss.

Chapter Fifty-Eight

The parking lot of the CIA's annex building was far larger than Frank had initially thought. When the building was constructed a few years prior it was originally intended to only be filled to one fifth capacity. The extra capacity would be filled over the course of ten to fifteen more years and the parking lot would be expanded as necessary to accommodate the additional workers. When the building—plus an additional hastily constructed wing— was nearly filled with new employees after just two years the parking lot that had been in front of the building was expanded to wrap around both sides as well.

While Frank had been frustrated by large parking lots before the annex parking lot took that frustration to a whole new level. He ran past the parked cars, mashing the lock button on the key fob as he tried to locate the vehicle associated with the keys he had picked up from inside the building. When he started going through the lot it hadn't occurred to him to start on one side and work his way around in a systematic fashion. Instead he spent twenty minutes running back and forth until he finally heard a light beep off to one side near the fence out in front of the building.

Frank ran to the vehicle that made the noise and reached for the door handle. As he opened it, though, he fumbled with the key fob and started to drop it. He grabbed for it and in the process mashed all of its buttons—including the alarm—with his fingers. The deafening alarm startled him and he dropped the keys again as he tried to push the alarm button again to make the sound stop.

Seconds passed by in panicked agony as Frank tried again to push the alarm button before realizing that he needed to manually unlock the car to turn off the alarm. He inserted the key and turned it, then opened the car door only to find that the alarm was still going off. Sliding into the driver's seat he jammed the key into the ignition and turned, then let out a sigh of relief as he was rewarded by blissful silence.

Laying partway on his side in the car Frank took a second to sit up and adjust himself before looking around at the interior. It was a small sedan not unlike one they had driven a few days earlier. The back had a few pieces of trash and odds and ends in it and one of the two cup holders had a thin travel cup sitting in it that was filled with a suspiciously fuzzy liquid. Other than that, though, the vehicle looked like it was in good shape and it was big enough to hold Frank, Linda and their two backpacks.

Frank shook his head as he put the car into reverse, lamenting the fact that their Humvee was still out on the edge of town with their rifles, extra ammo, food and other gear in it that they wouldn't be able to access. He briefly considered the possibility of somehow driving out of the cordon in the sedan, around to their Humvee and then taking it to find Linda's CIA contact, but abandoned the idea almost immediately due to how long it would take and the risks that would be involved.

As Frank wound through the parking lot towards the front of the annex a flash of movement in the rearview mirror caught his attention. He glanced at the mirror and his eyes grew wide as he saw the shape of three green camo vehicles racing down the road toward the annex. Frank twisted in his seat to get a better view and confirm that his eyes weren't playing tricks on him. Unfortunately, though, it was no trick. Two Humvees and one white police car were traveling together toward the annex at a high rate of speed.

The road in was narrow and twisty but the two Humvees didn't hesitate to go off-road to minimize the amount of time it would take to arrive.

"Shit!" Frank turned back around and slammed down on the accelerator, sending the sedan lurching forward. He turned the wheel and skidded to a stop in front of the annex, his foot throbbing from pressure as the antilock braking system kicked into overdrive. Frank jumped out of the car and ran into the building, not bothering to look behind him as he dashed into the lobby and over to Linda.

"Linda!" Frank shouted at her as he knelt down next to her. "Come on, we have to go! There's a patrol on the way and we have to go now!" Linda didn't respond and Frank leaned in, putting his ear to her face. He could hear and feel her breath on his ear but she didn't open her eyes or show signs of movement no matter how much he pushed, pulled, pinched and shouted at her.

After wasting several seconds trying to wake her up, Frank slid his arms under her legs and back, scooping her into his arms. He turned and ran back out of the building as fast as he could, all while trying to not let her or her clothes fall to the ground. He opened the back door of the sedan awkwardly and slid her inside before slamming the door closed. A quick glance out across the parking lot made his heart leap into his throat as he saw that the vehicles were nearly at the gate and guardhouse out front. The gate was tall and well-armored against vehicular attacks but Frank knew how well the Humvees were built and was certain that they would be able to win if the drivers wanted to smash on through.

Frank turned and ran back into the building faster than before to grab the scattered pieces of clothing on the floor and his and Linda's backpacks. He raced back to the car and threw open the driver's side door before tossing the backpacks and clothes across into the passenger's seat. He paid no attention to the sharp crack of glass as a piece of metal on the outside of one of the backpacks left a chip in the side window.

After getting in and closing his door Frank put the car into gear and quickly took off, heading around the side of the annex towards the back of the building. The parking lot came to an end on the side but there were wide walking paths behind the annex. The sedan jumped the curb with ease though the handling grew looser as Frank drove across the grass and gravel, turning sharply to avoid the well-manicured hedges and trees. He weaved his way through the park-like area until the opposite side of the parking lot became visible, then he turned away from it and headed towards the fence that ringed the perimeter of the annex grounds.

While Frank wasn't sure whether or not he could ram through the fence in the sedan he saw no other option at his disposal. Off to his left at the end of the parking lot sat the two Humvees and the patrol car with two soldiers standing in front of them at the gate with a pair of bolt cutters in hand. One of them glanced up at the sedan as Frank was watching and pointed as he said something to his fellow soldier.

Not waiting to see what they were about to do, Frank glanced back at Linda and shook his head. "Sorry about this." He double-checked to make sure his seatbelt was fastened and then accelerated toward the fence. He was heading toward the section set at the top of a small rise in the ground and aiming for the area in between the fence posts themselves. He hoped that if he hit the rise at the right speed the car would impact the middle or upper portion of the fence which would then tear it off of the posts and allow him to drive over the chain link.

Formulated in blind panic and executed with numerous flaws, Frank's plan somehow worked exactly as he had intended. The car's wheels momentarily soared above the ground by approximately three inches as he hit the rise at a speed of nearly sixty miles per hour. The nose of the car, angled upward, hit the middle of the fence above the mid-way point causing the most stress on the middle and top wire connectors that held the fence to the posts.

The fence, while effective at keeping casual intruders out and tearing up perfectly good jackets, was no match for the two-ton chunk of metal and plastic. A horrendous screech came up through the bottom of the car as the undercarriage scraped on the fence, making Frank wince as he imagined all of the bits and pieces beneath the car that could be damaged or torn off.

Much to his amazement the fence did not get caught on the car and the airbags didn't go off either despite the speed at which it was traveling when it hit the fence and then landed back on the ground. The wheels posed the biggest problem as they twisted to the right, sending the car into a spin that Frank was not expecting to have to deal with. While his first instinct was to hit the brakes and turn to the left, he instead did his best to keep the car steady while turning into the spin. The sedan weaved to the left and right as Frank fought with it on the soft grass until he finally got it under control.

Behind him past the deep ruts in the soft grass, the mangled fence and the parking lot in front of the annex building stood the two soldiers. They along with their companions still in their vehicles watched in disbelief as the sedan sped away, heading toward the bridge a short distance up the river. They scrambled to call the other patrols in the area to get them to divert to the bridge to stop the unknown intruders but by the time the call went out the sedan was already on the road and heading over the water.

Chapter Fifty-Nine

W ith the morning light comes a break in the rain over Pittsburgh, an easing of the rising waters and a chance for the military to enter the city and try to bring out any survivors. Transport vehicles equipped for dealing with high water levels roll out into the city, forming long convoy lines as they deploy along predetermined routes.

The soldiers in the back of the convoys wear thick waist-high rubber boots, rubber gloves and filters that are tightly affixed to their faces. All reports indicate that the disease has completely died out in the city but there are no chances being taken. It is suspected that some individuals may be immune to the virus or that it somehow jumped from human hosts to animals or insects. The disease could yet again spread unchecked if even a single soldier becomes infected so discipline is key.

Deep into the city the convoy begins to break up. Every vehicle is assigned to a small section of the city. Each one rolls through its assigned streets slowly, searching for signs of life visually and with the help of thermal scanners. The scanners penetrate the walls of most buildings, showing heat sources on the interiors. Most houses are empty but a few have people huddled in the top floors of their homes or in their attics.

When live survivors are found the vehicle stops and a four-man group exits the back of the truck and proceeds to the home. They announce their presence *before breaking down the door and search room by room until they find the survivors. The soldiers' weapons are kept shouldered and holstered with the safeties on. The city is not a war zone.*

Until it is.

The first attack comes from the western side of the city when five survivors are detected inside of a home. The group of soldiers that proceeds inside never comes back out. There are no shouts or gunshots or emergency calls over the radio. A few minutes pass before the man in the front of the truck operating the thermal scanner pans back over to the house with the tool, wondering why the soldiers are taking so long. The five survivors are still present but they are accompanied by the slowly fading heat signatures of four bodies lying on the floor.

More soldiers pile out of the back of the truck, leaving the already-rescued survivors in the back with instructions to stay perfectly still and not move. Before the soldiers can make it to the front of the house they are gunned down. One of the five figures in the house stands at a top window with an automatic weapon in hand.

The two soldiers in the front of the truck are shot next. Multiple weapons open fire on the back of the truck, wounding and killing the few remaining soldiers and survivors as they try to get out. One of the soldiers manages to croak out a message on his radio before he dies, calling out his location and reporting unknown sources of heavy gunfire.

While several vehicles converge on the location of the massacre, the rest of the rescue parties go on the defensive. Survivors are no longer greeted by friendly faces but by the barrels of guns, instead, as they are systematically searched before being escorted to the waiting transports. This matters little, though, as only a few more survivors are rescued before the attackers coordinate their next assault.

IEDs placed on the road ahead of a portion of the convoy on the eastern side of the city detonate, destroying three trucks and severely damaging two more. Dozens are killed in the blast and those that survived are almost immediately gunned down. On the southern side of the city near the perimeter border where survivors are being unloaded from trucks and passed through biological screening stations the screech of tires is heard. Two reinforced dump trucks speed in from out of nowhere, plowing into the crowd of survivors and the screening station. The drivers of the trucks go on a rampage for ten minutes before a Black Hawk can bring its weapons to bear and destroy both vehicles.

The chaos in the city is not isolated. Similar situations play out in eight more cities across the country that are all under lockdown thanks to the viral outbreak. While the attacks occur hours apart—more than enough time for the military to form an effective response under normal circumstances—the unique situation means that some cities don't hear about the first attacks until after their attacks have been dealt with. The loss of life numbers in the thousands split between military personnel and civilians. While the death toll isn't high compared to that inflicted by both the initial and biological attacks it does have an exponential effect on the response over the next few days.

Even without regular means of communication word travels fast through military channels and through select civilian channels. The impact of the first two attacks is well known even to those who were lucky enough not to be affected by either. The impact of the multitude of brutal terrorist attacks following the biological attacks is even greater.

People already afraid of vehicles exploding or dying to mysterious illnesses are now on edge about the possibility of being shot or stabbed by terrorist cells. It doesn't matter that the attackers are all dead. Their goal has been perfectly achieved. By adding additional worry and fear to that already existing in the populace they successfully encourage more people to migrate towards the survivor cities that the government has set up.

Those already en route to the cities move there faster. Many of those who planned to survive on their own second-guess their decision and choose to move to the cities instead. Heavy military and police presence in the cities along with power, running water and food rations are all strong motivators.

"The survivor cities are safe."

"The survivor cities are disease-free."

"The survivor cities will enable us to rebuild."

These are the words spoken by a government on its knees, gasping for breath after being punched in the gut thrice in a row. The words are truly spoken but they are hardly the truth.

Chapter Sixty

Two miles past the bridge and through a few neighborhoods later, Frank finally stopped the sedan to take stock of Linda, himself and the car. His hands shook as he pushed the shifter into the park position as his body tried to recover from the massive amount of adrenaline that was dissipating in his system.

After holding tight to the steering wheel for several seconds, Frank took a few deep breaths and turned around slowly in his seat to see how Linda was doing. She was still on her back but was moving around slightly as she tried to sit up. Frank unbuckled his seatbelt and turned to kneel on his seat so he could give her a hand up.

"What the hell?" Out in the afternoon sunlight Linda looked worse than ever. She was still sweating, her pants were still nearly down to her ankles and her jacket was down on the floor. She was weak enough that she couldn't sit up properly on her own but as she twisted and turned Frank could see the wound on her leg was oozing blood and pus onto the seat.

"Take it easy, Linda. Take it easy." Frank abandoned the idea of helping her sit up and instead pulled her back into a position where she could curl up across the back seats. "You need to lay still there, okay? We're on our way to find this friend of yours."

"Friend?" Linda's energy levels were so low that although she still wanted to sit up she had no choice but to stay still. Keeping her eyes open and staying awake was a difficult enough challenge and she started nodding off as Frank tried to talk to her.

"Yes. Sarah. The lady from the CIA?"

"Sarah." Linda gave a slight nod. "Where… where are we?"

"North of the annex somewhere. I don't know where."

"Head south of the mall. Westfield. Look for Wildwood. Don't know the house though. Maybe car in front green?" Linda's sentences started to fall apart and Frank touched her on the head.

"Dammit, Linda. You're burning up. Just be still back there, okay?" He turned around in his seat and buckled his seatbelt again. "We'll get there somehow. I don't know what this lady's going to be able to do to help you but we'll get there. Somehow."

Frank turned out of the neighborhood and headed back towards the highway, taking it slow and keeping his head on a swivel while he watched for any signs of the patrol that had nearly caught up to them at the CIA annex. The streets were quiet, though, and he drove on down the road as he looked for any signs indicating that the Westfield Mall might be nearby. Ten minutes of back-and-forth later and he finally noticed a giant billboard towering over the highway indicating that the mall was off the next exit.

The ease of driving on the roads near Washington surprised Frank but he quickly noticed that they looked like they had been cleared in the recent past. Much like the short stretch of road outside Pittsburgh there was a lane or two clear along the major roads he drove on since the debris and remains of destroyed trucks and cars had been pushed to the sides.

Frank took the exit towards the Westfield Mall and almost immediately had to drive off into the grass to get around a cluster of burned-out cars that were in the way. After going for a quarter of a mile on the shoulder and grass he finally saw the Westfield Mall off to his left. A glance at the sun told him that he was driving roughly in the easterly direction so he began looking towards the south for the Wildwood neighborhood that Linda had told him about.

Sure enough, as if on cue, an elegant sign for the Wildwood subdivision appeared next to a small two-lane road that disappeared back into the trees off of the main road. The layout of the area reminded him of the neighborhood he had driven through in Maine right before his first encounter with Linda and he grew wary of any people that might still be around. Each day that passed caused those that still clung to life to grow more desperate and Frank was in no mood to encounter anyone.

After passing through thick trees whose leafless branches formed a lattice overhead that nearly blotted out the sky, the sedan emerged into a neighborhood filled with rows of townhouses on both sides of the street. Short hedges dotted the curves in the landscape in front of and between the chunks of tall, narrow houses pressed up against each other. The homes were in chunks of five to seven with small gaps half a house's width in between the chunks. The exteriors were uniform for the most part with the only differences being in details like the color of the door, the trim on the windows and the color and type of doorknobs.

Most of the parking spaces in front of the houses were empty, their occupants having long since left for a destination they deemed safer than inside their own homes. None of the houses appeared occupied though with the interiors darkened and the sun still bright outside it would have been difficult to see anything anyway.

"What was that number again?" Frank racked his brain as he tried to remember the house number on the sticky note. He turned to look at Linda to see if she still had the note before he remembered seeing it fall to the floor. He couldn't remember if he picked it up or not and dug through his pockets before retrieving it with a triumphant shout. "Yes! All right, then. Twenty-eight fifty-four. Hmm." The numbers on the houses were going in the right direction but they ran out before he reached the specified number. He turned right at the next street and continued up through the next row until, around the middle of the road, he spotted the twenty-eight hundreds.

Frank felt unexpectedly nervous as he realized they were extremely close to arriving at the home of Linda's CIA contact. Scenarios flashed through his mind of all the ways the meeting could go wrong. What if she had set a trap for some reason? What if she never left the note, but someone else did? What if Omar had sent someone to wait for them there? Each idea that passed through Frank's brain was more outlandish than the last until, finally, he shook his head and clenched his jaw.

"No. This is stupid." He eased up on the accelerator and pressed down on the brake as he saw the house number appear on his right.

"Everything's going to be fine." Frank put the car into park and turned to check on Linda. Her condition appeared unchanged.

"Everything's going to be just fine." Frank got out of the car and pulled out his pistol. He pulled the slide back a few millimeters to ensure there was a round in the chamber and then tucked it back into his pants.

"I'll just walk up there." Frank mumbled to himself, narrating his actions as he went along as he tried to derive some sort of courage from his own words. "I'll walk up there, go up the steps, ring the doorbell and hope someone answers."

The fact that there was no power in the neighborhood didn't register with Frank until he had pushed the doorbell button, heard it ring and then stepped back a few paces from the door. His eyes narrowed and his expression changed to one of confusion as he realized that there must actually be power in the townhouse in order for the doorbell to ring. That fact didn't make sense, though, and it was in his confusion over what was going on that he nearly took a bullet to the face.

"Get away from here right now!" A woman's voice came from a window above Frank and he looked up just in time to see the barrel of a rifle pointed down at him. He scrambled to the side as a shot rang out and the round sent up a small puff of concrete dust from the top step.

"Holy hell!" Frank pressed his body up against the front door to take cover under the narrow overhang as he shouted up at the woman. "Calm down, lady! I just need to talk!"

"Get out of here now, dammit! If I have to come down there I'll make you look like a block of Swiss cheese!"

"I'm not here to hurt you! I'm here with Linda!"

The woman's voice hesitated for a second. "I don't know what you're going on about but if you don't get out of here now I'll kill you!"

"Linda Rollins is in my car out there! Look! You can probably see her lying there in the backseat!" In truth Frank had no idea whether Linda's form was visible but he hoped that the woman upstairs—presumably this Sarah person—would be persuaded to not take any more shots at the mention of Linda's name.

"Why the hell have you got her out there with her clothes half off?"

Ha! Frank thought to himself. *So you do know her after all!* "She's got a fever! I've been trying to keep her cool but we were chased!"

Frank listened intently, not daring to peek out to see if the rifle barrel was still poking out of the window. There was nothing but silence for several seconds and he spoke again. "Here, look! We were at the CIA annex. She told me we had to go there to find you. I found your note on your monitor, see?" Frank pulled the note back out of his pocket and held it out nervously, hoping that the illegible scrap of yellow paper would accomplish what his words and the sight of Linda's still form had not.

"You have a gun in your pants. Take it out, drop it on the steps, then walk back to your car." The woman's voice was firm, but sounded less panicked than it had before.

Fucking hell, Linda. Frank groaned to himself as he pulled out his pistol and looked it over. *I hope you're right about this!*

Frank dropped the gun on the ground and pushed it a few inches out onto the front step. He peeked out as he did so, noting with a small amount of relief that there was no longer a rifle barrel poking out of the top window. "There!" Frank shouted up at the woman. "Gun's on the ground."

"Walk to your car!" The woman shouted at Frank and he clenched his jaw, willing himself to take the first tentative step out of cover and into the woman's line of fire. He had only Linda's word to go on that the woman was trustworthy but the fact that she had changed her attitude towards him after he told her about Linda seemed like a step in the right direction.

Frank's first step was slow, but his second was faster as he started moving quickly down the steps, dodging to the left and right as he went. By the time he ran around to the other side of the car and crouched down he realized that the woman was no longer at the upstairs window. He scanned the third, second and ground story windows in confusion, wondering where she went when he saw the front door crack open and the rifle barrel emerge again.

"Open the back door of the car! Let me see her face!" The woman inside the house was still well-hidden by the shadows and Frank couldn't see her. Her gun, while poking out through the crack in the door, was angled down at the ground instead of in Frank's direction, though, so he decided to keep following her instructions.

"She's got a high fever!" Frank shouted back at the woman as he walked around the car and opened the rear door. "I think it's a deep infection in her leg or something!" In the back seat Linda was still unconscious but her face was clearly visible from the house. Frank heard the woman in the house say something in a muffled voice before the door slammed shut. There was a jingle of chains behind the door before it opened fully to reveal a middle-aged woman in a bathrobe and slippers holding a rifle.

"Linda?" The woman glanced around nervously at the neighborhood before leaning down to pick up Frank's pistol. She tucked the pistol into the pocket of her robe and hurried down the steps, keeping her rifle pointed at the ground but still in Frank's general direction.

The woman looked to be around five and a half feet tall and in her mid-fifties with short-cut Auburn hair. She carried herself well, gripping the rifle with steady hands and wearing a steely expression that indicated she wasn't to be trifled with. "Back away from the car." The woman motioned at Frank with her rifle and he took a few steps backward. "Good. Stay there and don't move."

The woman leaned in towards the car and glanced at Linda before looking back at Frank and shaking her head. "How do you know her?"

"Are you Sarah?"

"Who wants to know?"

"I'm Frank. Linda and I... we met several days ago. Right after all this happened. I helped her get out of a jam and we've been traveling together."

The woman eyed Frank suspiciously. "That doesn't sound like the Linda I know."

"Yeah, well, it took some convincing to get her to work with me. Like saving her ass, having her leave me in the middle of nowhere and then have to save her ass again."

Sarah snorted laughed. "Ha! Now *that* does sound like Linda. Hm." Sarah glanced back at Linda. "How long's she had the fever?"

Frank took a cautious step forward, glad to see that Sarah didn't object to him coming close to the car again. "Since last night or early this morning I think. She got shot a few days ago and hasn't exactly been taking care of the wound. I cleaned out a localized infection last night after we got through the patrols into the city but I think it's moved deeper into her body."

Sarah watched Frank carefully as he spoke and gestured, studying every nuance of his voice and movements. Before he finished speaking she made up her mind about him and held out her rifle. "Here. Hold this."

Frank grabbed the barrel of the rifle, his eyes wide as he tried to figure out what was going on. Sarah had gone from shooting at him to handing him her weapon in a matter of moments and the sudden change in attitude confounded him. Sarah leaned into the car and put her hand on Linda's head and chest. "Where's the wound?"

"Right leg, on her thigh."

Sarah turned Linda over slightly and peeled back the bandage from the wound before shaking her head. "Christ. Who patched this up? A drunk with no arms?" With a surprising amount of speed and strength Sarah lifted Linda from the car and shoved Frank out of the way. "Grab your gear and get inside."

Frank watched Sarah carry Linda up the steps to the townhouse for a few seconds before his brain kicked into gear. He grabbed the two backpacks from the car along with Linda's jacket and carried everything up to the door of the townhouse. Inside, Sarah was busy getting Linda down onto a couch just inside the door. Frank stepped in and started setting the bags and Sarah's rifle down on the floor when he caught a glimpse of Sarah holding his pistol across the room. She wasn't aiming the weapon at him but she had it in her hand and was watching him carefully.

Frank took his time setting the rifle down, then pointed at Linda's bag. "Her pistol's in there."

"Any other weapons or gear?"

Frank shook his head. "We left everything else in a Humvee on the other side of the city. I think the plan was for a quick in and out trip, not some long excursion."

Sarah nodded slowly. "Right. Stay here with her. I'll be right back." She disappeared up the stairs near the back of the house and Frank hurried over to Linda and knelt down beside her. Linda's breathing was shallow and sweat was still pouring off of her despite the chill both outside and inside the house.

"Hang in there." Frank whispered to Linda as he wiped sweat from her face and neck with the back of his hand. A moment later Sarah came back downstairs, carrying a large black suitcase with her. The pocket of her robe drooped and bulged with the shape of Frank's pistol and she pointed with her free hand at the wall behind him.

"Hit the light switch."

Frank reached for the switch, flicked it on and was surprised when the lights on the ceiling bathed the room in a soft yellow glow. "You have power?"

"Question time later." Sarah slammed the suitcase down on the floor next to the couch. She unzipped the case and flung it open to reveal a plethora of bandages, creams, ointments, surgical equipment and more. Frank watched as Sarah dug through the bag until she came across a steel case with a white label on the top. Sarah closed the suitcase and pushed it over towards Frank with her foot.

"You squeamish about needles?" Sarah posed the question as she opened the spring-loaded top of the steel case to reveal several small vials and three long needles inside.

Frank shook his head but gulped nervously despite his answer. "Not really, no."

"Good." Sarah plucked one of the needles from the case and put it between her teeth. She rifled through the vials after taking the needle, picking up and putting down three or four of them before settling on the one she wanted.

"What is that?"

"Antibiotics. Cefrriax-a-something or other. Very potent stuff."

"You really think she needs that?"

Sarah glanced at Frank as she popped the plastic protector off the end of the needle. "I'm not a doctor but I took enough first aid training to know when someone's at death's door. She's damned lucky to be alive right now. Whatever's inside of her needs to die and this stuff should do the trick."

Frank stood up and crossed his arms as he watched Sarah plunge the needle into the vial and draw out the liquid inside. "That's all she needs? Just one injection?"

"Hell no." Sarah shook her head. "I've got some ten-day general courses in here. She's going to feel like a truck's running her over for the next couple weeks but she should survive." Sarah flicked at the needle and gently depressed the plunger to remove any air bubbles inside. "Well." She paused and looked at Linda. "So long as she's not allergic to any of this stuff. I guess that's preferable to guaranteed death, though. Any objections?"

Frank shook his head. "You're more of a doctor than I am. Do whatever you think will help."

"Thanks for the vote of confidence." Sarah took Linda's arm and located the nearest vein. She pushed the needle into the vein without hesitation, moving ahead with what she thought was best in spite of the potentially disastrous outcome. The clear liquid disappeared as she pushed the plunger smoothly and quickly and she could feel Frank's eyes staring into the back of her head as she worked.

When Sarah finished she stood up, put the plastic protector back on the needle and slid it back into the steel case. "There."

"Now what?" Frank knelt back down next to Linda and touched her head.

"Now we try to keep her cool while this stuff works."

"I was trying that earlier, with minimizing her clothing and keeping wet socks on her head and stomach. It didn't seem to do much good."

"We'll need more than that." Sarah turned and looked behind her. "Go down the stairs to the basement. There's a small chest freezer in the garage. Near the top there are a few freeze packs. Grab two of those and bring them back."

"Two freeze packs. Got it." Frank turned and ran back towards the stairs down to the basement. Sarah, meanwhile, ran over to a nearby linen closet and grabbed two sheets and a thin blanket. She ran back to Linda and finished pulling off her pants, then took a pair of scissors and cut her shirt and bra free. Sarah draped one of the sheets over Linda's waist and legs and loosely wrapped the other around her chest, leaving her head, neck, arms and most of her torso exposed.

When Frank got back he handed the ice packs to Sarah and she nodded. "Good. Now grab me a couple of tea towels from the kitchen. Get a bottle of water and dampen them first. Not dripping wet, but wet enough to conduct heat and cold easily."

Frank jogged back into the kitchen and took a pair of hand towels from the counter. He held them over the sink and poured the remnants of a nearly-empty gallon of water onto them before mashing them together in his hands to distribute the water as evenly as possible. He brought them back to Sarah who took them and wrapped an ice pack in each one. She put one on Linda's forehead and the other across Linda's chest, then stuck a finger under both packs.

"Good. That's wet enough. They'll start cooling her off soon."

"Do you have a fan or something?" Frank glanced around the room as Sarah fiddled with the positioning of the ice packs.

"Only the ceiling fan. That circuit's not on the batteries, though." Sarah looked at Frank as she stood up next to him. "We've done everything we can for her. At this point we need to just keep an eye on her and hope the fever goes down."

Frank sighed and shook his head as he turned his back on Linda, not wanting to see her looking so ill any longer. "I should have cleaned the wound more. Done something else."

Sarah patted Frank on the back and gently pushed him towards a chair across from the couch. "You did what you could with what you had, I'm sure." Sarah flicked the light off and the room descended back into a state of twilight, neither fully dark nor light enough to see very well.

"Now then." Sarah sat down in a chair next to Frank where she could see both him, Linda and the front door. She pulled Frank's pistol out of the pocket of her robe and placed it on her lap with a flourish, ensuring that he noticed that she was still in possession of his weapon. She spoke softly but firmly, her dark eyes staring at Frank with an intensity and focus that made him uncomfortable.

"I think it's time you told me about yourself." Sarah cleared her throat and continued. "Such as your full name. And how you came to meet Linda. And anything else." Sarah shrugged. "Basically… just tell me everything."

Sarah flashed a smile at him which somehow managed to look both warm and cold at the same time. "Don't spare the details."

Chapter Sixty-One

O*ne Month Before the Attacks*

NATE SITS at his station at the Los Angeles port, dividing his attention between watching videos on his phone and glancing up at the radiation monitor on his desk every few minutes. His job, for which he receives a yearly salary of eighty-nine thousand dollars, consists of watching the radiation monitor and making a phone call if the radiation detected by the monitor reaches a certain threshold.

While Nate's job was relevant two decades ago he would have been replaced with a simplistic and far cheaper automated alarm had it not been for the tenacity of his union. Thus, for over thirty years Nate has functioned as one of the many gatekeepers in the port that helps protect our country. His effectiveness over those years has waned and he has only ever pushed the alarm button three times but he will fight tooth and nail to insist that his job is vital to the safety of all.

When the fourth radiation alert in Nate's career goes off he doesn't notice it at first. Mandatory equipment inspections rarely occur and when they take place they cover only the most vital parts of the systems. An alert bell for a system that has only triggered three times in thirty years is not, unfortunately, deemed a vital part.

When Nate glances up from his phone to check the monitor he freezes, momentarily taken aback by the red flashing light on the monitor. He sits still for several seconds before picking up the phone next to the monitor and dialing a four-digit number.

"Go ahead."

"This is Nate, down in bulk rad scanning. I've got a red light on the shipment passing through right now."

There is a pause on the other end of the line. "A red light? On the bulk cargo scanner?"

"That's right." Nate thumps the monitor with his fist, wondering if the alert could be a malfunction.

"You sure about that?"

"You want to come down and see the flashing red light?"

A heavy sigh follows another long pause. "I'm making the call. Stand by."

"Copy." Nate hangs up the phone and turns to his computer. He pulls up the cargo manifests passing through the scanners and locates the one that triggered the alarm.

"A rice shipment?" He frowns. "Who the hell's importing rice from Croatia?"

Nate is about to pick up the phone and call his superior officer to inform her of the situation when the phone rings first. He picks up the receiver and presses it to his ear while he continues skimming the computer screen.

"Rad scans. Nate here."

"Nathan Davis? Badge number eight nine seven five dash two six one?"

Nate's eyes grow wide as he tries to figure out what the formal-sounding call could be about. "Uh. Yes, that's me?" His voice cracks as he answers and he feels his palms starting to sweat. Perhaps the call is about the malfunction with the alert. Or someone ratted him out about his videos and naps on the job.

"I'll make this quick. The 'alert' on your screen is nothing more than a malfunction. One of the sensors had a bird crap all over it which shorted it out. It's giving false readings which is what's causing you to get radiation alarms."

"I... what? A malfunction?"

"Correct."

"I'm... I'm sorry. Who are you?"

"*Inspector Garcia. Badge two one six eight dash two one three. We're already on the line with your superior and the tech teams. They'll be fitting the new sensor in as soon as possible. For now we're moving to manual scans until further notice.*"

"*Manual scans?*" Nate starts to panic as he thinks about what that could mean for his job security. "*How long until the new sensor is in?*"

"*At least another twelve hours. Maybe twenty-four. I'll personally call you when the repairs are complete.*"

"*Okay... thanks, I guess. Do y*—" The line goes dead before Nate can ask his next question. He sits there for several minutes staring at the phone and the monitor, trying to work out exactly what just happened. While the explanation from Inspector Garcia sounded legitimate, Nate can't shake the feeling that something is amiss.

Although his analytical skills are rusty from years of idly sitting and doing virtually nothing in his small office, Nate decides to press in and see exactly what is going on. He taps away at the keyboard on his desk, slowly making less typos and mistakes as he digs into the software program that records the intricate details for each radiation scan. The records for the latest scan that tripped the alarm are extensive, consisting of dozens of pages of raw data that have to be carefully analyzed.

Nate pulls out a notebook from his drawer and tries three different pens before finding one that still works. He begins jotting down calculations, using his cell phone to look up long-forgotten formulae and constants that he used to know by heart. Lunch is quickly forgotten as Nate digs down into the data, checking and re-checking his calculations both by hand and through the computer system. Late in the day, when it's nearly time to head home, he finally puts down his pen and stares at the notebook.

"*Holy hell.*" Nate struggles to comprehend what he sees. The computer's calculations and Nate's own calculations do not lie, though. The radiation sensors which were working perfectly up until the alert earlier in the day show only two possibilities.

The first possibility is the simplest and conforms to what Inspector Garcia indicated. The sensor somehow suffered a malfunction and is showing radiation readings that are incorrect. This explanation is easy to accept on the one hand, but since the radiation sensors are regularly checked and replaced—unlike the equipment in Nate's office—it seems unlikely.

The second possibility is terrifying on a scale that boggles the mind. If the sensor is not broken then whatever was in the shipment that passed through and triggered the alert was not rice at all. The only thing that would have triggered the numbers Nate sees is weapons-grade nuclear material. The idea that someone would try shipping weapons-grade nuclear material in through a port that performs radiation scans on everything that comes in and goes out seems ludicrous on the surface. No one could possibly be that stupid.

But what if it's true? The shipment of rice that triggered the alert is already gone, having been sped through customs and picked up by the recipient mere minutes after it was marked as cleared. There are no records in the system of the manual radiation scans that Inspector Garcia performed, either, though that could possibly be explained by the fact that manual checks are so rare that it would take extra time to enter them into the database.

The more Nate considers the two possibilities, though, the more nervous he gets. He is normally one to make fun of conspiracy theorists but he finds himself thinking more and more like one. After several minutes of thinking he realizes that there's something else he can check.

He picks up the phone on his desk and calls to another department.

"Records."

"Ted? This is Nate down at scanning."

"What's going on, Nate?"

Nate instinctively glances around his small office and pulls his chair closer to his desk as he lowers his voice. "I need a favor."

"What's that?"

"Run a badge number for me, will you? I got an odd call earlier and want to make sure it's legit."

"A badge number? Can't you run it from there?"

"My system's down right now so I can't access it." It's a simple lie to disguise the fact that Nate doesn't want a record of him looking up the badge number in the system. Looking up badge numbers is not a prohibited activity but Nate wants to stay as far from the situation as possible while he's checking things out.

"Yeah, all right. What is it?"

Nate reads the badge number out that he had hastily typed into a text file on his computer when Inspector Garcia called earlier. Ted taps out the numbers on his keyboard and reads the text over the phone to Nate.

"Badge is registered to Jose Martinez."

"Is he an inspector?"

"Nope. He works off-site. General site security."

"Huh. All right, thanks. Appreciate it."

"No problem. Later, Nate."

The line goes dead and Nate hangs up the phone. He rubs his hand through his hair as he processes the new information and tries to decide what to do next. Making waves and drawing attention to himself isn't something he wants to do, particularly when it might involve him being tricked by someone impersonating an inspector.

"God dammit." Nate picks up the phone again and dials the number for his superior. When she picks up he starts giving her a summary of the events of the day when she interrupts him and cuts him off.

"I appreciate the call, Nathan, but there's nothing to worry about."

"But this inspector isn't—"

"Nathan." Her voice grows cold. "There's nothing to worry about. I've checked everything out and it was a sensor malfunction. A new one will be up tomorrow morning and you can resume your duties then. Understand?"

"I... okay. Sure."

"Great. Have a good evening."

The line, once again, goes dead and Nate sits in silence while he wonders yet again just what is going on.

Chapter Sixty-Two

"Welcome to the United States, Mr. Amari. Have a pleasant stay."

Farhad Omar smiles broadly at the immigration officer as he collects his passport from the desk and his luggage from the floor. Many would be nervous about traveling under a false name. Omar is not nervous in the slightest. Two dozen trips back and forth between the United States and other countries have left him feeling confident in his alias which, in turn, helps immensely when dealing with the immigration officers.

He passes the desk with a slight nod and another smile to the officer and continues on his way. Outside the airport, waiting near the front doors, a large black SUV pulls up. The back door opens and Omar climbs in, handing his luggage to a waiting assistant who loads it in the back before getting in as well.

Once inside the vehicle Omar's smile turns to a sneer. He stares out the window at the people walking and driving around, shaking his head as he mulls over all the reason he despises each and every one of them. A slight tap on his arm causes him to turn and look at the assistant seated next to him. The assistant wears a suit and a nervous expression as he holds out a phone for Omar.

"You wanted to call him when you arrived, sir?" The assistant speaks in smooth, accent-less English.

Omar nods approvingly as he takes the phone, speaking with the same elegant, flawless and accent-less English. "Your practice has gone well, I see. Good work."

The assistant's body visibly relaxes at the praise from Omar. "Thank you, sir!"

Omar turns back to look out the window. "What's the status on the material?"

"All shipments have made it through successfully."

"No problems at all?"

"None, sir. He was able to arrange for technicians to fabricate sensor malfunctions to ensure everything got through. Our men handled the scanning of the shipments and everything was cleared."

"What about the roaming scans? How are those being handled?"

"We had to change that some, sir."

Omar raises an eyebrow. "Nothing happened, did it?"

"No sir. He informed us that the roaming scans had an updated route just a few days after the shipments cleared customs. Three of our storage sites would have been compromised by the new routes so we moved them to new ones."

Omar nods thoughtfully. "You have the details prepared for me to examine at the hotel?"

"Of course, sir. Everything's ready."

Omar sighs with satisfaction and sits back in his seat. "Excellent. I'll call him now, then."

The phone rings twice before a voice on the other end of the line answers. "Stadwell."

"Mr. Stadwell. This is Amari. I am calling with questions and thanks. Is this a good time to speak?"

"Perfect. On my way out to get some lunch right now. What can I do you for, Mr. Amari?"

Omar glances at his assistant who leans in to listen in on the conversation and take notes. "I understand that there were some hiccups with the scanning routes that you helped sort out. You have my thanks for that."

Malcolm Stadwell glances around as he walks down the street, lowering his voice as he increases his pace. He has yet to suspect anyone even being suspicious of his duplicitous nature but caution has allowed him to remain active and he persists in exercising an abundance of it.

"Of course, of course. They change those randomly and it's been a while since anything was altered so I figured something would be coming down the pipe soon. Just glad I could help out you... and my pocketbook!" Stadwell laughs at his joke but quickly stops once he realizes that the man on the other end of the line is silent.

Omar pinches the bridge of his nose and struggles to keep his voice steady. "Your timely actions are most appreciated. As for my question, do you anticipate any problems related to the scanners? My assistant indicated that the matter was resolved but I want to ensure—"

Omar grits his teeth as Stadwell interrupts him. The American speaks quickly and huffs slightly as he is out of breath from speed walking. "No problem at all there, Mr. Amari. No problem at all. I was able to get your people into position with some legitimate documents and they handled it flawlessly. In a few days I'll have someone here flush the records of the incident and it will officially have never happened."

"You have an impressive array of resources at your disposal thanks to the Bureau, Mr. Stadwell."

Stadwell flashes an arrogant grin that Omar can very nearly hear over the phone. "Absolutely I do, Mr. Amari. Hey, listen, do you need anything else?"

"I believe that's everything."

"Fantastic! I'll be on for our usual call tomorrow. I need to run now. The day job awaits. Talk to you later!"

The line goes dead and Omar slowly lowers the phone from his ear. His nauseated expression betrays what he truly thinks of the man whom he bribed and turned to work for him years prior. He turns to his assistant and looks at the notepad. "What time is the call tomorrow?"

"Around eleven in the evening, sir."

Omar closes his eyes and lets out a slight groan. "Very well."

Malcolm Stadwell's position, like those of other double agents before him, affords him an enormous amount of leverage and power to assist with Omar's plans. Unfortunately for Omar, however, Stadwell requires an increasing level of attention and massaging to get tasks accomplished. The only reason Omar still puts up with the man is due to Omar's timetable. The first phase is nearly ready to begin. Once it starts Stadwell will be expendable and can be disposed of. Until that happens, though, Omar must tolerate and endure the man's attitude.

"Do you need anything, sir?" Omar's assistant has a concerned expression on his face.

"No, thank you." Omar resumes his watch out the window, staring off into space as he contemplates what is to come. *"I'll have everything I need soon enough."*

BOOK FOUR

THE TEMPEST

Chapter Sixty-Three

W hen most picture the country of Pakistan they imagine a harsh, sand-filled country. The idea of lush forests and green grass covering a large portion of the landscape does not occur to them and they will not hesitate to laugh at the notion.

Just north of the city of Islamabad, located near the northern tip of Pakistan, the harsh sandy desert climate is far from reality. The city sits near the Margalla Hills, part of the Himalayan Foothills. Margalla is filled with lush trees, green grass and vibrant landscapes. The elevation is such that some areas do, from time to time, receive snow during the winter months. The city of Islamabad itself is no desert city, either. It is filled with trees and grass that stretch between the houses and buildings and roads, filling the region with enough green that one might never realize they were in Pakistan in the first place.

It is on these green grassy paths, in view of the lush Margalla Hills, that a woman walks in the evening hour, heading for a nondescript building half a mile away. She walks alone, wearing a baggy pair of trousers and shirt and a simple scarf wrapped around her head. Her hands stay close to her waist and she constantly scans her environment, watching around her for any sign of danger.

As the woman passes by a bench on the outside of a nearby park a man sits up and stares at her. He calls out to her in Urdu, shouting in a slurred voice that betrays the fact that he has been drinking for the last few hours. She ignores the man, keeping her pace steady as she plods along. He tries to stand up from the bench but fails to remain upright, toppling over almost immediately and falling to the ground. His loud groans of pain will soon attract attention so the woman increases her speed to get away from him before the authorities show up.

The building the woman is traveling towards is one of many along a busy street in the heart of the city. It is several stories tall, made of brick or stone or some other material that feels to her like it is completely devoid of color and life. The building is designed to blend in and not attract attention but it is that fact that draws her eye directly toward it.

The woman walks past the building, heading for a bus stop on a nearby street corner. She checks her watch as she approaches the bus stop and speeds up, realizing that she is nearly thirty seconds behind schedule. The bus arrives as she reaches the stop. She gets on board, pays her fare and takes a seat at the very back. Four women and three men are on the bus as well, though two of the men depart at the stop where she got on board.

Once the bus is moving again she reaches under her seat and dislodges a white envelope that was jammed between the seat and the seat support. The envelope is thick, at least one and a half inches, and contains over two hundred sheets of paper. She eyes the people sitting in front of her carefully as she opens the envelope, making sure to hide it behind the seat in front of her so that no one else can look at it.

The pages are written in a mix of English and Urdu and each is marked with the logo of the Inter-Services Intelligence agency, the main intelligence agency of the country. With operations in most countries around the world, the ISI is well-known to other countries as a top-tier intelligence agency though most people have never heard of them.

It has taken months of work and a large sum of money to obtain the envelope she now holds in her hands and Linda Rollins can feel her heartbeat increasing as she thumbs through the pages. The ISI's intelligence assets on the ground inside Iran are second to none and she hopes that the price she paid and the risks she has endured are worth the information contained in the pages.

For the next half hour, as the bus winds through Islamabad, Linda skims through the pages, looking for the promised details about Farhad Omar, the person she so desperately wishes to find. Unfortunately, though, the more she looks through the pages the more she realizes that every piece of information about Omar is something she has already found out through other means.

She knows where he was born and she already knows each of his closest lieutenants by name. She knows the places where he has been and where he's likely to turn up even though he fails to do so each time it is predicted to happen. After reading through half of the documents she stuffs them back into the envelope with frustration and tucks it beneath her tunic.

She watches out the window of the bus, mulling over what to do after yet another dead end, when the reflection of one of the men sitting in front of her catches her eye. He is staring directly at her, unblinking. His expression is calm and plain, with no leering or devious thoughts of any kind written across it. It is the definition of an expressionless expression and she immediately hears alarms going off in her head.

Linda's hotel is two stops ahead but the fact that someone is watching her has changed her plans entirely. Instead of going back to her hotel for the night and leaving on a flight the next day she decides to head to the hotel, grab her things and go immediately to the airport. She also gives up any hope of making any calls home, as there is no chance she won't be constantly monitored until she's well out of the country.

When the bus finally stops in front of Linda's hotel she hurries out and heads inside. She glances behind as she opens the door and sees the man who was staring at her standing outside the hotel. He is making a show of looking at anything except for Linda which in turn causes what he is doing to become even more obvious than it was before.

Linda heads to the front desk and talks to the person on duty. Instead of leaving her bag in her room she left it at the desk along with a sizeable tip to ensure that nothing would happen to it. After she checks to make sure everything is inside she pays her bill and exits through the back of the building, running to catch the next bus that is about to leave a nearby stop.

The squeal of car tires from a nearby street tell Linda that her tail has discovered her subterfuge and is after her again. She briefly considers trying to make it to the American embassy but decides against it since they will likely ask the same uncomfortable questions that her pursuer wants to ask.

She watches out the bus windows with no small amount of nervousness as she heads for the airport. When she gets close she pulls the stop signal and gets out early, running across the street to approach the airport from a side entrance. She makes it inside the building and up to the ticket counter with no sign of any pursuers, then she quickly has her ticket changed to the soonest available flight. Leaving in two hours is better than twenty-four, but she still has to avoid her pursuer until the flight is ready for boarding.

The airport is quiet late at night and she passes through security in a matter of minutes. After she finishes she heads for the nearest bathroom and opens her bag, pulling out a pair of pants and scarf that are different in color than the ones she was wearing previously. She changes her clothing and exits the bathroom before making her way to a small restaurant inside the terminal. There she sits at a table, sipping on a cup of coffee as she pretends to read a magazine, all while observing the people around her.

She spots her pursuer just after she gets up from the table after the boarding call is made for her flight. The man is walking slowly through the terminal, one hand pressed against his ear. His lips move subtly as he speaks into a microphone tucked away in his sleeve. Linda considers turning around but knows that if he was going to stop her then he would have done it already. She wagers that he wants to catch her alone, steal the documents she has in her possession and get away without being caught. It's a risky wager but one that she has to make or else she may miss her flight.

Linda increases her walking speed, gliding past the man and nearly causing him to trip and fall as she brushes up against him. She drops a white envelope on the ground as she passes by, joining in with the small crowd of passengers waiting at the gate for her flight. The man is distracted from her twice: first by her pushing him and second by her dropping the envelope. He ignores her and scoops up the envelope, tears it open and finds it to be empty. He looks around, searching for her but she is already gone, having blended in with the crowd at her gate before he can look to search for her.

The man futilely tries to have the plane stopped before it can take off but given that he is working unofficially his pleas with the agent at the gate have no effect. Linda's plane is in the air in twenty minutes, winging its way towards Germany where she will change flights again and head towards home. After the plane levels out Linda gets up from her seat and walks down the aisle, observing the other passengers closely. None of them bother to look back at her, absorbed as they are in their own affairs. When she sits back down she breathes a sigh of *relief, glad to be rid of the man following her. Disappointment sets back in quickly, though, and she sighs again, wishing she hadn't taken the time to travel to Pakistan to chase yet another dead end.*

After a few hours Linda pulls out the stack of papers from her bag and flips through them once again. She re-reads the material she read previously on the bus and finds nothing new. When she gets to the pages she skipped, though, she begins to find bits and pieces of information that she hasn't seen before.

There are references in the documents to Omar's obsession with the United States, starting from when he was a young man working under his father in the government. A failed coup—believed by the ISI to have been orchestrated by the CIA and MI6—resulted in the death of the Iranian President's wife as well as dozens of members of government. Omar's father, mother and two brothers were slaughtered in the coup. The only reason he survived was because he was out of the country studying at Oxford when it happened.

Though the Iranian President's wife was killed the President himself was not. Forces loyal to his regime quickly pushed back the attackers and reestablished the rule of law but not before the damage was done. While the coup happened decades prior there are references in the papers to Omar's radical transformation shortly after it occurred. He poured himself into his university studies, earning a doctorate in physics and a second in chemistry.

After his education he returned home, heralded as a hero by his country due to being the sole surviving member of his family. His education and his family's former position quickly garnered Omar a place working in the military where his newfound tenacity and ruthlessness were allowed and encouraged to flourish.

Though the information in the documents is presented as speculation, Linda realizes that it matches up with information she received from several other sources and is most likely true. Whether the coup was indeed orchestrated by the CIA and MI6, Omar latched on to the United States as the chief instigator of the incident. This belief was no doubt fostered by the coup d'état in 1953 which the CIA admitted to having planned, though Linda knows of no such admission for the modern attempt.

When Linda finishes going through the paperwork she leans back in her seat and stares out the window, contemplating the newfound information. She is glad she went to Pakistan as the trip turned out to be useful after all but the information she gathered has created as many new questions as it has answered. Omar has an obsession with the United States, but what is his game plan? A man so dedicated as to use American military personnel as guinea pigs for his weapons and hide himself so thoroughly from detection from foreign intelligence services must have a long-term strategy.

What it is, though, she cannot imagine. She knows, however, that whatever it is will not end well. Not unless she finds him first.

Chapter Sixty-Four

A thick, syrupy molasses surrounded Linda on all sides. It pushed at her, reaching from her toes to her neck. She, in turn, pushed back, struggling against it with all of her strength. Her muscles felt like they were on fire and the substance was too dense for her to make any headway. As she continued to struggle against the molasses it began to thin out and the blackness that filled her vision gave way to the blurred sight of the inside of a building.

Linda was lying on her back on a couch, covered with a sheet. She prodded at the sheet, trying to pull it off but finding it impossible to do so. She finally freed her arms, though, and started to push herself into a sitting position when a pain in her leg made her flop back down. Her left leg was working properly but try as she might she couldn't get her right leg to bend upwards. She opened her mouth to mutter a frustrated curse but her throat was so dry all she managed to do was squeak out a hoarse gasp instead.

"What... the hell..." Linda put her head back, overcome with exhaustion. She blinked several times, trying to will the room around her to come into focus when she heard a noise nearby. Panicking at the sound she struggled more, thrashing her entire body against whatever was restraining her. A soothing voice cut through her fears, instantly filling her with a measure of tranquility that relaxed her.

"Linda! You're awake!" The voice belonged to Sarah, though it took Linda a long moment to realize that.

"S—Sarah?" Linda croaked out the words.

"Hush. Save your strength." Sarah retrieved a glass full of liquid and brought it over to the couch. She sat down in a chair next to Linda and held the glass up, putting a straw into Linda's mouth. The liquid was shockingly cold and sweet and Linda coughed, spitting it over herself before taking another sip. The second one went down and she began to suck it from the straw as hard as she could.

"I guess you were thirsty. I'm not surprised. We've had you on IV fluids for the last week."

"Week?" Linda's throat felt less raw after the drink and her mouth felt like it could move again, though she was still hoarse. "Where am I? What do you mean by a week?" She began to struggle at the sheet again and reached for her immobile leg when Sarah put a firm hand on her arm.

"Ha." Sarah shook her head and put the glass down on the floor. "Just relax. A lot's happened since Frank brought you here."

The mention of Frank brought Linda's memories back like a flash flood. They surged through her mind and her eyes opened wide as she looked at Sarah in a panic. "Frank! And Omar! And… wait, we're at your house, aren't we? This is where you live!"

Sarah nodded, keeping a strong hold on Linda's arms to keep her from unexpectedly moving around. "Yes, this is my house. Frank's out right now but he'll be back soon. We'll talk about Omar later. Right now you need to just relax and lay back down."

"Why can't I move my leg?" Linda struggled to do anything with her right leg but failed again. "Did something happen to my leg?"

Sarah shook her head. "No, no. Goodness no. Well, mostly not. You had a nasty infection. Quite severe, actually. You were an hour or so from dying when Frank brought you in here."

"So why can't I move my leg? Or this thing?" Linda pulled on the sheet again but couldn't budge it.

"We had to basically strap you down a couple days ago. You were rolling and thrashing around so much you fell off the couch a few times. Your leg's taped down to a board and the sheet's tied around the couch." Sarah gave Linda a shrug. "Sorry. We didn't want you to hurt yourself."

"How bad was the infection?"

"Bad. Very bad. I'm pretty sure whatever was in your leg got into your bone. You've been on heavy antibiotics and morphine for the last week."

"Christ." Linda closed her eyes and put her head back down on her pillow. "Wait." Her eyes snapped open again. "A week? I've been here for a week?"

"Technically I guess it's been six days."

"I've been here? For a week? You have to be kidding."

Sarah shook her head. "I'm afraid not. It's been pretty touch and go with you up until last night."

"Have I been out this whole time?"

"More or less. You were in a lot of pain so I had Frank scrounge up some morphine from a hospital. I put you on a drip of that and kept you out for the most part. How is the pain, by the way?"

Linda flexed the muscles in her right leg, feeling a twinge of pain deep in her thigh. "It hurts a little bit. Not much, though."

Sarah nodded. "Good. I'm going to put you on oral antibiotics for a few more days, just to make sure we killed everything off. Then you can start getting solids in your system again. You've mostly just been having broth a few times a day when you're coherent enough to sip from a straw."

"Is that why I'm so hungry?" Linda groaned. The longer she spent talking to Sarah the more coherent and aware of her own body she felt. Everything was sore, as it had been in her dream, but she also felt strength somewhere deep inside as well as a great relief to be alive.

"Ha." Sarah smiled. "Probably, yes. Don't worry." She patted

Linda's arm. "We'll get some good food in you soon. It's good you're up now, though. We can talk for a bit before Frank gets back."

"Where is he, anyway?"

"He went out yesterday on a supply run. He radioed in this morning and said he'd be back soon. We're running low on bottled water and he wanted to check out a little pharmacy a few miles away to see if they had been looted of everything useful."

"Frank's out by himself?" Linda nodded thoughtfully. "I'm impressed."

"You should be." Sarah gave Linda a sly smile. "I think you'll be surprised when you see him again."

"Why's that?"

"He's changed quite a bit since he drove here with you in the back seat. I'd never met him before that day but even I've noticed a change in him."

"Is that a good thing?"

"Oh yes. I think seeing you get knocked on your ass had a profound effect on him. We had a long talk the day he brought you in. I could tell he was still struggling with his decision to come with you and unsure of whether you were telling him the truth about Omar."

"Did you set him straight?"

Sarah stood up and went around to the back of the couch to untie the knots that were holding the sheet in place. "Try not to fall off this time. And yes. Once I heard enough of his story to establish he wasn't lying about knowing you I filled him in on everything you and I know about Omar."

Linda grunted and pushed herself up on the couch a few inches. "You told him everything? That's not like you, Sarah."

Sarah sat down in her chair, shook her head and sighed. "We live in desperate times. There aren't many people we can trust. I'm a decent judge of character and Frank appears trustworthy."

"I'm glad you think so. Makes my decision to trust him feel even more like the right one." Unhindered by the sheet Linda looked down at her bare leg and gingerly touched at the bandage taped across the bullet wound. "How's this thing looking anyway?"

"You won't win any beauty contests involving showing off your thigh and it's going to keep hurting for a while. I sewed it up as best as I could and the infection's been dealt with so as long as you don't get shot again you'll be just fine."

Linda snorted and smiled. "Yeah, thanks. I'll try to keep that in mind the next time I'm dealing with meth heads."

"Promise you won't move your leg around a bunch and I'll get you out of this splint."

Linda nodded and Sarah grabbed a pair of scissors and cut the gauze that held Linda's leg down on the board. Linda flexed her leg slowly once it was free, noticing a substantial difference in how it felt compared to her left leg. "It doesn't hurt that much. Mostly it's just sore."

"Mhm. We'll get you up and on it tomorrow and see how much weight you can bear."

"Tomorrow?" Linda shook her head. "If I've been lying here for the last week then we can't be delaying anything! We have to go after—"

Sarah put out a hand to keep Linda from getting off the couch. "Whoa, whoa, just calm down. There's nothing we can do today." Sarah was about to continue talking when there was a burst of static followed by a voice coming from the kitchen.

"Sarah, I'm on the way in. Thirty seconds or so."

Sarah got up and headed to the kitchen where she grabbed a two-way radio off the table. "Copy that. See you in a minute." She put the radio back down, went to the front door and picked up a rifle standing against the wall.

"Was that Frank?" Linda twisted her head to try and see out one of the front windows before she realized that they were mostly boarded up except for some thin slits that she couldn't reach to see.

"Yep, he's back. Hang tight, I'm going to help him get the stuff inside."

Sarah slung the rifle across her back and unlocked the front door. She stepped through the door and scanned the surroundings, looking both for movement and for signs that anything had changed since the last time she was outside. Once she was satisfied that things were safe she headed down the steps towards the station wagon that was pulling up in front of the house.

Frank stepped out of the vehicle and glanced around before nodding to Sarah. "Everything good here?"

"Better than good. She's up."

"She's awake?" Frank smiled. "Excellent! Is she doing okay?"

"She seems fine. She's sore still but the medications have done their work."

"Fantastic."

"How about you?" Sarah circled around to the back of the vehicle. "Looks like you found a decent stash."

"Yep." Frank walked to the back of the station wagon and opened the door. "I had to go a couple hours away to find anything, though. I'm pretty sure there are other people in the area who are scrounging."

"Of course there are. Did you pull these from a house or a store?"

"A house. Nobody was home and they were stacked up in a closet along with a bunch of emergency rations." Frank kept glancing at the townhouse as he talked, nervously shifting on his feet. Sarah glanced at him and raised an eyebrow.

"You have to take a leak or something?"

"Huh? Oh, no. No, just... wanted to say hi to Linda."

"Well come on, then. Let's get this stuff inside and get out of sight then you can catch up with her."

Frank and Sarah quickly unloaded the station wagon and carried everything to the front porch of the townhouse. Once it was empty they opened the door to Sarah's home and pushed everything inside, minimizing the amount of time that the front door was open. Linda watched as they worked and once they finished she grinned at Frank.

"Look at you, going out and getting food and water."

"Linda!" Frank grinned and walked to the couch, dropped to his knees and embraced her. "How are you feeling?"

"Like somebody shot me." Linda smiled. "I hear you've been keeping busy while I've been sleeping the last week away."

Frank shrugged and glanced at Sarah. "Your friend here's been keeping me on my toes. You had a couple of close calls with that infection but she did a good job keeping you alive."

Sarah rolled her eyes and started carrying the bottles of water and packets of food into the kitchen. "You two let me know when you're done patting everyone on the back. Then we can get to the real work."

Linda watched Sarah for a few seconds before whispering to Frank. "She's a handful, isn't she?"

"She is not at all what I expected when you talked about having a friend in the CIA."

Linda nodded and her expression grew serious. "How are you doing, though? Sarah told me she shared everything about Omar with you. Are you good?"

Frank nodded and sat in the chair next to the couch. "Yeah, I think so. It's been a lot to take in but we've had some interesting discussions about Omar and what we should do about him."

"Ugh." Linda groaned. "I hate that I've been out of the loop for the last week. What have I missed?"

Frank looked over at Sarah. "We were talking about that the other day, actually. Sarah agrees that Omar is behind everything, like you said. It's also obvious he's planning something even bigger that hasn't come to fruition yet."

"So what's the plan?"

"We'll have to talk to Sarah about it. She has a few things she needs to tell us."

"I think," said Sarah as she walked over to the couch with another chair in hand, "that we should have that discussion right about now."

Chapter Sixty-Five

"Come on, baby." A man wearing a dirty orange vest and bright yellow hard hat looks up at a bank of lights, pleading with them as though they'll respond to verbal encouragement.

"Anything?" The shout comes from outside the building and the man turns and shouts back.

"Nothing yet! Try the next one!" The man inside the building waits for a few seconds until he hears the sharp click of another breaker being flipped back on. He eyes the lights suspiciously, wondering if his eyes are playing tricks on him when the brief flicker of an electrical arc turns into a full-blown light show. The rows of fluorescent bulbs surge to life across the ceiling, bathing the room in a harsh off-white glow that hasn't been seen in many days.

"Anything?" The shout comes again. This time, though, the answer is given with a cheery tone of voice.

"Let there be light!" the man inside the building steps outside and grins at his partner. "That's all of them, right?"

The second man consults a clipboard in his hand and nods. "Lights are all a go in the buildings that are still intact."

"What's next, then?"

"Helping get new lines pulled from the main building to the ones near the docks."

The first man's cheery expression sags at this answer. "Great. Like that won't be a pain in the ass." He sighs and checks his watch. "Coffee first?"

"Better hurry before anyone notices."

━━

THE LOS ANGELES PORT, hard-hit by the initial terrorist attack, is once again abuzz with activity. Floodlights hastily rigged to the tops of buildings and power poles are connected to generators that ensure that repair and reconstruction efforts can go on through the day and night uninterrupted. Offers of foreign aid flood the United States though the government is cautious about how the aid is delivered. No foreign flights are allowed to touch down except in very rare and extreme circumstances. Food, medicine, repair equipment, emergency supplies and so on—anything that comes in large, bulk deliveries—must arrive via land or sea so that they can be inspected far from the locations where they are to be delivered to.

This draconian rule impedes the initial flow of supplies and causes more than a few deaths due to a lack of aid. With military and law enforcement agencies scattered and stretched thin across the country, though, the flow of everything into the country must be properly regulated. Allowing cargo planes to make deliveries directly to survivor cities would, in the eyes of the government, open up a whole new vector for the attackers to continue their assault. The effectiveness of this policy is… debatable.

As one of many main ports set to receive enormous amounts of aid, the Los Angeles Port must be repaired and prepared for the arrival of dozens of cargo ships. A lack of manpower necessitates the opening of only a small section of the massive port and the selected location is one of the ones damaged by a bomb during the initial attacks. The cleanup process proceeds smoothly, though, with debris pushed out into the water or piled high in two designated spots by a pair of bulldozers.

Once the debris is cleared the holding areas are cleared of any cargo containers that were left over from during the attacks. These containers are moved out by truck to different sections of the port, their contents unknown and forgotten as they are doomed to sit for an indeterminate amount of time before someone is able to open and search through them.

Fresh concrete and rebar is used to rebuild and reinforce key high-traffic areas of the port that were damaged, while at the same time the electrical connections to the massive cranes and lights are repaired. The blast from the ship and the pair of trucks that were at the port severed lines both above and beneath the ground but it takes the crew of workers less than a day to find and replace the bad lines and restore power to all of the key systems.

In a matter of days the critically damaged port is transformed and turned from a darkened and damaged maze of metal and concrete into a small, functional and well-lit miniature city. A group of military personnel consisting of soldiers from the Army and National Guard as well as a handful of Marines stand guard over the port. Their presence is, initially, solely for security but they soon begin to perform other functions as it becomes clear there aren't enough skilled civilians to handle the daunting task of offloading all of the ships. A few of the longtime workers at the port are located and brought to the port, exchanging their skills and labor for food, water and security that is so hard to come by.

Before any vessels are offloaded they are checked top to bottom by a group of soldiers outfitted with detection devices of every type. The delay in clearing each cargo ship is excruciating but the government refuses to budge on the issue. As the hours and days pass, the clearing team grows faster and more efficient with their work, leading to a glut of cleared ships waiting to dock so they can offload their supplies. The workers at the port, while initially left with little to do, must quickly spring into action.

Cargo containers are filled with nonperishable food, parts to repair key systems damaged during the attacks, medicine, portable shelters and more. Each container, once taken off the ship, is quickly unloaded into a warehouse where the contents are cataloged and marked with the location where they are to be delivered.

Convoys move between the port and the airfield multiple times per day, working based on the schedule of the aircraft that transport the goods to their ultimate destinations. Some goods are transported over land but the urgency involved in delivering food, water purifiers and medicine to key regions necessitates the use of air delivery.

The main transport aircraft consist of C-17 Globemasters due to their ability to take off from and land on runways that are short, damaged or otherwise inaccessible to large aircraft. C-5M Super Galaxies and C-130s form the *bulk of the rest of the transport fleet. Civilian airliners are strictly prohibited from being used due to fears that they may have been compromised.*

Despite the massive amount of transport vehicles in use there is still a clear shortage of men and machinery during the crisis. Dealing with the effects of the bombs and biological attacks leaves the military stretched thin. Tens of thousands of troops are brought home from overseas deployments and they are immediately reassigned to help deal with the situation on their home soil. Even with this influx of manpower there is still much to be done that goes unfinished.

Tens of thousands of civilian and military vehicles sit by the wayside, unable to be used in the rescue operation. The military struggles with checking and verifying the systems on their vehicles before allowing them to go out in the field. A few brave civilians take it upon themselves to use their vehicles to help transport emergency supplies and survivors but any vehicle that hasn't been checked by the military isn't allowed inside the survivor cities.

This situation leaves most cities with miles-long lines on the highways leading in as soldiers force survivors to abandon their vehicles. In the cases where vehicles may be useful inside the city they will check them from top to bottom to clear them for entry but the additional workload provided by these cases strains their resources even further.

At the end of the day the ongoing chaos caused by the attacks threatens to overwhelm the fragile response network set up by local, state and federal governments. Each new development pushes the response teams closer to their limit, stretches their resources even farther and destroys the lives of countless more souls. All it will take is one more large, coordinated attack and everything will collapse beyond hope of repair.

Chapter Sixty-Six

"So he's planning something bigger, huh?" Linda sighed. "I knew he would be. What is it, though?"

"I'm not certain." Sarah tapped away at her computer on her lap. "I've spent every spare minute since the start of the attacks reviewing the data dump I was able to make from the annex."

"You what? You dumped the data from the annex?" Linda's eyes widened. "How did you manage that?"

"I was in the chain of command to purge the databases. I realized pretty quickly though that if I did that then we'd lose a lot of valuable data pertaining to the attacks. So I falsified a purge command and went back a day later and pulled the physical drives and brought them here." Linda stared open-mouthed at Sarah for several seconds, not sure what to think or say. "You seem surprised." Sarah smiled.

"I… how… why would you do something like that? You were the most straight-laced person I ever met!"

Sarah shrugged. "Am I? I did help you, after all."

"Yeah, but you never betrayed classified information. You always just nudged me in the right direction."

"I'm loyal to this country, Linda. Once I realized that we were going to lose information vital to protecting our country I did what I had to do. Just like with you. I knew you were onto something important so I helped you where I could without betraying my oath because, at that time, that was the right thing to do."

Linda nodded slowly. "I suppose. What is it you've found in your database?"

"Like I was saying, I'm not certain. There are hints that someone has been trying to bring dangerous materials into the country."

"What type?"

"Nuclear."

"What?! Someone's been bringing *nukes* in? And nobody found out? How is that possible?"

"Well," Sarah said, brushing a loose strand of hair back over her ear, "there's a lot to break down to tell you all of that."

"I'm not going anywhere. Tell me everything."

"All right." Sarah resumed her typing and clicking. "So I've spent every spare minute possible looking for anomalies that could be related to the attacks. I've had some software assistance but I don't have the computing power here to crunch the data like the agency does. A lot of it's been guesswork, but…" Sarah spun her computer around to show Linda the screen. "A month before the attacks there was a strange little incident at the Los Angeles Port. Their radiation detectors went absolutely insane but it was filed as an equipment malfunction."

"And you don't think it was a malfunction?"

"If it was an equipment malfunction then it was the most specific equipment malfunction I think there's ever been in the history of the world. The sensors don't just detect radiation. They detect the type, the strength and the distribution throughout the container. If you ship a crate of bananas you'll trip a sensor but it won't sound an alarm because the distribution and type of radiation will match known readings. The sensor detected mass amounts of radioactive material in several crates that were shipped through. It was immediately taken offline, 'repaired,' and then a new one was put back in."

"That sounds suspicious." Linda nodded. "What was it, though? Nukes? That seems like it would be hard to get anywhere even if you did have someone on the inside to make a sensor look like it was malfunctioning."

"You'd think so. Unless the coverup came from higher up in the food chain."

"What." Linda's response was a statement, not a question, delivered flatly with stunned surprise. "How far up the food chain are we talking here?"

"High enough to remove almost all references to this incident. Which, by the way, is the type that *always* gets logged to multiple government databases." Sarah sighed. "Someone inside our government was helping Omar. And they probably still are."

"That's insane. How could they get away with it?"

"It wouldn't take much. Falsify a few documents here, erase a few reports there, push his men into certain positions over here. If it was spread out over a wide enough period of time it wouldn't show up as a pattern in the system, either."

"So someone helped him bring nukes into the country. What's he going to do with them?"

"Honestly, I'm not sure he did bring in nukes. Falsifying a sensor malfunction at a radiation portal monitor station is one thing. But there are mobile monitors driving all over the country—especially near borders and ports—and they would easily detect a nuclear bomb."

"So a dirty bomb, then?"

Sarah nodded. "A less concentrated radiation signature disguised inside a heavily shielded vehicle would work. Especially if someone gave them the routes of the mobile detectors so they could stay as far away as possible."

"Sorry, but this is the first I'm hearing about a 'dirty bomb.'" Frank finally broke into the conversation. "You didn't mention that before, Sarah."

"I wasn't sure about it, but I found some supporting clues last night. I'm still not convinced, though, but I think it's our best assumption so far."

"What's a dirty bomb?"

Sarah was about to respond but Linda started talking first. "The official term is radiological dispersal device but everybody calls it a dirty bomb because it sounds better. Nuclear weapons are hard to get your hands on and even harder to build. Getting access to radioactive material isn't hard, though, especially if you're someone in Omar's position. A dirty bomb is just a combination of radioactive material with ordinary explosives. It's easy to make, extremely deadly and spreads radiation over a wide area if created properly.

"What I don't get, though, is why he would be building a dirty bomb." Linda looked at Sarah. "Didn't some study show that the radiation levels from something like that wouldn't be high enough to kill very many people?"

"Ordinarily, yes." Sarah replied. "But this sensor data picked up a *lot* of material passing through before it was taken offline. If Omar packed enough material into the bomb then it could spread a lethal amount of radiation over a wide area. People would be dying in weeks and months instead of years and decades like they might if a more 'conventional' amount of material was used."

"The mass hysteria caused by a dirty bomb would be bad enough. If the radiation started actually killing people in a short amount of time, though…" Linda sighed. "Damn. If that's what he's up to then it's not good."

"No. It's not." Sarah closed the lid on her computer. "Which is why you two are going to do something about it."

Frank looked nearly as surprised as Linda when he heard what Sarah said. "You want us to do something about it? Why? Isn't this a job for some government agency or something?"

Sarah laughed, stood up and walked to the boarded-up front window to peek through one of the cracks between the boards. "Do you really think the feds have the resources or the desire to chase after something that sounds like a late night conspiracy theory?"

"I hate to be a voice of doubt here but I'm kind of with Frank on this one. What is it he and I could possibly do to help?"

"Something this sensitive requires eyes on the ground. Linda, you've had enough experience in field ops to easily handle something like this. Frank's more than capable of assisting you."

Linda paused for half a second before bursting out laughing. She started to cough from laughing so hard before she finally calmed down enough to speak again. "You want... *us* to go do field work? Sarah, have you seen the condition I'm in? Come on. You have contacts all over the place. You know more people than I ever did. Surely someone who's not crippled on the wrong side of the country can handle looking into it, can't they?"

"Remember what I said about trusting people? I wouldn't trust anyone but you with this. And getting across the country will be easier than you think."

"What?" Frank looked at Sarah. "How?"

Sarah smiled. "I have my ways. In any case, you two are going and that's that." She looked at Linda. "You'll be feeling better in another day or so once you start getting solids in you. Better enough to get on a plane, fly out and ask a few questions, at least. That's what you're going to do. Head to the port, ask some questions, get some information on these shipments and send that information back to me so that I can pass it on to the proper agencies."

Frank frowned. "Didn't you just say that the feds wouldn't go after conspiracy theories?"

"It's not a conspiracy if we have evidence. Also known as proof. Also known as the stuff you two are going to procure."

"Sarah, look—" Linda started to talk but Sarah cut her off.

"I'm not taking 'no' for an answer on this one, Linda. I know you're still recovering and this is going to be rough, but after all these years of my helping you get bits and pieces of information so that you could pursue Omar, it's time for you to get me some bits and pieces. If we don't do this then a *lot* more people are going to die. A lot of them have already died. Let's try to keep the count from going up, shall we?"

In any other circumstance, Linda's first response would have been to jump at the opportunity to further pursue Omar. Feeling as ill as she did, though, all she wanted to do was continue lying on the couch while she waited for her body to heal. If what Sarah said was true, though—and she had no doubt it was—then Omar's plans were far more serious than she had originally imagined.

"I can do it." Frank spoke up, interrupting Linda's thoughts. "Just send me out there. I'll take care of getting the information back to you." He looked at Linda. "I don't want you risking your life when you're just now starting to get better."

In the back of Linda's mind she wondered whether Frank was telling her that because he wanted to goad her into going with him. It didn't matter if he was trying to bait her or if he was genuinely concerned, though, since his statement lit a surging fire inside of her. She pushed herself up against the pain and swung her legs around to sit properly on the couch. "Frank, you have zero experience in the field. If anyone should be staying it should be you. No, we'll go together, though I sure as hell am not driving across the entire country."

"You won't need to." Sarah smiled. "I'm glad to see you sitting up and looking better, by the way."

"Same." Linda glanced down under the blanket on her lap and sighed. "Where the hell are my pants?"

Chapter Sixty-Seven

A fter another night's sleep and the consumption of several thousand calories worth of food, Linda was starting to feel better. After some stretches she found that her leg wasn't hurting as much as she had originally thought. It still felt weak though, and as she tested putting her weight on it, she found that she was limping a lot more than she would have wanted.

In between eating, sleeping and getting her leg back into a semi-functioning state, Linda sat with Sarah and Frank to discuss the details of their trip to the west coast. Sarah gave each of them printouts of the vital information they would need during the trip, along with the names of several contacts she knew of in the area in the military and local government.

"Remember, only talk to them if it's an emergency or if you have hard evidence and can't get in touch with me."

"Yeah, about that." Frank glanced up from his papers. "How is it we're going to get in touch with you?"

Sarah retrieved a small black plastic case from a closet and opened it up. Inside, surrounded by a sea of foam, was a large phone that looked like something out of the 80's. A short, thick antennae half the width of the phone itself was attached on its side. Linda pulled the phone out of the case and hefted it in her hand, turning it over as she examined it. "Sat phone?"

Sarah nodded. "Military grade. It runs on their network. Whatever you do, don't lose it or break it. You won't be able to transmit on their satellites without this."

"You have one too?"

"Yep." Sarah nodded and pointed upward. "There's a small dish mounted on the roof and it's integrated into the house's line. One of the perks of having friends in high places. My number's written on the inside back panel so you won't be able to lose it."

"How long does the battery last?" Frank took the phone from Linda and swiveled the antenna back and forth.

"Almost a month in standby. Probably three or four days of talk time. You won't have a place to charge it so I put two extra batteries in there just in case you need them."

"We'd better not need them." Linda took back the phone and shook her head. "If we're gone for that long then you'd better send the cavalry."

"That'll be pretty difficult considering you *are* the cavalry."

"Ugh. Don't remind me." Linda put the phone into the case and closed the lid. "We've got intel, a means of reaching you, a cripple and a guy with no field experience." She smiled at Frank. "No offense."

"None taken, cripple."

"Ha!" Linda laughed and stood up. She hobbled over to the counter and poured a glass of water for herself before continuing to walk around the small island in the center. "What about that plane you mentioned, Sarah? I'm curious to see how that's going to work since the people I talked to said that most of the military's vehicles are still grounded while they check them over."

"A lot's changed in the last week. One of the biggest is that there are cargo planes making runs back and forth to distribute supplies between the survivor cities."

"What kind of supplies?"

"From what I've heard we're getting shipments in from some of our allies overseas. Medicine, food, mechanical parts. Things to survive and rebuild." Sarah rolled her eyes. "It'll take more than a few boats with parts to fix what's gone wrong here."

"And these are coming in through the port, I assume?" Frank asked.

"Yep. The same port that was bombed during the initial attacks. I have no doubt that was done to both cripple the port and disguise the source of the attack."

"How's it up and running so fast?"

Sarah shrugged. "Who knows. It's not like they have just a single dock, though. I'm sure they're making it work somehow. Anyway, that doesn't matter right now. Once you touch down at whatever airport they're using—I'm guessing either LAX or Long Beach—you'll need to head for the port. You could take a military vehicle there if you want but I'd advise a civilian one instead, to be more discreet."

Linda nodded. "Wouldn't want to tip off the suspect that we're coming."

"No, you would not. Plus folks are getting pretty rowdy around there. A lot of people without anything next to a port jammed full of supplies is a box of dynamite with somebody throwing lit matches at it. Sooner or later it's going to go up in flames and you don't want to be a target."

"So we're going to go there on a military cargo plane?"

"Yep."

"How?"

Sarah opened a bag next to the table and pulled out a pair of small leather ID cases. She flipped each one open to reveal a gold badge next to a small card with embossed lettering, a barcode and an integrated computer chip. "These are emergency ID cards."

"What do you use them for?" Frank picked up one of the cards and turned it over before realizing what he had just asked. Both Linda and Sarah stared at him and he shrugged, then Sarah sighed and continued speaking.

"They're nigh-on impossible to get your hands on. Display these to the military and they'll identify you as working on behalf of the CIA. You won't be able to get into classified areas or access classified information with them but you'll be able to do pretty much everything else. You need to requisition a vehicle, borrow a weapon or get on a plane? These will do it."

Frank eyed the leather case with a healthy amount of respect. "That sounds incredibly insecure. Surely a foreign agent could get their hands on one and use it to get up to all sorts of bad things."

"Normally they're keyed to individuals with embedded DNA samples. In times like this, though, they're pretty much bearer bonds. If you hold one then you're assumed to be one of the good guys."

Linda looked at Sarah as she picked up her badge. "If we can use them like that, what about Omar's people? Could they?"

For once Sarah didn't have an answer.

———

THE NEXT MORNING, after packing a few days' worth of supplies and getting their things together, Frank and Linda said their farewells to Sarah and headed southwest, taking a wide loop around the survivor city to get back to their Humvee. They were relieved to find it and all of their supplies and weapons intact thanks to the fact that they had hidden the vehicle well before leaving it when they entered D.C. previously.

Upon hearing about their Humvee Sarah had recommended that they take it to Davison Army Airfield where it combined with their special access badges would ensure that they were able to get on the next flight westward. As Frank approached the airfield in the late afternoon he began feeling nervous about what would happen next.

"I can't imagine they'll be happy to see civilians driving one of their vehicles."

"We have the badges, Frank. We'll be fine."

"We pull up, I hand the guard our badges, then what?"

"What do you mean? We tell him we're on an assignment and need to get to Los Angeles as quickly as possible. We'll play it by ear."

Frank nodded and twisted the steering wheel nervously. Linda smiled at him and patted him on the shoulder. "Stop worrying. Besides, Sarah said you're a changed man now. All self-confident and gung-ho."

Frank laughed. "It's easy to be gung-ho and self-confident when you're looting houses. Dealing with the military is your line of work."

"I'd be happy to drive but my leg's not strong enough yet. The last thing we need is for me to crash into the fence or the guard himself."

Frank chuckled and the pair lapsed into silence for several minutes before Linda spoke again. "Hey, what's the deal with it being so quiet around here?"

"What do you mean?"

"I just... I guess I expected things to be louder. More boisterous. But we've seen, what, three cars since we left Sarah's? And maybe ten people total? All of them were heading into the survivor city, too."

"Heh. I forgot you wouldn't have seen the notices or heard the bullhorns a few days back."

"What do you mean?"

"There were people driving around posting flyers and shouting about how everyone needed to evacuate their homes and get into the survivor city. They were delivering relief supplies to a few places outside the survivor city but they're not going to do that anymore so they wanted people to know about that."

"Wait, so the only place people will get relief supplies will be inside the cities now?"

"Well, yeah. You were the one who was telling me about that when we were *in* the city."

Linda nodded slowly. "Oh I know, but... wow. They're really doing it. I'm moderately surprised. People are going to be rioting in the streets over it soon, I'm sure."

"You mean the ones who didn't go to the cities?"

"Exactly. Too unprepared to store up their own emergency

supplies but too paranoid to go into a survivor city. I'll bet you there's a fair number of them."

"I sure hope not." Frank sighed and pointed. "There's the base entrance. You ready for this?"

Linda pulled out her ID and waggled it in the air. "Ready as I'll ever be. You?"

Frank patted the breast pocket of his shirt. "Good to go."

A FEW MINUTES later Frank slowed the Humvee as they approached the gate. Several guards stood behind it, each of them holding rifles as they conversed with each other. At first they didn't react to the Humvee's approach but once they saw that the people driving it weren't wearing uniforms they snapped into action. Two of them drew down on the Humvee while standing to the sides of the barrier. Another ran to a nearby phone and picked it up while a fourth grabbed a nearby bullhorn and shouted.

"You in the Humvee! Halt or we'll open fire!"

Frank slammed on the brake pedal and the vehicle jerked to a stop. Linda raised her hands in the air and talked to him out of the side of her mouth. "Put your hands up. Keep them up till they get to the window, then slowly roll it down."

"Got it." Frank gulped nervously. The guard with the bullhorn put it down and shouted something to the one who had run to the phone. He then walked over towards the Humvee, tapping on the trigger guard of his rifle nervously. He stopped a few feet from the vehicle and looked at Linda and Frank intensely for several seconds before raising his hand and waving it in a vertical circle.

Frank slowly lowered his left hand and rolled down the window before putting his hand back up in the air. The guard didn't approach any closer but instead circled around to the side to get a clear view through the open window. "Identify yourselves, please." His tone was stern and no-nonsense with a hint of confusion.

"Frank Richards."

"Linda Rollins."

"What are you two doing here in a military vehicle?"

Frank pointed at his shirt pocket with his index finger. "I have identification here. Can I take it out?"

The guard stiffened slightly but nodded. "Move slowly."

Frank went far slower than he thought the guard wanted as he opened the flap on his shirt pocket and pulled out the identification that Sarah had given to both him and Linda. He opened it and held it out through the window for the guard to read. "We're on assignment for the CIA. Our contact sent us here to catch a flight to the west coast."

The guard's eyebrows shot upward at the sight of the badge. He stepped forward and plucked it from Frank's grasp, stepped back and examined it closely. "She has one, too?"

"Yes sir, I do." Linda replied. "It's sitting in my lap. Do you want me to get it?"

The guard stared at Frank's ID for several more seconds before snapping it shut. "No. Just hang tight." He walked back toward the guard shack where one of the other guards was still on the phone. The pair had a whispered conversation that went on for a few minutes and involved no less than three separate phone calls. There might have been more but Frank and Linda couldn't see what the pair of guards were doing very well. The two who had been aiming their rifles at the vehicle had, however, lowered their weapons which made Frank feel slightly better about the situation.

Several more minutes passed before the guard who had taken Frank's badge came walking back. His stance was visibly more relaxed and his rifle was slung over his shoulder instead of being held at the ready. He walked up to the driver's window of the Humvee and nodded. "Here you are, sir. You said you have one of these too, correct, Ma'am?"

Linda picked up her badge and passed it across to Frank who handed it to the guard. He flipped it over and looked at it for a few seconds before closing it and handing it back. "You two can lower your hands now. Thanks for doing that."

"No problem." Frank smiled. "Are we cleared to pass?"

"Yes, sir." The guard reached into his shirt pocket and pulled out two plastic cards with lanyards attached to them. "Put these around your necks and wear them at all times. You'll want to head inside to the main building and speak with the flight coordinator. They'll get you to your destination as soon as humanly possible."

"Thank you!" Frank smiled and took the cards, passing one over to Linda. "We appreciate the help."

The guard nodded and waved at the others to open the main gate. "No problem. Sorry about the delay there. It's been a while since we've seen an emergency ID so I had to call in and have it cleared." The guard stepped away from the Humvee. "Go on ahead. The main building's straight through the gate, just off to your right. We've let them know to expect you."

Frank nodded and put the Humvee back into gear before accelerating forward. The guards around the gate were already back to looking bored and their conversations had resumed as well. Linda watched them as Frank drove past, heading towards the main building.

"Nicely done there, Frank."

He let out a sigh of relief and rolled the window back up. "I'm just glad those badges worked. I've never heard of them before."

Linda shrugged. "They're relatively new. I'm surprised that they work at all without the DNA authentication but I guess it's like Sarah said; if there's a crisis and they can't access the database then they assume that if you hold one you're good to go."

"That seems like something that would be easy to abuse."

Linda nodded. "Under normal circumstances it wouldn't be but right now, yeah, it would. I suspect nobody ever really planned for what to do in a situation like this. We're lucky, though. Very lucky."

"I'll say. What do we do when we get inside?"

"We ask them for a plane ride. Simple as that."

Frank parked the Humvee in front of the main building. He and Linda got out and headed inside, leaving their weapons and gear in the vehicle until they found out more information about their flight. At the front desk they displayed their badges and went through another several minutes of phone calls before the person they spoke to told them what to do.

"You need a flight to the Los Angeles Port?" The man shook his hand as he flipped through a thick logbook that had past and upcoming flight numbers and times scribbled across its pages. "You part of the rescue operations?"

Frank and Linda exchanged a quick glance before Linda spoke. "More or less. We're on assignment from the CIA. Doing some recon. We have our gear and weapons in the Humvee out front."

"Fair enough. I know better than to ask too many questions about those spooks." He glanced around and shook his head before talking in a low tone. "I sure as hell wish they would have done something about this attack, though."

Frank shrugged. "Not my department, sorry. Now about that flight…"

"Yes, right. Sorry. We've got one arriving from Long Beach in about twenty minutes. We'll need an hour to refuel and offload the cargo then it'll be up in the air heading back."

Linda nodded. "Excellent. Where do we go?"

"If you want to put your feet up, you can—"

"No thanks." Frank shook his head. "We have some prep work to do beforehand. Where can we park while we get our gear in order?"

The man nodded slowly. "Right. You'll be looking for hangar six. Half a mile down the main road, on the right. You can't miss it. Make sure you've got those tags hanging where everyone can see them, though. We've had more than a few civvies jumping the fence. Wouldn't want you to be mistaken for one."

"Will do. Thanks for the help."

"Mhm."

Frank and Linda turned and walked out of the main building, both of them feeling the curious gaze of the man behind them, wondering who the strange pair was and what they were up to. When Frank and Linda got back to the Humvee they sat in it for a few minutes to talk.

"How's the leg holding up?"

"It's been better. And worse. Mostly worse."

Frank chuckled and looked out around the Humvee at the vehicles and people going back and forth. "I'm not familiar with the Los Angeles area. How far away is the port from the airport we'll be flying to?"

"Ten, twenty miles maybe. It's a ways inland so we'll have more than a bit of driving to do."

"Think we'll be able to find a regular car, like Sarah was saying we should do?"

"It sounds like if we don't then we'll just be setting ourselves up for a worse time than we'd otherwise have." Linda squirmed in her seat to make enough room to stretch her leg out straight. "We'll make do, though."

"I guess so."

There was a brief pause before Linda turned to Frank and patted him on his arm. "Nice work back there, by the way."

"You mean with the guy?" Frank shrugged. "When you've got a 'go anywhere' badge you don't have to do much."

"Nah." Linda shook her head. "You do. But I wasn't just talking about that. I heard you were the one going out and being the hero while I was sleeping."

"Oh. That." Frank glanced around, uncomfortable with the praise. "I just did what needed to be done."

"Good." Linda squeezed Frank's hand. "Hold on to that attitude and we'll get through this somehow."

Frank nodded slowly and they both sat quietly for another twenty minutes before Frank glanced at his watch. "We should probably get going, eh? They'll be ready for us to board soon."

"Yep, let's go."

Frank drove along down the road, counting off the hangar numbers until they reached number six. Out in front sat the massive body of a C-130 Hercules, its back door lowered as people swarmed inside and around it as they offloaded large crates of supplies. Frank pulled around to the side of the hangar out of the way and sat watching the ordered chaos for a moment, amazed at how something that appeared so messy could actually have so much order.

"It's weird, you know." He spoke, mostly to himself.

"What's that?" Linda opened a bottle of water from her backpack and took a drink.

"Outside the fences of this place are millions upon millions of people who are either dead, dying or struggling to survive. All that chaos and confusion and disorder and death seems so far away when you watch these people here."

"They're trying to help everyone out there, you know."

"I know." Frank sighed. "It's just surreal, you know?"

Linda watched the soldiers work for a minute before replying. "I guess I'm used to seeing order in the midst of chaos. Being deployed in the middle of a sandbox will do that to you."

"I guess that's true. It's still weird to me, though."

Linda smiled and opened her door. "Better get used to it soon, Frank. We're going to be living it for the foreseeable future."

Chapter Sixty-Eight

"Just find a clinic or a hospital, Frank. They'll have morphine locked up in a cabinet, Frank. Easy pickings, Frank." Frank Reynolds rolls his eyes as he stalks through the dark halls of the Washington Walk-In Clinic. "Thanks a lot, Sarah." He continues whispering to himself as he goes, wishing he had chosen a different location to search. His small flashlight cuts through the shadows in each room, though it fails to reveal anything of interest.

The walk-in clinic was looted days ago based on how much dirt and rain has accumulated through the holes in the windows and doors. Cabinets full of bandages, antiseptics, medicine samples and surgical tools have been stripped bare. The majority of what remains are the bones of the building. Most of the walls and furniture are intact but there are thick layers of spray paint on both. Gang symbols, obscenities, proclamations of the end of days and even a few small murals cover the interior and exterior of the building.

Frank takes this to mean that the place has been heavily trafficked by those looking to procure the same type of supplies he is after and thus he employs a healthy amount of caution during his search. In addition to the flashlight in his left hand he wields a pistol in his right, using it to sweep each room he passes by. Light and shadows from the mirrors and gleaming metal surfaces jump back at him, making him flinch every time he thinks someone is lying in wait.

Though Sarah had enough medicine on hand to put Linda under and start treating her deep infections she was blunt with Frank about what he had to do. "If you don't get enough of this antibiotic, Linda will die." Frank grits his teeth as he plays back the words in his mind. He picks up the pace through the clinic, searching for the back room he knows exists. After going to three walk-in clinics and two hospitals Frank is already well-versed in where the restricted medications are kept under lock and key. The problem, though, is that he's not the only one who knows.

The clatter of glass bottles makes Frank freeze in place. He shuts off his flashlight and shifts to the other side of the hall and ducks down in case anyone was watching him. A soft yellow glow appears out of the darkness a few doorways down, emanating from the room Frank has been searching for. He creeps up to the door slowly and peeks in.

Two figures stand in front of a tall metal cabinet. A large lantern rests on the table in between the pair and the doorway, giving off the yellow glow. Both of the men are thin and wear track pants. One has a light jacket on while the other wears a ragged and stained tank top. Both have tattoos across their exposed skin and curse at each other with every other word. The pair grunt as they struggle with a crowbar, trying their best to break open the metal cabinet without having the foggiest idea of how exactly to do so.

Frank watches the two for a moment, thoroughly absorbed in amusement by their idiocy. First they try prying the cabinet open from the top of the right door, then the bottom of the left, then from the sides and then from the middle. The double doors on the cabinet remain fast, though, and the lock is positioned in a way that they can't break it off or open without a key or a gun of some type.

"Dammit!" One of the men yelps as he turns on a portable cutting torch, burning off the hair from his left arm and very nearly setting his shirt on fire. He points the torch at the cabinet for a few seconds before his partner grabs it and turns it off before launching into a rant.

"What're you trying to do? Burn all the drugs?!"

"I thought—"

"That's what I'm here for!" The second man turns and throws the torch on the table next to the lantern. Frank, noticing the man's movement too late, is seen by the second man who backs up and grabs at the first man while speaking. "Someone's here with us!"

Frank stands up and starts to move in front of the doorway as he replies. "Hey! Sorry, I'm just here for some—" Frank's words are cut off by the sound of a pair of pistols firing wildly from inside the room out towards him. He swings back around the doorframe and ducks low, staying clear of the shots. The smell of gunpowder fills the cramped space as the two survivors quickly expend their ammunition reserves. When they run out of bullets Frank shouts again, hoping to reason with the pair. "I just need some morphine and antibiotics! Please, they're for my friend who's injured!"

"Fuck your friend!" The first man shouts. Two slides slam home, indicating that fresh rounds have been chambered and another hail of gunfire pours out into the hallway. Frank sinks into a sitting position on the floor and watches as the opposite wall is turned into what he considers a fairly accurate representation of Swiss cheese. He briefly considers abandoning the clinic and finding somewhere else to locate Linda's medicine when Sarah's words echo through his head once again.

In that moment Frank feels something grip his insides, twist them up and shake them around. Avoiding conflict wherever possible while letting Linda take point in any conflict situations that do arise has been his strategy up until this point. Any actions he has taken beyond that have been out of pure necessity and survival instincts. It is not necessary to engage the pair in the next room. He could easily slip away and find somewhere else to search. But he doesn't.

As he sits in the hallway watching drywall turn into puffs of white powder while his ears ring he feels something click inside his brain. It's similar to what clicked when he had to save Linda from the meth heads and when he bluffed their way out of an arrest in the D.C. survivor city except this time he is alone. There is no backup, no one to encourage him and no one to see whether he fails or succeeds.

In this moment he is completely alone.

Frank double checks the safety on his pistol and tightens the muscles in his legs. He stays still, waiting for the dual-firing pistols to expend their last rounds. As before there is the sound of frantic clicking once the two men finish emptying their magazines and they both go to reload at the same time.

Frank feels the rough texture of the wall as he slides upward, scraping his back and nearly tearing his jacket on the plastic sign glued to the wall. He turns and steps to the right, raising his pistol and leveling it with the first figure he sees. He squeezes the trigger twice in rapid succession, sees the first figure recoil in pain and performs the same action on the second figure.

While both men have a long and sordid history of using firearms on others *for some reason neither of them has ever been shot. The surprise at actually being shot is the first feeling they experience though the pain comes through a few seconds later. The first figure—who nearly had his new magazine fully inserted into his pistol—drops both to the ground in shock. The second figure stares down at his chest with wide eyes as the brownish white color of his tank top begins to turn crimson.*

Frank glances at both figures long enough to shoot each of them once more. He aims for their heads, wincing slightly as a mist of blood and a few pieces of gore are ejected into the air and onto the floor. The groans of pain and struggles to retrieve their weapons stop after these final shots and Frank steps over the men to examine the cabinet.

Twenty minutes later Frank steps out from the Washington Walk-In Clinic with a dirty duffel bag over his shoulder. The bag contains dozens of IV bags filled with life-saving and pain-relieving liquids. Frank walks to his car stiffly and puts the duffel bag in the passenger seat before heading back inside to retrieve a second bag filled with the rest of the cabinet's contents. As before he steps over the bodies of the two men without looking at them, doing his best to avoid stepping in the pools of blood that are slowly spreading through the room.

Once both bags are in the car Frank gets in, turns the key and starts it up. He grips the steering wheel with both hands and looks down at the bags that will save the life of his friend. He starts to ponder the cost of obtaining the supplies when he stops himself, shaking his head to try and physically dislodge the thoughts from his mind. With a slight nod and a deep breath he puts the car into gear and pulls out of the parking lot, heading for Sarah's townhouse and a reprieve from the day.

Chapter Sixty-Nine

After having their badges cleared yet again Frank and Linda boarded the nearly empty C-130 as it was undergoing refueling. All of the supplies had been offloaded and the only things left on board were the seats along the sides of the plane into which dozens of soldiers and other people were situating themselves. Frank and Linda sat by themselves down at one end of the aircraft, not wanting to have to face any unnecessary questions while they were in the air.

Halfway through the flight, as Frank began counting the rivets on the opposite wall for the third time, he heard a buzzing sound coming from beneath his seat. He reached down and pulled out the padded case holding the satellite phone and opened it up. The screen on the device was illuminated and a message flashed across indicating that two messages had been sent.

Frank pressed the button with an envelope on it and the messages appeared. They were sent by a number he didn't recognize but as he read the messages he realized they had been sent by Sarah.

1: Found someone in Long Beach. Will advise when I make contact.

2: Casey Schultz. Air Force, black hair, 5'5", working in admin at airfield. She will procure vehicle for you two. Best of luck.

Frank re-read the messages three times before putting the phone back into its case. *I guess that solves the car problem. Just how many people does Sarah know, anyway?* The thought drifted around through his head for a few minutes before he went back to counting rivets to pass the time.

The flight lasted for just under six hours and Frank was relieved to see Linda fall asleep shortly after takeoff. She stayed asleep until the plane started to descend toward Long Beach at which point Frank tapped her on the leg until she woke up. "Hey, we're a few minutes out from landing."

"Hm?" Linda rubbed her neck before collecting up a few loose strands of her hair and retying her ponytail. "Did I sleep the whole time?"

Frank nodded. "Yep. You were out like a light. How's your leg?"

"Doing okay." Linda flexed her leg back and forth. "I should be good to walk on it for a while. Did you sleep any?"

"Nah. I'll be fine."

"You sure?"

"Jet lag never really affected me. I'm good."

"Must be nice." Linda yawned and looked around at the other people strapped into their seats. The mood was somber and everyone appeared to be minding their own business, scarcely saying a word to one another. "Once we're on the ground we'll get directions to the port, get ourselves a vehicle of some sort and head straight there. I want to get this over and done with as quickly as possible."

"You expecting trouble?"

"I always expect trouble, Frank. Always."

"Well, you'll be pleased to know that we might not have as much trouble with the vehicle situation as we thought. Sarah sent us a message on the satellite phone. We need to look for a lady named Casey. She's in the Air Force and is working at Long

Beach. Sarah apparently talked to her and this lady can get us a car."

Linda smiled. "Excellent. We'll find her first thing after we're on the ground."

The plane touched down several minutes later and spent several more taxiing around to its designated spot. The crew chief came walking around to help the non-military personnel with unbuckling their straps before opening the massive back ramp at the back of the plane. Frank and Linda were two of the first to depart once their rifles had been retrieved by the crew chief. They headed straight for the closest building that had a swarm of people around it. Behind them, once all the passengers were off the plane, workers began offloading crates of supplies from trucks onto the aircraft so that it could head back out again for another run.

Frank and Linda expected to be stopped or, at a minimum, be greeted with stares as they walked in to the hangar that appeared to serve as the hub for the airfield. The amount of traffic that the airfield received meant that no one even bothered glancing at the pair except for the guard who checked the tags hanging from their necks and waved them through. The level of activity in the hangar was frenetic as people walked and ran to and fro all while talking and shouting at each other.

"Do you see anyone who looks like what Sarah described?" Linda cupped her hand around her mouth and talked directly into Frank's ear.

"Over there. Let's ask her." Frank pointed to a woman wearing an Air Force uniform who had a phone to one ear and her hand over the other. She matched the description that Sarah had sent so he and Linda walked over to the woman and waited until she got off the phone.

"Son of a bitch!" The woman cursed as she hung up the phone. She slammed it down on the receiver before glancing up at Frank and Linda. "Sorry about that. These idiots can't get maintenance parts in for another two days and I've got three birds grounded till then."

Linda nodded sympathetically. "Sorry to hear that." She

handed the woman her badge and Frank did the same. "We need to get a vehicle. Something discreet, preferably, without any markings."

The woman looked at the badge and did a double take, her eyes widening and her voice lowering to a whisper that was barely audible over the background noise. "You two know Sarah?"

Frank and Linda exchanged a glance. The woman smiled and stuck out her hand to shake both of theirs. "I'm Casey. Lieutenant Casey Schultz. I worked with Sarah a few times, helping her out with some of her projects. She called me a few hours ago and said you two would be here soon."

"Huh." Linda nodded thoughtfully. "I guess she really did make contact with you. Did she say what it was about?"

Casey shook her head. "Nope. She said you two were here and would need a car and asked if I could help. I asked her what it was about but she said she couldn't tell me."

"Can you?" Linda took her badge back. "Get us a car, I mean?"

"Absolutely!" Casey smiled and flipped through a large binder on her desk. "Give me just a minute and I'll find something for you. Are you sure you don't want something big, though?" She looked at the pair nervously. "The streets are pretty rough right now."

"Nah." Frank shook his head. "We'd rather blend in as much as possible."

"Having anything that drives is going to make you stand out like a sore thumb but I'll see what I can do." Casey continued flipping through her binder and touching various lines in the book with her pen until she tapped on one and looked back up. "This one belonged to Roberts. He was killed a few days ago during a rescue operation. It's a black SUV in decent condition."

"The guy who owned it died?" Frank blinked a few times in disbelief. "And we can just take it?"

Casey shrugged. "This isn't a normal situation. Every vehicle, including private ones, is counted and cataloged in case it needs to be used for something. You two are the something this one's going to be used for."

"Sounds good, Casey. We'll take it." Linda slipped into the conversation. "Where can we find it?"

"Look behind the second hangar down. Keys will be inside. License plate is JCV-790."

"Thank you." Linda smiled. "Thank you *very* much."

Casey nodded. "You're welcome. I hope you two are successful with whatever you're doing."

Frank and Linda turned and walked off as Frank mumbled under his breath. "Me too, Casey. Me too."

―――

"WHAT'S your problem with them using a dead guy's car?" Linda talked as she and Frank headed towards the area where Casey directed them. "This is an emergency. Every vehicle that still operates is needed for something."

"Yeah, yeah. I know." Frank nodded and waved away Linda's concern. "Sorry if I seemed weirded out by it. It just seemed odd in the moment, that's all."

"Good. Because there it is." Linda pointed ahead of them at a small parking lot filled with vehicles. "JCV-790, right there at the end."

"Perfect. Let's load up and go swing back around and talk to Casey. I want to see if what Sarah said about getting three days' worth of supplies will be true or not."

"Hey, nice idea." Linda took her backpack off and put it on the ground next to the SUV. "I had forgotten about that."

Frank looked through the tinted front window and pulled on the handle. The driver's side door opened with a soft whoosh. He reached around the steering column and nodded with satisfaction as he felt a small bunch of keys hanging from the one that was inserted into the ignition. "Looks like Casey was right."

"Fantastic. Let's get loaded up, go see her about the supplies and then get going." Linda looked at the sky and then at her watch.

"If we move quickly we might make it to the port before midnight."

"That'll be a stretch, but maybe."

Frank loaded his and Linda's gear into the car, tucking their rifles into the back seats along with their backpacks. They both got in and drove back to the hangar where Frank went inside to talk to Casey. Fifteen minutes later, when Linda was starting to get worried that something might have gone wrong, he came back out carrying a large duffel bag. He threw the bag into the back of the SUV and got back into the driver's seat with a smile on his face.

"I take it things went well?"

" I asked for three days of supplies, just like Sarah said. I'm pretty sure she gave us a week's worth even though I specified that we only wanted enough for three days."

Linda poked Frank in the arm. "Maybe she thought you were cute."

"Ha!" Frank laughed and put the SUV into gear. "We've got water, MREs and a box of protein bars. Add to that the stuff we brought and we're in good shape for a nice long stakeout."

"I hope to hell it won't come to that. Say, did you happen to get directions while you were in there?"

"I did one better." Frank pulled a thickly folded piece of paper from his pocket and handed it to Linda. "That's what took me so long. She was looking up the latest intel on the area to see what our fastest route would be. I told her we were going to a place a mile or so from the docks so that she wouldn't know exactly where we were going. Just in case."

Linda unfolded the map. "I'm impressed you thought of that. We'll turn you into a field operative yet."

"I'd settle for not having nukes go off all over the place, thanks."

The mention of the reason why the pair were in Los Angeles sucked all levity out of the conversation and Linda's smile fell. "Agreed. Okay, it looks like this should be fairly easy to follow. It's a roundabout route but we should be able to drive it in an hour."

"Sounds good." Frank pulled out of the parking lot and headed for the exit of the airfield. "Just give me directions while I keep an eye on the road."

"Will do."

———

WHILE FRANK HAD BEEN EXPOSED to the raw, post-attack world for over a week, Linda had been unconscious and had forgotten much of what things were like. The drive from Sarah's to Dulles had been spent with her dozing most of the time and while the airfields were chaotic they lacked any real sense of destruction or cataclysm. After being insulated from the apocalyptic landscape for so long it was a shock to her system when they drove out of the airfield and into the city.

Fires had ravaged the city, reducing many of the structures to piles of ash or leaving their steel structures leaning at odd angles. One of the overpasses visible from the airport had partially collapsed thanks to three tractor-trailers being at its apex when they all exploded. While the airfield had power thanks to the backup generators on site the power to the city hadn't been restored and likely wouldn't for months or years. The level of damage suffered by the area meant that while it had long ago been preselected as a survivor city there was no way it could support any large numbers of people. Tens of thousands perished in the explosions and subsequent fires that blew through the area, a scene that had been echoed across the country.

Frank wove in and out between the piles of collapsed rubble and the destroyed vehicles, making frequent turns as he followed each of Linda's directions. The main route straight down from the airport along the Long Beach Freeway was blocked by rubble and burned-out trucks so most of their time was spent weaving through densely packed neighborhoods and run-down strip malls. There were few signs of life amongst the houses, with most of them having burned in the fires. The few that remained looked as though they had been picked clean of everything but the foundation. Doors and windows were smashed in, graffiti was all over the exterior and there were bits and pieces of furniture and other household items strewn across the lawns.

In total Frank spotted three people during the drive from the airport to the port, and all of them looked as though they were out scavenging or looking for trouble. The fact that people were still managing to survive in the big cities that had been hit the hardest was astonishing to Frank. Anyone without significant reserve resources stashed away had either been forced to move to another city or had died from a lack of food and fresh water.

The wide highway that separated the residential neighbor-hoods from the port region marked a stark change in scenery. The flames from the densely packed homes hadn't spread to the port district but it had still suffered from its own set of problems.

Huge open asphalt lots spread out along the water, dotted by the occasional warehouse and other buildings belonging to both government entities and private organizations. Some of the lots were barren but most were still filled with the same goods that had been sitting in them on the day of the attacks. Hundreds of cars—most of which had been defaced by looters—sat parked in rows near a large ship that had carried them from their country of origin. Other lots had hundreds and thousands of eighteen-wheeler trailers and cargo containers sitting in them. Most of these had been broken into, though a few of the trailers had been rigged with explosives and were destroyed during the initial attacks.

The containers holding high-end electronics, clothing and other products were the first to be ransacked by looters as most thought the attacks were over and that normalcy would soon return. When days passed and the situation continued to deterio-rate, though, they soon returned to search for perishable goods that had been imported from overseas. Unfortunately the vast majority had been spoiled due to sitting out in the hot sun for days on end instead of being moved into refrigerated trailers and sent off to their destinations.

The abrupt disruption of complex transport systems hadn't stopped at cars, food, electronics and clothing. Cargo ships full of goods waiting to be offloaded at the port either turned around and headed back to their port of origin or dropped anchor where they were, depending on their cargo and whether their crew was from the United States or not. Those with captains and crew who were citizens of the United States by and large left their ships where they were and headed onto land in search of loved ones.

A few enterprising individuals had managed to get aboard the cargo ships and raided them for food and fuel, turning the transport vessels into temporary miniature floating fortresses. This strategy ultimately didn't lead to any significant improvements for those few on board, though, as the food and fresh water soon ran out and there were no easy ways to get the fuel out of the ship's tanks and onto land to use elsewhere. One person did try to navigate one of the cargo vessels out to sea in a foolhardy attempt to escape to another country but without tugboats to guide the ship out of the narrow passages around the port all he managed to do was scrape up the ship's hull along the shore.

While most of the Los Angeles Port was either filled with refuse, partially destroyed or out of commission, there were two docks that were up and running at maximum capacity. Ships carrying relief supplies from other countries had been using the docks for the last few days after emergency repairs were hastily made to the surrounding infrastructure. The National Guard was tasked with guarding the supplies in between the port and the airfield and shipments went back and forth at irregular intervals to make it difficult for looters to try and ambush them (as had happened with the second and third shipments).

Nonperishable food, water purifiers, medical supplies and temporary housing materials were sent in bulk primarily by ship due to the massive amounts of aid required to support those in the sanctuary cities. With two docks operational and only a handful of experienced workers available to oversee them the process of getting the supplies onto land wasn't as smooth as it otherwise could have been.

"Holy hell." Frank's jaw dropped open as he made the final turn on their approach to the docks. Several floodlights had been rigged to a nearby generator and hung from cranes near where the ships were being unloaded. People were running and driving around the area, working together to move large crates and sea containers out of the way so that they could be emptied. The contents of the containers were then checked by several people who drove around in golf carts while holding clipboards and occasionally shouting into two-way radios. Once the goods were checked they were then loaded onto large trucks with military markings and driven to the edge of the dock area to await transport to the airport.

"Wow." Linda whistled. "That's quite an operation they have going on." She pointed out across the water. "Look at all the ships they have lined up out there waiting to dock. It has to be a good dozen or more."

"Why do they only have two at the dock?"

"Probably because they don't have power at the others for the cranes, or something else is wrong with them. Look at all those people, too."

"Yeah, that's just… wow. There has to be one, maybe two hundred."

"At least. And that's just the workers. They've got an active perimeter established, too, with the National Guard and Army working as security."

Frank snorted in amusement. "I guess we didn't need to worry about not taking something with military markings, eh?"

"Yeah I don't think that would have been a problem." Linda's eyes flitted back and forth as she scanned the docks. "I think we'll be fine in this thing, too. I see several cars parked just inside the main gate. As long as we can get past the guards we'll be fine."

Frank drove the SUV around to the main gate, going slow enough to keep from drawing unnecessary attention from those inside. When he got near the gate one of the guards held up his hand and walked out to the SUV while another stood a few feet behind.

"You folks know there's a curfew, right?" The guard's tone was cautious as he wasn't yet sure what the pair were up to."

"Yep. We're here on business." Frank held up the ID tag he

received back at Dulles along with the badge provided by Sarah. While the guard had no prior experience with the badge Frank was wielding he did recognize the ID tag and, together with the official-looking badge, he decided that the pair were suitable to allow in through the gate. "Go ahead. Parking's over there. Try to stay out of the way."

Frank caught himself before saying something to the effect of 'are you sure' and drove through the gate. After he parked he looked over at Linda. "I can't believe that worked."

"I can. The badges look official enough and these ID tags are good for another few days. This isn't a military area so he would have no real reason to deny us entry."

"What if he's working with the person who's helping Omar?"

Linda shrugged. "What alternative did we have? Climb over the fence and hope nobody spotted us?"

Frank sighed and nodded. "I guess at some point you just have to roll with what you've got and hope it turns out okay in the end."

"That's the spirit." Linda smiled. "So, what's our plan going in there?"

"You're asking me?" Frank chuckled. "How the hell would I know?"

"Think of something. Be creative."

Frank scratched his chin and looked out the window at the people running around. "We need to look for someone low on the food chain. Whoever covered up the radiation detection couldn't have been a normal worker. It would have been someone higher up. I say we go in, figure out who's in charge and if anyone's still working here who *isn't* in charge and then we try to get them to help us."

"It makes sense, it's logical and not overly complicated. I like it."

"All right. Let's get out there."

Chapter Seventy

While Linda had been all over the world both during and after her time in the military she had never visited a place quite like the docks that she found herself wandering around in. Frank, on the other hand, had been to places quite like it several times during his month on the road as a truck driver and he quickly found himself taking the lead as they made their way through the hustle and bustle.

Once inside the walls they found themselves in a sort of miniature city with its own rules, hierarchy and quirks. While the Army and National Guard were providing security and overseeing the offloading and transport of the incoming supplies, they weren't technically in charge until the supplies reached the airfield. An eclectic collection of civilians—the few experienced dockworkers who had returned to help run operations—were the ones who handed down orders and kept things running smoothly twenty-four hours a day.

Identifying those in charge turned out to be quite easy thanks to the manner in which they carried themselves and Frank skillfully avoided them, preferring to stay out of their way as he and Linda searched for someone who appeared willing to answer a few of their questions. They found said person some thirty minutes later as he sat in a break room hungrily devouring the contents of a microwaveable TV dinner tray.

"Hey." Frank nodded at the man as he and Linda sat down, both of them careful to hide the military ID tags hanging from their necks. They had spotted the man talking to a pair of his superiors earlier and after witnessing his disgruntled attitude, Linda decided that he was the most likely candidate to give them the information they wanted.

The man glanced up at Frank and looked over at Linda before nodding in return. "I don't recognize you two. You new here?"

"Just passing through." Frank rubbed his nose and glanced at Linda. "We were actually hoping you could help us."

The man took another bite and chewed it slowly as he looked at Frank and Linda, trying to figure out what they were after. "Look guys, I'm just working here to try and get some extra supplies for my folks. You want anything you'll need to go through the suits." The man mumbled something as he shoved another bite of food in his mouth and Linda slid over a few chairs to sit across from the man.

"We don't actually need anything except a bit of information. We're looking for someone. Except we're not really sure who it is."

The man raised an eyebrow and wiped the corner of his mouth with his napkin. "Sounds like it's going to be tough to find them if you don't even know who they are."

"We're looking for someone who would have been monitoring some detection equipment about a month or so ago when it happened to malfunction."

The man stopped chewing mid-bite and abruptly swallowed, cringed, took a long drink of water and wiped his mouth on the back of his arm before replying. "You want… what? Who?" The man's relatively impassive face was suddenly wracked with nervousness.

Frank, sensing that the man was about to flee, stepped into the conversation. "It's okay, just relax." He flipped open his badge and held it up for a few seconds before closing it and putting it back into his pocket. "We're from the Department of Energy. It's part of our job to close out the books on any sort of radiation equipment malfunctions. Just crossing the t's and whatnot."

"You're… Department of Energy? What?" The man shook his head, thoroughly confused. "The world is basically ending and you guys are out here to check on a radiation sensor malfunction?"

Linda smiled at the man. "Radiation sensor malfunction, eh? So you know about it?"

The man stammered and sounded like he was going to make up some sort of excuse when he slumped down in his chair and shrugged meekly. "It's not my fault, okay? I was doing my job. I was sitting in my little office watching the screens and everything went to shit. I reported it just like I was supposed to do and that was that."

"Wait a second." Linda looked over at Frank with a raised eyebrow. "*You* were the one monitoring the equipment when the sensor malfunctioned?"

The man nodded slowly. "Yeah… I thought you guys knew that."

"Can you tell us what you remember about that day?" Frank guided the topic of conversation back to where he wanted it to go. "Our records are somewhat muddied right now due to what's going on."

The man took another bite of his food, feeling slightly more at ease with the pair talking to him. "I already filed a report but I can tell you what I remember if you think that'll help."

"Yes, please. Let's start with your name."

"Okay. I'm Nate. Nathan Davis." The man took another drink and sat back in his chair with a loud belch. "Sorry. Anyway, so it was a normal day. Just like any other. The sensors were fine, like I said in my report, and they had received their maintenance checkups just as usual. There was no reason to believe anything was wrong."

"But something was wrong?"

Nate rolled his eyes. "That's what my supervisor said at first. When I tried to ask more questions later it was like the whole thing was being ignored. I couldn't believe it, though. Not at those radiation levels."

"Were you the one that filed the report on them?"

He nodded. "I did. I caught shit for it but I did it anyway."

Linda glanced at Frank. "Why did you file a report?"

"Isn't it obvious?" He looked at Frank and Linda in disbelief. "You don't get those kind of readings from a broken sensor. No way. And I'm pretty sure a shipment of rice isn't radioactive."

Linda scribbled in a small notebook she had produced from her pocket near the start of the conversation. "Rice?"

"Yeah, that's what was passing through the scanner when it went haywire."

"Where was it shipping from?"

"Ukraine, I think? Maybe Croatia? Somewhere over there."

"Nate," Frank asked, "what happened after you initially saw the issue? Who did you talk to, besides your supervisor?"

Nate sat back in his chair and looked at the ceiling, trying to remember the name of the man who had called him. "There was a guy who called me and explained that the sensor was malfunctioning. I talked to another guy who works here and looked up the guy's badge number and it belonged to someone else."

"So someone called you, impersonating someone else, to give you the explanation that the sensor malfunctioned?"

"Yeah. It was really weird. But when I tried to talk to my supervisor about it she didn't want to hear a thing. She said everything was under control and to basically just mind my own business."

"Interesting." Linda nodded and jotted down a few more notes. While the decision to act like a couple of investigators had been completely off the cuff it was working surprisingly well and she continued to play her part. "We'd like to speak with anyone who you talked with. The person on the phone, your supervisor, anyone who worked on the sensors. Folks like that."

Nate shrugged. "Wish I could help you but nobody like that is still working here. They all left right after the attacks along with pretty much everyone else."

"Why didn't you leave?" Frank asked.

"I did, for a while. Then I heard they were reopening the port so I came down to see if I could get some work. I get food and a safe place to sleep so I don't mind being here."

"Hm." Linda wrote a few more lines in her notebook and stood up. "Excuse us for just a moment, Nate." Frank stood up and followed Linda across to the other side of the room where she whispered to him. "What's your read on this guy?"

"He seems like he's telling the truth to me. And it lines up with what Sarah said."

She nodded. "I agree. I don't think he's involved in this at all. So I think we need to take a calculated risk here. Are you okay with that?"

"Yeah. What did you have in mind, though?"

"Follow my lead." Linda walked back to the table with a smile and picked up her backpack. "I think that's all we have for you, Nate." She was about to put her notebook away when she stopped. "Oh, actually there was one other thing you can help us with since you've been working here consistently. Have you noticed anyone different around?"

"You mean all the guys in uniforms carrying big guns?" Nate nodded with a quizzical expression. "Yeah, I'd call them different."

"No, no." Linda smiled. "I mean anyone not part of the security and guard details. Maybe someone working administration who you don't recognize or who seems a bit off to you." Linda made a show of glancing around before sliding back into her chair and lowering her voice. "We have reason to suspect that the impersonator may be working with some bad folks. Ones who could put this operation here at the port in jeopardy." The more Linda spoke the paler Nate's face became. "If you've seen anyone around here who arouses any suspicions in you then we'd appreciate it if you helped us out by telling us about it."

Nate sat quietly for several seconds. Linda started to think that she might have gone slightly too far in her attempt to get his help when he finally replied. "There's this one guy. He's... odd."

"How do you mean?" Frank sat down next to Linda.

"He's got on the same clothing as the other guys who are

working here but I never see him doing anything but wandering around. And his shoes are *really* nice."

"His... shoes?" Frank repeated.

"Yeah. He wears dress shoes and slacks along with a big camo coat."

"What's his name?"

Nate shrugged. "I have no idea. He sounds and looks foreign but I don't know where from. He only comes around every other day or so, usually for an hour or two. He talks to a few people and then he leaves."

"Where does he go?"

"How would I know?" Nate got up from the table, taking his empty food tray with him and dumping it in the trash can. "I live here at the docks. Which is a good thing, otherwise I'd be out there on the streets or jammed into a survivor city like everybody else." He started sounding more agitated the longer he talked. "I don't make waves, I do my job and I try not to ask any questions. If you guys want to go around asking questions then be my guest but don't ask me to participate, okay?"

Linda smiled and stood up. "Don't worry, Nate. We appreciate your help. You won't be mentioned anywhere in this." Linda held out her hand and Nate grasped it tentatively.

"Thank you."

"No, thank *you*." Frank stood up and shook Nate's hand. The worker nodded to both of them and hurried out of the room, going back to his duties as he tried to forget his conversation with the pair. Frank and Linda were quiet for a moment as they were lost in their own thoughts until, finally, Linda spoke.

"Poor bastard."

"Hm?" Frank looked at her.

"Just... wow. The guy's at the center of the smuggling, then he's left homeless and now he's living here while working day and night with this supply operation. Talk about a rough time he's had."

Frank shrugged. "Yeah, but he's still better off than most. He could be dead, living on the streets or trying to find enough space to lie down inside a survivor city."

"True."

"Where do we go from here?"

"Our best lead seems to be this foreigner with the fancy shoes who comes around once in a while." Linda opened her notebook and looked through what she had written down. "I haven't seen anyone matching that description since we've been here."

"Does that mean a stakeout?"

"Unfortunately I think it does."

Frank let out a groan. "Great. Think we can do it from in here somewhere? Or should we get outside to a building nearby?"

"Outside, for sure. If this guy comes and goes at odd times then we'll be able to follow him and grab him for a little talk when he arrives or leaves next."

"All right. Let's get going."

Chapter Seventy-One

Frank sat motionless in a chair by the second story window, his body partially turned as he watched one of the world's greatest survivors crawl across the ceiling. The cockroach's antennae twitched as it felt the air currents in the drafty building, skittering along in sudden bursts as it searched for any trace of sustenance. Frank wasn't a fan of insects in general and while he wouldn't admit to it publicly cockroaches made him feel particularly squeamish. He didn't want to wake Linda, though, so he kept still and eyed the roach cautiously until it disappeared through a hole in the wall into the next room.

With his nemesis gone from sight Frank rubbed his bleary eyes and turned his gaze back out onto the street below. After leaving the port he and Linda parked their SUV in a nearby alley and walked back to the edge of the street separating a small group of apartment buildings from the port itself. The apartments hadn't been lived in for several years and they were filled with holes, mold, stray animals and—Frank suspected—at least a few thousand roaches. Linda chose the building due to its proximity to the port as well as how easy it was to get up and down the stairs without being noticed from the other side of the street.

After using a few emergency blankets to set up a sleeping area in a corner of the floor Frank had insisted that Linda get some rest. She had only argued for a moment or two before giving in and it didn't take her much longer to fall asleep. Frank pulled in a chair from another room and put it near the window before easing into it. After taking some time to get comfortable he began the hours-long tedium of watching out over the port and road nearby, both wanting and not wanting to see any signs of abnormal activity.

The long night eventually ended and Linda woke with the dawn, giving Frank a few hours of rest before he got back up and they both ate breakfast. The rest of the day was spent in quiet conversation as they took turns sitting near the window. Linda was careful to avoid any movement directly in front of it and made sure that neither of them made any noise that would give away their location in the structure.

The rest of the first day spent on watch revealed no sign of anyone matching Nate's description but it did offer a fascinating overview of what life at the port was like for those working there. The Army and National Guard lived inside the complex along with the workers, though each group was segregated into different quarters. The Army and National Guard each had their own groups of tents while the workers appeared to live inside one of the buildings previously used for storing goods.

None of the workers left or entered the port during the first day. The only movement was a convoy of twelve trucks that headed in the direction of the airport under the protection of six heavily armored and armed Humvees and one APC. On the night of the second day a helicopter with Coast Guard markings landed just inside the edge of the port complex and three people who turned out to be additional workers got out.

The second day was a mirror of the first, with nearly nothing interesting going on. Frank and Linda found themselves memorizing the individual traits of each of the "regulars" they could see from their position in the building. They began making up humorous stories about the people in an attempt to entertain themselves as the morning stretched into the afternoon, evening and night yet again.

When Frank took over for Linda just before dawn on the third day he thought that it was going to be uneventful and that they would have another day of nothing to report back to Sarah. Activity along the road in front of the docks was sparse, with emergency and military vehicles being the chief source of traffic. They had seen around a dozen civilian cars total since starting their stakeout but none of the vehicles loitered or even slowed down around the area.

Thirty minutes after taking over for Linda, though, Frank realized that the day was about to get a lot more interesting. A dark green four-door car came down the road, driving unusually slowly until it stopped near the gate. The guards at the gate—in contrast to how they had acted toward Frank and Linda—didn't seem to be bothered by the vehicle. A man with slicked-back black hair, dark slacks and a camo-patterned jacket stepped out of his vehicle and walked towards the gate. He waved at the guards and one of them waved back, allowing him through without the slightest delay.

"Hello. What have we here?" Frank's eyes widened and the fog of exhaustion on his mind evaporated instantly. Linda, who hadn't quite fallen asleep, heard him mumbling to himself and sat up in the corner of the room.

"What's going on? Something wrong?"

Frank turned to her and put a finger to his lips. "Shh." He continued talking quietly despite the fact that there was no chance anyone across the street could hear him. "Come look. This might be our guy."

The pair watched as the man slowly walked through the compound, stopping every so often to pull out a piece of paper from his pocket, jot notes down onto it and then carry on. Linda tried in vain to get a glimpse of what was on the paper but the distance was too far for her to make anything out through her binoculars. She did, however, note that the man took great care in avoiding any puddles or piles of dirt and debris and his shoes glistened brightly with the reflection of the rising sun.

"Oh yeah." Linda nodded. "That's got to be him. Foreign, nice shoes, wandering around making notes on the shipments going through. Yeah. Without a doubt."

"What do you want to do?"

Linda looked around at the small piles of her and Frank's belongings that they had scattered about the room. "You get everything packed up and ready to go. I'm going to head downstairs and make sure his car can't go anywhere."

Frank raised an eyebrow. "By yourself? Are you sure?"

Linda double-checked that there was a round chambered in her pistol and nodded. "As soon as you're done getting everything ready to go, meet me down at the bottom floor. I should be done by then."

While Frank got all of their things back into their packs Linda hurried down the stairs, trying to ignore the pain in her thigh. It wasn't enough to induce a limp but it was a constant, nagging reminder of her wound. When she got to the bottom of the building she looked outside, checking to see if the man or the guards across the road were looking in her direction. The bend of the road and the trees in the median were arranged such that she was shielded from anyone near the main gate, though, so she hurried across the street to the man's car.

Linda considered stealing the vehicle, but driving it around near the gate would most likely be both loud and attract a large amount of unwanted attention. If she waited in ambush near the vehicle she would likely be spotted and, even if she wasn't, all the man would have to do is shout and the guards would come running. *Need something better… something smarter.* She stared at the vehicle for a few seconds before her eyes opened wide with the thought of a particularly risky idea.

With their bags ready to go and a few extra magazines for their pistols in his pockets, Frank hurried back around the building to the front lobby. "Linda?" Frank whispered as he stalked through the open lobby, looking for any sign of his companion. "Where the hell'd you go?"

As he walked by the entrance to the building Frank glanced out at the car parked across the street and saw the back of the SUV open. He stopped short in surprise at the sight of Linda as she started to climb into the rear of the vehicle. *What the hell?* Frank dropped their bags in the lobby and darted out the door and went across the street, looking both ways out of force of habit. He reached the vehicle and crouched behind it just as Linda started reaching for the strap to pull the door back down.

"Linda!" Frank looked up at her with wide eyes as he hissed at her. "What are you *doing*?!"

Linda's eyes had a glimmer of madness in them that Frank had seen a time or two prior. "New plan, Frank. I need you to head down the street a couple blocks. I'm going to force him off the road, then we'll drag him out of the car and kick his ass."

"But—"

"Don't argue. We can't do anything here or we'll be in some deep shit. Just trust me, okay?"

Frank hesitated for only a moment before nodding at her. "Okay. I'll be waiting three streets down, on the left."

"Good. Oh, and make sure you're not standing in the street when we pull in. Find an alcove or something. Just in case."

Frank nodded slowly as he stood up and ran back to the other side of the road, not fully understanding Linda's instruction. He grabbed their bags from the front of the building and headed down the direction Linda had indicated. Once he reached the third street he turned in and waited at the corner. He could just barely see the gate to the docks but the man's SUV was out of sight so he had no idea when it would start driving his way. The minutes ticked by agonizingly slowly until a flash of light near the gate attracted his attention.

Sunlight reflected off the windshield of the car as it drove forward down the road in Frank's direction. He almost turned and ran farther down the street but the thought of Linda alone in the vehicle with the man they were pursuing spurred him to pause and wait to see what happened.

The SUV continued driving normally until it was about thirty feet from the street where Frank was waiting. Out of nowhere the vehicle surged forward and to the left, thumping over the median and careening directly toward the side of the cross-street where Frank was standing. He leapt backward and pulled himself inside the closest doorway just as the SUV drove past him, made a sharp right turn and collided with the side of a building.

Frank pulled himself up from where he had fallen and ran towards the SUV, arriving there just as the driver's side door started to open. He drew his pistol and circled around in front of the door, keeping it trained on the man who was trying to pull himself out of the vehicle. "Get down! Now!" Frank tried to keep the volume of his shouting to a minimum even though anyone within hearing range would be drawn to the scene by the sound of the crash.

The man getting out of the SUV looked up at Frank and tried to say something in a language Frank didn't understand. The man's face was covered in blood and his speech was slightly slurred. He shook his head as he stumbled forward, eventually falling to the ground in a heap. Before Frank could reach down to grab the man Linda was out of the SUV and sitting on top of the stranger. She grabbed his arms and pulled them behind his back before using a length of wire to tie the man's wrists together.

"Help me get him up, quick!" Linda didn't look at Frank as she spoke and only got off of the man once Frank leaned down to loop his arm under the man's shoulder. Together he and Linda pulled the man up onto his feet and he started speaking again, though this time it was in English.

"United States… State Department… you're assaulting a… government official." The man gasped for air as he spoke, and though his face was still soaked in blood his eyes looked like new life had sprung into them since he got out of the SUV.

"Shut the hell up." Linda pushed the man's back and nodded to Frank. "Get him in the back of the SUV."

Frank opened his mouth to ask Linda what they were doing with the man but the look she shot him told him that he needed to continue following her lead. Frank and Linda both shoved the man into the back of the SUV, and she slammed the door closed. Frank pulled on her arm before she could walk around to the passenger door. "What the hell are we doing with him?" He whispered to her, not wanting the man to overhear.

Linda growled in response, sounding more like a caged animal than a human. "I know him. He's one of Omar's lieutenants."

Frank could feel the color draining from his face. "Are you serious?"

"Very. Now get in and drive. We're going to head inland, find a cozy little corner and see if we can't extract some information from him."

IT TOOK JUST under twenty minutes for Linda's patience to run thin. She had originally wanted them to get clear of the city before stopping to interrogate Omar's lieutenant but once they got past the Long Beach Airport she abruptly told Frank to pull over into a small shopping center. The buildings in the center had been looted shortly after the attacks and the glass from their windows was scattered across the sidewalk and parking lot. They appeared deserted, though, and there hadn't been any sign of anyone in the area they were driving through.

"Pull up to that café. Park right by the entrance, back of the SUV up against the building. I want to get him inside fast."

Frank dutifully turned the vehicle around while Linda watched the man squirm in the back of the vehicle. His bonds around his wrists were tight enough and his clothes restrictive enough that he hadn't been able to maneuver his arms around under his body to free himself. Once Frank parked the SUV he and Linda jumped out. "You grab our stuff." He called out to her across the vehicle. "I'll get him inside."

"Don't be gentle." She growled again and Frank felt a chill run up his spine. He opened the back of the SUV and grabbed the man by the arm. His face had changed from one of confusion and defiance to one of abject fear and he whispered at Frank, pleading with him.

"Please, no. Don't do this! You have the wrong man! That woman is a monster! She's a monster!"

"If we have the wrong man," Frank said as he pulled Omar's lieutenant out of the vehicle, "then how do you know who she is?"

The man struggled against Frank's grip but he held firm, pulling the man along into the café. Linda was already inside setting up a pair of lights in the back of the building, far out of sight of the main entrance. She brushed dirt and debris off of a booth and motioned towards it. "Sit him down back there." Frank pushed the man into the far edge of the booth so that it would be nearly impossible for him to escape without an immense struggle. Linda then ensured that escape was a complete impossibility by taking out a length of rope and lashing his feet together around the center leg of the table.

"Are you done yet?" The man sneered at Linda, trying to feign bravery but Frank could tell that the man was still scared of what might happen to him.

"Aref Hawrami." Linda smiled at him as she sat down in a chair next to the booth. "It's been far too long."

Aref stared at her for several seconds, contemplating whether he should try to keep up his act or not. In the end, though, he decided on the latter. His body sagged slightly and he glared at her. "Linda Rollins. Omar always said you'd come back."

"It's a bit of bad luck for you, being here and all."

"What do you want?" He spat at Linda and she laughed as she wiped her cheek and chin with the back of her sleeve.

"A lot of things, Aref. Turning back the clock would be a good start but I'm pretty sure you can't do that." The position Linda was sitting in put strain on her leg and she felt a pain lance through it. She grabbed at it instinctively, sucking in a gasp of air.

"Looks like you've got a problem there." Aref's smile was more genuine, with some of the fear gone as he sensed his enemy's weakness. "May you die quickly and terribly from it."

Linda kept her composure as she stretched out her leg, feeling the pain slowly subside. "I'm sure I will, Aref. But it'll be long after you do the same." She glanced at Frank. "My colleague and I are here for answers. And you're going to provide some."

"Or else what?"

Linda's eyes narrowed and her tone grew cold again. "I didn't say 'or else.'"

Aref's face fell again and Frank started to wonder why he was so obviously afraid of Linda. It could have just been an act but Frank was starting to think that it was far more genuine than he first realized.

"Do your worst, bitch." Aref's voice wavered. "I know all about you and what you've done."

"Do you?" Linda smiled and leaned close to Aref. "Or do you know what Omar's told you?

The man responded by lashing forward with his head, striking Linda on the forehead and sending her bouncing back into her seat with a sharp groan of pain. Aref began struggling against his bonds as Linda was distracted, kicking and thrashing his legs to try and break free.

As Aref attacked Linda, Frank was near the front of the café checking their surroundings. Upon hearing Linda's cry of pain he ran back to the booth to see Aref thrashing back and forth with his arms and legs, trying to free himself. Feeling a surge of anger and the same "click" he felt several days prior in the walk-in clinic Frank jumped forward and slammed into Aref, battering and pushing the man against the back of the booth to keep him from succeeding in his escape attempt. Frank got in several hard punches on Aref's chest and face before Linda recovered her senses and pulled on Frank's shoulder.

"Frank! Ease up; that's enough!"

Frank stepped back, massaging his aching hands as he looked at Linda. "Are you okay?"

"Jesus, Frank." Linda looked at Aref, then back at Frank. "What got into you?"

An image of the two men lying dead on the floor of the walk-in clinic flashed across Frank's vision and he shook his head. The sight of seeing Linda being assaulted combined with Aref trying to escape had stirred up his rage and determination. He shrugged sheepishly and stepped back as Aref moaned and yelled.

"What the fuck?! You broke my nose!" Blood streamed from Aref's nose down around his mouth and his voice sounded congested.

Linda, seizing on the opportunity presented by Frank's outburst of violence, turned to Aref. "Try escaping again and I won't stop him. Understand?"

Aref leaned forward to wipe his nose on a part of his jacket that was caught on the table before glaring over at Frank. "Asshole."

Linda looked back at Frank, flicking her eyes to the side. He nodded at her and stepped back around the corner, leaving Linda and Aref to talk by themselves. He could still hear parts of their conversation, though, and kept his ears sharply tuned to pick up as much of what they said as he could.

"How long's it been, Aref? The last time I remember seeing you was through a scope in Baghdad."

Aref cleared his throat and spat a mouthful of saliva and blood onto the floor. "What do you want? I'm not giving up any information."

Linda chuckled. "No small talk. Fair enough. You know we already know about Omar, right? The CIA's been keeping a close eye on him."

"You're working with the CIA now?" Aref laughed, then winced as pain shot through his nose. "I can't believe you'd let yourself be muzzled by those incompetents. And that's bullshit, anyway. Omar's on no one's radar except yours."

"That used to be the case."

"Again, what do you want? Besides slitting throats and putting more notches on your belt."

"It's simple, Aref. I want to know everything about Omar's plans."

"I'm not—"

"You have a lovely wife, you know." Linda spoke over Aref. She didn't bother looking at him but could still tell that his eyes were growing wide at the mention of his family. "I never did figure out how she got into the country but I'm betting whoever you have working for you on the inside arranged that, didn't they?"

"What—" Aref tried to speak again, failing miserably to contain his surprise, but Linda continued talking over him.

"Your children, too. Bethany and Lee. Adorable names. Not very traditional, though. But that was to blend in, right? To assimilate. To keep them from being discovered by me." Linda looked at Aref, giving him a slight smile. "I watched all three of them for six months straight, you know. Learned everything about them. When they went back to Iran a year ago I thought it was odd but I kept tabs on them anyway. Three-story home, brown exterior, small backyard, silver trim on the kitchen cupboards. Nice tile on the floors, too. Omar pays his top men very well."

It took Linda less than thirty seconds to communicate to Aref what she knew about his family. Her tone was gentle, her voice soft and her face neutral. In that time, though, he underwent a series of radical transformations. His initial shock wore off relatively quickly and was replaced by anger which was replaced in turn by numbness and more shock. By the time Linda finished speaking Aref's shoulders were sagging and he shook his head slowly at her.

"He was right."

"That I'm a monster?" Linda shrugged. "I suppose. But I'm not the one who smuggled enough radioactive material into the country to kill millions of people with a dirty bomb."

"You—how… what?" Aref stuttered for a few seconds in disbelief. "How do you know about the material?"

Linda pulled her chair closer to him, well within striking range again. This time, though, he remained still instead of lashing out as he watched her pull a black case from her pack. She opened the case to reveal the satellite phone given to her and Frank by Sarah.

"You see this? It's a sat phone. It runs on the military's network. With it I can call anyone in the world." She picked up the phone and slowly rotated it in her hands. "There's a number I punched in while we were driving here. I didn't dial it but all it would take is a couple of button presses to make that happen. After that it'll take a few seconds for the call to connect and once it does someone will take a short walk to a three-story home with a brown exterior, small backyard and silver trim on the kitchen cupboards.

"Right now there's one person in this world who can keep me from pressing those buttons and dialing that number, Aref. And that person is you. So tell me—is Omar worth that? You know I'll find him with or without your help. If you help then that three-story home will be passed over and you can go to your grave knowing that the people inside won't be harmed." Linda stopped turning the phone over in her hands and looked Aref dead in the eye. "Or I can push the buttons."

———

"IT'S a terrible idea to hit somebody in the face with your bare fists, you know."

"No kidding."

Frank rubbed his hands, grimacing at the bruises that were starting to appear and trying to massage out the pain in his joints. He and Linda sat on the far side of the café as they talked, each of them keeping a close eye on Aref who was still tied to the table in his booth. The man's initially defiant demeanor had swiftly deflated to the point where he appeared to be a shell of the man who Frank had brought into the café a short time earlier.

"I'm surprised you didn't whale into him to get him to talk."

"Nah. That kind of interrogation doesn't work. You can pull someone's toenails out and waterboard them and do all sorts of other things but if they're trained properly they won't reveal a thing. Torture sounds nice and it gets the masses riled up but evidence proves it's not the way to get the information you need."

"I've never heard that."

Linda shrugged. "It never gets much press because everyone likes to grandstand instead of doing what works. Back in WW2 there was a Nazi by the name of Hanns Scharff. He was one of the grandfathers of the type of interrogation that actually works."

Frank raised an eyebrow. "A Nazi?"

"Oh yes. He was a sharp son of a gun, too. The FBI studied his methods extensively as they worked to develop new interrogation techniques."

"So what was his secret?"

"Getting to know them. Conversing with them. Treating them like human beings, no matter who they are."

"I didn't know threatening to kill his family counted as treating him like a human being."

Linda snorted, then nodded and laughed. "Yeah, well, I'm working on a minutes and hours timetable here, not days and weeks. It's not ideal but using his family as leverage seems to have gotten him to open up." She held up her hands. "It wasn't all threats, you know. That was just to get him to drop the braggadocio and have an actual conversation."

"It worked?"

"More or less. He doesn't know very much but I got everything I could. I think he's holding a few things back but I didn't sense that they were earth-shattering." Linda sighed. "I honestly don't think he knows anything earth-shattering."

"It's too bad you couldn't get more from him."

"Mhm." Linda nodded as she watched Aref. "Omar's been doing a good job Chinese firewalling his people."

"Doing what now?"

"It's a legal term. Chinese walling, or firewalling. You keep people isolated from each other and from information that they don't need to know. Like a cell in a terrorist organization. That way if they're caught then they won't be able to give out very much information because they won't actually know anything more than they absolutely need to."

"Clever. How can you be sure he's telling you the truth, though?"

She looked at Frank. "I've been following Omar and his people for years. If I thought this guy was lying we'd be having an entirely different conversation right now."

"But you said he was holding some things back."

"That's where having days or weeks to talk to him and try to make friends with him would have helped. I think the parks around here are closed for the season, though. Regardless I'm pretty sure I got everything from him I could."

Frank sighed and shook his head. "Whatever you say. So, what's our next move?"

Linda stroked her chin. "I'm not entirely certain. He confirmed that they brought in enough radioactive material to make a couple dozen dirty bombs that could contaminate large metropolitan areas. He doesn't know where the material was taken, though."

"Did he explain why he's been down at the docks? I missed that part of the conversation when I went outside."

"He's supposed to report back on the type and amount of aid supplies coming in as well as where they're going. Omar probably wants to know as much information about that sort of thing as possible."

Frank paused for a moment before asking his next question, not sure if he wanted to know the answer. "Do you really have someone near Aref's wife and children?"

Linda smiled and patted Frank on the arm. "Some questions are best left unanswered. Come on, let's go."

"What about him?"

"We take him with us back to the airfield. He's our proof. We'll deliver him to the commanding officer, phone up Sarah and she'll hopefully get the ball rolling on getting some help here on the ground to track down Omar."

"Shouldn't we call her now? Or at least send a message?"

Linda paused and nodded. "Yeah, not a bad idea. You get our stuff back in the SUV while I send her a message."

"Consider it done." Frank grabbed his backpack first and headed back to the SUV. When he walked outside the café into the light of the early afternoon sun he stopped next to their vehicle and cocked his head to the side. The area had been unusually quiet each time he had stepped outside throughout the day but as he walked out with his backpack in hand he realized that their situation was undergoing a rapid change.

The silence that had filled the air was overshadowed by a dull, distant roar that—at first—sounded almost like the ocean. As he listened, trying to identify the source of the sound, bits and pieces of it became more distinguishable. There was a voice here, the sound of crashing metal there and even a gunshot or two. The underlying cacophony was a raucous mixture of the screams and shouts of hundreds—perhaps thousands—of individuals as they marched together, heading south towards the port. While the crowd wasn't yet visible to Frank their tone made it clear that they weren't taking a stroll through town looking at the scenery.

Frank threw open the back door of the SUV and tossed his bag in before running into the café. Linda was sitting down at the table near Aref having a conversation with him when Frank skidded to a stop near the table, nearly tripping and falling over in the process.

"Frank, what's—"

"People. A lot of them. Heading this way."

"People?" Linda's eyes widened.

"Yeah. They sound pissed."

"Looters?"

Frank shrugged. "Looters, survivors, gangbangers… how the hell would I know which is which?"

"You didn't see them?"

"No. They sound like they're just to our north and they're heading this way. We need to get out of here right now."

Linda glanced at Aref. "Help me get him into the car."

Frank looked at the front door and the SUV just beyond. "I don't know if we have time."

"He's not getting away." Linda looked at Aref who was sitting very quietly with his head down, trying his best not to be conspicuous in any way, shape or form.

Frank rubbed a hand down the side of his face, dragging his cheek and the side of his mouth downward. "Dammit. Fine. Let's go, let's go!"

"I'll get my bag in then I'll help you with him."

"No, here, give it to me." Frank grabbed Linda's bag and

handed her his rifle. "Just remember," he said, speaking loud enough for Aref to hear, "his life's forfeit if we get into a bind."

Linda nodded and Frank ran back to the SUV. He threw Linda's bag in the back and glanced around, looking for any sign of the people he could hear shouting nearby. They sounded as though they were only a hundred feet away but he still couldn't see where they were. Given the location of the café, though, he assumed that they were walking on the street just to their west.

The only reason the SUV was hidden from their sight was due to a tall wooden construction fence that ran alongside the small plaza. While the fence provided visual cover from the crowd it would do nothing to conceal the noise of the engine when they started the vehicle up. Frank briefly considered recommending that they sit tight inside the café doing nothing until the crowd passed by but he soon dismissed the idea the more he thought about it.

We can't turtle up like that. Need to stay mobile. That's how we stay alive. He closed the door to the SUV slowly and ran back into the café. Linda already had Aref up and out of the booth, having cut the rope around his legs. The man was still passive, neither speaking nor trying to escape nor doing so much as looking at Frank and Linda.

"You ready to go?" Linda asked Frank.

He nodded and motioned at Aref. "You want him in the back again?"

"Yup. Same as before."

"Let's go, Aref." Frank took the man by his arm and pushed him forward. Aref shuffled along slowly, keeping his head down without struggling. Linda went ahead of the two men and opened the driver's side door to make sure everything was set when hell broke loose.

Aref jerked to the side, breaking free of Frank's grasp. He ran forward, barreling into Linda and pushing her against the inside of the open car door. Before Frank or Linda could get him out of the front of the vehicle he slammed his head against the steering wheel, setting off a loud honk from the SUV's horn.

The sound of a functional vehicle in a time when vehicles and the gasoline to propel them were both in such short supply was like presenting a wounded buffalo to a pack of starving wolves. The people who were walking nearby almost immediately broke through the wooden construction fence as they searched for the source of the sound. Realizing that they were about to be swarmed Frank grabbed Aref and threw him to the ground before helping Linda get into the back seat. He then jumped into the front of the car and locked the doors just as the first few people ran up and threw their bodies against the side of the vehicle.

Pieces of wood, garden tools and other blunt instruments struck the SUV as Frank turned the key and started the engine. He threw it into gear and lurched forward, turning sharply to the left to get away from the encroaching crowd. Their shouts of desperation and irrational anger intensified as Frank pulled away, leaving them—and Aref—behind.

A FEW MEMBERS of the crowd ran after the SUV for a few hundred feet before giving up. The rest began searching the nearby buildings, looking for scraps of food, clean water, clothing, medical supplies and anything else they could make use of. The half dozen or so that thought of themselves as leaders of the crowd spotted Aref as he was trying to stand up and get away and grabbed him.

"Who were they?!" A man with long, greasy hair and several tears in his jeans grabbed Aref by his shirt. "Where did they get the car?"

"Military! They're trying to protect the port, the supplies at the port!" Aref spat out the words as fast as possible, trying to direct the attention of the man from himself to Frank and Linda. "They took me captive because I was working there; please, help me!"

The man looked Aref over with wide eyes and nodded several times. "Yeah, yeah. But you gotta help us first."

"You need supplies, yes?"

The man nodded. "Desperately."

Aref glanced nervously at the crowd that was forming around

him. "The docks. The dockyard, just to the south. They're unloading a ship right now. Full of food and medicine. Enough for all of you and plenty more."

The man watched Aref closely for a few seconds before looking at the others with him. "To the docks! Now!"

Chapter Seventy-Two

"You can't do this!" The man shouts through the fence, clutching a bag in each hand. "Where are we supposed to go?" His pleas, like those of the dozens around him, are ignored by the guards inside. They stand watch, weapons in hand, striving not to look those outside the fence in the eye.

"Come on." A thin man, with long hair places a hand on the other man's shoulder. "It's no use."

"Just because we won't give up every single possession we have? And follow every single one of their inane rules?"

The long-haired man nods. "Follow me. We have a camp nearby. There's not much there but you're welcome to share. I'll tell you more once we arrive."

The walk from the airfield to the 'camp' takes less than an hour at a slow pace. Children and the injured are among those rejected passage through the airfield to the sanctuary cities beyond. The rejection comes not out of spite but out of necessity. Draconian rules are set to ensure the safety of those within the cities, rules that some refuse to follow.

With lines of people trying to get into the cities longer than ever those who break the rules are kicked out. No exceptions are made. Some are ejected from the cities for accidentally breaking the rules. Some purposefully break them. Of those that purposefully break them there are some who do so on a philosophical basis. These are the most vocal opponents of the cities, the ones who lead the crowds of people struggling to survive outside the sanctuary cities.

"Impossible." The new group led by the long-haired man arrives at the camp—established in a shopping mall—as a passionate argument is underway. "They wouldn't do that! Not to civilians!"

"I'm telling you, I have a brother who's in the Army. He said they were!"

"Bullshit. If you had a brother in the Army then you wouldn't be here. You'd be sleeping on a cot in a city somewhere instead!"

"It's not like that, not after the crackdowns. I swear what I'm telling you is true!"

"What's going on here?" The long-haired man wades into the argument. "What's all the groaning about?"

The man who shouted "impossible" earlier rolls his eyes. "Jack here claims that he has a brother who's in the Army who heard that supply drops for survivors outside the cities will be cut off in two days."

The long-haired man ponders the statement for a long moment before responding. "I'd believe it."

"Oh please."

"See? I told you!"

"Impossible!"

"Hold on!" The long-haired man raises his hands and his voice. "Just calm down for a minute. We've got a lot of new faces here. Before they have to sit through another one of these arguments let's get them some food and see if they need anything else, okay?"

A murmur of acquiescence ripples through the crowd sitting and standing in the center of the shopping mall. A few from the crowd break off and greet the new arrivals, showing them to a nearby clothing store that functions as the makeshift dormitory and kitchen. When the new arrivals have left the main room the long-haired man resumes speaking.

"As I was saying, I'd believe it. Before you start with the shouting, let me explain, okay?" The crowd grumbles and nods. "Good. Now, the rules have been rough lately on people but today they kicked out a whole new bunch from the airfield. Said that they had too many belongings on them. All you're allowed to bring in now is a single change of clothes, one book and one small bag."

"Christ…" One of the women arguing earlier shakes her head. "Why? What's the point?"

The long-haired man shrugs. "I don't know. But it doesn't matter. If they're getting stricter then they're probably preparing for riots. The only reason I can think of they'd be preparing for riots is if they're starting to consolidate the life-saving supplies around the survivor cities."

An older man with a thick salt-and-pepper beard nods sagely. "It would be easier on their infrastructure. And then they can stop worrying about anyone outside the cities."

The long-haired man shakes his head. "This isn't good. We're already running low on supplies as it is. We'll either have to find more or follow the rules and join the nearest city.

"That's well and good for you if you were never in the city in the first place." Another person shouts from the crowd. "What about us who were kicked out and told not to come back?"

"Then we have to start searching more. Aggressively. We'll go in a large group, leave a few here to help guard the children and anyone who's too sick or frail to go. We gather everything we can and come back here."

"Why not just send out a few smaller search parties?"

"Strength in numbers." The man with the long hair shakes his head. "This isn't a game. This is real life. There are people out there who will kill you for a can of food. If we go then we go en masse. Anyone who tries to hurt us won't stand a chance."

There are whispers of agreement amongst the crowd despite the radical nature of the man's idea. The man with the salt-and-pepper beard approaches the long-haired man and whispers quietly. "Do you really expect to find anything around here? Most everything burned up."

"I know. But these people need hope more than they need food or water or medicine. Hope will keep them alive. Without hope... they won't make it."

The man with the beard places his hand on the long-hair man's shoulder, sighing wearily. "I hope you're right about this."

The man with the long hair smiles. "Me too."

AFTER THREE DAYS of searching the few dozen people have found enough food and water to keep themselves alive—barely. Resources are dwindling and the "bullshit" rumor that the military was going to cut off the supply shipments outside the survivor cities is starting to look more and more real. After another day passes without any sign of emergency supplies the group realizes that they need to move on if they want to survive.

They begin moving south through the city, spreading out to comb every building they can find. They find only meager amounts of food and water, enough to keep them alive but not enough to survive on long-term. After a military convoy loaded with supplies passes by on the way to the airport the crowd grows angry. The next day they continue their march to the south, looking for the origin of the convoy.

After nearly giving up hope and starting to turn on one another they find a man left behind by a couple who drives away in a vehicle. The man tells them that one of the docks at the Los Angeles Port is back in operation and supplies are being offloaded from ships on a daily basis before they are transported to the airfield.

Because he has been visiting the port regularly he knows precisely how the crowd can get in and overpower the guards and staff working there. In return for the information the crowd leaves the man lying on the ground, still tied up, shouting at them to let him go. Their sole focus is on their own survival though, and they ignore his pleas.

A few hours later, as the sun turns orange over the horizon, the group storms the port. Those few with firearms in their possession lead the charge, killing several of the guards and half a dozen soldiers before an alarm is triggered. By the time a response is rallied it is already too late. The crowd controls the port.

———

IT TAKES Aref an hour of walking, stumbling, crawling and sliding to find a piece of metal that is both sharp and angled correctly to allow him to sever the bonds holding his hands. He rubs his wrists gingerly, wincing at the pain. After collecting himself for a few moments he widens the scope of his thoughts, switching his focus from escape and survival to his responsibilities to his leader.

His abduction by Linda and Frank has delayed his check-in with Farhad Omar which he knows will trigger certain protocols put in place to ensure that compromised assets do not jeopardize the overall operation. He looks at his *watch and shakes his head as he realizes he has only a few more hours before his window is up and he is as good as dead.*

Aref stands up and begins walking, increasing his speed as he goes along until he breaks into a fast jog. As he heads for his destination, unsure whether he'll arrive in time or not, he clings to the consolation that his mission was not entirely in vain. Directing the crowd of survivors to the port will no doubt throw a wrench into the fragile rescue infrastructure the military is attempting to set up. It may not change much but any chaos—no matter how large or small—is worth smiling about.

Chapter Seventy-Three

"Dammit!" Linda slammed her fists against the dash of the SUV again and again, taking out days' worth of frustration on the plastic. Frank kept his attention on the road, glancing at her now and again out of the corner of his eye as she cursed, growled, grumbled and shook with rage. When she finally sat still in her seat again, her arms crossed as she stared out through the windshield, Frank spoke softly.

"Feel better now?"

"Bite my ass, Frank."

Frank couldn't help but chuckle at her response. "This… is better than trying to beat up the car. Still not great but I'll take any improvement I can get."

Linda shook her head. "Do you have any idea who we had back there?"

"One of Omar's lieutenants, right?"

Linda sighed and reclined in her seat as she closed her eyes. "We were a step away from Omar and we blew it. We let him slip through our fingers." She sighed again. "That's not fair. *I* let him slip through *my* fingers."

"Eh. Omar keeps his people firewalled, like you were saying. He couldn't have told us anything anyway."

"Anything would have been helpful. Literally anything at all. A phone number, a name, a—"

"Hey! Phones!" Frank took his right hand off the wheel and fished around in the back of the SUV for a few seconds before retrieving the satellite phone case. "You were going to send a message to Sarah just before all that stuff happened, right?"

Linda sat up in her seat and opened her eyes as she remembered what Frank was talking about. "Oh!" She grabbed the case and opened it, then pulled out the phone and turned it on. "Screw sending a message. I'll just call her."

Linda punched in the numbers for Sarah's phone. After a several second delay the satellite phone finally connected and Linda heard ringing. The ringing went on for almost a minute and Linda was about to hang up and try again when she heard a click followed by a soft rustling.

"Hello?"

"Did I wake you up?" Linda glanced over at Frank and smiled as she spoke.

"Sort of." Sarah groaned as she sat up from the couch where she had been resting. "It's been a while since I heard from you. You have news?"

"Yeah." Linda spent the next few minutes explaining the events since they touched down at the airfield. When she reached the part of her story where the crowd arrived and they had to leave Aref behind she heard Sarah groan on the other end of the line.

"Of course he got away."

"Yeah, but the information I got from him is good, right?"

"What information?" Linda started to reply but Sarah continued. "As far as I can tell all you got from him was that they snuck radioactive material into the country—which we already knew—and that they're making dirty bombs from them—which was a logical progression from knowing about the material in the first place."

Linda, feeling defensive, shook her head in frustration as she replied. "But we talked to his lieutenant! That's what you needed, solid proof of what was going on."

Sarah sighed deeply, pressing her thumb and forefinger against the bridge of her nose. "Take a step back, Linda. That's not proof. If you had been able to bring him in then that would have been something. All you've got is confirmation of what we already suspected."

Linda closed her eyes and put her head back against the head-rest. "We can go after him."

Frank, having kept quiet through the conversation so far, nearly exploded. "Are you insane?! If that crowd didn't eat him alive then he's who knows how many miles away by now!"

"Give Frank my regards." Sarah chuckled, amused by his outburst. "He's right, though. Aref's undoubtedly gone." She hesitated. "However…"

"However what?"

"I presume you remember the young woman who helped you, one Casey Schultz."

"Yeah, why?"

"Head back to the airfield. I'm going to make a few calls. When you get there, find her and explain what's going on. I'm going to make contact with a few other people and see if Aref's name rings enough alarm bells to get some support out and about."

"Sounds good, we'll—" The line went dead in the middle of Linda's sentence and she pulled the phone away from her ear to see that the call had been disconnected. "Oh. Yeah. Thanks. Goodbye to you too."

"She can be blunt at times." Frank glanced at Linda.

"No kidding."

"Back to the airfield, then?"

Linda shrugged. "Yep, sounds like it."

"Fantastic. And then we get to do our best impression of *not* being paranoid conspiracy theorists as we explain a secret plan to detonate dirty bombs across the… wait a second." Frank's face turned ashen as what he was saying started to click in his mind.

"What?" Linda was only half paying attention to him but his abrupt change in tone got her attention.

"Linda. The dirty bombs. Did Aref specifically say that they were going to use the material to make dozens of dirty bombs?"

"He didn't use the word 'dozens' but he did say they were making multiple dirty bombs, yes."

"Get Sarah back on the phone. Right now."

"What's going on?"

Frank pressed down on the accelerator, pushing the SUV even faster as they wove their way through the city streets toward the airfield. "Just do it."

Linda dutifully dialed Sarah's number. The phone rang several times before she answered. "I hope to hell this is important, Linda, because I was—"

"Sarah?" Frank grabbed the phone and held it up to his ear. "Shut up and listen for a second. How detailed were the records you had about those nuclear materials that went through the port?"

"I don't follow."

"Is there any way to estimate how many city-covering dirty bombs could be manufactured out of the material that made it into the country?"

"I... I don't know. Maybe. My expertise isn't in that field but I could make some guesses. What's this all about?"

Frank took a deep breath as he glanced over at Linda's questioning face, answering the question that Sarah had posed and Linda was silently wondering.

"He's sending the bombs to the survivor cities."

Linda couldn't remember a time when Sarah had been rendered speechless and in the back of her mind she wished that she could see Sarah's face during the long pause that followed Frank's revelation. When Sarah finally responded her tone was unnervingly level. "Get to the airfield. I'll be in touch."

The line went dead again and Frank handed the phone to Linda. She took it and put it away in the case as she thought about Frank's statement. They rode along in silence for a few minutes before Frank spoke. "I guess she thought I might be right, eh?"

Linda nodded slowly. "Yeah. It makes everything else make sense, too."

"How do you mean?"

"If this is Omar's endgame then he's done a damned fine job of making sure that as many people will die from them as possible. First the attacks to cripple the infrastructure, then the targeted biological attacks, then he waits for the sanctuary cities to be established and survivors to populate them."

Frank finished her thought. "Then he detonates the bombs and kills… millions?"

"At least."

The scale of death and destruction that Frank and Linda were discussing was incomprehensible to him. His mind reeled as he tried to imagine the scope of what Omar was planning but found it difficult to form thoughts, emotions or even words to describe the situation. He and Linda drove on in silence until they neared the airport when she sat up in her seat, squinting out through the windshield.

"What's going on up there?" Though they were still a few blocks from the edge of the airfield Linda could see columns of smoke rising into the air. When Frank made a final turn onto the road leading along the edge of the airfield he abruptly stopped the SUV and stared at what was going on.

Several vehicles sat just inside the airfield's perimeter, having been driven through the fence a short time earlier. Most of the vehicles were riddled with bullet holes and were on fire after having been shot at by the soldiers and airmen on duty at the airfield. Unfortunately, though, this did nothing to stop the swarms of looters who descended upon the airfield from the cover of the buildings across the street. They used the holes in the fences from the vehicles to make their way onto the airfield where they spread out, heading to the various buildings and vehicles on the airfield grounds.

A few of the people shot at the soldiers and airmen but the

majority of the people ignored them, choosing instead to run and loot instead of risk getting into a firefight. While the guards felt justified in destroying the vehicles that had crashed through the fence they hesitated to open fire on those who were unarmed. The few that tried to open fire on the guards were instantly gunned down but once a handful of them had been killed the rest of the group that had been armed dropped their weapons and ran.

The group of people overrunning the airfield was separate from the group at the Los Angeles Port, but the people comprising both groups had very similar motivations. In both cases the individuals in the groups had either voluntarily refused to join the survivor cities, been refused entry or been kicked out for some reason. Driven by a lack of food, water and medicine the crowd swarmed through the base as they broke into any building they could in search of supplies.

With only a skeleton crew working at the airfield there aren't enough soldiers and airmen to bring the looting under control without slaughtering dozens or more. The commander, faced with the prospect of losing a key link in the supply line between the port and the survivor cities receiving aid, was at a loss of what to do. His short-term solution was to evacuate any non-critical buildings and pull everyone on the airfield into a central location where they could defend themselves. Once this was complete he radioed his superiors to get instructions for what to do next.

Frank and Linda watched the looters as they spread out across the airfield. Frank finally asked the question that both of them were thinking. "Any idea what we should do?"

"Not go in through the front entrance for starters."

"Great idea. What else?"

Linda scanned the perimeter of the airfield and pointed off to the right. "There's a side gate down there. We can probably get in that way."

Frank turned the wheel and accelerated as he replied. "You saw all those people in uniform running for the hangar, right? If we go in there and run up to the door they're liable to shoot us."

"They won't be there for long."

Frank looked at Linda, not sure if he heard her correctly or not. "I... wait, what? Why not?"

"Look at those people. There's more streaming in from the city beyond. There weren't enough weapons on that airfield to hold off that large of a group when we passed through a couple days ago and I doubt they've gotten any reinforcements in. They'll be forced to leave soon, probably to retreat to the east somewhere."

"So you want to wait for them?"

"Exactly. Pull in through the gate if it's open and we'll wait just inside. If it's still locked up we'll wait outside for them to leave, follow them and..." Linda trailed off.

"And what? Ask them to kindly not shoot us while we flag them down as they're running away from a bunch of looters?"

"You're always with the jokes, aren't you?" Linda sighed and nodded. "But yeah, basically."

⸻

LINDA'S INTUITION proved correct as it took just over thirty minutes for the commander in charge of the airfield to give the order to evacuate. Three more civilians died as infighting broke out among the looters and there was enough light and heavy weaponry sitting in the hangar with the military personnel that the commander knew he couldn't let it fall into civilian hands. After radioing for orders and not hearing back for what felt like ages he was about to give the order on his own volition when a response came through ordering everyone at the airfield to evacuate.

While the commander thought that the order was due to the looters overrunning the airfield the truth was that the situation happened to coincide with news that a separate group had overrun the Los Angeles port. With the port no longer available to receive emergency aid the airfield was rendered useless and everyone stationed there was ordered to proceed east to a rendezvous point where they would await reinforcements to go back and retake both the airfield and the port.

Linda and Frank watched as a convoy of vehicles sped out of

the hangar and headed for the gate near where Frank had parked the car. "Let them pass and get on the road. Once they're out we'll drive after them and try to get close enough to show them the ID cards and badges. With any luck they'll stop and talk to us."

Frank nodded and sank down into his seat, not wanting to get spotted by the convoy. Their SUV was parked just off of the road outside the airfield and he thought that they were hidden relatively well. Each of the vehicles in the convoy sped past the SUV without slowing down—until the end. The final two vehicles, a pair of armed Humvees, screeched to a halt in front of the SUV and a group of airmen wielding rifles jumped out and advanced on Frank and Linda.

"Get out now!" The one in the lead shouted at Frank and Linda while a pair of his companions hung back near their vehicles, keeping a nervous eye turned toward the looters still spreading out across the airfield.

Linda put her hands up, gripping her ID card in one hand and nodded furiously in response as she whispered out of the side of her mouth to Frank. "They must have seen us waiting here and thought we were going to ambush them. Just get your card and your badge, get out and keep your hands up."

Frank raised his hands and held up his card as well before reaching slowly for the door handle. "I'm getting really tired of having guns pointed at me."

Chapter Seventy-Four

The journey to Aref's safehouse is made all the more painful by his aching wounds and muscles. He mistypes the keycode three times before finally getting it right and barely managing to not lock himself out. He stumbles through the door and closes it behind him and is immediately drawn to the thin mattress in the corner.

No! Aref thinks, scolding himself for being weak enough to even consider sleep. He hobbles to a chair in front of a small desk and sits down, wincing at the new pains in his back even as the ones in his legs are relieved. He opens a bottle of water on the desk and downs it in a few seconds, each gulp bringing relief to his dry mouth and throat. He throws the bottle across the room and it clatters to the floor, rolling beneath the slats and cinderblocks that form the frame for his bed.

Located in the basement of a residential home purchased nearly a year ago by a shell corporation the safehouse is dirty and simple but it provides everything Aref needs to carry out his mission. A small generator with several cans of gas sits at the far side of the room attached to a metal pipe to vent its fumes up and out of the structure. A cluster of large plastic totes sit nearby, each containing essentials such as clothing, medicine, food and water that can be easily sealed in the totes in case of flooding or other emergencies.

Radio equipment hangs from the wall above Aref's small desk, connected both to the generator and to a set of large batteries hanging on the opposite wall. While the batteries are intended only for emergencies Aref flips a switch next to them and watches as the lights on the radios begin to glow. The generator, while relatively quiet, would still let off far more noise than he feels comfortable with.

Aref takes a deep breath and glances at a clock on the wall. He is over an hour late in checking in with Omar and knows full well that the delay may mean he will be cut off from all communications and supplies. Omar is exceptionally paranoid as the countdown to his final phase approaches and any deviances from established plans will not be tolerated. In spite of this Aref still feels an unwavering loyalty to Omar. Aref has worked closely with Omar for years and sacrificing himself to ensure that Omar's plan succeeds feels to him like a worthy end.

He picks up the transmitter, tunes to the appropriate frequency and keys in his authentication code on the radio. A few seconds later a light on the device glows green and he depresses the transmission button.

"LT-8 calling base. This is LT-8 calling base. Please respond."

The only response is static. Aref waits for a moment before trying again. "Base this is LT-8. I understand that I'm late with my report and that I've probably been burned. I have mission-critical information you need to hear. Please confirm reception and recording of my transmission."

Static again follows Aref's call, but it is suddenly interrupted to a squawk and a reply. "LT-8, this is base. Your status is burned. No further transmissions will be accepted."

Aref slams his fist down on the table, sending a few empty cans and a couple of pencils flying into the air. "If you don't listen to this information then the mission may be over before it even starts! Please confirm you are receiving and recording!"

Aref waits for the reply, but it doesn't come. Minutes tick by slowly and Aref puts his head down on the desk and closes his eyes. He leaves the radio on, hoping that someone who picked up his transmission from the base of operations will be lenient enough to let him tell them what's going on. He is just about to consider shutting off the radio when a new voice cuts through the static.

"LT-8 this is base. Your status is burned." There is a brief pause before the voice continues. "Confirming reception and recording. You have two minutes."

Aref raises his head, his eyes growing wide as his breathing intensifies. He *fumbles with the transmitter and pauses before pressing the button as he tries to compose himself and decide on the exact words to say. "They know about the bombs. She knows about the bombs. She… tried to break me." Aref stops talking and tries to remember what he told Linda. His knowledge about the bombs was minimal due to Omar's insistence on secrecy but he never thought he would tell Omar's nemesis anything. The way she spoke to him, though. Threatening his family, then speaking to his fears as she probed and twisted, pulling the bits of information from him. He shakes his head, deciding that a lie is better than the truth. "I resisted. Told her nothing of importance. But she knows somehow."*

Aref pauses to catch his breath and collect his thoughts. The voice speaks again, surprising Aref. "Shey'taan? She is back again?"

Aref nods before remembering he is using a radio. "Yes. It's her. And a man, someone who's helping her. There may be another, somewhere else, who they're communicating with. I'm not sure."

"She knows of the bombs? How?"

"I don't know."

"What did you tell her, LT-8?" The voice drops an octave and grows thin and sinister. Aref hesitates in his answer and in that split second of hesitation he knows that his failure will never be forgiven. There is a click and static returns. Aref slowly reaches for the switch to the battery bank and flicks it off. The lights on the radio go dim as the capacitors discharge and the room is again awash in darkness. Aref sits back in his chair and closes his eyes, no longer fighting the urge to sleep. His failure, though monumental, will not be the down-fall of the operation. Omar will ensure that the woman—the shey'taan—is dealt with in the harshest possible way.

A few hours later, long after Omar has dispatched men and vehicles to deal with the woman, Aref gasps as he awakens. He sits straight up in his bed, the hairs on the back of his neck standing on end. He looks around the room slowly. It is still dark, illuminated only by the soft glow of a few lights on the battery packs on the wall and a dim night light plugged in near the bed. The small lights cast shadows across the room, blanketing it in what a child version of Aref would find to be exceptionally frightening shapes. As an adult Aref has no business being afraid of the dark. Except, of course, when something else is in it.

"Why." The word is a question as much as it is a statement. It comes

from a dark corner of the room, where a figure has absconded with the chair from Aref's desk. The figure is masked in darkness, enveloped by it as though it is a physical blanket to be wrapped and draped around one's body.

Though the underground room is cold Aref can feel sweat pouring from his forehead and neck and dripping down his chest and back. His teeth chatter nervously, uncontrollably, and he feels the sudden urge to vomit. "Wh—what did you—" He tries to speak but the words are difficult to form. His tongue feels engorged, like its filling his entire mouth and is about to shatter his teeth.

The figure shifts slightly, uncrossing its legs and then re-crossing them in the opposite direction. "What did I do? Show you more mercy than you deserve." The words are spoken with raw emotion and Aref feels tears well up in his eyes though he doesn't know whether it's from what the figure said or from what the figure did to him.

"I—" Aref tries to speak again but the figure shushes him.

"Shh. Speaking will only make it more painful." Next comes a long sigh. "You were once strong. Able to resist. Why did you let her break you?"

"My… family." Aref chokes out the word, distinctly aware that the figure just told him not to speak before asking him a question.

"She threatened your family? That was all it took?" Aref can't see the figure but he can sense that it is shaking its head. "Someone so promising. So strong. So weak. So ineffectual."

Aref feels his limbs grow numb. He falls back on his mattress, not even bothering with trying to move. He knows it is useless. The poison—he doesn't know the exact type—has worked its way through most of his body. His brain remains relatively alert even as his internal organs and autonomic functions begin to shut down. His heartbeat grows erratic, his breathing slows and he feels his body slip away before him. He tries to move his lips to tell the figure he is sorry but it is far too late.

The figure stands slowly and moves out of the shadows. He places a hand on Aref's face and closes the dead man's eyelids. He shakes his head before sighing, turning around and leaving the dingy basement. Once outside a pair of men go back into the basement, each of them carrying a can of gasoline and a lighter. The basement and all of its contents are soon ablaze, snuffing out all traces of Aref and the fact that he was ever there.

As Omar watches the flames and contemplates the fate of his lieutenant he hears the soft padding of approaching footsteps. "Sir. They have fled. We are pursuing." The man speaks quietly with a smooth, accented voice.

Omar nods once. "Ensure you delay them as long as possible. I will see how fast the timetable can be moved up." He refuses to give in to the twinges of doubt that play at the edge of his mind and he dismisses them as swiftly as they appear. His upper lip curls as he speaks the nickname he gave to the woman long ago who still dogs him even after all these years.

"Stop the shey'taan. No matter the cost."

Chapter Seventy-Five

"What the hell are you two doing out here?" It had taken a couple minutes of shouting and swearing on both Linda's and the airmen's parts to get to the point where the airmen were no longer actively pointing their rifles at Frank and Linda. The one who had shouted at them initially—one Robert Brightman—was still clearly pissed off, though, and he wanted to know exactly what they were doing.

"We're working with the CIA, and we—"

"Your badges make that clear, but that doesn't answer my question. Why are you parked out here watching us?"

"Casey Schultz got us this SUV to help us get to the Los Angeles Port. We've been doing surveillance and left there a short time ago with a man connected to the initial attacks."

"The... attacks?" Robert shook his head. "You mean the bombs and biological shit?"

"Exactly."

He was about to reply when another airman ran up behind him and tapped him frantically on the shoulder. "We just got word that the port's being overrun. We need to get moving right now."

"The port?" Robert turned back to Frank and Linda. "That's

where you two were doing surveillance, right? Do you know anything about this?"

Frank and Linda both shook their heads and she replied. "No. We had a brief run-in with a crowd of survivors just north of the docks, though. That's when we lost the suspect connected to the attacks. The crowd started rushing us and we had to leave in a hurry."

"Brightman! We've got to go!" Another airman ran up behind Robert. "A few of them are dispersing from the airfield and heading our way."

Robert nodded and glanced at Linda and Frank. "Grab your gear and get into the Humvee. When we get to the rendezvous you can talk to my lieutenant and explain all this to him."

The ride through the city was bumpy and fast. As the landscape changed from thick walls of burned-out residential and commercial structures into more open areas Frank was the first to spot the cluster of military vehicles that were parked on a baseball field just off the road. Instead of stopping near the end of the line with the other vehicles Robert's driver took them to the center of the field where a few portable tables had been set up with maps and communications equipment.

Robert was the first out of the Humvee followed by Frank and Linda. They both had their packs on their backs and their rifles on their shoulders making them—aside from the lack of uniforms—blend in moderately well with the soldiers and airmen. They walked up to the table where Lieutenant Jackson was listening intently to a woman with a streak of blood across her face and her arm in a sling.

"We're still missing a few soldiers but we think they got out safely. They may have taken the long way around, though, so it could be another hour before they get here."

Jackson looked at his watch and furrowed his brow. "We'll give them and the others an hour more, max, then we're moving on the port."

"Sir?" Robert stepped forward, taking the mention of the port to jump into the conversation. "I have a couple folks here who have some information related to the port and the attacks in general."

Lieutenant Jackson, a short man with bright red hair mostly covered by a camo-colored cap, turned and looked Frank and Linda over top to bottom. "You two are?"

"Linda Rollins. Former Marine Raider." She held out the badge given to her by Sarah along with the ID card they received at Dulles. "We're working on behalf of the CIA to figure out what the hell's going on in the country and how to find those responsible for it."

Jackson glanced at the badge and ID before looking at Frank. "Frank Richards. Right?"

Frank nodded, somewhat unsure of what to say since he had no idea how the man in front of him knew his name. Before he or Linda could speak, though, Lieutenant Jackson turned to speak loudly to the men and women surrounding him. "All right, everyone. We're moving out in an hour. Check your gear and prepare for potential hostile engagements. Details will be coming before we head out." He then looked back at Linda and Frank and motioned at them. "Follow me."

Frank and Linda followed the lieutenant as he wound through the lines of vehicles parked in the middle of the field. He stopped in front of a large bulky truck that looked more like an RV than a cargo vehicle. He opened a door on the side and stepped in and the pair followed. Inside the vehicle were rows of seats placed near the walls of the vehicle on which were hung dozens of large and small computer monitors. A pair of keyboards and a mouse sat in front of each seat though only a few of them were filled, near the door where the trio entered.

Lieutenant Jackson made his way to the far back of the vehicle where he sat down in one of the chairs and pointed at a pair across from him. "Sit down." His tone was neutral but Linda could tell he was studying them carefully. She wasn't sure how he knew who Frank was but she decided to test a hunch.

"How do you know Sarah?" Linda eased into her seat, watching Jackson's facial expression. It stayed unchanged except for the slightest twitch of one of his eyebrows. He stared back at her, studying her as much as she did him until he nodded, relenting.

"I've worked with her on Agency business. Both officially and unofficially. She managed to contact me directly just before we had to evac the airfield. I don't know how she still has access to the Milsat network, but… yeah." He cleared his throat. "She told me you two found something out about the initial attacks. Said it was critically important and that I needed to drop everything and help you out." Jackson raised his hands and gestured to his general surroundings. "We don't have much to offer and I'm about to dedicate my men and resources to retaking the port. If you want anything then you'll need to make a compelling case that I can run up the food chain."

"What do you know about a man named Farhad Omar?"

Lieutenant Jackson's eyebrow twitched again. "I've heard that you have a history with him. You've been looking for revenge on him for something for years."

Linda ignored the undertone in Jackson's voice. "Omar's the one who set up this whole attack. The initial destruction of our transportation infrastructure, the biological attacks and the upcoming nuclear attacks."

"Nuclear?" Jackson's eyes widened. He glanced down the length of the vehicle and leaned in, lowering his voice so that the two soldiers and one airman near the front couldn't hear him. "What do you mean by nuclear?"

"Dirty bombs." Linda whispered back to him. "He's going to target the survivor cities with them. It's likely that they're already in place and he's just waiting for more people to keep filtering in before he sets them off."

"No." Jackson shook his head. "Impossible. We've got… countermeasures for that type of thing."

"Mobile detection units, yeah." Linda shrugged. "Doesn't matter when he knows their routes."

"How would he know that?"

"Someone's working with him on the inside. High enough up

to have access to all that kind of information and more. Someone who's been helping him plan his attack and give him and his cronies access to the country."

Lieutenant Jackson closed his eyes and sat back in his seat, trying to process the information Linda had just dumped on him. "I don't… it can't be true." He shook his head. "The alphabet agencies would have been all over this."

"Again, man on the inside. High up. High enough to hide enough of the pieces that Omar never showed up on peoples' radar."

Jackson opened his eyes and stared at Linda and Frank for a long moment before leaning forward again and speaking in a quiet voice. "I'm not saying I believe you and what I'm about to tell you never came from me. Got it?" Frank and Linda both nodded and Jackson continued. "We've had some incidents in a few cities."

"What kind of incidents?" Frank asked.

Jackson licked his lips, struggling with how to phrase what he was about to say. "In the cities that were biologically affected there were post-infection incidents. Attacks on the rescue teams. Groups of heavily armed men ambushed the search and rescue crews. It seemed as though their goal was to keep us from saving any survivors of the biological attacks."

Linda looked at Frank and shook her head. "It's all a diversion to push people toward the survivor cities. Corral as many as he can inside them, make everyone think the cities are the only safe places in the country."

"This is something I have to pass up the chain of command." Jackson started to stand up but Linda grabbed him by his shirt and pulled him back down into his seat with a thud. One of the soldiers up front turned and frowned at the noise but went back to his work after Jackson shot him a dirty look.

"No!" Linda hissed under her breath. "We can't be going around telling people about this willy-nilly!"

"I'm not telling people, I'm passing it up the chain! I'm trying to get us some help to stop this guy!"

"Did you miss the part where I told you he has someone on the inside? Maybe more than just one? Right now the only people who know the details of this are us three and Sarah. And she's the only one that has enough perspective on what's going on to decide who to tell."

Jackson arched his back and cracked his neck, bristling at Linda. "Don't tell me how to handle my business, Rollins. I've got a job—"

"Your job, *Jackson*, is to honor your oath." Linda leaned forward, nearly touching her nose to the lieutenant's as she snarled at him. "If you start shouting about this over channels that I guarantee you someone unsavory is listening to then you're going to have the blood of millions on your hands if he decides to set off those bombs prematurely."

Frank found himself nearly falling out of his chair after unknowingly leaning away from Linda due to the intensity of how she spoke. She sat back after finishing her fiery tirade and watched Jackson carefully. She hadn't gotten enough of a read on him to know whether he was going to let his pride get the better of him and do what he wanted regardless of what she said or whether he would actually listen to her. The seconds stretched on in agony as they stared each other down before he finally, mercifully, relented.

"Fine." Jackson shook his head as his shoulders slumped. "You'd better be right about this."

"We are." Linda glanced at Frank, a look of relief washing over her face. "And thank you."

"Save it for the court-martial." The lieutenant took a deep breath and looked at her again. "So what is it you want me to do?"

After shooing out the two soldiers and the airman from the vehicle Linda produced the satellite phone from its case and powered it on. She dialed Sarah's number as Jackson watched, trying to hide his surprise at seeing the phone connect to the military's satellite network.

"What is it this time?" Sarah wasted no time getting down to business.

"The situation's developing rapidly. A couple of big groups of survivors stormed the airfield and the port. We linked up with Lieutenant Jackson—"

"I know Jackson. Did he give you any trouble?"

Linda stifled a chuckle. "No, he's been very helpful."

"What do you need from me, then?"

"We need a game plan. If Omar's distributing these bombs to the survivor cities then we need to get at him."

"Which we might have been able to do had you not lost Aref." Sarah sighed. "I'm working on an alternative angle but you may be able to help speed it up. At the port, when you talked to the radiation detector operator, did you get any details from him on the dimensions or visual markings on the crates that tripped the sensors?"

Linda and Frank glanced at each other. "No, I can't say we did, though we didn't really think of it."

"I assume Jackson's been ordered to retake the port?"

"Yes, ma'am." Lieutenant Jackson leaned towards the phone as he spoke. "We'll be leaving in thirty."

"Good. You need to go with him there. Once they retake the port either talk to the operator or, if he's dead, search their records. If we know what the crates look like or at least get their weight and dimensions then I can shoot up a flare and get some searches started in the cities."

"Will do. Do you have any other leads we can pursue to track down Omar?"

"No. Especially not if Aref's made it back to him to alert him to your presence. Speaking of which, you need to prepare for that eventuality." Linda felt her stomach drop at Sarah's words. She hadn't thought about Aref making it back to Omar since, during her interrogation, he told her that Omar had his people split up into cells. With Aref's escape she had started to doubt all of the questioning she performed on him and wondered how much of what he said had actually been true.

"How cheery." Frank replied. Linda was about to ask Sarah another question when the door to the vehicle flew open and a soldier breathlessly ran inside.

"Lieutenant! We have a problem, sir!"

Lieutenant Jackson jumped up and glanced at Frank and Linda. "We'll continue this later." He hurried down to the soldier. "What is it?"

We just lost contact with the patrol on our northern flank, sir. The loss of communication was accompanied by a brief burst of gunfire."

"Any visual on the patrol?"

The soldier shook his head. "No, sir. They were two blocks away. Last check-in was 5 minutes ago when they were turning east."

Sarah, who had been able to hear the conversation spoke quickly to Frank and Linda. "You two stay safe. Get to the port and get me whatever information you have. I'll be in touch soon." The line went dead and Linda quickly put the phone away before joining Frank near Lieutenant Jackson.

"Get everyone on alert," Jackson said, "but do it quietly. We may be under surveillance right now and I don't want them knowing that we know what's going on. Move everyone into a defensive position with extra gunners facing north, but ensure all sides are covered. Get me an exit strategy from this field, too."

The soldier nodded. "Yes sir!" He ran out and Jackson turned to Frank and Linda.

"Keep your heads down and stay in here. Got it? We're going to roll out soon and this is the best place you—"

Jackson's words were cut short by the sharp, shrill whistle of an incoming projectile followed immediately by the deafening blast and intense heat of an explosion. The end of the vehicle where the three had been sitting while talking to Sarah was torn apart by the blast, sending a shower of hot metal and flames into the air. Frank felt pain in his right side as bits of metal and plastic caught him on the side of his body, cutting through his pants and shirt and burning his skin. The concussive force of the blast knocked him, Linda and Jackson over but aside from a few minor burns and cuts they escaped relatively unscathed thanks to their distance from the explosion.

"Move!" Linda responded to the blast on instinct, shoving Jackson through the door and pulling Frank behind her. She pushed and dragged the two of them down to the next closest vehicle and flipped the safety off on her rifle which she and Frank had thankfully thought to bring with them when they got up from their seats just a moment before. Shaking off the ringing in her ears and the shouts coming from every direction around her Linda crouched to look up and over the vehicle they were hiding behind as she tried to locate the source of the gunfire.

On the northern edge of the baseball field a group of soldiers were firing at a row of abandoned buildings across the street. Flashes of yellow light illuminated the interior of several of the windows of the buildings as those inside shot back, keeping the soldiers pinned down and unable to move from their position behind the field's concession stands.

Off to the west toward the airfield a cluster of airmen were bringing the most heavily armored vehicles around as they worked to form a half-circle covering the west and north side. They were being engaged by a group of hostiles that had some sort of high-caliber weaponry. Linda crouch-walked to the far end of the vehicle and looked out to the west when the whistle of another rocket-propelled grenade sounded out over her head. She instinctively dropped to the ground just as the projectile exploded a few dozen feet beyond the convoy, sending up a shower of pulverized grass and dirt.

"Move out! Move out!" Jackson shouted at his subordinates, pointing off to the east. "Get off the field and move out to the secondary rendezvous! Get your asses moving!" He turned and bellowed out the orders at every man and woman he could see before pushing Frank and Linda to get into the vehicle the three of them had been hiding behind.

"Where's the backup site?" Linda slid behind the wheel before Frank or Jackson managed to do so. She started up the engine and pulled out, weaving a path between the other vehicles that were either just starting to move or which were still stationary.

"East, half a klick."

"In the city?"

"A big parking lot. Drone footage showed it being mostly empty."

Linda shook her head. "I don't like the sound of that. We should go farther and spread out amongst the buildings. Force them to work to get to us."

Jackson looked at Frank then back at Linda, shaking his head vigorously. "No way! We'll set up a defensive perimeter there and use the surrounding buildings as cover. These looters aren't going to catch us with our pants down a second time."

Linda slammed on the brakes and jerked the wheel to the right, careening wildly around the Humvee in front of them that abruptly turned into a glowing yellow ball of fire. Metal raked against the windows and armor of their vehicle and she gritted her teeth as the rough movement sent a shockwave of pain through her leg. "Seriously, Lieutenant? You think these are looters? Where'd they get the RPGs?"

"From… the airfield?"

Linda took her eyes off the road just long enough to give Jackson a death stare, sending him shrinking back into his seat. "Who do you think they are, then?"

"It's got to be Omar's men." Linda glanced in the side mirror, silently screaming for the others in the field to move faster. The soldiers and airmen were dealing with both the attack and with trying to move off the baseball field without suffering heavy losses. Three more vehicles went up in flames by the time Linda got to the edge of the field and decided to make her move.

"Jackson!" Linda shouted at him in the back seat. "Get your ass on that gun!"

Lieutenant Jackson, while initially taken aback by Linda's takeover of the situation, had adjusted to the course of events and understood immediately what she wanted to do. "Strafe the north side, then head down the westerly flank?"

"Damn right! We'll be bobbing and weaving to avoid those RPGs so make sure you strap in!"

Jackson nodded and unbolted the hatch to the mounted

machine gun on top of the Humvee. A cross between a new and old model, the turret was completely enclosed on the top and all sides to protect the gunner but it required manual control to operate versus the remote-controlled systems in the newer vehicles. It had been a few years since Jackson had last used one of the turrets but as he fastened the leather straps around his shoulders and waist he felt his muscle memory engage.

"Now!" Linda shouted from below and Jackson swiveled the gun to the right. Flashes of gunfire from the buildings showed him his primary targets and he squeezed the trigger on the gun's handle. A spray of .50-caliber rounds flew forth from the barrel of the gun and into the front of the building in a long arc. A combination of phosphorous and armor-piercing rounds made for a stunning—and painful—show for those both inside and outside the building. The roar of the Humvee's engine was too loud to hear anything going on outside but as Frank clung to his seat to avoid smashing into Linda or the passenger door he could imagine the screams of agony coming from the attackers.

Linda kept the Humvee moving both forward and to the sides, alternating between slow side-to-side motions and quick ones. She alternated the speed of the Humvee too, applying the brakes and the gas at random intervals to try and keep the attackers from hitting them with an RPG. The counterattack was swift and surprising enough for the attackers that they didn't get a chance to return fire on the Humvee, but pulled back instead to avoid being shot.

It took Linda less than a minute to circle around the north and west sides of the field as Jackson laid down suppressive fire, but the distraction was more than adequate. Soldiers and airmen who had been pinned down by the incoming fire and RPGs quickly loaded into vehicles that roared off the field heading east. A pair of Humvees broke off from the convoy and followed in Linda's path, spraying the buildings with fire before following the rest of the vehicles in a hasty retreat.

For a moment Lieutenant Jackson considered ordering a halt to the retreat so that they could launch a counteroffensive but as they drove past the field and approached the tail end of the convoy he realized that they needed more time before they could hope to be successful enough to minimize their casualties.

Several vehicles had either been destroyed or damaged enough that they were left behind on the baseball field and Linda could see that more than a few of the ones that were driving away with the convoy had sustained light and heavy damage. Gunfire mixed with the imprecise RPG fire had wreaked a moderate amount of havoc on the convoy but thanks to Linda's quick thinking and Jackson's skill on the machine gun far more people survived the surprise attack than otherwise would have.

"Jackson!" Linda shouted at the lieutenant. He unbuckled himself from the gun and slid back down into the back seat as she continued. "When we get there you need to get everyone ready for another assault!"

"Understood." Jackson nodded, still breathing heavily from the adrenaline pumping through his veins.

After a moment's pause Frank spoke up. "We were right about these guys being from Omar. I caught a look at some of them in one of the buildings when Jackson was lighting them up. No way in hell are they looters."

Linda glanced at Jackson in the rearview mirror. "Aref must have alerted Omar to our presence. We have to repel their attack and get to the port as soon as possible. If we don't…"

Jackson nodded as Linda trailed off. "We'll make it happen."

Chapter Seventy-Six

As Frank pulled into the parking lot Jackson jumped out of the Humvee and began bellowing out orders. A defensive line quickly formed on the open side of the lot while squads of soldiers and airmen took cover behind their vehicles and in the buildings around the edge of the parking space. Frank parked the Humvee near the edge of the lot by an alley that Linda had pointed out would offer easy emergency egress should they need it.

As the soldiers and airmen ran back and forth setting up their defensive positions Linda and Frank headed over to Jackson who was busy watching as a small surveillance drone was being prepared for launch. "How high can that thing go?" Linda pointed at the drone.

"We usually fly these at five hundred to a thousand feet. They're still fairly new so there aren't that many guidelines for them yet. Mostly we're just—hey! Get that truck moved over!" Jackson cupped his hands and shouted at a soldier who was backing a truck up near the entrance to the parking lot. He shook his head and sighed as the soldier hastily moved the vehicle. "What I wouldn't give to have my old guys back. Anyway we started using these overseas to get real-time info on enemy troop movements."

"Sounds like just what we need."

"Yeah except this urban environment isn't the best for them. Fly too high and we lose good resolution on the thermals. Too low and we're liable to hit a building or power lines." Jackson and the others stepped back as the drone's four propellers spun up and it jumped into the air, soaring high above the parking lot and quickly out of sight and sound.

"Fast little thing." Frank whistled.

Jackson looked at Linda and Frank. "Either of you two have any experience piloting these things? My main pilot caught a couple rounds in the chest and shoulder while we were evacuating. He'll be fine but he can't pilot for shit with his arm all jacked up."

Linda shook her head while Frank shrugged. "I toyed around with them a few years back but never to any serious degree."

"Good enough." Jackson pushed Frank in the direction of a nearby table where a pair of soldiers were working with a joystick and what looked like a game controller. A small screen displayed two views from the drone, one from a camera pointed out from the drone's front and the other a view from the thermal camera mounted on its belly. "Michaels, get up. Frank's got some experience with these things."

"Oh thank God." The soldier holding the controller stood up and handed it to Frank. "Last thing I want to do is crash this thing."

The soldier holding onto the separate joystick with his left hand glanced up at Frank, the motion pulling at the bandages around his chest and arm and making him wince. "Frank? You flown these before?"

Frank looked around at everyone with wide eyes and shook his head. "Years ago I played around with one for a while. I was looking for some new hobbies and figured a quadcopter would be fun."

"Yeah, well I'd be flying it if I had been sitting in the back seat. As it is all I can do is work the thermal camera here."

Jackson pushed Frank down into the seat that Michaels had been occupying and patted him on the shoulder. "Williams is our go-to pilot for this baby. He'll help you with whatever you need." A shout from across the parking lot drew Jackson's attention and he turned and ran off to see what was going on. Linda leaned down and whispered to Frank.

"You've got this, okay? I'm going to go see what's going on with the defenses. Jackson's having a rough time holding things together and I want to make sure he didn't miss anything. As soon as you have info on anyone approaching our position you need to let us know."

Frank nodded numbly, his eyes glued to the screen in front of him as his thumbs played with the sticks on the controller. The drone was highly sensitive to the inputs, zipping back and forth like an over-energetic dog. Memories of standing in an open field with an RC controller in his hands while a quadcopter zipped around overhead came back to him and he soon found himself handling the drone like an expert.

"Nice work." Williams nodded. He rotated the joystick controlling the thermal camera. "Take it up another two hundred feet and let's do a sweep of the route we took from the baseball field."

Frank nodded and pushed the drone upward. With Williams guiding him Frank made several fast passes of the area around the parking lot over the course of ten minutes. It was on one of the last passes before the drone needed to be brought back and get new batteries when Williams shouted for Jackson.

"Lieutenant!" Williams stood up and looked around before pointing at an airman standing nearby. "Get Lieutenant Jackson right now!"

The airman nodded and dashed off. Jackson ran up a moment later with Linda following close behind. "What is it? You have something?"

Williams nodded and pointed at the screen displaying the thermal camera's view. "Frank, bring it back around like before." Frank pushed on the sticks on his controller and the drone zipped to the side. The cold blacks and dark blues on the thermal camera were suddenly punctuated with large rectangular blocks of orange and yellow.

"Are those trucks?"

"At least a dozen of them, yes sir." Williams nodded. "Looks like a good fifty, maybe seventy-five men. The vehicles appear to have mounted weaponry, too."

Jackson groaned and rubbed a hand across his face. "How far out are they?"

"Four or five blocks. We'll be hearing their engines soon."

"Okay. Keep an eye on them and let me know what their movements are."

"Sir," Williams said, swiveling in his seat to look at Jackson, "we need to bring the drone in and swap out the batteries. We've got five minutes of flight time left."

"Fine, but do it fast. We need those eyes in the sky."

Williams looked at Frank. "Bring it home. We'll get the batteries changed and get it back up in no time."

While Frank and Williams focused on getting the drone ready for another flight Jackson pulled Linda away from the others and spoke to her in a low voice. "This urban bullshit's going to be the death of us unless we have someone guiding us who's actually experienced. I know about some of the action you saw during your deployment in Iran, deep in their urban jungle. Any advice you can give would be appreciated."

"Keeping the drone up is going to be top priority for the initial assessment of where they're going to be. Once they get inside buildings, though, the drone's going to be next to useless unless they're moving around outside a lot." Linda turned and pointed at a tall building back behind the parking lot. "I would get a sniper team up there so they can provide intel as well as have a firing position on anyone across the street from us.

"If they're bringing in mounted weapons then my guess is they're going to push an initial assault from the front to cover a flanking maneuver through the buildings and alleys. If you have any claymores you should set them up at chokepoints and make sure we've got plenty of elevated fire to take out their mounted gunners. Oh, and Frank and I left our rifles in the Humvee. Have somebody get us guns with plenty of spare mags."

"Third truck down has spare weapons and ammo." He hesitated for a second before nodding to her gratefully. "Thank you." With that the lieutenant hurried off to give the necessary orders required to carry out Linda's suggestions.

Before Jackson had asked for her advice Linda had managed to avoid thoughts comparing her time in the streets of Iran to what they were currently going through. Jackson's reminder and her instinctual evaluation of what was going on made her glad she could help while at the same time bringing back more than a few unpleasant memories.

Ultimately the thing she hated most about what was going on wasn't the fight against Omar's men. It was the knowledge that each moment they delayed in getting to the docks and continuing their search for the bombs would mean another moment closer to Omar's plan being fulfilled. That—more than anything else in her past—terrified her the most.

BOOK FIVE

THE GAUNTLET

Chapter Seventy-Seven

"They're almost here!"

Linda turned around at the sound of Williams' shout and called back to him. "Copy!" She held a two-way radio up to her mouth and depressed the microphone, looking up at the twelve-story office tower behind the parking lot. "Sniper team, are you in position?"

The answer was accompanied by a burst of static. "In position and ready to rock. We've got eyes on targets."

"Wait to engage until their trucks roll in."

"Copy."

Linda jogged over to Jackson, who was standing at the front of a Humvee along with several soldiers and airmen. "Snipers are in position. They've spotted ground troops moving in. Are the choke-points ready?"

Jackson nodded and pointed to a crude drawing on the hood of the Humvee that outlined the parking lot and surrounding area. "We've got wreckage blocking this side alley and the building entrances are lined with claymores."

"Good. They'll likely start with sending in ground forces, then they'll graduate to vehicles or RPGs once they test our strength. Whatever you do just make sure you don't throw everything we've got at them up front."

"What's the split between the elevated firing positions and boots on the ground?"

"Sixty-forty, like you said."

Linda nodded. "Good. I'm going to watch the drone with Frank and Williams."

"I'll be over in a second."

Linda patted Jackson on the back and ran over toward where Frank and Williams were sitting. Frank's eyes were glued to his screen as he guided the small military drone above the city, watching the incoming troops. She sat down next to him and watched the images of the vehicles and individuals moving around, appearing as white-hot images against a cold black and blue background.

"How much longer?"

"Five minutes. Probably less." Williams answered as Frank executed a low dive over the troops, biting his lip as he slipped the drone between a pair of dangling power lines hanging over the street. "This sucker's maneuverability is incredible." Frank mumbled to himself. Next to him, Williams toggled the thermal camera off, giving them a more detailed view of the soldiers.

"Looks like rifles and a few RPGs. Trucks with mounted guns." Williams pointed at the screen as Frank flew the drone over the enemy's heads before pulling back on the stick, sending the small craft rocketing up into the air before any of the men on the ground noticed it was there.

"There's a lot of them. More than we saw earlier." Linda looked at Williams. "Any estimates?"

"We guessed seventy-five or so last time. I'd say another fifty on top of that. And half a dozen more vehicles."

"A hundred and twenty-five men and eighteen vehicles?" Linda groaned. "What hole in the ground did these guys all crawl out of?"

"Beats me." Williams shook his head.

"Hey!" Frank took one hand off the controls in his hand and pointed at the screen. "They're almost to the perimeter!"

Linda jumped up and looked around. She was about to start running toward Jackson when she saw him heading in her direction, a concerned look on his face as he saw her standing up. "What's up, Rollins?"

"They're here."

Jackson nodded and spoke into his radio. "Attention all units. Enemy forces are outside our perimeter. Hold fire until you are otherwise ordered to do so. Ground units, you have clearance to engage at will."

Jackson waved an arm in the air and shouted at the soldiers who were milling around the cluster of vehicles in the parking lot. "Move out! Get to defensive positions right now!"

While Williams and Frank moved their equipment to the back of the parking lot behind a ring of heavily armored vehicles, Jackson and Linda helped round up a few stray soldiers who were still moving vehicles and checking their weapons. The five minutes predicted by Williams came and went without incident and Linda was about to run back to them to see if they had any further updates when her radio crackled and Williams' voice came over the line.

"Here they come!"

The chaos began approximately seven seconds after his warning.

Private Dan Tucker crouched in the dark hallway of a building on the far side of the street, just across from the parking lot. The doorway at the far end of the hall had long since been torn off, making it the perfect entrance for anyone trying to sneak up on the parking lot without being seen. The hall, like many of the entrances of the buildings in the area around the parking lot, had been rigged with explosive devices that would go off if their laser tripwires were crossed. The soft red beams coming from the explosives were just barely visible down the hall thanks to the light amount of dust gently floating through the air.

Footsteps and whispers in a foreign language drifted down the hall, alerting Tucker to the imminent arrival of the enemy. He looked back at the three soldiers crouched behind him and motioned for them to get ready. They, like him, were all young, low in rank and had barely seen any combat since joining the Army less than a year ago. The ambush a short time earlier had been their first real combat experience and they were more than a little nervous about what was to come.

Tucker was about to whisper a few words of encouragement to the others when nearby footsteps were immediately followed by a deafening explosion. With the laser tripwires on the Claymores having been crossed by some unfortunate soul, a combination of metal spheres and conventional explosives rocked the hallway. The spheres acted like slugs from a shotgun, blasting out from the device and tearing through flesh and bone like tissue paper. The conventional explosives sent out a massive shockwave, tearing apart eardrums and vital organs as a small ball of fire plumed outward.

Despite the hearing protection worn by Tucker and the soldiers with him, all four men found their ears ringing after the explosion. Tucker peeked out from his cover after the Claymore went off to see three bloody bodies on the floor down the hall with several more men beyond them, still on their feet. With a shout, Tucker and the other soldiers took aim and added a healthy dose of lead to the mix.

Similar scenes took place nearly simultaneously in the buildings around the parking lot. The dull explosions echoed out from the buildings, breaking the tense silence that had settled around those in the lot, the elevated positions and in the tower. The time for hasty preparation was over and Linda was about to find out just how well her strategy was going to work.

Jackson and a pair of airmen worked the radios as the explosions went off, keeping in touch with the soldiers in the halls. Bursts of gunfire made Frank flinch but he kept the drone steady, trying to get an eye on what the enemy was doing next. Linda stood near Frank and Jackson, her rifle hanging from one shoulder while she idly chewed on the thumbnail of her free hand. Each shot and explosion made her want to go get involved in the fight more than ever before and she had to resist the temptation so that she could continue handing out advice and orders to Jackson and the others.

Taking a leadership role hadn't been Linda's desire. On the contrary, during her time in the sand she had vastly preferred carrying a rifle and a hundred-pound bag on her back to sitting in an armored vehicle or an office trying to decide who would live and who would die. Formulating a plan, strategizing and deciding who would go where and do what was something she was good at. What she preferred, though, was carrying out those orders. There was no responsibility for dozens or hundreds of lives hanging over her when she was another pair of boots on the ground. There was only her duty to obey her orders, help the members of her squad and her responsibility to complete her mission.

A tap on Linda's shoulder pulled her out of her reverie. She blinked several times and turned around to face Jackson, nearly forgetting where she was for half an instant. "Rollins? You okay?" Jackson's eyebrow was raised and he shook his head, dismissing his own question before continuing. "Ground teams are holding. Minimal causalities. It looks like the initial assault was repelled."

"Good," Linda nodded. "They'll probably pull back for a minute, regroup and then try to break through with the trucks. Is everyone in hard cover?"

Jackson was about to respond in the affirmative when a loud crash of metal on metal came from the far end of the parking lot, along the road. Several engines accompanied the crash as a group of trucks rammed the makeshift barricades set up by the soldiers and airmen. Another crash came from the opposite end of the road a second later as a second group of trucks came through. Both groups converged on the parking lot, stopping at the perimeter of vehicles parked near the road.

Gunfire from the vehicles began as soon as they stopped in front of the parking lot. Fifty-caliber rounds sprayed from the guns mounted in the backs of the light pickups, their operators swaying and rocking as they twisted the weapons back and forth. The gunfire was intense but lacked direction or focus and Linda almost immediately realized what they were doing.

"Jackson!" She shouted at the man crouched nearby, hiding behind a nearby armored vehicle.

"What is it?" He yelled back, straining his voice over the thundering booms of the guns.

"They're trying to sneak people in under cover of fire! We need to take out those gunners right now!"

Jackson turned toward the buildings to the sides of the parking lot, shouting into the radio as he watched the positions where the elevated shooters were still in cover. "Open fire on the trucks! Ground units, watch our flanks! Snipers take out the gunners and call out anyone you see trying to get in behind us!"

With everyone in cover, the trucks had nothing in particular to shoot at. As the majority of the troops began to return fire on the trucks, though, the gunners began directing their fire as they focused on those in elevated positions. Two machine guns swept across the right-most building, shattering glass and shredding particleboard desks and tables. Several other vehicles began moving forward, pushing against the parked vehicles to make a path through into the parking lot as they focused on keeping the soldiers at ground level pinned down.

Linda sat next to Frank, watching the video from the drone as she contemplated joining in the fray when a loud crack cut through the roar of the machine guns. She smiled coldly as the video showed one of the gunners in the trucks slump over to the side and fall out, his head having been turned into a fine pink mist. She looked up at the tower behind the lot and saw muzzle flashes from inside one of the floors, evidence that the sniper team was working their magic. The number of gunners in the trucks quickly dwindled until it was just three left who were out of sight of the tower. Half of the drivers of the trucks whose gunners had been killed were also dead, either from the sniper team or from the other soldiers clustered around the area.

With the battle looking like it was starting to reach its conclusion, Linda looked back at the video screen and tapped Frank on the shoulder. "Pull it up; get a wider angle on us, would you?"

Frank glanced at Williams who nodded in agreement. Frank pushed the throttle on the craft and it rose higher into the air, turning the people-shaped blobs on the thermal imager into smaller, less distinct blobs. Linda scanned the screen carefully before shouting at Jackson. "I think it looks clear here! Any word on flanking movements?"

Jackson shook his head. "Nothing." He depressed the button on his radio and was about to send out a request for everyone to check in when the sound of a loud hissing made Linda dive forward, screaming at everyone within earshot to get down on the ground.

The rocket-propelled grenade hit one of the large trucks, turning it into a fireball and throwing everyone near away with the force of the blast. Jackson was knocked onto his side, the radio falling from his hand and smashing against the rough asphalt. Linda jumped onto Frank's back, pushing him down to the ground and shielding him from any shrapnel that might be heading in their direction.

Linda's reflexes upon hearing the activation of the rocket were lightning-quick and were the only reason she and Frank didn't— literally—lose their heads. She felt a *whoosh* overhead as the hood of the truck sailed through the air, clipping the top of Williams' head and sending him falling to the ground with a gut-wrenching crunch. Intense sound and heat flared up for a few seconds before dying down, and while all Linda wanted to do was lay still in the fetal position she still had a job to do.

"Move!" Linda screamed as she staggered to her feet, looking around to try and figure out where the rocket had come from. Based on the sound and the orientation of the impact it looked like the origin was on the southern side of the lot, perhaps from one of the buildings where troops had been established on the ground floor and in elevated positions. Remembering back to when she had called out the trucks as a distraction, Linda realized that the troops in the southern buildings must have been overrun by the attackers who then set themselves up in an elevated position to fire down on the parking lot and across to the other buildings.

"Get to cover! Attackers to the south!" Linda screamed again as she pulled Frank to his feet. Another rocket hissed by overhead, slamming into the face of one of the northern buildings. Faint screams of pain and surprise accompanied the deafening explosion, and Linda realized that unless something was immediately done they would suffer even heavier losses.

Linda picked up her rifle from where it had tumbled onto the ground and slapped at her pockets, checking to make sure she still had spare magazines. A hand caught her from behind just before she ran out from cover and she stopped and turned to find Frank staring at her. He was breathing rapidly and bleeding from a long scrape down his head and face from where she had pushed him onto the ground.

"You going after them?" Linda nodded and he took a deep breath. "Good. I'm coming with."

Linda started to argue, but as he grabbed his rifle off of the ground she realized that it would be both pointless and a waste of precious time that they did not have. "Keep up, stay close and don't get shot. Got it?"

Frank thumbed the safety off on his rifle and nodded at her. "Go."

———

LINDA AND FRANK advanced quickly through the southern building, stopping only for a few seconds to check half a dozen soldier and airmen whose bloodied bodies lay strewn near a stairwell. Linda grimaced as she moved between the men. "All dead. Damn." She crouched near the bodies for a moment before beckoning Frank to continue following. "We can't do anything for them. Come on."

Another RPG hit the far side of the parking lot as they ascended the stairs, the explosion muffled by the walls but still loud due to its close proximity. Frank adjusted his grip on his rifle, nervous sweat dripping from every pore on his body. "How close are they?" he whispered at Linda.

"Next floor up," she pointed at the ceiling and held a finger to her lips. He nodded and followed her up, keeping his rifle aimed low at the ground to avoid any friendly-fire incidents.

At the top of the stairs Linda put her body against the edge of the doorframe and slowly rotated her head around until she could see down the hall. The door had been blown off of its hinges either by the Claymores or by the attackers, giving her a perfect view down the hall. Several more bloodied bodies of fallen soldiers and airmen lay strewn on the floor. She clenched her jaw as she saw them, then her whole frame tensed up as she looked beyond.

A dozen men or more stood in the hall, clustered together in two groups. She could see that every man was armed with a rifle, though one man in each group also wielded an RPG that his comrades were helping to reload after he fired it upon the people in the parking lot below. While leaning out into the hall and opening fire would—under any other circumstances—be a ludicrous suggestion that she wouldn't dream of carrying out, each RPG that the men were allowed to fire down at the parking lot was potentially another cluster of deaths that could be avoided if she were to act quickly.

Linda was just starting to turn and raise her rifle when Frank's hands grabbed her around her arms and chest. He pulled her back sharply, nearly causing her to drop her rifle. The noise of their scuffle was masked by the noise of the men down the hall and she cringed as another RPG was fired through a window and it was followed by a nearby explosion.

"What the hell, Frank?" Linda hissed in his ear as she broke free of his grip and whirled to face him.

"Stop!" Frank's eyes were wide as he replied. "If you open fire now they'll just send one of those things down the hall at us!"

Linda was too embarrassed to admit that Frank was right and she fought back against a sick feeling in her gut that she had just narrowly avoided death thanks to his intervention.

"Don't you have a grenade or something?" Frank whispered at her again.

"No," she shook her head, "but I think they might have something even better." Linda turned and peeked around the doorframe again, her searching gaze flitting across and around the feet of the attackers in the hall. A dark green canvas bag sat behind each of the RPG wielders and she smiled coldly as she watched one of the men reach into the bag closest to her and Frank and pull out the familiar black RPG and pass it to the man holding the launcher.

"Cover your ears." Linda spoke with a grin that bordered on the maniacal. "This is going to be loud."

Rocket-propelled grenades, like many other types of explosives, are designed to be extremely stable at all times before they are used against a target. Explosives that detonate prematurely or from rough handling just aren't very good in a combat situation. Under normal circumstances, a direct shot from a bullet would either bounce off of or harmlessly penetrate through an explosive since, without the fuse or primer going off, there wouldn't be enough energy from the bullet to cause the explosive to detonate.

Firing at a cache of twenty-five-year-old RPGs sitting clustered together in a canvas bag after they've been hauled around for an indeterminate amount of time by people who don't really understand their destructive capabilities is not a 'normal circumstances' type of situation. When Linda squeezed the trigger and sent several rounds into the bag, she half-expected her plan to fail and for the men to send an RPG hurtling down the hallway to engulf both herself and Frank in a ball of fire. Fortune, however, was on her side.

The third bullet to enter the bag slipped between a seam in the metal around one of the RPGs, tearing it open and igniting the fuse inside. The initial explosion would have been devastating to the cluster of men around it but the detonation of a few dozen RPGs simultaneously generated enough force to blow a swimming-pool-sized hole in the side of the building.

The flames and the force of the explosion sent the men farther down the hall flying, gravely injuring two and killing the rest.

Those who were standing near the first bag were virtually disintegrated, their bodies and clothing liquified, burned up or thrown far enough from the source of the explosion that they would never be able to be identified.

Though Linda and Frank were down the hall and in good cover compared to the attackers, they too felt the force of the explosion. Frank's teeth and chest rattled from the blast and Linda covered her ears and turned away from the doorway, feeling a blast of wind and debris pass by inches from her back. The majority of the force of the explosion went out the sides and top of the building but there was enough energy in the blast that most of the soldiers in the area not only heard but felt the rumble of the explosion as well.

Linda stood a few seconds after the explosion was finished and she felt a familiar hand on her shoulder. Frank stood behind her, his face covered in dirt and grime, looking her over from head to toe. "You okay?" Frank spoke loudly though Linda was still having trouble hearing him due to the ringing in her ears. She nodded slowly and pointed at him, silently asking him the same question.

"I'm fine," he said. "But I can't believe that worked!"

Linda looked around the doorframe, peering down the hall alongside Frank and nodding with satisfaction. "Same here. No time to dawdle around, though." Linda took her radio off of her belt and keyed the mic. "All units, this is Rollins. Attackers in the south building are down." She crept down the hall, looking through the massive hole in the wall out into the parking lot while being cautious not to fall through down into the next floor. "I still see stragglers along the north side and a couple at the vehicles. Jackson, I suggest we try and capture them for a little bit of intel."

Down in the parking lot, Jackson grabbed a radio from a nearby airman and listened to Linda's broadcast. The explosion in the building had caught everyone off-guard but they were all thrilled to hear that the attackers were dead. Their joy was short-lived, though, due to the number of wounded and dead they had to deal with.

"Rollins, this is Jackson," he replied back, looking around the parking lot at the devastation wreaked upon the men and women under his command. "Nice work up there. I've got a team chasing down the stragglers. All units, anyone not currently chasing down those bastards needs to be working triage right now!"

With ringing still in their ears, Frank and Linda made their way back down the stairwell and out into the parking lot. While the pair of them had nearly died from the RPGs during the attack, neither realized the sheer magnitude of the destruction until they were out walking amongst it without being under fire. Vehicles of all types were blown apart, their components twisted, blackened and scattered to the winds. Large craters in the asphalt denoted spots where the RPGs hadn't quite hit their mark while dark red puddles next to Army-green blankets draped over still forms told sadder tales.

Linda and Frank walked through the rapidly-growing crowd of soldiers and airmen as they searched for any injured that had been overlooked. A groan from beneath a half-destroyed truck drew Linda's attention and she crouched down to see a man pinned beneath the vehicle, still alive but covered in blood and breathing heavily.

"Son of a…" Linda cursed under her breath and turned to scream at a few soldiers running nearby. "Help me get this off of him!" With help from Frank and Linda, the soldiers managed to get the truck lifted off of the injured man and a medic moved him to the side and began tending to his wounds. The sight of the gravely injured man made Linda's blood boil and she left his side, heading to the north side of the parking lot where a few stray attackers had been spotted. Frank followed behind her, keeping quiet as he tried to figure out what they were doing until he couldn't contain his question any longer.

"Linda? Where are we going?"

"To find them." Her response was a guttural growl, containing the fury of a woman who had been dragged through hell multiple times and was finding herself being pulled back in once again.

"Find… who?"

"Any of those assholes. If they're still alive."

Frank shook his head as he trailed behind Linda, sidestepping soldiers limping along and carrying stretchers with their injured comrades. The pair passed through the northern set of buildings and heard several men shouting a short distance ahead. They both readied their weapons and broke into a run, weaving down the alley until they saw the source of the commotion on the open street ahead.

A group of soldiers were clustered around a body on the ground, and for a second Linda thought it was one of their comrades who was down. When one of the soldiers kicked at the legs of the person on the ground, though, she realized that it must be one of the attackers.

"Hey!" Linda shouted as she ran toward the soldiers, Frank still doggedly keeping up behind her. "What happened here? You were supposed to get one of them alive!"

The soldiers spread apart and one of them shrugged as he gestured to the corpse on the ground. "We tried, ma'am. He had other plans."

Linda looked at the man lying on the ground and ground her teeth together when she saw the self-inflicted bullet wound in the side of his head and the revolver lying on the ground a few inches from his right hand.

"We tried to stop them, but once they realized they were cornered they just… yeah. All of them at once." The soldier knelt down next to the body and shook his head. "Damnedest thing I've seen, too."

"They had orders," Linda said, shaking her head in disgust. "There are more, though?"

"At least two. Maybe three?" The soldier shook his head. "They're down just a bit, with the next squad."

Linda nodded and motioned at Frank. "Stay here, search this guy's body. Look for any clues you can. Phones, notebooks, wallets; anything at all that could help us. I'll go search the others."

Frank grimaced as Linda ran off. He knelt down slowly and reached for the body before pulling his hands back in disgust. He repeated this motion twice more before there was a gentle tap on his shoulder. He looked back to see one of the soldiers looking at him sympathetically as he held out a pair of black disposable gloves for Frank to take.

"Here, try these."

"Oh thank goodness," Frank sighed with relief. The soldier nodded in response before turning away to talk with the others. Frank pulled on the gloves and began picking at the dead man's clothing which was already starting to absorb the blood that was pooling out onto the asphalt. The man's jacket pockets contained no documents, electronics, keys or anything that Frank would normally expect to find on a person and he found the same in the man's pants and shirt as well. He stood up and took off the gloves, threw them on the ground and hurried off to find Linda, only to have her nearly barrel into him as she ran out of an alley.

Linda's face was ashen and in her right hand she held a small bundle of papers with an iron grip. Frank looked at her with concern. "What's going on? Did you find something?"

"Did he have anything on him? The one you checked, I mean."

"Nothing," he replied.

"Neither did the others. Except for one of them. And he had these." Linda held the papers up and shook them at Frank.

"What are they?"

Linda flipped through the pages of text and handwritten maps and spoke with a lowered voice, glancing around to see if any of the soldiers were listening in. "They're orders, Frank. Orders from Omar himself telling these guys to track us down. *Us.*" Frank felt a chill run up his spine as Linda continued. "This wasn't just an attack on the military or the country or anything like that. It was an attack directed specifically at us. Omar wants both of us dead."

To emphasize her point, Linda pulled out a small shiny piece of paper from the bottom of the bundle. On the front of the glossy page were two color photographs. The first was of Linda, dressed in her Marine uniform and smiling at the camera. The second was of Frank, taken a few months before he had been let go from his job when HR had gone around with a cheap camera to update the company's website. Frank gulped hard at the sight of his picture, both confused about why it was in the bundle and wondering how on earth someone could have gotten their hands on it.

"Linda?" Frank spoke nervously, asking a question that he never imagined he'd be asking. "Why did one of Omar's men have my picture?"

Chapter Seventy-Eight

"I don't know what else to say." Jackson shook his head as he leafed through the small stack of papers Linda had taken off of the body of one of the attackers.

"How can you think they're fake?" Linda scoffed at him.

"Why would Omar, a master tactician and someone who's clearly very good at what he does, leave something like *this* with one of his men? Why not just give them orders to kill you two and leave it at that?"

"Because," she scooped up the pages as she replied, "he knew that if they succeeded then it wouldn't matter. And if they failed he wanted to send a message to us, telling us that he knows we're onto him."

Jackson rubbed his eyes and ran a hand through his hair as he tried to make sense of the situation. Frank, meanwhile, stood off to the side as he nervously chewed on his thumbnail and tried not to completely freak out at the thought that a terrorist had managed to find out who he was and obtain a picture of him. The back and forth between Linda and Jackson did nothing to calm his nerves and their latest exchange had him on edge.

"Jackson?" Frank stepped forward and spoke with a hesitant tone. "Question for you."

"Shoot."

"If this is fake, then how do they have a picture of me from so long ago? This was taken back when I worked as an accountant. Just... can you explain that one to me?"

"Easy," Linda interjected herself into the conversation before Jackson could reply. "It's not a fake."

"That still doesn't tell me how they got my picture. Yours I understand. You've been chasing this guy for years. But why me? I never even *met* you before all of this crap started!" Frank didn't realize until his last few words that he was steadily increasing in pitch and volume. He cleared his throat and looked at Linda and Jackson expectantly.

"Rollins?" Jackson looked at Linda. She, in turn, pulled out the photo of herself and Frank and stared at it for several seconds before responding.

"There's a leak somewhere."

"No kidding!" Frank shook his head. "Sarah told us that much!"

"No," she shook her head, "I don't mean a leak at the top. I mean someone on the ground. Someone who met us, got your name, passed it on to them and they did background research on you."

"How would they even pull something like this? It's from my old accounting firm's website."

"From what I've heard a decent portion of the web is still up and running." Jackson rocked his head back and forth as he thought aloud. "Most of the US-based web is down but there are plenty of caching services and non-US sites are still functional. Anything that was in the US but replicated or hosted in other countries could be accessible." He scratched his chin and plucked the photo from Linda's hand. "Still, the level of access this guy would have to have just to get your name is ridiculous. How do you even stop a spy operation like that?"

Linda felt her blood run cold as another possibility presented itself. "Maybe they don't know they're part of the operation." Both men looked at her silently, wondering what she meant. "What if," she continued, "The people who have been passing on the information are just doing their jobs? They're following instructions given to them by people higher on the chain of command than they are…"

"But in reality they're just passing along information to whoever the traitor is." Frank finished the thought and shook his head in disbelief. "That…would be insane."

"It's also a lot simpler than turning a bunch of low level people and risk having them divulge what's really going on."

"This doesn't really help us figure out what to do next, though." Jackson handed the photo back to Linda. "Especially since Omar knows you're after him."

"Oh we know what to do. We stick to our plan." Linda folded the papers and photograph and tucked them away in her jacket. "We get to the docks, look for information on the crates and get that to Sarah so she can have anyone with a functioning pair of eyes start looking for them."

"And what about Omar?"

"What about him?" Linda snorted in response to Jackson's question. "So he knows we're after him. Big deal. All that's going to do is accelerate his plans. We can't do anything about that except work twice as hard at finding him and stopping said plans."

Jackson stared at the ground for a long moment before nodding slowly. "All right. We'll do it."

"What's the status on the injured? Do we have enough people to head out to the docks?" Linda looked around at the soldiers and airmen in the parking lot, many of whom were injured or assisting those who were.

"We're getting reinforcements in a couple hours. They won't be much but they'll have enough vehicles with them to get the injured out to some real hospitals. Once that happens I'll take anyone still able to walk and carry a rifle, load them up and we'll head to the docks."

"A couple hours?" Linda looked at her watch.

"It's the best I can do, Rollins. As important as this is, my people come first. You know that."

Linda took a deep breath and nodded. "Absolutely. How can we help?"

⊏⊐

WITH NOTHING TO do until the reinforcements showed up, Frank and Linda busied themselves with assisting the injured soldiers and airmen who still required attention. Most everyone had suffered some small injury, whether it was a cut or abrasions due to the RPG fire, but many had sustained far worse injuries. The total number of dead was sixteen with another eight critically wounded. Of the original group that had left the airfield there were only thirty-five men and women who were still in good physical fighting condition.

The strain of being out in a hostile environment—especially when it was on American soil—wore on the morale of the survivors, as did seeing what their enemies had managed to do between the two attacks. Jackson, Frank and Linda were the only ones who knew the full extent of the details about the man responsible for the attacks and none of them wanted that situation to change.

With Williams dead, Frank took over the drone and sent it back into the sky. He swept the area with thermal cameras, helping to cover gaps in the defenses and provide an early warning for any more potential aggressors. Splitting his attention between the drone's location and the live video feed took some getting used to but keeping the craft flying high above power lines and buildings made controlling the craft somewhat easier.

Linda, meanwhile, stuck close to a medic by the name of Gutierrez. The two women wore white plastic gloves and moved between patients as they evaluated injuries, dispersed medication and tried their level best to keep the most seriously injured from bleeding out until backup arrived. Working on the other side of the hospital bed was a change of pace for Linda after her experience being shot and she was grateful for the fact that she wasn't lying on her back wondering when she'd feel well again.

It was just over three hours later when the sound of distant diesel engines sent up a shout of joy from the survivors in the parking lot. The reinforcements had broken off from a larger force moving into San Diego in an attempt to establish control of port facilities in that location after the Long Beach port and airfield were both compromised. Over a hundred soldiers and Marines descended on the parking lot, encircling it and quickly transporting the injured to a pair of advanced trauma vehicles. Miniature hospitals on wheels, the trauma vehicles were equipped with state of the art equipment and supplies that would allow the injured to be treated for their wounds on the spot, since the chances of any of them making it to a hospital were slim to none.

As everyone worked, Linda and Frank stood together off to the side until they spotted Lieutenant Jackson in the middle of a heated discussion with another officer from the reinforcement convoy. They wandered toward the pair until they were close enough to hear what was going on.

"Jackson, this is insane. You're low on supplies, your people have been through hell and we're here to reinforce you! Let us take point on this!"

"I appreciate the offer. Truly, I do. But this is our fight right now."

There was a long, uncomfortable silence before the other officer sighed in resignation. "You won't change your mind on this, huh?"

Jackson gave a slight smile as he shook his head. "Nope. Sorry."

"Yeah, I'm sure. Look, have your guys take what they need from us. Make sure you have enough ammo, food and water to last you however long this secret mission will take. We'll get your people taken care of and back to safety."

"Thank you." Jackson nodded at his counterpart and the pair shook hands before parting ways. Jackson looked around with a grim look on his face as he walked through the parking lot until he spotted Frank and Linda, both of whom were doing a terrible job of looking nonchalant. Jackson rolled his eyes at them as he approached. "How much did you hear?"

"Enough." Linda reached out and put a sympathetic hand on Jackson's arm. "We appreciate you staying with us. I know what it's like to lose people."

Jackson sighed and shook his head, dismissing the thoughts before they could overcome him. "There'll be a time for remembering, later, once this is settled. We have a job to finish first, though. You two ready to get moving?"

———

TWENTY MINUTES LATER, as the reinforcements were still working to treat the wounded and collect the remains of the fallen soldiers and airmen, five vehicles rolled out of the parking lot and headed back toward the west. Four Humvees and one APC—the only one that had survived the attacks undamaged—traveled backwards along the path they had taken not too long ago, winding their way toward the Long Beach dockyard and whatever awaited them there.

Linda, Frank and Jackson rode in the second Humvee and another twenty troops were spread out across the rest of the vehicles, each of them armed to the teeth and looking to exact vengeance for their fallen brothers and sisters. Jackson sat behind the wheel as he, Frank and Linda conversed, trying to decide what their moves would be once they entered the docks. A short time ago Jackson had been the outsider but as far as Linda and Frank were concerned he was one of them.

"She wants what, the general description of the crates, right?" Jackson spoke loudly over the roar of the engines.

"Any and every detail we can get. Weight, dimensions, color, patterns; anything that can be broadcast out and be used as a way to start searching for them."

"I hope to heaven that kind of info is even available at the dockyard." Jackson shook his head. "Though that might not matter much if the people who overran the port destroyed everything."

"How far out are we?" Frank checked his watch and looked up at the sky. The new day had brought with it a dazzling array of purples, pinks and blues as the sun lazily rose into the sky. A feeling of general exhaustion washed over Frank as he focused on the outside world, but he fought against it with thoughts of the fights that were sure to come and with the help of another mouthful of stale, lukewarm coffee. His short stint as a trucker hadn't adequately prepared him for going so long and hard without sleep, but he wasn't about to be the one holding everyone else back.

"Five minutes," Jackson replied. He picked up a radio and held the microphone to his mouth, scanning the buildings around them as they drove along. "Look alive, people. We're five minutes out. Gunners keep eyes on the windows and rooftops. When we get to the port keep your safeties off and be ready for a fight. These might just be civvies who overran it but it might be more of the bastards from before."

A chorus of acknowledgements came back through the radio and Jackson nodded in satisfaction. "All right, you two. Listen up. Keep your helmets on and your eyes on a swivel. Once we've secured the perimeter of the dockyard we'll move inside. I'll make sure any records or computer rooms are cleared first, then I'll have a couple of guards with you while you do your searches."

Linda nodded. "We'll be fine, Jackson. Just get us inside."

The relatively calm atmosphere that had pervaded the ride west toward the dockyard was quickly being replaced with tension. Frank could feel his heartrate start to rise as he recognized the streets they were driving on from when he and Linda had been in the area earlier. In the front passenger seat Linda re-checked her pistol and rapped her fingers against the side of her rifle, her right leg drumming up and down in an expression of nervous energy.

When the port drew into view, Frank's first sight of the dockyard made him gasp. Smoke billowed from buildings and vehicles alike, one of the ships waiting out in the water beyond the port was clearly on fire and there were large pieces missing from the wall and fence that surrounded the area. Frank stared slack-jawed while Jackson shouted into the radio at the soldiers in the other vehicles.

The four Humvees pulled off to the side of the road as the APC raced past, accelerating as it smashed over and through any vehicles and other obstacles in its path. The driver of the APC expertly guided it through a portion of the brick wall surrounding the dockyard with expert precision, taking advantage of a weak spot and hitting it at an angle to ensure the Humvees would be able to follow behind. It drove through the dockyard at full speed in a wide circle, the single machine gun turret on top swiveling around as the gunner prepared for an assault from any direction.

There was no assault, though. In fact, there was little of any sort of response to the APC's entry whatsoever. Jackson watched from outside the compound as the APC swept through, listening to the stream of reports coming in from a soldier inside the APC.

"No contact, sir. We've got a few people fleeing on the western side through holes in the fence but they're unarmed and appear to be civilians. Should we engage or pursue?"

"Negative." Jackson replied back immediately. "Do not engage unless they appear to be hostile."

"Copy that." The APC rumbled across an open stretch of the dockyard and another transmission came through. "We've got no one at the far end, sir. Doing another pass by the near buildings. If those are clear you should be good to go."

Jackson watched the APC turn again, half the wheels screaming in protest while the other half lifted a few inches off the ground. The armored vehicle zoomed past the wall and around the main dockyard building. Frank and Linda watched the scene from inside the Humvee, and Frank whispered to Linda without taking his eyes off of the APC. "I wonder if that guy's still there."

"The radiation monitor tech?"

"Yeah."

"Doubt it. He probably ran for it when those people overran the compound."

"Where did all the people go, anyway?" Frank scratched his chin.

"I don't know," she said, shaking her head slowly. "But I don't like it."

Jackson jumped back in the Humvee and glanced at Frank and Linda. "Get ready. We're heading in."

The other three Humvees went in first, splitting up as the drivers took soldiers to three separate entrances into the main dockyard building. Jackson drove the vehicle with himself, Frank and Linda in last, watching and waiting as the groups of soldiers moved out of the Humvees and the APC and worked to secure the building. He wanted nothing more than to be in there with his men but protecting Frank and Linda was the most important task he had on his plate.

"When do we go in?" Linda asked as he eased the Humvee to a stop near the building.

"Soon. Once they've swept the entire building and given the all-clear."

Linda slowly turned her head to look at him, raised an eyebrow, rolled her eyes and reached for the door handle. "Yeah, sure. You have fun with that."

Linda pulled on the door handle and jumped out, rifle in hand, and began jogging toward the nearest entrance. Frank and Jackson watched her for a few seconds before Frank fumbled with his door, opened it and jumped out after her. Before running off he paused and looked at Jackson. "Aren't you coming with us?"

Jackson looked at the pair heading toward the building and groaned as he unbuckled his seatbelt and got out of the vehicle. "Son of a...."

Chapter Seventy-Nine

E ven without the benefit of heavy equipment or tools, the civilians who overran the port did a marvelous job at tearing the place apart from top to bottom. Holes in the walls and fences surrounding the dockyard were only the tip of the iceberg and the damage was far more extensive than anyone from the convoy thought when they first encircled the main building.

Locks on shipping containers had been broken and the contents of the containers were spilled out onto the ground as looters searched feverishly for food, medical supplies and other necessities. While some of the containers did contain useful supplies, the vast majority of them were empty at the time the looters stormed the dockyard due to the fact that the military was being exceptionally aggressive with transporting the supplies out to the airfield as soon as they arrived at the port.

The main building and warehouses in the dockyard had nearly all of their windows broken out and the doors were broken and hanging from their hinges. The guards and staff on duty had done their level best to barricade themselves inside the buildings when the looters arrived, but they were far too outnumbered to put up any sort of a real fight. Some of the guards shot and killed a few looters but the sheer number of people storming through the dockyard meant that anyone who acted in an aggressive manner quickly faced brutal mob justice.

A few of the braver looters took small boats out to the waiting cargo ships. Some were dispatched by a group of soldiers whose job was to check the cargo ships before they were allowed to dock. Others boarded a ship whose crew barricaded themselves in the cabin, at which point the looters began tearing the ship and the containers on board apart in a frenzy to find much-needed supplies. The small craft the looters used to make it to the vessel was quickly torn apart by gunfire from the soldiers. Then, not wanting to risk the looters traveling to any more cargo vessels and finding it too risky to try and board the ship, the soldiers ended up using shaped explosives to punch a hole in the ship's hull so that it began to slowly sink. They then evacuated from the area in their small vessel, leaving the looters and crew on board the sinking ship no choice but to try and escape by swimming back to shore.

After the actions by the offshore military team and the discovery that there were little to no supplies in the dockyard, the looters began to disband after only a few short hours spent at the port. A few stayed behind to pick through the buildings and look for anything of use but the arrival of the convoy prompted them to flee without looking back.

While the main complex of the dockyard looked bad enough due to the actions of the looters, the interior of the buildings were a whole other matter entirely. Linda entered the main structure first, remembering how it had looked not that long ago and scarcely believing that she was in the same building. Frank and Jackson followed her in, with Jackson hurrying over to a nearby cluster of soldiers who were talking with some people that looked like they had gone through hell itself.

"What's going on here?" Jackson straightened his back as he approached the group.

"Sir, these civilians were working here when the looters attacked. They've got more in the back room and some are seriously injured."

"That's right," one of the staff members replied, stepping forward with a cough to clear his throat. "We were working here when those... *people* attacked us. If you can even call them that. They forced us into the conference room, killed several guards and started tearing everything apart."

"Is Nathan Davis here?" Linda spoke from behind Jackson, watching the faces of the staff members carefully.

"Nate?" The staff member scratched his head and shook it slowly. "I don't think I've seen him since the attack. He wasn't in the conference room with us, was he?" The other staff members shook their heads. Linda was about to reply when Jackson cut her off with a wave of his hand.

"Show my men to your wounded. Lindon, make sure they get treated and debriefed. I want to know everything they know." The soldier Jackson was speaking to nodded and turned back to carry out his orders. Linda stood silently next to Jackson for a few seconds as the soldiers and staff members walked out, heading for the conference room.

"All right, Rollins, who's this Nathan fellow?" Jackson turned to look at her.

"He was the tech who was working the radiation monitors when the crates came through. I figured he would be a good source of info, but if he's not here then we'll need to start searching through their database and any paper records."

Jackson waved at a nearby soldier. "Figure out where the server room is and get us there."

"Yes sir, we found it a few minutes ago. Down this way."

Jackson, Linda and Frank followed the soldier down a hall as Jackson continued talking. "Why didn't you two get all this info when you were here before?"

"Hindsight's 20/20, Jackson," Linda replied. "We didn't have all the facts at that point. I'm not convinced we have all of them even now."

"Are we sure their records will have descriptive information on the crates?" Frank asked from behind Jackson and Linda.

"They'd better," Linda shook her head, "Or we're going to be in trouble."

After another moment of walking the soldier leading the trio stopped in front of a door and motioned at it while holding out a flashlight. "In here, sir. You'll want this."

"A flashlight?" Jackson looked at it and switched it on. "Why would we need a flashlight? The place has pow—oh." Jackson walked into the room and sighed as he panned around with the light. "That'll be all for now. If anyone needs me I'll be in here with these two."

"Yes, sir!" The soldier saluted and ran off to attend to his other duties. Jackson slowly spun in a circle as he looked over the contents of the room while Linda and Frank walked in. "Well, Rollins? Thoughts?"

The server room looked like a bomb had gone off in one corner. Dark black scorch marks ran up the side of one wall while a pair of discarded fire extinguishers lying on their sides in the middle of the floor told the story of what had occurred. Linda pulled a flashlight from her pocket and pointed it at the tall metal rackmount cabinet that housed what used to be several fully-functional computers. It was one of four such cabinets in the room, but something had happened to cause it to catch on fire. The flames would have spread across the building if not for a staff member's diligence in the aftermath of the looters leaving the dockyard.

"Can we get the overhead lights back on?" Linda pointed her flashlight at the ceiling. "Is the breaker tripped or did something more serious get damaged?"

Jackson stepped back out into the hall. "Stay here while I go check." He ran off, leaving Linda and Frank alone in the quiet, dark room. Frank wandered slowly around the room, running his hands across the computers and furniture as he spoke.

"You think we'll be able to get anything off these machines?"

"I don't know." Linda sighed. "But it's the best place to start. Hopefully whatever happened in here didn't destroy all their data."

After a few minutes of waiting the lights in the ceiling suddenly flickered on and the room was filled with the sound of dozens of computer components powering on. The sound of rushing air quickly dominated and the pair had to raise their voices to be heard over the din.

"You want to wait for Jackson to come back or get started now?"

"Might as well do it now." Linda looked around the room as she slipped her flashlight back into her pocket. Over in one corner sat a small desk with a pair of chairs in front and a monitor, keyboard and mouse on top. "Let's take a look."

Linda switched on the power button for the computer, expecting that it would go through a short bootup process and then present her with a login screen that one of the staff members at the dockyard would be able to get through. Unfortunately, though, after going through the bootup process the monitor switched to all black with white text scrolling by along the left side. A series of error messages displayed in rapid succession. Linda skimmed the messages and shook her head. "Hoo boy. This doesn't look good."

Frank leaned in and caught sight of words like "no connection," "system error" and "data fragmentation" on the screen. "No it doesn't."

"I'm no expert—and jump in if you are—but it looks like their database is corrupted. Probably as a result of... well, *that*." Linda gestured to the burned server cabinet in the corner.

"You can't get any data out?"

"I dunno." She swiveled around in her chair at the sound of footsteps out in the hall. "Maybe Jackson can find someone here who knows this system."

"Rollins?" Jackson poked his head in through the door and glanced up at the ceiling. "Excellent. This is Jim Ward. He was the onsite IT guy; I figured you might be able to use his expertise."

Linda stood up from her chair and crossed the room with her hand extended. "Jim? I'm Linda, this is Frank. Good to meet you."

Jim nodded and shook her and Frank's hands. "You too. Not the best circumstances, though."

"That's why we're here, Jim." Linda steered him toward the computer and motioned at the seat. "We need to access records relating to some shipments that went through here a while back. They were crates that triggered some radiation alerts. We need to know any and everything about them but it looks like—"

"Yeah, the servers are down." Jim finished her sentence as he tapped out commands on the keyboard and read the return information on the monitor. "Looks like one of the surviving racks is offline and a few machines on the other two either have corrupted drives or they just aren't spinning up." Jim looked over at the blinking lights on the stacks of machines and sighed. "It's been a mess here, as you can see."

"What happened in here?" Frank asked. "With the fire, I mean."

Jim shrugged as he continued tapping out commands. "We've had all sorts of power issues ever since they brought it online. Something blew and started a fire which someone noticed and put out."

"Huh." Linda glanced at Frank. "So why are you here, anyway? I didn't know they needed an IT admin to stay during emergency operations."

Jim swiveled in his chair and gave Linda a look of exhaustion. "Look, lady, I'm just trying to survive this nonsense as much as the next person. A call went out, I answered and I've been doing cataloging and manual labor ever since. Though it's mostly been the latter instead of the former." He tapped a few more keys and sighed as he pointed to a line displayed on the monitor. "And there you go. The data from the timeframe that your Lieutenant said you'd want is gone."

"Gone?" Linda leaned in and looked at the monitor. "What do you mean by 'gone'?"

Jim stood up and walked over to one of the server cabinets. He looked at the labels taped to the side of each machine until he found the one he was looking for, then leaned in close and pressed his ear up against the case. "Gone as in dead." With a quick motion he popped the front off of the unit and slid out the tray inside, revealing the components of the machine including the half-dozen disk drives. He pointed to the drives with a grimace.

"Looks like the motherboard blew. Probably too much juice during a surge. The drives are most likely dead."

"Most likely?" Linda moved in with Frank close behind. "Can't you put them in another machine and see?"

"I'd love to, lady, but this is one of four servers that still supports drive interfaces this ancient."

"What about the other three?"

Jim turned and gestured at the burned server cabinet. Linda rolled her neck and her eyes, groaning loudly. "Great. So we're at a dead end."

"What about paper records?" Frank piped up next to Linda. "Don't you all have those anywhere?"

Jim scrunched his eyebrows and pursed his lips as he thought over the question. "You know, we did have a paper retention policy. Every few weeks there would be a data dump that they'd store for six months or so down in the basement. I guess it's possible that what you're looking for might be down there."

Linda forced herself not to growl as she replied with a simple statement that came out sounding like an order. "Show us to the basement."

———

OUTSIDE THE MAIN DOCKYARD BUILDING, Lieutenant Jackson glanced around as he stood by himself off to one side. After double-checking to ensure he was alone, he reached into his pocket and pulled out a tattered packet of cigarettes. He flipped open the box and mumbled something incoherent over the fact that he had only three left. He plucked one from the box, put it in his mouth, retrieved a lighter from his pocket and was just about to flick it on when a sharp call startled him so much that he nearly dropped the lighter and cigarette on the ground.

"Jackson!" Linda shouted at him as she and Frank ran up. She glanced at his fumbling hands as he tried to shove his lighter and cigarettes back into his pockets before giving him a wink and a devilish grin. "Don't worry, I won't tell."

Lieutenant Jackson cleared his throat and straightened his back. "Bad habit that comes back to bite me sometimes. What've you got?"

Frank stepped up and handed a thick manila folder to Jackson. "Actual physical descriptions of the crates. Weight, color, dimensions; we got the works."

Jackson felt an enormous weight fall off of his shoulders and he closed his eyes and breathed a sigh of relief. "Thank goodness. Finally some good news for once. Have you called this in to Sarah yet?"

"That's next on the list." Linda looked around for their Humvee. "Come on, let's go."

The trio ran for the Humvee and once they arrived Linda retrieved the case containing the satellite phone and opened it on the hood of the vehicle. After powering it on and dialing Sarah's number, she tapped her foot impatiently as the device connected to the military's communication network and began the long, complex process of reaching out to Sarah's phone.

"Did you finally find something?" Sarah sounded as if she had been woken again and Linda couldn't resist mentioning it.

"Are you sleeping round the clock now?"

"Until you two idiots get some solid intel I'm about as useful as a screen door on a submarine, so yes, dammit! I *am* catching up on some much-needed sleep!"

Linda choked back a laugh before replying, a wide grin still plastered across her face. "Good to hear it, because you're about to get a lot less."

There was a shuffling noise in the background on the call and Linda could tell that Sarah had just sat up from wherever she was lying and was fully focused on the call. "You got information on the crates?"

"You could say that. We've got dimensions, weights, colors and everything else you need to put out an alert for them."

"About time. Hold on, I'm grabbing a pen and paper." Linda could hear the phone at the other end of the call being placed down, then a set of footsteps echoed in the background. Instead of footsteps back toward the phone, though, what Linda heard next was the sound of Sarah saying something unintelligible far in the background followed by the unmistakable sound of a rifle's safety being flipped.

"Sarah?" Linda spoke into the phone as she pressed it against her ear and bumped up the volume on the device. "Hey, you still there? What's going on?"

There was silence for a few seconds before the faint sound of wood and glass breaking came through. Shouting and gunfire followed, as did the shouting of at least three different people before there was a scuffle near the phone and the line went dead.

"Sarah? Sarah!" Linda shouted into the phone, feeling her heart skipping a beat as a wave of nausea hit her stomach, threatening to bowl her over. Gunfire didn't normally phase her but the thought of it going on around—and potentially targeting—Sarah brought her old team back to her mind and what had transpired when she lost them. She grabbed onto the front of the Humvee to keep herself upright as she called out Sarah's name repeatedly. Frank took the phone from her while Jackson took Linda by the arm, helping her sit down on the ground.

"Sarah?" Frank spoke into the phone and listened for anything on the other end. Once he realized that the line had gone dead he redialed the number only to hear a rapid beeping coming back through the phone. He tried several more times but was greeted by the same result before he crouched down next to Linda. "What happened? What'd you hear?"

Linda's face was a cold mask of fear and she shook her head slowly. "There was shouting and gunshots. Someone must have broken in."

Frank sat down next to Linda and took her hand. "Hey, look at me." She glanced up at him.

"Don't tell me it's going to be okay."

"I don't know if it'll be okay, but I'm sure she'll be fine. She's tough. You know that better than I do."

Linda closed her eyes and took a deep breath as Jackson crouched down next to her. "What is it you heard, exactly?"

"Gunshots and shouting and what sounded like a door being broken in. Didn't she say something in our last conversation about there being incidents up there?"

Jackson swiveled away and spoke quietly into his radio as Frank nodded. "I think so, yeah. But I'm pretty sure that if looters broke in to her house they'll be in more trouble than she will."

"Why'd the line go dead, then?"

"Somebody stepped on the phone?" Frank shrugged. "I don't know. She'll be okay though; I know tha—"

"You can't know that. Nobody can know that. She might be or she might not."

"Back in a minute; stay put, you two." Jackson stood up and walked away, still talking quietly into his radio. Linda and Frank watched him having an animated conversation several feet away, picking up only a few of his words here and there. When he came back there was a determined expression on his face. "I called in a favor. Don't know if it'll actually go through but we'll see."

"What favor?" Frank asked.

"To see if someone can check on her, see if she's okay. No promises but they'll do their best."

Linda nodded once. "Thank you, Jackson. I appreciate it."

"Hey, this isn't just about you. Sarah's the one with the million connections. We need her in this. Badly."

The trio was silent for several seconds until Frank cleared his throat and broached the topic the other two didn't want to bring up. "Until we hear back from Sarah, shouldn't we be operating under the assumption that she's out of the picture right now?"

Jackson nodded, but Linda was the first to respond. "Yes. We should." The wave of nausea and the feeling of being back in Iran had subsided and she pushed herself to her feet, shrugging Jackson's hand off her arm and squaring her shoulders in the process. "Jackson," she said, turning to him, "What are the chances you can get someone up the chain to pay attention if you call this in?"

"Halfway decent, I'd say. But that'll just alert the person on the inside. I thought the whole point of going through Sarah was to avoid that?"

"Of course it was. But with Sarah out of the loop for the time being we have to push forward. Omar already knows we're looking for him so I can't imagine him finding out we know what the crates look like will speed up his timetable all that much."

"I suppose not." Jackson hefted his radio in his hand, then paused and looked at Linda closely. "You sure about this?"

Linda glanced over at Frank. "What do you think?"

Frank spoke slowly, carefully selecting each word. "I think that if Sarah's potentially out of the loop... then we need to move forward. Stalling and waiting for her isn't going to get us to the next step of solving this problem."

Linda nodded and looked back at Jackson. "Do it. Make as much noise as you possibly can. Get anyone and everyone's attention and make sure to emphasize how serious this is. Maybe, *maybe* if we scream loud enough then the traitor will be forced to back off and play ball just to stay in cover."

"And if not?"

"Then we burn that bridge when we come to it."

Jackson took a deep breath and nodded. He took the papers Frank was carrying that described the crates and stepped away to start making his calls. Frank and Linda watched him walk away for a moment before Frank stepped closer to Linda and spoke in a quiet voice.

"You okay?"

"Hm?" She looked at him, knowing full well what he meant.

"The thing a few minutes ago, with you going all pale at the phone call."

"Oh. No, I'm fine. Just... yeah. Losing Sarah's not something I really want to think about. We need her."

"Absolutely. What should we do in the meantime, though? I'm guessing Jackson's call is going to take a while to go through."

"Good question." Linda rubbed her hands together, trying to think of an answer but coming up blank.

"What about... well, no."

"Go on, cough it up."

"Well." Frank shifted on his feet, trying to decide if his idea was worth saying or not. "Would there be any records of where those crates went? So we could maybe try to start going after some of them ourselves?"

Linda had been idly playing with the strap of her rifle as they talked but her hands froze upon hearing Frank's question. "You know, that's a really good question. I don't know the answer but I bet I know someone who does." She looked at Frank, her eyes suddenly possessed with hopeful exuberance. "Come on. Let's go talk to Jim again."

———

TWO HOURS of searching resulted in a shout of glee from Linda as she held up a piece of paper with one hand. "Got it!" The physical copies of the shipping manifests were stored in a separate location from the other paperwork and the disheveled file system left much to be desired. The switch to digital copies of everything meant that processing, data lookups and most day-to-day operations were more efficient. Paper backups had nearly been done away with except for obscure regulations that required them to be kept, though no organization system was specified in the regulations so the paperwork was dumped into rooms of the main building in random piles with no easy way to tell what was what. The discovery of the shipping manifest was a minor miracle in and of itself, and one that Linda and Frank were elated about.

"Where'd they send them?" Frank stood up from where he had been searching and hurried over to read the paper over Linda's shoulder. Jackson, half-buried into piles of discarded papers, shuffled through the mess and stood on Linda's other side.

Linda ran her finger across the lines of the paper, nodding and mumbling to herself as she read the obscure acronyms and documentation bit by bit, not wanting to miss anything in the process. "They were processed through successfully minus the radiation detector 'malfunction.' At that point they were put aside for pickup by a private shipping company by the name of Wayne Shipping." Linda blinked a few times and shook her head in exasperation.

"Seriously? Did anybody pay enough attention to this nonsense to see that apparently Batman himself owned the shipping company?" She sighed again and continued. "They were picked up twenty minutes after processing—seems fast—then it has their destination address as…Perris? Where's that?"

"East of here; inland," Jackson said. "Probably fifty, sixty miles as the crow flies."

"Is it a big city?"

"Moderately. About eighty thousand people spread out over the desert."

"Is it close to any military installations?"

Jackson shook his head. "Nope. None that I'm aware of, at least."

Linda looked at Frank and nodded. "I think this is our place."

"Sounds like it," Frank replied. "Out of the way, enough traffic to blend in and close enough that they could get the crates secured without setting off radiation detectors elsewhere."

Jackson took the sheet of paper from Linda's hand and passed it off to a soldier standing outside the room. After speaking with the soldier for a few minutes he returned to Frank and Linda, rubbing his hands together. "We'll be ready to roll out soon. Twenty minutes tops, unless you think we need anything else from here."

Linda shook her head. "If that info's good then that's all we need. Frank and I'll talk with a few more of the staff to see if they know anything else, but we should move as soon as you're ready."

"Copy." Jackson nodded and headed out the door and up a flight of stairs to get his men ready to move out.

⸺

"WE'VE GOT a way through over here, Lieutenant." The soldier's voice was garbled, both by radio static and by the sound of heavy breathing.

"Copy. All units, proceed through. We'll take up the rear-guard." Lieutenant Jackson sat in the gunner seat of a Humvee, watching as the three Humvees and the APC slowly rolled past, heading for the break in the debris that the soldier had called out. Linda sat in the driver's seat while Frank sat next to her, his head constantly rotating as he scanned their surroundings.

As soon as reinforcements arrived at the dockyard to secure the facility and continue treating the staff and workers, Jackson loaded everyone up and set out for the town of Perris, California. The drive took just under three hours, most of which was spent getting out of Long Beach and onto roads where they could drive at reasonable speeds instead of simply crawling along.

Unfortunately, shortly after they crossed into Perris they soon found themselves crawling along once again. The city looked like the others that Frank and Linda had seen, with collapsed buildings, destroyed vehicles and the aftereffects of desperate survivors trying to loot and salvage. Some of the roads in the Long Beach area had been cleared by the military so that convoys could easily move between the port and the airport, but no such clearing had been performed in Perris. Thus, Jackson assigned a pair of soldiers to scout ahead of the vehicles for paths that were relatively clear. Any obstacles were then pushed aside by the APC, making enough room for the Humvees to follow behind.

"How much farther do you think we have to go?" Frank asked.

"We've got another mile or so. I think things will open up soon since we're circling around to the southern edge of the city."

"Is the warehouse not inside the city proper?"

Jackson squatted down through the hole in the roof and tapped Linda on the shoulder. "Go on ahead. And no, Frank, it's part of a big industrial complex based on satellite imagery." Jackson stood back up, swinging the gun around to scan behind them as Linda pulled their vehicle in line behind the rest.

"Sounds like fun," Frank sighed.

Linda glanced over at her companion, a slight smile playing at the corners of her mouth. "You getting tired of this, Frank?"

"Nah," he shrugged, "Just tired in general. It feels like it's been years since I've had a full night's sleep."

"Buck up," Linda replied, giving him a pat on the shoulder. "We'll be through this soon. I hope."

Though the gunners on the vehicles and the soldiers leading the way were all vigilant for any attacks, the city offered no surprises to the weary group. There were signs that a few survivors still lingered in the area, subsisting off of stocked food and water or scavenging for what they needed in the ruins, but for the most part the city was clearly deserted. As they approached the southern edge and the going became smoother again, the pair of scouts got back into their vehicles and the convoy picked up the pace.

The afternoon sun was slowly falling in the sky when Jackson climbed down from the gun and closed the top hatch. He grabbed the radio from the front seat and sat back, stretching his shoulders as he radioed the convoy. "All units, listen up. We're approaching the location. Break up as we previously planned. The APC will hold back while the rest of us divide into two groups. Drive like you're performing a basic patrol and nothing more. Once you reach your designated positions I want the APC rolling in like a bat outta hell. We'll follow them in, using it for cover until we reach a location where we can deploy further."

A chorus of confirmations echoed back over the radio and Jackson leaned forward between the front seats. "All right, Rollins. We're on point. Take us in nice and easy."

AS LINDA DROVE ALONG, she focused on keeping her breathing steady. Her mind wandered to thoughts of driving through the narrow streets in Iran, passing between homes and businesses all while wondering when the next mortar or ambush would come. Dealing with survivors who were trying to scrape together food or water to survive was one thing. Coming up against terrorists from the country she had been to before was quite another.

After the first attack on the baseball field and the subsequent annihilation of the attacking forces at the parking lot a short time later, Linda had been on edge about further encounters with

Omar's people. Chasing after the crates was certain to draw no small amount of attention and even if the bombs themselves weren't at the warehouse, Linda knew that she was stirring up a lot of potential trouble.

"Group two report." Jackson kept his voice quiet in the back seat, his eyes trained on the large industrial compound to their north. Once a raw materials processing facility for computer chip manufacturers, the compound had operated on a skeleton crew for the last six months as they dealt with impacts from trade negotiations and more companies moving their business to foreign countries. The push from a few years prior to manufacture more complex goods inside the USA hadn't lasted for long as Asian markets pushed back, lowering manufacturing prices and offering attractive tax-related deals to US companies.

"Nothing here, sir. All appears quiet."

Jackson tapped the radio against his leg as he watched through the window. "I don't like this. We should have seen something by now. Some sign of something going on."

"Maybe they abandoned the place?" Frank unscrewed the top of a canteen and took a few sips before passing it over to Linda. She gratefully accepted it and took a long drink before handing it back to Frank.

"I don't know," she said, "But we're coming up on a break in the wall. Want me to slow down, Jackson?"

"Yeah, take it easy around this next corner," he replied, lifting a pair of binoculars to his eyes.

Linda nodded and took her foot off of the accelerator as they wound their way around a curve in the road. The reduction in speed didn't last for long, though, as Linda glanced out the window and saw a puff of smoke off in the distance near one of the buildings.

"Shit!" Linda shouted as she slammed the pedal back down, sending the Humvee surging forward. Frank and Jackson both shouted, wondering what was going on, but the explosion of the RPG masked any words they were trying to get out.

The slight increase in speed meant that the RPG didn't hit the

Humvee dead on, but impacted on the back left wheel instead, striking the center of the wheel and completely obliterating it and the tire as well. Linda felt the Humvee begin to roll over and fought the motion futilely, twisting the wheel back and forth to no avail. As an intense heat enveloped the vehicle and it began a violent roll off the road and across the sand, Linda closed her eyes, waiting for the kiss of death to brush against her lips.

Chapter Eighty

"Idiots." *Malcolm Stadwell mutters the word to himself as he stalks through the halls of the J. Edgar Hoover Building. He just left a three-hour meeting where his presence was completely unnecessary and he had to decline a call to his personal cellphone that he very much needed to answer.*

Malcolm Stadwell has worked with the Bureau for less than a year and already he feels as though the walls are closing in around him. His gambling habits that he managed to successfully hide during his interviews and background checks have come back to haunt him as his indulgence in the 'sport' grows in an attempt to cope with the stress placed upon him by his new job.

Stadwell's office is only a few feet away when he feels his phone buzzing in his pocket. He presses a hand against his pocket, trying to muffle what feels like the loudest vibration on the planet. After he ducks into his office he closes the door and pulls the blinds, then stands near his window as he pulls out the device. The screen is bright with a picture of two young children and a woman behind a transparent box with a phone number and photograph that he knows far too well.

"Mickey." Stadwell taps the green button on the phone and says the name with as little emotion as possible. He can feel sweat dripping from beneath his armpits and traveling down his sides.

"Malcolm?" Mickey's voice is surprisingly pleasant. It almost sounds like

the bookie has had a reasonably good day. "What's shaking, Mr. Eff-Bee-Eye?" The man speaks with a thick New Jersey accent, drawing out each letter in the acronym as long as possible.

"I know, Mickey. I've got most of it together. Enough to satisfy you. I'll bring it tonight."

"Most of what?" Stadwell's face creases into a frown at the sound of genuine confusion in Mickey's voice. "You're all paid up! That packet you sent earlier today cleared and you're zeroed out. Better than zeroed out, though; you've got a balance! I just wanted to call to confirm that it arrived and you're good. See you tonight!"

Stadwell's mouth falls open as he tries to think of which question to answer first, but Mickey hangs up and the line goes dead before any words come out. He stands in the corner of his office, a stunned expression on his face with a feeling of intense confusion saturating his mind. "Twenty grand?" He mutters to himself and shakes his head. "No, that can't be right. I sent him three, I thought. I know I did!" He's about to look down at his phone when he feels the device vibrating in his hand again. The screen lights up and reveals the caller as simply 'Unknown.'

Under normal circumstances Stadwell would simply ignore the call and then, when his voicemail was completely filled up, go through and listen to each message in rapid succession. He is still somewhat confused by the conversation with Mickey, though, and answers the call without thinking much about it.

"Hello?"

"Mr. Stadwell?" The voice is crisp and clear with hints of a foreign accent playing around the edges. "You can call me Mr. Amari."

"Amari?" Stadwell is confused. "I'm sorry, I don't think I know you. How did you get my number?"

"Our mutual acquaintance—you know him as 'Mickey' I believe—provided it."

Stadwell's mind races as he realizes that whoever is on the phone has just paid off his twenty thousand dollar debt. "I'm sorry, but I really don't know who you are. Have we met before?"

Mr. Amari ignores the question and continues speaking. "I was glad to be of assistance, Mr. Stadwell. If you need anything further, I'll be in touch." With that, the line goes dead, leaving Malcolm Stadwell to stare at his phone and try to discern what on earth is going on.

━━

SIX MONTHS LATER, Malcolm calls in sick to work on a Friday morning. He is ill, though not because of a bacteria or a virus or anything of that nature. After months of promising himself that he would not get himself caught up in gambling debt he has nonetheless found himself in the red to the tune of nearly six figures. His bookies are growing more impatient with each passing day and he needs a day off of work to try and relax while he attempts to figure out what to do.

He's three beers deep into a twelve pack when the doorbell rings. He looks up from the television and stares at the door, trying to make whoever's there go away by sheer force of will. A moment passes and he thinks he was successful, then the bell rings again. The third ring comes a few seconds later, followed by staccato knocking.

"Son of a…" Malcolm gets up from the couch, brushing crumbs from his undershirt and pulling his robe around his form to try and adopt some semblance of modesty. He hasn't been expecting any packages and he knows his bookies don't have his home address. When he opens the door he's taken aback by the people standing on the other side.

Three middle-eastern men are standing in the hall to his apartment, all dressed in bespoke suits with dark glasses, gold watches and smelling like they bathed in cologne. The man in the middle steps forward as the other two take a step back. He extends his right hand as he takes his glasses off with his left hand. "Mr. Stadwell. I'm Mr. Amari. Might we talk for a moment?"

Malcolm Stadwell's mouth moves but he can't form words to respond to the request. The two men with Mr. Amari move forward, gently pushing Malcolm aside and the three men enter the apartment, closing the door after they are inside. The sound of the door clicking shut snaps Malcolm out of his stupor and he shakes his head.

"Wait, no! Get out of my apartment!"

"Mr. Stadwell." Mr. Amari's voice is cool with the same hint of an accent that Malcolm heard six months prior. "I'm here to make you an offer. I under-stand that you've gotten yourself into a bit of a bind. I would be happy to help you with that."

Though Malcolm Stadwell is a gambler he is not a fool and he knows a quid pro quo when he sees one. He briefly considers making a break for his weapon that is sitting in a drawer on the other side of his living room but the two men accompanying Mr. Amari make that a challenging proposition. He watches Mr. Amari closely before replying.

"I appreciate the offer, but I don't need any help with anything."

"Ninety-eight thousand, four hundred and thirty-seven dollars. You don't need help with that?"

Malcolm feels his blood run cold. "How do you know that?"

"My job," he says, taking in a deep breath as he settles back into a chair, "Is to know things, Mr. Stadwell."

"Oh." He understands now. "Let me guess, you want to pay off my debts in exchange for information from the Bureau, right?"

Mr. Amari smiles. "That is such a crude, rough way of putting it. I don't want any information that would break any laws or force you to do anything that goes against your better judgment. Think of yourself as a consultant. My position requires that I have intimate knowledge of the law enforcement system and I find myself in need of an expert whom I can contact from time to time when I need help dissecting the finer points of certain matters."

Malcolm doesn't know what to say. He expected to be told that, in exchange for paying off his debts, he would have to give up every secret he knew. Being a consultant, though? It wasn't kosher to consult while working at the Bureau but if that is the only thing he's going to be doing wrong then he figures it would be worth it to ensure that he won't wind up with broken fingers or kneecaps.

"ANOTHER?"

The dark-skinned, bikini-clad woman looks down at Malcolm Stadwell as she holds a tray filled with drinks. He opens his eyes and looks up at her, smiling at her as he sits up in his chair. "Absolutely."

She smiles back at him as she hands him a glass filled with ice and an orange-colored liquid, then takes his empty glass and places it on the tray. "Anything else?"

He leans back in his chair and shakes his head. "That's all. For now."

Malcolm Stadwell's annual two-week vacation is nearly over and he's trying to enjoy every last second of it before he has to fly back to the United

States, exchange his swimming trunks for a suit and tie and return to the gray, featureless halls, conference rooms and offices of the J. Edgar Hoover Building. While a Bureau man like himself would not normally be able to afford vacations like the one he's currently on, his 'consulting' work pays quite well and has afforded him luxuries that he has taken full advantage of. He's been careful not to be too ostentatious when anyone from the Bureau is watching, but after three years of doing outside work for Mr. Amari without anyone catching on, Malcolm is feeling better than ever.

Two days later, Malcolm rubs his bleary eyes as he waits for his bags at the Dulles airport. He still feels the effects from his last night on the island and wishes that there was some way he could have extended his stay for another two weeks or longer. As he sits on a bench, yawning, he catches movement out of the corner of his eye. A man dressed in an ill-fitting suit sits down on the bench, holding a small white envelope in his hand. Malcolm pays no attention to the man until the man scoots closer to Malcolm and begins speaking in a soft voice.

"Good afternoon, Mr. Stadwell. Mr. Amari sent me to give you this."

The mention of Malcolm's 'client' sends a wave of excitement through his body. He takes the white envelope and opens the flap before thumbing through the bills as the man who handed him the envelope stands up and walks away. Every new payment for Malcolm's 'consulting' services means another chunk of money put into his secret savings account, more cash for his safe and more simple tasks to perform for Mr. Amari. The slip of folded paper nestled between the bills contains his instructions and he plucks it from the envelope before placing the wad of cash into his pocket.

Mr. Amari's requests have always been fairly straightforward and simple —almost too simple at times. A request for advice on how to deal with foreign diplomats, an introduction to certain private corporations, help with ensuring certain shipments aren't unnecessarily delayed. Each request is more complex than the last, but none of them have stepped so far over the line of reason that Malcolm feels like he can turn them down. None of them, that is, until today.

He opens the slip of paper and reads the small words printed upon it and his smile begins to shrink. **A client is shipping in some food products through the port in New Orleans, but the crates they used are slightly radioactive. The food products are still good, but we require assistance clearing the items through customs. Contact information follows.**

While the request is framed as a mundane one, it is odd enough that Malcolm re-reads it just to make sure he isn't missing anything. The contact information included at the bottom of the instructions is meant for sending a confirmation text message once the request has been fulfilled, but on occasion Malcolm has used it to get further clarification on the requests.

Malcolm glances around, trying to spot the man who gave him the envelope, but the figure is long gone. He sighs and pulls out a cheap cellphone from his pocket along with a battery. He inserts the battery into the phone, powers it on and dials the number on the slip of paper. There are three rings before a voice answers.

⸻

"DO I need to get agents down here? Because I will if I have to." Malcolm sneers menacingly at the operator, keenly aware of the large volume of sweat trickling down his face. Louisiana is unbearably hot in the summer and Malcolm would rather be just about anywhere else. Instead, though, he's standing inside a cramped office with no air conditioning at a small port in New Orleans, threatening a radiation tech with federal charges if the tech doesn't cooperate.

While the tech stood up to Malcolm at first, the threat works and he backs off. Malcolm nods and relaxes his posture, taking a step back from the man. As the tech works, Malcolm tugs at his collar, wishing he could douse himself in a bath filled with ice water. The heat isn't the only thing bothering him, though. There's still a nagging feeling in the back of his head about the requests he's been fulfilling for his contact, Mr. Amari. The requests seem to be benign; Malcolm visually inspected the contents of the crates that came through the port and found nothing irregular. Still, though, he knows in his gut that what he's doing must be a precursor to something larger.

What choice does he have, though? He became a slave to Mr. Amari the day he didn't report the payoff of his gambling debts. Every time he's 'consulted' in exchange for more cash to pay for more debts or luxuries in his life he's sold another piece of his soul. Whenever he thinks about how deep he is with Mr. Amari he pushes the thoughts away and focuses on something else. Even if he wanted to get out—and with the way the money is he doesn't—he couldn't.

Shaking off his feelings of apprehension, Malcolm finishes up his work at *the port. When he's done he heads to his car and leaves the port, dialing the temporary number on his burner phone. After a brief conversation with the person on the other end of the line, the call ends and he removes the battery from the burner phone and disposes of both the battery and the phone in a nearby dumpster.*

While the 'consulting' job at the port is the first of its kind, it is not the last. More jobs are assigned to Malcolm and he is soon tasked with instructing associates of Mr. Amari in how to deal with the imports on their own. Each new job brings a new, brief twinge of worry in the back of Malcolm's mind, but he pushes it aside, consumed by his own greed and inextricably trapped in a web of his own design. Unfortunately, though, it is a web that not only endangers himself, but countless others as well.

Chapter Eighty-One

The last thing Frank Richards could remember was intense heat, light and sound before everything faded to black. As the world pushed through the darkness and everything took on a fuzzy tint, he first became aware of an intense ringing in his ears. After a few seconds—or minutes, he couldn't tell which—the ringing started to die down, though it was immediately replaced by what sounded like distant shouting.

"Get up! Frank, get up now!"

Frank Richards forced his eyelids to open as he awoke in hell. The sound of gunfire came through in the background followed by another explosion and the shouts of Jackson who was standing nearby.

"Get him up! We have to move right now!"

Linda pulled Frank up and checked him over, nodding with satisfaction before pushing him toward Jackson. "He looks fine! Just a little banged up!" Frank stumbled forward, glancing briefly at what looked like an enormous amount of blood on the side of Linda's face.

"Are you hurt?" He yelled without realizing it, his ears still ringing.

"Just a scratch; keep going! We have to get to cover!" Linda pushed Frank forward again and he looked around, his memory suddenly flooding back to him. They had been in a Humvee when an RPG hit one of the back wheels, the force of the explosion sending the vehicle rolling over. The Humvee's back left section was in tatters but the interior was mostly intact thanks to its armor plating.

A piece of glass nicked the side of Linda's head causing the bleeding that looked far worse than it actually was. Jackson had survived relatively unscathed but Frank had suffered the worst as he briefly lost consciousness and was dealing with a pounding headache from the concussion suffered when his head met the roof of the vehicle with an overabundance of speed.

Another rocket whistled by and exploded several dozen feet behind the trio, prompting Frank to break out into a run before he tripped and fell next to Jackson who was taking cover behind a building. Linda helped Frank back up and sat him down next to Jackson before handing her wounded companion a rifle and grabbing the sides of his face to direct his attention to her.

"Frank!"

"What?"

"You took a nasty hit on the head. We have to clear the path and once we do we'll get a medic to check you out, okay? Just stay here and keep safe!"

Frank nodded slightly, then winced in pain as the throbbing grew worse. Linda tapped Jackson on the shoulder as she spun around to crouch behind him. "Where the hell is unit two?"

Jackson pulled out his radio and shouted into it as a small cluster of soldiers crouched behind a nearby wall began laying down suppressive fire on the main warehouse. "Unit two, report!"

There was a squelch and a burst of static before the breathless voice of a soldier came back through the radio. "Almost there, sir! Thirty more seconds!"

"Don't wait for my order to engage; as soon as you see those sons of bitches you open fire, understand?"

"Copy that!"

Jackson slid his radio back onto his belt and peeked out from behind the building, peering through the scope on his rifle and firing off a few shots at a pair of exposed heads looking out through windows in the warehouse. Linda did the same, all while Frank sat next to them, his right hand pressed against the side of his aching head while cradling his rifle in his left arm.

Just over thirty seconds later, a hail of gunfire erupted from the direction of the main building and Jackson stood to his feet though he still kept himself hidden behind their building. "That's them! Everybody get ready to move out!" He grabbed his radio and shouted into it. "Take in the APC now!"

The thrum of an enormous diesel engine filled the air, punching through the still-present ringing in Frank's ears and causing him to sit up to see the source of the sound. The APC had been parked behind a nearby brick wall, out of sight of the soldiers and the ambushers in the main building. With the enemy distracted by the advance of the second unit, the APC roared to life and smashed through the bricks like they were made out of tissue paper. Frank scooted over near the edge of the building, behind Linda and Jackson, and watched the scene unfold, his headache all but forgotten.

After taking an RPG from the main building, the other Humvee traveling with Jackson, Linda and Frank had laid down suppressive fire on the source of the RPG while the APC provided armored cover for them to escape. As soon as Linda and Jackson had pulled Frank from the wreck, the APC drove off, both to ensure it wouldn't take any serious damage and to make the attackers think that it had gone off to circle around from another direction.

The other two Humvees on the opposite side of the compound, meanwhile, had not been spotted by the attackers and stopped just outside the industrial complex. The soldiers moved in swiftly and on Jackson's orders opened fire on the warehouse, both to provide a distraction and thin the herd of attackers as much as possible.

With the enemy engaged the APC pushed forward, racing

toward the warehouse at full speed. It didn't slow down until the front end of the vehicle smashed through the side wall, rattling the entire structure and tearing huge chunks of sheet metal from where they had been so carefully riveted into place. Soldiers who had been forced to wait out the brief ambush inside the safety of the APC burst forth like a tidal wave as they moved through the warehouse. The enemy's two-dozen-strong advantage of superior numbers—and a surprise attack—meant nothing against the fury of the trained soldiers, and the mass of enemies in the warehouse was quickly put down.

Jackson and Linda raced forward as the APC plowed into the building but by the time they arrived most of the fighting was over. As soon as they started moving Frank pushed himself to his feet and took off after them, not wanting to be left behind. He lagged far behind, though, as he walked forward over the open ground at a slow but steady pace, feeling particularly vulnerable since he was out of cover.

He reached the warehouse as Jackson and Linda were talking to one of the soldiers who was in charge of the second unit. The rest of the soldiers were going through the various rooms in the place, calling out when each area was clear. After the brief gun battle that ended when Linda and Jackson arrived there was relative silence in the warehouse. As Frank stepped up through the hole the APC made, though, there was a flurry of shouts from somewhere down below which were immediately followed by the sound of heavy gunfire.

Linda whirled around, instinctively checking her surroundings and saw Frank leaning up against the APC, looking like he might collapse at any moment. "Frank?" Linda rushed to his side and helped him into the armored vehicle where he slowly sank down into a seat. "We told you to stay put!"

"And let you have all the fun?" he cracked a smile. "Fat chance."

"Rollins!" Jackson called for her out in the warehouse and she patted Frank on the leg.

"Stay here, okay? I'll be right back." She ran out as Jackson shouted for her again.

"Rollins! You need to see this!"

"Sorry," she said, hurrying up to him, "Frank came over and I was getting him situated in the APC. What's up?"

Ignoring the update about Frank, Jackson pointed toward the far end of the warehouse. "They found something."

JACKSON WALKED QUICKLY through the mess of bloodied bodies, toppled-over boxes and twisted metal as he wound his way back through the warehouse to where one of the soldiers had told him the stairs were. Linda followed close behind, keeping a wary eye on the second level of the warehouse even though she knew that it had already been checked for any more attackers. At the back end of the warehouse stood a wide set of double doors, one of which had been blown off of its hinges. A soldier stood at the top of the steps, holding a radio in his hand and carrying a nervous expression on his face.

"Is it down there?" Jackson stopped and addressed the soldier.

"Yes, sir. Down and to the left. Some of the lights were broken in the firefight so watch your step." He glanced at Linda and nodded at her. "Ma'am."

Jackson and Linda descended the stairs, each of them pulling out their flashlights and switching them on. While the smell of gunpowder pervaded the upper section of the warehouse, the first smell that reached Linda's nostrils from the bottom level was that of sweat. She wrinkled her nose in response and cast her light about, trying to find the source of the odor.

"It smells awful down here." Jackson was the first to mention it and Linda nodded in agreement.

"What could be the cause?"

Jackson shrugged. "I don't even know what they found. They just said that you, Frank and I needed to see what was down here."

Jackson took a deep breath and made a face. "I bet they've been living down here, underground so that they wouldn't get spotted."

"How many were there?"

"A couple dozen."

"Yeah that would explain it. I wonder what they've been doing, though."

"Sir!" a soldier ran up to Jackson. "It's over here, sir."

"What is 'it' exactly?" Linda asked.

"One of the crates, ma'am. The ones you've been looking for. We found one."

Jackson and Linda looked at each other with wide eyes and broke into a run as they followed the soldier back to where he had come from. The floor of the warehouse basement was concrete, though it was filled with cracks and crevices from years of use and abuse. The place had originally been used to store raw materials before they were processed in other areas of the compound but the virtual abandonment of the structure meant that the basement was more or less empty—aside from everything brought in by the attackers.

A few makeshift stoves and cookpots sat in a corner, their exhaust vents leading into rickety-looking lengths of pipe that stretched up through the ceiling so that the smoke could vent out into the top floor of the building. Thin, ragged mats covered with dirt and grime were laid out along one wall, and the blankets and pillows that rested atop them seemed like they could give Linda head lice or fleas if she merely glanced at them for too long. In one corner, far from the makeshift kitchen and sleeping quarters, sat a pair of blue portable toilets that had been stolen from a nearby distributor. Linda cringed upon seeing these, not wanting to imagine what they looked or smelled like on the inside.

At the end of the basement, tucked into a corner behind what looked like hastily-constructed walls made from scrap metal, sat a large metal crate. It was roughly four feet on each side with dull red paint that was peeling and chipped on all sides, a healthy amount of rust on the bottom and a top painted blue, of all things. As an object unto itself it had no mysterious, unusual or extraordinary properties but when Linda laid her eyes on it she felt a shiver run up her back as the hairs on her neck and arms stood on end.

"This one of them?" Jackson spoke to a soldier standing nearby, holding a digital display in one hand and a small green wand in the other. He was waving the wand across the device as he stared at the screen, and looked up as Jackson spoke.

"It sure looks that way, sir. Radiation's off the charts compared to background. Whatever's in here is smoking hot with radiation."

"Huh." Linda replied. She walked up to the crate and opened the top as Jackson and the soldier holding the radiation detector both shouted at her to stop. She looked back at them and rolled her eyes. "Please. I've been exposed to enough bad stuff that a few seconds of this won't matter." She peeked inside the crate with her flashlight, waving it around before stepping back from the crate and nodding.

"There something in there?" Jackson asked.

"Mhm. Something big. Lots of wires. I'm not going near it again."

"Perhaps next time, ma'am, you could wait until I give the all clear before messing around with an explosive device." The soldier reached out and gingerly closed the lid, doing his level best to keep the majority of his body as far from the crate as possible. Linda took another step back and looked at Jackson.

"You know what this means?"

"What?"

"Proof." The response came from behind Linda and Jackson. They turned to see Frank standing behind them, hand out against the wall as he walked along. He looked somewhat better than before but Linda could tell that he was still in pain.

"Frank, what the—I told you to stay still!" She walked over to him and tried to help him sit down but he waved her off and sniffed a few times.

"It smells like crap down here. Were they all living down here?"

"It seems that way." Linda looked back at Jackson. "What do you think? Is this thing enough proof for your superiors?"

Jackson snorted with amusement. "Are you kidding me? We'll

have everyone with a working pair of legs and eyeballs out searching for these crates."

"Good. They shouldn't be hard to find if they're all leaking like this one." He looked over at a pair of soldiers who were moving the bodies of a few of the attackers to one side of the basement and shouted. "Cooper! I need the camera and radio!"

"On it!" The soldier ran off and Jackson turned back to look at the crate while scratching his chin.

"I'll get some pictures of this thing and we'll send it up the chain. Of course you know that your traitor is going to pick up on it, right?"

"Doesn't matter," Linda replied. "We already alerted them when you called in before. This is just going to make an even bigger splash."

"How many of these things do you think there were?" Frank stood next to Linda, swaying slightly as he fought to stay upright.

"Good question," Jackson replied. "If they were keeping them back here then… a dozen? A couple dozen? I'm not sure."

Frank looked at Linda and swallowed hard. "That's a lot of cities that could be in danger."

"Yeah, plus it sort of leads to an obvious question."

Jackson glanced in her direction. "Which is?"

"Why didn't they move this one out?"

The trio was quiet as they pondered Linda's question. Cooper appeared a moment later, bearing a radio and the camera that Jackson had requested. He got to work documenting everything about the crate that he possibly could including some of the radiation readings, pictures of the crates from all sides and a few photos of the device inside. When he was done he gave the equipment back to Cooper along with orders to broadcast it. Once Cooper was gone, Jackson spoke to the soldier who had been scanning the crate with the radiation detector.

"How dangerous is it to be down here with this thing leaking like this?"

"Not terribly, but I wouldn't stay down here any longer than necessary. You won't grow a third eye in the next fifteen minutes but you probably don't want to dose yourself up with this stuff for no reason."

"Understood." Jackson nodded. "We need to think about containment, though. I don't like that we're messing around with this thing without knowing what could set it off." Jackson paused. "You got some bomb defusal training, right?"

"Yes, sir."

"Good. I want you in a radiation suit checking this thing over for a trigger. Don't mess with it any more than you have to, but figure out what makes it tick. Anything we can send up the chain to try and make it harder for the bad guys to set these things off is going to be another point for the good guys."

The soldier nodded and ran off. Jackson looked at Linda and Frank. "Let's get everyone out of here and get upstairs. I'll follow up on that call and you two can try to get in touch with Sarah again."

As they headed back up to the main floor of the warehouse, Linda had mixed feelings about the situation. On one hand she was elated that they had finally found one of the devices they were chasing, but she also had a nagging feeling that they were missing something. "Jackson?" Linda stopped on the stairs and peered back into the basement level. "What if they left this one here because it was damaged, and that's why it's leaking?"

"Then the sooner we disarm it the better. As soon as I call this in I'm sure we'll have some nuclear guys out here to take care of it."

"No," she shook her head, "No, that's not what I mean." Linda looked at the soldier ahead of them who was heading to find a radiation suit in the APC. "Hey, hang on a second!"

"Ma'am?"

"Can you tell how long that thing's been down there? By measuring the radiation levels and whatever in the soil around it?"

He cocked his head to the side and raised an eyebrow. "Maybe... but why?"

If that's the only one left behind, then if we know how long it's been sitting there alone—with no other crates to block the radiation from hitting the ground or walls or whatever else—then we'd know how long ago the other crates were moved out from here to the cities."

Jackson nodded vigorously. "That… is a good idea. Might come in handy in tracking them down." He pointed at the soldier. "Figure that out if you can, too. I'm going to go follow up on the call and see how fast we can get reinforcements here."

"Yes, sir!"

"Linda." Frank took Linda's arm and pulled her off to the side. He had managed to follow most of what was going on despite the pain in his head, and he was growing more and more concerned about one particular aspect.

"What's up, Frank?" Linda looked him over, still worried about his condition.

"We need to try calling Sarah. I don't like how we haven't heard from her."

"Agreed. You still have the phone?"

"Oh yeah, I forgot." Frank slipped off the backpack he had been wearing since before they arrived and opened it up. He pulled the black case out of it and looked in horror at the long crack that stretched across the shell of the plastic. "What the…" Frank opened the case and found the phone inside to be damaged as well, bearing a broken screen and a large dent on the number pad.

"Looks like the case took the brunt of the damage when that RPG hit us." Linda gingerly pulled the phone from the case and gently depressed the power button. There was an electronic whine from somewhere inside the phone before it grew so high pitched it became inaudible. A small puff of smoke came from a crack on the side of the device a split second later and Linda dropped it back into its case with a grimace.

"Hm." Frank grunted and placed the case down on the ground before putting his pack back on. "So much for trying to call her on that."

Linda sighed and looked around. "I'll see if Jackson can get someone to get a phone for us. We have her number so we can try calling her again."

Frank stared at the phone on the floor for a few seconds before looking at Linda. "Do you think we'll catch a break sometime soon? Or are we going to be perpetually one step behind?"

Linda sighed again and shrugged, her silence the only appropriate answer to Frank's question.

Chapter Eighty-Two

"I don't see what the damned problem is. You've got your money, so why—" The man talking on the phone pauses and rolls his eyes as the person on the other end of the line interrupts him. After a few seconds he speaks again. "Look, fine, whatever. I don't care anymore. Just get it taken care of. Yes. Yes, it's still working. Yeah, great. Thanks. Later."

Malcolm Stadwell throws his satellite phone onto his bed and rolls his eyes again. "Asshole." He tilts back his head as he finishes another bottle of beer before chucking the bottle into a nearby trash can.

Though the apocalypse has come to the United States, Malcolm Stadwell barely feels a thing. With a backup generator, a large stock of food and drink and a healthy amount of security, he is both safe and comfortable in his four-bedroom home on the northern outskirts of Washington, D.C. The home is small but has a spacious basement, a built-in generator, whole-house battery and solar panels and is set up in a discrete neighborhood off of the beaten path and surrounded by ten-foot-tall steel fencing.

It is Malcolm's sanctuary and fortress and home, allowing him to remain in denial about the events in the outside world while he relaxes, watches old movies and drinks himself to sleep every night.

As Malcolm trots down the stairs from the second story to the first, he opens his mouth to shout at his housekeeper. "Maria! Did you get around to that mopping today? The cellar's in awful shape and I don't… what the hell?" As his right foot hits the bottom of the stairs, it nearly slips out from under him. He looks down and lifts his foot up, grimacing as he realizes that it's covered in some sort of sticky substance. "Dammit, Maria! What did you spill?!" He shouts at her again, but there is no answer.

He shakes his foot gingerly, not bothering to look very closely at the substance as he hops over a puddle of it and rounds the corner of the stairs. He stops, frozen in shock as he sees a dark form lying on the ground in front of him. A pool of dark red blood covers the floor, having flowed from the body's head and collecting at a low spot at the bottom of the stairs. Malcolm gulps hard, not sure how to process the sight of his dead housekeeper until he remembers that there's a small .380 revolver tucked away in the pocket of his robe.

Malcolm pulls out the revolver and snaps back the hammer, holding the weapon out at arm's length with a slight tremor. He glances down at the body again, confirming that what he is seeing is real. "Someone broke in?" He whispers to himself as he steps forward, cringing as his wet foot hits the dry floor with a slight squelch. Fear seizes at his stomach, causing his arm and hand to shake even more as he steps forward. The edge of his robe catches in the thick liquid, pulling it slightly back and startling him.

"Who's there?!" He whirls around and shouts at the empty room, nearly firing at a shadow in the corner cast by the grandfather clock. He takes a few steps backwards, heading into his living room when his left ear barely catches a soft rustling off to the side. He turns again, ready to fire, but an olive-skinned hand reaches out and grabs his arm, bending it to the side and snapping the bones in his wrist.

Malcolm cries out in pain as the gun slips from his fingers and clatters to the ground. He reaches for the weapon with his left hand but the assailant gets to it first, pulling it away before Malcom can get to it. Recoiling in fear, a small scream of pain escapes Malcolm's lips before another assailant approaches from behind. In less than thirty seconds he is seated in a chair in his kitchen with his arms and legs bound.

"What the hell do you want?! Just take whatever it is you want, please! Anything! Just take it!" Tears run down his cheeks, partially from the pain in his wrist and arm and partially from the abject fear running through his mind. His home north of Washington was supposed to be secure; after all, he designed it that way intentionally. Paranoia fueled by his traitorous actions against his *country led him to spend money on unnecessary security measures for his home. When the unexpected happened and the country fell to the attacks, the home became a fortress. The first few days were traumatic as he realized that he was partially responsible for what had occurred. Justification and alcohol quickly took away the trauma, though, replacing it with a sense of self-righteousness and egotism.*

'Anyone could have done it.'

'If I had said no then they would have found someone else.'

'At least I'm safe and have food and water.'

'Idiots. They should have thought ahead and prepared themselves for something like this.'

"Mr. Stadwell." The voice is smooth and cuts through Malcom's thoughts. He opens his eyes, blinking several times to clear away the tear-filled clouds. An olive-skinned man stands before him, dressed in casual clothing. His features are masked by shadows but he bears the attitude of a man who is in complete control of a situation and has no fear or anxiety whatsoever.

"W-who are you? Just take whatever you want, please! But don't kill me! I beg you!" Malcolm chokes out the words.

"Take whatever I want?" The man smiles coolly and sits down in a chair a few feet away from Malcolm. "You've already ensured that I have everything I want and need, Mr. Stadwell."

The way in which the man says his name makes Malcolm realize who he is. He squints, trying to make out the man's features to confirm his suspicion. "Amari?! Wh-why are you here? What's going on?"

"My name is not 'Amari,' Mr. Stadwell. My name is Farhad Omar."

"Why are you here?" The momentary indignation slips out of Malcom's voice as he realizes that he is most likely not going to leave his kitchen alive. While he doesn't know who this 'Farhad Omar' is, the way in which Amari says his true name makes it clear that Malcolm is involved in a game in which he is destined to be the loser.

"To deliver your final payment, of course." Omar flashes a warm smile. "You have provided invaluable assistance to me and for that you have my thanks. You are, however, a supremely disgusting individual. You have betrayed your country for coin. I have no love for your country but it is yours, and you have given it up because you cannot control yourself. I find that to be… intolerable."

Omar stands up and nods to one of the men standing next to him. Malcolm opens his mouth to protest, to try and defend himself and prolong his existence for a few more seconds. Before the first syllable can slip past his lips there is a loud snap as the suppressed pistol fires. Malcom's head sags down on his chest, blood spilling from the gaping wound in the back of his head and trickling out the hole in his forehead.

"Goodbye, Mr. Stadwell." Omar turns and heads for the front door to the house, taking care to step gingerly over the housekeeper whose body still lies on the floor. As he exits the house and heads toward a pair of vehicles parked out front, a man runs up to Omar from one of them, a phone clutched in his hand. "Sir, they're mustering at the mouth of the river. They're awaiting your arrival."

Omar smiles and nods. "Tell them I will meet them in six hours. We will commence then."

Chapter Eighty-Three

It was early the next morning when the distant rumble of diesel engines woke Linda from her slumber. She sat up from a sleeping roll and threw off a rough green blanket, looking around to get her bearings. After Jackson placed multiple calls with those higher in his chain of command, everyone at the complex settled in as best as they could with the threat of a dirty bomb lurking beneath their feet. The APC was moved out of the warehouse and the hole in the wall was patched up, the intact Humvees were moved to key choke points at the entrances to the complex and another soldier who had some basic bomb defusal training worked with Cooper to defuse the dirty bomb.

It took a few hours, but Cooper and his comrade finally emerged from the basement, sweat pouring from their faces as they pulled off the hoods of their radiation hoods and smiled in triumph. The bomb was relatively simple to defuse, but they had taken extra time to carefully document each step and each component of the device with photographs and notes which Jackson then passed up the chain for use once the other devices were discovered.

With the threat neutralized shortly before sundown and the promise of a large convoy of reinforcements on the way, the group dug in at the warehouse and prepared to wait out the long night. A fire was built in the middle of the warehouse, its smoke disappearing through holes in the roof, and meals were heated and passed around. Linda had kept close to Frank throughout the night, watching him carefully for any signs that his concussion or potential internal injuries might be leading to further issues.

The night passed without trouble, though, and when Linda woke up and looked around Frank was already up and about. He was moving slowly, his body still aching from the rolled Humvee, but the fire was back in his eyes as he leaned over to hand Linda a steaming metal cup filled to the brim with a black liquid.

"This is supposed to be coffee," he said, sniffing suspiciously at his own cup. "But it tastes like… I don't even know."

"Turpentine?" Linda grinned as she sipped from the mug, winced, smiled and took another big sip. "It's sort of an acquired taste. Spend a few years in the sand and you'll grow to love it."

One of Frank's eyebrows shot up as he watched Linda drinking the brew. "You can keep it." He held out a hand and she grasped it, stood up and looked around. A small cluster of soldiers sat around the fire eating breakfast while a couple others stood guard near the back entrance of the warehouse. The rumble of the patrolling Humvees reminded her that they were still at risk of being attacked. She put her coffee on a nearby barrel and took her rifle, vest and backpack from the ground. Once her vest and backpack were on she took a long drink from the cup before nodding at Frank.

"Thanks again for that. Any word on when the reinforcements will be here?"

"Jackson said he'd come by soon and let us know. I'm not—oh, there he is."

Frank and Linda looked over toward the APC as the back door opened with a clang and Jackson jumped out and came jogging over to them. He wore an expression of concentration and determination, though Linda thought she detected a note of glee in his voice when he spoke.

"Nice to see you finally up, Rollins. I need you two in the APC now. We've got new orders from command." There was a sense of urgency in Jackson's tone and Frank and Linda glanced at each other before Linda responded.

"What's going on, Jackson?"

"This way," he replied, ignoring her question. He turned and jogged back toward the APC with Frank and Linda close behind. When he arrived, he leaned in and gestured at the soldier sitting inside with headphones on. "Take ten."

The soldier nodded, took off his headphones and left the APC. When he was gone, Jackson climbed inside and sat down near the front. Frank and Linda followed suit and Jackson pointed at the back of the vehicle. "Close up the hatch, Rollins." She complied and took a seat next to Frank who was looking uncomfortably at the short ceiling. "You okay, Frank?"

"Just remembering what happened the last time the three of us were sitting inside a vehicle."

Jackson snorted and nodded. "We'll keep it brief." He picked up a few papers covered with scribbled writing and flipped through them before continuing. "As you know, reinforcements are on the way. We received orders an hour ago to await their arrival, at which point they'll secure the device." Jackson gritted his teeth as he read the next line. "We're then going to proceed with them to the east where we're going to be joining with a task force to respond to a fire that's broken out near a sanctuary city."

"What?!" Linda exploded as she leapt out of her chair, banging her head against the roof of the APC. She rubbed her hand on her head as she shook it, not believing what Jackson was saying. "What is this, some kind of sick joke?"

"I'm afraid not, Linda." Jackson spoke softly, using her first name in a show of genuine sympathy.

"Didn't you tell them about the crates? The devices?? The fucking *attacks by Omar's men*?!" Sitting next to Linda, Frank tilted his head and winced slightly as she screamed at Jackson.

"Of course I told them!" Jackson raised his voice, though he stayed still in his seat. "I told them everything multiple times, talked to all sorts of people! I've been on the horn on and off since last night. No dice."

Linda stopped and stared slack-jawed at him for several seconds before slumping back down into her seat. "Unbelievable. Just… unbelievable."

"They acknowledged it and said they're going to investigate, but they're not treating it as a priority."

"Dirty bombs in the survivor cities aren't being treated as a priority." Linda closed her eyes and tilted her head back. "What a load of crap."

"Does this mean they're not going to search for the devices?" Frank asked.

Jackson shrugged. "I have no idea. I told them in no uncertain terms that this was a huge deal but they've got a lot on their plate and I don't have any special pull."

"That's why we needed Sarah," Linda groaned. "If she was there she'd have every last man, woman and child out searching for those crates."

"I know. But she's not, and we have to deal with this as best as we can. I'll keep calling and trying to get through to someone who understands what we're dealing with, but… oh, wait. Here. Someone's calling back." Jackson turned at the sight of a blinking amber light on a radio mounted to the wall of the APC. He picked up the telephone-like transmitter/receiver and spoke into it.

"This is Jackson." For a few seconds his expression remained neutral and Frank and Linda could hear the staticky voice of a woman talking on the other end of the line. Jackson's expression suddenly changed, though, and his eyes grew wide and he sat up in his seat. He looked up at the mount on the wall as he spoke again. "Hang on. I'm putting you on speaker. There's a couple of people here who want to talk to you."

Linda's stomach did a somersault and she felt a shiver run through her entire body. Even though she hadn't recognized the voice on the other end of the line, Jackson's face and what he said told her all she needed to know. She glanced at Frank who, like her, had obviously figured out who Jackson was talking to as he had the same look of disbelief that she was bearing.

"—the hell are you talking about, Jackson?" The annoyed voice came through a speaker on the radio. The person on the other end sounded like they were sitting in a bathtub while wearing a bucket on top of their head but to Frank and Linda's ears it was the sweetest sound they could imagine hearing.

"Sarah?!" Linda nearly shouted.

"...Linda?" Though Sarah tried her best to keep the emotion in her voice contained, it was clear that she was somewhat taken aback to hear Linda speaking.

"I thought we lost you!" Frank spoke next, grinning from ear to ear. When Sarah replied, her gruffness returned, though there was still a certain note of elation leaking there from time to time.

"These idiots were doing door-to-door sweeps. My solar panels caught their attention and they decided to try and no-knock me. Ha! Didn't go so well for them. We got it sorted out in the end, though."

"Wait, so you... you're with the military now?"

"Darned right I am," Sarah sniffed. "And as of this moment I'm the one in charge of this little shindig." Sarah's voice faded briefly as she turned to glare at a few high-ranking officers who were standing nearby. "These walking sacks of dog feces have managed to see the error of their ways after tearing the crap out of the front of my home. After I made a couple of calls their bosses let them know what was going on and they got all of my data transferred here to their servers in D.C. The initial intel you gave me was enough to sway them to believe us, though Jackson's latest calls apparently fell through some cracks—asscracks is more like it. Which is also why it took so long to get a call back out to you. Anyway, long story short is that I'm in charge and you have new orders now. Jackson, you still there?"

"Yes, ma'am!"

"Good man. Listen carefully, all three of you. You've been through hell but you're about to go through worse. Omar's in the country."

The announcement caught Linda off-guard and she sat back in her seat, momentarily stunned. Frank looked at her, then at the radio as he replied. "Are… are you sure about that, Sarah?"

"As sure as I can be about anything. We've had…" Sarah paused, lowered her voice and scooted closer to the microphone on her end, amplifying her breathing and making her easier to understand. "Unusual events. A few patrols have gone missing, there's been some odd firefights north of the city. It's nothing big but it feels wrong. Like there's trouble waiting to happen."

Linda felt a chill run down her back again. "What can we do to help?"

"First off, you've already done a damned fine job. I saw what Jackson sent through early this morning and I had people start searching. They already located three crates in the last hour thanks to some video and satellite surveillance. We've got people on the ground and a bunch of eyeballs reviewing images and videos to find the rest. We're also working on a way to keep the bombs from being remotely detonated, but that doesn't mean jack if they're being guarded."

"Were the three you found being guarded?"

"Zealously. It was only thanks to an overwhelming response that we were able to take them down before they set off the bombs or sent out a transmission about what was going on."

"What do you think's going on with this?" Jackson asked.

"Good question. Hold on." There was a scuffle on the other end of the line and the sound of Sarah walking. An electronic squeal came through and another light appeared on the radio. Jackson looked at it, then punched in a series of numbers. The squeal stopped and Sarah's voice came through again. "There. I had to step away. There are some theories that are best left unspoken around others for now."

"What do you mean?" Linda leaned forward, speaking in a conspiratorial tone.

"I think Omar's planning on attacking D.C. directly once he bombs the other survivor cities."

"What?" Linda blinked rapidly a few times. "Why would he do that?"

"Call it symbolic retribution. You know how I said we had missing patrols and firefights? That's not all. I can't go into details right now but there are other signs that something big is going to happen soon."

"Ma'am, this sounds bad." Jackson paused, realizing what an understatement that was and then continued. "What do you have for us to do, though?"

"It just so happens that you're close to where a crate was spotted recently. You're going to take on reinforcements from the units arriving there soon and proceed to Phoenix, one of the survivor cities. Once you're there you'll meet units who are sweeping the city for the bomb and assist in the search."

"That's it?" Linda said. "Shouldn't we be coming to D.C. if—"

"No, not yet. That's one of the only cities where we don't have enough people to search for the bomb. You need to help them find that first. Once that's done we'll talk about getting you up here so you can find Omar and beat him to a bloody pulp."

The mental image made Linda smile. She forced down thoughts of her fists whaling on Omar's bloodied face and nodded. "Copy that. I can't wait."

"Good. Also, I presume your phone's either lost, out of batteries or destroyed so you'll get a new one from the unit arriving shortly. Keep it on you at all times, got it?"

"Will do."

"Good. Now take me off speaker, Jackson. I'll pass you off to someone who'll fill you in on the technical details of everything."

"Yes, ma'am." Jackson reached for the button on the radio, but before he could push it, Sarah spoke again.

"Oh, and Frank? Linda?"

"Yes?" They both replied in unison.

"It's good to hear your voices again."

IF THE MOOD of the group in and around the warehouse could be described before Sarah's call it would best be done so as somber. After the call, though, word spread like wildfire that a new mission was at hand that would take the fight to those responsible for the ambushes and potentially save tens of millions of people from a dirty bomb attack. While the soldiers had no knowledge of the complexities of the situation surrounding Omar and his attacks on the country, the promise of revenge for their fallen comrades and being the source of salvation for their countrymen was enough to electrify them.

Linda and Frank sat on the sidelines as Jackson gave orders to groups of soldiers, whipping them into shape and preparing them for the journey ahead. Frank's gaze flicked back and forth between the soldiers, taking in their acronym-filled conversations and odd habits with wide eyes. Linda, on the other hand, was quite used to the scene unfolding in and around the warehouse and she instead spent her time thinking about the conversation with Sarah and the various emotions it stirred up inside of her.

Relief was by far the deepest one she felt, though it wasn't just over the fact that Sarah was alive. A journey that had been years in the making was, at last, looking like it might be coming to a close. While she initially thought she might feel excitement, joy, elation or even grow jittery at the thought, she instead felt the simple, sweet wash of relief.

"You look happy." Linda started at Frank's voice and looked over to find him staring at her, a curious smile on his face. She realized that she had been grinning as she stared out across the warehouse, her eyes unfocused as she was lost in thought.

"Hm?" She took a deep breath. "Yes. Yes I am."

"About Sarah?"

"That's part of it."

Frank was silent for a few seconds before speaking again. "Are you ready to find Omar?"

The question was simple, but it stirred up another wave of emotions in Linda, and not all of them good. She locked eyes with Frank, watching him intently as she thought back to the first time she had seen him back at the gas station that she barely escaped from with her life intact. If he had asked the question at any other time, she would have had to fight the urge to snap at him. This time, though, something was different. Frank was no longer just some person she met and was putting up with to try and survive so that she could achieve a goal. He had risked life and limb for her, saving her on more than one occasion. They shared a bond that had continued to keep them together in spite of their disagreements and Linda no longer looked at Frank as a stranger. He was a friend.

"Yes." Her answer was deliberate. "More than anything else in this world."

Frank nodded and patted her on the back. "Good. We'll find him."

"I know."

The pair sat in silence again as they continued watching the soldiers working. It was another hour before the rumble of the vehicles around the warehouse and industrial complex was dwarfed by the sound of a convoy approaching. A dozen Humvees, four large tracked vehicles that Frank didn't recognize and a trio of APCs rolled down the road toward the complex, throwing up a thick trail of dust behind them. Gunners sat on all of the vehicles that had mounted weaponry, the turrets rotating slowly as they scanned for threats. The power of the engines made Frank grin and he felt like a child again as he grew giddy with anticipation.

After a brief exchange between Lieutenant Jackson and the head officer on the convoy, several soldiers clad in radiation suits hurried down to the basement of the warehouse and began packaging the defused dirty bomb for shipping. While they worked, Jackson began the final preparations to combine the forces that had secured the warehouse with the freshly arrived reinforcements so that they could head to Phoenix. The group securing the dirty bomb would take one of the tracked vehicles—a light tank variant designed for urban combat—along with a pair of LMG and TOW missile equipped Humvees and move the device to a secure location.

The rest of the vehicles and manpower would then move out to Phoenix with the expectation of arriving early the next day and immediately getting to work on locating the bomb that was undoubtedly hidden somewhere in the city. The departure preparations were complete in less than an hour and, before Frank realized what was going on, he was sitting in yet another Humvee with Linda and Jackson.

As the convoy pulled away from the compound, Frank glanced back in the rearview window before snorting and leaning forward in his seat to talk to Linda. "Never thought I'd be glad to be getting back into one of these things."

"Just try not to crack your skull wide open if we crash again, okay?"

Frank grinned and patted Jackson on the shoulder. "That's not a problem so long as Jackson here doesn't get us into another ambush."

"Keep cracking wise like that and I'll have you sitting on the back bumper all the way to Phoenix." Jackson's tone was flat and serious but there was a twinkle in his eye that made Linda and Frank both chuckle.

With their numbers bolstered by the reinforcements and the new mandate from Sarah in hand, they were all feeling elated to be moving on to the next step in their journey. The fact that they would have to search for a dirty bomb while under the constant threat of it detonating nearby was of little consequence and the threat of D.C. being overrun by Omar's men meant nothing in that moment. They had their health, they had each other and they had the determination and drive to see their mission through to the end.

What end it would have, though, was anyone's guess.

Chapter Eighty-Four

T welve soldiers run down an empty street, their bootsteps echoing against the walls of the buildings on both sides. Each man wears a backpack, though not the one they are used to carrying. Instead of carrying extra ammunition, supplies and gear in large bags they wear small ones, weighing only a few pounds each. A small piece of electronic equipment rests in each bag, and from the bag stretches a braided wire that leads to a small computer screen. Each soldier wears their screen on their arm, attached by way of an adjustable strap. The screens display a constant stream of data provided by the sensors in the backpacks but the soldiers don't know what most of the numbers and words on the displays mean. All they know is that they need to look for one particular word, symbol, reading and color.

The vehicles that used to cover the streets and parking lots of the city have been moved, towed away and taken to scrap heaps and junkyards so that every square meter of flat land is usable. Temporary shelters are constantly under construction, being assembled from kits as quickly as they are delivered. They have not yet reached the section of the city where the soldiers are searching, though, and the only other people in the area other than the soldiers are civilians who own the local homes and businesses. Some of those individuals have chosen to relocate to shelters closer to the center of the city where they can be near the routes taken by the trucks that deliver aid supplies. Many have stayed in their homes and businesses, though, and the soldiers can feel the peoples' eyes on them as they march down the street.

The soldiers take care not to give any outward indication of their mission. Public knowledge of what they are searching for would incite panic that would lead to countless more lives being lost. The grim reality is, though, that the object they are searching for will end everyone's life in the city unless it is found in time.

"We've got something over here, Corporal." One of the soldiers adjusts the screen on his wrist and turns to look at the man he is speaking with.

"What is it?" Corporal Anderson glances to his left and right, scanning the tall apartment buildings on both sides for any sign of hostiles. A few dirty faces peer back at him, hiding in the shadows of the apartment windows as they watch the soldiers marching by. Such patrols are frequent in the sanctuary cities and new arrivals find the constant presence of soldiers to be unnerving, to say the least.

"Readings are increasing."

Anderson checks the screen on his wrist and nods in confirmation. "Yes they are. All right, everybody spread out so we can start triangulating this." The soldiers break formation and spread out across the street. A few head down a nearby alley to an adjacent road while others enter an apartment and exit out the other side. Corporal Anderson taps on his screen, entering the necessary commands to start the automated triangulation calculations. The process takes readings from all of the devices in the area and feeds them back to a central system that processes the levels to determine the approximate location of the target.

It doesn't take more than ten more minutes of wandering for Anderson to receive a call over the radio. "Corporal, you initiated the program a short time ago, did you not?"

"Confirmed; that I did."

"All radiation readings confirm the device is in your neck of the woods. Keep searching and find the exact location. Question anyone in the area to see if they noticed anyone hauling in crates. We're sending all available units to your vicinity to help sweep and secure."

"Copy that." Anderson tucks his radio back on his belt and feels an uncharacteristic surge of butterflies in his stomach. The orders to begin searching for metal crates of a certain size and color came down a short time *ago. The initial order merely stated that the crates needed to be found, without expounding on why. The 'why' came a short time later, though, and turned a reluctant search into one driven by fear and necessity.*

A dirty bomb, designed to spread as much radiation as possible across as wide of an area as possible, was sitting somewhere in the Chicago sanctuary city. That much had been confirmed by drone and satellite footage showing the crate sitting in the back of a pickup truck that had arrived days ago. The exact location of the device inside the crate was unknown, though, as it vanished from the vehicle that was abandoned outside the city. Whoever was in charge of issuing orders for the search did not believe that the device was taken away, though, as the instructions were crystal clear: find the device before it detonates.

Anderson, like many others in the search parties, had initially responded to the revelation of the device with determination and dedication to finding it. There were more than enough troops in the city that they could easily canvass the area with portable radiation detectors disguised inside backpacks. What had been initially estimated as a quick search ended up taking far longer than anyone anticipated and morale was beginning to drop. Until Anderson's group stumbled upon the first credible radiation signature, that is.

A breathless soldier runs up to Anderson, his cheeks splotched red and sweat running down his face. "Two hundred meters ahead, Corporal. We found something."

Corporal Anderson follows the soldier down the street, into a parking garage and down the ramp into the first underground level where several other soldiers are standing around a closed metal door. Anderson motions at the door with the butt of his rifle. "It's behind here?"

"Yeah, that's the place. It's closed up tight, though. No way are we getting in with anything less than a blowtorch or a bulldozer."

"Somebody ask for a blowtorch?" A soldier from a nearby squad appears at the top of the ramp and lifts a large blue case in the air. Twenty minutes later the locks are broken, either from the torch or from the excessive amount of foul language hurled in their direction by the soldier wielding the torch. Once the door rolls open the soldiers grow serious as they double check their weapons and descend into the bottom floors of the structure.

Radiation readings spike as they pass through the door at the bottom of the ramp and Corporal Anderson affixes a mask over his face and motions at the other soldiers to do the same. They move slowly through the dark parking garage, checking behind and between the few scattered vehicles that are still present. With the first underground level clear they continue moving down even farther, descending another level before arriving at a second locked door. This door stands between them and the bottom of the parking garage.

Corporal Anderson whispers to the soldier carrying the blowtorch, asking him to get to work on the locks and bolts on the door. The soldier nods and begins setting up the torch, but as he goes to light it he stops and leans close to the metal.

"Does anyone else hear beeping?" The question comes an instant before the explosion. Plastic explosives affixed to the door at the ramp in several locations explode outward, killing several soldiers and sending several others flying back from the force. A hail of bullets rain forth from beyond the shattered door, piercing through the soft tissues and brittle bones of the surviving soldiers. The attack is strong and pushes back against the soldiers, but it cannot last forever.

More reinforcements converge on the parking garage to help assist with the securement and disarmament of the device. They instead find themselves drawn into battle with a foe that rapidly becomes outnumbered. The tactical advantage offered by the chokepoint of the ramp and final floor of the parking garage becomes moot in the face of grenades, tear gas and a continuous stream of suppressing fire.

The number of assailants in the lowest floor of the parking garage diminishes until there are no more attacks coming from the room beyond the shattered door. The soldiers advance slowly, using night vision goggles to cut through the smoke and darkness until they spy a lone figure half-hidden behind a car. The figure is one of the attackers, dressed in plain clothes that are soaked with blood.

One of the soldiers reaches out to touch the attacker, to locate his wounds and try to slow the flow of blood, but Corporal Anderson stops him. "No. Back up, now!" The command is stern and the soldier obeys, taking a few steps back from the attacker, who slowly lifts his head and forces out a slight smile. He mumbles something in a foreign language before his head sags and hits the ground with a dull thump. A radio falls out of his hand, tumbling across the ground before stopping at Anderson's feet.

"Hostiles are down," he shouts, "Move in and secure the crate right now!"

As the soldiers hurry to secure the crate, Anderson takes a step back and breathes a sigh of relief. He picks up the radio and slips it into his pack, hoping that there's some way it can be used to help identify the attackers and their *accomplices across the nation. As the soldiers crack open the crate, they turn to him, their eyes wide with alarm.*

"It's empty, Corporal."

"What?" Confusion clouds Anderson's face as he steps forward to peer inside the crate. "Where the hell is the device?" As he speaks, he hears a sharp squeal from the radio in his pack. He doesn't have time to even reach for the radio before the world explodes around him.

At the very top of the parking garage where the elevator has been marked as "Closed for Maintenance" for an unusually long period of time sits a device that used to be located inside the red and blue crate resting in the bottom of the garage. While the device itself emits a low level of radiation, it used to emit far more due to a problem that was recently fixed. As a result, the empty crate is saturated with radiation and is the primary source detected by the military's devices.

Unfortunately, though, because the crate is empty, there is nothing that can be done to stop the detonation of the device above.

Everyone within a few blocks of the parking garage is killed nearly instantly, though each person's exact cause of death depends on where they were and what they were doing. Some die from the heat while others die from the shockwave. People further out are severely injured by the blast but they survive for a short time only to succumb to their wounds later on. They are trivial in the grand scheme of things, though. The explosion of the dirty bomb sends a massive amount of radioactive material into the air, spreading it far and wide across the city.

Those closest to the explosion who are not killed by it die in a matter of days. Others take a few days longer while more still take a week or two. Those who are not injured by the explosion feel nothing at first, but that does not matter. They are the walking dead. And their killer? He is still free.

Chapter Eighty-Five

Seeing a large number of armored and heavily armed military vehicles driving down a highway can be an intimidating experience, regardless of whether it's wartime or peacetime. Being a part of said convoy as a civilian whose prior experience with military vehicles—up until a short time ago—was watching them on the TV or from the sidelines was both exhilarating and awe-inspiring.

Frank swiveled around in his seat for the hundredth time since they had left the industrial compound, looking back on the rows of vehicles behind them. Ten other Humvees, three tracked tank hybrids and four armored personnel carriers were arranged in a staggered, two-column formation behind the lead vehicle driven by Jackson. The roar of the vehicles' engines and the black smoke belching from their exhaust was an impressive sight and Frank couldn't help but grin as he turned back around in his seat.

"Calm down, Frank. You're going to overexcite yourself if you keep doing that." Linda looked back at Frank from the front passenger seat, smiling at his enthusiasm.

"We're about twenty minutes out," Jackson said, glancing at the rearview mirror. "Right on time with the estimates."

"Good," Linda nodded, "That's a rarity."

"The highway's getting a lot more open," Frank noted, sitting up in his seat as he looked out through the windshield. "Why are they clearing the vehicles and debris off so far out from the city?"

"From what I understand they're trying to get the backbone of the interstate system back up and running," Jackson replied. "They're working with bulldozers and repair crews to spread outward from the sanctuary cities so they can start getting trucks back on the road again."

"Trucks? Back on the road again?" Frank shook his head. "Where are they going to find the people to do that?"

"There's a lot of people sitting around twiddling their thumbs right now. I imagine that a decent number of them are itching to do something."

"Yeah, but so soon after what happened?"

"All we have to fear," Linda intoned, "Is fear itself."

"Yeah, but with Omar still running around out there…" Frank trailed off.

"We have to rebuild at some point," Jackson said. "If we can get some basic infrastructure repairs completed then we can start getting goods on the road again. That'll open up the possibility of getting repairs started on a much wider scale. If we do that… well. The sky's the limit."

"It'll take years to rebuild," Linda sighed. "But we have bigger problems to worry about right now."

"Indeed." Jackson nodded. "If we don't stop those bombs then it doesn't really matter." There was silence in the Humvee for the next few minutes before Jackson hefted his radio and spoke into it. "Phoenix base, this is Lieutenant Jackson, do you copy?" Static was the only reply so Jackson spoke again. "I say again, this is Lieutenant Jackson calling anyone at Phoenix base. Do you copy?"

Linda glanced over at Jackson. "Why wouldn't they be responding?"

"Good question." He glanced at the convoy behind and depressed the switch on the radio again. "All units, we're not getting a reply from Phoenix base. We're only a few minutes out so keep your eyes open." There was no reply to his transmission to the convoy behind, and he, Frank and Linda all looked back as they wondered what was going on.

"Should we stop and see what's going on?" Frank asked.

"No, I think we're about to find out," Linda replied. She pointed out the windshield and down the road to where the first exit from the highway into Phoenix was blocked off by a small group of soldiers. The convoy slowed as it approached the blockade before finally stopping a short distance away. Jackson hopped out of the Humvee along with Linda and Frank and approached the soldier who stepped out from behind the blockade and saluted.

"Sir! Are you Lieutenant Jackson?"

"That I am," Jackson replied, returning the salute. "What's going on here? We radioed about our arrival a short time ago but got no response. Local channels seemed down, too."

"That'd be because of the signal jammer, sir."

"Signal jammer?" Linda raised an eyebrow.

"Yes, ma'am." The soldier nodded at her. "We have signal jammers set up across the city to keep the devices from being remotely detonated. You must be Ms. Rollins, and you're Mr. Richards, correct?"

Frank and Linda nodded before she replied. "How did you know we were coming?"

"We got word a short while ago that you'd be joining us to search for the device. I have orders to escort you in, get everyone with you detector devices and assign you to the grids where our manpower is low. We have a lot of ground to cover and not a lot of time to do it in."

"Why don't we have a lot of time?" Frank furrowed his brow. "If you're blocking any sort of signal from getting in, shouldn't that give us enough time to get this thing found?"

"We..." The soldier hesitated and glanced at Jackson before continuing. "We believe that there are enemy forces near the device. They could manually detonate it if we don't find them quickly, before they realize something's going on."

Linda ground her teeth together and shook her head as she looked at Jackson. "We need to get moving, then."

"Agreed." He turned to address the soldier again. "Tell us where to go so we can get to work."

———

HALF AN HOUR LATER, after following a small pickup truck along the western edge of the city, the convoy finally arrived at a large forward operating base that had been set up in the structure and vast parking lot of a large mall. Stores inside the mall had been hastily converted into offices, makeshift operating rooms and storage areas for supplies while the parking lots were divided up into sections for barracks, vehicle parking and maintenance areas. A small section of the parking lot appeared to have the light poles cut down and a large white circle was painted onto the pavement, enabling helicopters to land and take off close to the base.

"All right, listen up!" The officer in charge of the search operation looked out across the troops from Jackson's unit as he pointed at a large map hanging on the side of the mall. "We've searched most of the eastern side of the city and haven't located any trace of the device. At this point we're leaning toward it being on the western side, as we think they may be trying to take advantage of winds to carry radioactive materials across the city once they detonate it. You'll be divided into four search groups and be assigned to the northwestern and southwestern corners. Each search member will have a radiation detector, but we won't be able to link them up to command here due to the signal jammer that's in place."

"Crap," Linda whispered to Frank, "That's going to make this more challenging."

"Two members of each search unit will be designated messengers. We've outfitted a few light vehicles for the messengers to get around the city quickly, but we're also going to work off of a flare system." The officer gestured at a group of flare guns sitting on the table. "Green means the sector is clear, red means you think you've located the device and are calling in reinforcements. Don't fire off the red unless your rad detectors are going off the charts. We've already had a couple of false alarms and we don't need to be rushing around letting these assholes know we're onto them until we're ready to go in.

"Once the device is located, you're to use lethal force to secure it. We believe that the terrorists have orders to manually detonate the devices if they're located, so you'll have one chance at it before the city is covered in radiation. Try not to screw up, okay?"

"Jeez." Frank shook his head as he whispered to Linda. "Way to be positive, eh?"

Linda shrugged. "It's reality and they're not about to sugarcoat it." She turned to look for Jackson who was moving toward the officer to speak with him and figure out how his troops were to be divvied up across the search areas. "Come on," she said, motioning at Jackson, "Let's keep up."

After receiving more detailed instructions on how to use the radiation monitoring equipment, the group of soldiers led by Jackson divided into four teams and headed out to the northwestern and southwestern edges of Phoenix to start their searches. The radioisotope identifier (RIID) devices carried by each member of the search teams were small in size and fit into discrete backpacks that were strapped onto the normal packs worn by the soldiers. A special emphasis was placed on appearing like regular patrols in the city so as to not spook any of the terrorists that might be watching the search process unfold.

As Linda, Jackson and Frank headed out with a group of soldiers to a grid in the southwestern section of the city, Frank pointed at a section of the parking lot that contained a cluster of remote-controlled drones. "Why aren't those up in the air searching, too? They have the same kind of detectors on them that we do based on the logos."

Linda peered out the window at the drones. "They can't take them up with the signal jammer in place. My guess is they're doing a wide-spectrum jam that's blocking all radio and satellite signals coming in or out. We're effectively cut off from the outside world right now until this situation gets resolved."

"Wow," Frank whistled softly and looked at the cluster of small packs next to him in the back seat. "So these things will tell us where the bomb is, huh?"

"That's the hope."

"Oh, they'll tell us, all right," Jackson said. "Whether or not we'll stop it from going off is another matter entirely."

Ten minutes later, after the search party arrived at their designated location, they were all on foot and moving down the streets. The group stayed spread out, moving into buildings periodically as they watched the radiation readings on the wrist displays, looking carefully for any signs that levels were increasing. Jackson had gone on ahead with a group of soldiers while Frank and Linda stayed together near the middle of the group, talking quietly as they went along.

"Why can't they just do this search on vehicles? Get some Humvees or something rolling and search the city really fast?"

"I'm sure they did, but this device probably isn't leaking radiation like the one back at the warehouse. With only trace amounts of radiation to pick up, doing a street-level sweep is the only way we're going to be able to identify the exact location."

"I don't know how we can possibly hope to find this thing anytime soon."

Linda smiled and patted Frank on the back. "Have a little faith. We may be cut off from the rest of the world and searching for a needle in a haystack but at least we're not being actively shot at, right?"

Frank chuckled. "That's true, I guess. It's way better than it was yesterday." His smile fell and he stepped closer to Linda and spoke softly, not wanting his words to carry to the soldiers nearby. "How are you doing, by the way? We haven't had a chance to talk much since the ambush and everything that followed."

"What do you mean?" Linda kept looking straight ahead, feigning ignorance.

"I mean about you and dealing with all of this urban fighting and the fighting in general. This can't be easy, even what we're doing right now. I have to imagine it's bringing back a lot of memories so… I just want to make sure you're okay."

Linda opened her mouth, ready to snap at Frank and tell him to mind his own business before closing it and physically biting down on her tongue to keep from saying anything. Her initial reaction was to brush him off and tamp down on the plug she had put over the emotional and physical responses she had been feeling over the last couple of days. In truth, though, he was right, and more so than he would ever know. Jackson's push for her to lead their counterassault against the ambush had taken a lot out of her and while resting at the warehouse the day before had given her a momentary pause, walking down the tight streets of an urban environment with hostiles potentially waiting around any corner was something she had never wanted to do again. Engaging with hostiles in an urban environment and then moving into two more urban environments was infinitely more challenging, and as she thought about Frank's question she realized that her answer was simple.

"No." The response was soft, and came out so quietly that Frank barely noticed she spoke at all. He glanced at her, raising an eyebrow.

"Huh?"

"No, Frank. I'm not okay." She still spoke quietly so that the others around them wouldn't pick up on the conversation but loud enough for him to hear. "I don't really want to get into the details, but this isn't easy. At all." She hesitated, taking a deep breath before continuing. "But I appreciate you asking."

"What can I do to help?" Frank's voice was filled with compassion as he reached out to take her hand and squeeze it tightly with his own. She smiled at him, squeezing his hand in return.

"Nothing, for the moment. The fact that you're thinking about this means a lot."

Frank watched her carefully before nodding. "You tell me if you need anything, okay?" Linda nodded in return and Frank patted her on the back before looking forward again. Linda's gaze lingered on him for a moment, and she felt something turning inside of her. The wall she had laid so carefully around herself over the years, piling brick upon brick, was suddenly punctured by a hole. It was a small hole, but a noticeable one nonetheless. Through it came a wash of emotions and feelings that she had kept locked away, ignoring them as her pursuit for Omar completely dominated her life. She had never expected a stranger—whom she had abandoned at the first chance—to be someone who would punch a hole in that carefully constructed wall and frankly, she didn't know what to think about it. As she started to get lost in her own thoughts, though, the situation once again changed in an instant.

The roar of a motorcycle engine was distant at first, growing louder by the second until a crotch rocket tore around the corner a block behind the group. They all turned and looked at the motorcycle as it roared toward them, the camo-clad rider's face hidden behind a large black helmet and facepiece. The motorcycle stopped with another squeal and the rider sat up, unbuckled his helmet and pulled it off to reveal the sweaty face of a private who was having more fun than should have been allowed.

"Lieutenant!" The soldier stepped off the bike and ran through the group, looking for Jackson. "Lieutenant Jackson!"

"What is it, soldier?" Jackson turned around and eyed the private closely, biting his tongue at the young man's haggard appearance.

"We've got something, sir. To the south, next grid down. We found a building that looks occupied and we're seeing triple the normal amounts of radiation in the area around it."

Jackson's face hardened and his eyes narrowed. "How many other units have you informed?"

"Yours is the first, sir."

"We'll head there immediately. Get moving and inform as many others as you can. Did you put up a red flare yet?"

"Not yet, sir."

"What the hell are you waiting for!? Get a flare up and get moving!"

"On it, sir!" The private ran back to his bike and slid his

helmet back on before gunning the engine, turning the bike with a quick squeal and dashing off down the road.

"All right, listen up!" Jackson raised his voice as he addressed the group. "Everybody back to the vehicles now! We're heading out! Everyone load up and follow me!" He had considered informing everyone of what was going on, but if they were wrong about the location and the terrorists were in the vicinity then they'd be tipped off. *Not that they wouldn't already be tipped off by the fast arrival and departure of the motorcycle, though*, he thought.

Jackson ran back the way the group had been walking, heading for the Humvees that were following a short distance behind, providing both cover and extra security for those on foot. Linda and Frank, who had been close enough to Jackson to hear what the private said, jumped into one of the Humvees with him as the soldier who was driving slipped into the back seat next to Frank.

"Sir, where are we going?"

Jackson glanced at the young man in the rearview mirror as he waited for the rest of the soldiers to get into their vehicles. "To stop this before it gets out of hand. I hope."

TEN MINUTES LATER, after traveling to the far southwestern edge of the city, Jackson's group slowed to a halt as they encountered a pair of soldiers standing by the edge of the road. The soldiers ran up to Jackson's vehicle and saluted as he rolled down the window.

"Sir! You're the first units to arrive."

"What's going on? Which building are they in?"

One of the soldiers turned and pointed at a large grey building a couple blocks down the street. "It's a building that's under construction. A library or something, sir. It's mostly finished on the outside, but apparently there's a lot left unfinished on the interior. We've encircled it as discreetly as possible and have all the exits covered."

"Any movement inside?"

"We caught a glimpse of two men walking by a window a while back, but nothing since then. They still have to be inside, though."

Jackson nodded and turned off the Humvee's engine before glancing at the soldier sitting behind him. "Spread the word down the line; I want everyone getting into supporting positions, ready to breach the entrances. Hand signals until we go in, got it?" The soldier nodded, his eyes wide, and Jackson turned to look at Frank and Linda. "You two come with me."

Jackson, Frank and Linda followed one of the two soldiers that had greeted him, slipping away down a side street and entering a small storefront across from the library. Construction on the southwestern edge of the city had been ongoing for several months and was part of an attempt to revitalize the area. Residents who worked in the city proper but couldn't afford to live there were moving in droves to nearby housing that was far less expensive, but the city officials could see that things were going to take a turn for the worse unless the area had some major upkeep. New parks, streetlights and public works—such as the library—were all investments in the area that were providing employment and leisure activities to residents in their local neighborhood.

The library was a massive, gray monolith that was nearly constructed. Tall pillars stood out front at the top of a wide staircase while long, stained-glass windows were still being installed on the other three sides. A side entrance to the lower floor of the library was visible from the storefront, and though it appeared boarded up a quick glance at the building with a pair of binoculars told Jackson what was really going on.

"Somebody broke in through there, eh?" He whispered to the soldier they had followed, Private Faulks, as all four of them crouched in the shadows behind the shop counters to stay out of sight.

Faulks nodded and gestured at the door. "We haven't been any closer to the building than this, but we have soldiers in place all around the perimeter. The entrances on all sides look like that one. Clearly broken into and sloppily fixed up to look like they weren't."

"Any signs of IEDs behind the doors?"

"No, sir. Scans with the wall imagers showed nothing around the door or frame."

Jackson nodded approvingly. "Good. Do you have orders yet from command on what to do?"

Faulks gulped and shook his head. "No, sir. You're the ranking officer here."

Jackson hissed an inaudible curse and Linda gave him a half-grin and punched him lightly on the shoulder. "Time to step up, eh, Lieutenant?"

"Bite me, Rollins." Jackson rolled his eyes and turned to Faulks. "Got your watch?" The private held up his wrist and nodded. "Good," Jackson continued. "We go in in seven minutes from my mark. That'll give you just enough time to inform everyone. I want a few more with us on this side, just to bolster our numbers. When everyone goes in, we're going to use standard breaching formations. Shoot to kill anything that moves and isn't wearing a uniform. Our sole priority is the device. Once we secure it then we can worry about whatever else these assholes might throw our way. Got it?" Private Faulks nodded and Jackson stared at his watch. "And... mark. Go!"

Faulks dashed out of the back of the storefront, heading out to give verbal instructions to anyone he could reach and hand signals to those he couldn't. Jackson groaned quietly as he sat back from his squat, taking the weight off of his legs and ankles so he could sit down on the ground for a couple of minutes. Next to him, Linda double-checked that her rifle had a round in the chamber and that there were a trio of spare mags in her vest ready for easy access.

"What do you two want me to do?" Frank was looking over the counter at the library as he spoke, trying to keep any hint of nervousness out of his voice.

"Stay—" Jackson started to speak, but Linda cut him off.

"Stay behind me." She glanced at Jackson as he opened his mouth to argue, her expression making it clear that it wasn't a subject up for debate. "You and I are going in last, after Jackson. We don't have uniforms on and we're not going to get into a potential friendly fire situation. If something goes wrong, just shoot at anyone except me who's not wearing a uniform."

Frank took a deep breath and nodded. Hearing that he and Linda would be going in last made him feel somewhat better, though there was a twinge of regret over not being part of the group that was going to storm in and—hopefully—save the city. The sound of footsteps in the back room of the store distracted Frank from his thoughts and he turned to see a pair of soldiers he recognized walking in.

"Sir." The soldiers knelt down next to Jackson, looking at him intently as they took deep breaths to recover from their run over.

"You get the word on what we're doing?" Jackson asked.

"Yes, sir. Ready to rock and roll."

"Good." Jackson checked his watch and rolled his head around, cracking the tendons in his neck. "Thirty seconds, people. Everyone get ready. I'll go in first, you two after, Linda and Frank to follow." He glanced at the pair and gave Linda the same mischievous grin she had given him just moments earlier.

"Time to step up, eh, Rollins?"

━━

FOR THE DOZEN TERRORISTS SITTING, lying and walking aimlessly throughout the interior of the library, life had never been more dull. After slipping the crate into the city and getting it inside the target building without a hitch, they had set to work on rigging the structure with explosives tied to the device to create an explosion that would be guaranteed to spread the radioactive material inside as far and as wide as possible. Once this setup was complete, though, there was nothing left to do except guard the building. The predictions provided to them by their leader turned out to be accurate, though, and the building and surrounding area had been left largely alone by the soldiers and civilians inhabiting the city, though that also meant that boredom was left to grow at an ever-increasing pace.

They never got a chance to be bored again.

Four teams—one at each entrance on each side of the library
—went in with breaching charges and flashbangs at the exact same
time. Five terrorists who happened to be in the general vicinity of
the entrances went down without being able to even reach for their
weapons. Two terrorists who were in the bottom floor of the
building trying to sleep were able to get up, get their rifles in hand
and start moving toward the noise when they were gunned down in
a hail of rifle fire from Jackson's team.

The remaining five terrorists, on the top floor of the library,
were able to get into cover before the team that went in through
the main entrance of the library could get to them. Two soldiers
from the front team were dropped in the initial gunfight and the
rest had to back off as the group of terrorists dug themselves in to
a makeshift barricade they had constructed around the device. The
other three teams, upon clearing the bottom floors of the library
and hearing the gunfire from above, raced to the top as they
followed Jackson's bellowed orders. As he shouted them, though,
he realized that they were likely too late.

As four of the terrorists crouched behind cover and fired
blindly at the soldiers pinned down near the main entrance to the
library, shards of glass and plaster and marble rained down from
the walls and ceiling. The fifth terrorist, meanwhile, worked feverishly on the device as he tried to remember the sequence for
arming and detonating it. He wasn't the man who was supposed to
manually trigger it; he was merely the third backup. The one who
spent the least amount of time learning about the device. His lack
of knowledge and the delay that ensued was the only reason that
Phoenix was not consumed by fire and radiation.

Jackson's boots thundered up the steps as he lead the teams
forward and they emerged from two lazily spiraling staircases, one
on each side of the library. He spotted the soldiers first, pinned
down near the front and reduced to taking potshots at their attackers. With a quick shout he directed the team across from him to
move forward and engage, laying down suppressing fire on the
attackers while he and the group with him moved around to the
side in a flanking maneuver.

"Miss me?" A voice from behind Jackson startled him and he glanced back to see Linda running alongside him and Frank just a few steps behind.

"I told you two to come in after us!"

"For the record, we did."

Jackson shook his head and waved her off, having neither the time nor the patience to deal with her. He spoke to his unit as they ascended a small staircase on the side of the library, gaining elevation over their targets and providing a perfect line of sight. "Take them out, but don't hit that device!"

Linda was the first to fire, bringing her rifle to bear and squeezing the trigger with a practiced hand that had sent tens of thousands of rounds downrange. The head of the man fiddling with the device flopped to the side as a pink mist consisting of blood and brain matter sprayed across the device. Jackson and the other soldiers with him took aim next, quickly dispatching the remaining four terrorists before they could figure out where the new fire was coming from.

"Cease fire!" Jackson bellowed out as he stood up, before turning his attention to the unit that was pinned down near the door. "Get a medic over there, now! The rest of you, secure this area!" As the soldiers scrambled to obey the orders, Frank and Linda raced back down the short staircase and headed toward the device.

"You got this, Rollins?" Jackson looked at her expectantly, knowing that she and Frank had been listening in on the debriefing given to him by the techs who had dismantled the device in the warehouse. He would have preferred to have one of the techs who had performed the original dismantling perform this one, too, but one of the soldiers being tended to by the medics was that same man.

"Hell no." Linda shook her head firmly and pointed at Frank. "He does, though."

"Richards?" Jackson looked at Frank and raised an eyebrow. Frank nodded and took a deep breath. "Yeah, I can handle it." He gingerly stepped over the dead man lying in front of the device and opened a small panel on the side. As he worked, Jackson stepped close to Linda, hardly believing the sight before him.

"How is it he knows what he's doing better than you do?" He whispered to her, trying to keep Frank from overhearing.

"You saw him with that drone. He may have been an accountant but he's good with this kind of stuff. Way better than you or me." She glanced over at the wounded soldiers near the front entrance and grimaced. "And way better than him, at least in his current state."

Before Jackson could answer, Frank stood up and put his hands into the air. "Done!" He stepped back from the device as the small screen on the front slowly faded and shut off as the capacitors discharged.

"Already?" Jackson asked, stepping up to look at the side of the device.

"Yeah, it's actually pretty basic to disarm. They never put any sort of failsafe mechanisms on them to protect them from tampering."

"So if they turn off the signal blocker this thing won't explode in our faces?"

Frank kicked at a small part on the floor. "Unless that receiver hops back onto the device by itself... no. We should be good."

"Nice work, Frank." Linda patted him on the shoulder. "You just kept us from being nuked."

As the adrenaline started to fade and Frank realized what he had just done, he felt his body shake and he sat down on the edge of the barricade. Linda crouched near him while Jackson headed over to check on the wounded soldiers.

"You okay there?" She asked.

"Yeah... yeah, I think so." He nodded and gave a weak smile. "That was... intense. I didn't really expect to step up and do that."

Linda shrugged. "You got put on the spot and you didn't crack under pressure. Can't ask for any better than that." She watched as he trembled again before standing up and helping him off of the barricade. "Come on, sit on the floor. Don't need you passing out from all this excitement and cracking your head open on the floor."

Frank managed a slight laugh as he sat on the ground and put his head back. He closed his eyes for a moment before opening them and staring up at the half-finished skylight above. Outside, in the street, the roar of diesel engines echoed faintly as the next sets of reinforcements arrived. Drawn by both the messenger on the motorcycle and the flare, they arrived expecting a fight but were overjoyed when Jackson's unit described the quick and decisive way in which they had been able to take out the enemy.

Over the next hour, after more techs arrived and confirmed that the device was indeed disarmed and enough officers higher up on the food chain were satisfied that it wasn't going to explode, the signal jammers across the city were switched off. Signals of all types flooded into the former dead zone, both military and civilian alike. Some were standard communication channels giving updates and keepalive codes, but the majority were talking about something else. A city that hadn't been as fortunate. A city whose operation hadn't gone quite as smoothly.

As Frank and Linda milled around in the library, watching the soldiers go back and forth on their assignments, they spotted Jackson walking toward them. Instead of the cheerful, celebratory expression he wore earlier, there was only anger and pain in his eyes. Linda recognized the cause by instinct and her gut twisted in fear.

"Jackson? What happened?"

He swallowed hard and fought to keep his voice steady, though all he wanted to do was scream to the heavens above. "Chicago's gone."

The announcement was simple and silence followed in its wake as Linda and Frank digested the news.

"What do you mean by 'gone,' Jackson?" Linda finally asked.

"They had a nuke go off. Dirty bomb. Whatever. Initial causalities are in the tens, maybe hundreds of thousands. Millions more'll die before too long. They had the device planted in the perfect place to do the maximum amount of harm." He looked at the device sitting on the ground next to them, partially dismantled by the techs. "Just like this one."

There was silence again for a moment until Frank finally worked up the courage to ask the question that was on the tip of his tongue. "What do we do?"

Jackson glanced at him before staring Linda dead in the eyes. Her expression had turned as ice cold as his and she nodded at him in agreement, knowing what he was going to say before he said it.

"We're going to find that son of a bitch you've been chasing and take him down."

Chapter Eighty-Six

"I just heard we lost Miami, too."

"Chicago and Miami? How is that possible?"

"Don't know; they're not telling us anything."

"But we got the one here, right?"

"Hell yeah. And they killed all the assholes guarding it, too."

The whispered conversation between a group of soldiers surrounded Frank and Linda as they waited for Jackson. Frank tried to ignore the whispers, dismissing them as rumors and hearsay but a quick glance at Jackson as he jogged back toward them confirmed that everything was true.

"Sorry about that, you two. Took a hot second to get in touch with D.C. You're both confirmed, though. Nobody'll question you again."

Linda nodded and took back her ID, as did Frank. "Thanks, Jackson. Is it true what they're saying about Miami?"

"I'm afraid so. I haven't been briefed but Miami and Chicago are all everyone's talking about." He looked around, trying to see through the crowd of people and makeshift buildings before motioning at a large structure a short distance away. "Come on, let's get to the command post so we can try to get Sarah on the line."

The celebration over the location and disarmament of the device in Phoenix had been short-lived once the news about Chicago came over the radio. With the device gone, units were being redeployed both through Phoenix and to other portions of the country. Jackson's unit, as the ones who spearheaded the attack against the group at the library, were summoned to the local command post to undergo a debriefing before being reassigned.

After all of the traveling with the convoy and working on the fringes of cities for the last few days, Frank and Linda received a shocking reminder of just how bad things really were as they drove toward the more populated section of the city, near the command post. People sat in droves along the sidewalks with jackets zipped and blankets pulled tightly around themselves. They were largely quiet as they watched the soldiers driving and marching back and forth, having lost most sense of self after being stuck in the city for so long. In some areas, where relief supplies were being distributed, there were disagreements, shouting and even a few minor fistfights, though those were quickly clamped down on by nearby soldiers.

A sense of perpetual dread seemed to hang in the air, its tendrils tugging at Frank as he hurried to keep up with Jackson and Linda. Every time he bumped into another person standing or sitting around with a vacant stare on their face he grew more uncomfortable with how eerily quiet they were. Far from the screaming and shouting he had witnessed and experienced during the opening days of the attacks, these people were largely calm and quiet. Somehow, though, that was scarier. The end of the world was supposed to be loud and noisy and violent as people fought tooth and nail against it. It wasn't supposed to be accepted with a shrug and a sigh and an outstretched hand for another day's rations.

"What's wrong with these people?" Frank caught up to Linda and leaned in close, whispering in her ear. "This is worse than what we saw in Washington. At least the people there were actually animated."

Linda kept her voice low as she replied. "A loss of hope and no sense of direction will do that. They've been here for quite a while. A lot have lost family or friends. There's no timetable on when they can get back to their homes and without anything to do they're just… stuck."

Frank looked back at the people they were passing with a newfound sense of compassion. "When *will* they be able to leave?"

Linda glanced at Frank, not sure whether he was serious or not. She motioned at a nearby apartment building that had most of the interior lights on. "You think they're moving people into these places by the millions just to send them back out to their homes again anytime soon?"

"You mean… they're going to live here?"

"What else are they going to do?"

Frank opened his mouth to reply before closing it, cocking his head and contemplating the question. He hadn't considered what tens upon tens of millions of people would do after the entire country ground to a screeching halt. "There's always cleanup, right?"

"You don't need the entire population of the United States on cleanup duty."

"What about repair work?"

"To what? The electrical grid? Building new trucks? Repairing complex machinery and other systems? Those are all skilled jobs, requiring a lot of education and expense. Anyone still left alive who can do those jobs will be able to name their own price. But that's still a miniscule fraction."

"Farming? We need food, don't we? Plus all of the other stuff. Blue collar workers, managers, waiters…." Frank trailed off as he realized what he was saying. "I guess… if things are that bad… huh."

"As of a few years ago," Linda screwed her eyes shut as she tried to remember what she had read, "The most common jobs in the United States by number of people employed in said jobs were retail salespeople followed by cashiers, office clerks, chefs and waiters and then nurses, if I recall correctly. Not a lot of in-demand positions there, except nurses, and I guarantee you that anyone with any skills in that area is already working overtime."

"What will everyone do, then?"

"Try and stay fed, dry and warm, I imagine. Once all the dust clears I suspect the feds will implement some sort of programs to get people back to work. Rebuilding roads, getting farms back to work and things like that. Stuff that virtually anyone can do if they're given a bit of direction." She paused. "It's a monumental task, though. An entire country upended, untold numbers dead and no clear way forward."

Frank was quiet as he contemplated Linda's words. They continued pushing forward through the streets, occasionally bumping into people nearby. The crowds were growing thicker and more animated the closer they got to the command center and as the trio approached the security line around the structure they could see that there were a dozen or so people lined up nearby waving wrinkled cardboard signs and shouting slogans that none of them could quite make out.

Jackson presented his ID to the guard at the gate, as did Linda and Frank. As Linda took hers back she threw a thumb in the direction of the people standing a short distance away. "What's up with them?"

The guard rolled his eyes. "Bunch of idiots if you ask me. They're protesting about who-knows-what."

"Huh." Frank took back his ID and slipped it into his pocket. He eyed the protestors carefully as he followed Linda and Jackson through the gate before whispering to Linda again. "Protestors? That doesn't sound good, no matter what side they're on." Linda nodded in silent agreement before stopping as the three of them once again had to present their IDs.

Frank took a moment to look around, noticing for the first time that they were standing in a relatively open area with trees and grass around them and a large, unusually shaped building in front. Frank took a few steps back and looked at the large sign hanging from the building.

"The Temberly Theatre." He looked back at the entrance as

the guard standing before the door held out his ID. "The command post is in a theater?"

———

BUILT a few years prior thanks to a multi-million dollar donation by local businessman and philanthropist Gordon Temberly, the Temberly Theatre was designed to be the most sophisticated, elegant, modern and up-to-date theater establishment in the entire country. The building's exterior design came about after lengthy consultations with top modern designers and evoked images of the Sydney Opera House. The interior was crafted by computer algorithms and designed to carry sound from the main stage to every single corner of the auditorium thanks to a system of automated wall and ceiling sections that changed position and material based on what type of performance was taking place.

In addition to the main auditorium there were two smaller auditoriums, one on ground level and one below ground in the main basement. These were often used for community plays, musical performances and other projects while the main auditorium was reserved for larger performances. Even the smaller stages were impressive, though, and featured as many modern amenities as the main one.

Unfortunately, due to the state of the city—not to mention the country—the theater had been repurposed as a command post for the military forces working to keep the city safe and secure. The pristine walls and floors were marred with grease and dirt, the wide airy halls were filled with desks, supplies and equipment and even the auditoriums and stages had been turned into living quarters and offices.

Though the number of people inside the theater was far less than the number out in the streets surrounding it, Frank felt much more cramped as he walked down the halls—and he was certain it had nothing to do with being indoors. If the mood outside the building was best described as depressed and downtrodden the mood inside was best described as desperate and panicked. Most of the civilians in the city had no clue that bombs had gone off in Chicago and Miami, though the few that did seemed to be less interested in that fact and more interested in staring blankly into space.

For the men and women in uniform, though, things were radically different. With the device in Phoenix dismantled a large portion of the forces in the city were being sent out to other sanctuary cities, either to bolster flagging forces or work as replacements for troops being sent to Chicago and Miami. There was a sense of chaos in the building, but not the ordered kind.

"This way, you two. Keep up." Jackson turned to look at Frank and Linda, both of whom had slowed to a walk as they looked around the interior of the theater, taken in by both the building and the people in it. The pair hurried to catch up with him and they eventually found themselves in a quiet corner of the building surrounded by a group of men and women seated at desks speaking into headsets.

"Is this the comms nest?" Linda asked.

"You got it," Jackson pointed across the room. "They should be getting a line set up for us to D.C. If they remembered, that is." Jackson, Linda and Frank crossed the room and Jackson got the attention of one of the women who was wearing a headset.

"This is Linda Rollins and Frank Richards. We're supposed to have a secure line to D.C. set up for us?"

"Yes, sir, Lieutenant." The woman nodded at him. "Right this way." She led the trio into what looked like a repurposed green room and motioned at a communications setup on a table. "You're all set to go in here." She eyed Linda and Frank carefully on the way out and closed the door behind her.

"Right, then," Linda rubbed her hands together and sat down at the table, not keen on wasting any more time. "Let's see if we can get Sarah on the horn."

It took sixteen minutes to get Sarah on the line, including the time to have the call actually established—Jackson's suspicion was correct—and get through the layers of bureaucracy between the person at the other end of the line and Sarah herself. When

Sarah's voice finally came through, both Frank and Linda grinned as they heard her typical annoyance shining as bright as ever.

"…the hell would you wait so long to tell me they called?! I said I was expecting a call and I meant it! Go find a crayon and stick it in your ear you great buffoon!" There was a sigh, the sound of someone putting on a headset and her voice again, though louder and more clear this time. "Linda? Frank and Jackson with you?"

"Sarah." Linda smiled. "It's good to talk to you."

"You two, dear; now's not the time, though. We have developments. Have Jackson make sure the line's secure." After a quick squeal and the input of a few numbers on the radio's keypad, Sarah was back. "Good. Now, are all three of you there?"

"We're all here, ma'am." Jackson spoke as he and Frank stood next to each other, hovering on either side of Linda.

"Good. Now listen close. I'm guessing you heard about Chicago and Miami, but you haven't heard everything. This isn't to be shared, understand?" Frank, Linda and Jackson all replied in the affirmative and she continued. "The bombs in those cities were triggered remotely and the only reason it hasn't happened in more cities is because we have broad-spectrum signal jammers set up in every other location where the devices are believed to have been delivered."

"Triggered remotely?" Jackson asked. "Through a radio signal?"

"Could be anything. The jammers block everything from radio to television to satellite. The cities that are still standing are keeping their jammers enabled until the devices are contained."

"What about manual detonation?" Jackson spoke again. "Why aren't the terrorists guarding them just blowing them up?"

"Unknown. We're guessing that they were put in place solely to guard the devices and act as emergency triggers. Their orders are likely to just guard the bombs until they're vaporized by them. Hell of a way to go."

Frank crouched down next to Linda, leaning in closer to the microphone as he closed his eyes and spoke. "How many people died?"

"No clue; not in my department. We're mostly focused on getting the other devices found. Houston's clear, Cincinnati's clear and Richmond's clear. That's about it for now, though, other than you all."

"Sarah," Linda said as she adjusted her chair, "I get the feeling that you didn't just call us on a secure, encrypted frequency just to give us the details about which cities are gone and which aren't."

"Darned straight." There was a rustling again as, on the other end of the radio, Sarah got up and double-checked that the door to the room she was in was closed and locked. "The jammers have local unlock codes, but there's also a master signal on a specific frequency that can punch through the noise. The unlock code is here in DC, in the sanctuary city, at the command post."

There was a long pause while she waited for them to catch up with what she was suggesting. "I'm… not sure I follow," Frank finally answered.

"Remember how I said I think that something odd's going on around here?" Another pause. "This is going to sound crazy which is why I haven't told anyone yet, but I believe Omar's planning an attack here."

"Yeah, we talked about that, didn't we?" Linda replied.

"I don't think he's attacking *just* to get revenge, though. With those jammers up his plan's foiled unless he can get runners on the ground inside the cities to hand-deliver a message to the terrorists guarding the devices. Every minute that passes is a minute that we're closer to disabling the devices once and for all. If he could pull down all the jammers at once while simultaneously dealing a death blow to D.C. all while our military's in disarray trying to respond to the devices…."

Sarah trailed off and Linda finished the thought. "That would be it. Tens of millions or more would die in the first few moments. Countless more after."

"Forget about rebuilding," Sarah replied. "Whoever was left would be trying to get passage to some other country so they could live away from all the hot zones."

"What do you want us to do, ma'am?" Jackson cut in, his voice firm and authoritative in spite of the dire news.

"Get your asses back up here. Whatever's going to happen next isn't going to happen down there." There was another pause and the sound of footsteps. "You three need to get on a plane to D.C. It's time to end this once and for all."

"Uh, I have a question," Frank said, raising his arm partway in the air like he was attending a lecture. "Why isn't the military up there doing something about Omar? You were able to get through to someone about the devices, clearly. Why not just tell them about Omar?"

"Because if she does," Linda answered before Sarah could, "Then if the traitor's still around and listening in then he would have that much more information."

"Exactly. Screaming at the top of our lungs about the devices worked, but I don't know that we can risk it a second time. We'll— hang on." Footsteps came through the radio again, followed by the sound of a door opening and Sarah shouting at someone down a hall. A low rumble cut through the noise, making Frank's ears perk up at the sound.

"What was that?"

Another rumble came through the speaker, though it was followed by the sound of an enormous explosion that filled the room, making Frank, Linda and Jackson all cover their ears in pain. "What the hell?!" Linda reached for the volume knob to turn down the sound and called out into the microphone. "Sarah? Sarah! Are you there?"

As the ringing in their ears died down, they realized that there were no longer any transmissions coming through the radio. Whatever had just happened at the D.C. command post had disrupted the line.

"Here, move out of the way, Rollins." Jackson sat down in Linda's seat and began working the transmitter as he spoke quietly into the microphone, trying to reestablish contact. After a few minutes of fruitless work, he turned in his seat and pointed at

Frank. "Richards, get out there and tell them we have a situation going on in D.C. We need them to get our channel back up now!"

"On it!" Frank ran out of the room, at first feeling bad for making so much noise as he burst through the door as he remembered the relative silence the people in the next room had been working in. The feeling didn't last for long, though, as he saw that everyone who had been quietly tapping away at a computer or speaking softly into a microphone was now fully animated, loud and in a moderate state of panic. Looking around at the chaos and wondering what to do, Frank grabbed the nearest person he could find by the shoulders as they tried to dodge past him.

"Hey, we need help back here. We were on the line with Washington and—"

"Washington? D.C.?" The man's eyes widened. "Something's going on up there. We lost comms and can't get them back. There was some gunfire or something before that happened and—"

Linda and Jackson came through the door as the man was about to finish his sentence. Jackson glanced at Linda and nodded. "Be to the intersection in ten."

"We will," She nodded back at him before turning to Frank. "We're heading to Washington. Jackson's going to get seats on the next flight out. We need to get our gear and some spare supplies and get ready to go."

The noise in the room was loud enough that Linda waved at Frank to follow her as he shouted in response. "What did you find out?"

"Same thing everyone else here did, I assume. A surface to surface missile just took out the main comms array at their command post. There's some kind of fighting force heading into the city."

"A fighting force? What does that mean?!" Frank broke into a run to keep up with Linda and the pair moved quickly down the street, pushing aside soldiers and civilians alike as they ran for where they had stowed their gear.

"It means Sarah's suspicion about Omar was right. All of it. He's there in D.C. with enough people to start a fight."

"Can't the military just… fight back? He can't have all *that* many people, can he?"

"Guerilla warfare, Frank. It's a bitch and a half to fight against and Omar's people are the best of the best. With his people and resources, whoever's still stationed there won't last very long." As Frank and Linda hit the main road leading to a nearby airfield, a fleet of trucks racing by seemed to confirm what she was saying. "All the cities that are still searching for their devices don't even know what's happening in Washington so they can't send any aid." Linda shook her head. "This is bad. Really bad."

The squeal of tires made both her and Frank turn and they saw Jackson at the wheel of a camo-painted truck that roared alongside the convoy before squealing to a stop in front of them. "Get in!" Jackson shouted at them through the rolled-down window. Linda jumped into the front middle seat and Frank clambered in after her. As soon as the door was shut Jackson took off, honking the horn to alert the civilians and soldiers walking nearby to stay out of the way.

"Do you have a flight for us?" Linda shouted over the roar of the engine as Jackson accelerated sharply around a corner.

"They're sending five hundred soldiers and Marines along with some supplies in fifteen minutes," he shouted back, not daring to take his eyes off of the road. "We've got three seats in the cargo section if we can make it there in time!"

"Drive faster, then," Frank mumbled as he clung to his seat and braced himself against the door.

The drive to the airfield took just under ten minutes and when they arrived Jackson stopped the truck on the tarmac and jumped out. "Hurry up! Get your gear and let's go!" He threw a backpack on and grabbed his rifle from the back of the truck. Frank and Linda jumped out and grabbed their backpacks and rifles from the back of the truck as well, then ran after Jackson across the tarmac.

A pair of C-17 Globemasters were parked on the tarmac with both of their cargo doors open as dozens of soldiers and crates of supplies were loaded in. The energy on the airfield was electric as troops from all branches ran back and forth on various assignments. Jackson, Frank and Linda ran up to the rear C-17 and Jackson had a brief conversation with the loadmaster.

"Airman Bradley! I'm Lieutenant Jackson and this is Linda Rollins and Frank Richards. I'm escorting these two to Washington. I radioed in a few minutes ago; you have three seats for us, correct?"

"Absolutely, sir!" Bradley nodded and glanced at Frank and Linda. "Seats are in the front, ahead of the cargo. We need to get you on board right now, though; we're on a tight schedule and need to get in the air within minutes."

"Absolutely; just point us there and we'll get seated."

"Follow me, sir."

After following Bradley to their seats, Jackson, Frank and Linda secured their weapons and bags before strapping themselves in. A flurry of activity continued around them as crew and cargo continued to pour on board in preparation for takeoff. While Jackson and Linda took the opportunity to drink a full bottle of water each, Frank sat slack-jawed at the coordinated chaos before a tap on his shoulder drew his attention.

"Here," Linda said, holding out a bottle of water to him. "Hydrate up. It's going to be a long flight."

"How long?" Frank took the bottle of water and unscrewed the top.

"Four hours, give or take."

"Holy crap," he choked on the first sip of water and coughed loudly. "Are we even going to be in time to do anything?"

Two seats down, on Linda's left, Jackson leaned forward and looked at Frank. "They'll hold out, don't you worry. There'll be plenty of fight left for us when we get there."

Frank nodded as Jackson sat back in his seat, then he turned and looked at Linda, wanting to hear her opinion. She leaned in and spoke quietly to him. "We've got zero intel on how things are going up there. You saw how it was before we left, though. The place was practically a warzone already."

"So you don't think they'll hold out?"

Linda shook her head. "I didn't say that. They'll hold out,

yeah. But if Omar's really directing the assault and he's got a decent-sized fighting force, they're going to be hard-pressed to hold out for more than a few hours without getting in reinforcements."

"Surely there are more troops from closer cities going there, though, right?" Frank had to speak up as the whine of the engines and sound of the closing cargo doors began to grow louder. A few airmen ran down the line of people seated on the sides of the aircraft, passing out hearing protection in the form of earplugs and earmuffs.

Linda didn't answer for a moment, then she shook her head. "I don't know. We're going to be one of the only cities sending troops, and that's because we verified that the device here was dismantled and our jammer is down. The cities that are still searching for their devices aren't about to give up on that search—hell, they won't have even heard about Washington if their jammers are active." Linda took a deep breath and sighed in exasperation. "Who knows what we're going to find up there or how we'll find Omar if he's in the neighborhood. But we'll try. We'll try our damnedest."

Frank nodded and sat back in his seat as he put on his earmuffs. Further talking was impossible as the whine of the engines turned into a scream as the Globemaster accelerated forward, taxiing toward the runway. Designed for short takeoffs and landings, the Globemaster lurched forward as soon as its sister aircraft was in the air, the four massive jet engines propelling the craft forward and upward into the sky. Frank closed his eyes as he was pushed around in his seat, moving only half an inch or so back and forth as his restraints kept him from flying out of his seat and turning into a pink smear on the far wall.

His last flight on a military aircraft had been stressful enough, with the assignment of heading out to California to try and locate some mysterious devices that had been smuggled into the country. This flight, though, was different in a whole host of ways. The devices had been found, some had been detonated, he had been through firefights and car wrecks, Sarah was missing and the District of Columbia was under siege by a force led by Linda's nemesis. He cracked his eyes and turned his head to look at Linda.

She sat still in her seat, the large black earmuffs covering half of the side of her head. Her hair was still tucked away in a neat ponytail that seemed to never come undone. Her face was a mask, betraying no hint of emotion to the normal observer. Though Frank hadn't known her for long, he knew her well enough to know that it was a face of raw determination. The same face that had taken them into the depths of hell and back. The face of a friend whom he had never dreamed he would have and someone who he would do anything to protect—and knew that she would do the same for him.

As Frank sat on the loud, bumpy flight, his eyes closed and his thoughts a swirling mess, he felt a small, calloused hand wrap around his, clasping it tightly. Opening his eyes he looked down to see Linda's hand in his, her fingers gripping his so tightly that her hand was turning white. He squeezed back, feeling a warmth spring up in his chest that radiated peace and tranquility through his whole body. The feeling filled him with something that could outshine the terrible darkness, bring order to chaos and transform his swirling mind into one that was calm and relaxed.

Hope is a simple, ordinary-seeming thing. But it can change the world.

Sitting there, squeezing tight the hand of someone whom he had never imagined he would meet in a situation he never imagined he would find himself in, Frank Richards had hope. Fierce, determined, unwavering, unflinching hope.

And that would be enough to turn back the darkness.

Chapter Eighty-Seven

D ressed in casual winter clothing with a tan scarf wrapped around his neck and leather gloves protecting his hands from the bitter cold, Farhad Omar stands tall on the bow of the riverboat as it motors slowly up the Potomac River. The intense precipitation for the past few weeks means the river is deeper than usual, an unexpected bonus for the man planning the most daring operation ever to occur on United States soil. He had been concerned at one point about the eleven riverboats behind him, as running even one of them aground would compromise his already fragile operation beyond repair.

Everything is running smoothly, though. He smiles as he looks out across the darkened city, basking in the fact that most of the area is without power. Its residents are displaced and in no small amount of discomfort—if they are even alive.

Omar takes one last deep breath of the frigid air before opening the door to the cabin of the riverboat and stepping back in. He casts his gaze across the men seated in the boat, each of them wrapped in a thick coat and long pants. They are all cold in spite of this and they are shivering uncontrollably, as are the men seated in the other eleven boats farther down the river. It is a necessary discomfort, though. Thermal imagers are undoubtedly in use by the patrols and keeping the boats as cold as possible will reduce the chances that someone spots them sailing slowly up the river.

"Report, please." Omar's voice is smooth and steady, the cold having no effect on him.

"Spotters report all clear. One foot patrol is nearby, on the port. They'll be passing by in two minutes."

"Have the spotters ready. Take them out if they look like they've spotted us or if they're alone."

The man seated near the pilot of the boat nods and speaks into a radio. Lying on top of each of the boats, pairs of men dressed in black shift positions, turning their long suppressed rifles in the direction of the approaching patrol. Six men and two women dressed in Army camouflage walk near the bank of the river, speaking quietly as they keep their eyes open for threats. It's been days since they last encountered looter activity, though, and they are at ease as they talk and crack jokes with each other.

Four of the eight die within the same half-second as fifty caliber rounds enter and exit through their skulls, turning their heads into gelatin and a fine pink mist. The other four only have enough time to realize that something has gone horribly wrong before they, too, are executed. Two die to gaping chest wounds, one bleeds out in under a minute after losing her leg and the final man takes a round to his lower spine as he tries to run to cover.

The sounds of the rifles are loud across the water in spite of the suppressors, and Omar flinches internally with each shot. There are no other patrols close enough to hear them, though, and the man seated next to the pilot looks up at him with a nod. "The patrol is down. We're clear all the way through to Hains Point."

Omar pats the man on the shoulder and smiles. "Excellent. Give me the radio and patch me through to the boats." It takes a moment for the man with the radio to prepare things, but once he does he passes a microphone to Omar who takes it and begins pacing at the front of the boat.

"My brothers, our path is clear. In less than one hour we shall arrive at our destination. We shall disembark and dissipate into the city as instructed, setting up safe houses and staging grounds for the eventual assault." He feels the next words catch in his throat as he continues.

"The assault on our people shall be returned in kind very soon, my brothers. The torment and misery and degradation felt by our people shall be visited back upon those who call this place home. Many of us will die. But we die with honor and truth in our hearts, knowing that we are performing a worthy *deed and executing a finishing blow upon those who desired to do the same to us." Omar's voice grows louder and more emotional as he finishes his speech.*

"So lie in wait, my brothers. For days or weeks if necessary. Pick at their flanks, find their defenses and then—when the time is right—we shall rain down upon them with hellfire! None of them shall be considered worthy to be spared our righteous wrath! For our vengeance is mighty and our cause is just!"

Muted by the thick walls and windows of the riverboats, the cries of joy and agreement from the men on the twelve craft are nothing more than shallow murmurs to anyone on the banks of the river. The dark craft wind their way forward, carrying nearly one thousand soldiers ready to lay down their lives for their cause. Their leader is a man filled with darkness. A swirling storm of hatred and retribution who will take nothing short of vengeance as a satisfactory answer to wrongs both true and perceived.

Like a storm, Farhad Omar descends upon the vulnerable like a ravenous lion, ready to carry his plan forth to the end, no matter what that end may be.

BOOK SIX

THE BATTLE

Chapter Eighty-Eight

"*P*lease *be warned that what you're about to see is graphic, and may not be suitable for all audiences.*"

A young man watches the television screen in the small living room of his off-campus apartment. A stack of textbooks and a laptop computer sit on the table nearby, the battery for the computer nearly drained. The ice in a glass of soda has nearly melted, and condensation from the glass drips off the table to the floor. In the kitchen, the oven ticks as the heating element turns on and off, and on the counter sits a warm tray of once-frozen macaroni and cheese, having long since been forgotten as it slowly thawed.

He is not concerned with the state of his apartment or anything in it. A young man, living in the country for just over two years, it has been many months since he's traveled back home to visit his parents. His country occasionally pops up in the news, but in spite of America's general distaste for his country, the students and teachers he sees on a daily basis have nothing but smiles and curious questions about his foreign lifestyle.

While the young man often imagines being back home, surrounded by his family, old friends and familiar sights and smells, he never dreamed he would see his country on the television in the state that it is in. The volume on the broadcast is unexpectedly loud, startling him and making him reach for the remote on the table. He knocks the glass over and it tumbles to the carpet, soaking it with watered-down sugar water, but the young man pays little mind.

Farhad Omar turns down the volume on the television and stares, transfixed in horror, as his home burns.

"What you're seeing now is video taken moments ago by civilians trapped in buildings just outside the main government buildings in Tehran. Internet service in the country is very spotty, and most reports making it out of the country are coming from satellite uploads as the main transmission lines have been physically severed.

"You can see there, near the bottom, several persons from this unknown group as they rig some sort of explosive device to the main security gate. We understand that there are dozens, perhaps hundreds of these individuals both in and around the main government buildings. The military's response was sluggish at first, but they are on the scene and doing their best to stop what appears to be an attempted coup of the Iranian president."

A phone rings off to Omar's side and he reaches for it out of instinct, slides the green answer symbol across the front and puts it up near his ear. Before he can answer, though, the line is filled with the sound of screams, gunfire and chaos.

"Farhad!" The voice is hoarse and full of pain. Omar's trance is broken, and he looks away from the television as he recognizes the voice on the other end of the line.

"Father?!" He presses the phone hard against his ear as his father coughs and speaks again.

"Listen to me, Farhad. They've gotten into the main buildings. The military's on the way, but I don't know if they'll make it in time. Your mother and brothers are here with me. We're trying to stay hidden, but… I just wanted to tell you we l—"

The line goes dead. There are no more voices, no screams, no sounds of gunfire and no indications as to what has happened to Omar's family. His breathing grows quick as he dials the number that called him, only to be met with a notice that it is no longer in service. He tries again, a dozen more times, but the result is the same.

On the television, the military pours into the government buildings like water, sweeping away the unknown band of individuals who sought to overthrow and kill the President. Minutes and hours tick past, and the broadcast *switches between the cold, formal faces of experts and analysts and scenes of sheet-covered bodies being carried out from the government compound.*

It's impossible to know who the bodies once were, but Omar doesn't need to see the images of his family to know that they are dead. Victims of assailants sent by an unknown source, they were once his rock and stable foundation. Now, though? He is alone.

Chapter Eighty-Nine

"Hold on!" Jackson's voice echoed through the cabin of the Humvee as it sped along, bouncing on the uneven terrain of the highway median. Sitting in the passenger seat, Frank held on to his seat with both hands, the expression on his face grim as he tried to keep from being thrown from side to side. In the back, Linda sat sideways in a seat, bracing herself against the front seats and the back door all while silently hoping that the latch wouldn't fail and send her tumbling out onto the ground.

The vehicle was one of the last operational ones at Davison, as all of the working vehicles of all types had been taken north to the Washington sanctuary city to help fight off the assault. Jackson had nearly gotten into a fistfight with a group of soldiers who were preparing to get into the Humvee until Linda distracted them and the trio managed to get away before they could be stopped.

The drive north into Washington was another stark reminder of the reality of the world. Abandoned cars, burned buildings and the smell of smoke and decay were everywhere, and Jackson frequently had to take the vehicle off-road in order to maintain their speed. While the light in the sky was soft, indicating that it was either soon after morning or near the evening, Linda and

Frank weren't entirely certain what time it was anymore. The rapid, rushed trips back and forth across the country and the frantic pace of their efforts to stop the dirty bombs had taken a heavy toll.

Linda felt the sting of exhaustion in the back of her head, noticing her slowed reflexes and decreased response times. There was nothing she could do about it, though, except to press on and hope that she had enough energy to keep going. She and Frank had both slept for most of the four-hour plane ride to Washington, but "sleep" in the back of a military cargo jet is more like torture than actual rest.

"Oh my…" Frank whispered from the front and Linda struggled to maneuver around to see through the narrow front windows at what he was gaping at. As Jackson crested a hill, taking them out of a shallow valley, they could see plumes of smoke and an orange glow off near the horizon. Unlike much of the smoke and fire they had seen on the drive thus far, though, what appeared in the distance was fresh and recent, caused by a source that was no doubt still very much present. "Is that… is that the city?"

"Looks like it." Jackson shook his head before jolting the Humvee to the side to miss the twisted edge of a crumpled guardrail. "I hope to hell they've held out. Frank, try the radio again. Maybe we're close enough."

Frank reached for the radio but Linda shook her head and put a hand on his arm. "It's no use. Whatever the assailants did in the initial attack knocked the transmitters in there offline. We're not going to get anything from them until we get close enough for the two-ways to be in range. How much longer till we're there, Jackson?"

"Fifteen, maybe twenty minutes." Jackson's voice raised an octave halfway through his answer as he jerked the steering wheel yet again, sending the Humvee onto the road for a few seconds to avoid a fence before going back into the median. "If we even make it. Whoever was in charge of repairing this piece of crap needs to be taken out and shot."

Frank and Linda said nothing as they concentrated on keeping themselves from being slung around the inside of the vehicle while Jackson did his best impression of a rally car driver. Linda kept one hand on Frank's shoulder as they went along, and Frank reached up and grabbed it, clutching it tightly in his fingers. He and Linda hadn't gotten a chance to speak privately since boarding the plane in Phoenix, but the moment they had shared while the plane was taking off had been stronger than either one of them had realized.

Since being woken in their seats by the jostle of the aircraft hitting the ground, they had moved more smoothly as a unit than they had since meeting each other. Working in tandem they had helped Jackson secure the Humvee, helped plot a route north to the city and generally kept each other and Jackson encouraged despite the grim circumstances. Neither of them were sure about what was going on, but both of them were determined more than ever to see things through to the end, if only so that they could find out.

"All right, ladies." Jackson swallowed hard as a long, wide turn in the road appeared in the distance. "We're nearly there. Make sure you're ready to bail out at a moment's notice. I'm going to skirt the edge of the barricades and try to get us north and as close to the command center's location as possible. My guess is that we'll have to bail out, but we might have to do that early."

"Jackson." Linda patted him on the shoulder and spoke in a calm, steady voice. The Lieutenant was putting on a brave face, but his voice was unsteady. "We're going to be okay."

"It's not me I'm worried about. If he gets his hand on those codes and shuts down the jammers remotely…"

"It's not going to happen." Frank replied with a matter-of-fact tone. "He *will* be stopped. We'll do it."

They sat in silence for another moment as they rounded the wide turn in the road, following the highway in toward the sanctuary city. If the smoke and flames from afar had offered a disturbing glimpse of what was to come, the up-close view was far, far worse. Fires were actively jumping between buildings and thousands of flickers of light appeared near the southern and eastern sides, evidence of the people fleeing with flashlights in hand, trying to make their way from the burning portions of the city to the portions still intact.

There were hundreds of thousands—maybe more—who were undoubtedly trapped in the city, left with nowhere else to go but away from the flames, and unless the military could direct their attention to the fires, the buildings—and the people—would soon be completely obliterated. The moderate-sized military forces that Frank and Linda could still vividly recall avoiding while walking through the city were otherwise engaged, though, and a quick look at the northern edge of the city revealed why.

Flashes of light and trails of smoke extended from the north beyond the river, signaling mortar and rocket fire that was raining down on the soldiers and civilians. Bursts of orange and yellow light flashed across the buildings as hundreds of attackers and soldiers attempted to suppress each other with small arms fire. Tracer rounds from atop Humvees parked near the edge of the city flew through the sky, setting small fires and punching holes through buildings in an attempt to drive away the attackers. Occasionally, one of the rockets or mortars would make contact with something other than bare metal or concrete, sending a fiery explosion into the air as yet another cache of supplies or a vehicle went up in flames.

"Have they really been under this kind of assault for four hours?" Frank whistled softly in disbelief.

"Look at how the fire's spreading." Linda leaned forward as Jackson slowed the Humvee to drive over a curb to get around a group of parked cars. "Nearly half of the buildings are in flames. How are they going to get that under control?"

"Cut a line around the edge of the fire, demo the buildings and stop it in its tracks," Jackson replied, "but they can't do that if they're dug in like that."

"Let's get in there and free them up."

Jackson stifled a laugh as he drove around the edge of the city, looking for a clear path in through the barricades. "You expect the three of us in this banged-up old thing with only limited ammunition and weapons to do what, exactly?"

Linda smiled from the back seat. "Strategy trumps numbers, Jackson. You ought to know better than that."

"I'd still rather not go charging in with a rifle and nothing else against what could be hundreds or more enemy combatants."

Linda pointed out the window again, highlighting the rows of buildings along the north end of the river. Their windows were still lighting up with yellow and orange flashes, and occasionally trails of smoke came from atop and behind them. "They've got half a dozen mortars back there, plus some rockets in the windows. If we can secure a couple of those mortars then we can flip the script and start targeting their buildings. That'll give the forces inside the city enough of a breather to move up and start taking buildings back, or get some heavy counterfire going."

"Huh." Jackson grunted and nodded slowly. "That could work. They're going to have more than just a few people manning the mortars, though."

"We can handle it. Trust me." Linda reached forward and adjusted the settings on the radio, turning the volume up so that she could hear the static squealing loudly inside the vehicle. "We need to get in communication with someone, though. If Sarah or someone else is still around, they need to be able to direct units to move in."

Jackson keyed the microphone and called out their location and disposition as he flipped through the channels. Finally the static turned into hurried, frantic speech as various units tried to speak to each other and to what was left of the command structure. Jackson was about to radio in when Linda put a hand on his arm and shook her head. "Give it a second; I want to hear what's going on, first."

In between the low quality of the transmissions, the static, the acronyms and the initialisms, Frank couldn't make out any of what was going on. Linda and Jackson listened intently, though, and when Linda noticed Frank's confused expression she began whispering to him. "They're not doing well. Mortar and rocket fire has taken out a lot of their static emplacements and they're starting to weaken. They also just spotted a small group heading for the command building." Linda glanced at Jackson and spoke louder. "They must be going for the codes to shut down the signal jammers. We need to get in there right now!"

Jackson threw a hand up from the wheel and gestured at the road ahead. "If you happen to see a way in, feel free to point it out! All we've got so far are walls, fences and barricades."

"Oh for—turn in there!"

"Through the fence?"

"Yes, through the fence! We're not in your wife's minivan, Jackson!"

The Humvee's wheels dug deep into the grass, kicking up clods of dirt that intermingled with bits of cheap, poorly-reinforced wood. The fence offered almost no resistance to the vehicle's assault as Jackson tore through it, heading into the backyard of a long-abandoned home that had yet to be occupied by refugees in the city. The yard was, thankfully, clear of any obstacles, and they smashed through another fence, went down a slight slope across the front yard and skidded into the quiet cul-de-sac out front. The brake pedal squeaked noisily as Jackson slowly lifted up his foot, and he turned to Linda as he slowly accelerated into a turn to head out to a main road toward the command center.

"Just FYI, she drives a truck. Not a minivan."

Chapter Ninety

T he drive through the city was eerily quiet, as they had taken the Humvee in through the eastern side, where most of the residents were either hiding in their homes and shelters or had already retreated to the south and west. Jackson kept them moving at a quick clip, though, and within a few moments they arrived at the outskirts of what was left of the command center.

What was left of the buildings housing the military and support staff were barely standing. Smoke billowed from the wreckage and fires still burned fresh, fed from lines of fuel leaking from hidden storage containers. Men and women in uniform ran back and forth, carting weapons, pouches with large white and red X's on them and crates of ammunition and other supplies. The gun and mortar fire had clearly slowed from how it had been when the attack first started, though, as most of the explosions from the shells were distant, at least a few hundred meters or more.

Jackson pulled the Humvee up against a nearby structure that was still relatively intact, trying to shield it from any potential incoming fire, and the trio grabbed their weapons and packs before jumping out. Set up in a series of large, portable, multi-story buildings, the command center was grey in color, and looked to be made of a combination of steel and some sort of high-strength plastic. Piles of sandbags were scattered across the outer edge of the second story of the structure while HESCO bastions lined the bottom story, providing both structure and security.

The upper of the three levels had been completely destroyed and melted bits of the command center were scattered across the ground as Jackson, Frank and Linda jogged toward it. Their presence was either unnoticed or disregarded by the military around the command post, and it didn't take long to see why. Injured service members, many of them dead or dying, lay on the ground near the barriers on the south side of the command post while medics desperately tended to their wounds.

Presuming that Sarah or someone else in charge would be in what was left in the command center, the trio ran through the open doors and into the main room on the bottom floor. Rows of tables that once held neatly arranged computers had been pushed aside to make room for cots for the more gravely injured. Near the back of the room, at the north side, sandbags were piled high around the narrow windows and soldiers stood near them with scoped rifles, firing rounds at targets in buildings beyond the river. If the atmosphere outside the command center was complete chaos, the atmosphere inside was slightly more organized, but disarray still reigned supreme.

"Sarah!" Linda shouted at the top of her lungs as she looked around in all directions. Jackson and Frank looked as well, though Jackson had his eyes open for anyone who was high enough in rank that they might be in charge of whatever operations were left.

"Linda?" The response was weak, with a hoarse cough following after, and the three turned and rushed toward the source. A pair of medics stood near an elevated cot where a figure was half-covered with a blanket. One of the figure's legs stuck out from the blanket, though it was mangled and covered in blood and iodine. The medics talked loudly as they worked on the figure's leg, and Linda had to put a hand to her mouth to conceal her shock.

"Sarah? What... what happened?"

"That?" Sarah lifted her head and smiled weakly. "Just a flesh wound. They hit the command center hard about twenty minutes ago and I got caught in the blast. Precursor to an infiltration attempt but I think we held them off. Sergeant?" She turned and called loudly and a woman whose uniform was streaked in sweat and soot ran up to her.

"Yes, ma'am. That group that crossed the barricade is down. The mortar fire is lessening, so they're probably preparing another assault like last time."

"Is the second floor evacuated and—"

"Everyone's out and we've tripled the sandbags. It should keep us safe until we can get all the wounded moved out of range."

"Good." Sarah nodded and waved at the woman before turning back to Linda. "Are Jackson and Frank with you?"

"We're here, ma'am." Jackson and Frank both stepped up next to Linda.

"Listen up. He's here. Drones spotted him before they were shot down. He's north, beyond their line of fire, likely where those skirmishes were coming from a while back. You have to get to him and stop him."

Linda shook her head. "Not while you're in this condition. No. Not a chance."

Sarah reached out and grabbed Linda's arm, her grip like a vice despite her weakened condition. "Listen to me, girl. None of us are worth that much. You go and you take him down."

"Ma'am, if I may?" Jackson interrupted and Sarah gave him a long look before nodding at him to continue. "While we were on the way here we saw the rocket and mortar fire coming in. The units here can't keep hunkering down and taking that kind of a pounding. At some point the enemy's going to cross the barricade en masse and everyone's going to be slaughtered, to say nothing of the jamming codes."

"You got a suggestion, Jackson? Or did you want all of us to say something completely obvious?"

"If we take a small group—three or four at most—we can slip across the river, get back behind the buildings that they've got barricaded and take out the mortars. Once those are down you can order the units to move forward and start pressing a counterattack."

Sarah nodded, almost without hesitation. "You're right. Linda, you take Jackson and Frank with you. We'll give you fifteen minutes then hit them as hard as we can to provide you with cover and a distraction so you can hightail it across the bridge. They'll ignore one lone car, especially if we can hit them with all that we've got. I'll coordinate here and—agh!" Sarah's whole body tensed in pain and one of the medics swore and turned to look at her.

"Listen, lady, if you don't hold still then you're going to bleed out! Just lay still and keep quiet!"

"Sarah, just—look, is there anyone else here who can help coordinate?"

Sarah's eyes were screwed shut and she whispered her response, trying to hold herself together as the medics worked on what was left of her leg. "Most of the officers were taken out when they hit command. I have to coordinate it."

Linda looked down at Sarah and took the older woman's hand, gripping it tightly in her own. Sarah's hand felt cold and weak, losing much of the strength she had shown only a moment earlier. "Jackson?" Linda kept her eyes on Sarah as she spoke.

"What is it?"

"I need you to take over here. Keep an eye on Sarah and start rounding people up to get that distraction ready."

"Linda, I—"

"Save it, Jackson. Frank and I are heading across the bridge in that Humvee we took in. Once we get across and disable the mortars we're going to immediately go after Omar. As soon as the mortar fire stops, rally the troops and kick these assholes in the teeth!"

"Can't you just take a couple more people with you?"

"Nope." Linda shook her head and looked back down at Sarah. "Do you have any of the high-gain trackers left?"

Sarah nodded again. "Storage. Yellow boxes."

"That's enough!" One of the medics shouted and pushed Linda back. "If you want your friend here to live, you need to go!"

Linda didn't fight the medic, but looked at Jackson as he stepped back as well, giving the medical personnel room to work. "Make sure she lives, Jackson."

"Will do. When do you want the fifteen minutes to start?"

"No need; I'm going to pick up a tracker so you can monitor us. Just keep the receiver pointed at the bridge and as soon as you see us waiting, get the distraction started."

"Those things have such a narrow field of view that it'll be useless once you get very far—"

"Jackson? Just do it. Okay?"

Lieutenant Jackson nodded and gave both Linda and Frank a pat on their backs. "Stay safe. As soon as those mortars are down we'll hit 'em like they never thought possible."

"Make sure you do." Linda smiled at him before motioning to Frank. "Come on, let's get moving."

"WHAT ARE THESE THINGS, ANYWAY?"

Linda fiddled with a small, matchbox-sized device she had pulled out of some thick foam padding in a large yellow crate. The device finally emitted a soft amber glow on one side and she slipped it into her pocket. "Tracking devices." she said, grabbing a laptop-sized black rectangle from the box and depressing a switch on the side. The top of the device flipped open and a small screen appeared, along with several buttons. Linda handed the device to Frank. "Press the green button in the middle and point it at me."

Frank pressed the button and the screen on the tracker lit up. As he angled it toward Linda the screen brightened, showing a blinking icon along with an estimated range between the tag in her pocket and the tracking device. "Huh. Nice. Why are you carrying that, though?"

Linda took the tracker back from Frank and shoved it into her pack and they started moving toward the Humvee. "Comms are a mess right now, but nobody uses these things anymore and they're super easy to pick up. They'll be able to track our approximate location and use that to help coordinate the counterattack."

"Seems… crude."

Linda shrugged. "Whatever works. If we can get through on the radio, great. If not, though, we've got a backup. Plus, there are other uses for these things, too."

Frank started to ask what she meant but was distracted by the whistle of an incoming mortar that exploded a few dozen feet away, sending shards of concrete and asphalt spewing in all directions. Linda's hurried but calm demeanor changed in an instant and she broke into a run, shouting at Frank as more whistling became audible in the distance. "Let's go, let's go!"

They reached the Humvee and threw their gear in the back, then Linda jumped behind the wheel and Frank climbed in next to her. The engine coughed and sputtered as it started, but after a few choice words from both Linda and Frank it finally roared to life. Linda threw the vehicle into drive and took off, winding around the command center and the maze of HESCO bastions and sandbags to get to the north end of the barricade. A chain link fence had been placed across the road, and she pressed down on the accelerator as they approached it, ignoring the shouts from the soldiers positioned behind barriers on either side.

The fence split open with a loud crash and the metal scraped and screeched against the Humvee as the vehicle pushed forward, heading into what was essentially no-man's land in between the city and the nearest bridge north over the river. The bridge had several large trucks parked at the southern end, with the rearmost one only half there, having been nearly completely destroyed during the initial attacks. The other trucks were abandoned by their drivers at the time, but the way in which they were positioned offered excellent concealment and cover from the attackers to the north.

Linda pulled up next to the trucks and grabbed the radio from the console, switched it on and started talking loudly into the microphone. "Base, this is Rollins and Richards. We're at the bridge. Start the diversion, over." A squelch of static and a torrent of voices called back and she shook her head, trying to pick up any trace of a reply from Jackson. After a few seconds she called out again. "Jackson, this is Rollins! We are in position! How copy?"

No discernable response followed yet again, and Linda shook her head as she put the radio back down. Frank looked at her with a raised eyebrow. "Now what?"

"We wait and hope that Jackson heard us but either can't reply or his reply's getting lost in all of the…" She trailed off and turned around in her seat, looking behind at the barricade in the distance.

"What's that?" Frank asked as he turned around, noticing the same thing she had. The sporadic fire from the northern edge of the city had stopped, and the only sounds of battle to be heard were from the attackers across the river. A few moments later, though, the situation drastically changed.

An explosive amount of fire erupted from behind the barricade as every able-bodied soldier threw all that they had into suppressing the enemy's attack. Small arms fire focused on pinning down snipers in the building windows while large-caliber machine guns and even a few rockets spread their damage out, spraying bullets and explosions across the breadth of the area where the attackers were entrenched.

So great was the amount of fire that the enemy forces were momentarily taken aback. Most of the attackers ducked for cover, moving into back rooms of the building as they tried to find a location to stay alive. Knowing that the heavy level of suppressive fire wouldn't last for long, Linda threw the Humvee back into gear and sent the vehicle lurching forward. The right side scraping noisily against the metal of the trucks and Frank winced at the sound, pulling away from the door for fear of it tearing off in the commotion.

The drive across the bridge took less time than Frank thought as Linda deftly wove a path back and forth both to avoid obstacles and to keep from presenting an easy target to anyone who might be watching them. Across the bridge the road diverged to the right in a long, arcing turn as it dove back down toward ground level. Linda followed the path of the road until the concrete guardrail vanished, at which point she took a hard left, crossing over through what used to be carefully manicured grass and flowerbeds. The Humvee bumped and jostled over the soft ground, throwing their heads up against the roof and then slamming them back down into the poorly-padded seats.

"Do we *have* to go this way?" Frank shouted over the noise of the vehicle. "There's a perfectly good road right next to us!"

"They're not going to stay distracted for long. We need to get back behind the buildings and find the mortar locations before they start firing at us!" Frank groaned at her reply and did his best to stay in his seat, the straps over his shoulders doing little to help.

A moment later, after an exceptionally hard *thump* followed by the sound of some part of the vehicle's frame being put under enormous strain, they bounced up a short flight of stairs and passed through the space in between two of the buildings where much of the attacker's fire had been coming from. Frank craned his head around to see through the window, trying to catch a glimpse of anyone in the buildings, but it was impossible to see between their speed and bumping along.

"Get ready, Frank!" Linda shouted at him and he glanced at her before looking out through the windshield. "Mortars were coming from just beyond the back of the buildings somewhere. As soon as I stop, get your gear and get to cover. Shoot anything that moves, got it?" She looked at him and he nodded in response. "I'm serious, Frank. You have to kill anything that moves, otherwise you're going to die."

"I got it!" Frank replied, trying to convince her that he would be able to handle himself, though the assurance was more for his benefit than anyone else's. He would have followed her past the gates of Hell and beyond if she asked him, so he hadn't even blinked an eye when she pulled him along on what was rapidly starting to seem like a suicide mission. Handling himself in the field, though, in spite of his willingness to do anything to help, was a different matter.

"Let's go, go, go!" The Humvee lurched to a stop, Linda opened her door and Frank was suddenly thrust into the middle of the fray. His hesitation and reluctance melted away, reminding him of when he had turned a corner all those… days? Weeks? Months? It felt like years ago when Sarah had sent him out to scout for supplies to save Linda's life, and he had undergone a transformation during that time. Each day, before heading out, he felt nervous and afraid, wondering how he could possibly do the things he was being asked—no, *demanded*—to do. Yet every single day, without fail, as soon as he got into the thick of it, he performed flawlessly.

The change in his attitude and mindset was instantaneous. He threw off his straps and jumped out of the vehicle, dropping low as he grabbed the pistol from his leg holster and pressed his back up against the open door of the vehicle. No threats were immediately visible off to the right side of the Humvee so he kept moving, standing up and opening the back door, retrieving his pack and his rifle. The pistol went back into its holster and he flicked the switch on his rifle to single-fire.

"On me!" Linda shouted and Frank ran around the back of the Humvee, hurrying to catch up as she headed for a series of large concrete blocks behind the building filled with plants and a single large tree in each one. The smell of gunpowder grew strong as they approached the nearest block, and they both circled around the same side, slowing their approach with Linda in the lead and Frank just behind to her left.

A shout from up ahead was instantly followed by a scream of agony as Linda squeezed her trigger, sending a 3-round burst into the upper torso and head of a man standing in front of her. Frank continued moving to Linda's left, firing several times at a second man who had been near the first before finally dropping him. The pair had been standing in front of a portable mortar resting on the ground, with dozens of spare shells scattered about on the ground. Linda turned and looked down the length of the series of concrete planters they were behind, seeing another half-dozen portable mortars set up, one behind each of the concrete boxes.

"Looks clear down that way," Frank said, taking a few cautious steps out from the planter as he looked down his scope, trying to make sure that there weren't any other enemies hiding the way he was looking.

"Clear this way, too." Linda lowered her rifle slightly and looked down at the tube and mortar shells on the ground. "Must have just been these two running back and forth between the tubes."

"Okay, so now what?"

"We destroy them so they can't use them again."

"Uh, quick question."

"What?"

"Why don't we lob a few shells at the buildings here? Angle them down enough to go through the windows and hey presto, take some of these guys out."

Linda stopped and thought for a moment, trying to recall her basic training on the small, 1-man portable mortars from her time in the Marines. With propellant contained in the bottom of each shell, dropping a mortar into the launch tube would ignite the propellant and send the shell on a high-arcing, relatively slow trajectory. The mortars in use by the attackers didn't appear to be adjustable to low enough trajectories to fire directly into the sides of the buildings, but Linda couldn't think of any reason why they couldn't make it happen anyway.

"Yeah. Yeah, okay, that's not a half-bad idea." She looked up and down the row of concrete planters and pointed off to the left. "Go grab all of the tubes and bring them back here. I'll get one rigged up so that we can destroy them all after we fire off a few shells into the buildings."

Over the next several minutes, Frank retrieved the other five tubes and as many shells as he could carry, all while silently praying that he wouldn't drop one in a way that could set it off. While he was busy with that, Linda rigged one of the tubes to fire directly up into the air and gathered all of the mortar tubes and shells into a cluster around it. She then rigged the other five tubes to fire in low arcs, angling them so that the shells would impact at various spots in the buildings.

"All right, Frank, pay attention." Linda waved for him to join her and they squatted together behind the square planter. "Get on one knee, drop a shell down into each of the tubes that are aimed at the buildings. As soon as you drop it, duck down next to the tube and do *not* get anywhere near the front or top of it, got it?"

"Got it. I assume this one's for destroying everything once we're done?" Frank pointed at the sixth tube which was pointed directly up into the air

"Yep. Let's put two shells through each tube pointed at the buildings and then I'll drop one into this tube. We'll only have a few seconds to get away before it comes back down, but when it does it should set the whole thing off and destroy all of their mortar equipment. That'll be the signal for the counterattack. I just hope Jackson's paying enough attention to see it when it goes off."

Frank nervously picked up a shell and held it atop one of the tubes before dropping it down. He barely remembered to duck down, and as he did he felt a whoosh of air and heard a light *ka-thunk* as the shell was ejected out. Instead of the long, trailing, whistling arc of the mortars that had been fired at the city, though, there was almost no delay before a large explosion sounded, coming from the buildings directly next to them. Glass, plaster and metal sprayed outward and Frank scrambled to get behind the planter. Two more shells went off simultaneously as Linda dropped them in, and two more explosions quickly followed.

Emboldened by the success of his first drop, Frank quickly chewed through several more shells, dropping a total of eight across three of the tubes before a smattering of gunfire ricocheted across the ground, sending him diving for cover yet again. "I think they're onto us!" Frank shouted at Linda as she let loose one final shell which was followed by both an explosion and more gunfire.

"You think?!" Linda pointed at Frank's pack as she scooped up her pack and rifle. "Get ready to go!" Frank grabbed his rifle and pack, quickly securing it on his back, and nodded at her.

"Ready!"

She glanced around, making sure that the coast behind them was still clear, and pointed out at the next set of buildings a good fifty feet away. "We've got to make it across there and hope they don't hit us along the way!" Frank groaned, but nodded, and readied himself as Linda held a shell at the top of the tube. She shouted as she dropped it, yelling at him to "go!" and they both took off at a sprint as the muffled *ka-thunk* echoed behind them.

Linda ignored the chatter of bullets hitting the ground around her and Frank, focusing solely on running as fast and as far as she could. While firing the round directly up into the air would, in theory, mean it would come straight back down, she knew perfectly well that there were enough variables involved that it could deviate enough to potentially hit them. A slight miscalculation in the angle of the tube, a gust of wind or an imperfect propellant charge on the shell could cause such a mishap, or potentially lead to the cache of mortars being left undestroyed.

Fortunately, however, not everything went wrong in what felt like the first time in quite a while. The whistle of the returning shell screamed out behind Linda and Frank, and they ran around the corner of the next building down just as it impacted with the outer edge of the pile of tubes and shells. A massive explosion rocked the courtyard between the buildings, shattering what few windows were still intact and catching anyone standing in the open with a blast of wind and heat. Frank wanted to peek back out to see what the damage looked like but Linda pulled on his backpack, urging him onward.

"No time for gawking. Let's keep going. We need to get away from that area before our troops swarm it and kill every living thing in the area. Plus, we've got someone to hunt down."

FAR BEHIND FRANK AND LINDA, across the bridge inside a half-destroyed command center, Jackson stood next to Sarah's cot, watching over her while listening to field reports streaming in over the radio. The mortars had stopped firing a short time after Linda and Frank had crossed over the bridge, allowing the troops inside the city to regroup and intensify their counterattack. Jackson continued to hold off on sending them across the river until he got some sort of signal that the mortars were down. The signal—in the form of a massive explosion behind the buildings—was all that he needed. Orders went out and troops loaded up into the few remaining intact vehicles they had, as well as on foot. Squads moved up in stages, keeping suppressive fire on the buildings while others crossed the bridge, until there were enough men on the northern side of the river that they could finally begin clearing the buildings that held the attackers.

Jackson stayed in the city, helping to coordinate the assault, all while watching over Sarah, ensuring that any change in her condition was instantly addressed by the medics in the command center. The attack on the city may have been pushed back, but there was far more to the battle than a gunfight.

Chapter Ninety-One

Frank sighed and shook his head as he jogged along next to Linda. It had been two hours since they left the chaos of battle behind, though they could still hear the occasional explosion and sound of heavy weapons fire. Thick, acrid smoke drifted through the air, blotting out the sky and making it impossible to tell what time it was. The streets were quiet apart from the battle raging off to the south, and while Linda had initially been hopeful about their ability to find Omar's location, she was starting to feel more than a few doubts.

She had assumed that once the mortars were taken care of, she and Frank would be able to take the Humvee and continue north in search of Omar's location. The gunfire from the buildings had prevented them from taking the vehicle, though, and they ended up having to go on foot instead. Linda's optimism hadn't wavered at the start of their journey, expecting that they could pick up some sort of hint of Omar's location from clues left behind by the attackers as they had made their way south to their emplacements in the buildings.

Block after block revealed nothing, though, and as Linda grew more discouraged, Frank's upbeat attitude began to grate on her.

He was surprisingly positive, asking questions about Omar and his past that seemed wholly irrelevant to the situation at hand. She bit her tongue, though, until they were sitting down inside a small bookstore on the corner of an intersection taking a breather and getting a bite to eat.

"Any idea what his—"

"Frank." Linda's reply was wrapped in frustration and weariness.

"What?"

"Enough. Okay? Enough with the questions. None of this matters for finding Omar. Nothing about his parents or his history or his living arrangements or what kind of shirts he likes to wear will matter in the slightest when it comes to actually finding him." She caught herself raising her voice at him and sighed before reaching out to pat him on the arm. "Sorry. I'm just frustrated by all of this."

"No kidding." Frank smiled and passed her a canteen filled with water. "We'll find him, though. It's a big city, but we'll find him."

"How is it you're so certain?"

"I dunno. I just get the feeling we'll run into him sooner rather than later."

She shifted in her seat to face him, crossing her legs and putting on an expression of curiosity. "All right, Frank. You've been asking me non-stop questions. Why don't you answer one for me? Where do you think we should look to find him?"

"Well," he furrowed his brow, "it seems to me that you've been thinking he would be close to the action. Right in the thick of it. But I don't necessarily think that's true."

"And why not?"

"He's been very involved in all of this mess from the start, but how many times has he actually been in the middle of it when there's been a risk of him being caught?"

"Hm?" Linda cocked her head to the side, not seeing what Frank was meaning.

"Okay, so like, he created that virus that killed a bunch of people. But he didn't personally deliver any of it. He worked to get the nukes into the country, but he never planted them in the cities."

"That we know of."

"That we know of, yes. But you see what I'm getting at? It seems like he's been directing all of this from backstage. He's letting his minions do the dirty work while he sits back and bides his time for... something."

"For what?"

"That's the million-dollar question, isn't it?"

Linda sighed, growing frustrated. "I don't see what this has to do with figuring out where he is."

"It wouldn't make sense for him to be anywhere close to the attacks on the survivor city. He's got to be somewhere to the north. Heck, even Sarah said something along those lines."

"So where do we look for him, then? We're a couple hours north of the fighting and there hasn't been any sign of anyone around here. It's just abandoned building after abandoned building."

Frank looked out through the window of the store and nodded. "That's our problem. We need to get some perspective on the situation." He stood up and headed out the front door, with Linda hot on his tail.

"Perspective? What are you, a philosophy major or something now?"

"No, you—how is it you're a Marine Raider when *I'm* the one to realize that we need to get to high ground?"

In a flash, Linda knew what Frank's ramblings all meant. With the tall buildings all around them, they had a limited view from which to see signs of Omar's men coming and going. For all she knew, they could be walking by a block or two away and she wouldn't know it if they were on foot. Searching for evidence of their passage could take days or longer on foot, but if they got to an elevated position, they'd be able to see anything out of the ordinary.

"Up there." Linda pointed to a tall, twenty-story hotel that was the highest point in the area. "If we get up there we should be able to see anything unusual in the area."

Frank grinned and slapped Linda on the back. "Good idea. Let's get moving."

———

HALF AN HOUR LATER, Frank held his side as he wheezed for breath. A large '15' was painted on the wall in front of him, and half a floor up Linda leaned over the railing to look down. "You okay there, Frank?" Her face was red and her limp had been more pronounced while walking up the stairs, but she wore a smile that irritated Frank more than he wanted to admit.

"Oh, yeah," he panted, "doing just fine. Never better. Not annoyed at all to be outpaced by someone with a leg injury."

"Well hurry it up, would you? Just a few more floors to go and then we can take a breather."

"You know what?" He struggled to talk as he kept moving, taking the stairs one by one in a plodding, methodical fashion. "I think you're taking this whole 'perspective' thing too seriously. Why couldn't we just look for signs of him from the tenth floor?"

"The roof's better. Now quit talking and hurry up!"

Frank groaned and shook his head but kept going, somehow overcoming the burning pain in his legs that made them feel like they were about to catch fire and shatter into a million pieces. Several minutes later, as he neared the top of the building, he heard a metallic thud and a bright beam of light cut through the dark shaft. The sound and light spurred him on and he reached the final floor just as Linda finished ascending to the roof via a ladder. Frank shut off the flashlight that he had been using and followed her up, glad that the access to the roof was large enough to accommodate him while he was wearing his backpack.

Up on the roof, Linda was already heading toward the edge when she glanced back and gave Frank a wave. "Take a look over there." She pointed to the opposite side of the building. "Look for anything suspicious." With Linda heading to the east side of the building and Frank to the west, they began scanning the streets and buildings, looking for signs of life in what had—from the ground— looked like a dead city.

Frank leaned up against a tall air conditioning vent as he scanned the city, trying to give his aching legs a rest. The cloud cover from the fires was clearer where the pair had stopped, but the air was still thick with the smell of smoke. Light—he still couldn't tell whether it was morning, afternoon or evening—shone through the soot and dust in the air, casting rays onto the ground that moved and vanished and reappeared at the whim of the breeze.

He looked back at Linda and called out softly, not wanting to be heard by anyone who might be nearby on the streets below. "Hey. What should we be looking for?"

"This was your idea, remember?"

"Yeah, yeah. What are we looking for?"

"Anything out of the ordinary."

Frank rolled his eyes as he turned back to look out at the city, muttering under his breath. "Out of the ordinary, she says. Sure. That's just incredibly helpful."

Visibility across the city was low, but the most defining characteristic of it was a complete lack of movement. No cars or people roamed the streets, and even the firefights carrying on to the south were far enough away that they were nigh-on impossible to see. He scanned out to the west, where the city gradually turned into apartments and then condos and then homes with yards. All of the people living in them were no doubt to the south, wondering what was going to happen to them, and whether or not they would survive the fight.

"Frank, here. Now." Linda's voice was low, too, but had a sense of urgency about it. He took one final look out to the west before turning and walking over to her. His legs felt like rubber and every step was excruciatingly painful.

"I really wish I had worked out more before all of this."

Ignoring his groans, Linda pointed out to the northeast. "Look out there. Notice anything?"

Frank followed the path of her finger, starting close and gradually looking farther and farther until he spotted what she was talking about half a mile away. "Is that a light?"

"Sure as hell looks like it, doesn't it? I saw it a minute ago, bouncing and bobbing all around. I think it's coming from inside that building and somebody doesn't realize they're giving us a light show."

"It's not far. You think it's him?"

Linda looked back to the south then swept her gaze back to the northeast where the light was located. "It's far enough away from the action to keep him safe but close enough that he can be involved." She looked at Frank and nodded. "I think it's him."

"Huh. I guess we're heading out, then." He turned and took a step, then groaned again and reached out for her hand. "If my spaghetti legs can make it."

Linda snorted in amusement and took his arm around her shoulders. "You know, it's a good thing you're halfway smart. Otherwise you'd be useless right about now."

Chapter Ninety-Two

Anticipation. The word didn't seem strong enough to describe the feelings coursing through Frank's entire body, and he could feel himself shaking. Each new building they passed through, each new corner they turned and each new step they took toward the place where they thought Omar might be brought greater and greater feelings of nervousness, fear and excitement. His legs, though they were still sore and felt detached from his body, were no longer of concern to him as he carefully followed behind Linda.

She had set an aggressive pace from the get-go, going first and taking the stairs down through the building two at a time and slamming into the walls as she rounded each flight, not bothering to even slow down. Frank had tried to keep up but ended up stumbling out of the front entrance to the building to find her standing across the street, crouched low and waiting for him with an annoyed expression on her face.

They said little as they went along, except to discuss possible routes that would keep them concealed as they approached the office building where they had spotted the light. The first sign that they were on the right path came as they were just half a block from the building in the form of the sound of a diesel engine starting up. The low rumble was quickly accompanied by the sound of a second engine, both of which sounded like they were quickly drawing closer to the pair.

Linda and Frank ducked down a nearby alley, crouching behind a pair of dumpsters as they watched the road with a limited field of view, waiting for the vehicles to appear. It only took a moment for the pair of large box trucks to roll by, both of them heavily weighed down based on how they bounced on the road. They went along slowly as the drivers avoided debris in the road, and Frank could see that there were three armed men in the front cabin of each vehicle, though the contents were a mystery.

"They're heading south," Linda whispered, "probably more reinforcements for the fight at the city."

"Must mean things are going our way, you think?"

Linda shrugged. "Who knows. Not our concern right now, though. If they were loaded down with fighters then this is the perfect time to make our way inside."

Frank took a deep breath and nodded to her. "I'm ready."

Linda's smile was genuine. "I appreciate you being here. I know this isn't what you signed up for when you helped me out at that gas station."

"I'm just happy to be here, with you. Helping to take this guy out, I mean." Frank stumbled over his words, swallowing hard and avoiding her gaze.

"You've done way better than I ever thought you'd be capable of. Not bad for an accountant-slash-trucker." She patted him on the arm and he smiled at her.

"Listen, Linda, before we go in, I wanted to ask—"

"Sh!" Linda put a finger to her lips as the smile and relaxed look disappeared, replaced with a wide-eyed expression of concern. "Hold the questions till later. You hear that?"

Frank cocked his head, listening intently until he picked up what she was talking about. A conversation drifted across the wind, coming from somewhere close by. It was loud and intense, in some language he didn't understand, though the emotion behind the words told him more than enough. "Sounds like arguing."

"Someone's getting chewed out." Linda peeked out from behind the dumpster and motioned with her head. "Come on. I need to get closer. I can't make out everything they're saying."

The pair slunk out of the alley and down the street toward their destination. The building in question was illuminated softly from within, and the sound of a cluster of voices grew louder the closer they got. Linda and Frank slipped behind a row of rectangularly-trimmed hedges just outside the building before crouching down and holding still so they could hear what was being said inside.

"...not possible that they're still holding out." The first voice sounded tinny and had a slight staticky quality, and Linda realized that the person was somewhere else speaking through a radio.

"Possible or not, it's true. We just sent two more groups to the front line. Without the mortars, we can't advance."

"Pound them with rockets, then!"

"We have been, but they're ineffective at that range."

A frustrated growl was followed by the sound of something breaking. "We need those codes! Direct the two groups you just sent down to come in from the east and west. Force their defenders to break off from their northern line to protect their flanks. Once they do, have the main force push across the river and attack them head-on!"

Linda's eyes widened and she whispered in Frank's ear. "We have to get word to Jackson. Warn him of what's coming."

"I thought we needed to get Omar first."

"If they break through into the city and steal those codes..." Linda shook her head. "No. We need to make contact with Jackson."

"How? We don't have a radio."

"No," she said, "but they do."

"So we're going to walk inside and ask to borrow it?"

"After we kill them all, yes."

Frank was about to argue with Linda over her 'kill first, ask questions later' approach when she started creeping behind the bushes over toward the door without saying anything else. *Son of a...* he screamed internally as he followed behind, wishing they could have come up with a better plan. She reached the edge of the bushes where the stairs met the building and peeked out at the half-open door. A sliver of cigarette smoke drifted out and Linda reached up to grab the rail on the stairs. She glanced back at Frank with an expression that asked if he was ready, and he nodded in affirmation.

In a smooth, catlike motion, Linda pulled herself up over the railing. When her feet hit the ground she pushed into the door with her shoulder while drawing a knife from its sheath on her chest. A faint gurgle was the only sound the man inside the door made as she slashed clean through his throat and grabbed his gun to keep him from pulling the trigger and alerting others to his condition.

Frank, feeling especially exhausted after all they had been through, exited the bushes and took the conventional way up the stairs before slipping inside the doorway. He gave the bleeding, quivering man on the floor a quick look before turning away to face Linda. She had already cleaned her blade and replaced it in its sheath and had her rifle up to her shoulder, waiting for his arrival. With a quick wave of her hand she signaled for Frank to follow her into the next room.

Based on the voices they had heard while crouching outside the open window to the building, Linda had expected there to be no more than two men in the room talking to someone on a radio. Supporting that assumption was the fact that they had said that two groups were on their way, so she figured that even if there were more people in the building, there couldn't be too many. As Linda charged through the door into the room where she and Frank had heard voices, the sight of half a dozen faces turning to look at her made her heart skip a beat and she realized that she had made a dreadful miscalculation.

"Oh, shi—" Linda backpedaled out through the doorway while she fired at the men standing around a table in the center of the room. They were nearly as quick with their weapons as she was, though, and by the time she had dropped two of them the other four were already firing back as they maneuvered for cover. Linda pulled the thick oak door shut as a hail of bullets hit it and she ducked out of the way and looked at Frank who was wincing as he stood on the other side of the doorframe.

"Okay," she said, "so I might have slightly underestimated how many there are."

Shouts from inside the room were met with more shouts from upstairs in the building, which were swiftly followed by the sound of footsteps as several more people began running for the staircase located down the hall. Frank looked up at the ceiling then back at Linda as she shook her head.

"Make that drastically underestimated."

"Do we stay and fight?" Frank fought to keep the panic out of his voice.

"No." Linda made the decision quickly, without hesitation. "It's a suicide mission. Besides, I haven't heard Omar here, so who knows if he's here or somewhere else."

The clatter of feet at the top of the stairs spurred the pair on and they both turned and ran through the front door just as the men in the side room opened the door and fired out into the hall, just barely missing Frank and Linda. Linda led the way across the street with Frank hot on her heels. Linda fired her rifle from the hip at a large window sitting in the front of a small restaurant, shattering the glass. She leapt through the open window, skidding along the glass and pulling herself behind the bar. She stood and fired at the building as the front door opened, bullets whizzing past Frank said as he jumped through the window and slid across the glass until he, too, was in cover behind the bar.

"Now what?" Frank shouted as he shouldered his rifle and fired alongside her. Bullets smashed through brick and wood as they hit the front of the building across the street, sending the men who were about to charge out through the door reeling back inside.

"Give me a second to think!" Linda shouted back at him as she fired slowly and steadily, trying to conserve ammunition while at the same time ensuring that their enemies would be penned in long enough for her to think of a plan.

"Better hurry; they're coming around the side!" Frank swiveled and fired at the corner of the building across the street, tearing chunks out of brick. Two men who had charged around the corner retreated behind a large truck sitting by the side of the road and began taking potshots at the restaurant.

"Dammit, they're going to flank from the other side and converge; we need to escape out the back!"

Frank turned and glanced into the darkness at the back of the building and shook his head before taking a few more potshots at the two men off to the side. "That's not gonna work."

"Why not?" Linda mentally counted down her last three rounds, firing them in rapid succession before fingering the magazine ejection lever to dump out the empty one. She slapped in a new one and the bolt slammed home and she began firing at the door again.

"Well, half the building collapsed in on itself so unless you can dig through a bunch of rubble…" A bullet sang as it cut through a glass on the counter just a few inches away from Frank's face and he yelped and ducked down, rubbing at the cuts on his cheek and forehead. "We've got to do something, though… maybe we should just run out the side over there? The ones at the front of the building can't see us there so we'd just be dealing with the two on the side."

Linda considered Frank's suggestion for a second before shaking her head. "No. Here." Linda shrugged off her backpack while firing one-handed and tossed it over to Frank. "Pull three more mags out for me."

Frank unzipped her bag and tossed the requested magazines onto the bar counter before zipping it back up and handing it back to her. "Nope," she replied, "you're keeping it."

"Huh?" Frank looked at her quizzically before dropping the bag and taking a few more shots at the pair off to the side of the building.

Linda looked at him, weighing the option of telling him the truth versus lying to him, wondering which would be more likely to get him to listen to her. In the end, she opted for a mixture of both. "Frank, someone has to get back to Jackson and warn him about what's going on with the impending attack." That was true. "Based on how these guys are acting and what I know about Omar, they're not going to kill me." That, however, was not guaranteed. "If you argue with me on this I swear I will make you regret it."

"You want me to get out while you cover me, get to Jackson and then come back for you?"

"It'd be nice if you came back, yeah." Linda snorted in amusement.

"How am I supposed to find you?"

Linda kicked at the bag at her feet. "I've got a tracker tag on me and the tracker's in my pack still. Get to Jackson, get some reinforcements and hone in on the tag. By the time you do, they'll have taken me to Omar. Even if I—even if I'm wrong about what they'll do, you'll still be able to stop Omar."

"Not a chance. What the hell makes you think I'm going to just leave you here to get captured? They'll kill you, Linda! *He'll* kill you!"

Linda stopped firing for a moment and stared Frank dead in the eyes. "You're going to do this for the same reason you started it. What matters is the mission; stopping Omar matters more than you or me or any other single person."

Frank felt his stomach tighten into knots as he struggled with the choices laid before him. Capture and certain death next to his friend? Or having a very high probability of stopping the madman responsible for so much death and destruction.

"But..." He spoke softly even as the fire from outside the restaurant intensified. "Some people do matter more. To me. I can't leave you here by yourself. Not even if it means stopping Omar."

"Frank," she said, running a rough, dirt-covered hand down the side of his face, "get to Jackson. Then get back here to me. If you don't, then we both die and the city—and the country—falls. If you do, and you make it back in time... then you can ask what you were going to ask earlier, and—"

"Get them! But don't kill the woman!" The bellowed call came from the front of the building across the street, confirming what Linda had told Frank.

"See?" She shoved him toward the side of the room, kicking her pack over to him. "Now get going, Frank! Move!" He stumbled as he grabbed her backpack and ran for the side of the store, spraying the window with his rifle to shatter the glass. He jumped out as Linda leapt over the bar and advanced toward the entrance, firing at the two men on the side of the building and gunning them both down. Her movement, screams and gunfire distracted the group emerging from the building, focusing their attention on her instead of on Frank. She fired on them as they dove for cover, wounding three before her mag ran dry. She dropped the rifle and continued advancing as she drew her pistol, turning to her left and taking potshots at one hiding behind an overturned dumpster until the trigger pulled back with a solid *click*.

Off in the distance, as Frank struggled to run down the street with his legs still in pain and overloaded with two backpacks, he fought every urge in his body to turn around and go back to help Linda. Even as her shouts of rage and the gunfire suddenly stopped, he continued forward, propelled by the slightest bit of hope given to him by what he had heard shouted by their enemies.

"*Don't kill the woman!*" It was the only thing keeping him going; the only hope he had of seeing Linda again. It was a faint hope, a mere sliver, but it was there. The city and country would stand—he would be sure of that. But if she fell, he wasn't sure if he could live with himself and his choice to run instead of dying by her side.

Frank Richards ignored the screaming of his legs and the thumping of the extra weight against his side and chose to run even faster.

Chapter Ninety-Three

The funeral for his parents and brothers is brief and unusually muted. In spite of the dangers involved in traveling back to his home country, Omar jumped on the first available flight, abandoning his classes and exams so that he could bury his family. Dressed in all black, he is surrounded by distant relatives who are wailing and gnashing their teeth in a home outside Tehran, grieving for the loss of the ones they loved. In Omar's heart, however, there is no grief or sorrow or sadness. Anger burns bright, fueling an intensity that he has never before known in his comfortable life.

On the third day of mourning, as he sits quietly in a corner, a pair of men appear before him. They sit down and give their condolences, and tell him that they are with the government. His father, it seems, had spoken quite widely of his success in his studies and with the loss of so many officials and scientists, they have come to offer him a job once he concludes his studies. He sits and listens to their offer, speaking only when he has a question or wishes to clarify a point. They soon move outside the house where the two men speak more candidly, disclosing details about the attempted coup in an effort to further motivate Omar to commit his life to his country.

They speak of how the Americans were behind the coup, with specific instructions to kill dozens of scientists and government officials before executing the president himself, but how his parents were merely collateral damage. They *speak of the heroic actions of the soldiers that burst in only a few moments after his parents and brothers were killed, and how doctors desperately tried to save their lives. They speak in cynical tones about how the truth will be swept under the rug because any finger pointing may give the Americans just the excuse they've been looking for to invade.*

Then they speak of how he can help. How, because his family was never on a list, he can continue his studies in America, develop his craft and talents in a field that will help his country, and return to it after graduation. He will be offered a prestigious position in military research and development, helping to shape the future of Iran to ensure that no one can ever try the same thing again. The offer is more than simply enticing. For a young man whose life has been overturned and virtually destroyed, it is impossible to resist.

In the late afternoon, with the wails of family mourning their dead in the background, he agrees with a handshake, and the two government men disappear as quickly as they appeared. Omar spends the next four days with his extended family, though unlike the first days he feels anger instead of grief. The anger is tempered with hope, though it is not a happy, joyful hope. It is a hope of revenge, a hope that his life can be spent finding ways to exact revenge for the death of his mother, father and brothers.

After his brothers and father and mother are buried, Omar heads back to America and immediately plunges himself back into his education. He doubles his scholastic workload and eliminates all forms of extracurricular activities even as his advisor protests and tries to insist that he needs to take more time off to grieve. Deposits still arrive in his bank account on a monthly basis, though the origin is an unknown name instead of his father's. He does not question the deposits, assuming they are coming from someone connected to the two men he spoke with. His only focus and thought is his work, which he excels in.

Over a period of four years he blows past his peers, earning a master's degree and a doctorate. The title of his thesis is unintelligible to anyone but an expert in his field, and combines chemistry and bio-engineering in new ways that turn him into a veritable rock star in a few small, niche scientific communities. He is cautious, though, to ensure that any and all research he performs and papers he produces do not cross lines that would raise eyebrows with military officials or attract the attention of national security agencies.

With his doctoral degree in hand and a swirling mass of new ideas and information fresh in his head, he completes his move back to Iran within days of graduation. Four years of keeping to himself, forgoing a social life and turning down any attempts at friendship with other students mean that he has no ties to cut, and integrating back into life in his home country is painless and simple. He spends a few days at home with grandparents and other extended relatives before he is contacted by the same two men who spoke with him four years prior. They thank him for his hard work and tell him that he has a job that he can start as soon as he is ready. He leaves for Tehran the next morning, promising his grandparents that he will call as often as he can, though he knows that is a lie.

On the military campus he is introduced to his new colleagues, all of whom are eager to hear about his theories and research projects. As he is introduced to his new work, he begins to realize that his position will afford him more than just the opportunity to protect his country. His desire for revenge has smoldered for years, and he has resisted fanning the flames until being in a position where he can effect some real change.

In his new position, with the resources and mandate he has been given, he realizes that—for the first time—he doesn't care about his country at all. The only thing he wants is revenge. And he will take it, no matter the cost.

Chapter Ninety-Four

When Linda's pistol ran dry she tossed it aside, pulled her rifle back up off of her shoulder and ejected the magazine. She was just about to pop in a fresh one and continue her assault on the men when a shadow loomed from behind and she felt the force of hard wood and metal slam against her lower back. She cried out in pain as she toppled forward, dropping the new magazine to the ground. The rifle clattered down as well, spinning as it slid a few feet away before coming to rest. She reached for it but another blow landed on her upper back, sending her to her hands and knees. She reached for the knife on her chest and pulled it out, then twisted and lunged at the figure she sensed behind. Her reactions were slowed, though, and the knife passed harmlessly through the air before a gloved hand grabbed her arm, twisting it sharply so that she dropped the knife in pain.

A boot rammed into her back, forcing her to the ground and another hand grabbed her other arm, wrenching it behind her where a large zip tie was quickly applied to her wrists. Whoever bound her made the tie exceptionally tight, and even through her hazed pain she could already feel her fingertips begin to tingle.

"Get...off of me...assholes!" Linda grunted and tried to roll over, to kick and lash out at her attackers, but two other figures accompanied the first, holding her tightly as they picked her up. They remained silent as they brought her inside the building that she and Frank had briefly entered, then threw her down on the floor in the room with the large table. She groaned in pain and rolled over on her back again before slowly pushing herself into a sitting position just as the doors to the room slammed shut.

"Linda Rollins. *Shey'taan* herself, in the flesh." The voice was smug, full of pride, and located somewhere close. She squinted, trying to clear her blurred vision. A figure standing at the far side of the table from her swirled into view, and though he knew her name, she didn't recognize him.

"Who the hell are you?" Spittle flew from her lips as she spoke, mustering up all the courage and outrage she could. "One of Omar's dogs?"

The insult intended to provoke the man had no effect, and he merely smiled as he watched her struggling on the floor. "He will be most pleased to see you. Plucking the thorn from his side after it has irritated him for so many years will, I imagine, be an enormous pleasure.

"Bite me." Linda snarled at him and he gave her a thin smile.

"By the way, your associate—the one following you around— we killed him."

Linda's heart jumped, though she kept her expression sour. "Liar."

The man stood up and raised his hands. "It's true. He took a bullet in the back. They're dragging his corpse back now, I'd imagine. Such a pity, for your friend to die like that. Running like a coward."

"What do you want from me? Shouldn't you be calling your master and letting him know I'm here?" Linda ignored what he was saying about Frank, though her certainty that he was lying was lessening as she wondered whether they really had managed to gun Frank down.

"Your defiance is admirable, *shey'taan*. He is already on his way." The man stepped close to her and she kicked out at him but missed by a hair. He laughed and kicked back at her, savagely, his steel-toed boot crunching into her chest. She felt a burst of pain as multiple ribs fractured and she gasped for air, each breath full of agony. "You should calm down," he hissed at her, grabbing her by the arm and pulling her to her feet, "or else you'll be in multiple pieces when he does arrive."

⸺

LINDA LOST track of how long she was lying on the floor of the closet. Her breaths were shallow and she tried to keep her arm off of her left side, but with her hands still bound behind her back the extra pressure on her chest made the pain in her ribs nearly unbearable. The room was dark, with the only light coming from a crack beneath the door. As she drifted back and forth between consciousness and not she heard muted voices and footsteps from various parts of the building around her. None of what she heard was clear enough to completely understand so she gave up trying and focused on staying alive.

Breathe in. She winced.

Breathe out. She ground her teeth to keep from groaning.

Breathe in. Stars flashed across her vision.

Breathe out. She tasted blood in her mouth from nicking the side of her tongue as she clamped down with her teeth again.

Minutes and hours blurred together until the footsteps and voices that had been muffled began to grow louder. Shadows passed in front of the light beneath the door and the voices grew soft as a conversation of some sort was held outside the closet. She squinted her eyes, preparing for the door to open, which it did a moment later. She squeezed her eyes shut as a blinding light was thrust into her face and a rough hand turned her head this way and that. Linda kicked out, sending shock waves of pain through her chest, but her leg was stopped before it could connect, held in place by a powerful hand.

"*Shey'taan.*" The voice was smooth and deep, with an oiled tone of sophistication and deadliness. She recognized it at once and felt her heart quicken. She opened her eyes slowly, adjusting to the light. Her worst enemy squatted over her, her hand in one hand and her leg in his other. He smiled at her look of recognition, flashing perfectly straight, white teeth against his olive skin.

"So you're really, finally here." His chuckle was genuine, as if he found her presence legitimately amusing. She said nothing in return and he nodded at her before glancing back over his shoulder at the cluster of men behind him. "Take her upstairs." He turned back and smiled at her again. "We have much to discuss."

"I HEARD ABOUT YOUR PARENTS, out in Tennessee. Such a tragedy." The voice came from somewhere behind Linda, still soft and smooth as it had been two hours prior when she was dragged from the closet. Her head sagged down to her chest and her breath came in ragged gasps as blood trickled from the corner of her mouth down her chin and onto her right pants leg.

The pain from her fractured ribs no longer bothered her, as it had been overshadowed by what Omar had done to her over the two-hour period. His voice had remained calm and steady as he moved from tool to tool, beating her across her whole body, twisting her extremities into painful knots but never crossing the line of breaking anything more than her already fractured ribs. She felt as though everything was broken, though, and wondered when he would tire of playing with her and simply end it.

"Freezing to death is a terrible way to go, isn't it?" Omar walked around her, a small baggie of ice held against the knuckles of his right hand. "Especially when you know you're trapped in a nursing home, knowing you're too weak to escape, having to figure out how to cope with your imminent death."

"Screw. You." The words were quiet, but defiant. She wanted to break her bonds, to leap from her chair and slam Omar against the wall, push him down and throttle his throat with her bare hands.

"Come now, *shey'taan.*" He tossed the baggie onto a nearby

table and massaged his hand, the knuckles red and raw. "Aren't you curious about how I know about your parents?"

"Mole. I assume."

Omar walked by her again and she braced herself for the blow she knew would come. A second later it did, into her right side through the gap under the arm in the chair. She spasmed and coughed, spitting more blood out onto her pants and the floor.

"Moles, actually. Plural. More than one. You can't pull off something like this with just one source." Another blow, with something more solid than a fist, this time to her right shoulder. "I've been watching your family for quite a long time, you know. You were harder to track down, but I picked up enough bits and pieces of your trail to make sure you were always a few steps behind me."

"Why."

"Why what?" Omar circled around to the front and crouched down just outside of spitting range. "Why do all of what I did? Or why keep you here, alive, for as long as possible?"

Linda raised her head slightly, meeting his gaze. Her eyes were bloodshot and she could barely keep her eyelids open. Each and every breath and word were pure pain. "Why. Alive."

"You've haunted me," another punch, "for so long," another kick, "so I'm going to keep you alive long enough to give you a taste of what I've had to endure." Omar's smooth voice wavered ever so slightly as he kicked at the side of her chair, knocking her over onto the floor. Linda couldn't do anything except lay still and wait for his next attack. Instead, though, he waved to one of the other men lurking in the corner of the room who quickly ran over, picked her and the chair back up and then returned to his place.

"Now," Omar intoned, walking over to a nearby table on which Linda's sparse assortment of possessions had been strewn, "can you tell me why you were so underprepared when my men brought you in? You had a single spare magazine for your pistol, a few for your rifle, some odds and ends in your vest pouches and not much else."

Linda's eyes flicked over to the table, roving over the belongings there until she caught sight of the small tracking device mixed in with the rest of the odds and ends. She was surprised that Omar hadn't noticed or thrown out the device, then she realized that he likely had no idea how significant the small piece of metal was. This suspicion was confirmed when she watched him pick up the device along with her flashlight, knife and multitool and slip them all into his pockets.

"Guess I was… packing light." She forced a crooked smile as a few more drops of blood fell from the edge of her mouth to her pants leg.

"And what of your friend, Frank Richards? My men tell me he ran down the street, leaving you alone to defend yourself. I didn't realize he was such a coward after everything you two had been through."

"He got… scared." Another wave of pain shot through her body and she shivered involuntarily.

"Hm. Somehow I doubt that. In spite of his relatively uninteresting past, his actions alongside you seem to indicate that he is more likely to be running for help than running away."

Linda started to raise her head, but stopped and let it hang against her chest. Her mind, however, was racing. One of the men who had bound her earlier had told her that Frank was dead, shot in the back. But Omar's account was different, telling her that Frank had apparently escaped. She thought for a few seconds and decided to feel Omar out. "Then he'll be back. With reinforcements."

Omar chuckled and shook his head, and Linda wondered if he was about to come over and begin the torture anew. "Oh, I'm afraid not. We've added several security measures since your arrival. Anyone attempting to assault us here will fail, and, it doesn't really matter either way. My forces are converging on your city and the deactivation codes will be mine before the day is out."

Linda couldn't help but smile ever so slightly,

Omar leaned in close to Linda, grabbing her roughly by the chin and pulling her head up to force her to meet his gaze. "Your attempt was noble, but in the end it failed as miserably as your other attempts over the years. You came close, but couldn't seal the deal." He let her head fall as he walked back to the table, taking her pistol in hand and gently seating in a new magazine. He aimed the pistol at her stomach, his fingers slowly tightening around the grip. "But, as much fun as this has been, I think you've just about served your usefulness in venting my frustrations."

As Omar walked closer to Linda, she put all of her remaining energy into one last defiant gesture. Bracing her legs and rocking herself forward, she tipped the chair up and swung her head upward, smashing her skull into the bottom of Omar's chin. There wasn't much force beyond the maneuver, but she could hear his teeth rattling together and his cry of pain as he shuffled back, letting her topple over to the floor with her arms and legs still bound to the chair. He aimed the pistol at her head, wiping a streak of red off of his bloodied lip and gave her a cruel smile before lowering the weapon.

"On second thought, perhaps I've not completely finished venting *all* of my frustrations."

"YOU SURE NOBODY SAW US?"

"I'm pretty sure they'd be jumping down our throats right now if they had. Now c'mon, just two more blocks to go."

"You sure you want to do this?"

"Absolutely. You try to put me at the back and I'll shoot through you."

"Ha. I'll bet. Just stay to the side if it gets bad."

"No promises."

"I hope to hell she's still alive in there."

"You and me both. You and me both."

WHILE LINDA HAD MANAGED to buy herself a temporary reprieve from death, she wasn't sure if it had been worth the price she was paying. Omar had rolled up his sleeves and gone to work on her, no longer concerned with making sure she survived to the end of the session. Black leather gloves adorned his hands to protect his already raw knuckles, and they were quickly becoming slicked with her blood. His face contorted with every blow, his mouth twisting into shapes of anger and hatred all mixed with pleasure and joy. His intent was no longer to seek mere revenge—he intended to beat her to death. Linda withstood the blows as much as possible, and even though he avoided hitting her in the head to avoid her blacking out earlier than she otherwise might, she felt as though she was going to pass out at any second.

A sudden bang from the floor below stopped Omar mid-blow and he turned to look at one of the men standing off to the side. "What was that?" His voice was ragged and he breathed heavily from the exertion he was putting out. Another bang turned into a muffled explosion and Omar turned to look at Linda. Her eyes were open and she forced the edges of her lips up into the slightest of smiles as she whispered. "Told you... he'd... come back." Omar's confident expression wavered as he glanced between Linda and his men, trying to cope with the idea that a situation had sprung up that wasn't entirely within his control.

SIX FIGURES STOOD TENSED outside the entrance to the office building, weapons held at the ready position and their eyes roving over the windows and doorway, looking for any emergent threats. "Three. Two. One. Go." The countdown and command were whispered, but what followed was anything but quiet.

The door to the building burst open under the weight of the portable battering ram, the wood and metal splintering and twisting with just a single blow. The bang of the doors flying open and rattling against the interior walls echoed through the halls of the building. As soon as the doors opened the two figures holding the battering ram dropped it and stepped back, allowing the two men behind them to step forward. They dashed inside the building, their weapons held loosely in one hand as they each cradled a small metallic object. They threw the objects into the two rooms just off of the entry hall to the building and dashed back out to the front steps. A few seconds later, amid the surprised shouts and call-outs from those inside the building, a pair of loud bangs and flashes of light went off.

"GO!" Jackson's voice was loud as he bellowed out the command, no longer bothering with any pretense of stealth. Four men dressed in black and dark olive green charged past Jackson and Frank, dividing into two teams and entering the rooms that had been flash banged. Bursts of gunfire erupted as Jackson and Frank passed by the rooms, heading for the stairs at the back of the hall.

Jackson took the lead as he and Frank headed upstairs, checking each corner and potential blind spot as they went along. Frank tried to imitate Jackson's movements as much as possible, though he knew full well that in a true firefight he would be just slightly more than useless.

"First floor clear." A staticky voice came through Frank and Jackson's earpieces. "No sign of her. Sanders was hit but still alive."

"Copy. Move up ASAP. Out." Jackson whispered back, his reply coming through loud on the radios thanks to his throat mic. "Richards," he continued as he glanced over at Frank, "watch right. I've got left. Shoot anything that moves unless it's her."

Frank nodded and shifted his attention from the hall in the center of the room to the right-hand side, depending on Jackson to cover his back. They moved lockstep with each other, peeking around the corner of each room before dipping inside, scanning the corners with their rifle lights and then dipping back out into the hall. It took less than thirty seconds of slow, stealthy movements for them to near the end of the hall, at which point Frank ducked into the next room and nearly dropped his rifle in shock.

"Linda!" He shouted and ran forward as he saw her still tied to the chair, head slumped over on her chest. As he ran toward Linda, Frank felt a presence from the side and turned to see a man leaping out through a window, shouting in a foreign language as he went.

One other man followed behind him, but Frank paid them no mind, focusing on Linda instead.

"What the hell happened to you?" He knelt down next to her and gently pushed her head up, sighing with relief at the sight of her still drawing in ragged breaths. A rattle of gunfire came from the room across the hall and Frank turned to see Jackson run in a second later.

"Three made it out the windows; get outside and see if you can run them down. Out."

"Make that five; there were two more in here with her."

"Copy. All units, correction: make that five targets. Out."

"One… of them… was him." Linda's eyes were still shut as she whispered to Frank. He slid a knife from its sheath on the belt at the small of his back and quickly cut the zip-ties that held her hands, arms and legs. She started to fall forward and he caught her, lowering her gently to the floor. She smiled faintly as her eyes fluttered open and caught sight of his face.

"Jackson!" Frank called out to Jackson who was peeking out one of the windows to see if he could catch sight of the fleeing enemies. "She said he was here."

"Who, Omar?" Jackson turned and advanced on Frank and Linda, stopping short and giving a shallow gasp at the sight of her.

"Yes." Linda replied weakly as she tried to nod.

"Holy hellfire…" Jackson dropped to his knees and craned his neck to activate his microphone. "All units, change of plans. Get back and secure the entrances and make absolutely sure this building's clear. I've got Rollins here in bad shape. She's our first priority."

"No," Linda started to speak again, then winced as pain shot through her side, "leave me and get him!" She wheezed the words out amid a smatter of coughs and groans.

"Not a chance, Rollins. Now shut up before you make this worse." Jackson dropped his rifle on the floor and whipped off his backpack and large medical bag attached to it and spread them out on the floor. "Frank, ease her down and go stand guard by the door."

"But—"

Jackson looked up at Frank with fire in his eyes, nearly snarling as he barked back a reply. "*Now*, Frank! I've got it from here!"

Frank nodded and gently lowered Linda to the ground, squeezing her hand as he stood up. Jackson took a deep breath as he removed his combat gloves and slipped on a pair of powdered latex ones from his medical bag. "Give me a report, Linda. Where'd you sustain the worst of it?"

"Didn't get me in the head except once or twice. Mostly in the chest, sides, extremities." Her words were whispered but determined as she worked to give him as much information in as short of a time span as possible. "Couple of cracked ribs makes it hell to breathe. Maybe some light internal injuries but most of it is exhaustion and pain. Lots of pain."

While Linda was talking Jackson had been busy gently probing her from top to bottom, checking for anything that was broken or didn't feel right. "Okay, here's the deal." He sat back on his knees and feet and looked at her. "I think you're right, and you do definitely have a couple of cracked or broken ribs. I want to evac you back to the city where we can start treatment as soon as possible."

Looking bloodied, bruised and utterly helpless as she did, Jackson didn't expect a vicelike grip to latch onto his arm and twist, sending pain shooting through his wrist and hand. "Jackson." Linda's voice was hoarse and rough, her face twisted into a mask of pain and anger. "If you try to ship me back there I swear to you I will gut you and hang you by your own intestinal tract."

"Ow, dammit, Rollins!" Jackson tried to shake his hand free but her grip was too strong. "You need attention! I can't just have you trotting around out here; you can barely stand!"

Linda nodded at the medical bag as she pursed her lips tight. "You confirmed nothing's broken except a couple of ribs. Everything hurts but that's manageable. Give me a speedball and I'll be back on my feet long enough to help finish this."

"A speed—are you kidding me?!"

"I know they're standard issue in the kits. For use in emergency situations only. I'd say this counts."

"Rollins, those things are dangerous as hell!" Jackson tried to argue, but Linda only squeezed harder on his wrist, prompting him to grunt with pain as he tried to pry her off. "Okay, okay! Fine!" He relented and she let go, sighing as though she had just expended nearly all of her energy on him.

"You," he mumbled as he dug through the bag, "are insane. You know that, right?"

Linda closed her eyes and snorted in amusement. "Part of the job, Jackson. Part of the job."

After several seconds of searching, Jackson pulled out a black case from the depths of the bag. He cracked open the case to reveal three small, thin syringes sitting in plastic holsters that both kept them safe and from being affected by any movement. He pulled one of the syringes out and held it aloft after removing the plastic sheath on the end, tapping on the side of the syringe while gently depressing the plunger to remove any potential excess air.

"You sure about this?" He looked down at her. "These are fairly low dosage but in your condition who knows what could happen."

Linda's eyes shifted over to Frank, who was still standing by the stairs with his rifle at the ready. "I'm not going back to the city. I'm going to finish this, come hell or high water."

Jackson tapped the syringe one last time and took a deep breath. "He's going to kill me if your heart ends up exploding because of this."

Linda smiled again. "Just make sure you don't do that, 'k?"

While the technical term for the cocktail in the syringe wasn't "speedball," the name had carried over from illicit drug usage and become lodged in popular lexicon among the medics who were still getting used to the new drug. A potent combination of a stimulant and a painkiller, speedballs were popular amongst druggies who liked to mix drugs like cocaine with heroin or morphine to achieve a high that would just as often kill them with an accidental overdose.

Some versions of the speedball had uses in legitimate medicine, such as giving terminal patients both relief from pain and enough lucidity to spend time with their loved ones before death. The use of the drug in combat situations was relatively new, though, and was reserved only for certain cases where soldiers needed to be able to move on their own two feet but required both pain relief and a stimulant in order to make that happen.

As good as the potential results were from the mixture of painkillers and stimulants, the possibility of an overdose was greatly magnified due to how the drugs interacted. Even with the cocktail Jackson was injecting into Rollins being highly refined and measured, there was still the chance that she could die from it. As afraid as he was of Linda if he didn't comply with her request, he wondered if he shouldn't be more afraid of Frank's response if she did end up dying.

As the drugs wound their way through Linda's bloodstream, they had a remarkable effect on her disposition. She went from lying on the floor, gently wheezing for air to starting to push herself up in a matter of minutes. As she tried, though, Jackson held her down and shook his head. "Not yet. I want to watch you for a few more minutes."

"Jackson," she replied, in a voice that was remarkably loud and clear, "stop being such a sissy."

"Rollins." Jackson growled as he forced her back down to the ground again. "Your ribs are cracked and you have severe bruising pretty much everywhere. You might be feeling fantastic right now but we need to at least bind your chest with some bandages before you start throwing yourself around all over the place, okay?"

Linda nodded slowly and sighed. "Fine."

Jackson eased off of her, helping her slowly rise to a sitting position on the floor. "How are you feeling?"

"Like I'm three miles high and nothing can stop me."

"You still with us?"

Linda nodded. "I experimented once or twice in my youth, Jackson. If I start losing it I'll tell you, okay?" With a slight groan she lifted her arms and nodded at the medical bag. "Hurry up and get those bandages around my chest. I want to get up and going before any of this stuff starts to wear off." Jackson pulled her shirt up and began winding tight layers of bandages around her ribcage. She winced at every pull Jackson made to tighten the bandages, but soon the discomfort began to subside thanks to the combination of the wrap and the painkillers.

"Linda!" Alerted by her talking, Frank hurried over and knelt down next to her as Jackson finished up. "Should you be moving?"

Linda smiled and patted Frank on the shoulder, surprised by the lack of pain involved in the movement. "I'll be fine, for a while. Once these painkillers start wearing off I don't know what's going to happen, though, so let's get moving, okay?"

Frank stood and took her hand, helping her to her feet while simultaneously giving Jackson a concerned look. "Is she—are you sure she can do this?"

Jackson shook his head. "Nope. But the alternative was to have her break my wrist and string me up by my entrails so I figured I'd do what she said."

"Quit your whining, Jackson. I'll be fine. This stuff'll keep me going for long enough for us to find him."

"We're going to go after Omar now?"

"You'd better believe it." Linda nodded. "He doesn't get to use me as his personal punching bag for hours on end and just get away. Besides, he's scared." She smiled at the thought and Frank nodded.

"All right. Where do you think he went?"

"All units, I need reports. Any sign of where those targets fled to?"

"North somewhere, sir, in a militarized vehicle. We got a few shots off on them and we may have punctured their oil pan. There's a pretty sizable leak in the road heading north. We were going to take one of their vehicles from out back and pursue, but you had us pull back."

"Understood. Get ready to move out. We're going to finish up and move out in pursuit."

"Yes, sir." There was a pause accompanied by several seconds of static, then the soldier's voice came through again, though a hint of panic accompanied it. "Sir, we may have a problem."

"What is it?" Jackson secured his packs and grabbed his rifle as he ran to the window overlooking the front entrance to the building. Although the glass in the window was still present, he could hear the faint rumble of engines as they drew closer. "All units, we have incoming forces from the south! Assume them to be hostiles, take up defensive positions and prepare to engage on my signal!"

"Jackson." Linda approached him from behind and tapped him on the shoulder. "We can't stay here; he's probably diverted forces from the south to try and hold us off until he can retreat. If we don't leave right now then we're going to lose him—possibly for good."

"I can't just abandon these men! They volunteered to come up here and search for you with Richards and I!"

"Who said anything about abandoning them?" Linda replied. "Just pull everyone back, we'll go out the back door, take the vehicle they spotted and head out after Omar."

"Rollins, I'll chalk this moment of idiocy up to the drugs; just how in the hell do you expect them to let us get away unless there's someone here to hold them off?"

"Sir, it's two trucks full; they're disembarking! Should we open fire?"

"Yes, dammit! Open fire! Open fire!" Jackson yelled back as he looked to see the waves of enemy men running across the nearby street like so many ants. Gunfire burst from the windows below and several of them fell to the ground, though others found cover and began returning fire on the office building.

"Jackson!" Linda pulled on his jacket. "Omar is the *only* objective here! If we can get him, then we can cut off the head of the snake!"

"I'm not aban—"

"Jackson!" Linda pulled him away from the window and bellowed in his face. "These men volunteered to give us a fighting chance to get Omar. We have that chance right now! You, me and Frank can take him down!"

"Sir, she's absolutely right." The voice came through Jackon's earpiece and he realized that the microphone had been inadvertently triggered when Linda was spinning him around. "There were only five of them; the three of you can push up and be on them before they know what hit them. We'll hold these guys off. We've got more than enough ammo and superior positioning."

"I—" Jackson hesitated, struggling between his unwavering loyalty to those under his command and the need to capture or kill Omar. "You four stay safe and send up a flare for reinforcements; we'll be back as soon as we get him."

"Yes, sir; you got it. Stay safe, all of you."

Jackson turned to Linda and shook his head at her. "You sure you're in a condition to move out?"

She rolled her eyes and snorted at him. "Just get me a gun and point me in the right direction."

Chapter Ninety-Five

I t only takes Farhad Omar two years to rise from relatively low on the totem pole in his work to being one of the most powerful men in the Iranian military. His family's reputation combined with his education, hard work, breakthrough weapons developments and becoming close friends with the Iranian president have put him in a position where he wields an enormous amount of behind-the-scenes power. He does not use the power to further himself, choosing instead to use it in small places here and there, shaping the course of a program here and influencing a foreign policy there.

By ensuring that he remains distant and does not personally profit or benefit from the seeds he is sowing, Omar ensures that he remains in a position to reap long-term rewards, no matter the outcome. And the outcome is fierce. Through careful manipulation, falsifying of evidence, targeted hacking and advanced intelligence-gathering and disseminating actions, he is able to bring about an invasion of his home country by a potent enemy.

The orchestration of the USA's invasion of his country is the culmination of years of work. As the Iranian military works to fend off the invaders, Omar is given free reign and unlimited amounts of resources to develop ways to beat them back. Programs that would have been taboo before the invasion are encouraged and lauded, allowing him to test the initial versions of both weapons and strategies that he will use as part of his master plan years down the road.

As American tanks crush the streets to rubble under their treads and soldiers bleed and die in the mountains, fields and alleyways, Omar deploys each of his carefully planned projects. Each one violates half a dozen international rules but desperate times call for desperate measures, even when the desperate times have been generated from within. As the Americans slowly realize that they have been pulled into a war without an endgame they start to form plans to withdraw, all while the top brass quietly panics over the alarming usage of nonconventional weapons. Whispers fly both on the battlefield and back at home, speculating about the true nature of the conflict.

It takes nearly a full year for the last boots to leave the ground in Iran, crossing over the border and heading back to US bases in Iraq and Afghanistan. In that amount of time, Omar completes over seventy separate weapons and strategic tests, fifty-seven of which are unprecedented successes. The Iranian government is only aware of twenty of the tests, though that is enough for them to declare him a state hero. He declines public ovations and continues his quiet life, continuing to exert influence in the background as he studies the results of his tests, refines them and performs small-scale experiments on willing and unwilling participants.

It takes years for Omar's tendrils to fully unfurl and wind their way into all of the different corners and crevices necessary for him to carry out his desired attack on the United States. Relationships are carefully formed with key players needed to get supplies and people into the country to build bombs, plan out attack strategies and distribute virus containers to where they need to go. His slow, methodical, unwavering planning is rewarded when the country is brought to its knees in a single day.

Thanks to those in government and civilian life who are on his payroll, no one was able to anticipate an attack of such magnitude. Whispers of bits and pieces of the attack leaked through beforehand, as he suspected they would, but any information that leaked out only served to confound and befuddle law enforcement and national security agencies. The bloat of government that was put in place ostensibly to protect the country proved, in the end, to be a key factor in its downfall.

Chapter Ninety-Six

"*Shey'taan*! Damn her!" Omar's usual calm façade was completely shattered. The driver of the truck kept his eyes on the road as Omar pounded on the dashboard, howling with rage. For years he managed to keep himself focused on his task with singular devotion and purpose, but the attack at the building was the first time in years that he had such a large setback. He survived the attack and got away, but that mattered little to him due to the fact that the thorn in his side once again slipped through his fingers.

"She was *there*! She was there and I had her and now they're going to be coming after us!" Omar's scream was guttural and he slammed his palms on the dashboard again, causing the plastic to crack under the force of the blows.

"Sir, they'll never find us, you know. Even if they left right after we did, the northern safe house is far enough out that they won't locate us."

Omar growled as he rubbed his palms, trying to coax some feeling back in amongst the stinging numbness. "Just get us there now. Take every precaution along the way. We'll switch vehicles up ahead, at the depot, just to be safe."

"Absolutely, sir." The driver gulped nervously, glad that his superior was starting to calm down even while fearing another potential outburst. The three men in the back of the truck kept their weapons at the ready as they scanned the area forward, behind and to the sides of the vehicle, all while trying to ignore the shouts and screams from Omar. It had been only on the rarest of occasions that he had shown any emotions, so seeing him fly off the handle merely served to reinforce the notion that things weren't going as well as they thought.

In the front passenger seat Omar pulled a large handheld radio from his bag and thumbed the controls, first to enter his encryption code and then to key the microphone. "Sarraf. This is Omar. What's the status of the attack?"

The reply was nearly immediate. "Not good, sir! It took longer than expected to cross over the river because the rafts weren't properly secured. By the time we got across and began moving in, we took heavy fire and had to dig in."

"You haven't even made it into the city?"

"No sir, not yet. It's like… like they knew we were coming, sir!"

The driver of the truck winced, anticipating another explosion from Omar. He glanced over at his superior and saw Omar's face twisted into a mask of rage, though he made no sounds as he ground his teeth together in an effort to get himself under control. Finally, when he responded, his voice was calm and neutral, though his face was still red and twisted. "Her companion, the one these idiots let get away, must have gotten word to them." Omar took a deep breath and rubbed a hand across his weary features. "Push up as hard as you can; try to draw most of their forces to one side and see if you can get a splinter group through the perimeter. We need the codes more than anything else. Ignore all other priorities and get the codes!"

Whatever response came back through the radio was muffled by Omar throwing the device back into his bag with a heave strong enough that the driver thought it might have broken into more than a few pieces. He thought about saying something to Omar, trying to reassure him that their plans would succeed, but wisely decided against it. Omar sat in silence for the next several minutes as the truck wove a meandering path through the city.

After getting out of the tight city streets the driver headed for a nearby big box retailer that they had taken over shortly after everyone evacuated from the city proper. Large corrugated steel overhangs off the back of the store allowed them to easily hide several vehicles, and the interior of the store was used to store supplies, fuel and weapons for combatants in the area.

With the assault on the city underway, the depot was manned by a skeleton crew, and as the truck slowed to a halt Omar jumped out and gestured at the three-man group standing behind the store. "You three! Get a transport ready, load it with emergency supplies and get ready to move out!"

Though the three men were curious about why they were being ordered to abandon their post at the depot, they were well aware of the consequences of questioning an order from Omar. They moved quickly to load several crates of supplies, weapons and ammunition from inside the depot into the waiting transport, then they got in the back. At the same time, Omar and the driver of the pickup got into the front while the three men riding in the back of the pickup moved to join the other three in the back of the covered transport.

"Anything else you need, sir?" The driver looked at Omar, his hand on the ignition switch.

"No." Omar looked straight ahead and the driver pushed the button. The throaty diesel engine roared to life and they took off without a second's hesitation, continuing to head north out of the city. Once they cleared the city proper they moved to get onto smaller back roads as quickly as possible, both to avoid any possibility of being trailed and to enable them to travel at a faster rate. The main roads were still clogged with vehicles in large patches and the long, wide military transport needed more room than was offered.

The safe house had been established in the rural areas north of

Washington many months prior, purchased from a few local residents for an exorbitant amount of money funneled through three layers of shell organizations. By purchasing four different small farms and homes adjacent to each other, Omar's operatives had been able to quickly build up a cache of weapons and supplies that could sustain them indefinitely, all without anyone in the area being the wiser.

It took a solid hour for the transport to make it to the safe house, and Omar spent the time in between the depot and the safe house in complete silence, as did the driver. In the back of the covered transport the six men spoke in hushed tones with each other, speculating on what Omar was doing and how well the mission was going. Each man who worked for Omar was connected to him in some way, either owing him for an obligation or having some sort of familial connection. This helped ensure loyalty and silence, though he had used other methods to keep their mouths shut.

A steady paycheck, life-long payments to their wives and children if they were to die and a leader who was both fearless and inspired meant that Omar's followers would march after him no matter where he went. On the drive out to the safe house, though, the seven men accompanying Omar were feeling less than certain about their leader and the situation in general.

"Sir?" The driver cleared his throat. "Sir? We're here." Omar sat quietly in the passenger seat, staring off into space, until the driver tapped him gently on the arm.

"Hm? Oh. Right. Yes. Good." He jumped out of the transport and looked around at the surrounding landscape. A pair of large red barns stood nearby along with a large home that had been hastily remodeled and expanded. A pair of armed guards stood near the home, watching the transport closely in case they were needed. Woods wrapped around three sides of the home and barns while a large field extended out in front, joining up to the other three nearby properties that had been purchased. Off in the distance were pairs of guards walking the perimeter of the properties, keeping in constant communication with short-range encrypted radios.

While the home and two barns were the main location of the safe house, the other homes and outbuildings on the other three properties were by no means ignored. Food, weapons and spare parts for vehicles and machinery were spread out across the properties and each home had several cots inside both for the guards and for anyone who might need to use the safe house in the short or long term.

ATVs and small pickup trucks were used to haul large quantities of people and supplies back and forth between the buildings, but most travel across the properties was performed on foot. It was quieter, used no fuel and helped keep everyone on their toes, watching for anyone who might try and intrude.

Since the mission began there had only been two instances of people trying to cross over onto the properties, and both had been handled discreetly and without gunfire or bloodshed. Omar's instructions on that point had been very clear—the safe house couldn't remain safe long term if people started disappearing nearby. People would eventually come looking for missing loved ones, he reasoned, even during the apocalypse, and it was better to not give anyone a reason to look at the safe house.

"Sir, it's good to see you. Are you here for a quick checkup? Or something more long term?" One of the two guards near the house approached Omar and extended his hand as he spoke.

"I don't know yet." Omar ignored the proffered hand. "Help get the supplies we brought inside. Double the guard and make sure this transport and anything else that looks remotely military or different is put under cover immediately."

"Is everything all right?" The guard's question was out of curiosity, but his face turned white as Omar fixed him with a murderous gaze.

"Do what you're told unless you want to find yourself face-down in a ditch. Got it?"

The guard nodded numbly and jogged to the back of the truck to speak with the men in the back. Omar's hand fell on the pistol that he had stuck into his jacket pocket and he pulled it out, his lips twisting into a sneer. "*Shey'taan*," he whispered, "this isn't the end of things between you and me. Of that, I promise you." He slipped the pistol back into his pocket and walked toward the safe house, determined to do something about what was going on.

Chapter Ninety-Seven

"They had a weapons depot right under our noses! How the *hell* did this happen?!" Frank and Jackson stood off to the side next to the truck they had taken while Linda stormed around the vehicle they had been pursuing which was still dripping gasoline from its tank. "A weapons depot, Jackson! How did no one realize they were setting this up? Is the entire US government inept?!"

Jackson wisely chose to remain quiet during Linda's rant and rampage, choosing to look at the ground and wait for her to calm down before figuring out what to do next. Frank, on the other hand, was more impatient and spoke up. "Linda, I know this is bad, but shouldn't we be focusing on finding Omar right now instead of worrying about a weapons depot?"

Linda stopped her pacing and stared at Frank for a long moment, her jaw working furiously even as she remained quiet. Finally she took a deep breath and nodded at him as she sighed. "Yes. You're right. Sorry."

"Not your fault," Jackson replied, walking over to the other truck and peering into the front cabin. "And I hate to be the bearer of bad news, but unless you managed to punch a hole in whatever vehicle's gas tank that they took from here, I don't know how we're going to find them."

Linda glanced at Frank. "That part's easy. Frank? I need your backpack."

"My b—"

"Backpack, not twenty questions."

Frank turned and grabbed his pack from the floor of the passenger seat in the truck and held it out for Linda. She took it and set it down on the ground, unzipped it and began rifling through its contents while mumbling to herself. "If you dumped it on the ground... swear I'll skin you... ha!" She grabbed at some-thing near the bottom of the pack and pulled it out. "Here we go!"

Jackson looked over at the device in her hand and shook his head. "A tracker? Are you... you put a tracker on their truck? How is that going to help us? And how did you do it in the first place? And why weren't we following *that* instead of a freaking trail of spilled gasoline?!"

Linda chuckled and shook her head as she opened the device to reveal the screen and controls. "Jackson, I'm still half as high as a kite. It slipped my mind. But in answer to your other question, no, I didn't get a tracker on their truck." She pushed a button and the screen lit up, and she began turning the device slowly in her hands. "Omar did, however, take all of my things that were in my pockets. My knife, gun, flashlight and the tracker that was in my pouch."

A wide smile spread across Frank's face as he knelt down next to Linda and saw the indicator on the screen begin to flash. "There it is. To the north."

"Mhm." Linda tapped a few buttons and frowned. "Only problem is that it's way out there."

"How far?"

"No way to tell without moving around a bit to get some trian-gulation of the signal. It's to the north, probably a long way out of the city. Maybe at some safe house or another depot or something."

"You still want to go through with this?" Jackson stood over

Linda, looking at her with a concerned expression. "We could fall back, get reinforcements and then go after him."

"No." Linda shook her head as she closed up the tracker and stood up, cringing from a sudden pain in her chest. "We're already falling further behind. The longer we wait, the more distance and time he'll have to figure out a way to get away or to get the codes. No, we're going after him right now." She bent down to put the tracker back in the bag and couldn't stifle a groan. Frank took the device and the bag as she leaned against the truck, taking a long, slow breath.

"Meds starting to wear off, eh?" Jackson eyed her closely. "If they're far outside the city you could be coming down off the high and the meds right as we arrive."

"There's a reason why the speedballs come in threes, Jackson." Linda replied with her eyes shut as she tried to regulate her talking and breathing to minimize the pain.

"You're not taking another one of those things, Rollins!"

"We'll discuss it when we get there." Linda arched her back and pressed lightly on her chest, feeling the thick layers of bandages wrapped around her. "I'll get in the back seat and take a rest while you two get us to wherever he is."

"Linda," Frank replied with a concerned voice, "I think he might be right. We don't know how many men Omar's got with him. It could be us three against dozens of them. I think we should at least try to get a call in to the city, see if we can reach anyone and get some reinforcements sent up after us."

"I'm not wai—"

"I'm not saying we have to wait for them. But let's at least try to make a call, okay? See if we can get some people heading our direction as backup?"

Linda hesitated a few seconds before nodding. "Fine. Just do it fast." She opened the rear door on the vehicle, climbed inside and pulled the door closed, leaving Frank and Jackson to stand out on the pavement watching as she tried to find a comfortable position to rest in.

"Well, you heard the lady." Jackson nudged Frank in the side. "Let's see if anyone's still listening down there."

"I'm pretty sure I saw a radio setup inside the warehouse. It'll probably work better than the handheld units we've got."

"Good eye." Jackson nodded. "Use those cans and get the truck gassed up, then put whatever extras you can find in the back, along with any and all weapons and ammo you see lying around. I'll get on the radio and see if I can get in touch with anyone."

Fifteen minutes after heading inside the building, Jackson reemerged as Frank was finishing up tossing boxes of ammunition into the bed of the truck along with a couple of spare cans of gasoline. In the back, Linda had her eyes closed, but her facial expression made it clear that she was agitated and wanted nothing more than to get on the road.

"Everything ready?" Jackson looked in the back of the truck.

"All set. Just need to secure these cans and we can leave. Were you able to contact anyone?"

Jackson shrugged. "I'm not sure. I picked up bits and pieces of transmissions from the city but as far as actually talking to anyone? No. They had a nice little setup in there, though, so I set up a repeating loop broadcast. Hopefully our guys hear it and come after us before the bad guys do."

"I guess that's the best we can do for now."

"Are you two really going to have that conversation out there?" The door to the rear cab of the truck cracked open and Linda's voice came from within. "Let's go already!"

Jackson and Frank glanced at each other and Frank headed around to the driver's door while Jackson tried to argue in protest. "Wait, why are you driving?"

"Because I'm tired of riding shotgun on this little excursion."

Chapter Ninety-Eight

Building and successfully detonating a bomb is not an easy task. There are a hundred different factors at play and a hundred different ways that the entire process can go south. The first obstacle is often in the planning process, before materials to create the bomb have even been acquired. Aspiring bomb-makers either give up, end up killing themselves or inadvertently making contact with undercover law enforcement in their quest.

If the materials can be acquired, the bomb must then be successfully assembled. This offers yet another opportunity capture by law enforcement or death in the process of creating the weapon. While there are numerous guides and resources available for aspiring bombmakers, those that work in isolation—as many do—will often miss key aspects of the process. This can lead to failure or working with someone who turns out to be carrying a badge instead of successfully creating their explosive device.

If the device can be successfully built without causing the capture or death of its creator, the next problem is just as daunting as the previous ones: how to deploy it. Sophisticated devices involving timers or remote detonators are not only harder to build, but they involve an even greater risk since they have the potential to either be discovered or to malfunction. Deployment of an explosive device is not, contrary to what television and movies seem to think, easy. At all.

For a single individual, building and deploying explosives in a way that *doesn't involve them getting killed or caught is extremely difficult. For a small group of individuals, some parts of the job are easier while others—such as the risk of getting captured—increase.*

Unfortunately, all of these assumptions apply to situations where a single individual or small group is working in isolation and trying to stay hidden in the shadows while they assemble their materials. For someone who has virtually unlimited resources and connections, none of these assumptions apply.

It has taken years for Omar's men inside the United States to build up their cache of weapons and explosives, but they have not lacked for anything even in their isolation. Split up amongst a few dozen safe houses around the country, they have been given every luxury to ensure that they are comfortable while they work around the clock. Hundreds upon hundreds of devices are built and stored, stashed away in places that—even if the safe houses were somehow compromised—they would not lead back to the overarching plan put in place by Omar himself.

Funds are funneled into the country through shell organizations and charities while materials are either crafted on-site or come from caches that have been slowly built up over a long period of time to avoid any hint of suspicion. Morale is a chief concern for Omar, and he ensures that not only are the operatives paid well, but that their families are taken care of and that they all have every possible convenience at their disposal.

Once the devices are built, they must be deployed. This ends up being far easier than anyone could have predicted. Truck stops and weigh stations are targeted and devices are secured in place with magnets far enough inside the vehicles that they won't be discovered unless a full-blown repair was undergone. With as many targets as there are, this is a possibility, but the timetable is kept short between deployment and detonation of the bombs, and none are found.

Once enough trucks have been outfitted with the explosives over a four-day period, the plan is put into action. Each device is outfitted with a cellphone receiver cannibalized from a "burner" phone. En masse, using a simple piece of computer software, each number is dialed at the same time. The results are catastrophic. When carried out in conjunction with targeted infrastructure and viral attacks, there is no time for law enforcement on any level to carry out a response that can even begin to cope. Panic grips the throat of three hundred and fifty million people as they see millions of their own begin to die in the chaos.

The death of millions and the collapse of a country's infrastructure and sense of self was not brought about by a war or by an asteroid or by a solar flare or by an electromagnetic pulse. It was orchestrated by one man whose sheer force of will, drive and determination to seek revenge for his family drove him to commit mass murder.

One person started it all. And three now seek to end it.

Chapter Ninety-Nine

Green grass had long since given up in the face of the cold and the trees that lined the country roads were barren aside from the occasional pine that stuck out amongst the bonelike limbs of the other, leafless species. Asphalt changed to gravel which changed to dirt and then back to asphalt, stirring up stone and dust as a lone vehicle crisscrossed the back roads north of Washington.

While Omar's trip to his safe house in the rural hills and plains was relatively quick and painless, the trip carried out by those trying to follow him was anything but. It had been over an hour since they took off from the depot, and they had no solid way of knowing how close they were to locating Omar's hiding place.

The tracking device was still giving off a signal, though the unspoken worry between Frank and Jackson was whether or not it would die before they arrived. It still amazed Jackson that Omar had pocketed the tracker, and though he wondered if they might not be driving into a trap, he had to concede that it was altogether possible that the man had simply not ever seen one before.

"You thinking about the tracker again?" Frank spoke softly from the driver's seat as he glanced over at Jackson. In the back, Linda had finally fallen asleep and was snoring intermittently.

"That obvious, huh?" Jackson shook his head. "This is the only lead we've got on the man singlehandedly responsible for all of this crap and here I am looking a gift horse in the mouth."

"You're just doing your job. What you're trained to do."

"What do you think, Richards?"

Frank snorted in amusement. "I think that questions like that are way beyond my pay grade and skill level. But if Linda thinks that he's not trying to double-cross us, then I'd go with her gut instinct. She knows him better than anyone else does, I'd guess."

"What a hell of a way to live. Spending years hunting someone and he ends up doing all of this. It's a conspiracy theorist's best dream and worst nightmare all wrapped up into one."

"Heh. I just hope she can handle what's coming up next." Frank looked at Linda's still form in the rearview mirror. "He really worked her over."

"Oh, she'll be able to handle it. His best case scenario at this point is to put a bullet through his brain before she gets to him."

"No kidding."

A slight smile crossed Jackson's lips. "What's the story with you and her anyway?"

Frank felt his heart rate increase at the question. "What do you mean by story?"

"How you two managed to link up. I mean, you're not exactly… well, I mean…" Jackson fumbled with his words.

"I'm not exactly a soldier or a Marine? It's okay, Jackson. You won't hurt my feelings." Frank shook his head and smiled. "I was an accountant for years. The only trade I knew. Then, when things started going south I was laid off and spent a while out of work before I took the only job I could find—driving trucks across the country."

"Was yours one of the ones that they hit?"

"Oh yes. I happened to be getting a bite to eat—and ruining my driving stats at the same time—when it just… yeah." Frank shivered at the memory. "I was stuck up in Maine and my parents live in Texas, so I hoofed it to the closest town to try and find a way to get down there. One thing led to another, I saved her from a really pissed-off group of people at a gas station, she abandoned me in the middle of nowhere, I saved her again, yada yada yada, here I am now. Driving a military vehicle around north of D.C. searching for a terrorist."

"Not exactly what you'd pictured doing, is it?"

"It never made my top ten list, no."

Jackson chuckled and looked back down at the tracker. "Take a left up here at this next road." Frank nodded, and as they turned off onto yet another road, Jackson continued. "She likes you, you know."

Frank froze mid-turn at Jackson's words, nearly driving them off of the road before he managed to recover amidst Jackson's fruitless attempt to stifle his laughter. "What's that supposed to mean?" Frank kept his eyes on the road, trying to keep his voice level and natural and failing on both counts.

"She likes you. It's obvious. Plus I've gotten a couple earfuls from Sarah."

"I... I don't..."

"Hey, you don't have to talk to me about it." Jackson turned and looked at Linda, still sleeping in the back seat. "But it's true. She's got a thing for you."

"This really isn't..."

"There's never going to be a perfect time, Frank." Jackson's smile turned sad. "This whole mess has torn everything apart. We've all lost a lot. Just... don't waste any opportunities. Okay? She may act like she's all about the mission and the goal but there's still some emotions buried under those layers of scars and callouses. If you want to say something, then do it."

"I..." Frank struggled to find the right words before settling on the best thing he could think of. "I will. And thanks. I appreciate that."

"Yep. And hey, look at that!" Jackson jabbed a finger at the tracker's screen. "Signal's coming in way louder. I think we can get a proper triangulation on it." He pushed a few buttons on the device before looking up at the road. "Swing the next right you can. I need to get a few more readings from a different location."

"Got it. Taking a right."

AN ADDITIONAL FORTY-FIVE MINUTES PASSED, with only the occasional "take a right" or "take a left" punctuating the silence. Each time they made a new turn, Jackson would scribble on a scrap of paper lying on the dashboard, recording the signal strengths from various locations as he worked to figure out the precise location of the tracker. A map of the area was folded over next to him and had red X's in various spots.

"Which way now?" Frank eased the truck to a stop at a four-way intersection and looked over at Jackson.

"Gimme a sec." Jackson mumbled as he looked between his scrap of paper and the map before closing the tracking device and spreading the map across his legs. He used his red pencil to draw a circle around a point just to their northeast and looked up at Frank. "There. We're going there."

"You sure?"

"We've taken double the number of readings needed. So yeah, I'm sure."

"Double? You mean we could have been there by now?"

"Call me overly cautious, but I'd rather not go in with guns blazing to the wrong address."

"I... okay, yeah. So I hang a right here?"

"Yep." Jackson unbuckled his seatbelt and turned around, throwing the tracking device onto the back seat next to Linda. He dug through his bag next, pulling out spare empty magazines and lining them up on the floor in front of his seat. "I'll let you know when we get close. We need to pull over and get everything in order before we go in."

"How are we going in, exactly?"

"Good question. We don't have any satellite or drone reconnaissance of the area so we'll be going in relatively blind. It's not ideal but if he's there then we need to try to get to him. Linda's got more experience with this sort of thing so as long as she's up to it, she's going to take point and tell us what to do."

"She can certainly improvise well. Do you think she'll be up for it, even if you give her one of those shots again?"

"A speedball? Yeah. That'll get her going again for a while. It's hell on her system and terrible for her, though."

"You're not my mother, Jackson." A voice from the backseat made both Frank and Jackson turn and look at Linda.

"How you feeling?" Jackson shifted in his seat to get a better look at her as she slowly pushed herself into a sitting position.

"Like somebody spent hours punching me repeatedly."

"How're the ribs?"

"About the same. Hurts like hell every time I take a breath. How close are we? Did you find the location yet?"

Jackson folded the map over on itself and passed it back to Linda as he pointed at the red circle. "The tracker's there."

"You're certain?"

"He had us drive around long enough to take double the number of signal strength and directional readings. I'm pretty sure he's sure." Frank answered.

"Good man." Linda nodded as she examined the map. "We're almost there, I take it?"

"Ten minutes out, probably. We're going to stop soon and get everything in order." Jackson took the map back and laid it out on his lap again.

"Good, good. What's the strategy?"

Jackson and Frank exchanged a glance before the soldier turned back around. "I figured you'd want to take lead on that. You've got more experience in that sort of thing than I do, plus if I try to take point on this you'll probably end up killing me."

Linda didn't respond to the joke as she stared out through the windshield. "Well, let's see. Without recon we're going to be going in blind."

"Jackson already went through that." Frank replied. "He said we'd probably be improvising the whole way through."

"Absolutely we will. He's bound to have guards around the

property he's on, and we don't know how many buildings might be there or which one he's in. We should ambush one of the guard patrols and extract that information from them before we go in any further. The key is going to be doing it without alerting him that we're there. If we do, then he could escape again."

"Ambushing a guard patrol? What is this, some kind of spy movie?" Frank snorted in amusement as Linda began to stretch her arms and legs, groaning at the myriad of pains that made themselves known with each and every movement.

"We need info before we move in on Omar," Jackson replied, "otherwise we'll be sitting ducks."

"It sounds crazy."

"Frank, we're driving a military truck north of Washington in search of a foreign terrorist after we destroyed a mortar attack on a city, defused a nuclear bomb and survived numerous attacks. We're a little beyond crazy at this point." Linda couldn't help but crack a slight smile at how absurd it all sounded when it was jumbled up together.

"Fair point." He nodded and sighed. "Just tell me what to do."

⊏▭⊐

HALF A MILE from the location on the map, tucked behind a small shed near the edge of the road, Frank, Jackson and Linda stood around the back of the truck. They spoke in low, conspiratorial tones as they pushed bullets into magazines, checked and re-checked their weapons and carefully organized their gear in their vests and backpacks. Linda took the small black pouch containing the two remaining needles and tucked it into her pocket, promising Jackson that she would only use it when absolutely necessary. Her pain was still severe, but the brief rest she took in the back of the truck left her feeling less groggy and more alert and energized.

"The layout of all of this area seems to be the same. Fields with small patches of woods here and there." Linda looked around, confirming what she had seen during the last few minutes of their drive. "So I say we go in on foot from here, sticking to the opposite side of the road and keeping to the low points of the fields and in the trees as much as possible. As soon as we spot the first guard patrol we'll lie low until we find a good way to take them down, then I'll get as much information from them as possible."

Jackson tightened the straps on his backpack and checked that the safety on his rifle was on. "You lead and we'll follow, Rollins."

"Frank, I want you sticking to me like white on rice. Where I go, you go. Walk in my footsteps, breathe when I do and don't shoot at anything unless I tell you to. Jackson, you provide rearguard. Hang a few meters behind us and make sure we don't get surprised by anything."

Frank and Jackson both nodded and Linda picked up her rifle. Her face was rigid and she was still clearly in pain, though Frank could see a sparkle of joy in her eyes for the first time in a while. She flashed them both a grin and turned from the truck, heading toward the road.

"All right, boys. Let's go bag ourselves a terrorist."

"PERIMETER GUARDS JUST CHECKED IN, sir. They've not spotted anything abnormal."

"I want updates every ten minutes starting now." Farhad Omar sat on the edge of a folding chair in front of a table, his legs bouncing nervously. "Something doesn't feel right."

"Sir, with all due respect—"

"I suggest you choose your next words *very* carefully."

"Sir, I just... how would anyone know where we are? We weren't followed and I don't think even *she* could—"

"Assumptions are what get people killed." Omar's voice is steady, but there's an unmistakable streak of anger building at the edges. "Assumptions kill us and wreck our plans and destroy years of ceaseless work. We will *not* assume. Not about her. Have them check in every ten minutes. Understood?"

"Yes, sir. I'll let them know now." Omar's eyes track the man as he walks away, talking into his two-way radio in a low voice. In the house, Omar studies a map of the city to the south as though the bird's-eye view will give him some insight into how his rapidly depleting forces can somehow take it. Reports from those attacking the city have grown sporadic and the latest ones are not on the positive side. The man who escaped—who his men somehow allowed to escape—is more than likely responsible for warning the city about the flanking attacks. The attacks that, if they had succeeded, would have meant the final stage in his plan would have been carried out.

So many cities and so many bombs but with no way to activate them, all he could do is sit in frustration and wish that everything wasn't collapsing around him.

Chapter One Hundred

A bath. A warm bath. With bubbles, some scented candles, music and a glass of red wine, with the bottle sitting nearby. And maybe someone rubbing her feet. More than anything else in the world, Linda just wanted a bath. She had forgotten the last time that she had a proper shower under steaming hot water with something better than a bar of plain, unscented soap. Relaxing in a warm bath and letting her aching muscles relax while the water soothed them sounded like the most divine experience in the world.

"Linda." The whisper from just to her right side dissolved the daydream and returned her to reality. The cold, stiff, bruised, constantly painful reality that she was living in was in stark contrast to what she had been imagining.

"What is it?"

"Up ahead on the left. You see that guy standing out there?"

Linda hadn't been paying much attention during their half-mile walk, but at the first mention that someone else was nearby she instantly snapped into a focused, analytical state. "Good eye," she whispered to Frank and held up a fist, signaling for both him and Jackson to stop.

The man Frank had spotted was walking slowly on the inside

of the barbed-wire fence bordering the property to the left. He
wore a camouflage jacket and blue jeans along with a baseball cap.
A black rifle was balanced in his hands as he walked along, slowly
meandering alongside the fence, looking very much like he had no
particular destination or goal in mind.

"Well, well, well. Doesn't he look out of place." Linda whispered to Frank and Jackson as they both knelt down next to her
and watched the man.

"Could just be someone who lives out here," Jackson replied,
"but I wouldn't expect most folks to be dressed and armed like that
just to take a stroll around their property."

"Especially not when there's more than one." Linda pointed
out beyond the first man to another pair of figures emerging from
the trees. They were dressed in dark-colored clothing, like the first
one, and they both carried what looked like the exact same
weapons, too. The pair stopped in front of the man and one of
them pulled a radio off of his belt and held it up to his face for a
moment while looking around before finally replacing it. The three
stood there for a few more minutes before breaking off again, the
lone man turning to retrace his steps while the pair vanished back
into the woods.

"Definitely not someone who lives here. Looks like you two
found the correct place, all right."

"Is it just me," Frank asked, "or is it odd that he's by himself?
Those other two were together, so why's he alone?"

"It looks like he might be assigned to a small patrol area. They
may have a limited number of people and if they're on high alert
they could be spread too thin."

"Here," Linda slipped out of her backpack and dropped it on
the ground, "watch this. I'm going to take him down."

"No." Jackson put a firm hand on her shoulder and she
winced. "You are *not* in good enough shape to do this. I'll grab him
and bring him across the road, up there to that little barn. You two
wait for me there." The lieutenant pulled off his own backpack
and handed his rifle to Frank before drawing and checking the
ammo in his pistol.

"Good idea. Come on, Linda." Frank nudged her and she picked up her pack again as she sighed at Jackson.

"Just don't make any noise, okay?"

"I know you think I'm just a grunt, Rollins, but give me a break here." Jackson smiled. He looked across the road, watching the guard carefully. When there was a thick row of trees—including a pair of pines—in between the guard's sightline and the road, Jackson charged out at full speed, boots pounding on pavement as he crossed over and slunk into the ditch on the other side. He slowed his pace then, taking each step carefully and deliberately as he listened and watched for the guard through the branches.

The telltale sound of slow, methodical footsteps through grass and dead leaves grew louder on the other side of the trees, and Jackson could just barely make out the shape of the man through the branches as he walked along. While Jackson's OCP uniform didn't blend in perfectly with the surrounding lack of vegetation, the pair of pine trees nearby provided enough cover that he was invisible to the guard.

When the crunch of leaves grew the loudest, Jackson sprung from his crouched position and pushed through the pine branches. There was the faintest cry of surprise from the guard before Jackson bowled him over, knocking his rifle away, planting his left hand over the guard's mouth and pressing the barrel of his pistol up against the guard's temple.

"Listen to me *very* carefully. If you make a sound, you die. If you try to get away, you die. If you answer our questions, you won't die. Understand me?" Jackson had expected the guard to be old and grizzled, a hardened veteran with complete loyalty to Omar who would need to be subdued before he could be taken back across the road. What he saw instead was a young man no older than eighteen or twenty, his face a mask of pure fear and his whole body trembling. The young man nodded frightfully and his body relaxed as he submitted to Jackson's commands.

Not taking any chances, Jackson roughly pulled the man up and shoved him back through the trees. Constant, unceasing movement was necessary to keep the man off guard, confused and distracted so that he didn't try anything. Linda and Frank watched from the ditch on the side of the road as Jackson pushed the man forward, causing him to trip and fall into Frank's waiting arms where he pinned the guard down. Linda crouched next to him, her pistol pressed up against his temple. His gaze flashed between her and Frank until he finally realized who she was and he gasped and his eyes widened.

"You... you're...."

"*Shey'taan.* Yes. I am. And you are going to answer every single question I ask of you, or else I'm going to—" She growled at him and Jackson put a hand on her shoulder, interrupting her as he knelt down in the ditch.

"Rollins. Take it easy. He's just a kid."

"He's not just—"

"*Rollins.*" Jackson snapped at her and he pointed at the guard. "Look at his face."

Linda looked down at the young man, studying his expression for a long moment. Instead of the battle-hardened face of someone like Omar, she saw the panicked and terrified face of someone who had gotten caught up in something far larger than he had ever anticipated. Someone who, while certainly responsible for his decisions that led him to be working for a mass murderer, was not her direct enemy. His whole body shook under her gaze and she realized that threats would not be necessary.

"Are you going to answer my questions?" She asked him again, more forcefully than she intended. He nodded furiously, his short-cropped hair rubbing against the barrel of the pistol still pressed up next to his head.

"Good." She shifted positions, planting a knee on his chest to keep him still. She pulled the gun away from his head and aimed it down at his neck to help remind him who was in charge. "Is Omar in there?"

Another frantic nod.

"Where at?"

"Big house. Quarter of a m—mile back or so. Next to a r—red and white barn."

"How many guards are patrolling?"

"A d—dozen."

"Including you?"

"Yes."

"How many are solo, like yourself?"

"Most of them. Th—there aren't enough people to patrol everything properly."

"Is there another fallback location he might try to retreat to?"

"I… I don't know. I'm just a—"

"What types of weapons does he have on hand? Any RPGs or mounted LMGs?"

"A few RPGs in storage, yes. A pair of surface to air launchers, I think."

"Good. Last question. And this one's going to be the difference between a long stay in a cell and a bullet in your brain. You want the bullet in your brain?"

A frantic, panicked shaking of his head came next.

"What's the most direct route to the house where he's located? How do we avoid the patrols and get there undetected?"

"I don't know the routes, I—I'm sorry. Please don't kill me. Please!" Tears formed in the man's eyes and Linda rolled her own in response. "Jackson, tie him up and gag him. Leave him here. He'll be hidden from anyone who goes by, at least long enough for us to take care of our business."

Jackson nodded and dug through his bag as he traded places with Linda to guard the man. Linda whispered to Frank as she moved away from them. "You think he was telling the truth?"

"I think he probably pissed himself at the sight of you. What's that shay-ten thing he called you?"

"*Shey'taan*. Arabic for Satan. Omar's called me that for years." She snorted and grinned. "I can't say that I mind it too much, all things considered. Especially now that we're about to catch up with him."

"Don't get cocky, okay? We've still got a lot more ground to cover. Plus a dozen guards on patrol, and who knows how many more at the house with him."

"Mhm." Linda nodded slowly. "I think I might have an idea for that. I'll need to talk with Jackson first, though."

"Talk to me about what?" Jackson slunk over to Linda and Frank, then glanced back at the man who was thoroughly bound and had a thick gag shoved into his mouth with tape wrapped around his ears and face, leaving just a pair of holes for him to breathe through his nose.

"You have C4 with you, right?"

"Two blocks with a pair of detonators."

"What's the range on them?"

"Well, they're remote detonators so... whatever you want, within reason. Why?"

"Eleven more guards is going to be a lot to deal with. We can try sneaking past them, but I think we could do something a little more flashy and have a better chance at success."

"Rollins..." Jackson's voice was full of trepidation. "What are you thinking about?"

Linda smiled, all of her pain and discomfort temporarily forgotten as her mind churned with the final details to the plan she was thinking up. The hardest part of it, she realized, would be convincing Jackson that it could work.

Chapter One Hundred One

"Let's do it."

"Look, just hear me—wait, what?"

"Let's do it." Jackson repeated his statement as he shifted positions on his knees, all three of them still crouched in the ditch on the opposite side of the road from the property on which Omar was hiding.

"I... okay, I didn't expect that." Linda shook her head, wondering if she had suffered some sort of brain injury that was making her hallucinate Jackson's agreement with her admittedly borderline insane plan.

Jackson slunk back down the ditch and grabbed the legs of the guard they had captured and pulled him toward Linda and Frank. The guard's eyes went wide with fear and he started shaking his head, fully expecting that his captors had changed their mind about letting him live. Instead, though, Jackson removed the man's gag and roughly pulled him into a sitting position.

"Listen up. I want the exact location of the house where Omar's staying. I want to know the lay of the land between the edge of the road here and the house. Is it a field? Are there trees?

Any big holes? Any fences? What's around the house itself? You tell me everything you know, got it?"

The guard nodded and began talking at a rapid pace, telling them everything he could think of that might be relevant to Jackson's demand. The trio listened closely for a few minutes until the guard wound down, then Jackson roughly put the gag back in. "Good job. Stay here and don't try anything stupid."

Jackson, Linda and Frank all moved down away from the guard and Linda spoke first. "You still sure about this, Jackson?"

"It sounds like a straight shot between here and the house. By the time you two get into position I'll be back with the truck and we can get this show on the road."

"Honk three times before you turn in, okay? Let us know that you're starting your run."

"Three times, yep. Will do."

"Good. And stay safe. That thing's not bulletproof."

"Relax, I'll be fine."

"See that you are. We'll start moving out now." Linda looked at Frank, who nodded at her.

"I'm ready when you are."

With one final exchange of looks between the three, Jackson turned and began jogging back toward where they had left the truck. Frank and Linda, meanwhile, headed in the opposite way down the ditch. Frank was in the lead and continued on while Linda took a few seconds to stop and kneel down next to the guard, whispering in his ear before getting up and following after Frank. The guard's face, which already looked like he was scared half to death, turned pale. As the trio split up he stayed motionless on the ground on the ditch, too frightened to do anything but blink and take shallow breaths through his nose.

Frank glanced back at the guard as Linda caught up with him and raised his eyebrow. "What on earth did you say to him?"

Linda gave a coy smile and shrugged. "They call me *Shey'taan* so I'm just embracing it."

"You're terrible."

"Not nearly as much as they are. Now come on; we need to

pick up the pace if we're going to get into position before Jackson gets back."

━━━

THE TRUCK BARRELED down the road, the engine roaring as Jackson kept the accelerator pressed down against the floor. There was no more pretense of stealth as he followed the curve of the asphalt, preparing to make his move from on-road to off-road. His rifle sat on the floor of the passenger seat nearby and his backpack was in the rear seat. His vests were stuffed full of mags for his rifle as well as a small plastic and metal device with a handle, short antenna and pair of buttons.

Sitting on the dashboard—secured against the movement of the truck by several strips of tape—was a tan block with a small antenna and electronics housing mounted to one end. A pair of wires led from the housing to a detonator buried in the tan block. Despite the fact that the C-4 was incredibly stable, Jackson couldn't help but feel nervous and glance at it with each bump and sharp turn he took in the truck, as though they could somehow trigger the blasting cap.

"Here goes nothin'." Jackson turned the wheel and guided the truck at an angle over the ditch on the left side of the road, cringing as it groaned from the bumps and jostling. Saplings and tall, brown stalks of grass slapped the underside of the truck and the noise from the road vanished, replaced by the soft thumping of dirt and debris as the wheels fought for traction amid the leaves, sticks and loose earth.

"Straight across the field, take a left at the first fence." Jackson mumbled to himself as he drove along, repeating what the guard had told them about the location of the house. Trusting an enemy combatant for information on said combatant's superior wasn't the most reliable way of getting intel, but given their situation and the time crunch they were under, it was all that they had to go on.

Jackson kept the truck moving at a slow but steady clip as he tried to keep from rattling the vehicle apart. There had been no sign of guards near the road or in the field, and as he approached a line of trees with a fence nearby he turned to the left to swing around the fence and had his first direct encounter with a patrol.

Gunfire exploded out from the trees, punching holes in the doors on the passenger side of the truck and shattering the glass in the rear right window. Jackson ducked low in his seat and pushed hard on the accelerator, trying to get out of the line of fire. Two men stepped out of the line of trees as the truck roared by, rifles to their shoulders as they continued to fire, though most of the rounds failed to connect. Those that did plinked harmlessly off the back of the truck.

As the trees thinned out into brush and saplings, Jackson pulled the wheel hard to the right, intending to go around the trees and use them as cover as he continued speeding toward the house. The sight of a trio of armed men running across the field made him spin the wheel back in the other direction as he veered away from them. They opened fire, sending more rounds into the truck, and he felt a searing pain in his right arm as one nicked him near the shoulder and two others hit the dashboard, with one slicing through the upper portion of the tan brick of C-4.

"Dammit!" Jackson shouted as he pushed the truck to go even faster while he swerved back and forth to try to make himself harder to hit. As he crested a small hill, he saw a large house and barn that the guard had described loom into view and a rush of fear seized his gut. Somewhere inside was the man that they had been hunting, the one who had caused so much damage and destruction, and Jackson wasn't nearly ready enough to face him.

Pulling the wheel to the left, he pointed the truck toward the nearby woods just as the doors to the barn off to his right flew open, revealing a small tracked vehicle with a heavy machine gun mounted on the top. The vehicle pulled out of the barn with surprising nimbleness and speed and the gun rotated around at the direction of a man standing atop the vehicle and opened fire on Jackson's truck.

Unlike the smaller 7.62 rounds fired from the guards' weapons, the vehicle-mounted gun fired .50 BMG rounds which tore through the truck like it was made out of tissue paper. Jackson yelped in surprise and veered off to the left, driving away from the house and barn as the vehicle and several guards from patrols and from near the house followed in pursuit. His truck slowed as it neared the woods and turned again, to the right, before continuing onward and smashing around a tree. A few seconds after the impact, the smoking and bullet-riddled vehicle exploded with a deafening roar that shook the trees for miles around.

Even though those in pursuit of the truck were a fair distance away, they couldn't help but shield their eyes and pull back a few paces as the truck vanished in a massive fireball. The tracked vehicle, having driven too close to the truck after it crashed, was caught in the blast and torn apart as the gunner went spinning off of his perch out into the field. Pieces of metal flew in all directions, and several nearby trees virtually disintegrated as they split apart at their bases, sending wood and sap raining down for a good hundred feet in every direction. The heat from the blast was intense, and it made it impossible for the guards to get close.

They formed a half-circle around the truck at a distance instead, keeping their weapons closely trained on it as though the driver could have somehow survived the impossible and might come crawling out at any second. Minutes ticked on as the flames slowly spread through the trees, prompting the guards to fetch water hoses and fire extinguishers to try and slow its spread, but there was still no sign of Lieutenant Jackson.

AS JACKSON WAS NEARING where they had left the truck, Frank and Linda were already deep inside the boundaries of the property where Omar was hiding. They had made a beeline along the road to the north, slipping past one two-man patrol and venturing toward what they hoped was the northern side of the main house. The guard had described the house as having thick woods on nearly three sides, and up ahead in the distance Linda and Frank could see the trees growing thicker as they angled back toward the south.

Both Frank and Linda walked along in silence, saving their energy for their quick pace that occasionally sped up to a jog before winding back down to a walk. As the brush and trees grew thicker the closer they got to the woods, the slower they were forced to go. It seemed like no one had taken care of clearing out the area in years, and every step was one filled with scratches and scrapes.

Linda took the lead as they closed in on the house, and as they left the field and smaller trees behind for the mature woods, she suddenly stopped and knelt down, motioning for Frank to do the same. He squatted down just behind her and whispered in her left ear.

"What's going on?"

She shook her head at him, wanting him to keep quiet, then motioned up ahead with a tilt of her neck. Frank straightened his back, looking over her to get an eye on what she was seeing, then immediately ducked back down as he saw it. He nearly muttered under his breath but kept quiet instead, cursing silently instead.

A pair of men dressed in thick jackets, camouflage pants and carrying rifles were walking through the forest, heading directly for where Linda and Frank were kneeling. The brush in the woods had thinned out, making it easier to walk through and offering less options for concealment. As the men got closer, Linda adjusted her grip on her rifle, unsure of what to do. Firing her rifle so close to where Omar was supposed to be would alert him, but if she didn't do something then the men would see her and Frank before they got much closer.

Just as she was about to stand and fire on them, the two guards stopped in their tracks and turned around, leaned up against a pair of trees and began quietly talking to each other as they broke out a pair of cigarettes and a lighter. Their behavior made it obvious that they weren't supposed to be taking a smoke break, but Linda didn't mind a bit. She slipped her rifle strap off of her shoulder and passed the weapon to Frank before she crept forward, her right hand going to the knife strapped to the small of her back.

With the breeze already creating a fair amount of background noise, Linda's quiet steps through the damp leaves and dirt underfoot were barely audible, and neither of the guards noticed her presence until the one closest to her had his throat slit from one side to the other. His partner fumbled with his rifle as he dropped his cigarette, but Linda was on him in a flash, covering his mouth with one hand while plunging the knife between his ribs and deep into his heart. She sat atop him for a moment, holding him down until he stopped thrashing, then she slowly stood up and put a hand against her chest.

Frank was about to speak when the sound of a huge explosion made him instinctively duck down. A brief flash of light shone through the trees and he turned to Linda. "Holy…" Frank's eyes were wide as he whispered to her. "You think that was Jackson?"

Linda nodded, closing her eyes and taking another slow, deep breath. "Probably."

"I hope he's okay." Frank looked out in the direction of where the sound had originated, then he looked back at Linda and saw the look of pain on her face. "What's wrong?"

"It hurts. Bad." She held out her hand, motioning with her fingers. "Get in my pack and get out the black case, the one with the syringes."

"Are you sure? Jackson said—"

"I swear if you don't hand me that case you're going to wake up on the ground a week from now wondering what hit you."

"Okay, okay!" Frank shrugged in surrender and leaned her rifle against a nearby tree before unzipping her backpack and retrieving the black case containing the two remaining syringes. Linda nodded her thanks as she opened the case, rolled up her sleeve and got a syringe ready.

"The house can't be much farther ahead. Give me two minutes to deal with this and then we'll move in." She glanced at her watch. "Jackson should be in position to assist here in a few minutes, too."

"Just tell me what to do if you need help." Frank watched as she pushed the tip of the needle into her vein and slowly injected the potent mixture. She pulled the needle out and put it back in the black case, which Frank put back into her pack, and it only took another moment for her to feel the effects. She leaned against a tree to steady herself as a feeling of euphoria rushed through her head. The pain in her chest began to melt away and she felt energized and ready to conquer the world. She took her rifle and looked at Frank, giving him a determined nod.

"Let's finish this."

Chapter One Hundred Two

W hile the lack of gunfire involved in taking out the pair of guards on their smoke break helped to hide the advance of Linda and Frank at first, the massive explosion did most of the work in keeping them concealed. All of the guards on the property came running toward the noise, and though Frank and Linda had to duck down and stay still a few times to avoid being seen, they were able to make progress toward the house in a safe and fast fashion.

At the edge of the woods they pushed up against a pair of large oak trees, keeping low and behind scraggly brush and bushes. The flames from the explosion were licking at the trees farther away in the woods, down to the south and west of the house, and the source of whatever had blown up wasn't visible.

What was visible, however, was the house itself and the collection of guards wearing military-style gear who surrounded an unarmed man. The guards and the man were staring at something off in the distance, and the man was gesticulating wildly as he shouted orders. It took Linda a moment to realize that the man was, in fact, Omar, but when she recognized him she raised her rifle. Frank saw the motion out of the corner of his eye and turned to warn her not to shoot. It was too late, though, and a single shot rang out just as Omar began to turn back to the house with his entourage.

One of the guards who had been standing just next to Omar toppled to the ground, blood spilling from a hole in his head. The other five guards turned in unison toward the direction of the shot and opened fire without hesitation, sending their shots wildly into the woods. Frank pulled Linda back just before she could be spotted and they sat behind the oaks as rounds whizzed past.

Frank looked over at Linda with wide eyes, not daring to speak as the guards continued to fire. She shook her head at him in return and he shrugged, not knowing what to do. She motioned with her hands and head, pantomiming returning fire, then held up five fingers and began to mouth out a countdown. Frank took a deep breath, waited until she mouthed "one," peeked out from behind his tree and opened fire.

Linda was able to drop two more guards and Frank winged a third before the surviving three guards made their way back around the house and into cover. The few seconds of respite from the hail of gunfire was immediately punctuated by more from the southwest, off toward where the explosion had occurred. The patrols and guards near the house that had been focused on the wreckage of the truck were drawn up closer to the house by the gunfire and the shouts from the three survivors still behind the house.

Frank dug his back into the oak, shielding himself from the house as he began firing on the enemies advancing through the edge of the woods, sending them scrambling for cover as they split up and branched out, looking to flank the pair. Linda, meanwhile, stayed focused on the trio around the side of the house and managed to take another one of them down with a round through the head before a spray of heavy fire from an upper floor of the house drove her back behind the tree.

"Linda!" Frank shouted at her over the staccato gunfire. "We're getting surrounded! There's too many of them out in the woods!"

He fired again, grunting in satisfaction as he finally dropped one of the advancing guards.

"Don't stick your head out around the trees; Omar's got someone upstairs shooting down. We can't fight that kind of elevated fire until we get the ones in the woods cleared out!" She squeezed one eye halfway shut and aimed down her sight, trailing the scope across a runner in the woods before firing three times. He fell with a scream and she ducked down into the scrub as return fire peppered the area. Even as the man fell, three more took his place, and soon all Frank and Linda could do was press themselves to the ground and take a few potshots all while hoping that a stray round wouldn't slice into them.

"We're in trouble here!" Frank shouted at Linda.

"No kidding!" She rolled her eyes as she fired from a prone position, tearing bits of bark and wood from a distant oak. The guard she was firing at crouched out of sight and she crawled forward into some thicker brush. "Just try to keep them pinned down! Maybe we'll get lucky or something!"

The heavy thumping and snapping of the 7.62 rounds continued unabated for another moment until, off in the woods, Linda's ears perked up at a new sound. Lighter and snappier than the guards' weapons, it came in bursts a few seconds apart and seemed to be changing position rapidly, like the bearer of the weapon was moving through the trees at a breakneck pace. Shouts went up a moment later and the gunfire that had been solely directed at Frank and Linda's position was suddenly redirected, offering them a welcome reprieve.

"Frank!" Linda shouted at him as she pushed herself up on one knee. "Start taking them out!"

"Are you crazy? They're just going to shoot us once we stand up!" Frank lifted his head, but still kept his body pressed to the ground."

"It's Jackson! He's coming in on their rear! Come on!" She stood and fired, then ran forward to a nearby tree and fired again, taking out two of the guards who had spun around to hide from the surprise attack, exposing themselves to Frank and Linda's position.

Frank stood up, took aim and fired at another guard who was running and downed him, then Frank joined Linda and they began to advance, each covering the other while they advanced. The rapid-fire bursts of their weapons soon drowned out the heavier fire from the guards, and in less than a minute they had managed to down the last of the guards in the woods, all while staying in cover from the ones still at the house.

"Rollins! Richards!" A familiar voice came from farther out in the woods.

"Jackson?" Linda shouted back as gunfire from the house cracked through the trees. She and Frank both ran forward before a hand reached out for Frank to grab and pull him down to the ground. Linda skidded to a halt and dropped as well, then crawled forward to sit next to Frank and Jackson.

"Glad you two are still alive." Jackson smiled broadly as he ejected a near-empty mag from his rifle and slammed a new one home. "I was worried you might not make it."

"Everything went according to plan for us, or close enough for government work at least." Frank looked Jackson over. "You look like you had it worse than us."

"Ha." Jackson rubbed his face, wiping off a mixture of sweat, soot and blood. "The explosion was larger than I thought. I jumped out without being seen, but I should have gotten farther away before I set off the C-4. A piece of the door nicked me on the head; that's why it took me so long to get back to you."

"You did great, Jackson." Linda leaned around the tree. "And the best part is that Omar's still in the house."

"He'd better be. I blew out the tires on the couple of vehicles they had around the front of the house before I started my run through the woods. If he's going to flee, it'll have to be on foot."

"We still have three around the front of the house to deal with, plus an unknown number guarding him inside." Linda looked around the tree again. "We should split up and flank through the woods. You head back southwest with Frank while I go around the other side. We'll meet on the field side of the house." Linda took off without waiting for a confirmation, heading through the woods to circle wide around the house.

"You got it, ma'am." Jackson smiled again and looked at Frank. "Let's get moving and try to get a few shots in before she merc's them all."

<hr>

"*KILL HER!*" The absence of gunfire in the woods had driven Omar's rage to new heights. His eyes were wide, veins on his forehead and neck were bulging and his voice cracked as he screamed at the six men who were still inside the house. The three outside could hear him and they opened fire as well, though peppering the trees at random was the best they could do considering they had no visual on their targets.

"Sir, we need to get you into the panic room." One of the guards pleaded with Omar, speaking to his superior in a calm tone even as gunfire drowned out most of his words.

"I'm not hiding in a damned hole!" Spittle flew from Omar's mouth as he shouted. "Not today and not any day! There's only two or three of them out there! Why can't you just *kill them*?!"

"We think one of them died in the vehicle explosion, sir. So there should only be two left alive."

"That's not very comforting, considering one of them is *her*!" Omar threw his hands in the air and stalked over to a nearby window that overlooked the woods. A short distance away, down from the house and barn, the wrecks of the truck and tracked vehicle still burned, as did a portion of the woods and grass. The ground was heavily laden with moisture, keeping the fire from burning fast and hard and reducing the risk of the home being turned into an inferno.

"Sir, please." The guard pulled Omar away from the window. "You need to stay away from the windows. We're watching them carefully. If they move close, we'll know."

"What word is there on the city assault?"

The guard who had been talking to Omar nervously glanced at another guard at a nearby window. News from the city had not been good, but he was loath to admit that fact to Omar. "No word yet, sir." The guard lied through his teeth, forcing a slight smile. "But no news is good news, as the Americans say."

"Not for my operations it isn't." Omar growled at him. "Keep watching. I'm going to make a call to the forces myself." As he left to head downstairs to where the radio equipment was kept, the guard who had been speaking to him breathed a sigh of relief and headed over to the window.

"You shouldn't have told him that, you know." The guard at the window whispered.

"I'm not about to take any more heat over this… what do they call it?"

"A 'cluster' I think?"

"It most certainly is."

"You think we'll make it out of this alive?"

The first guard sighed and leaned his head against the window frame, closing his eyes in frustration. "I don—"

His reply was cut off by the sound of shattering glass and a second later he dropped to the floor with a bullet hole cutting through his right eye.

⬛▭▭▭▭⬛

"TWO DOWN INSIDE, ONE DOWN OUTSIDE!" Frank as he and Jackson took cover behind the barn. A smattering of gunfire peppered the corner of the barn and the ground, but none hit either of the men. Return fire erupted from the far side of the house and Frank peeked out to see another one of the outside guards fall over, his rifle spilling from his grasp. "Make that two down outside. There's got to be four, maybe five or six more inside though."

"You move up next, I'll provide suppressing fire. How's your ammo situation?"

"I've got a few mags left."

"Good. Once you get to the edge of the house, stay low and hit the upstairs windows with whatever you can so I can make it across."

"Got it."

On the count of three, Frank sprinted across the short distance between the house and the barn while Jackson popped out from behind cover and peppered the upstairs windows with automatic fire. He didn't see anyone in the windows who might have been hit but didn't have time to look for long. As soon as Frank reached the side of the house he began firing upward, sending rounds smacking against the window frame while Jackson followed in a sprint.

A shout came from around in front of the house, followed by a burst of gunfire, and a figure staggered out from cover, clutching at a spreading stain of red growing across his chest. A second figure came out behind the first, stumbling backward with his hands in the air as rounds tore through his stomach and chest, sending him to the ground howling in pain. Linda came stalking around the corner, rifle held at the ready against her shoulder, dropping the barrel as she spotted Frank and Jackson.

"You two all right?"

"We're good. Is the front clear?"

"Clear. Time to head inside." She turned around before Frank or Jackson could respond and headed toward the front door. "I'll lead the way. Jackson, help me check corners. Frank, stay behind us and watch our backs. If anything moves, shoot it."

Jackson fell in behind Linda, grateful that she was taking point. It had been a long time since he had last gone through a training course on how to clear a structure, but his muscle memory was good. She swept to the right while he stayed a step behind, sweeping to the left as they pushed through the front door, staying in a staggered formation.

The house was dimly lit, but there was no initial sign of enemies as they pushed forward, cheeks pressed against their rifles and fingers hovering close to triggers. Linda swung to the right, checking inside a small half bath while Jackson covered to the left, checking a corner of a living room. "Clear." She and he both whispered to each other as they moved along, keeping their steps light as they checked behind furniture and around edges of walls for any threats.

"There!" They had been in the house for less than a minute when Frank suddenly shouted and fired a burst between Jackson and Linda. They whirled to see where he had been aiming as a body fell off of the last few steps of a staircase, a pair of rounds through the man's face. Linda moved forward to get a different angle on the stairs while Jackson nodded at Frank.

"Nice work."

Frank started to thank him when Linda opened fire and ran back around to the side of the stairs, screaming at the top of her lungs. "Grenade! Get down!" She flung herself to the floor on the far side of the room as Jackson pushed Frank over on top of her, then laid himself flat on both of them. The explosion came a second later in the form of a blast of heat and shards of metal, wood, cloth and carpeting went flying in all directions. Frank was stunned by the blast but Jackson was already up nearly before it was over, moving down the living room to change angles on the staircase and get a view on what was going on.

Gunfire erupted from the base of the stairs and Jackson shouted in pain as three rounds lanced through his shoulder. His rifle dropped from his grasp and he fell to one knee behind a sofa as a group of men descended the stairs, firing in Jackson's direction. Frank pulled himself off of Linda and helped her sit up as the group continued firing, and Linda grabbed her rifle as she tried to orient herself after the loud explosion.

"A little help here!" Jackson's cries for assistance attracted her attention and she turned to see rounds tearing through the sofa, then directed her attention at the assailants. Three men stood at the base of the stairs, all in a row, and she took down two of them herself while Frank fired on the third. As they collapsed, the sound of metal scraping on metal came from the room behind them and Linda looked over at Frank.

"Go get Jackson!" She whispered to him and crept forward through the room, stepping over the bodies and through the door next to the base of the stairs. It looked like the room beyond had once been a sitting or reading room, or perhaps a second living room, at least until Omar got his hands on the place. The floor, walls and ceiling had all been torn apart, and in their place were thick pieces of plate steel that formed a large box that consumed a good two to three hundred square feet of space.

"What the…" Linda raised an eyebrow as she looked at the welded and riveted steel plates in front of her. It took a moment for her to realize what she was looking at, and she chuckled with no small amount of delight. "It's a safe room. He put in a safe room."

"Linda!" Frank's call sent her hurrying back to the main living room where Frank was working to get Jackson up onto a chair. The lieutenant's face had gone pale and his shoulder, arm and half of his torso was stained dark red with blood.

"Holy crap, Jackson; you look awful." Linda knelt down next to him and glanced up at Frank. "The house should be clear but I need you to stand guard at the stairs and make sure nobody comes down them, or out of the room next to them, got it?" Frank nodded and backed off while Linda fished a medical kit out of her backpack and used her knife to cut open his uniform, exposing his wounds.

A pair of rounds had passed through and through his right shoulder while the third had nicked the top of it. The damage wasn't bad but the bleeding was still heavy and she worked with gauze and bandages, stuffing them into and around the wound to slow the bleeding. When she had thoroughly packed the bullet holes she wrapped the bandages in tape and Jackson opened his eyes, breathing heavily.

"How bad is it, Rollins?"

"You're going to hurt like the dickens for a while. But you'll live."

"What about Omar?"

She turned to look over at Frank and the bodies that were next to his feet. "I'm pretty sure those three were distracting us while Omar got to his safe room."

"Safe room? You mean he's trapped?"

"Could be. Only one way to be sure, though."

"Linda." Jackson reached out and grabbed her arm, shaking his head. "Wait till backup arrives. If he's in there then he won't be going anywhere."

Linda shook off Jackson's grip. "Not happening, Jackson. I don't know if he's in there and we're not going to stand around for who knows how long waiting for backup if there's a chance he might escape. No, I'm blowing it open."

"Are… you mean with… you'll take down half the house!"

Linda shrugged. "Maybe. Still worth it." She turned to Frank, ignoring Jackson's protests. "Frank, I need you to get Jackson outside, okay? Get to the far side of the barn."

"What's going on?"

"That big steel box in there is a safe room. Omar's inside and we're going to crack it open like a can of tuna."

"Only if you open your tuna with a stick of dynamite!" Jackson protested, his voice weak and full of pain. "Rollins, come on, be reasonable!"

Frank stared into Linda's eyes for several seconds before nodding. "Fine. I'll get him to a safe spot. Then I'm coming back in to help you."

"Frank, I don—"

"Argue with me and I'll shoot you in the knees and drag you out, too." Frank growled at her. "You're not doing this by yourself. Got it?"

She sighed and rolled her eyes. "Fine. I'll get started, but you'd better hurry."

As Frank helped Jackson hobble back through the house, outside, past the bodies near the front door and over on the other side of the barn, the lieutenant spoke sparingly. "Have her cut down on the amount she uses. If she uses the whole block she'll kill him if he's inside. And make sure you watch that the timer's set properly; they can be a little bit finicky. Also, target a weak spot or a corner, so it'll crack open instead of just tearing and twisting the metal like it would if you hit it in the center. Look for the door and plant it there if—"

"Holy cow, Jackson, just take a deep breath." Frank lowered Jackson into a sitting position just at the edge of the barn and gave him his rifle. "She's been after this guy for years. She won't screw this up. I'm sure of it."

"Give 'em hell, Frank. From all of us. Make sure she doesn't kill him, though. He needs to answer for everything he's done."

INSIDE, in front of the steel box, Linda whistled cheerfully as she worked with the pliable block of C-4. She cut into it with her knife, pulling off several large slices until it was small enough that she didn't think it would kill Omar when it went off. As she placed it on the thick steel door built into the box she began humming to herself, stopping only when she heard footsteps in the next room. She stopped working and aimed her pistol at the doorway only to put it back away when Frank appeared.

"How's it going?" He walked into the room and stared in awe at the steel structure.

"Nearly done."

"Jackson said to make sure—"

"Jackson's a great guy, Frank, but I've been doing this kind of thing a lot longer than he has, okay? Just relax."

"So what's going to happen when you trigger the explosive?"

"It'll go off, hopefully blow the door here off and concuss the rat inside long enough for us to get back in and grab him before he dies from whatever injuries he might sustain."

"You sure you're okay?" Frank patted her on the shoulder and she looked up at him.

"I've been chasing him for years, Frank. And now he's finally here, trapped inside this room. I'm better than okay." She grinned at him and stood up to admire her handiwork. "Good. We're all set. You ready for this?"

Chapter One Hundred Three

The explosion was more muffled than Frank had expected it to be, especially when compared with the one that had destroyed the truck earlier. That one had been massive, sending out a wave of sound and heat that could be heard and felt for a huge distance. The one inside the house was different, though. It was quieter, more subdued—as much as an explosion could be—and contrary to what he was expecting, it didn't appear to do any damage to the house itself.

Standing out in front of the house, Linda turned and charged inside as soon as the explosion went off, not even waiting to see if the structure would withstand the blast. Frank hesitated to go in after her and looked over at Jackson, who had pulled himself up and was leaning against the entrance to the barn.

"Get in there!" Jackson shouted to Frank, who nodded and ran in through the front door after Linda. Smoke filled the entire house, growing thicker the farther they moved toward the back room, but Linda paid it no mind. She pushed forward with a purpose and moved past the stairs to see what the explosive had done to the safe room. The sound of someone coughing echoed against metal and Linda inched forward with Frank on her side.

"Omar!" Linda roared, ignoring the stinging in her eyes and throat. "Farhad Omar!" She took a few more steps deeper into the smoke and dust, all but vanishing from Frank's sight. Seven shots rang out, one after the other, and they were immediately followed by a burst of three rounds and a howling cry of pain.

"Linda!" Frank rushed into the smoke after her, fearing the worst. In the thick of the smoke he made out a form standing tall over another lying on the ground. The standing one turned to him and he saw a flip of hair and he lowered his rifle, glad he had taken the extra second before shooting. "Are you all right?" He asked her as he stepped closer, dust still swirling in the air."

"Yep." Linda held out her rifle to him and he accepted it, then she took a step forward and he heard another cry of pain in a language he didn't understand. "He's not doing so hot, though."

Frank squinted, peering through the smoke-laden air, and saw a figure lying on the ground with Linda's boot on his chest. A red stain was spreading across the figure's shoulder and leg and he began talking in Farsi. Linda leaned over and grabbed his injured arm, pulling him to his feet even as he screamed and bucked against her.

"Get your filthy hands off me, *shey'taan!*" His injuries didn't seem to matter much to him as he thrashed and kicked against Linda's pull. She lashed out with a boot to his injured leg and he cried out again, nearly collapsing to the floor as she pulled him out of the safe room and into the living room, then outside just beyond the front door.

Free of the smoke, dust and darkness of the house, Frank could see that the injured man was in rough shape. He was bleeding from a head injury sustained during the explosion, his breathing was ragged, his clothes were stained with dirt and blood and all he could do when Linda threw him to the ground was writhe around, unable to push himself even into a sitting position.

Linda drew her pistol from her holster and stood over Omar, aiming it with a steady grip at his head. His defiance knew no limits and he spat at her, then groaned and coughed from the effort, trying to crawl away. She put her boot back on his chest and pressed down hard, leaning over to keep the pistol pointed at his forehead.

"Farhad Omar. Nice to see you again."

"Bitch." He wheezed out the word in between shallow breaths that were growing more painful as she dug her boot deeper into his chest.

"Oh come on. Surely you can do better than that." She put more weight on her foot, grunting with satisfaction as pain spread across his face and a faint cracking sound came from his chest. The pistol wavered ever so slightly in her grasp as rage began to build inside of her, borne of years' worth of frustrations and fruitless pursuits. Her finger began to tighten around the trigger when a shout from behind made her turn.

"Rollins!" Jackson came out of the front of the barn, rifle slung over his shoulder. "Don't shoot him!"

"Why the hell not?!" She turned back to look at Omar.

"Backup's just a few minutes out! We need to take him in, Rollins!" Frank hurried over to Jackson's side and put an arm around the lieutenant, helping him walk over to Linda. "They have a radio setup in the barn and I used it to call the city." He placed a hand on her back, but she made no motion to lower her weapon. "It's over."

"Over?" She asked.

"Yes, over. The last of the forces he sent failed. They're all dead or on the run." Jackson tried to reach for her arm but she pushed him away, keeping the gun aimed at Omar's head.

"You... think that means this is over? No. It's never over. Not until he's paid." Tears of intense anger and sadness were beginning to form in her eyes.

"It's over, Linda." Jackson spoke softly, trying to reason with her. "And now he needs to be taken in so we can get information from him and then put him on trial."

"Trial? What trial? The country's in shambles, Jackson! It'll be years—decades maybe—before we're put back together enough to even function, much less have a trial for someone like him." She looked down at Omar, adjusting the grip on her pistol. "No.

We do this now and make sure he doesn't get to see another sunrise."

"If we don't uphold the law for men like him, then he wins. We are who we are because no matter how bad things get, we still hold to our principles."

"Ha." Frank shook his head. "Been a long time since we acted like that, even before all this."

"But," Jackson shot Frank a look, "we need to do it now. We have to uphold justice, even for him."

"Justice right now means a bullet through his head." Linda growled. "Besides, what does justice matter when he's already won?"

"He hasn't won. Not if you put the gun down."

"She's right, you know. I did win." Omar's eyes fluttered open and a thin smile spread across his lips as he looked at Jackson. "I didn't have to kill everyone. I just had to incite enough terror for you to tear yourselves apart at the seams. It's been done before, just not to this degree. I didn't create this apocalypse. You did. *You* were the fuel. I merely lit the match."

"Close your trap." Linda pushed down harder on his chest and he spasmed, coughing violently under the pressure and pain. "He's right, though, Jackson."

"It doesn't matter." Jackson still kept his voice level and calm. "You have a choice to do the right thing or the wrong thing right now."

"*Years*, Jackson!" Linda yelled, her voice carrying across the open fields. "I've been after him for *years*! My unit was slaughtered! He's experimented on countless others and he brought us to our knees! And now you want me to let him *live*?" Her arm wavered more and the pistol swayed back and forth, still aiming in the general direction of Omar's face.

"When the darkness is at its thickest and the night has closed in around us… that's when we need to be the strongest." Jackson took his hand off of her arm and stared at her, silently pleading with his eyes.

Linda's jaw worked furiously as she clenched and unclenched it

before finally sighing and looking over at Frank. He was tired—
exhausted—but still standing, his rifle in one hand while he
supported Jackson with the other. His face was one of concern.
Not for himself, but for her. The stranger who had become her
closest ally, following her blindly based solely on faith and devotion
and a desire to make things right. Her friend who had stuck with
her even when given every opportunity to leave. Someone who had
supported her decisions even when they had been blindly made
and was there to help pick up the pieces and keep pushing forward
even when she had been unable to do so on her own.

In the distance she could hear the sound of Humvees and helicopters closing in; the backup that Jackson had spoken of. Linda
looked at Frank and felt her tension, fear, jitteriness and years of
pent-up frustration disappear. The corners of her mouth began to
curl as she remembered the first time she had seen him and
wondered what his angle was and how he would try to take advantage of her and how, in the end, he had been one of her fiercest
allies. She smiled at him as her arm suddenly steadied, the barrel
still trained on the face of the man she had spent far too much of
her life hunting down.

"So, Frank. What do you think we should do?"

Epilogue

Life is fragile. Whether it's human life or the complex machinations of a society that relies on complex interdependence, even the smallest things can turn it upside down. Life is also resilient. Call it the human spirit, the will to go on or whatever you want, but life is resilient. From the organisms that live at the bottom of the ocean as they feed off of volcanic vents to the child in a hospital who fights for survival, life is resilient and strong.

"Got the ice machine working. It still needs some work, but this should cool you off."

Frank Richards pulled a checkered cloth from his back pocket and wiped it across his brow and short-cropped hair. He smiled as Linda walked up to him holding a pair of tall plastic cups that were already dripping with condensation. The weather was hot— brutally so—but it wouldn't be long before it turned cold in the fall and winter.

One more heave of the maul split another piece of future firewood and Frank dropped the tool to the ground as he gratefully accepted one of the drinks. The water was cold, with small ice cubes floating at the surface, something he hadn't seen in many, many months. "I can't believe you got it working."

"Took a bit of cannibalizing a few other things, but it was worth it."

"Absolutely."

They both drank in silence as they looked out across the fields and woods that had grown from a strange environment to one that was familiar, safe and comforting. The property was small, with a modest-sized home nestled in the trees and a fertile field large enough for farming out in front and another house far on the other side of the field. Out behind the house, near where the neatly trimmed grass turned into overgrown clumps at the edge of the woods, sat a small plot surrounded by a short fence. Two small slabs of stone sat inside the plot, and around each were the beginnings of a pair of rose plants that had been freshly watered and fertilized.

A tractor slowly wove its way through the field, turning up soil for new plantings and a figure inside waved as he saw Frank and Linda watching. Linda raised her glass and pantomimed drinking with her other hand, and the figure shook his head in response. "Your dad still planning on doing the planting next week?"

"Last I heard, yeah." Frank crunched on the last of the cubes, delighting in the pain they caused his teeth. "I forgot to ask this morning but they're going to come over and help out with the barn roof tomorrow so I'll double check then."

"Thank goodness. It'll be nice to store some things out there without the rain ruining it all." Linda held out her hand, a narrow gold band on one finger, and Frank passed over his empty cup. "Give me a few minutes and I'll be back with the trailer to start loading this all up."

"You got it. Take your time." Frank smiled and wiped his brow again as Linda turned and walked away, her ponytail bouncing with each step. He watched her all the way back to the house where she took the steps up two at a time and went back inside. A sense of refreshment—and not just from the water—surged through him and he hefted the maul, stroking the edge of the blade before swinging it in a wide arc, letting the weight of the head do most of the work on the next piece of wood.

TWO HOURS LATER, as the sun was growing high in the sky, the pair were still hard at work. Wide-brimmed hats were on their heads to shield them from the heat as they stacked the split wood onto a long trailer, ready to be transported into the barn for storage. A light breeze had manifested, offering both a welcome relief from the heat as well as a mask against the distant sound of an incoming aircraft.

Twin blades spun in a flurry, pulling the silver V-22 Osprey through the air at over three hundred miles per hour. The craft soared low over the Texas plains and hills, banking to follow the curve of the ground. Inside, hunched over a map, a man dressed in Army ACUs shook his head as he spoke loudly into his headset.

"Are you sure this is where they are?"

"Of course I'm sure." The woman answering him was dressed in a casual pantsuit and her eyebrow arched in amusement. "You having trouble there, Major?"

"No ma'am, just… a little lost."

"Ma'am, is that it?" The pilot tilted the aircraft and pointed to a pair of houses below.

"That's it. Bring us around and set us down." The woman allowed a slight smile to escape. "And make it look fancy, if you could. I've got an old friend down there who'll appreciate it."

"You've got it, ma'am. Better strap in tight."

On the ground, Frank and Linda stopped loading firewood into the trailer and looked up to the sky, watching the craft circle loudly around the house. It came in low on the final turn and the rotors transformed, shifting to tilt the blades from a vertical position to a horizontal one, effectively turning the craft into a lumbering, twin-rotor helicopter. Finicky to control at best, the craft tried to buck and twist in every direction but the pilot was more than a professional and he controlled his craft with seasoned expertise, bringing it down just a few hundred feet from the house and letting it coast to a stop while the engines wound down.

Clouds of dust swirled in the air as the dry ground surrendered in the face of the intensity of the blades, but Frank and Linda both walked toward the craft as it rolled to a halt, shielding their mouths and noses with cloths. "Who on earth is this?" Frank kept his eyes locked on the craft, resisting the urge to reach for the revolver he had strapped to his upper leg.

"Are you kidding?" Linda dropped the cloth from her face and immediately coughed before grinning with delight. "Who else *could* it be?"

The back ramp of the Osprey slowly lowered as the pair walked closer, revealing two figures standing side by side at the back of the craft. They began walking forward just as the ramp hit the ground with a soft thud and Frank shook his head and raised his hands as he called out to the pair standing in front of him and Linda.

"Nope! Whatever you're selling, we don't want any!"

Linda backhanded him in the stomach and he choked on a laugh as she jogged forward, wrapping her sweat-stained arms around Sarah Callahan. Sarah returned the greeting, breaking from her usual professional demeanor to smile and laugh at the sight and embrace of her friend.

Frank, meanwhile, walked forward and stuck out his hand. "Lieutenant? How's it—wait. Major? Major Jackson now, is it?"

Jackson couldn't repress a smile as he shook Frank's hand and pulled him into an embrace. "Richards. You're looking good for being an old farmhand."

Frank chuckled, his eyes sparkling with happiness at the sight of Sarah and Jackson. "Hey, I went from accountant to truck driver to terrorist killer. I'm enjoying the off-time."

"Mhm." Sarah walked over to Frank who ignored her proffered handshake and went straight for a hug while Jackson and Linda embraced as well. When the greetings were settled, Sarah spoke.

"Are you sure you're enjoying it?" The question immediately set off alarm bells in Linda's head and she crossed her arms.

"Sarah."

"Mhm?"

"Why did you two fly all the way out here? You could have called, you know."

"We could have, yes." Sarah raised an eyebrow. "If you had phone service. Which you don't. And your satellite phone goes directly to voicemail, oddly enough." She ran her tongue over her teeth as she glanced at Frank. "And your parents, who have phone service, always seem to not know who either of you are when we try calling them."

Frank and Linda looked at each other, sharing a mischievous smile. "Eh," Frank shrugged, "we like our privacy."

"So I see." The faintest shadow of a smile was back.

"All right, Sarah." Linda took a step closer to Frank. "What's this all about? And why are you here with Jackson?"

"DOD assigned him to me at my request."

"I'm her errand boy." Jackson replied with a grin. "We're working on reconstruction efforts, passing off law enforcement work back to local officials, gathering evidence of the whole plot."

"You're *still* gathering evidence?" Linda's eyes widened. "How's that possible?"

"Omar turned a lot of people, including those in senior positions." Sarah reached into the bag on her shoulder and retrieved a thick manila file folder. "And that's why we're here."

Jackson took the folder and handed it over to Linda, who immediately handed it over to Frank. He cracked it open and they both looked at it while Jackson spoke. "We're pretty sure that we've got nearly all of his accomplices and the people that he's turned rounded up. Trials are starting in three months and the government would like for you," he gestured at Linda, "to act as a key witness. Frank, you'd also be helping with some testimony given how closely you worked with Linda after the event occurred."

Linda opened her mouth to respond, but Sarah cut her off. "I know your first response is going to be a 'no' but hear me out. We're obviously not allowed to offer you anything in exchange for your testimony, but as your actions—and yours, Frank—have come to the attention of those higher up the food chain, they've authorized me to offer you a few things as a thank you for what you did to stop Omar before he could detonate the bombs."

"Without you two," Jackson interjected, "there would be nothing left."

"What kind of 'thank you' are we talking about here?" Frank asked.

Jackson pulled a few small documents from his breast pocket and passed them over for Frank and Linda to see. "A bank account with the details there has already been created in your names, with that balance applied to it. If you look at the second card you'll see an address and a satellite picture of some land in Maine and in Tennessee that belonged to—"

"My parents and I." Linda spoke softly as she finished his sentence.

"Yes. Everything's been taken care of, fixed and upgraded to be self-sufficient at both locations. Both properties are in your names, just like the bank account."

"Thank you again for what you did, Jackson." Linda looked up from the cards with tear-filled eyes, then cast a glance to the small plot with the pair of gravestones behind the house. "You didn't have to bring them here."

"Sarah insisted on it and it was the least we could do. But now we can do more."

"So this," Frank raised an eyebrow, "is what? Some kind of a bribe for her—for our—testimony?"

"It's a thank you. From an old friend to another old friend." Sarah looked at Linda, then over at Frank. "And to a new one."

"What if they ask what happened to Omar?" Linda's eyes were dry, a fire slowly burning in them that made them sparkle in the sunlight.

"You tell them the truth." Sarah replied. "Nothing more and nothing less. You tell them that a man who slaughtered millions was brought to justice, and anything that happened to him during his capture couldn't be avoided."

Frank wrapped the fingers of his left hand around Linda's right hand and squeezed as she took a deep breath before responding.

She looked Sarah dead in the eye, looking for any hint that the request was anything but genuine and forthright. "Is this legitimate, Sarah?"

"It is. No strings. No traps. No tricks. I'll be with you both the entire way. Regardless of your decision, though, the properties and money are yours to keep, along with the thanks of a grateful nation."

"I don't know, Sarah. We're building a life out here. The country's doing its own thing but we're self-sufficient, near Frank's parents—who, to be fair, are a bit of a pain in the ass but still fantastic."

"Hey!" Frank shoved her in the side with his elbow as she laughed. "Be nice!"

"My parents are resting properly and things…" she looked at Frank and smiled. "Things are good."

"Things will still be good, Linda." Jackson looked at Sarah. "I promise you both that things will still be good. And better. It'll be a long process, but you'll be helping to solidify cases and ensure that every single person behind this plot is brought to justice."

Linda nodded slowly, then turned and looked at Frank. His hand was still in hers and she rubbed the band on his ring finger, turning it as she considered what Sarah and Jackson had to say. The offer was tempting, but it was one that she couldn't make on her own.

"So, Frank." She asked with a slight smile.

"Oh no." He groaned. "Don't you put *this* on me, too."

The wind picked up again, sending the scent of fresh cut grass, fertilizer, earth and warm sunshine cascading over her face. Linda broke out into a grin as she closed the folder and looked at him, seeing her helper, her equal and her friend standing before her.

"What do you think we should do?"

THE END

Author's Notes

Author's Notes

No Sanctuary has been an interesting series. It started out as a by-the-books post-apocalyptic adventure and turned into a cross between post-apocalyptic and a thriller somewhere around the halfway mark. I don't know how or why the story took that turn, but I sure am glad that it did because it has been *crazy fun* to write.

Building up to Linda meeting Omar was tough and I hope that I did it justice. Between the final set of backstories for him and his initial encounter with Linda, I wanted him to feel like someone who was both deeply troubled and deeply, unreservedly evil. I didn't base him off of anyone in particular; he's a creation formed completely internally, and he represents what I think someone could really become and do if they were given sufficient resources and motivation.

If you're wondering about the ending and why I don't definitively say whether or not Linda killed him or let him live... that's a hard question to answer. I've been planning the ending for a few months now and I just couldn't decide whether I wanted to have her kill him or let him life. The former felt like a "good" ending where the bad guy gets killed by the person he tormented and who was chasing him. Letting him live, though, felt like it would show growth on Linda's part, because she would be giving up her personal revenge in favor of having proper justice performed as he was brought forward to answer for his horrendous crimes.

In the end, I couldn't decide. So I left it ambiguous and that ended up feeling right—but not in the way that you might be thinking about.

See, once I decided to leave it up in the air about what she did, I realized that something more important came forward: her relationship with Frank. She started as an adversary of his, leaving him in the middle of the night after he rescued her. As she grew to trust him, though, a bond formed, and the story wasn't about two separate people traveling alongside each other, but about how they worked together. One pushing when the other was falling behind. One pulling when the other was struggling. Ensuring that, no matter what, they would make it to the next goal. Together.

I wanted to really reinforce this in the epilogue, again by leaving Omar's fate ambiguous, but also by showing the pair together. Working side by side. Two imperfect people helping each other to become better each day.

In stories of the apocalypse, a great deal is made about the events that happen. The bombs or the viruses or the solar flares or the weapons or the political drama.

None of that matters. None of it. They're all just set pieces.

What matters—what *always* and *only* matters—are the stories of the people. Their struggles. Their hopes. Their dreams. Their nightmares. Their road from disaster to survival that reflects in us our belief that, no matter what, we can press on and survive whatever happens. Those stories speak to us and connect with us and make us feel a connection with the characters in the story because we see them and shout and cry and sing and feel sorrow alongside them. The characters matter more than anything else.

I love Frank and Linda and the small cast of supporting characters that I built up around them. And I hope you do as well. I'm not a Marine or an accountant or a trucker or a soldier or a CIA spook. But I am a human, and I feel a human connection to these characters.

I hope, on some level, you felt some sort of connection to them as well. And if you did, then I did my job.

I love my job.

All the best,
    Mike Kraus

P.S. If you enjoyed this story and/or any of my other stories, please leave a review for them on Amazon. Just go to the book you purchased or checked out through Kindle Unlimited, scroll down to the review section and click the button to write your own review. It only takes a minute, but it seriously makes a world of difference to an independent writer like myself.

You should also really sign up for my newsletter. I send out quick messages a few times a month and I take a totally different approach to my newsletters than other authors. Where other authors see a newsletter as a selling tool first and foremost I see it as a way to connect with my readers first and foremost. I've met some terrific people (like my AWESOME beta readers) and really enjoy talking to folks who email me.

Don't like email newsletters? I also keep my Facebook page

updated and you can message me through there as well if you prefer FB to email. Feel free to drop me a line via email/FB. I'd love to hear from you.

Catch you in the next book!

Made in the USA
Lexington, KY
11 May 2019